D1452595

Home at Last

Roy Taylor

A novel

First Printing

Printed in the United States

Published by J Mark
203 North Cone Street
Wilson, N.C. 27893

Library of Congress Catalog Card Number 89-90422
ISBN 0-9613485-2-6

For my daughter, Kay,
her husband, Marshall,
And grandsons Jason and Andy

HOME AT LAST

Foreword

This is a work of fiction. In a few instances actual names of persons have been used to give to myself, at least, a sense of realism. However, there is nothing said in such instances that would have any bearing on the character of the individuals mentioned. Such names are only casually mentioned and are not a central part of this work. All the major characters are purely fictitious.

The setting is the 1930s and 1940s, a time now regarded as the most crucial period in our history, because of the trauma and devastation wreaked by the Great Depression and World War II. There is much material available on the Depression and the war both in the written word and pictorially. Many books show pictures of hopeless people during the Depression and accompanying captions tell of their plight across the nation.

Most of those doing research on such projects were far removed from the subject and had no conception what the reality of those days really was. To have been there is to know. To be told by others leaves one to wonder.

History leaves many unanswered questions about those days. Generations have grown up who know nothing about those decades except for what is recorded. Left out is the most important element - the people - and their lives. Stories are recorded of the society group of those days - celebrities and the famous people known the world over. But little is recorded about the everyday lives of the little people who made up ninety nine percent of the population. And when such stories were told they accentuated the poverty and suffering of the people in books of that era.

There was suffering and poverty and hardships that we would consider intolerable today. But there was a pattern of life, as strong as there is today.

Much was happening in those days, although many of the events were

overshadowed by major happenings in the world. For instance, it was during this era that some medical discoveries were made that have had a tremendous impact on the world. Those discoveries paved the way for modern medical advances that are making it possible for people to live much longer than in the past.

The drug ACTH that is one of the drugs of the modern age, was discovered in 1949 by Armous & Company. Aureomycin was discovered in 1948 by Dugger of the United States. Cortisone was discovered in 1936 by Kendall of the United States.

The practical use of penicillin was discovered in 1941 by Florey of England.

Streptomycin was discovered in 1945 by Waxman of the United States. Sulfanilamide was discovered in 1934 by Domagk of Germany. Sulfadiazine was discovered in 1940 by Roblin of the United States.

Terramycin was discovered in 1950 by Finley of the United States. And the polio vaccines were discovered in the 50s by Doctors Salk and Sabin. These were no less than modern miracles. Before their discoveries we had no "miracle drugs" working for us. These discoveries have no relevance to this story but serve as an example that the world wasn't stagnating during those years.

New cars were being manufactured. The World's Fair was being held. Great movies were being filmed. It was an exciting era.

Events occurred during those years that had an impact on all Americans. They are still remembered by millions when they are mentioned, such as the Lindbergh story, both the trip across the Atlantic and the kidnapping of his baby; the birth of the Dionne quintuplets; Will Rogers' death; the activities of the Ku Klux Klan; the "chain gangs" and the mass executions at our state prisons.

Bear Grass is a fictional community and has no resemblance to the neighborhood in which I grew up.

Book 1

Chapter 1

I t was the kind of resting place intended for those who have made their walks through life, with only memories of the past for the living to reflect on.

Serene. Isolated. Lonely. The burial ground was far from the highway, on a windswept hill where the drainage was good and where caskets were protected when wet spells came. It was a sprawling cemetery that had been donated to the community by an area landowner almost a century earlier.

Any white person in the Bear Grass area could be buried there. No permit was required.

There was a variety of trees that shaded the graves in summer and brought comfort to loved ones when the hot sun bore down. Yet there was room to allow sunshine to bring out the flowers in spring.

Dew still sparkled on the new foliage and a peach tree sheathed in thousands of fragile pink blossoms dominated the area on the outer edge of the cemetery. Jonquils were yellow in little plots and wild violets with miniature purple blooms grew on many graves.

Hobby Turnage stood beside the grave of Wilbert Lee Turner on a sunny morning in 1948. Tears were in his eyes.

It was almost total silence in the graveyard. Only a bark from a dog occasionally and the ringing of a bell around a cow's neck interrupted the tranquility. A cardinal and a bluebird vied for a worm on one of the walkways and other birds sang in the trees, unaware that their cries for recognition went unnoticed except for the times when people gathered at the resting place for a little while or went there, as Hobby Turnage did on this day, to meditate and reflect back on life. Reflection was his mission on this day, although it seemed like a place to pray.

It had been two years! Dirt on the grave had long settled, forming a mound as all the other graves did. The only distinction between the graves was the newness of the head stone that was brighter, giving the appearance of having been polished. This stone and others in the cemetery that had been erected in recent years made the other stones appear dull. The inscription on the monument read: W.L. Turner. 1920-1946. The epitaph read "Gone But Not Forgotten."

Hobby had not been to Wilbert Lee's grave before. He had wanted to go many times but it had been too painful, too personal, for him to cope with. The tragedy still seemed as close as yesterday in a sense. It had changed his life in a matter of days. And the change was what he always knew he wanted, but the circumstances that brought about the change were something he tried to keep out of his mind.

It seemed that his entire life was parading before him as he stood on the hill where the wind played among the trees and the long-leaf pines whispered their secrets that held no meaning for the inhabitants. Bear Grass was the most beautiful spot in all the world to Hobby. It was in Bear Grass that he had his first awareness of life and he learned to love and appreciate the simple people he knew and a tranquil way of life outside the mainstream of America. Although quaint, it mirrored thousands of rural areas across the nation.

There had been the long line of sharecropper shanties along Beston Road where he and many of his friends lived and played together. There had been the leisurely days when they were small and were able to explore their entire domain and dream the dreams of childhood. He and Wilbert Lee, Buddy Stone, Jimmie Joe Smith, LaBeth Sims, Violet Shaw, Minnie Mae Moore, Lisker Johnson, Tom, Billy Earl, Robyn, and Arlene Finch, Philip Stroud and some of the colored children roamed the fields and woods and played in the streams and lived in a child's paradise.

Hobby thought of the way fate had twisted their lives, sending them in different directions. Who would ever have thought that the little simple girl, Robyn Finch, would have captivated his heart and become the dominant force in his life? Who would have thought that he would ever have left the land he loved best and return there still as a young man to live out his life? He hadn't determined his leaving although it was his greatest desire to return to the quiet life Bear Grass afforded him.

He thought of the struggle of the sharecroppers to survive as far back as he could remember, even before the Great Depression struck.

He remembered the brawny faces and sad eyes of the older generation whose real thoughts he never knew. He was aware that time had weathered them and hardships had made them old before their time. But it was strange that he had never heard them complain. Most were easygoing and took a keen interest in life.

As a child he would study the faces of old colored men with snow white hair and beards and eyes that appeared to be looking beyond the range of visibility. But they were always smiling, often dressed in ragged clothes with large safety pins holding their coats and shirts together as they traveled the roads in shackly one-horse wagons, often carrying an old plow and maybe a roll of wire discarded by others. He remembered the long lines of wagons on the road in fall going to the gin to have the cotton ginned. He could see goldenrods blooming beside the road and people sitting high above the sheets of cotton. He visualized the weigh-horses at sunset when the cotton was being weighed with a golden sun slowly sinking below the horizon.

But there was an awareness of many blessings during those years. Southern farmers were blessed with home-grown food and there had been no starvation in Bear Grass. Food was grown in family gardens, and the neighborliness of the people would not have allowed any hungry person to perish. Although money was out of the picture, the farming community had come through the poorest years in the nation's history and could lift its head in pride when the economy began a slow spiral upward.

Hobby's thoughts returned to Wilbert Lee who had been Hobby's idol as a child. He had loved Wilbert Lee above all the other neighborhood children. He had almost been a young god to Hobby. He wanted to be with Wilbert Lee every moment possible and since they lived next door to each other they sometimes played together when none of the other children were around. It was Wilbert Lee's expertise at swimming and running and assuming the leadership role among the children that appealed to Hobby so much, for Hobby was unable to indulge in some of the children's activities. Wilbert Lee was all the things Hobby couldn't be.

The two boys' personalities were entirely different. Hobby was a happy child and wore a smile on his face and a grin that people noticed and he enjoyed talking with his elders as well as children. Wilbert Lee was more constrained. He had a temperament that often got him in trouble with the other children. There was something troubling about him that you couldn't put a finger on. He often appeared aloof and sometimes acted as if he felt superior to his playmates. He would act bully with those smaller than he, although he was careful not to tackle boys larger than himself.

The morning dew dried up and the sun became a brilliant fire in the heavens. The hillside beside the cemetery sloped down to a little stream and beyond the stream was a swamp where leaves were showing hues from light yellow to brilliant green. The horizon looked the same as he remembered from childhood with some trees standing taller than others. The sweet gums were stately, the walnuts towering over all the others and the oaks spread out and bushy. The tall trees dominated the horizon and brought reminders to Hobby of how he had picked out objects among them when they were only a silhouette on the horizon. And beyond the trees were more fertile fields where farming operations were carried out daily.

Hobby never ceased talking about Bear Grass and the beauty of the life he had left behind as a twelve-year-old boy in Tennessee. He saw the mountains with their panorama of color year-round with the rhododendron blooming in spring along with many other mountain flowers and the millions of trees merging into a solid background that became marvels of nature in autumn. But somehow he couldn't see that beauty in the same light as what he remembered in Bear Grass. A single sassafras bush on a ditchbank with brilliant red foliage captured his fancy more than the mass of color he saw in the hills.

Why couldn't they see the picture as a whole? he thought. Why did they have to label the area he knew and loved as flat country with nothing but old shanties and fields of corn, cotton and tobacco and paths leading to nowhere and with hundreds of hands in the fields - a land of ignorant rednecks.

Throughout his high school years he discussed "back home" with his friends but somehow he was never able to convince them that he had a special place on earth above any other, but he wasn't discouraged. He did the same thing during his college years and in medical school. He was always homesick, always aware that something was missing in his life that only the environs of home could cure.

But time passed and he became so involved in his medical studies there were few hours to reflect on Bear Grass.

The most beautiful memory of his lifetime was when he was eighteen and returned to Bear Grass to visit his old friends. He had been away six years. A miracle had occurred in the interim and he had two straight legs and was able to get about in a normal fashion. He wanted to see everybody he had known, but learned that quite a few of his former playmates had moved away. But he made an effort to find them, and the reunions were more than he could hope for.

He knew the Finches were going to move to Jones County before he left, but he had lost contact with them, and wanted to see all the family. They had been close when they lived only two doors away and Hobby had eaten at Miss Cora's table many times. He remembered the kindness of Miss Cora and Mr. Tobe and how he and their children had gotten along so well together. But he was totally unprepared for what he found at the Finch household. One look at Robyn and his fate was sealed forever. It was like being in a cloud and completely out of the realm of reality. How could it be? He had liked all the children - Arlene as well as Robyn - and the boys as well as the girls.

Hobby had sat on the front porch with Miss Cora and they had laughed and talked about their days in Bear Grass and Hobby had remembered the delicious pies and dumplings he had eaten with the Finches and a feeling of euphoria had settled over him. The afternoon would soon end. It had been a sunshiny day and the air was comfortable. He had watched the purple martins as they entered their nests in the gourds assembled on poles at the edge of the yard, a sight he hadn't seen in six years. Then he saw a figure coming up the path with the setting sun behind her.

"It's Robyn getting home from work," Miss Cora had said, and Hobby said, "Robyn?"

As she came closer he observed the simplicity of her dress. A white v-neck blouse and a checked, billowing skirt and saddle shoes. But it was only when he saw her features close-up that he was overwhelmed with her loveliness.

His heart was racing as she approached the porch. He was speechless. Oh, what eyes! Had they changed so much? It was Robyn, all right, but her countenance had changed somehow. All the beauty he visualized in an instant had been hidden behind the mask of childhood, waiting to be expressed when nature performed her wonders as it transformed adolescents into adults.

"Robyn!" he exclaimed, and she responded, "Hobby!" and they embraced. And so it had begun.

As Hobby squatted and took a handful of soft clay from the grave and ran it through his fingers, a rabbit darted across the cemetery and headed for the briers in the lowlands and a jaybird carried a twig to a cedar tree in the distance. It was all lost to Wilbert Lee. All of a bright future given up in a moment of passion. Every hope, every dream lost forever when hope was so bright. Change was evident everywhere - change that would benefit the poor man who had sacrificed so much and who had dreamed of the good life. If he could only see the rabbit and the jaybird and could observe the tranquility of the scene, that in itself would be enough to live for.

Childhood was the only time in life Hobby had to remember about Bear Grass - years in which the values that would shape his life had been formed, regardless of his being away during his years of growing up. He knew that not only the place, but the people with whom he had associated, played an equally important role in his feelings about an unknown community hidden from view of the general public.

He remembered the night Rev. Otto Pell had called him and the impact it had had on him. He could see the Baptist minister going about the community ministering to the people and how they looked up to him. He could not imagine what had possessed the man of the cloth to go astray. And a few months after his conversation with Rev. Pell he had seen in the back section of a paper that the minister had walked out into the Atlantic while his wife and children stayed ashore and just kept walking until he was overcome by the rough waters and just yielded himself to the ocean; an apparent suicide. He wept when he read of his death.

And they were still electrocuting people regularly at state prisons across the nation. Reading of all the executions, Hobby puzzled over what made people do the things they did - always with malice in their hearts - to have it all end in death. What possessed people to make them have no regard for their own lives, to say nothing of the lives of others?

And the miracle of his own mother's good fortune, blessed with the undying love of a great man, as well as his own benefactor. The greatest gift is love, and Nick Staphal would always shine brightly in the memory of those who knew him.

Years in which a world turned topsy-turvy; years of change as is always the case. Years of talking about war and people picking themselves up and trying for a new beginning after being humbled by a depression.

Years in which he had lived the idyllic life as an innocent child when he believed in all people; a world in which he had no prejudices; when he saw only the good in people, to have that world shattered by the realities of life when boyhood fades and manhood confronts you.

How sweet the days of innocence as he recalled them in the lonely setting.

Visions of childhood flooded his soul. Suddenly there were tomwalkers with children standing seven feet tall on limbs from hardwood trees that accommodated their feet and made walking easy, although he had never been on the tomwalkers himself; chicken feathers attached to a band of cloth that children wore around their heads and pretended to be Indians doing a war dance. He could almost hear the war chant; bows made from stiff limbs from hardwood trees, notched at the ends and shaped with strong cord and arrows made from smaller hardwood with homemade flints added at the ends to kill their prey; bean shooters made from reeds and green cherries used for ammunition; sling shots carved from tree limbs and rubber from old innertubes and tobacco twine shaping the sling shots into weapons used by all the neighborhood boys; wheels from small machinery parts and sticks with nails in the ends providing hours of play rolling the wheels along the paths and even into the fields. He remembered the slobber from the mouths of the children as they imitated the sounds of automobiles; the homemade carts and the labor of love in getting them ready for riding and running over the countryside; toad frog houses, using the naked feet to shape the mound and banking damp sand over the foot so that when it was removed the house was there and the little green animals were found and placed in their domains; paths made under the houses when the children played on hot afternoons with cans of water taken there to make cement out of the powdery earth. Beautiful, nostalgic scenes that Wilbert Lee could never reflect on again.

A man in a field across the marsh was plowing corn just large enough to show green in the rows and a little cloud of dust swirled around the plow as it turned up the soil. Hobby stood and spoke softly and no one heard except the animal world about him.

"I'm so sorry, Wilbert Lee, sorry that I wasn't there to protect you from yourself and my beloved Robyn. If I could only have been there I would have saved your life as you saved mine that day when I was drowning in the creek. You could be with the dear boy and girl who still grieve for their father. You could be shaping up an impressive career as a banker. I can visualize you becoming the president of a bank someday and exerting great influence over a community. Banks are big business now, Wilbert Lee, but they're only in their infancy. We saw the dawning of the atomic age, World War II; and that was only the beginning. The Giant is awake now and beginning to show His strength. It's just starting to build, like the storm clouds that produce powerful tornadoes. If you had only waited, Wilbert Lee, everything would have worked out.

"I think about all the changes we have seen during our short lives and the little events that have shaped our lives and the larger things that affect our world, and I grieve that you ended it all at this stage and can never know what the tomorrows will bring. And despite all the sorrow, all the heartaches, all the trauma that you caused, I would breathe the breath of life into your body again if it were in my power. I would give you a second chance to become the man you could be.

"Consider this as my reunion and my goodbye to you, Wilbert Lee. I am finding new strength every day to face life with a smile and with hope in my heart. I see your Will and Beth occasionally. They are lovely children and my heart goes out to them. They loved you more than you ever realized.

Whatever I may be able to do to make life pleasant for them, I will do happily. I must get on with my life and I leave you here among the trees in the quietness of the setting, a place typical of where all of us rest when our lives have ended. It is a fitting place and I hope you have found the eternal peace that eluded you in life.

"But I know that coming here has opened up the floodgate of memories that I must relive in their entirety. I will have to do that in order to be able to fit the entire picture together. May you rest in peace, Wilbert Lee."

Chapter 2

Thunder rumbled across the heavens like a boulder rolling over railroad ties. The flashes of lightning were muted by a waning moon. Rain was falling in sheets, sounding almost like hail as it hit the window panes and the wind rattled the tin roof and caused a barn door to swing to and fro as if it were a plaything for the summer storm. The old chaney ball tree near the house bowed its branches, some scraping the rusty tin roof.

The boy was awakened by the noise. He raised up and looked out the window, then lay back down and drew the sheet close about him. He smiled.

From the next room came the snores of his grandparents, and during the quiet intervals, he could hear the clock ticking on the mantel.

Blessed with a unique gene from some unknown ancestor, he saw a beauty in life few people bothered to look for. He was secure from all the storms of life in his own little room, whether stars studded the sky or lightning flashed in the heavens. Life was beauty to him. He reflected on it from morning till night, with each day a new experience.

He was usually up when the morning stars still hung low in the skies and roosters welcomed a new day from their perches in neighborhood henhouses. He was waiting for the sunrise when it came over the trees and glistened on the morning dew. On fair days, it was a large ball of orange that welcomed him and his world. When clouds were on the horizon he watched as they were painted in colors of purple, orange and red with a rosy hue where the sun shone through.

He welcomed all the seasons, from the time spring brought new growth after the dormancy of winter and green dominated the countryside and brought out the flowers and the smells of spring, till the days of summer with a relentless sun and people busy all day in the fields; to fall with its display of foliage that painted the picture he loved best; to winter when the ground froze over sometimes and when the earth spewed up after the thaw, to the silent snows that whitened the fields and clung to the unpainted houses and accumulated on farm implements scattered around the shelters and barnyard.

His world was touchable - not a fantasy land filled with elves and fairies and things many little boys' worlds were composed of.

Home was his first love. It was humble enough; a sharecropper's shanty with four rooms with weatherboarding the only material enclosing the structure. There was the "front room" where his grandparents slept and where the open fireplace gave warmth in winter and where they sat and watched as the fire was replenished and the wood burned to embers with little sparks rising up the chimney occasionally.

There was his bedroom with a bureau for his clothes, nails on the studs where he could hang items, an old trunk at the foot of his bed and a straight chair between the door and his bed. There was the bright patchwork quilt that decorated his bed and the thick goosedown feather bed underneath that warmed him in winter. There was the back room where Grandma stored all manner of things. He loved to roam in the room and look at the many old things stored for no apparent reason except that they held some fond memory for her and which she couldn't part with.

Then there was the kitchen that he loved as well as the "front room." With an old oilcloth covering the table and a safe as old as time it seemed, where the food was kept and the flour barrel over in the corner and the bread tray straddling the barrel, the strings of hot pepper and popcorn and the small sacks of sage and dried apples and peaches behind the stove and the cooking utensils hanging on nails driven into the weatherboarding. There was the slop bucket beside the stove, and the side table, also covered with an even older oilcloth and a kerosene lamp and a shelf on the back porch where the washpan sat and where they washed their hands and dashed the water into the yard and dried their hands in the salt-sack towel hanging beneath an old looking glass so they could see themselves as they "primped up" for meals.

And Grandma's cooking was so good! Buttermilk biscuits every meal.

Sausages in season and country ham after the meat had mellowed for months, fat back when the cured meat gave out, homemade butter and black molasses and peach, pear and grape preserves and vegetables cooked to a tender delicacy.

Better yet were the pies and dumplings and jacks Grandma made and fed to him with a smile on her face and a love that showed in her every mannerism.

He loved the two old people who ministered to him and supplied all his needs. They'd often take him into their laps and he'd lay his head on their shoulders and they might not say anything; just pat him gently on his hips and he'd go to sleep sometimes and they'd undress him and place him in his bed and he'd sleep throughout the night.

The premises were his domain, where chickens ran during the day and birds pitched in the yards and in the trees and sang and bathed in mudholes in the yard. There was the stable where the mule was kept, and he loved old Kate. He love Smut, the black cow, and Sam, the shaggy dog that always licked his face when he came up to him. He loved to hear the ducks quack and he laughed when they waddled across the yard with their babies tugging behind. He loved the white ganders and the gray geese that habitated the yard.

He was intrigued by the hogs in the pasture down the path. They squealed for food and rooted under the fence sometimes and Grandpa and Grandma had to get out and run them back in, with Grandma shaking her apron as if that would turn them around. And when the old sow had babies he'd sit and watch for hours as the little pigs cuddled up to their mother and nudged her udders for nourishment.

When the nannie goat had a baby, the little animal became his plaything and the goat would come up to him and let him rub his face. When the cow had a calf, it was the same routine.

He played with butterflies that pitched sometimes and moved their colored wings up and down.

He habitated the plum trees along the ditchbanks when the fruit ripened. He picked brierberries for his grandmother and she made them into jelly. He did all the things any normal boy would do. And he was happy in his world.

He lived along a gravel road where almost all the houses were of the same design and construction - four or five rooms with a front and back porch, unpainted with no underpinning, weatherboarded but with no interior finish, allowing the winds of winter to invade the houses and with knotholes in the weatherboarding through which stars could be spotted at night and cracks in the floors that let the wind in and chilled the rooms. There was a well in every yard, a privy, a smokehouse, a barn and shelter of various descriptions; a woodpile, a wash pot, a clothesline, and trees that shaded the houses and grounds in summer and stood with naked limbs uplifted in winter.

There were endless acres of farmland on which crops were grown. The fields were separated by ditches or thickets or hedgerows with lush growth on the ditchbanks or any other untended place. And there were the forests, always the forests, forming the horizon with pines predominant, but with other species vying with the pines for recognition.

It was flat country with little elevation and few valley-like areas. The land was fertile and hundreds of sharecroppers and tenants tended the land for the landlords, although a very few people owned their own land. Both white and colored people worked in the fields side by side. There were long hours of toil in the fields growing tobacco, cotton, corn and soybeans along with sweet potatoes, and some truck crops that added a few dollars to farmers' income during the summer season.

It was a picturesque sight for the boy to observe the traffic along the roads. There were many wagons and carts on the move as farmers hauled crops from the fields in harvest season, and tobacco trucks raising the dust along the roads as they hauled the golden weed from the fields to the barns.

It was especially beautiful as day ended. From every house smoke rose from the kitchen chimney as women prepared supper for hungry families. Fireflies dotted the yards as darkness fell, giving an appearance of a miniature constellation at ground level. Then the stars appeared and sparkled like diamonds in the sky.

It was a simple land and a simple people. The time was the early 1930s and the world was gripped by the Great Depression, although its effects on the rural community were less evident than in metropolitan areas. There were no bread lines out in the country. People grew their food, and in that respect, were especially blessed during the years when many people felt the pangs of hunger.

Most people were uneducated, and those that had some schooling were generally in school through the seventh grade. And although lacking in educational values, the populace was far from ignorant, and kept up with world, national, state and local events through newspapers and farm magazines.

The boy spoke as a child and acted as a child, yet, in many ways he reasoned far beyond his years. And if he saw the beauty of his secluded world far from the eyes of the general public, he realized that there were others who viewed life differently than he. He respected their views and there were some children who said they wanted to get away from the solitude of back-country life and go to new places. There were those who spoke about life differently than he; who poked fun at themselves and all other poor people; who complained that the sordidness bothered them. He loved his playmates and made himself comfortable with them, whatever their views or attitudes.

It was a time when the "Giant" was still sleeping, barely able to move. The "Giant" appeared to be on the verge of expiring. The "Giant" was the economy, that had almost ceased to exist as the Depression deepened. But it hadn't been a sudden drop from prosperity to near-starvation. Rural people generally thrust off the word "Depression" for it had had little impact on their lives. There had been no millennium for them, even before the Depression.

As the boy reflected on life at such an early age, he had no forewarning of all the events that would transpire to change his own personal world and the world about him as time unfolded.

His name was Hobby, and he was a little crippled boy.

Chapter 3

Abie Turner was out on the front porch with a water pitcher. The geraniums, sitting in pots on the edge of the porch, were beginning to turn yellow and the climbing vines growing to provide shade to the porch were wilted in the summer sun. It was hot and dusty and corn was head-high and cutting off most of the view of the community.

Abie saw a commotion down the road and wondered what was happening. A man was in the road and several women were around him motioning their hands and then they suddenly left and the man came on up the road. What in the world could it be?

As she was entering the house and knocking at flies trying to enter the door she heard a man call, "Abie, wait a minute." It was Luby Sauls.

Abie turned around, straightening her apron, when Luby came up to the porch.

"Have you seen anything of a run-mad dog Abie?"

"Lord no!" Abie replied. "Oh my God, where is Wilbert Lee?" Wilbert Lee was her five-year-old son. "I have pleaded with that boy not to run off and not let me know where he was going. I bet anything he's playing with Hobby somewhere and they ain't no telling what they're into. Oh God, please don't let nothing happen to my boy." She failed to mention anything happening to Hobby.

"Now don't git all riled up, Abie," Luby said. "You know run-mad dogs don't go searching for something to attack. They're mad and don't even know what they're doing. They usually go in a fairly straight course and don't bother nothing unless a human or animal gits in their way. That dog hain't been near your boy, Abie."

"Lord, I hope not," Abie replied as she stepped from the porch and began running toward the Turnage house. "Which way was he traveling?" she asked as she was getting farther away from Luby.

"Come from the swamp," Luby yelled. "Billy Smith saw him come out of the woods and head this way. A dark, grizzly looking dog, big and ugly. I hain't never seen that dog around here."

Wilbert Lee and Hobby weren't in the Turnage yard and Abie saw Viola in the garden and she ran as fast as she could, becoming short of breath and finding it hard to talk. "Where are Hobby and Wilbert Lee?" she asked.

"Lord, I don't know Abie. Why?"

"A run-mad dog is on the loose and I'm scared to death he's going to bite my boy. I couldn't stand it if he had to take them fifteen or so shots they give them right in their bellies when they are bit. Come help me look for them, Viola."

"Now there ain't no need to panic, Abie," Viola said. "I know how protective you are of Wilbert Lee and all that and God knows I don't want no run-mad dog biting your young'un or mine either. But I know how you go all to pieces about Wilbert Lee and all it does is git you so riled up you go into hysterics."

"You know very well why that is Viola. I've had 10 babies for Gant Turner and every one of 'em lost except for Wilbert Lee, and the last at that. I'm too old for more. Already been through the change. Seems like I worship that boy for all them pretty babies that died or were stillborn."

"Well, I love my grandson as much as if he were mine," Viola said. "I shore don't want nothing to happen to him or Wilbert Lee. But I'm placing my faith in God to protect them. There ain't nothing else to do Abie. And you're one of the most Christian people in the neighborhood. Where is your faith, Abie?"

"When it comes down to my boy, I reckon I don't have faith," Abie replied. "And I know that ain't Christian, but I feel like nobody else, not even God, will protect my boy but me."

They walked across cotton rows and a stinging worm got Abie on the leg and she cried out and took snuff from her mouth and plastered over the sting where little bumps had risen. "I'd love to set down and cry it hurts so bad, but I just don't have the time," she said. They entered a corn field after leaving the cotton patch and the debris from the tassles got down their necks and they itched and sweated as they searched for the boys.

They were not under the tobacco barn shelters, nor in the barns. They searched stables in people's yards and asked everybody they saw whether they had seen them. Nobody had seen the boys that day. And Abie was beginning to wring her hands, when Viola spied them at the edge of a ditch under the shade of a tree playing with toad frogs.

"Have you seen anything of a run-mad dog Wilbert Lee?" Abie asked as she took the boy into her arms.

Viola bent down and patted Hobby's head.

"No ma'am," Wilbert Lee said and Hobby confirmed Wilbert Lee's statement.

"Let me look at you," Abie told Wilbert Lee. "Mama just wants to be sure nothing has happened to her boy. Let me see your hands."

Wilbert Lee opened his hands and Abie saw several red places where briers had pricked the skin. "Oh Lord!" she cried out. "Look at his hands, Viola. That dog has bit my boy as sure as the world."

Hobby came up to Abie and placed his hand on her apron. He looked up into her face with a smile not even Wilbert Lee could duplicate. "Miss Abie that was where we got into briers coming to the ditch. Honest, we didn't see no dog."

Abie thought how pitiful it was for a boy as pretty as Hobby to be so crippled he could never be a whole person. Tow-headed with sky-blue eyes and white teeth and a mouth as shapely as a girl's. But Abie had never been able to have the depth of feeling for Hobby she might have had if he had not been conceived and born out of wedlock. That was a cardinal sin and could never be forgiven and such children just had to bear the brunt of their mothers' mistakes. That Perline, his mother, was a hussy if there ever was one. But one thing about it. Nobody could ever say she was not a "looker." The prettiest girl that ever lived in the community. Could have had her pick of the neighborhood boys. Had everything going her way except respectability. She felt outrage for Perline, and that extended to her offspring.

Abie's heart finally stopped pounding after she was convinced her boy hadn't been bitten by a run-mad dog, and they walked back home at a leisurely pace. Abie watched Hobby as he tried to keep up with Wilbert Lee, and his good leg was bent so badly it was a genuine effort for him to keep up, but he looked at Wilbert Lee as if he were an idol.

"You reckon anything can ever be done for Hobby's leg?" Abie asked.

"I hope and pray so," Viola replied. "Perline says she's saving every dime she can to have an operation on his leg."

"What's Perline doing now?" Abie asked.

"She's working in a mill in Tennessee. She worked in the cotton mills in Hallsborough before she went away, you know. And they said she was good with them spindles, too."

Abie was thinking that Perline was no doubt picking up dollars on the side as well as working in the mill, knowing her to be the easy woman she was. But she didn't mention this to Viola.

"I tell you, that boy's leg is so ill-deform I just don't know whether the doctors can ever straighten it out. And if they can, he will be left a cripple it seems like."

"They're learning how to do a lot of things these days," Viola replied. "But I don't know when we'll ever be able to git anything done about it."

Abie was deep in her own thoughts as they traversed the path beside a long field of corn. Gnats were swarming around her eyes and the little bit of wind that was stirring was hot and a haze was over the fields. She was thinking that she'd have to wean Wilbert Lee away from Hobby and she didn't know how to go about it. Hobby was not the kind of boy she wanted Wilbert Lee to associate with. Oh, not his character or anything like that. But he would call attention to Wilbert Lee if Hobby was always around him and looking up to him as if he were some kind of god. What would it be like if the two boys were seen together in town? People would think of Hobby as they did those crippled beggars on the street. She wanted better than that for Wilbert Lee.

Philip Stroud was the one boy in the community she really wanted Wilbert Lee to associate with. Now that boy had a future in front of him. His daddy had a lot of land and Phil was a nice-looking boy and showed a certain "class" the other neighborhood young'uns were lacking. Phil was a year or so older than Wilbert Lee, but there was not enough difference in age to matter. And Wilbert Lee did go up and play with Phil sometimes.

"What are you so quiet for?" Viola said. "You act like your mind's a thousand miles away."

"I was just thinking about our community and how things are," Abie said. "I reckon we're like communities everywhere with the good and the bad all mixed together, and the good outdoes the bad enough so that we keep some kind of balance. They's good people and bad people all mixed together and it's up to us to weed out the chaff from the wheat. A lot of people don't even go to Whispering Pines Church and we are told that where one or two are gathered together in His house He will be there amongst us. We've got busy-bodies and news-toters and whoremongers and harlots among our midst and it seems like a whole lot of folks ain't giving God much thought."

"Abie, I don't quite understand you," Viola said. "You were just saying a little while ago that you didn't even trust God to look after Wilbert Lee, and you come right back and talk like this. Just where is your faith, Abie?"

"Folks just don't know the depth of my feelings," Abie replied. "My heart bleeds for lost souls and I want people to walk the straight-and-narrow path. But it seems like people don't understand me that way."

Viola thought to herself that of all people at Whispering Pines Church, no person needed to take a closer look at herself than Abie Turner. Why she was the news-totingest person in the neighborhood, the most gossipy, the first to suspect the worst in everybody else but never seeing the things she did that caused people to wonder about her. One of these days she was going to get Abie straight about her own self. But Abie would probably never speak to her again if she did that.

Wilbert Lee was following behind Abie and Viola, and Hobby was a few steps behind Wilbert Lee.

"Hurry on boys," Viola said. "It's time for us to git dinner on the stove. The people in the fields will be hongry in an hour or so."

"I'm just too shook-up to cook today," Abie said. "I'm going home and take me a nap after I wash this dirt and corn tassles off. Gant will just have to fend for hisself today."

"If I didn't have something on the table Craven Turnage would have a fit," Viola said. "And I wouldn't blame him. He works hard in them fields and he needs plenty of vittles to keep him going."

As they left the path and entered the graded road, several of Cora Finch's children were playing by the side of the road. One of the boys was chasing a butterfly and some of the girls had a tin can filled with water and broken pieces of glass and were making mud pies.

Tom, the oldest boy, asked Wilbert Lee and Hobby to play with them and Abie and Viola told them they could if they would keep their eyes on the lookout for any strange dog, and the women headed for the house.

"I heard a little bit of gossip yisdiddy," Abie said, unable to keep any kind of shady news to herself. Viola thought: Lord, what now?

"Speaking about Luby Sauls, and it's strange that I would see him the very next day after hearing the news, that he's had his eyes on a certain woman in the neighborhood. But I'm not going to say who, Viola. And I don't know how far it has gone, but I'm told that the woman has got eyes for him, too."

"Abie, if I were you I'd put that mess out of my mind right now. People in this neighborhood run their mouths all the time and half of what is said ain't worth repeating. Luby always seemed to be a good man to me, and Rhepsie certainly acts like she's happy."

"But where there's smoke there's usually fire, Viola. And that's not the worst I heard. I hate to even mention this, but there has been talk that preacher Otto has his eyes on the women, too."

"Hush your mouth Abie," Viola answered. "Don't you carry this one step further. Otto Pell is a fine man and has the respect of the entire community. Please let whatever it was you heard rest right here."

"I didn't want to believe what I heard," Abie said, "but I got to thinking that it just might be the truth. You know how sickly Vicey is and how Otto has to wait on her so much. And Otto Pell is a strapping, healthy man, and a handsome one if I must say so. He'll weigh 200 pounds at least and is as muscular as a boxer and is brimming with life. There ain't no way Vicey could satisfy his "man" needs."

"Abie, you talk about purity and chastity and say you think men's and women's relations outside of marriage are unforgivable sins, but it seems like you'd rather talk about them things than anything else. I declare I think sometimes somewhere down deep inside of yourself you want to be a philanderer too. I think talking against it is your way of trying to clear your own conscience."

"No, no, it's not like that at all Viola. I want our community to be perfect I reckon, and we're just like all the rest. I look for the good in people and it seems like there's just not much good there."

"You need to look at your own self, Abie," Viola said. But Abie didn't reply for they were now in front of Viola's house. The women parted and Viola wiped her face with her apron and shook her head for a long time. It had been quite a morning.

Chapter 4

Rev. Otto Pell shook hands firmly with Wilbur Stroud as the preacher entered the large, sprawling store filled with most any kind of goods anybody could want, from thread to farm implements, fat back, sausage, country hams, flour, molasses, coffee, sugar, vinegar and kerosene.

"How are you doing today Wilbur?" the preacher asked. "And Miss Callie?"

"Fine, fine preacher," Wilbur replied.

"Hot out today," Otto said as he wiped his brow.

"Here, have a seat preacher," Wilbur said as he pulled up a chair.

"How's everything going in the neighborhood?" Otto asked.

"As usual," Wilbur replied. "Our team beat Sandy Cross last night, and that's something to brag about." Wilbur sponsored a community baseball team and even bought uniforms for the boys.

"Good, good" Otto replied. "Sports are good for young men and boys to participate in. Keeps their minds and their time occupied and builds character as well."

"By the way, how is Vicey doing these days?" Wilbur asked.

"She's about the same," the preacher replied. "It seems like Vicey just can't get her strength and the doctors can't seem to find out why. She has been ailing for such a long time it's beginning to get discouraging."

"Sorry to hear that," Wilbur said as he went behind the counter to wait on John Blount, a member of the Board of Deacons at Whispering Pines Church.

"Haven't seen you in church recently Wilbur," John said as Wilbur weighed out nails. "We miss you at services Wilbur."

"I know," Wilbur said apologetically. "You know how we get careless sometimes and how easy it is to get out of the habit. You know, attending church is a habit, John. When you're attending regularly, you're really into the swing of it and look forward to church services. But just get weaned off and it's hard to get going again. But I've got to start back."

"Yeah," John said, adding that he noted that Callie was there almost every Sunday as well as prayer meeting on Wednesday night.

Hobby Turnage hobbled in as Wilbur finished waiting on the minister, wearing a big smile and holding a penny in his hand.

"I'll bet I know what Hobby wants," Wilbur said as he squatted down and patted the boy on his head.

"A penny won't buy nothing but a sucker Mr. Wilbur," Hobby laughed. "You know that."

"What color? Wilbur asked.

"Chocolate if you've got it," Hobby said.

"Tell you what," the storekeeper said. "I'll give you two suckers - one chocolate and one lemon."

"For a penny?" Hobby asked.

"Yep, just for you Hobby," Wilbur said.

"Thank you sir," Hobby said with a grin.

"You're welcome son," Wilbur said.

"Hello preacher," Hobby said as he turned toward the man of the cloth.

"Hello yourself," Otto said. "You're in fine fettle this morning."

"What's fettle?" Hobby asked.

"You know, in fine shape, bright-eyed and bushy-tailed and all that."

"Oh," Hobby replied.

Otto noticed the boy as he left the store and how deformed his leg was, and he was moved by the boy's spirit and friendliness and his upbeat attitude about life despite his condition. He thought it a pity that Hobby's attitude didn't extend to many of the people he ministered to. Whispering Pines was the only white church nearby and it served a pretty big rural area.

As he walked back toward the parsonage a mile or so up the road, Rev. Pell thought about the beauty around him; the rolling fields with crops shining and the blue skies overhead and the landscape and the people that made up the Bear Grass section of the county, and he was moved. He was not a native of the area, having grown up in the coastal section of the state where he still missed the seabreeze and the boating and fishing and the solitude he found in just standing and watching the mighty Atlantic for hours. But his eight years in the Bear Grass community had drawn him to the people and he felt a closeness toward them he had not felt toward any of the people he had known in other places he had pastored over the past twenty years.

For the most part, they were God-loving, dedicated people trying to live exemplary lives, striving to attain spiritual values that would transcend their hardships and crude lifestyles and give them a hope beyond the fields of eastern North Carolina. Yet they had an insight into life far beyond their educational levels.

He tried to reason within himself what man's soul longed for; what he hoped to gain by adhering to Christian principles; how they affected him in his everyday living and his actions. Was it something of deep faith in the heart of man or was it fear that if he succumbed to his own desires he would reap the results of sinful living?

Otto Pell knew the temptations of man as well as any other person. He often prayed to God to deliver him from sin and to keep his thoughts pure and his mind set on Godly things. But Otto Pell realized that he was as human as any other person and was subjected to the same temptations as all other people. He was a man with a man's perception of life. That was designed by nature from the chemicals that regulated his body and made him male as opposed to those chemicals that regulated the bodies of women and made them female with feminine traits, all designed by God. There was supposed to be a magnetism between the two that drew the two species together. And that magnetism was not reserved just for marriage. Those body chemicals could not distinguish between the sanctity of marriage and pure male lust that by nature was designed to conquer and fulfill the mission of the male. That was where man's spiritual values entered the picture and if he listened to the voice of his conscience, refrain from acts that made him an animal more than man.

During his sermons, Rev. Pell did his utmost to keep his thoughts on his text and never let them waver to the carnal instincts of man, but he was unable to keep his eyes off some of the women among the congregation. He caught himself feeling funny sensations in his groins sometimes, and he felt like a backslider when that happened. He attributed his feelings to the fact that Vicey was not able to be a wife to him in the physical sense. But he could not justify his feelings and told himself it was because he didn't have a close enough walk with God.

The preacher nodded and spoke to Abie Turner as he passed. "How are you this morning?" he asked as he stepped up to the porch and propped a foot on the doorstep.

"Fine preacher," Abie replied. She didn't really feel comfortable in the presence of Otto Pell. Something about him disturbed her. She couldn't help wanting to touch his red beard and feel his sinewy body and those thoughts were against everything she preached to everybody she talked to. But she had never known him to wink at her in church, if he really did such things.

"Coming to prayer meeting tonight?" he asked.

"I'm going to try to be there," Abie replied. "Since I sing in the choir I feel like I ought to be there for the song service if I can. But sometimes it's just not possible to attend."

"We need all the people we can get for Wednesday night services," the preacher said. "Seems like this time of the year it's hard to get a good crowd to attend. I reckon work in the fields keeps a lot of people away."

Otto noticed Wilbert Lee and Hobby playing under a tree in the yard. He said, "There are two fine boys, Abie. I know you're proud of Wilbert Lee and everybody just loves little Hobby. He's about the brightest thing around and is an inspiration to all of us."

"Yeah, they're fine boys," Abie replied, "and it's amazing how that Hobby gets about on that bad leg. And I want to say something to you I've been meaning to say for a long time but just didn't find the right time. And I ask God to forgive me if I'm wrong. But preacher I just can't feel the closeness to Hobby that I ought to because of what Perline did. I'm blaming Hobby when he didn't have a thing to do with any of it. The poor boy was the result of some man's lust and Perline's too. It's no different than seeing dogs doing the same thing when the old female is in season. There ain't anything else you can say about it preacher, and when a baby is the result all that can be said is that it is a bastard, and that name don't never wear off. Hobby will be called a bastard from the day he starts to school. And it affects me too. I just can't feel the same about babies conceived in wedlock as I do such babies as Hobby. And the Lord only knows who his daddy is. Perline shore hain't never said and there has been all kind of speculation about it and Perline may not know herself."

"May the Lord have mercy on you Abie," the minister replied when he got a chance. "Whatever his mother may have done or whatever the circumstances of his birth, little Hobby is as innocent of all that as your Wilbert Lee. He had no part in his creation and you shouldn't feel that way about it at all Abie. Besides, there is lust in the marriage bed, too. I don't know how you could deny that."

"I reckon I'm all mixed up preacher," Abie replied. "I knew I was wrong about Hobby, and I reckon in some ways I'm jealous of him. He gets more attention than even Wilbert Lee, and is just as handsome except for his leg."

"I'm going to pray for you sister," Otto said as he started to leave. "You need to pray about this too, and I mean hard."

"Thank you for your lecture," Abie said as the preacher was leaving. "I think that's what I have needed for a long time."

Chapter 5

Cora Finch had a hard time bending over the washtub to rub the clothes over the washboard. She was heavy with child. There were already four children - Tom, Billy Earl, Robyn and Arlene - and Cora and Tobey were looking forward to their next baby. They loved children.

Cora watched as the children ran over the premises. Tom was running a frysized chicken and the other chickens in the yard were darting about to get out of the way. A Junebug was singing in the oak tree that shaded the wash bench and Billy Earl was rolling a wheel and the girls were playing in their playhouse.

The house in which they lived was more a shanty than a house, with open places in the weatherboarding and cracks in the flooring that let cold air in in winter and provided peepholes for star-gazing at night. Some of the windows were covered with pasteboard and where there were small pieces of window lights broken out, rags were stuffed in the holes. There were only four rooms, including the kitchen. It was already crowded and as the family grew it would become more crowded.

Some of the sheets were ragged. The children wore ragged clothes during the week. The flour barrel was often empty. The summer vegetables were a life-saver for the Finches. Cora worked long hours when the fruits and vegetables were ready for canning, preparing and getting them in jars and processing them for winter use.

Times were hard and there was little hope of things getting better any time soon. But Cora was hardly aware of this. Things had always been tough for her and the other people she knew. Cora Finch viewed life with beauty and dignity, even under such circumstances.

And Tobey worked equally as hard in the fields as she did at the house.

He was a fine man and reasoned far beyond his time and his ability to comprehend all the factors that had contributed to their poor status in life. He too had been bred and born to the hard life.

The Finches were an inspiration to other people in the neighborhood. They observed life at the Finch household and there was always some activity going on. Cora was never caught resting or taking time to chat with the neighbors. She was liked but neighborhood women realized that her time was occupied and they respected that and didn't bother her from her work. Cora often wished she had the time to visit Viola Turnage. She considered Viola a fine person, but she shunned Abie Turner at every opportunity, even at church.

What was most-amazing to the neighbors was the drastic change in the appearance of the Finches on Sunday from the way they looked during the week. Come Sunday morning, the family walked to Whispering Pines Church looking spick and span. The little girls wore starched dresses and hair that had hung in shreds during the week was braided and tied with ribbons. The boys were in white shirts and ties and short pants in summer and knickers during the winter months.

Cora had a navy blue skirt and a tan one. Whenever she could accumulate a few pennies she would buy material and make blouses to go with them. She always looked nice on Sunday and the hair that had dangled about her face during the week was rolled Saturday night and done in a becoming style on Sunday. Cora Finch was a fine looking woman and took pride in herself. Although exposure to the sun had an adverse effect on her skin, she rubbed a little rouge on her face and brought out the color to her advantage. She even had a faint tint on her lips, and one Sunday she heard Abie Turner comment to the woman sitting beside her that Cora Finch was using make-up. Cora thought to herself that if Abie would do something to herself, including getting that ball of hair off the top of her head and shedding twenty-five or thirty pounds and get some of that belly off of her she would be doing herself a favor and everyone else around her as well. But that was only thinking, for Cora Finch didn't talk about people.

Cora was proud of Tobey when he donned his blue serge pants on Sunday morning and the white shirt she starched as stiff as a board every week and had ready for him with not a wrinkle anywhere. He had a blue polka-dotted bow tie and a navy blue necktie, and he reversed them every week. They'd forget which was worn the Sunday before sometimes and the children would get them straight as to which neckpiece to wear.

Cora was proud of her man when he paraded before the public on Sunday.

During the week he was often in bare feet with his overalls legs rolled up, wearing a straw hat to shade his face, often with a three-or-four-day growth of beard because he worked in the fields until sunset and came home and ate supper and washed off and soon went to bed to get his needed rest. At dinner time after he ate, he took a quilt for a pillow and lay on the front porch for a rest spell and the children climbed all over him and he seldom got the needed rest. But Tobey loved his children and was tender with them unless punishment was necessary. At those times he put his foot down and his children were obedient.

They were hard-working, proud people. They stood tall and never let adversity cause them to lose their positive attitude about life. Both had grown up in the Bear Grass community, although in a different area than where they were living. Tobey had rented the place from Wilbur Stroud the year he and Cora were married.

There was one advantage to tending Wilbur's land. He was a large landowner and with his store he could run the sharecroppers for a year until crops were housed. With money so scarce, it was easy to go to the store and get items when there was no cash on hand. People said Wilbur Stroud cheated his tenants, but Tobey had never taken any account of that. Some said if you went to the store and asked for a five-pound piece of white side the clerk would throw it on the scale and it was never cut. And the piece of meat always looked small for five pounds. Some said a pound of sugar would hit three-quarters of a pound on home scales. But Tobey gave the storekeeper the benefit of the doubt, for he doubted the accuracy of the home scales that were always rusty and had to be reset for every weighing.

Tobey was comfortable with Wilbur and the land he tended was rich except for one sandy area in one field. Not enough guano was put in the soil to grow the best crops possible, for it was expensive and there just wasn't the money available for heavy fertilization.

The soil was easy to tend, rich and loamy, and the fields were separated by ditches with about the same amount of land in each field.

It was a pretty area with a heavy growth of trees surrounding the fields and with a canopy of green in summer, shading to a rust and brown landscape in fall with the many species of trees in the background shading into any color you might wish to see, all forming a beautiful background to the serene setting.

There was a little creek nearby where he went on the rare occasions when he had a little time off, to catch bass and bream and catfish. It was where the neighborhood children went to bathe and swim in the warm waters of summer.

Wilbur must have had twenty-five or thirty tenants in all, sprawled along several roads in the Bear Grass community. Tobey knew most, but not all of them. The Negro families lived mostly on the road behind the store that led to Greene County. Wilbur said something about getting all the tenants together for a barbecue one Saturday, but it had never come off. Some folks said it was because the white folks didn't want to associate with the "Nigras" and the "Nigras" didn't want to associate with the whites. It may have been such conversations that caused the idea to be dropped. But many of them were at the store on Friday evening and Saturday to pick up supplies, and they conversed outside the store.

Blacks and whites worked side by side in the fields and children of both races often played together. But beyond that, there was no socializing. Whites attended white churches and coloreds attended colored churches. Some blacks in the community were of high standing with the white people and a sign of stature among blacks was to be called "Uncle" or "Aunt" for the aging blacks. Black men always removed their hats when they entered public places or white people's homes. There was little on the exterior to show any appreciable difference in the way whites and blacks lived. Everybody was poor and everybody carried his own load.

Chapter 6

The neighborhood children were playing down by the little creek that was their usual meeting place. Wilbert Lee Turner and Philip Stroud, as usual, were dominating the games and telling the others what they would play. Wilbert Lee told Tom and Billy Earl Finch to find the horseshoes and put some of the young'uns to pitching them. Philip told the girls to find something else to do; that some of the boys were going to play baseball and they didn't want girls messing up the game.

Robyn Finch stuck out her tongue at Philip and he started chasing her, finally catching up and pushing her head toward the ground.

"Stop that Phil, or I'll tell on you," Robyn said and Wilbert Lee said "shit" and Robyn put her hand to her mouth and swore she'd tell Miss Abie and Wilbert Lee said, "You just do, Miss Priss, and I'll whip your ass."

Tom, Robyn's brother, came up to Phil and Wilbert Lee and told them to lay off his sister, and they did, for Tom was larger than either Phil or Wilbert Lee.

Hobby Turnage came up to Wilbert Lee, looked up into his face and asked what he could do.

"It don't make no difference what you do, Hobby," Wilbert Lee answered. "You can't do much nohow, the shape you're in."

"Just show me," Hobby said, "and I'll do it. You can throw me in the creek if you want to. You can box with me if you want to. Come on and hit me Wilbert Lee. I can take it. Wrestle with me. Knock me down if you can and I'll just get up and jump on you again."

"Oh, go on Hobby," Wilbert Lee said.

All the children were growing. The year was 1929 and the older ones were ten and eleven years old. Wilbert Lee would be eleven in a month or two, and Phil was already eleven. Both boys were beginning to feel superior to the other neighborhood children.

Abie had continued to urge Wilbert Lee to pay more attention to the higher-up young'uns and not pay Hobby and the Finch's too much attention. And Wilbert Lee was beginning to be bored when all the young'uns congregated down at the creek. He had his mind on bigger things.

The boys began playing ball, and Roscoe Gooch came up to the field.

"What you doing here?" Philip asked.

"Just happened by," Roscoe said with a broad smile on his black face. He was thirteen and a big boy.

"The reason I asked why you are here is that you've not been before," Phil said, and Roscoe told him he liked to throw a ball and asked them to let him see that ball. Wilbert Lee tossed the string ball to Roscoe and he rubbed it in his hand for a minute. Then he said, "I can throw the shit out of that ole ball, boys." Wilbert Lee stepped off some distance and told Roscoe to throw it to him, and the black boy wound up and shot the ball by him so fast he didn't hardly see it.

"God!" You sure can throw that ball," Wilbert Lee said. "We'd love to have you on our team when we play the boys at Shine if we could. Course they wouldn't let us have a Nigra on the team."

"The color of the skin hain't got nothing to do with throwing a baseball," Roscoe said as he took in the crowd at a quick glance. "If'n we work together we ought to be able to play together, hadn't we?"

"Yeah," Phillip said, realizing that his father would have a fit if he heard him say that.

"Most Nigra boys wouldn't even come up and say anything about playing ball," Wilbert Lee said. "You're different, ain't you Roscoe?"

"Yeah, I'se different," Roscoe replied.

"You want to be a white boy don't you?" Phil asked.

"Naw, I don't want to be no white boy," Roscoe said. "I just want to be able to do like they do. I just want to be free to play my old guitar and roam about and do like I want to and have fun. I don't like workin' in them fields and Mr. Wilbur's already got me out there plowing whenever he sees me doing nothing and he says I'm going to git out and crap backer next year just like the grown men."

"We've already been doing that," Billy Earl said. "Me and Tom crapped backer this summer and hung it in the barn too."

Neither Wilbert Lee nor Phil had done any cropping tobacco during the summer. Abie had warned Gant that Wilbert Lee ought not to be sent out in them hot fields; that he hadn't been used to all that hard work and she'd just about die if anything happened to him in a backer field. She said it ought to be a sin to grow the mess anyhow and allowed that folks just worshipped it the way they catered to the weed during the summertime. Rather than listening to a constant cry from Abie, Gant had put Wilbert Lee at the looping shelter to hand the tobacco. And of course with Wilbur Stroud owning all the land around and running the store and Phil being his last-born, and the last young'un, he did pretty much as he pleased.

"How come your houses smell funny Roscoe?" Wilbert Lee asked.

"What you mean smell funny?" Roscoe replied.

"You know - that greasy smell when you pass the kitchen and a piss smell in the yard. What you all do, piss out the windows?"

"No more so than you do," Roscoe said. "White folkses houses smell funny too."

"And what makes you so rank smelling?" Phil asked. "You can raise your arms and it near bout knocks you down."

"Musk boy," Roscoe answered.

"And why does your hair feel like wire?" Wilbert Lee asked. The boys were giving Roscoe the third degree and all the other young'uns were listening with their mouths wide open. Roscoe didn't have an answer about the wiry hair.

"And why do Nigras call white folks "White soda crackers?" Hobby finally spoke up.

"Cause they call us niggers," Roscoe said. "We ain't no more niggers than you are white soda crackers. When you say "nigger" we knows you'se putting us down, so we come back with the soda cracker even if you don't give a damn about what we say."

"Where's your papa?" Wilbert Lee asked Roscoe.

"I hain't got no papa," Roscoe replied.

"Oh come on Roscoe, everybody's got a papa. Hain't you learnt nothing yet?"

"I knows what you'se talkin' bout," Roscoe said, "but I ain't the only one. Hobby ain't got no papa either."

Wilbert Lee then realized he had asked Roscoe the wrong question. But Hobby just grinned as he always did and smiled about the whole thing, making no comment.

Billy Earl said it was time for them to go home, and the others said they had to go too and Roscoe headed for the path that led to the road, swinging a stick at weeds beside the path and taking his time as he left.

"I like Roscoe," Wilbert Lee said as he and Phil were heading toward home.

"Me too," Phil replied. "But I know Pa will have something to say about us messing around with niggers when he gets the word. But there's something funny about Roscoe. He's different from the other niggers. He's not satisfied being with them. And if we could just have him as a pitcher we could beat the shit out of that crowd at Shine and Cross too."

"Yeah," Wilbert Lee replied, "but Ma will just about strip a gear when she hears I've been messing around with a Nigra. But I'm getting tired of Ma's messing. I've had just about enough of her. That woman torments me."

"Pa gives me a hard time too," Phil said. "Pa's good to me and lets me do what I want to, but he wants me to think bigger than I want to. He tells me who to look up to and who to shun and he's already talking about when I will be going to Hallsborough High School. He's got it all figured out for me to get in with the town doods and all that."

"Ma's got the same thing planned out for me," Wilbert Lee said.

On that day in the summer of 1929, children playing in rural areas as well as those across the nation could not know of the events that were soon to come that would trigger the Great Depression. It was on Oct. 29 that year that the Stock Market crashed that signaled the beginning of the Depression. Stock losses for the 1929-1931 period were estimated at fifty billion dollars.

But as the Depression set in, it had little effect on the rural population in eastern North Carolina as well as rural dwellers across the nation. There had been years of little prosperity and the farming class people were especially blessed, for most were able to have adequate food since most everybody had gardens and a hog or two to salt down. In that respect farmers fared better than their counterparts in the cities.

The boys chased butterflies on the road to home. It was peaceful along the country road and chickens were roaming in the fields and dogs were barking in people's yards. The sky was a deep blue with specks of white clouds occasionally casting a shadow over the area as they sped across the sun. A cow-bell tolled in the distance and a mule neighed and birds sang from the trees. Buzzards soared overhead and in the thickets some foliage had taken on a yellowish hue. It was the earliest sign of approaching autumn when children would return to school.

Chapter 7

Viola Turnage sat on her front porch with a newspaper to fan herself. The air was oppressive and she said she believed she could wring water out of it like wringing it out of a dishrag if she could capture it in her hands. Her grandson, Hobby, was out in the yard playing. She was thinking that it would soon be time to start to school again and she dreaded the thought of the boy having to walk a mile and a half each way morning and afternoon. It was bound to be torture for him with his twisted leg.

He was a fine boy and the best-natured young'un in the neighborhood. Good-looking too and was getting more handsome every day. His hair was turning rich blonde where it had been almost white when he was younger. His head was well-proportioned and his hair was manageable and his eyes seemed to get bluer every day.

She hadn't heard from Perline, Hobby's mother, in quite some time and it was getting time for a letter. Viola thought a lot about Perline, and although she and Craven had borne the brunt of neighborhood scorn because Perline had become pregnant and left the neighborhood to get away from all the criticism, Perline was still her daughter and she loved her. Such a pity, she thought, that a girl as beautiful as Perline got her life messed up at such an early age. Only seventeen when it happened, and she had been the belle of the community. Everybody had raved about her looks and she had held the world in the palm of her hand. Then to have such a thing happen. She hadn't believed it when she first began to notice Perline's stomach with a slight bulge. Her breasts had filled out more too.

There had been crying and praying and Craven cussing and you just knew that everybody in the neighborhood was talking behind your back, although they never got around to saying all the gossip and unkind things to your face. But they had talked it over and Perline decided to get out of the community and go up to Tennessee where she knew a girl that had worked with her in the mill in Hallsborough. She had offered to let Perline live with her until she could find work in the mill there and get her own place to stay.

Perline had gone through labor with Viola knowing nothing about it until the ordeal was over, and Perline had had a hard time and the baby had been breech. It was good Viola didn't know about her suffering until it was over.

Then the poor girl had dropped the baby and it had landed on a piece of iron bedstead lying on the floor, and the baby had cried for a while but appeared to be all right after that. Perline had wanted to take him to a doctor but there was not a penny of money with which to pay the bill, so she didn't bother with it. But within a week or two the baby was holding his leg in a peculiar position and Perline had been mortified. She had taken him to the local hospital as fast as she could get there and after the doctors examined him they told her his leg had been badly damaged and that it would require major surgery to straighten the leg but that she would have to wait until he was at least two years old to begin treatment. The baby was only a month old when the accident occurred.

But the lack of money prevents many noble deeds from being performed. Hobby crawled over the floor and laughed and played and didn't have a care in the world, and Perline felt better about his leg. And time slipped up on her. The boy was walking everywhere but he was having to accommodate his bad leg by bending the good leg in order to be able to walk. There was no money when he was two either.

Viola and Craven hadn't seen their daughter since she left, and had never even seen a picture of the baby, and Perline was able to save up enough money for bus fare the second year and she came home to see her parents and for them to see the baby. Both Viola and Craven fell in love with the boy at first sight and they were too glad to see Perline to scold her. It was a reunion of love and Perline was glad to be back home again.

Viola talked it over with Craven and they decided to ask Perline to let the baby stay with them. Perline had all she could manage just trying to make a living, and the boy needed special care and Viola knew she would be able to give him that care. And Perline agreed to let them keep Hobby, after a long crying spell. She had grown foolish about the boy and couldn't see herself living without him. But she couldn't see herself continuing on as she was either. So after a ten-day vacation ended she flagged the Trailways bus down right in front of the house and Craven and Viola saw her aboard as all of them wiped tears from their eyes; that is, all except Hobby. He was observing the bus and saying "choo choo" and pointing to the monster with its loud engine. Perline opened the window and waved until the bus rounded a curve and her parents and Hobby were out of sight. Viola had saved up five dollars from egg money and she had placed it in Perline's hand before she left.

"Don't do that Mama," Perline had said. "It's just as tough with you all as it is with me. You need the money and I'll be all right." But Viola had insisted that Perline keep the money.

That began a new life for Viola and Craven. It had been many years since a child had been in the house and it was all new to them. But Hobby was never a burden. He was the joy of their life and although they fretted over his poor lame leg, they let him live a normal life and the fresh air and sunshine and open country made the boy happy and carefree. He was bright and inquisitive and made friends with all the people in the neighborhood.

The years had passed swiftly and now Hobby was getting to be a big boy. It was time to start thinking about his future, although there was no way of planning for it, for times were hard and money was non-existent and farmers reaped little for their labors except for subsisting by cutting corners and doing without most material things.

Perline had said something to Craven about thinking about leaving the farm and going out to Tennessee and trying it out there. That way they would all be together and Craven would stand as good a chance at finding something to do there as in Bear Grass. He wasn't getting anywhere farming anyway, what with tobacco selling for eight and nine cents a pound and cotton no better. Giving half to Wilbur and paying up at the store left him owing Wilbur every year.

Craven said he had already been thinking about leaving the farm, but didn't know anything else to try. He liked to tinker with machinery and tools and was a jack-of-all-trades and Perline had said if he could just get his foot inside one of those mill doors and get a look at the things that had to be constantly fixed or repaired, he'd be able to fix them in no time. And Craven had said yeah, that might be true, but gitting a foot in the door would be the main thing, that people everywhere were out of work and labor was the cheapest thing there was. And if they didn't have a garden to tend and they got off somewhere like that they might end up near 'bout starving to death. Perline reminded him that just about everybody in the mill community had gardens too.

But that's as far as it went.

Chapter 8

Wilbert Lee and Hobby were fishing on the edge of a pond that had been the site of a mill in former days. It was a fall day in 1930 and the colorful foliage reflected in the waters that caught the afternoon sunshine and sparkled and gave the feeling of a magical setting. The autumn breeze was cool and the sound of shotguns in the distance gave evidence of men hunting for doves. Some of the somber-colored foliage had fallen from the trees, leaving limbs already bare and stretching toward skies that had turned a deep blue.

It was at such times that Wilbert Lee was willing to be Hobby's friend, for they were away from prying eyes and Wilbert Lee didn't have to feel a challenge to his superiority. Hobby loved to fish and he was busy concentrating on his pole and awaiting a tug on the line. And Wilbert Lee, despite his feeling about Hobby, had a guilty conscience for some of the things he had done to him over the years. Only last weekend he had asked Wilbert Lee if he could go with him to town, and Wilbert Lee had told him he already had everything planned and that he would be with some other boys and Hobby would feel out of place with them. He just didn't want to be seen in town with Hobby.

And Hobby had asked to attend a party with Wilbert Lee earlier, but excuses were made, as they always were, and Hobby never got to go with Wilbert Lee any place where there were people. Hobby pestered him at school, and there was no getting around that, but that was as far as any public closeness went between them.

Wilbert Lee could almost see hero-worship in Hobby's eyes whenever they were together, and as much as Wilbert Lee appreciated admiration from other people, he thought of Hobby's outlook in an entirely different light. But there was one saving grace, despite Wilbert Lee's rejection of Hobby. It didn't dampen Hobby's feelings for Wilbert Lee.

Hobby looked toward Wilbert Lee since he was getting no strikes on his hook. "What you thinking about?" he asked.

"Oh, nothing," Wilbert Lee replied.

"I was," Hobby said. "Grandpa and Grandma have been talking about moving away and going out to Tennessee and giving up farming. And I don't feel like I can stand to leave, Wilbert Lee. I love this place and nowhere else on earth could ever make me as happy as living in Bear Grass. I love all the children I've played with, and especially you, Wilbert Lee. I know I've pestered you and aggravated you a lot of times and wanted to do things that I couldn't do because of this bum leg, but I've really meant it when I've wanted to be with you and do all the things you've done. I couldn't run; couldn't play baseball; couldn't jump from the banks into the water; couldn't stand up and fight like you and some of the other boys have done. But you know I've jumped in whenever any of my friends were being beaten and done all I could. We have had so much fun, Wilbert Lee. And I just can't stand to give it up. I'm twelve and you are thirteen, and it will soon be time for high school. We will soon be grown up and that is when we could do so many things. I'll have to adjust to people I never saw in a place I know nothing about, and I'm so unhappy I could cry." He took his arm and held it up and rubbed his eyes on his shirt sleeve.

"I can't imagine you leaving Bear Grass," Wilbert Lee said. "You've been here as long as I can remember." But Wilbert Lee was thinking that this would be the best thing that ever happened to him (Wilbert Lee) for as they grew older, the problem would become more sticky with Hobby around.

Wilbert Lee was thinking that his mother would be ecstatic when he told her Hobby wouldn't be around to pester them any longer. But he didn't say anything like that to Hobby.

They gave up on fishing and started back on the road toward home. Hobby mentioned how pretty the trees were around them and Wilbert Lee said the colors would be even prettier in Tennessee where there were a lot of mountains and Hobby said he didn't want to see the pretty colors in Tennessee; that he wanted to see them in Bear Grass.

As they approached the Tobey Finch house, they saw two of the girls playing in their playhouse under a big oak tree near the road. They had the house roped off and divided into rooms, with fish boxes draped with cloths to represent beds and bottles and jars in the kitchen and blooming goldenrods as the centerpiece. Robyn and Arlene were busy working in their make-believe home, and Wilbert Lee got the urge to upset their little domain. As they approached the girls, Wilbert Lee bent and pulled up one of the stobs supporting the tobacco twine that formed the outline of the playhouse, and the rooms were no longer separate.

"Don't do that Wilbert Lee," Arlene cried. But Wilbert Lee was determined to completely upset their housekeeping. Robyn was sitting on one of the fish-box beds, cradling a rag doll in her arms, and Wilbert Lee side-swiped her and she fell off the box and landed on the ground. He looked around and saw her with her skirt almost up to her face, and he saw two or three drops of blood on her underwear, and was shocked. He thought: God, they sure grow up early, don't they. Robyn wasn't twelve years old yet. And Wilbert Lee was thirteen and was just beginning to get a growth of hair in his groins.

As he observed Robyn in such a position, he looked into her eyes and suddenly realized that he'd never seen eyes like that on any person. He couldn't explain it. In some respects they looked like some animal's eyes he had seen. They were dark, maybe a violet color with gray specks and they seemed to be impenetrable. Strange that he had never noticed her eyes before.

Robyn was crying silently. She just looked up at Wilbert Lee and said, "Why did you do that, Wilbert Lee? We weren't bothering you."

Wilbert Lee didn't even bother to reply. Hobby had not stopped at the playhouse, so he didn't know what had gone on. Wilbert Lee walked casually past the Finch house on his way home. He noticed Roscoe up the road a piece and as they met he stopped to talk with the Negro.

"How you doing Roscoe?"

"I'se all right. I saw what you done back there and I laughed my head off when you tore down that playhouse. Tickled the piss out of me. You my kind of boy, Wilbert Lee."

"What you mean your kind of boy?" Wilbert Lee asked.

"You know, into mischief and stuff. You acting old for your age, Wilbert Lee. I bet you can even come."

"Yeah," Wilbert Lee said.

"You jiving me, white boy," Roscoe said. "You ain't old enough to come, boy. You'se just thirteen, ain't you?"

"Yeah."

"Hell, I'm fifteen, Roscoe said. "You had any Wilbert Lee?"

"Yeah."

"You lying like a dog Wilbert Lee. You don't know nothing 'bout no piece. You want some black nooky, Wilbert Lee?"

Wilbert Lee blushed a deep red. "Naw, I don't want to mess with no black girl Roscoe. Why you asking such a thing? You want to mess with a white girl?"

"Uh uh," Roscoe replied, although the way he said it didn't convince Wilbert Lee. "If you do, you'd better get that out of your mind, Roscoe. White folks wouldn't tolerate that and you know it."

"You got me wrong Wilbert Lee," Roscoe said. "I was just thinking about you and how grown-up you are and all that. I just thought you could git broke in with one of them sweet little colored things. Pig meat. All it would cost you would be a ten-cent box of snuff Wilbert Lee. I didn't mean nothing 'bout me messing around with no white girl. The black girls' goin' to mess around wid somebody, whether black or white. It's just nature wid us, Wilbert Lee."

"I got to get home," Wilbert Lee said, anxious to change the subject. His manhood was being challenged by a nigger. "See you around Roscoe."

"Yeah," Roscoe replied as he turned with his stick and meandered on up the road, hitting at blooming goldenrod along the way.

And Wilbert Lee was thinking that he had to be initiated into manhood. He had to know what it meant for boy and girl to mate. Sex consumed his thoughts much of the time, and from everything he had observed from nature, it was a pleasant experience.

Chapter 9

Lester Finch, Tobey's uncle, was a landowner down in Jones County. He had a hundred-acre farm and had managed a little better than many people since the Depression had set it. Fortunately, he didn't have his fairly meager savings in a bank when they closed. Instead, Lester chose a few spots on his property to bury his money. And he had detailed, written instructions as to where every cent was and how to locate the burial sites. Lester was going on seventy-five years old and had become feeble. His wife had died several years earlier and they had remained childless throughout their marriage. His closest kin was his nephew, Tobey Finch.

Lester felt no real closeness to Tobey, since they hadn't visited each other for years; not since Tobey's father had died when Tobey was just a teen-ager.

Lester had a good, solid house and a fairly solid tenant house also. His home was dated with furniture he had owned since he and Hettie were married. Beds with high headboards and curlicues at the top; a heavy wardrobe; an old hall rack; a wood-burning kitchen stove with a reservoir for heating water; a homemade dining room table with benches on each side; two old safes and such items.

There was a big orchard and several large grapevines and four tobacco barns along the path leading into the fields. He kept a few hives of bees. There were several outbuildings that housed mules, cows, sheep and even a couple of goats. There were turkeys and chickens and geese and ducks that roamed over the premises and wildlife habitated the pond at the back of the farm. Lester's surroundings were peaceful and tranquil. He would often sit under the shade of a large willow tree in his yard and observe his domain. But there were thoughts of having to give it all up too. Lester knew that he would no longer be able to look after the farm and his animals as he had done in the past. He had depended on Les Best who had lived in the tenant house for fifteen years and tended his land. But Les had decided to give up farming and try something new. Like all sharecroppers, he was working from year to year and getting nothing from his labors except food and shelter. This upset Lester and set him to thinking. He wondered about Tobey and what had happened to him. The last he had heard Tobey was living in the Bear Grass community in Waynesborough County. He'd have to see about getting up to see if he could locate Tobey. He just might persuade him to come down to Jones County and tend his farm for him. At least there was some blood kin there and if Tobey had turned out all right he'd have to trust him with his business, and it might help Tobey out too. If Tobey was like most all other farmers he needed all the help he could get.

Lester's eyes were failing, and he was almost afraid to tackle the roads. But there was no one else to call on. His model T Ford was in good shape for he had driven it very little, and he decided to risk the trip. He'd just take his time and if he had to spend the night he might be able to stay at Tobey's or get a room for fifty cents in a Hallsborough rooming house.

He made his way safely to Hallsborough and stopped at filling stations and asked how to get out to the Bear Grass community and didn't encounter great difficulty in finding where Tobey Finch lived. He asked several people going down the road if they knew Tobey Finch. He'd hold a hand cupped around his left ear as he waited for an answer, for he was getting hard of hearing.

Lester finally rolled into the Tobey Finch yard about dinner time where there were several children playing. They ran for the porch as Lester turned into the yard. They weren't used to having company driving cars.

Cora came to the door and Lester said, "Ma'am, I'm looking for some of my kin, Tobey Finch. I was told he lives here. That right?"

"Uncle Lester," Cora said as she placed her arm around his neck. "I've heard Tobey speak about you many times. It's so nice to meet you. And you're just in time for dinner if you can put up with our fare. Tobey will be home in a little while. He's working down in the mash."

Lester was thinking that here was a smart woman. One that acted nice. One that acted like she held her head high and looked good too, considering that she was in everyday clothes and cooking for a family.

"How many children do you have?" Lester asked.

"Four," Cora answered. "Quite a bunch of children to look after. But we get along fine."

"Yeah, it looks like you do," Lester replied.

"How's your wife?" Cora said as she hastened to get the biscuits in the oven.

"What did you say about life?" Lester said as he cupped his hand around his ear.

"Your wife," Cora said in a louder tone.

"Passed on," Lester said. "Two years ago. Been mighty lonesome since. Course I've done all right and got no complaints."

Tobey had driven up in the wagon by then and the small children who were not in school ran out to tell him about their company. Tobey ran to the house and grasped Uncle Lester's hand firmly. "My, my, it's good to see you Uncle Lester. Why I've not seen you since I was a boy. How have you been and what on earth brings you to Bear Grass? How did you know where to look for me?"

"I knowed your daddy settled in the Bear Grass area and I figgered you'd still be around after growing up around here. And you need to speak up to me Tobey. I can't hear good no more."

"I can't believe it," Tobey said. "I hadn't heard from you in so long I didn't even know if you were still living. You settled down in Jones County, didn't you."

"Yeah," Lester replied. "Got a pretty good old place down there too. Land is sort of poor but I've had pretty good crops. Course things git tighter and tighter with this what they call "Depression" on. Been depressed for me a long time before they declared it a depression though."

"You didn't go and lose all your money in the banks when they closed did you Uncle Lester?" Tobey asked.

"Not on your sweet life," Lester said. "I hain't got much money nohow, but I shore God didn't have it stuck in no bank. No sir ree. I didn't lose nary penny in them banks."

"And I might as well tell you right off what I'm doing here." He said this as Cora put the food on the table and took the steaming biscuits from the oven.

"Come on, dinner's ready," she said and told Uncle Lester there was a basin and water on the porch and a towel to wipe in. Lester and Tobey went out to the porch together and Lester washed his hands and tossed the water in the yard and Tobey did the same thing.

Tobey blessed the food and it was passed and Lester took a hot buttermilk biscuit and bit into it instantly. "Don't git nothing like this since the Missus left me," he said. Then they were silent for a little while while savoring the food.

"Now, what I come for Tobey is to talk to you about going down and tending my farm for me. I can't look after it no more Tobey. And the man that's been tending it is quitting farming. It has really put me in a bind and I don't feel like I could move away and leave it in somebody else's hands. I thought and thought and finally came up with you."

"What size farm have you got, Uncle Lester?"

"A hundred acres of cleared land and fifty acres in timber. Not a bad farm either, Tobey. I'd love for you and the Missus to go down and take a look at it and see what you think. And you'd fare better than just being a sharecropper. 'Specially since you're my nephew. You look like a fine, solid man and better looking than your Pa or me were at your age I must say. I believe I could trust you with running things Tobey. Course, I don't know what kind of roots you've got here and maybe you don't want to leave. Anyhow, if you can, you and your wife - what's her name? can go back with me and look things over and I'll pay your bus fare back to Hallsborough. And what I've got would be yours at my death."

"Well, I don't know about going, Cora said. "We've never left the children alone overnight. But the older children are large enough to trust with the younger ones. What do you think Tobey?"

"I don't know what to say either," Tobey said. "This has dropped on us like a bomb out of a clear blue sky. And it gives us something to think about too. I tell you, we ain't even paying out the way things are now and there's not a chance of getting ahead. I'd sure like for us to better ourselves if we could. I think we ought to go down and take a look Cora."

"Tom and Billy Earl can look after things and we'll be back tomorrow. We'll get ready and go on back with Uncle Lester if you want to," Cora said. "But I don't want the young'uns to mention a word about where we are or that we've even gone anywhere. Nobody needs to know our business, and if Abie Turner found out we had gone off and left our children overnight she would broadcast it up and down Beston Road."

Uncle Lester got to meet the children when they returned from school and he was pleased with them. They seemed to be mannerly and well-behaved. He was hoping Tobey and Cora would decide to go and farm on his place in Jones County.

It was a treat for Tobey and Cora to get out of Bear Grass and the community for a change. They seldom got farther away than Hallsborough.

Tobey drove. As they traveled down the highway the slant of the afternoon sun cast a golden glow over the countryside. There was the painted background with the trees on the horizon shouting for recognition. The cirrus clouds floating across the heavens posed no threat of rain. There were fields of hay stacked uniformly with the ground appearing clean-swept from the mowing machines. Corn stalks were a golden brown; lifeless after their mission was completed with abundant grain showing on the stalks. Cotton patches were white and people were busy in the fields. Children played in yards and cows and mules still grazed in pastures along the highway. The skies were deep blue and the setting was peaceful, despite the stagnant economy and the poor plight of farmers.

Soon it would be the Thanksgiving season, and pumpkins added to the beauty of the landscape. They were massed in some yards while a single pumpkin would adorn the front porch at some homes. There would be an occasional display of pumpkins on bales of hay and around them, or shocks of corn tied together so they stood with the pumpkins arranged around them.

The three travelers took in the scene and there was something stabilizing in what they saw. Somehow, they felt things would work out all right.

Chapter 10

Rev. Otto Pell conducted a revival at Shady Run Free Will Baptist Church in Lenoir County. It was customary for churches to invite pastors from other churches to conduct revivals. Church officials felt ministers from other churches could have a greater impact on congregations than the local preacher.

Otto didn't have any problem in leaving his wife. Vicey's mother lived with them and looked after Vicey, who was in bed more than out. Vicey seemed to be in a stage where she didn't improve, nor did she go downhill. She was listless and short of breath and just sitting up was a problem for her. And Otto sympathized with her, but her condition had become something to be tolerated without causing undue worry.

Shady Run was in a grove of trees on a graded road some four miles from the county seat and in a community typical of Bear Grass. Otto had been told the people there were anxious for the Word and that he could expect many converts during the revival. The preacher had looked forward to the revival.

The church was overflowing on Sunday night as the revival began.

Looking out over the congregation, Otto saw a representative group of rural people and as always, he paid special attention to the women. Some of them were attractive.

Members of the church took care of visiting evangelists and invited them into their homes, provided sleeping quarters and did their washing and accommodated them as best they could. The minister would usually spend one night with a church member.

The singing was good, with old-fashioned hymns featured with some good bass, alto and tenor among the choir members. Otto preached a rousing sermon Sunday night and people flocked to the altar. Seven were converted that night. People praised the Lord and there was some shouting and speaking in tongues. Otto was ecstatic with the reception.

The first night was spent with an elderly couple, Joe and Hattie Pace. They were dyed-in-the-wool Baptists and their lives dedicated to God. Otto and Joe had a long conversation at breakfast Monday morning and later on the front porch.

On Monday night Otto preached what he called his "stepping-on-toes" sermon. He told about all the sins people committed and still called themselves Christians. He touted hell-and-brimstone before them and exhorted them to come to the Lord before it was too late.

When the offering plate was passed, poor people who had little to give, did the best they could, and there was a sizable offering. Preachers were not paid specific amounts for their services. Their pay was determined by free will offerings.

There were ten converts on Monday night and the congregation realized that there would be a big baptizing after the revival closed. People loved to attend baptizings.

Monday night was spent with a younger couple, Max and Mildred Scott. They were not as religion-oriented as the Paces, although they attempted to be good Christians. Otto enjoyed his stay with them.

There was special singing Tuesday night and the congregation got into the spirit of the revival with several renditions by a local quartet. Hands were clapping and amens were heard throughout the church. And despite the cool weather, Otto became saturated with sweat during his sermons as he emphasized his words with movement of his hands and body. He even pounded the Bible on the lectern and told about hell and damnation and the pit where the fire was not quenched and the worm didn't die.

His invitation to altar service brought hordes down the aisles, some crying and wringing their hands in supplication. Church members gathered around those seeking God and prayed aloud. The offering was good again. The night was spent with a brother and sister who had never married but had kept the house they grew up in and had been pillars of the church for many years.

On Wednesday night before services began, a woman came up to Rev. Otto and introduced herself as Maybell Aswell, a member of the church. She said she was a widow woman with a grown son living with her, and she would like for him to spend the night with them.

A broad smile came over Rev. Otto's face for here was a very attractive woman, no older than her late thirties at the most, voluptuous and radiant. Something sounded a warning bell, but the sound was distorted by the woman's mere presence. He knew he should decline, but realized at the same time that he could not as a man, decline such an invitation.

"Why, I'll be happy to visit with you Sister Aswell," Otto said as he shook her hand vigorously, at the same time feeling an electrical current between them. He lost sight of God for a moment and allowed the flesh to dominate his thoughts.

Otto asked the minister of the church, Rev. Donald King, to deliver the sermon that night; that he wasn't feeling quite up to par and was drained out from the three previous nights.

Otto was nervous as he accompanied Maybell Aswell home. She smiled and talked as they drove to her house and told him he needn't call her Sister Maybell; that Maybell was fine, although in deference to his title she would call him Reverend Otto rather than Reverend Pell.

The minister's thoughts were in turmoil after they reached the house where Maybell fixed a glass of tea for both of them and brought out cake she had baked that day. She crossed her legs (and they were shapely) and Otto's hands shook as he took the tea and cake. He noticed her mouth and there was a sensuousness there that was unmistakable. In her he saw adult womanhood at its height. He learned that her husband had been dead for fourteen months and he saw desire in her eyes and he knew she was able to observe the same thing in his.

They retired some after 11 o'clock and Otto immediately began praying. He had never before felt such remorse as he felt at this moment. His mission was to lead people to God. His thoughts were supposed to be above the average man's. He, like all men, was tempted by the devil. But everything in Biblical teaching indicated that the men of God who were Christ's leaders among the people were supposed to be able to put carnal thoughts behind them and concentrate on the Word of God for sustenance. Everything about this visit was wrong. Yet he felt helpless to intervene. It seemed to be inevitable from the beginning of time. His pillow was washed with tears and he felt that his prayer was bouncing off the ceiling and hitting him in the face.

An unknown magnetism was drawing them together. He could feel it, even before the bedroom door opened without making any sound, and she stood beside his bed.

"You think I'm terrible, don't you? she asked.

"I think you're beautiful," he replied. "You're one of the prettiest women I've ever seen and your womanhood enthralls me. I am consumed by your magnetism. I feel like a real man more than I have in many years."

"Why?" she asked softly, careful not to awaken her son.

"You see, I have a sick wife," Otto explained. "In fact, she is in bed all the time. She has been sick for years, so that should explain why I have felt like less than a man for a long time."

"I see," she said, "and I'm sorry. I didn't know your wife was sick. Do you have any children?"

"No, there were eight born to us, but they all died as infants. Bad blood between the two of us I suppose. They were all jaundiced at birth and the doctors said they couldn't do anything to get the bad blood out."

"Poor man," Maybell said. "You've had a big burden on your shoulders. More than I've carried. But I've suffered too, Rev. Otto."

"In what way?" Otto asked.

"In the physical sense," Maybell said. "And that's ridiculous I know. I have not had a burden of the kind you have carried. And I know all of us are made differently, but I always enjoyed sex Reverend Otto and it makes me blush to say this, but I'm only stating the truth. I need a man in my life and being denied that since my husband died instantly has had a profound effect on me. And I don't want you to feel that I'm just a cheap woman. My morals are high and I believe in clean living, and I've had all manner of chances to go out with men, but you know how most of them are."

"I understand your position," Otto said. "I fit into the same category."

"I have prayed about it over and over," Maybell said, " and my prayers get nowhere. And the moment I saw you I knew that there was a magnetism between us and it sounds cheap, even to me. But as God is my witness, I am not able to control it. Please don't think of me as being cheap, Reverend Otto."

"How can I think of you as being cheap when I have the same feelings?" Otto asked. "I am a man of the cloth Maybell, and I should be able to withstand such temptations better than you. I preach repentance and morality and walking with God, yet I find myself in the same position as the worldly person whose thoughts are on carnal things and are not expected to think in terms of the Christian."

A pale moon cast a faint shadow inside the room and Otto could see Maybell as she stood beside the bed. She couldn't resist the temptation to lay a hand on his arm. Just the touch of her hand sent spasms of passion coursing through his body, and she felt the hard muscle in his arm and placed her hand on his chest where his pajama neck was open and felt the heavy mass of hair. Otto only realized at that moment that he wasn't wearing anything but the pajama top. It was warm in the room and he slept in the nude in warm weather and considered pajamas a necessary evil. He felt Maybell's hand sliding slowly down to his pubic region and his stomach stiffened. He suddenly turned on his side away from her and groaned.

"Please don't," he begged. "I can't stand it Maybell and this is nothing less than lust. We hardly know each other and we just want to satisfy our lust without thinking about the repercussions. I want to love the woman I make love to in a spiritual sense as well as the physical. And I know that I could love you in every way that a man is supposed to love a woman. But we need time Maybell."

"I understand," Maybell replied. "I'm sorry Otto. I got carried away and I wouldn't offend you for anything in the world. Please try to think of this as something that you dreamed. I won't bother you again."

"You're so sweet, Maybell," Otto said as he turned back toward her, "but I do want to kiss you goodnight."

She bent over and placed her lips on his mouth and his lips became hungry and he placed his tongue in her mouth and there was a moment of bliss with nothing more going on than kissing.

"Good night Reverend Otto," she said as she rose and stood erect. "And sweet dreams."

Otto lay in quietness after she left the room, his thoughts in turmoil. He felt his heart palpitating. Sweat broke out all over his body. Guilt weighed heavily on his conscience. He thought of poor Vicey back home. But none of that quieted the deep passion consuming him. Sleep didn't come. He heard roosters crowing in the neighborhood before dawn appeared. He sat up on the bed and observed a beautiful fall morning come alive. He watched the sun as it made its appearance over the horizon, sending its rays into the room.

Otto dressed and went to the living room and sat quietly on the couch, dreading to face Maybell in the light of day. He had escaped this time, realizing that it was only postponing the inevitable. They would come together in an unholy union. The only puzzle was when.

Maybell was pleasant and radiant at breakfast, showing no signs of the brief moment of closeness so soon past.

That night Rev. Otto Pell took as his subject "The Pitfalls of Mankind." He was a different evangelist that night. There was none of the vim and vigor of his other performances. He called to the attention of the worshippers a quote in scripture which he didn't even both to identify: "There is a way that seemeth right unto man, but the end thereof is death." He pointed out that man can justify his actions by believing that what he does is right and proper. He can ignore the written laws from the Bible and really believe that what he does is right, even in the sight of God.

The minister always placed a handkerchief on the lectern and a glass of water was provided. He took a sip of water and wiped his eyes with the handkerchief. He sobbed as he told of man's transgressions, and no one in the audience knew he was relating more to himself than the congregation except Maybell Ashley.

Rev. Pell spent that night with a bachelor, Henry Butler, who was a dedicated Christian and a big supporter of the church. Otto observed this man who appeared to be without temptations that most men encounter and wondered whether his nature was that of a typical man. He wanted to broach the subject, but realized this would be improper.

Rev. Pell was in a daze the last two nights of the revival. He questioned his own sense of values and determined that he was not a Christian at heart. He had been too easily tempted. It had come about so suddenly he was unable to comprehend its meaning. But he realized his vulnerability more than at any time since he had dedicated his life to preaching the word of God. Certainly he realized that his spiritual values often left him with a guilty conscience where women were concerned. But he hadn't realized how easily he could be moved to violate his Christian beliefs because of lust of the flesh.

He could not blame Maybell Ashley. Many would point a finger at her if it were known just what had transpired and refer to her as a "Jezebel" seeking to tempt men with her wiles. She would be categorized as no more than a streetwalker with a mission of ruining men's lives, breaking up homes and manipulating them with their bodies. But Otto didn't think of it in those terms at all. He was the guilty party for allowing his emotions to overcome him.

Rev. Otto decided to forgo baptismal service on Sunday, telling the pastor of his need to return home to see about his wife. But he had to speak to Maybell before he left. So after the service ended he went up to her as she stood apart from the group talking out in the yard. That should arouse no suspicion since it was known he had spent the night with her and her son.

"I'll be going home in the morning," he said.

"I thought you might be," she replied.

"I need to know how to contact you," he said. She found a piece of paper and a pencil in her purse and scribbled her name and address and handed it to him. He also wrote the address of Whispering Pines Church and told her to write to him there.

"Maybe we should just let it end here," she said.

"It is what we should do," he admitted, "but I can't do that. Can You?"

"No," she replied. "I feel so guilty Reverend Otto. But I've thought about it and it was something beyond my control. I can't explain it, even to myself and I've never done such a thing in my life before."

"Goodbye for now," he said and as he looked into her eyes he saw a tear run down her face."

"Goodbye," she replied. As they stood without speaking she wondered how this could have happened in the course of one day. He was asking himself the same question.

"We will meet again," he said, and she just nodded her head.

Otto caught the 9:30 a.m. Seashore Transportation bus on Sunday morning for Hallsborough. It was a pleasant morning, neither hot not cold. The landscape was still beautiful and he saw people walking to church and others driving their cars and parking them under the trees in the various churches that dotted the countryside. But inside, Otto Pell was troubled. He knew that he would eventually disgrace himself and the church he had pastored for eight years. He would bear the brunt of criticism from those who had placed their trust in him and his life would take a one hundred-eighty degree turn - for the worse.

Chapter 11

Perline Turnage was at her wits' end. After working ten years in a cotton mill in the little town of Clyburn in the Tennessee hills, she was no closer to reaching her goal than she had been the day she began work. It had been a struggle every step of the way and trying to save money was a far-fetched dream.

She had spent her days within the confines of a cotton mill where dust accumulated, clinging to windows and finding its way to the ceiling where it formed into little strings of lint. She feared it would injure her health, and like other employees, wore a mask on the job.

There were endless hours standing at a spinning wheel and working the spindles. It was a mechanical process and required no real knowledge except to understand the process of spinning thread into cotton fabrics. There was no challenge to the mind; no way of improving intellectually.

Dressed in coveralls with her hair hidden behind a bandana, she was indistinguishable from hundreds of other workers. She entered the plant at 3:15 p.m., punched the time clock at 3:27, and was on the job from 3:30 till midnight, with half an hour break for supper.

Lint accumulated on her eyebrows and the blue coveralls she wore. At break time she went to the dining area, opened her brown bag containing a sandwich and fruit, and drank coffee from a large urn furnished by the mill at five cents a cup.

She sat with other girls in her section, as well as men who worked on the machinery. They might have been convicts as far as appearances went. They were all look-alikes, men and women, dressed in the coveralls.

Perline had a few good friends at the mill, but for the most part, she found their conversations boring. Few thought beyond the life of a mill-worker and their conversations were about their men or their children. Some dipped snuff. Many smoked. Alot of them drank. Most of them lived in the mill village, which actually made up the town. Everything was company-owned and workers paid their rent to company officials at the first of every month.

Whatever feminine traits the women were endowed with, they were hidden behind the garb they wore in the mill. There were no second looks at the women.

There were times when Perline and some of her girl friends went to the movies on Saturday night and over to Sutton's, the town's only decent restaurant, for a meal and other workers in the mill didn't even recognize them. They would have makeup on with their hair washed and curled, showing full figures and shapely legs, and men would swarm around them. But Perline wasn't interested in the men. Her thoughts were on Hobby. Always Hobby. He had to have surgery and it was already long past due. Whenever she thought about pretty clothes or vacations or better living quarters, she had to put them out of her mind. Hobby came first. He was the great love of her life and she accepted the responsibility without any ill feelings toward her son. Rather, it was constant guilt. It had lived with her since the day she dropped the tiny baby. It would not go away. It consumed her. She never excused herself for her mistake because of her age. She had not been shielded from life. She knew responsibility as a sharecropper's daughter. She had helped with all the farm chores in Bear Grass. Her mother had taught her well.

Perline had been reading the ads in the local newspapers, hoping to find work that would offer promise of something better. She realized the odds were against her.

That night after taking her bath she took a good look at herself. Twenty-eight years old. She had noticed a thin line in her face and checked it out carefully in the mirror. She undid her hair and it dropped into waves to her shoulders. She scrutinized her face and was satisfied with what she saw. There were dimples in her cheeks. The skin was still soft to the touch and showed a pink tint, although she was exposed to very little sun. Her teeth were white and even, and her eyes were large and sky-blue. Her mouth was shapely and her neck thin, with no veins showing. She wore a cup B bra and there was cleavage and her waist was small - 24 inches. Her hips were small and her calves shapely, particularly when she wore high heels.

"I can do better than this," she told herself during the examination. "I must beat the odds. I must find other work and get out of the mill before it's too late. I must find a better way to help Hobby and my parents. I can't do it in a cotton mill."

Then she realized that she didn't really have a wardrobe, and clothes were essential if she hoped to better her position in life. There had been no need of a sizable wardrobe in Clyburn. She had one black sheath dress and a belt that she used as a staple. She had a navy wide-bottomed skirt and a light blue one for summer. She had a v-necked blouse and two white ones. One of the white blouses had ruffles at the neck and sleeves. That was all she could claim as presentable clothes to wear when seeking employment. And, if she should get a job, what then?

There was a restaurant out on the major highway that was advertising for a dining room hostess, and she gave a lot of thought to the ad. The job probably didn't pay all that well, but it offered the opportunity to meet people of a different stripe than those she was associated with daily. Too, the restaurant was on a scenic route and many tourists traveled through Tennessee to see the scenery in summer, with the highway becoming crowded in the fall when the foliage was in full color.

On Tuesday she went to the pay telephone in the drug store across the street and called the restaurant. She told the lady that answered she was interested in the hostess job, and the lady got the proprietor on the line. Perline asked for an appointment on Saturday, if possible, in case the job hadn't already been filled. The restaurant owner told her he had several applications but had not made a decision, and said she could come in at 3 p.m. Saturday for an interview.

Perline was elated. She could make the half-day shift, dress and catch a bus out to the restaurant in plenty of time. That night she got out the black dress and the matching jacket and looked the outfit over carefully. She retrieved a small brooch from a box in the dresser drawer and lay it over the dress to see its effect. It was inexpensive but it looked good, and she found the small pearl earrings her mother had given her one Christmas. Her black patent leather pumps were in good shape, so she would feel comfortable about her appearance when Saturday came. Nobody would know that her underpants had runs in them.

She dressed carefully after pulling her half-day shift at the mill. She groomed her hair until it shone in the light and was meticulous in applying lipstick, pressing her lips together to ensure a smooth application. Her eyelashes were long and her eyes clear and sparkling. But her heart beat faster as she rode the bus out to the restaurant. She was a little apprehensive.

She had never been in Joe's Dining Room during all the years she had been in Clyburn. She was impressed as she entered. Fresh flowers were on all the tables, overlaid with white cloths and with afternoon sunshine coming through the windows.

She announced herself and the proprietor came immediately and introduced himself. "Joe Peterson," he said.

"Pearl Turnage," she replied. She had always hated the name Perline, and she determined that in the future she would be known as Pearl.

"What do you do now?" Peterson asked.

"I work in the Clyburn Mills," she replied.

"You work in the mills?" he asked in an inquisitive voice. "I didn't know girls like you worked in the mills."

What does he mean? Pearl thought.

"I mean you've got class," Peterson said. "Nothing about you looks like a mill worker. How long have you worked there?"

"Ten years."

"Ten years, my gosh! Where are you from?"

"Waynesborough County, North Carolina."

"And what did you do there?"

"I was a sharecropper's daughter. I worked in the fields - helping harvest tobacco, picking cotton, plowing sometimes if necessary."

"I am amazed," Peterson said. "I've had seven applications for the hostess job, and I haven't been satisfied with any of the applicants. The others just didn't show the qualities I am seeking in a hostess. This is a high-class restaurant and we have all kinds of patrons. Even during these hard times, some come through who are still living far beyond the level of the average person. I need a hostess who is attractive, capable, and who takes an interest in our customers. And I believe you fit the bill, Miss Turnage, or is it Mrs."

"Miss."

"When can you start?"

"In two weeks."

"No sooner?"

"I have to give notice at the mill."

"Two weeks from Monday then."

Pearl had expected an application form to fill out and a check into her background. She couldn't believe he had not even asked for references. She was glad she had answered his questions truthfully and that he knew about her rural background.

The Trailways bus was late on its route to Western Tennessee and its stop at the drugstore in Clyburn. It always stopped at Joe's Restaurant momentarily to pick up passengers returning to Clyburn. Pearl sat on a bench and thought about what had just happened could be the turning point of her life.

She asked herself why she should think on a higher level than most of the people with whom she was associated. After all, she came from a sharecropping background, which was on the same level as mill workers. She only had a seventh grade education, so why should she think of herself as being different from the others? But she reasoned that every person was an individual with individual talents and perspectives. If she were placed in the same mold with all those who presumably thought only in terms of life experiences, there would be no possibility of rising above that kind of life. And this was America where anything was possible.

Pearl was also concerned about her own feelings. She offered no apologies for her humble background, nor did she feel disadvantaged because of it. She had found life pleasant in Bear Grass and enjoyed the rural atmosphere. She had had plenty of friends, male and female, and plenty of boys who were interested in her. She had enjoyed the expansiveness of the outdoors and the freedom it offered. She had taken all that for granted until she moved to the three-room apartment in Clyburn with its outside entrance and shackly steps to climb. There was no room to plant a bed of petunias or pansies and there was another apartment that was a clone of hers within eight feet.

There were times when she felt she would be happier if she thought as most of the mill workers thought. But there had always been something in her nature demanding that she think tall and try to learn about the finer things in life. She had never been content to accept the status quo and although her life had been isolated in the mill village, she had continued her learning process. She looked at all the catalogs and dreamed about having clothes like those displayed in beautiful color. She had read the women's magazines and books and newspapers. But all this gave her no feeling of superiority. She would have done the same thing if she had remained in Bear Grass.

The next two weeks were spent in preparing for her job at Joe's. She would have to find a place to live, for another mill worker would take her apartment. She had noticed a small empty house not far from the restaurant. It had been painted in time, although it was shabby in appearance now and some windowpanes were out. She asked about it and found it was for rent for three dollars per week. She paid the three dollars when she looked at the house, although dissatisfied with what she found. A lot of work would have to be done inside and the yards cleaned up. But it was near her employment and that was a distinct advantage. There were four rooms and she hoped to eventually get her parents and Hobby to come and live with her. Her father was getting too old to farm and she felt he could find something to do around the Clyburn mills. But she was making plans far in advance.

Her salary in the mill was ten dollars a week, and she would be earning fourteen at the restaurant, which was a forty percent increase in pay. That would be a big help.

Pearl got settled in the house before she began work at the restaurant. She spent every spare moment cleaning and washing walls and doing everything possible to make the place presentable. And she was excited the day she began work at Joe's. Dressed in her red blouse and navy skirt, she entered the restaurant exactly on time. It was only a ten-minute walk from the house to the restaurant.

Joe Peterson turned the money box over to her without any kind of instructions. He put her on her own at the very beginning, apparently feeling that she was capable without having to go through a long rigamarole of rules and regulations. Pearl appreciated that.

She felt at ease from the start and the proprietor watched her without her knowing it. He noticed her graceful walk and the smile she gave to customers. He was dumbfounded. She was open and friendly and patrons would strike up conversations with her and there would be laughter when she was around.

All manner of customers came into Joe's, from mill hands - mostly men - from Clyburn out on the make, to white-collar workers and quite a number of tourists. Some men made passes at her but she just smiled at that kind and got herself out of those situations without offending the patrons. Some tourists asked her for dates and one man asked her to marry him outright only a few weeks after she began work, although she didn't take him seriously. But she did enjoy the attention after being isolated in a cotton mill village for ten years.

Pearl managed with her wardrobe very well. She combined the skirts and blouses and wore the black suit with all the blouses and laundered the clothes in off-duty hours. She would have to sacrifice a few dollars to buy a new dress when she got her pay, after dipping into her five-hundred dollar savings, for moving expenses. It had cost her twenty-five dollars to move.

Pearl found life as a dining room hostess pleasant and exciting. She felt she was in an entirely different world. Although hostesses didn't usually receive tips, sometimes customers would leave a dollar on her table and one customer actually left five dollars and his card on top, listing his name, residence and telephone number. A five-dollar tip was almost unheard of. But it paid for a dress she had been dreaming about since she saw it in the window of the only dress shop in Clyburn.

In time the house looked good inside and Pearl felt comfortable in her new quarters. There was an open fireplace and plenty of wood from limbs that had fallen in the yard and sometimes when the weather was cool she would light a fire and dream about life in Bear Grass and remember how cozy it had seemed with a big fire going on winter nights; how the smoke smelled and how it spiraled up the chimney; how the churn had sat on the hearth and the oil lamp on the bureau shedding dull light over the front room. There were pleasant memories and she was happy in remembering them.

Lucille, her best friend at the mill, came to see her sometimes and they would have long conversations and Lucille told her she was also looking for work outside the mill. She was trying to get on at the library as a helper. Lucille would catch Pearl up on what was happening in the mill. For one thing, a group was trying to unionize the mill and there was a big stir about that. But many mill workers were in favor of a union. They felt it would mean better working conditions and more pay also. A woman had been raped on the way home from work a few days earlier, but the rapist hadn't been apprehended. One of the girls that had worked with them was going with a married man and there were tales that she was pregnant, but nobody was sure about that. But it all seemed far away to Pearl after only a short time at Joe's.

Pearl wrote and told her parents about her change in jobs and that she was planning for them to come and live with her in a year or two. She told all of them how much she loved them and that she was happy in her new job.

So life settled down and Pearl went to work each day exuberant and looking forward to meeting and talking with patrons of the restaurant.

One day a man entered the restaurant that set Pearl's pulse beating faster before a word was spoken. She couldn't explain. He apparently was a foreigner - Greek or Syrian or Arab perhaps. He wasn't especially handsome, although there was something that made you look twice. His nose was slightly hawkish, but not excessive. His hair was black and wavy and he had expressive brown eyes. There was an odor of cigar smoke about him. He was tall and well-built and he wore a warm smile on his face. Pearl took him to a corner table where he could gaze out on a countryside tinted with the golden hues of fall, with hills rising in the distance.

He said, "Thank you" when she seated him and when she showed him the menu he ordered the most expensive dishes. She noticed a diamond on his finger that must have been two carats at least.

As Pearl went about her duties, she noticed his eyes following her and it made her self-conscious. But she was pleased that he noticed. He ate leisurely and in silence and lingered on after he had finished with his meal. She brought several cups of coffee and finally sat down at his table for a moment.

"New in the area?" she asked.

"I guess you could say that, although I've stopped here a number of times. I like the food and the service, although I must admit it's better this time than ever."

"Just passing through?" she asked.

"Yeah, I guess you could say that. But I don't have a set time to arrive or leave any place. It's possible I might stay around for a few days. If rooms are available at the hotel up the road I think I'll stay around and take in the scenery. It's beautiful around here."

"That would be nice," she said. "If you stay around for a while maybe we can become acquainted, and we'll feed you well."

"No doubt about that," he replied. "By the way, what is your name?"

"Pearl," she replied. "Pearl Turnage."

"Married?"

"Nope."

"Why?"

"That's a little personal, don't you think? And what is your name?"

"Nick. Nick Staphalopoulous if you can imagine such a name. Greek."

"Well it's nice meeting you Nick. I won't even attempt the surname."

"Nobody does," Nick said. "That's why I call myself Nick Staphal."

Nick stayed on until time for the dining room to close. Pearl was about her duties and checking with the waitresses before going home. She finally came to his table and said, "It's time to go, partner."

"I'd like to talk with you further," Nick said. "Could I take you home?"

"Not tonight. Perhaps some other time. But we can talk at the restaurant. You'll be back for breakfast, won't you?"

"Sure."

"I'll see you then," she said as she went to the rack, took his hat and handed it to him."

"I'll look forward to morning then," Nick said.

He was smiling as he entered the dining room the next morning and he thought Pearl was more beautiful than she had been last night. He said, "Hi" and Pearl smiled and said, "Hi" as she took him to the corner table again.

"Big breakfast?" she asked and he said yeah, that he was hungry.

"I'll get a waitress to serve you in a moment."

"Do you have tenderloin? If so, I want that with biscuits and two eggs and jelly and plenty of coffee."

"My, you are hungry, big man."

"Will you be able to sit with me for a while?" he asked.

"You know better than that Nick. Look at all the customers and here comes another."

"Then I'll just have to go to your home to talk. When can we arrange that?"

"Soon," she replied. "I want to talk with you too. A man walks into my life out of the blue and I know absolutely nothing about him. I'm sure you have plenty to tell and I'll bet it's a humdinger of a story."

"Not all that big," Nick said. "No kidding, when can I see you?"

It was Friday and Pearl would be off on Sunday. "How would Sunday afternoon be?" she asked.

"Any day, any time," he replied. And as Pearl went about her way visions were dancing in Nick's head and the morning sunshine sparkling on the autumn foliage and the blueness of the water in a lake across the way made him feel as if he were in a fantasy world. He ate and looked out on the scenery and felt the greatest sense of belonging he had ever known.

On Saturday Pearl cleaned the house meticulously but wasn't satisfied with the result, no matter what she did. She felt it wasn't good enough for the big man with the diamond ring that spoke something about a higher plane that she knew nothing about. It was the first time in her life she wished she were able to meet a person of the higher echelon on equal ground. Then she said to herself, "What the heck. If he can't accept me for what I am and who I am, he's not worth associating with anyway."

It was very chilly in the mountains on Sunday, and Pearl lit a fire and the room was cozy when Nick arrived. Two plain rockers were on each side of the hearth and the coals were glowing and clouds were coming in and it was an ideal day to dream by the fire.

Pearl greeted Nick warmly and he was smiling and there was the faint smell of tobacco smoke mingled with an odor of perfume she wasn't accustomed to and she said to herself: "Oh, boy, I'm in class for once in my life."

"Nothing is more beautiful than a warm fire glowing in a fireplace," Nick said. "I could sit in an atmosphere like this forever and just dream my life away."

They commented about the weather and the possibility of rain and perhaps a killing frost and each became more comfortable with the other.

"You haven't told me about yourself," Nick said.

"Nor you me" she replied.

"You begin," he urged.

"Why? So you can get a negative impression of me from the start?"

"Not at all," Nick said. "I doubt that anything could give me a negative impression of you."

Pearl decided she would give it to him in the belt with the first punch. "I'm fresh from the Clyburn cotton mills, seven miles away."

"Go ahead," Nick said, although he was astounded.

"Ten years in the mills, wearing coveralls and getting lint all over me. Living in a three-room apartment with an outside walk-up. Toting in buckets of coal morning and evening. Low pay and little incentive. A drab atmosphere and not much to look forward to."

"That all?" he asked.

"Come from sharecropper stock back in North Carolina. Lived that life until I was seventeen. Helped my daddy farm. Grew tobacco, cotton and corn. Chopped and helped to harvest the crops. Even plowed in the fields sometimes. Seventh grade education."

"How did you migrate from a sharecropper to a mill worker?"

"Worked in the Hallsborough mills for a year and had a girl friend from Tennessee that worked there. Ma and Pa said I'd be better off working in the mills than on the farm for there was no money out there. I was seventeen then. My friend moved back to Tennessee and told me to come and live with her if I ever wanted to leave Bear Grass. And I had no plans to go to Tennessee at the time, but it became a way out later." She decided now was the time to give him the killing punch. "Then I became pregnant and I took my friend up on her offer. I had to get away to escape the scorn of an unforgiving public. And I wanted to spare Ma and Pa as much embarrassment as possible. So I have a ten-year-old illegitimate child that I simply adore and who lives with my parents in Bear Grass. Now Nick Staphal, can you top that?"

"You are the most adorable human being I have ever known," Nick replied.

"Now about you, Nick."

"You know I have a restaurant background. What else is there for Greeks to do in America? There are Greek restaurants strewn all across the nation, even in the smallest towns. My parents were immigrants. Learned to speak in broken English but never learned to write the English language. They never became naturalized citizens. But my parents were so happy to be in America they never complained. They had fared worse in Athens. And my daddy was a miser, a penny-pincher. Our humble home in Memphis consisted of four rooms, two on each side of a wide hall. My daddy put me to cooking by the time I was ten years old. And he'd say, "Son, you've got to learn to be a good cook and carry on the family business when I'm gone. Start at the bottom and save your money and gain the respect of the people.

Squander it away and you'll be a nobody. Don't try to be as big as the higher-ups you'll come in contact with at school. Don't get above your raising."

Nick paused and took the fire poker and stirred the wood and noted that more wood was needed to keep the fire going. He rose and went outside and brought in an armful of broken limbs. Pearl thought he seemed as much at home as if he had been there forever.

"Can I ask you something," Pearl said as Nick returned and replenished the fire.

"Sure."

"There is such a pleasant odor about you that I can't associate with anyone else. There is the aroma of spice and other exotic smells, coupled with the odor of cigar smoke. It fascinates me. What is it?"

"Old Spice," Nick said. "It's a man's cologne that has become very popular."

"Well, I don't get around that class men so I trust you will pardon my ignorance. Incidentally, it's all right for you to smoke your cigar. It doesn't offend me. No farm worker who has worked in tobacco would object."

"Thank you," Nick replied as he took a cheroot from his inside coat pocket, removed the wrapping and bit off the ends and retrieved a large-stem wooden match, ignited it and drew on the cigar. "I don't want to offend those who don't smoke, most of all, you."

"Now back to you, Nick."

"My dad insisted that I go to college, so I went to Tennessee State and worked my way through college. Dad didn't give me a penny. He said I'd need a college education in order to be able to cope with life in the future. But after getting my degree I went right back into the restaurant with my father. And if I haven't mentioned Mother's contribution, she was as much a part of the restaurant as were my father and me. It was a team. I was twenty-two when I graduated and business went on as usual until 1926 when Dad died. It was sudden and we knew nothing of his legal arrangements. And it was a real shock to learn what that little Greek man had accomplished. He was afraid of banks and he had never deposited any money in them. Instead, he hoarded it away in a tin box in a bureau drawer in the house. And those were hard times, Pearl, and they got ten times harder after the Depression struck in earnest.

"I didn't know what to do about the money, but I talked it over with Mother and we decided to leave things just as they were, at least for the time being. So the money was not deposited in any bank and I thanked my God a million times after the bottom fell out that the money was in that little tin box.

"Dad had saved fifty thousand dollars in that tin box, and it was a staggering amount of money in 1926, but it became more staggering after the banks closed and people lost their life savings. They lost their property and were reduced to paupers almost overnight, and you know that many simply committed suicide rather than face the consequences. Property was the cheapest thing in Memphis. Large estates were selling for a pittance - beautiful homes with large grounds as well as land holdings.

"Mother died two years after Dad's death, and I was left sole owner and decision maker. It seemed the worst time in the world to invest in property, but I reasoned that the nation would rise from the ashes of the Depression and America would prosper again. I decided to invest some of the money in Memphis property as well as farm property. I didn't know whether I was doing the right thing and many of my friends felt I was saying goodby to my hard-earned money.

"It didn't work out that way and my investments paid off handsomely. So I have a nest egg, Pearl, but I'm not what you could call rich. But right now I'm not interested in all that. I'm interested in you. You see, I've been swept off my feet almost suddenly, and that's something that has never happened to Nick Staphal before. And I've been with many women, Pearl. Incidentally, that is not intended as boasting; just stating the facts."

"I'll just bet you have," Pearl replied. "Ever been married?"

"Once," Nick said. "Married a Memphis woman and things went well for a year. Then everything began to unravel. We didn't have the same interests. She was society-oriented. Wanted to run in the social circle and none of that appealed to me. She tired of my old-fashioned ideas in a hurry and filed for divorce. Got a nice settlement too."

"No children?" Pearl asked.

"No children."

The fire had died down to embers and Pearl looked at the clock on the mantel. It was almost midnight.

"It's getting time for you to go, Nick," she said, yawning. "Time for me to get my beauty sleep."

"If that is what has made you so beautiful, I will go immediately," Nick replied. "And let me say this has been a genuine pleasure to sit and talk with you tonight. I feel like a gawky teen-ager again with all the passions I remember from those days."

"I've enjoyed it too, Nick." Pearl said. "But there's a lot more to your story and we'll take that up next time."

"Tomorrow night?" he asked.

"No, Wednesday night," she replied.

They stood and he took her into his arms and kissed her tenderly at first, becoming more aggressive as she snuggled in his arms. She was so soft and feminine and he felt the firmness of her breasts and she again noticed the aroma about Nick and with his command of the situation she felt he was the sexiest man she had ever known.

The wind was blowing his overcoat around him as he left and a soft rain was falling over the Tennessee hills.

Chapter 12

It was 1931 and the depression was deepening. Its effects were felt everywhere. It was a period that tested America as well as nations around the world. There was nothing with which to bargain. People remembered the roaring 20s when the world seemed to be in a spin and life was being lived at a fast pace. It had been a nation on the move before the mighty economy crumbled. People were willing to stoop to lower levels than they had been used to in order to survive. In the cities, many people had no place to turn except the soup kitchens that dished out food to untold thousands whose eyes told the story of the depression era. There was no hope. Everything was lost. Many who had prospered saw everything they had worked for go into receivership, leaving them paupers with nothing to cling to.

Goods were produced under sweat-shop conditions. Labor was available for a pittance. Manufactured goods were available at giveaway prices, yet those who needed those things so badly had no money with which to purchase them. And no man had ever been cursed as had Herbert Hoover. He became a victim of the times and the hard times during his presidency ensured that he would not be re-elected.

Al Smith and Franklin D. Roosevelt were conducting presidential campaigns across the country and the people debated and argued the merits of both men. In the predominantly Protestant areas of the country Al Smith's name brought loud cries from the people: He's a Catholic. He's under the dominion of the Pope. If he wins we'll have to bow to Catholocism. There is no way we can have a Catholic in the White House.

The people seemed to see a savior in Roosevelt. The name had a charisma all its own. Many had admired Teddy Roosevelt when he was president and FDR was a family relative who had served as Governor of New York from 1928 to 1932 and whose work had been hailed by many. And he was a Democrat. Hoover had caused many Republicans to change their party affiliation after his disastrous years as president. Roosevelt was nominated because W.G. McAdoo who was pledged to John N. Garner threw his vote to Roosevelt. The Depression and Roosevelt's promise to repeal prohibition ensured his election. And a nation breathed easier.

People tried to piece their lives together as best they could. Whatever the circumstances, life went on. Newspapers were read avidly for they were the source of the news of what was happening in America. Radios were on the scene but very few people owned one. And there were many headline catchers besides the everyday stories concerning the Depression and its effects on the lives of the people.

One of the wire services put out a story about a woman who was pregnant and who burned her Bible. The story said that when the baby was born it had the characteristics of the devil; the image we have in our minds of the devil. In the conservative Bible Belt that story gave the people something to talk about for weeks. The general public was more concerned with the daily serial in the paper, the Katzenjammer kids, Lil Abner, the Willis' antics in Out Our Way, Maggie and Jiggs and other daily features than they were in front-page news. Visits in the various areas of the papers' readership were also read avidly, although the same visitors were listed over and over, week after week. The poor people in rural areas were looking for something to laugh about instead of dwelling on poor conditions across the nation.

The things city dwellers were experiencing were things they had dealt with all their lives except for those who were going hungry. Few rural dwellers could identify with real hunger, although it wasn't always allayed with the food of their choice. If people were hungry, they didn't complain about the diet that sustained life. Many a young'un in the South would be given a cold biscuit to munch on while the mother hoed long rows of cotton or corn or tobacco, leaving the baby in a little pen under the shade of a tree, or working at a tobacco bench when green tobacco was being housed.

The babies would heave sometimes from the accumulation of biscuit in the roofs of their mouths and the mothers would reach inside and remove the soaked bread and the babies would start the process all over again. They would brush away the flies, take time to put a clean diaper on the babies and resume their work. It was a way of life in the rural areas, even before the Depression.

Mothers would masticate table food in their mouths and feed it to their babies. This supplemented milk from their own breasts and most babies were fat, with two chins and accumulations of fat around their wrists.

But life moved on and people saddened by hardship learned to smile through it all and hope for a better tomorrow.

The relationship between Pearl Turnage and Nick Staphal deepened. Winter came with its snows and the mountains became white and the fire in Pearl's parlor burned brightly. Nick would return to Memphis for a week or two to attend to business while Pearl continued working as a hostess. She awaited Nick's return with anticipation and continued dreaming about all the things that had happened to her since he came into her life. He had told her about his home in Memphis with fourteen rooms, tree-shaded, grounds with sloping lawns and a brook that ran through the grounds and the little bridge that spanned the stream, and Pearl thought of it as being like something she had seen in the movies. She was more impressed than she admitted to Nick. But Pearl was realistic. She had learned to love him, but there was still a reserve that kept her within rational limits.

Somehow, she couldn't trust Nick completely. She asked herself what his motives could be; why he had chosen a plain country girl over the higher echelon of women he had been associated with; how he could hold her up as a model over other women; whether his intent was purely physical or whether there was the genuine love she would expect in any man she loved completely? Pearl realized that background was all-important to many people. She had made a big mistake as a teenager, but experience had been a wise teacher, and she would have to profit from that mistake whether it was a man of the world like Nick Staphal or a farm boy from Bear Grass.

Pearl had to admit that Nick affected her physically as well as intellectually. She could easily give herself to him in a moment of passion. And he had certainly made his desires known more than one time. If she let her guard down once, that would be her fatal mistake. Pearl Turnage had taken life's hard knocks but she had tried to profit by them. She had to depend on her own intuitions for survival and maintaining her self-respect. If she didn't look after her own interests no one else would. She just didn't want to be taken advantage of ever again.

During one of Nick's absences when the mornings were still frosty and snow capped the higher elevations, when the winds howled and tree limbs creaked, she reclined by the fire one night and thought about Nick and herself. She realized that they were near the extremes in lifestyles and she didn't know whether they could come together on common ground. If they couldn't, she wouldn't blame Nick. She devised a plan that would put Nick to the ultimate test. If he met the test, then she could accept him. But beyond the test she would give him, he would also put her through a test of his own.

She would take Nick back to Bear Grass where the lifestyle she had known was still intact; where the bare facts of life were lived every day; where all the things she had told Nick about "back home" were still evident. She would put him through the paces, expose him to raw country living, let him know what life as a poor farmer was all about. She would see that he worked two weeks in the fields, helping her father and doing all the things that were done on the farm during the busiest season of the year - "puttin' in backer" time.

She would choose mid-July if she could arrange it with Joe. It would be the busiest time of the year in Bear Grass. People would be barning tobacco every day, curing it at night, suckering the weed, and doing other chores as time allowed. The gardens would be laden with vegetables. She'd expose him to "real" Southern cooking and let him get the feel of being a sharecropper. Nothing would be left out.

Nick was a healthy man and could endure the rigors of country life without any permanent damage. She would get into the act again herself. The thought excited her and she laughed. "I'll kick off my shoes and go "splinter" barefooted again just as I used to do. I'll don an apron and put on one of Ma's loose dresses and let my Nick know me as I was and without apology," she said to herself. "That's who I am anyway at heart. I can't be a pretender, although I do want better things than we had at home. But I'm no better today than I was when sharecropping was my world."

"If Nick Staphal can accept all that and can say in all sincerity that he loves me beyond a doubt and that he wants to make me a part of his world for as long as we live, I'll marry him the next day if he wants me to. And if he turns me down I'll just dry up and let my life end now and cry myself to death. But I can't pull anything over him. He has to know and accept me and all my family for what we are if we are to have a happy life together."

She thought about how happy she'd be to introduce Hobby to Nick, and when she thought about the boy tears came to her eyes. She loved him so much, yet he had been only a small part of her life. She longed to see him every day, but when the blue spells came and loneliness crept in at best, she grieved at his absence. But she smiled when she realized that at last things were beginning to shape up so Hobby could have the surgery he so desperately needed if he were ever to become a normal person.

She had no doubt that Hobby would like Nick. He liked everybody. Nor did she fear that Nick might not like Hobby. If she were any judge of human nature, Nick would take to the boy instantly. She pictured Hobby being beside her, looking up into her face and she could almost see the infectious grin on his face and the freckles showing on his nose. What a treasure, she thought.

Nick had invited Pearl to visit him in Memphis a month or so after they became acquainted. He had told her he wanted her to see his home but he reminded her that everything was strictly above-board, for Mrs. Gardner, his housekeeper, would be there as chaperone. Mrs. Gardner was a sixty-nine-year-old widow who had kept house for him since he had moved to his present quarters. But Pearl had declined saying that she felt it a little improper for a lady to accept such a visit at that stage in their relationship. But she told him she wanted very much to see his "mansion" and to observe what life was really like on the other side of the tracks. And as she planned Nick's visit to Bear Grass, she realized that if she had visited such a place as he had described she would never have the heart to ask him to visit her humble home.

She longed to hear from Nick during his absences, yet she had declined his offer to have a telephone installed in her home. To allow that, she thought, would be an invitation to accept other offers that could lead to problems. And Nick realized that if he got into the habit of calling her at work it could jeopardize her job. When he planned to return after his absences he would call the restaurant and tell the person that answered to let Pearl know when she could expect him.

Nick had offered to have wood cut and stacked on the porch so it would be no bother to Pearl to have plenty of wood for the fire. She had declined that offer also, so when Nick was around he'd spend half-a-day sometimes chopping limbs and stacking them between the porch posts. He'd rake the yard and make things tidy outside.

"I want to pay for Hobby's surgery," he had said out of the blue one night as they sat at the table eating a coconut pie Pearl had made, and drinking coffee. Nick Staphal loved food as good as anybody Pearl had ever seen and she had often wondered why he didn't have a pot belly and weigh half a ton. As it was, he was well-proportioned and weighed 203 pounds. Nick's words shocked her.

"Before you have a chance to get your breath, allow me to explain, Pearl," Nick added. "I have never met your little boy but I already love him, and if it were any other child and I knew the circumstances, I would pay for the surgery as quickly as I would pay for Hobby's. I'm a pussycat, honey. I have the softest heart you can imagine. And if I paid the bill and you never spoke to me again there would not be one regret on my part. There is absolutely no obligation involved, Pearl, and please don't feel that I'm trying to take unfair advantage in the things I offer to do for you. What do I have to do to prove to you that I am completely above-board where you are concerned? If I'm selfish, it is not with the little money I have. I am selfish about you, my dear, and if it were another man, I'd be ready to kill. As it is, I'm only trying to do a good deed and whatever I have offered to do before, you have turned down cold. What is wrong with me, Pearl?"

"I believe I'll be able to handle it," Pearl had replied and they had let it go at that. Nick had already learned that it did little good to argue with Pearl.

Nick left for Memphis the next day and Pearl continued her work at Joe's. Business had been off during the winter months and the people were looking forward to spring. Pearl began to feel cramped in and she'd stand at the window sometimes and look out over the rolling hills and dream about summer and the outside freedom it allowed. She also thought a lot about what Nick had said about paying for Hobby's surgery. However she might feel personally about declining help from Nick, she realized that she had to think more about what was best for her son. In the hands of an expert orthopedic surgeon, he would stand a better chance of making Hobby whole than if he were operated on by a general orthopedic surgeon. Hobby would need the very best if his leg were to be repaired and made reasonably whole. She would have to talk further with Nick about his offer.

Pearl had planned to try to get Hobby entered in the North Carolina Orthopedic Hospital at Gastonia in 1932. She had looked into the situation and learned that as a resident of the state he could receive surgery there at no cost to her. She had entertained the idea of entering him and hoping for the best, but somehow she wanted him in the hands of a recognized expert.

She knew that Duke University had a good orthopedics program and that Duke was recognized worldwide as a great medical complex. But Johns Hopkins in Baltimore was uppermost in her mind, since she had read so much about the work done at the hospital. She was hoping that if he could be given the best surgeon possible, it would be recompence for her carelessness that resulted in Hobby's lameness.

So Pearl thought about these things while Nick was away and her thoughts were also occupied with getting her family moved to Tennessee. Her parents were growing old. Hobby would never be happy in Tennessee if they remained in Bear Grass and she would feel more responsibility toward them if they were left alone back home than if they were with her. She would talk with them about that if they made the visit to Bear Grass in July.

It was a period when Pearl felt the heavy yoke of responsibility on her shoulders when she would have preferred a time of freedom to enjoy the warmth she was feeling in her relationship with Nick. There was no doubt in her mind that she was desperately in love with him. She wanted to pick up the pieces of her life she had left behind as a teen-ager and had to become an adult before her time. She felt cheated.

Then the phone call came to the restaurant saying that Nick would be back on Monday. It was now Friday. So there would be a lonely weekend when she would remain inside and read a book or do her laundry; anything to pass the time.

Then there was the knock on her door early Monday evening. She was at home since Monday was her day off. Her heart fluttered as she opened the door and they embraced instantly. She felt Nick's maleness as he embraced her and her nipples grew firm and she was aware her bosom was pressed close to him. She drew back but he gathered her close again and they kissed passionately. It seemed like heaven.

They finally came back to reality and Pearl helped Nick get his topcoat off and they seated themselves by the fire. Pearl had rearranged the furniture and placed the couch where the chairs had sat in front of the hearth.

"Gosh, it's good to be back," Nick said. "That big house of mine is the loneliest place in the world Pearl. I'd give anything if I could feel as cozy at home as I feel when I am with you. Of course it isn't the house that makes your place cozy. It is you and the woman's touch you give it. I will treasure this place for as long as I live."

"It costs all of three dollars a week, Nick."

"To hell with the cost. A house doesn't make a home. Love is what makes a home, my dear, and we are two people head-over-heels in love."

"Sentimentalist."

"Do you deny it?"

"No," Pearl replied. "And I have no regrets. I am floating on a cloud and expecting it to dissipate any minute. I feel as silly as a teen-ager. What have you done to me, Nick Staphal?"

"Whatever I could to make you love me, Pearl. I fell in love with you the moment I saw you. I knew right then that my life would never be complete until you were mine. We've got to do something about it."

Pearl drew near him and lay her head on his shoulder. "Silly boy," she said. "You're talking to a woman labeled a whore back home. You're talking with a woman who has a bastard son. You're talking with a chorewoman, a sharecropper-turned millworker. A slut, in so many words."

"You're beautiful. You're lovely. You are all the things my heart has longed for all my life," Nick said as he pulled her face to him and kissed her on her lips.

"It's getting to the point where I can't stand to leave you, Pearl," Nick said. "It's so interminably long when I am in Memphis and I might as well be here anyway, for you are all that I think about."

It was warm inside. The fire had burned down to embers except for a knot that still flickered among the ashes. Pearl had lighted an oil lamp and placed it on the table and turned off the electric light before Nick arrived. The tick of the clock seemed to be magnified during their silent moments. The dimness of the light in the room allowed the stars to shine through the windows and all the world seemed to be peaceful and they the central players on this very special night.

Nick took her chin and pulled her face up to him. They kissed again and suddenly his mouth was on her breast, caressing her and sending waves of passion through her body. His hands were exploring her and she wanted him so much she was no longer able to resist him. They came together in a passion so great they gave themselves to each other with abandon and there was the moment of bliss in which they felt they were animals acting on instinct in the greatest of all human experiences. Time stood still. Caution was thrown to the winds. It was lust enjoyed to its fullest extent.

She shivered as gushes of sperm entered her body. Nick was panting, almost becoming hysterical as his orgasm exploded in her.

They were spent, fatigued, lethargic. Shadows from the flickering fireplace played over her body and she looked into Nick's face and there was a look of complete relief. Whatever their later regrets might be, sleep was overtaking them and they were caught up in the pleasures of the moment. Pearl gazed out the window as a star was falling and Nick saw the lamplight as the flame ebbed and flowed as a whiff of wind played on the shade, causing soot to accumulate on the chimney. They slept.

Nick's hand on her shoulder roused Pearl from her slumber. A fire had been laid and Nick had placed his overcoat over Pearl. It was still dark outside.

"I'll be going back to the hotel now," Nick said. "I don't want to give the wrong impression to the neighbors. And I can't say I'm sorry for what happened last night, Pearl, but I want to make amends. We can find a justice of the peace and be married this morning. I don't want to cause you any worry, my darling. I love you more than life and if you will marry me this morning I will be the happiest man in the world." He reached down and kissed her tenderly.

Pearl placed her hand on Nick's arm and he sat beside her on the couch. "You're too sweet Nick," she said, "and I do want to marry you. But right now isn't the time. It's too late for what may have happened last night. I wanted you as much as you wanted me. We were irresponsible and if we have to pay the consequences, there is no need to regret that now. We can't act in that manner again and both of us realize that.

"As to marriage, we would be jumping into something in which we didn't know all the facts. You haven't met my family, not even Hobby. You don't know anything about them or our way of life. You must meet them and get to know them before we entertain the idea of marriage. I want you to go home with me this summer and get to know them, Nick. That may change your mind about me and my family. But you have to know. If you had a family I would have to know about them also. But it would be unfair to you to do otherwise."

"I'm dying to meet your people, Pearl," Nick said. "I've thought about that boy of yours a thousand times and I already feel as if he were mine. I want to meet your mom and dad also. You have nothing to fear in me meeting them. Nothing on earth could change my mind about you, my darling."

"I appreciate your not questioning me about the circumstances of Hobby's birth, Nick. I know you must have wondered as to who his father is. I have never told who he is, and Hobby will be the first to know. But I must wait until he is old enough to understand. You will be the second to know. Until then, you can be assured that it was nothing like we experienced last night. There was no love involved Nick."

"That is the least of my concerns," Nick replied. "You were only a child when that happened. You need never tell me if you don't want to."

"Will you go home with me in July?" Pearl asked.

"You name the day and I will have my bags packed." Nick said.

He kissed her again and departed for the hotel.

As the days of winter gave way to the dawning of spring, Pearl and Nick watched as warm sunshine brought out green buds everywhere and the mountains were carpeted with wild flowers. They walked in a wonderland in their free hours and took long hikes along mountain trails. The scenery was spellbinding, and sometimes they would embrace as they took in the beauty of gushing streams or viewed scenic landscapes in which objects became miniatures and they were the lords over their domain. They were youths again, enjoying all that life had to offer.

Pearl told Nick that she had been thinking about his offer to bear the expense of Hobby's surgery. But she said their affair had nothing to do with her decision to take him up on his offer. "I have to think in terms of the best possible care for my boy," she said. "He must have the opportunity to know all the things we are sharing now. He must have his chance in life, and I can't think selfishly where he is concerned. I would like for us to take him to Johns Hopkins if that is all right with you, Nick."

"I'll take him anywhere on earth you choose," Nick replied. "I want the best for him also, and I think Johns Hopkins is a good choice."

"I was thinking that maybe we could bring him back with us when we go home and get the ball rolling a year ahead of my schedule. I had planned to try to get him hospitalized next year." .

"I'm so happy you have changed your mind," Nick said.

Pearl sang through her days and hummed songs of the day when she was at Joe's. She added a few pieces to her wardrobe, now that she didn't have to count every penny for Hobby's surgery, and Nick noticed.

"You grow more beautiful every day," he said, and Pearl relished his words. "No other woman can match your beauty," Nick would say as he embraced her. "I am the happiest man on earth and consumed with jealousy. I couldn't stand for another man to look at you."

"Don't be silly," Pearl said. "If I didn't attract other men you wouldn't want me either."

"Yeah, I want them to be attracted to you. I just want them to leave you alone beyond that attraction."

"Who knows. Maybe I'll fall for some other dark, tall and handsome man just as I did you," Pearl teased. And Nick's face became red.

Chapter 13

Viola and Craven Turnage sat on their front porch on a Sunday afternoon in mid-July. The air was stale and the humidity high. Little trickles of sweat ran down her neck into the crevice between her breasts. Beads of perspiration were on Craven's forehead. They were shelling butterbeans.

Craven had just returned from the tobacco barn after opening the doors to allow moisture to enter the barn when night came. The tobacco would have to be taken from the barn in the morning, for Monday was "puttin'-in-day" for him. He wanted the leaf to be in good order so it could be handled easily.

Both were a little uncomfortable. It was common practice to undress after church and put on more comfortable clothing, and Craven did remove his suit and don a pair of pin-checked cotton pants but he still wore his white shirt with the gold-colored stud where it held the collar together. Viola kept on the cotton print dress she wore to church.

They were expecting Perline and her "Yankee" boyfriend sometime in the afternoon, and that had them in a state of expectancy as well as anxiety. They called all people from other areas "Yankees."

"I just don't know why Perline had to pick this very time to bring a foreigner here," Viola said. "It's the busiest time of the year and I work myself half to death as it is to pick the vegetables and cook and try to work at the backer shelter when I can. I'm about as put-out as I've ever been. And Perline knows that there's nowhere to sleep a stranger and she knows what life is like during puttin'-in-backer time. It would be bad enough if it was somebody that knows about country living, but for it to be a man that's never lived in the country and knows nothing about how poor farmers live, it's pure ridiculous to me."

"Perline told you not to worry about a thing," Craven reminded her. "She said everything would be fine and for you not to go to a lot of extra trouble. I'd take her at her word if I was you Viola."

"I'm scared to death a chinch will bite him," Viola said. "Now won't that be something if Nick - whatever his last name is - gets bit by a bedbug? I'd be so ashamed I couldn't hardly stand it if such a thing happened."

"You don't have to go out in the sticks to git tangled up with chinches," Craven said.

"And if that man was to see me picking them little green worms off of the collards before I cook them he'd swear I cooked some in the collards, and I couldn't swear I didn't, but Lord, I hope not."

"Do you know what's worse than finding a worm in an apple?" Craven asked, laughing.

"No, what?" Viola asked, "and don't try to be funny Craven. I'm not in a laughing mood."

"Half a worm," Craven said and he roared with laughter.

Hobby came up and joined them. He was wearing a pair of overalls and a blue shirt. "When do you reckon they'll get here?" he asked. He kept looking up and down the road for signs of cars.

"I don't know that that man can stand any of the things I cook," Viola said. "Yankees" are peculiar eaters, I've been told. The mess I cook is as plain as you can cook. But that ain't what's bothering me. It's having to put him on a pallet on the floor and nowhere to go but outdoors to relieve hisself. Not only that. You have to keep the doors open to let the air circulate. If all the doors were shut we'd sweat ourselves to death. We'll all be traipsing through this rabbit box and it will be one time, let me tell you."

Chickens had crossed the road and were foraging among the cotton rows. The field of tobacco on the right was wilted from the summer sun. The mules in the lot swished their tails and stomped their feet as they tried to rid themselves of the large horse flies that settled on them and drank their blood. A yellowjacket buzzed around Viola's face and she stood and dislodged the pan holding shelled beans and Hobby got on the floor and picked them up one by one.

Viola became more nervous as mid-afternoon came and Perline and the "Yankee" still hadn't arrived. Hobby was in a state of excitement also. Craven showed no emotion. He couldn't quite figure it all out, but he suspected Perline wanted the man to know what life was like in the sticks. Well, he'd shore find out.

Then Hobby saw a cloud of dust far down the road and a car coming toward the house. "It's them, it's them!" he shouted.

"You don't know it's them," Viola said, but by then the car was slowing down and all of them stood and waited until it came to a stop in the yard. They ran out to meet them.

Hobby was suddenly in Pearl's arms and she was crying and kissing him and Viola had her hand on Pearl's shoulder and Craven went around and introduced himself to Nick. "Craven Turnage," he said, offering his hand. "It's a pleasure to have you visit us."

"Thank you sir," Nick replied. "I'm Nick Staphal, and it's a pleasure to be here. I've heard a lot about you people."

"Not too bad, I hope," Craven said, and Nick said it was as good a report as you could get.

Hobby was still in Pearl's embrace and Viola went over and told Nick who she was and that she hoped he would enjoy his visit. But her heart was pounding like there was a hammer beating inside.

Pearl finally released Hobby and they stood before Nick. "I want you to meet the finest young man in the world," she told Nick.

"It's a real pleasure to meet you, Hobby," Nick said as he squatted and looked the boy straight in the face. "You're a handsome young chap," he added.

"Thank you sir," Hobby replied. "And I'm glad to meet you."

"I see Mama and Papa have already introduced themselves," Pearl said as she began pulling suitcases from the trunk of the car, with Nick lending a hand and the others waiting to help get everything in the house.

"He's nice looking," Viola whispered when she and Pearl got to the bedroom.

"He's a nice person," Pearl said. "And Mama, I can see that you are all to pieces and I want to get your nerves settled right now. I know you think I'm crazy to bring Nick here at such a busy time, but there's a reason for it. You see, we may get married, but not before Nick knows about us, just as we are. I'm not about to try to pull anything over on him, and he knows all about my background. And you know something Mama, I'm not in the least ashamed of it. Nick can accept me for what I am, or he can find someone else. I brought Nick here to work for the next two weeks, and I really mean work. He's going to know what farm life is all about. So don't you go making any excuses and apologizing for what we don't have. Can you do that, Mama?"

"I don't know," Viola said. "If we just had a bed to put him on I wouldn't feel so ashamed. And I put every quilt and bolster and pillow on the line and let them air for a full day, but I'm afraid he'll say there's a quare smell to the bedclothes and things like that."

"You let me worry about Nick's sleeping," Pearl said. "Hobby and I would sleep on the floor and give Nick Hobby's bed, but Hobby just wouldn't be comfortable on the floor all night. So Nick can sleep on a pallet and it won't hurt him."

"I 'clare, you get prettier every day," Viola said as she placed her arm on Pearl's shoulder. "I want everybody in the neighborhood to see you while you're here."

"I certainly want to see everybody," Pearl said, "and I appreciate your compliment on my looks, Mama. I try hard."

"You always did," Viola replied. "I'm mighty proud of you, honey."

Nick came by with two large bags and Pearl took him to the storage room and told him to leave them there. "This will be your room," she said.

After things settled down Viola, Pearl and Hobby sat on the front porch and Craven asked Nick if he would like to walk over the farm and Nick said he would. They started with the eight-acre field of tobacco.

"Don't reckon you ever had anything to do with farming?" Craven said.

"No sir," Nick replied. "But I certainly want to learn."

"Not a bad crap of backer this year," Craven said. "There have been better years, but we're planting backer a little closer than we used to and the leaves are bigger too. Went for years and planted Bonanza and it always had peaked and sort of small leaves. But they've come out with strains that git bigger and it is increasing the yield. They'll be a right good crapping tomorrow too. If you gaze down the rows you can see three and four ripe leaves on most every stalk. It'll take two barns this week. So far I've been gitting by with one barn, but it's really turning loose now."

They moved on down to the hog pasture where several shoats were standing at the gate, squealing for food. A sow was standing nearby.

"Old Sooky is supposed to find pigs in two or three weeks," Craven said. "It's bad to have a fire of pigs in real hot weather and bad in real cold weather too. But the pigs stand a better chance of living in hot weather cause the sow don't have to be in close quarters. "When they're close-in they lay on a lot of the pigs."

The cotton patch was shiny with blossoms in shades of pink, white and some with a yellowish tint.

"It's been sort of a dry year," Craven said. "If that continues there should be a good cotton crop. Cotton's a dry weather crop. But if it gits rainy the boll weevils take over and they can ruin a crop of cotton in a little while.

"We won't go to the corn fields today. I speck you're a mite tard after all that driving, so we'll head back for the house. Where is it you live?"

"Memphis, Tennessee," Nick replied.

"A lot different than here I speck," Craven said.

"Yes sir, a lot different,"Nick replied. "But it's still in the South, you know."

"What do you think?" Pearl asked when they reached the porch.

"Pretty crops. Pretty hogs and a nice farm," Nick replied. "And I couldn't help but notice the chickens roaming all over the place. They were a pretty sight in all colors, scratching and with the roosters crowing and hens and biddies roaming everywhere."

"I'll make a farmer out of you yet," Pearl said.

"Not a bad idea," Nick replied.

"Mama, your zinnias are really pretty this year," Pearl said as she looked across the road at the flowers on the outside of the garden fence. "You always did have pretty summer flowers, and I missed that when I worked in the mill. There wasn't any room to grow even a tomato plant. I never got used to that."

They had an early supper and Viola was a little squeamish about the stranger eating her food. She had plenty left from dinner and only had to warm it up. But Nick ate as if it were as good as any other food, and she knew if he liked chocolate he couldn't resist her chocolate cake made into six very thin layers with the juice seeping through. Nick asked for two servings and that pleased Viola.

There was little air stirring after dark, and it was nearing bedtime. "Got to git up at 4 o' clock to take out backer," Craven said. "That'll come 'fore you know it. You and Nick can sleep as late as you want to," he told Pearl.

"Papa, we're getting up when you do," Pearl said. "We're going to help you take out that tobacco."

"You don't have to do that," Craven said.

"We didn't come here to loaf," Pearl said.

"I've got a problem tomorrow," Craven said. "Joe Riley's boy, Sam, has been helping me crap backer, and that boy's done come down with mumps and can't help this week. I reckon I'll have to use three crappers stid of four."

"Nick and I will crop the other two rows," Pearl said. "I haven't forgotten how to crop tobacco. Nick can carry one row and me the other. So don't you worry about that at all."

"Well, I'll be obliged to you," Craven said, "But I shore don't expect that."

"We'd better hit the sack too," Pearl said. "We're not used to getting up a 4 o'clock either." She went to the storage room and placed two quilts folded in half on the floor, put a clean case on the pillow, bunched the feathers together then spread them out. She placed a sheet over the quilts while Nick watched.

"Enjoy your night," Pearl said. "And by the way Nick, if you have to answer the call of nature during the night you will have to do like the rest of us. You will go out to the edge of the yard, and you will walk lightly and try not to wake everybody else up. And let me give you a word of caution. Take a good look at that old trunk sitting on the porch that you'll have to pass, and don't get your toes tangled up with the corner of the trunk and have them spread apart so wide you'll feel like you're dying. And don't walk on the edge of the porch for the floor is rotting where the rain has settled on the boards."

"Let's go back to the porch for a little while," Nick said. "It's so pretty outside and that Carolina moon is outdoing itself out there. It looks like a fairyland."

Wherever Pearl and Nick were, Hobby was right under them. Nick wanted to tell Pearl how impressed he was with the boy but there had been no opportunity. He also wanted to discuss his crippled leg, but that was out of the question also. The boy needed treatment as early as possible.

The curve of the road made it possible to observe four other sharecropper houses within view of the porch. Nick could see lamplight in every window, casting a yellow glow, and he was touched by the scene. He thought to himself that the lights represented a safe harbor and a signal that everything was all right.

A whiff of air brought a pleasant aroma and Nick asked what it was.

It's from a cluster of honeysuckle somewhere nearby," Pearl said.

"It's romantic," Nick replied. "In fact, the entire setting is romantic."

"Well, I've heard it expressed in a number of ways," Pearl said, "but I can't say I ever heard it referred to as romantic before. Thank you, Nick. But I do know something romantic I want to show you."

"What Pearl?" Hobby asked. "Not the knothole I reckon."

"Yeah the knothole," Pearl replied.

"I wanted to show Nick," Hobby said and Pearl told him he could. They went into Hobby's bedroom and he told Nick to lie down on the bed. "Now look to your right and glance up about half way from the floor to the ceiling and there is a hole where you can see moonbeams, and if the night were dark you could pick out a star and go to sleep gazing at it."

"Well I'll be darn," Nick said. "I wish I had seen those sights when I was growing up."

"Something else you ought to see is powdery snow coming in through the eaves of the house and settling on the quilts in winter," Hobby said. "That's as pretty as stars and moonbeams."

"You love this place don't you Hobby?" Nick asked.

"Better than anything on earth except my mother and my grandparents, and now you," Hobby answered.

"Why do you love it so much?" Nick asked.

"I don't know how to say it," Hobby said, "but it's like a baby blanket I reckon. I remember Grandma used to wrap a blanket around me when she was rocking me to sleep and I felt like that blanket made me safe from everything else in the world. And I feel the same way about where I live. I'm safe from everything here and it's so pretty and fresh and I know all the people and they're nice and they know me and if heaven is any prettier I can't imagine what it is like."

Nick thought to himself that the boy would never be happy any place on earth other than Bear Grass.

They went inside and Pearl and Hobby retired to Hobby's room and Nick lay on the pallet. He was tired from the long day and a cricket was singing nearby and an owl screeched in the woods and he was asleep within seconds.

He slept fitfully for a while, although he didn't know how long since there was no light to check the time on his watch. He was disoriented and at first wasn't aware of where he was. He reached out and his hand was on the floor and he realized he was on a pallet. It was almost unbelievable to him that he was on a floor in a sharecropper's house in North Carolina. Then he felt a sense of guilt. His home in Memphis was a mansion. Yet, by comparison, there was a warmth in this humble house that was missing in his rambling home. He felt that he had just gone back to sleep when Pearl stuck her head in the door and told him it was time to get up. He rubbed his eyes and yawned and rose from the pallet and put on the new overalls Pearl had bought for him and an everyday work shirt. He had never worn overalls before and they felt bunglesome and stiff.

Craven hitched the mule to the truck and drove it to the tobacco barn door. Pearl climbed on the tier poles and separated the cured tobacco to make room for Nick to go to the top and hand the tobacco down to her.

It felt strange to Nick to have his legs separated as he straddled the tier poles. Pearl took the tobacco from Nick and handed the sticks, two at a time to her father, who placed them on the truck where it grew into a neat pile.

By the time the barn of tobacco was taken out and packed down in the packhouse, Viola had breakfast ready, and as soon as they finished eating they went to the fields. Pearl showed Nick how to crop the leaves and told him to get only the leaves that were beginning to turn yellow. The dew got their feet wet at first and the morning was comfortable, but by the time a couple of trucks had been filled and taken to the looping shelter it was humid and perspiration was showing on all their faces. Nick's face soon became red and he took the rag Pearl had torn from an old sheet and given to him to put in his pocket and wiped his face. Gum had accumulated on his hands and they felt stiff and the odor of the green tobacco almost nauseated him. Hot water came up in his throat and he spit it out. Pearl was feeling the heat too, but neither of them said anything about it. They were ready for a siesta by the time the bell rang at Miss Smithy's signalling the neighborhood to dinner.

Pearl took the kerosene can and poured some of the oil over Nick's hands and the gum came off easily. They ate ravenously and Viola was happy that they found her cooking edible.

The new overalls had caused Nick's legs to become sore just below his groins. "What's wrong?" he asked Pearl.

"You're galded," Pearl replied. "Mama," she called to Viola who was washing the dishes, "parch some flour for Nick to use on his legs. These overalls have galded him. Nothing on earth is better when you're galded than parched flour. You can put that soft flour on your legs and it's instant relief."

The temperature was in the 90s when they returned to the field and the dirt was almost too hot for Nick to bear. He was barefooted like all the other workers. He'd stand in the shade of a hill of tobacco as he pulled the leaves from the stalks. Pearl tied a band around his forehead to catch the perspiration, torn from the same ragged sheet. Pearl placed a band around her forehead also.

A cloud began to make up in the south and the sky became dark. Thunder was distant at first, but it soon began to rumble louder and flashes of lightning lighted up the sky.

It was too far to reach the house before the storm struck, so the workers went inside the tobacco barn.

"Don't touch the flues," Pearl cautioned Nick. "Lightning plays on the flues sometimes during electrical storms. Tobacco barns seem to be perfect conductors of electricity with the smokestack running up the end of the building and the flues going around the inside of the barn." As Pearl was saying this a deafening clap of thunder and a sudden flash of lightning seemed to have struck the barn, although a pine tree outside the barn was the victim.

The storm passed in about half an hour and they returned to putting in the green weed and everybody became soaked from the water on the leaves.

It was approaching dark when the tobacco was hung in the barn and

Craven went to the field and cut green corn and dragged it to the barn to feed the mules as well as taking some to the hogs in the pasture. Pearl and Nick went to the house, almost too tired to get to the porch where they sat for a little while.

"Hard work," Nick said. "I never realized farming was such hard work. I don't know how they do it day after day."

"They're used to it." Pearl replied. "It's a way of life, Nick."

"Yeah," was Nick's only reply.

Nick observed Craven as he went toward the tobacco barn and followed him. "Got to build a little fire in the furnace," Craven said. "Takes a couple of days for the backer to yaller before putting high heat to it. Day after tomorrow I'll get the heat up to around 180 and it will have to stay there until it is cured. That'll mean firing it day and night."

Nick drew up water from the well and put it into a tin tub and took it to the shed room, stripped off and washed as best he could. He had never been without the advantage of a bathtub before. Afterward he, Pearl and Hobby went out to the porch for a little while before retiring. Hobby chased fireflies while Nick and Pearl talked for a few moments.

"How's it going?" Pearl asked.

"Oh, all right," Nick replied. "Interesting to say the least. I really feel bad when I think about all the advantages I have while they have none. It seems a little unfair, Pearl."

"Now don't go feeling sorry for them," Pearl said. "They certainly don't feel sorry for themselves. They're as used to this way of life as you are to yours, and may be just as happy."

"I won't argue with that," Nick said. "But if you thought this would change my mind about you, you're dead wrong, woman."

"Really," Pearl replied. "But you may be speaking a little prematurely. Before two weeks have passed you may feel a lot differently. When Papa has to stay at the tobacco barn at night to fire the furnaces, you will stay and help him Nick. I want you to know the entire routine before we leave."

"Why? Planning on making me a farmer, I reckon."

"I might. You never can tell," Pearl replied.

"Might as well get used to it," Nick said. "If I know what I'm talking about, Hobby will be a farmer when he grows into manhood."

"I hope not," Pearl said. "Whatever they may be able to do for Hobby's leg, he'll never be able to actually do the farm work. I'm going to try to persuade him to become a doctor. Do you think that is possible, Nick?"

"Perhaps, but I wouldn't bet on it. That boy is so much in love with this way of life I don't think he can see beyond it. And if that's what he wants there isn't a thing wrong with it."

"Time for bed now," Pearl said as she rose and called Hobby in. "Go on to your pallet, Big Boy, and sleep well. And I just wonder what's going on at Joe's right now? If you had known what you were getting into, I'll bet you'd never have looked at me twice."

"One kiss," Nick said as he embraced her in the doorway.

Nick awakened again during the night. Even with the door open it was hot inside and he was perspiring. He went and sat on the edge of the back porch and listened as two cats shrieked while carrying out their mating act. A dog with a deep voice barked from a house up the road and distant lightning revealed a faraway thunderhead. A cow bell jingled in the distance and an owl screeched somewhere in the woods. They were lonely sounds, unfamiliar to a man whose life had been spent in the city. But there was a certain comfort in the sounds. This was the total reality of life, he thought. There was nothing fictitious about the world he had suddenly been thrust into. There were many lifestyles and many kinds of people, but each was individual and deserved a place in life.

Nick returned to the pallet and slept soundly until Pearl's voice aroused him. It was time to return to the fields and fill another barn with tobacco.

Abie Turner saw Viola rubbing clothes on the washboard in the yard and walked over to where she was. When Viola saw Abie she knew Abie had heard about Pearl being home, and with a man at that, and that she had to get first-hand information as to what was going on.

"Howdy Viola," Abie said. "Heard Pearl was home for a visit."

"Yeah," Viola replied, "and brought a man with her at that."

"A man!" Abie exclaimed. "Don't tell me Perline has done got married."

"No," Viola replied, "but she's talking about it."

"My, my," Abie said. "Well, I reckon Perline's old enough to know what she wants. And what is the man like?"

"As fine as you please," Viola said. "And a Greek at that. I was really worried about him before they got here. Thought I couldn't cook to suit him but I was worried more about having to put him on the floor to sleep. But I declare he's doing just fine and is even helping put in backer."

"Is Perline as good-looking as ever?" Abie asked.

"Gets prettier every day," Viola said. "You know as well as me that she was always pretty, but womanhood has really made her shine."

"I don't know when I'll get to see her," Abie said, "but I shore want to see her while she's here."

"You'll get to see her," Viola said. "I expect they'll be at church Sunday and they'll be here two weeks, so there'll be plenty of time."

"Has Perline decided to do anything about the boy's leg yet?" Abie asked. "It's shore gitting time to do something if she's going to. That Hobby is gitting to be a big boy."

"Yeah, Perline's planning to take him to a hospital later on this year. She mentioned to me taking him back with her to Memphis, but she's not broached the subject to Hobby yet and I expect there's going to be a time when she talks to him. And I don't know what me and Craven will do. That boy has filled our lives. But we know he's got to be operated on and given his chance in life."

"Well, I'll see you," Abie said as she left. "And don't you let Perline git away without me seeing her, you hear?"

"I hear," Viola said, thinking that Abie would have to say something to embarrass Perline before she left.

After the second barn of tobacco was finished, Craven began suckering the weed, and Pearl, Nick, Viola and Hobby joined him. "Now talking about hard work," Craven said, "this is one of the worst jobs of all to me. Pulling out all them suckers from between the leaves is a job and the backer smells rank and it will make you sick to the stomach sometimes. Gits your hand sore too if them suckers are big. I've had my hand so sore from suckering backer I couldn't hardly stand it. It's slow too. When you look at a field of backer filled with suckers it seems like you won't never git across that field. And if you don't git them out they'll git the strength of the guano and the backer won't fill out like it ought to. But you don't have to do this mess Nick. I feel like Perline is expecting too much from you. You hain't been used to none of this mess and if you want to go up to the house and rest feel free to do so."

"No sir," Nick said. "I came here to find out about farming and I'm going to learn all I can."

The slow heat in the barn had yellowed the tobacco and Craven filled the furnace late Wednesday afternoon and got the bunk and a tobacco truck ready for napping. "Can't fix nothing comfortable at the backer barn," he told Nick. "Sleep comes too easy as it is and if I had a soft pillow and a mattress to lie on I'd sleep the night away and the far would go out in the barn."

"I'm going to help you Mr. Turnage," Nick said. "Fix my bunk just like you do yours."

"All right," Craven said. "I'll put a piece of backer wood for you to rest your head on and we'll throw a quilt over that. You shore won't find that very comfortable. But like I said, you ain't out here for comfort. You sleep a couple of hours and then I'll show you how to fire the furnace and I'll git a little cat nap."

And so the week went. Craven was still curing the second barn of tobacco at midnight Saturday. "Don't usually cure backer on Sunday," he said, "but the Bible say if the ox gits in the ditch on Sunday, git him out. And the ox is in the ditch with this backer. I'll have to keep firing the furnace until sometime tomorrow."

"Let me do the curing after midnight Mr. Turnage," Nick said. "You see, I'm not very religion-oriented and it won't bother my conscience to cure the tobacco on Sunday. You've already taught me all I need to know about keeping the furnaces filled with wood and how often to tend the barns."

"All right," Craven said. "But we are expecting you and Perline to go to church Sunday. Everybody in the community will be wanting to see both of you and that's the best way to get to see them."

So Nick kept the furnaces stoked with wood until sunrise Sunday morning when Craven said the tobacco was "killed out," meaning the stems were dead and there was no danger of the tobacco rotting because of green stems.

As they were preparing to go to the house for breakfast, Nick noted an aroma that filled the air about him. "What in the world is that odor that smells so good?" he asked.

"Country ham," Craven replied. "The old lady kept the last one for Perline. Perline's crazy about country ham too. Says it's the best stuff she ever et. That's what you call poor folks eatin' high on the hog. That's food fit for a king. Ain't you never et country ham Nick?"

"Sure," Nick said, "but nothing that smelled like whatever that is I'm smelling now."

"Gravy's better than the ham," Craven said. "Viola will have rice I know and a spoonful or two of gravy over the rice makes it taste like something out of this world."

Breakfast was on the table when they arrived at the house and Pearl was already pressing their clothes for church. Nick's suit had a few wrinkles in it and she had the flat iron going, using a cloth over the suit material to prevent a shiny finish. Hobby's shirt needed touching up, and the dress she was wearing to church had to be gone over too.

"I don't believe in "arning" on Sunday," Viola said, "but as busy as everybody's been all week there's been no time for such things, so I hope God will forgive us."

"Mama, you just worry too much about some things," Pearl said. "What kind of God would it be that would hold us accountable for doing things that are necessary on the Sabbath? It's them big sins I worry about."

"But He said remember the Sabbath Day to keep it holy," Viola reminded her. "I know they's times when things have to be done, but if we git into the habit of doing just anything on Sunday, we'll soon forget what it's all about. I'm shore glad they ain't allowing none of them moving picture shows to operate in town on Sunday. If they did, every young'un with a dime would git to town and set in them theaters and see all that carrying on all evening."

"Mama, you're as old-fashioned as ever," Pearl said, "but you know something? I'm proud of you for it. We just don't know how to appreciate people like you enough. You're holding the world together for us."

Viola was busy preparing dinner and flour was on her face as she made apple dumplings to get in the oven. The chicken was already fried and the "tater" salad made. The string beans were tender and swiveled with liquor just coming to the top of the beans.

"Do you need to have anything pressed Mama?" Pearl asked.

"Lord no," Viola replied. "I just don't wait until Sunday to do things like that."

Pearl began dressing early for she wanted to look her best at church. It had been a long time since she had seen all the people she knew in the Bear Grass community and this was sort of a reunion. She had washed her hair Saturday night and put it in curlers. Nick's clothes had been placed on a chair in his room and Hobby's on his bed.

Nick used the wash pan and a rag torn from one of Craven's worn-out shirts and took a "rag" bath. Pearl did the same thing, using a pan from the kitchen. Hobby used a washtub for his bath.

Everybody was ready for church except Pearl. Nick looked distinguished in his light blue suit, white shirt and darker blue figured tie. Hobby wore his short tan pants and matching shirt with a brown-figured tie. Craven always wore his blue serge suit, white shirt and a stud in the shirt collar. He never wore a tie. Viola wore one of her three print dresses and white shoes. She had bought her first white shoes the summer before after wearing black patent leather shoes for many summers. She kept a bottle of Griffin's polish to use on the white shoes.

"Hurry up Perline," Viola called from the porch where the sun was already bearing down. "I'm already sweating and I'll be wilted down before I even get to Whispering Pines if we don't get started."

"Coming Mother," Pearl yelled back. Then she emerged through the door and Nick's heart skipped a beat. She wore a light blue, simple dress and a string of pearls with matching earrings and carried a white purse and spike heeled white pumps and her hair was golden and the blue dress accentuated her blue eyes and she was lovely.

"My, you're pretty," Craven said and Viola reminded him that Perline took after her mother.

"You sure look nice," Pearl told Nick. "You're a real knockout. And my boy is the handsomest young man around." She took her hand and rubbed it over his hair. "Go bring Mommy the comb. Your cowlick needs to be brushed down."

Craven, Viola and Hobby were excited as they rode in the back seat to Whispering Pines Church. It was a real treat for them, since they usually walked the mile from the house to the church.

Hobby held his arm out the window to get the full effect of the breeze and to wave at people walking along the road to church. Nick was a little apprehensive. He had attended church very little during his lifetime and when he did attend it was the Greek Orthodox Church. He knew nothing about the Baptist religion. Pearl had told him that sometimes people got "happy" and shouted and spoke in unknown tongues. This was totally foreign to him, but he determined to maintain an open mind about the religious service.

There was a commotion in the church when they entered and took their seats in a pew about midway of the sanctuary. People turned to look at them and a few nodded their heads. Abie Turner saw them as they entered and nudged Eliza Brown who sat on her right. She held up the fan supplied by the church and shaded her face. "See who just came in?" she asked.

"No, who," Eliza asked.

"Perline Turnage, with a man. And I hope it won't start tongues wagging and cause people to look down on poor Viola and Craven. They're good people and try to do right." Abie was using the fan to cool herself and she spoke in whispers. "But having a man in the house for a whole week and I hear they will be here another week, there's no telling what will be told before they leave."

"I don't see anything so unusual about that," Eliza whispered back. "Viola and Craven are right there with them and God knows we're narrow-minded enough in these parts. But I don't think you have all that much to worry about, Abie. We're ignorant enough but we ain't all that bad."

"Well, whatever they may say, there's one thing about it," Abie said. "That Perline is one good-looking woman. I'd say there's never been another woman in the Bear Grass community that could measure up to her in looks. And I declare I believe she gets prettier as she gets older."

Pearl had noted Abie talking and shading her face, and she was aware that Abie was talking about them. She had known Abie Turner all her life and idle talk was Abie's trademark.

Nick could not believe the transformation he saw in the congregation. He had seen some of them throughout the week toiling in the fields, wearing old worn-out clothing and getting themselves gummed up in the tobacco fields and having rags tied around their foreheads just as he had done. But today they were dressed well with the men's white shirts shining and the women's voile and print and eyelet dresses giving a variety of color to the sanctuary. And the people were friendly. Several had risen from their seats and come to where they sat and introduced themselves and welcomed them to Whispering Pines Church.

The choir opened the service with "At the Cross," followed by "Whiter Than Snow." Nick detected an off-key voice but the harmony was good otherwise. Rev. Otto Pell asked whether there were requests for prayer, and a number of hands were uplifted. A rousing prayer followed, led by Wilbur Stroud. Rev. Pell took his topic from the Beatitudes - "Blessed be the Peacemakers." He preached about how people around the world, and certainly some in the Bear Grass community, went about trying to destroy the peace rather than working to bring peace among the people. He mentioned back-biters and news-toters and Abie Turner cringed in her seat. He exhorted the people to strive to bring harmony among the people of the community and rather than putting those down who were already at the breaking point, lift them up and say kind words and do good deeds to bring them back into the mainstream of life.

There were a few hallelujahs and a few amens heard, but there was no shouting and talking in tongues and this disappointed Nick for he had been looking forward to such an outpouring.

After the service the people gathered on the grounds and Pearl and Nick were surrounded by those who knew Pearl. It was a genuine homecoming for Pearl who had not seen some of them since she had left Bear Grass. Some of the girls she had grown up with were there with their families and there was a lot of talk between them and the women showed off their children to Pearl and Pearl showed off Nick to them. Everyone knew that Hobby was Pearl's boy.

Miss Callie Stroud came up to Pearl after the crowd began to disperse and told her a chicken fry was being planned for them the following Saturday at her home. "There's plenty of room in my back yard," she said. "There's a lot of shade and it will be like old times to have you back, Perline. I know most of the people in the community will be there." Nobody in Bear Grass called her Pearl.

"My, that's nice of you, Miss Callie," Pearl said. "We will be looking forward to that."

"How did you enjoy the service?" Viola asked Nick as they were returning home.

"Very much," Nick replied. "I found the people friendly and I thought the preacher did a good job with his topic. He certainly said a mouth full about the way people are."

"Did you tell the women what you have been doing during the past week?" Viola asked Pearl.

"I sure did. I told them I'd been helping barn tobacco and suckering and taking it out and all the things I had done before I left."

"Were they surprised?" Craven asked.

"Of course not. People who know me know that I'm the same person I was then."

Then there was the usual Sunday dinner with a variety of vegetables and apple jacks for dessert. It had been worth the week's work to Nick just to sup at Viola's table. He had never tasted such food in all his life. He had learned the true value of Southern cooking at its best. He wondered whether he had gained ten pounds during the week and told himself if he hadn't it was because he had toiled and sweated in the fields and used up the excess calories.

The family reclined on the front porch for a while after dinner. There were areas of sunshine but shady places as well that allowed them a place to sit protected from the sun. Pearl had told Nick she wanted to have the afternoon alone with Hobby; that it was time to talk with him about going back with them to make plans for his surgery. Nick said he would go up to Stroud's store and get acquainted with the men in the neighborhood. He invited Craven to go with him but Craven said he didn't habitate the store on Sunday but that that was no reason for Nick not to go.

Pearl called Hobby who was out in the yard playing with a homemade cart. "I want to have you all to myself this afternoon," she said, and Hobby smiled. "Let's go down to the old log barn that is not being used. The one between here and the store. I noticed the weeds had been cut and there is a table under the trees and an old chair or two. It looks like a place that has been cleaned up for picnics and things like that. Come to think of it, somebody may be using it today. But I hope not."

"Anybody uses it that wants to," Hobby said. "Mr. Wilbur had it cleaned up for the public to use. It can't be used for curing backer no more."

"Good," Pearl said. "We'll get Nick to take the watermelon under the bed to the barn and we'll swill on watermelon and spit seeds and have fun."

Pearl had told Viola what she planned to do and that she wanted to take Hobby back with them to Tennessee. But Viola had told Pearl it would be a big shock to Hobby, as well as to her and Craven, for him to leave with such short notice. "I don't feel like I could hardly stand it, and I know Craven feels the same way," she said. "And there's no telling how Hobby will react. You just don't know how crazy Hobby is about this place Pearl. And if I must say so, that boy thinks a lot of Craven and me too. I hate the thought of the whole thing, but I know something has got to be done about Hobby's leg and Hobby knows that too."

"It's not easy Mama," Pearl answered. "It's something I've dreamed for years and now that it's about to happen I really don't know how to deal with it."

"I know," Viola replied. "And Hobby is beginning to ask questions Perline. He may put you through the third degree, so be on the lookout for whatever he might ask."

"I know," Pearl said with a sigh.

The area beside the barn was completely shaded by sweet gum and pine trees, and a few pine needles had fallen over the ground. Pearl removed the needles from the table and Nick brought the watermelon and Hobby was looking forward to cutting the melon. He loved watermelon. After Nick left and they were settled Hobby said, "What did you want to talk with me about Pearl?" He was already beginning to look like an adolescent, Pearl thought. His features had changed a lot in the year since she had seen him. Childhood was so fleeting it brought changes almost daily that were unnoticed by those who were not in close proximity with children during that special age.

"About your leg and that we have to prepare to have it operated on."

"Oh," Hobby replied. "But I'm used to that Pearl. It's something I have lived with all my life."

"But it must be repaired," Pearl said. "They can straighten your leg Hobby and then you will be able to get about like the average person. It is a pity it has had to go on this long and you've missed a lot during childhood. It can't continue through your adolescence and into young manhood."

"When?" Hobby asked.

"I want you to return with us to Tennessee next Sunday and let us set up an appointment."

"No, not that soon," Hobby said defiantly. "I couldn't stand to leave before having a chance to tell all my playmates goodby and playing with them. Please, Pearl, don't make me go like that. And how long will I have to be away?" He was beginning to cry.

"Darling," Pearl replied, "You may never return to Bear Grass to live. Mama and Papa are growing old and getting beyond the years of being able to carry on farm work. I'd like for them to move to Tennessee also to be near you and me. We could all be a family together out there."

"This is the worst day of my life," Hobby said. "I've always been happy and I never had anything to worry about and all of a sudden everything is falling apart."

"Well, maybe it won't work out that way," Pearl said. "But I have to think in your own best interest, little one. We could let things remain as they are and you could grow up with a crippled leg and the world would pass you by and you'd never be able to become a part of the mainstream of life. Just think what you'll be like when you have two good legs. You're already the handsomest boy around here and you'll tear girls' hearts apart one of these days. And not only that. If you were allowed to put this off now there would come a time when you would hate me for not carrying out my duties."

"Nothing could ever make me hate you," Hobby said, "I have loved you every day I have known you."

"You are the sweetest person that ever lived," Pearl said. "Now will you agree to return with me to Tennessee without going all to pieces and making me very unhappy?"

"I'll go to Tennessee," Hobby replied. "But please, Pearl, give me a month or two to tell all the other children and to think this thing out. Give me time to cry all of it out of my system for it seems right now that I've lost everything I ever had in the world. Give me until the end of summer, Pearl. Give me until October and I know school will be started then, but if I'm going in the hospital it won't make any differences about school being started. I expect I'll have to stay in the hospital for quite a while and somebody will teach me while I'm there. It has gone on this long and another month or two won't make that much difference."

"Let's cut that watermelon," Pearl said and Hobby took the knife and placed it in the center of the melon and pulled and the watermelon split in two, showing deep red meat and hundreds of black seeds. Hobby calmed down as they ate and laughed when Pearl began spitting seeds. "I'll bet I can spit them farther than you," she said, and Hobby took her up on the challenge.

Hobby suddenly asked, "Are you and Nick going to get married, Pearl?"

"I don't know," Pearl replied. "That depends on a number of things. Why did you ask?"

"I hope you will. I like Nick and he seems like the kind of man I'd think of as a father."

"I'm so glad to know that," Pearl said. "Your opinion will have a lot to do with whether I marry Nick or not."

They sat for a while and looked over the countryside. A few people passed along the road and they spoke to them as they passed. An occasional car would go by. Otherwise it was quiet in the area.

"Why did you go away?" Hobby asked and this caught Pearl off guard. She shivered and realized that this wasn't going to be the pleasant afternoon she had anticipated.

"I needed work," Pearl replied, "and I had a friend in Tennessee that offered to let me live with her. That's how it came about."

"I've missed you more that I can ever tell you," Hobby said, and tears came to Pearl's eyes.

"No one can ever know how good Grandpa and Grandma have been to me. No one can ever know how much I love them. But I have always felt that there was a vacant seat where you ought to be. I know when we have had something at school like Christmas parties and maypole dances and commencement Grandpa and Grandma were there just as if they had been my parents, and when others clapped they clapped just as hard for me. When I would get promoted and my name was called out they would stand and clap just as hard as other children's real parents. But I could always see in my mind an empty seat next to them and I even pictured you there clapping."

Pearl was sobbing now and Hobby tried to console her. "I'm sorry I caused you to cry Pearl. Here I am calling you Pearl when in my heart I want to call you Mom. But you know something Pearl. I felt that if I called you Pearl it would make it seem like it was not my actual mother."

"I can't stand this Hobby," Pearl said. "There are a lot of questions I can't answer for you today. You just aren't old enough to understand. But as soon as you reach that age, I will explain everything to you. Just keep on loving me and everything will come out all right in the end."

"Have I got to go to Tennessee next week?" Hobby asked.

"No," Pearl assured him. "I understand how you feel and I hadn't thought about it in the right sense. You can stay on until October and we'll make arrangements about moving you to Tennessee. Until then, have all the fun you can here in Bear Grass."

"Thank you Pearl," Hobby said. He placed his arms around his mother and planted a kiss on her face. Pearl felt relieved now that the tension had been broken and she had been able to get her point across to Hobby, even though it wasn't working out just as she had hoped for. But she realized, after thinking about it, that she shouldn't have expected Hobby to be ready to leave Bear Grass so suddenly. His life was here. This was his world, the only world he had ever known. But it wasn't over yet. She was dumbfounded by Hobby's next question.

Hobby had started to ask the question when a group of people in an old Chevrolet truck passed along the road, raising dust with children singing and hollering in the back.

"I'll bet they're going to the swimming hole," Hobby said. "They're not from around here."

"It's a good day for swimming," Pearl said as she wiped her forehead with her hand. "The humidity's high and it's pretty hot too. Not too comfortable, even in the shade. It will probably be hot in the fields tomorrow."

"Yeah" Hobby replied. Then he looked out over the fields and appeared to have his eyes cast toward the sky and said, "Who is my father?" Pearl felt as if she had been struck by a bolt of lightning.

"Hobby," Pearl said as she drew him to her, "I can't tell you at this moment, for you aren't old enough to understand fully. But I promise that when you are old enough I will tell you first. Okay?"

"I really want to know, Pearl. I have wondered about that since I was five years old. I knew there was something funny about it all, but I couldn't put it all together. I knew it was something I was not supposed to talk to Grandpa and Grandma about. I knew I couldn't talk about it to the other children. I knew I was different from the other children but it was something I had to keep to myself. I always felt like if you had been here everything would have been all right. But I've stood up for you Pearl. I've heard a few people say things that really hurt me - about my crippled leg and the funny way I walk and I remember a few bigger boys at school would come up with something ugly about me sometimes. I pretended that I didn't hear them and just acted like nothing had been said. But I didn't forget. And things like that helped me to learn to love Bear Grass even more. If I wasn't playing with Wilbert Lee or some of the other children, I was walking along the paths beside the woods or going back into the fields and learning about the plants and animals that lived in the back fields. I learned to love the trees and the plants and bushes that grow here and I learned to love the skies above me and they became a big part of my world. After all, they hover over me day and night and I think of them like an umbrella."

"What would they say?" Pearl asked, dreading to hear the answer although feeling compelled to know what was bothering her son.

"I'd rather not talk about it," Hobby said. "Let's just talk about something else."

"No, I want to know," Pearl insisted.

"I can't" Hobby said. "It might make you cry again and I can't stand to see you cry."

"I really feel that I should know," Pearl said. "Please tell me, Hobby."

"Well, for one thing, they called me bastard a few times."

"Who?" Pearl asked.

"Oh, some of the bullies at school. I remember Walter Scott always showing off. He was two or three years older than me, but he was just one grade ahead of me. To tell the truth, I was scared of Walter and Jacob Eubanks and Earl Radford. They were big with pimples on their faces and mustaches beginning to show and they'd cuss and laugh and pick on the smaller young'uns.

"And I tried to get on their good side, especially after Walter came up behind me and tripped me one day. I was walking as fast as I could and it really hurt me, but I didn't let them know it. I got up and smiled and dusted off my overalls and went on as if nothing had happened. When I was leaving I heard Walter say, ".... little crippled bastard." I turned around and went back to where the boys were standing, laughing. I looked up at Walter and said, "What's a bastard," Walter, and he said, "You, that's what," and I said why and he said because your mammy fooled around and when that happens and a woman hain't got no man and a young'un comes along, it's a bastard."

Pearl was sobbing now and Hobby began to cry also. They were in each other's arms and Hobby was snubbing and clear water was running from his nose and Pearl took her dress hem and wiped her eyes.

"I told you, Mommy that I ought not tell you," Hobby said between sobs. "Now I've hurt you real bad. Please stop crying Mommy. I love you just as much as any young'un loves his mother. You're better to me than a lot of mothers are to their children."

"I'm so sorry, Hobby," Pearl said. "I made a mistake when I was a very young woman and you are the one who has been hurt most. I can't ever make that up to you, but the greatest love I ever had was for you, my darling, and I will do everything in my power to be all the things you'd like me to be. And I'm sorry that I haven't been able to keep you with me through the years. You see, my dear, times have been very hard and when you're so limited in education you can't get a good-paying job. And there aren't any good-paying jobs now anyway. That is why Mama and Papa asked me to bring you to them and let them raise you. And during all this time I have been trying to save for your surgery and it has been impossible to save enough. But things are finally working out. I won't rest until your leg has been corrected and you are able to walk normally."

"Was I born with my leg like that?" Hobby asked.

"No, my dear," Pearl responded. "I made another mistake, but as God is my witness I couldn't help it, Hobby. When you were one month old I dropped you and you landed on an old bedstead lying on the floor. I didn't have any money to pay a doctor and you didn't act like you were hurt very much, so I just didn't do anything until a few weeks later I noticed you weren't holding your leg right. I became frightened and took you to the doctor, whether I could ever pay or not, and he said you had been injured badly and that it would be a few years before surgery should be attempted. My God, I've suffered the tortures of hell over that."

"Please don't worry," Hobby said. "I'm as used to that leg as I am breathing. Don't let that ever bother you again. If I never had surgery I could go through life without feeling badly about my leg."

"That's easy to say now," Pearl said, "but life is just beginning for you son. When you're grown-up you will feel different about that. You will want to be popular and to have girl friends and to be a part of society. You could be a part of life as you are but you wouldn't be able to reap the rewards like you'll be with two good legs. Later on you'd be embarrassed."

"I reckon you're right," Hobby said. "I'm too young to understand for I'm not getting much out of what you are saying. What I want to know is does Nick like it down here?"

"He loves it," Pearl said, "and he hasn't had the time to be with you like he wants to, for we're too busy in the fields now. He wanted to take you fishing and to Hallsborough to visit the park and see the animals there and go up in the woods with you and a lot of things that he hasn't been able to do. But Nick definitely likes it here and he has fallen completely in love with you."

"I wonder what it would be like to have a real father?" Hobby asked. "But I reckon I'm getting too old now for him to feel like a real father to me."

"Not at all, Pearl said. "Let's hope he can become that father one of these days. Say, let's get this watermelon rind to the woods and clean up. It's getting late and I want to just sit here for a while and think things out all by myself. You go on back to the house and Nick will be back from the store soon and you and he can do whatever you want to. I just feel like I need a little time to myself."

Pearl was consumed with guilt - guilt for all the things Hobby had said to her in such a short span - guilt that she had already felt in a thousand ways before she had heard the words from her son. She thought of her determination to acquire knowledge to compete with that part of society that had had the advantage of education and in looking back upon her actions realized that she had acted as a person without a modern outlook on life in neglecting Hobby when he was injured so soon after birth. But she had realized later that she had only begun to think about trying to reach a higher educational level after the accident. Before that, she had only been a child, thinking and acting as a child without being aware of all the possibilities that existed, even in her circumstances.

The afternoon sun was dropping lower and all was quiet until the 5 o'clock train shrilled its whistle at the crossing and the cars rolling over the tracks made their clackety-clack sounds as they crossed the ties. The same old train that had whistled when she was a girl and heard the sound that always made her feel a little sad. Eleven a.m., 2:30 p.m., 5 p.m. and 9:30 p.m. every day, becoming a part of Bear Grass for a few fleeting moments then moving on into the world of commerce. So few in Bear Grass who saw the passing of the train ever anticipated riding on one, content to hear the sounds and see the cars passing and an occasional hobo sitting on top getting away from one scene and searching for another, always moving like the trains.

It was a beautiful land, although dilapidated and run-down with no signs of progress; with poverty ever-present and tomorrows that would continue in the same pattern. But it was better than a mill village where there was no outdoors to explore and nothing to build dreams upon.

Being poor was a way of life, no matter where people lived. In the most beautiful cities where some people lived in luxury, even during hard times throughout the land, most people lived in squalor and merely tried to exist. To see the disparity between those who lived well and those who lived in hovels and scavenged for wood to burn and robbed trash cans for food made those who lived that life in the cities far more discontent than for the masses in the rural area to live under such conditions.

There were no comparisons in Bear Grass, although some people lived on a higher plane than others. After all, landlords were expected to have a little better homes and a few more clothes than the sharecroppers. She was glad she had been exposed to that life in order to be able to appreciate the finer things, if they ever came her way.

She couldn't get Hobby off her mind after all the questions he had asked. He was such an intelligent child he would have seen into the circumstances of his birth and she should have realized that. But in her heart, he was still the baby she had always worshipped. He would be into puberty in a year or two and his entire body process would change. She couldn't visualize him as a man in the sense that Nick was a man. She couldn't visualize Hobby in a sexual light. She wished she could keep him the boy always, innocent and without the impulses that drive men and women to commit sexual acts. To be without temptation was the ideal, she thought, particularly where Hobby was concerned.

But Pearl came to terms with herself that Sunday afternoon as she thought about her life and all the things that had happened. She said to herself, "I can't help what is past. Nothing on earth can ever change that. I can't now make recompence with Hobby for what I have done to him. We have both suffered and his suffering has been a result of my actions. But if God will help me, I will make him proud of his mother and do all that I can to make his life happy. I can't grieve over the past, not when the possibility of a new life for both Hobby and me may be opening up. And I can appreciate the good life as well as any person. But God, please don't let me ever feel above what I see before me at this moment. Don't let me ever feel ashamed of my heritage and the good people I have known here in Bear Grass. Don't let me ever be ashamed of Mama and Papa or any of the people I've known here in this little out-of-the-way place that most people have never seen. I would like to be all the things Mama and Papa want me to be and I know in my heart they are right. But you know that I want more than that.

"Let me know something of that life but keep me in my place so that I may not become a bigot or feel distaste for the life I have known. I will not let the shadow of a sharecropper stand in the way of accomplishment. I will not let the lack of education blind me to those things that we call "culture." Let me learn the ways of the elite so that I may be all the things Nick wants me to be as well as for my own personal satisfaction. I will be all that Nick wants me to be so long as it is within reason.

"There is nothing left to him to wonder about my past and I'll be damned if I'll bow down to him or any other man because of such a humble background. I have done an almost impossible thing in bringing Nick to Bear Grass, but there was no other way to show him what my life has been all about. And if he were ever to throw up my past to me I'd leave him almost before he knew it. But that won't be with the Nick I know. Thank you God, for Nick Staphal."

She was preparing to return to the house. The gnats were beginning to annoy her as they swarmed around her face. She tried blowing them away with her breath but had to resort to her hands to fan the tiny insects away.

The sun had become a red ball in the sky and the heat was oppressive with no sign of air stirring. The leaves on the trees were still and the smell of green tobacco hung heavy in the air. As she was wiping off the tobacco truck again where the watermelon had sat she saw a boy coming up the road and as he drew nearer she realized it was Wilbert Lee Turner. She hadn't see him since she had been home although Hobby had talked about him a lot.

"Hi Wilbert Lee," she said as he approached the barn.

"Hello," Wilbert Lee said. "I knew you were home but Pa's had me out in the fields helping put in backer. You know how it is this time of year."

"Yeah, and I'm beginning to learn all over," Pearl said. "I've been out in the fields for the past week and will be out there again this week. But it's not too bad. I'm just not used to the sun and I've had to try to cover up when I was out in the fields and that makes it all the harder. I've been wearing a pair of Mama's old black stockings on my arms and one of her old bonnets and I tell you they have just about smothered me. Say, how are things going? Hobby talks about you all the time and that boy looks up to you like you are some sort of god. I can see how he likes you, but you must have put some sort of spell over that boy."

"Ah, you know Hobby," Wilbert Lee said, careful not to say all the things he'd like to since he was talking to Hobby's mother. "No, I've not done anything to Hobby. We see a lot of each other and since Hobby can't do a lot of things I can I reckon he looks up to me and wants to be like me. If it's not that I don't know what it could be."

"Well I'm glad he has you Wilbert Lee," Pearl said. "I hope he hasn't upset you with his hero worship. He's a little crippled boy, you know, and it's easy for him to look up to boys like you to try to pattern his life after. But I hope that it won't be too long before Hobby will have the surgery he needs to make him a regular boy."

"Me too," Wilbert Lee said. "Hobby is a good boy but he's a little bit nerve-wracking sometimes. He wants to do all the things all us other young'uns do and he just can't do them and that bothers him. But he just don't give up."

"I'm sorry to hear Hobby gets on your nerves Wilbert Lee," Pearl said. That statement disturbed her and she took a closer look at Wilbert Lee. He was a very handsome boy but there was an arrogance about him that bothered her. She told herself it might be better to get Hobby out from under his influence as early as possible.

"I've got to be getting to the house," Pearl said. "I'm glad I got to see you Wilbert Lee. You be good to my Hobby now, you hear?"

"I'm always good to Hobby," Wilbert Lee replied.

Nick had returned from the store when Pearl arrived at the house. "Well, did you learn about Bear Grass and all its deep dark secrets?" Pearl asked.

"I was caught up on more of what life is all about than any half-day in my life," Nick said, laughing. "I heard some of the tallest tales and the wildest things that men in these parts have done than you can imagine. I almost feel like I grew up here and helped the boys make moonshine whisky and run from the law and gallavanted around and got pissy-assy drunk and raised hell." He laughed openly.

"Oh, that's nothing but a country store for you," Pearl said. "The men at those places strip every woman naked and look into her soul and pass their judgment on her and all that mess. That's why a women always hates to pass the store. She knows the men are looking at the way she walks and look for a hint of teasing in the way her hips move. It's sickening, but that's life."

"No, really they were very nice," Nick said. "And boy, they asked everything they could think of concerning Greeks. It must have been the first time they had had a person outside the community and of a different nationality around. They must have thought I was different from the kind of people they are. But we got along fine."

"I almost wish we had planned to stay for just one week," Pearl said. "The next week will be long, and Hobby isn't going back with us. He pleaded with me to stay on in Bear Grass until October and I was able to understand his point of view. He has to have time to adjust to the change and to see all his playmates and say goodbye to them and play with them a few more times. And he asked a lot of questions I wasn't able to answer at this time, but I think everything will work out all right in the final analysis. I am carrying around an awful lot of guilt right now, but I've come to better terms with myself and I know better how to plan for the future."

"I'm just sorry I haven't been able to spend any time with Hobby," Nick said. "You know all the things I had hoped to do."

"Yeah, I told him," Pearl said. "He understands, but he sure is high on you Nick. He thinks you're great."

A heavy cloud was making up in the west and lightning began to flash and loud thunder rolled overhead as they were eating supper, and the trees in the yard seemed to be bending over the house with their heavy branches raking the roof and the rain fell in sheets.

"There's hail in that cloud," Craven said. "Whenever you see a cloud with that yaller tint you can look out for hail." But no hail fell on Craven's land.

Nick felt an uneasiness when the old house shook from the storm and for a little while wished he were in a more stable house. But then he realized that this old shell of a house had withstood the elements for many decades.

The storm lasted for about an hour and after the skies became calm and the rain was a soft pitter-patter on the roof, the family retired for another long week lay ahead in the fields.

It was a repetition of the first week, with all the family in the fields from sunup till dark and Craven and Nick firing the tobacco barns at night. Nick learned to appreciate the hour for dinner when he could take a quilt and roll it up for a pillow and place his straw hat over his face to keep the flies away and get a few moments' sleep. He had found the floor a more comfortable place to sleep that he had thought of it as being. In thinking about all that had happened since he had met Pearl, it was almost like being in another world. The experience would give him something to think about for many years to come. His private world had disappeared in the past week and he had been drawn closer to other people than he ever had before.

He had passed through the darkened hall one night, and with all the doors open, he was able to see into the rooms without trying to pry. An oil lamp was giving only enough light to detect objects in the room. Apparently the wick had been turned to its lowest point to shed a ghostly shadow over the room, and he had seen Miss Viola kneeling at a chair. He didn't hear any words but he was aware she was kneeling in prayer, and it touched him. Oh, to have such faith, he thought. Nick Staphal knew that night that he would forever hold in his heart a very special feeling for the people in Bear Grass.

The days were long and hot and the nights short and humid. The crickets chirped. The mosquitoes hummed around the ears and put their stings into human bodies. Chickens scratched holes under canna bushes or hills of tobacco and scratched the dirt over their feathers in an effort to cool off. Hogs lay in any mudhole they could find. Cows stood in the shade of trees and chewed their cuds and switched their tails at insects that plagued them. People toiled in the fields with sweating bodies and gummy hands, working in the almighty weed that was revered for its money value.

Nick and Pearl worked with the other farm hands with little time for any other activities. There was no socializing and actually little conversation. It was a time of work to harvest the golden weed. It was a complete reversal of Nick and Pearl's way of life. The week was long but it seemed that Saturday came soon enough.

Miss Callie's back yard was filled with tobacco trucks, and chairs from one of the funeral parlors in Hallsborough. Tablecloths were spread over the trucks where the food would be spread. A wooden washtub had been scrubbed and filled with lemonade. The yard had been swept and the sun filtering through the trees cast spots of sunshine among the shaded places. A nest of mockingbirds in a mulberry tree provided a varied musical program and barks from neighborhood dogs let it be known they were aware of something different going on in the neighborhood.

There was more traffic than usual along the road, raising dust that settled over the neighborhood. A few people meandered along the road with fishing poles, going down to the creek for an afternoon of fishing. And people were also gathering to honor Perline who was one of their own and had been away for a number of years. Some of her friends with whom she had been close before she went away to Tennessee had not seen her when she would come home to visit. Most all of them had married and had families. Many of them made a special effort to attend the chicken fry.

Pearl arrived early, along with Nick, Hobby and her parents. She greeted guests as they arrived and her old friends would introduce her to their spouses and hold up their small children for her to admire as well as those that stood around them. In turn, Pearl introduced them to Nick. There was a lot of laughing and reminiscing and catching up on events over the past ten years.

There were around a hundred people there, according to one or two who tried to get a head count. Pearl was the center of attention, and Nick eventually gathered with the other men under one of the many trees in the yard, talking and joking while the women spread the food on the trucks. There were bowls of collards, cabbage with cornmeal dumplings, half grown stringbeans cooked full length with country meat, snapped, chopped up and even yellow wax beans to satisfy most any appetite; potato salad, corn on the cob as well as "rosen ears." There were squash and beets and cucumber pickles sliced into four pieces lengthwise with hot pepper, salt and vinegar added; freshly made chow chow and pepper relish, pies of all descriptions as well as cakes, some with six or eight very thin layers with all manner of fillings. And there were platters filled with fried chicken. It was a veritable feast.

It was a day of renewing old acquaintances for Pearl. She smiled through it all and received many compliments on her appearance, and she handed out a lot of compliments also. She was especially pleased to see Lonnie Strickland and his family. Lonnie had been one of her "flames" when she was a teen-ager. He was handsome as a boy, but had grown into a very plain farmer, although she still found something about him attractive; perhaps as a result of the feelings she had had as a girl.

The sun had gone beyond the horizon when the party broke up. It would soon be twilight and many of those in attendance had other things to do Saturday night. Pearl was anxious to leave also, for they had to pack and prepare to return to Tennessee on Sunday. They planned an early start in order to get back home sometime Sunday night. She had to report to Joe's Restaurant on Monday.

Chapter 14

T hen came October. On the first Monday of the month Nick came for Hobby. Joe needed Pearl at the restaurant and she and Nick had talked it over and decided Nick going alone would give he and Hobby a chance to really get acquainted with each other.

Hobby had cried until there were no tears left; only snubs when he talked with Craven and Viola, as they awaited Nick's arrival. To make matters worse, the skies were threatening and clouds hung low on the horizon and Hobby's world was obscured by a mist that isolated the community. He sat around the boxes that had been packed and securely tied with tobacco twine. Every item he possessed was around him. Everything had been taken from the nails on the walls. His sling shot and bows and arrows were lying atop one of the boxes. Viola was teary-eyed as she sat and looked silently out of the window. Craven walked around the premises to pass the time.

Nick arrived about mid-morning and Hobby's heart skipped a beat when he heard the car drive up in the yard. This was it. This was the end of his life in Bear Grass. But Nick came in with a smile on his face and was so cheerful Hobby actually smiled while they were preparing to leave for Tennessee. Pearl sent Viola material to make two dresses for herself and two shirts for Craven and Nick told Hobby that his mother had gifts for him when he got to Tennessee. Nick also gave Craven and Viola twenty five dollars each which they tried to decline, but he insisted that they keep it. He told them how much he had enjoyed his visit during the summer and they felt good about that.

Then came the parting. Viola stooped and put her arms around the boy as violent sobs shook her body. "I love you son," she said and Hobby couldn't speak. He just held his head on her shoulder and sobbed. Craven didn't sob but tears were in his eyes. "I'll miss you boy," he said with a pat on Hobby's shoulder. "You let me hear from you now, you hear?"

Then they were off for Tennessee.

"Now cheer up," Nick said as he placed his large hand on the boy's knee. "You're going to find everything's going to be all right. I'll admit there are big changes in store for you. But they happen to all of us Hobby, in one way or another. Life doesn't always just go on in the same pattern. It would eventually become boring if that were the case. But look what you have to look forward to."

"When do I go to the hospital?" Hobby asked.

"A week from today," Nick replied. "And you'll be there for quite a while Hobby, so just accept that as part of the healing process. You've never been to a large city, and Baltimore is a large place. They have one of the best medical complexes anywhere at Johns Hopkins. It's recognized the world over. And I know a hospital isn't the greatest environment in the world to look forward to, but it is all for your own good, son. Just flow with the tide and it will all be over before you know it and you can go on with your life."

"You just don't understand," Hobby said as he gazed out the window, not really seeing the countryside. His thoughts were in turmoil.

This boy beside him had such an effect on Nick he couldn't understand it himself. He had been around him such a short length of time, yet he felt that this boy could be his own flesh and blood. Pearl had told him so much about the boy and his love for Pearl was so great he felt more than a kinship for him.

"No, I'm sure I don't understand Hobby," Nick said. "But I'm trying to and I can certainly see things from your point of view. But I feel very close to you son and I would do as much for you as I would my own son. I just hope you can think of me in the same light."

"I can," Hobby replied.

"There are a million things I want us to do together," Nick said. "And we'll do all of them Hobby. We'll just have to put them off for a while. There'll be the period of surgery and recuperation and maybe more surgery, but time will take care of all that, and then we'll be the pals I want us to be, you'll see."

"I'm glad," Hobby replied, "but it won't be in Bear Grass, and that will make a difference. If we could do those things in Bear Grass I'd be the happiest person in the world. I feel like I've lost home forever and I know I'm selfish, but I don't think I'll even try to like any other place as well. It might cause me to hurt again. I don't want to ever be hurt like this again, Nick."

"I hope not," Nick replied and in that moment he knew that whatever plans he or Pearl might have for the boy, whatever opportunities might come his way, there was a longing in his young life that nothing would ever satisfy except the environs of home.

Chapter 15

I t was a time to pause, to get life's priorities in order, to reflect on all the events that had brought them to this point. It was a time for play and relaxation.

The trauma of Hobby's initial surgery was over. The prognosis was good for a successful series of operations that could make the boy reasonably normal. Dr. Robards had gone into detail with Pearl and Nick about the procedures necessary to correct the deformity. It would require at least three operations, and possibly four, and the boy would be hospitalized for a year at the least, and possibly a year and a half. He would be tutored while hospitalized and would not get behind in his studies. During convalescent periods between surgery he would be allowed in a wheelchair after the first surgery and could participate in a number of activities in the hospital gym. At the present time Hobby was wearing a cast up to his waist and it was grotesque and bulky. He was confined to bed with the leg held up by an overhead pulley.

Pearl and Nick had stayed in Baltimore for the first two weeks after Hobby entered the hospital, standing by his bedside after he came from the recovery room and attending to him as he vomited yellow liquids, wiping his mouth and chin and placing wet towels on his forehead to try to allay the nausea.

"It tastes so bad," Hobby had said. "Ether is the worst thing I've ever had anything to do with. Just to smell it makes me sick all over again. And I tried so hard to swallow when my face was covered with that mask. I knew if I could just swallow I would be all right."

"Yeah, you were trying to swallow all right," Pearl said...."your tongue. You've got a bruise on each side of your throat and that's what you felt when you couldn't swallow."

"I'll be durn," Hobby said drowsily. "If I'd a done that there wouldn't be no Hobby around now, would there?" By now he was tired and drifted off to sleep. But after the nausea was gone the boy recuperated quickly. There was a good deal of pain at the outset, but pain-killing drugs were administered. He was soon jovial and adjusting to hospital life.

After two weeks he was his old self again, although confined to bed. "You're doing fine," Pearl said as she leaned over and kissed him, running his blond hair through her fingers. "And we're going to have to be going, sonny boy. We've got a lot of things to do, and you're in very good hands. You already know that you're going to be here for a long time, but everything is looking good sonny, so I know you're going to be all right. And just think! The end result will be a straight leg! I'm so excited I feel like I'm floating on a cloud."

"I know you can't stay," Hobby replied. "I'm glad you and Nick came and I know you'll be back. That's all that matters. You and Nick need to relax and have some fun for a change. Grandma will write to me regularly and that way I'll know what's going on in Bear Grass. I'll be all right."

"Yeah, you're going to be fine," Nick said. "And we'll be checking on you regularly, and when something important comes up we'll be sending you telegrams, since you can't get to a telephone at this time."

"Telegrams!" Hobby exclaimed, as if they were too important to waste on a boy like him.

"Sure," Nick said. "And remember all the things we talked about on the way to Tennessee."

"I'm so glad you and Pearl are married," Hobby said. "I wish it could have been a big church wedding and all that though."

"It sure would have been nice," Nick said, "and that's what I wanted, but the urgency of the situation took precedence over that. This thing had to be right, Hobby, and I didn't want anybody to be able to cast a reflection on your mother's character. We've got to get everything organized, and then we can really start living."

"It didn't matter about a church wedding in the least," Pearl said. "We are as married as if we had been married in some large cathedral. I don't care about all the frills anyway."

On the morning after Nick brought Hobby to Tennessee the three of them had driven downtown, first to the only jeweler in Clyburn and Nick insisting on a two-carat ring for Pearl, then to a justice of the peace and were married quietly, with Joe from Joe's Dining Room serving as one witness, and Lucille, Pearl's friend at the mill, as the other. Pearl had been dressed in a simple white shantung dress with a V neckline and a string of pearls.

"What are you going to do now?" Hobby asked as they were preparing to leave.

"We're thinking about going back to Carolina for a week or so, down to the coast," Nick said. "I know it's too late for swimming and all the usual beach cut-ups, but we want to go some place where it's quiet so we can laugh and talk and just relax and make some kind of plans for our future."

"Gosh, I wish I could go," Hobby said. "I've never been to the beach. Mr. Sam took a bunch of young folks down to Wilmington last year, but Grandma and Grandpa though it would be dangerous for me crammed on a big truck with so many other young'uns."

"You'll get to go," Pearl assured him. "Just wait until all your surgery is over and you'll be able to do anything you want to do."

Nick extended his hand. "Bye now, young fellow. Have fun and don't be running all over this complex, you hear?"

"Silly," Pearl said as she stooped and kissed the boy on the cheek. "Take care, old buddy." She patted him on the head.

Hobby wanted to cry but he knew this would be the worst thing he could possibly do, so he just said, "Bye" as they left the room. The tears came after they were gone.

"You've haven't said a word to me about going to the beach," Pearl said as she slid onto the seat while Nick held the door open.

"Now didn't I," he remostrated. "I thought I'd told you about that, dearie."

"Calling all the shots, I see," Pearl pouted but with a wry grin on her face.

"It just seems the exact thing to do at this time," Nick replied. He looked at his woman with pride swelling inside. "We're not having a normal beginning for a marriage," he said, "so we've got to do something to help make up for the void."

"You're making such a big deal of what we're missing by not going through a long rigamarole of a formal wedding and all that. Boy, if you only knew how marriages are carried out back home, you'd stop running off at the mouth about it. Just about everybody either goes to the justice of the peace or a minister to get married. Some go to Dillon, South Carolina. That's very popular, especially with girls too young to get their parents' consent and those who are forbidden to see the "sorry scoundrels." I don't think you're being very practical about it Nick."

"Honey, I know I sound crazy," Nick replied. "But you see, I'm so crazy about you, woman, and so overwhelmed that you're actually mine, I feel like a teen-age boy about the whole thing. You're just going to have to put up with a little of my foolishness until one day I'll settle down and try to act like a man of my age. Don't you understand, honey?"

"I know that you're silly and all that," Pearl said as she placed her hand on his leg, "but if I must tell the truth, I'm thrilled to death with it all. I'm walking on air too, fearful that I'm dreaming and that I'll wake up and be back in the mill any time."

"You have no idea what thoughts have run through my mind about us," Nick said. "Remember, we still haven't been to Memphis, and after our beach vacation, we're going there. That's when the celebration begins."

"What celebration?" Pearl asked.

"Well, you've got to be properly introduced to Memphis society. I'm not going to take a plum like you and hide you. They're going to know you in Memphis, you can bet on that."

"I'll tell you one thing, buster. You'd better not try something to embarrass me, or I'll turn the tables on you so fast it'll make your head swim. I'm not high society, and you know it. Never have been. Never will be. So you had better tread very carefully with me Mr. Nick Staphalopoulous."

"Damn, you called me by my full name. That little ole country girl is gitting on up there ain't she? If you want to call the entire name as it was before I had it shortened, you would say Nicholas Adolphus Staphalanopoulous. But that's too much to put on any human being."

"No worse than Perline," Pearl replied with a grin. "Say, when are we going down to the Carolina coast? I don't have any kind of beach wear, never having had access to or the privilege of beachcombing; not that I didn't want to but simply because I had no one to take me and no money for extra indulgences. I've got to have beachwear."

"We can go shopping tomorrow," Nick said, "and head for the beach the next day. I just can't wait and I wish there wasn't another soul down there. I want you to myself with all that ocean and sand."

"So you can drown me?" Pearl laughed.

"Yeah."

The beach was almost deserted. It was Tuesday and most people had had their last fling of the summer season on Labor Day weekend. However, there were a few still lingering beside the blue Atlantic. When Nick and

Pearl left their cottage and made their way down to the water's edge, they saw a young man and woman running briskly across the sand, then stop suddenly and embrace, after which they resumed their frolic, running out into the water and retrieving shells.

The ocean was calm, as if it carried no malice in its might, with gentle waves lapping the shore on a low tide and the blue of the sky mingled with the waves and the two became one in the distance.

They placed a large towel on the sand and lay down facing each other.

"It's the most ideal time I can imagine to come to the beach," Nick said. "The breezes are cool, but not cold. The sun is warm, but not hot. I feel like I could lie here forever."

"It's lovely," Pearl agreed. "I think this is just what the doctor ordered for us, after the rush of summer and all we've been through." She was thinking of the two weeks in Bear Grass when she had put Nick to the ultimate test. And the fact that she was now his wife made her feel guilty somehow.

"I'm so happy darling," she said as she gazed out over the expanse of water, her eyes following a seabird as it flew beyond her vision. "But I feel like you've downgraded yourself, Nick."

"Now just what in the hell does that mean?" Nick asked, raising himself up on an elbow.

"Somehow I feel like you're allowing yourself to wallow with the hogs," Pearl said.

"Are you calling yourself a sow Pearl?" Nick asked as his eyes flashed angrily.

"I don't mean that Nick. But as I think about it more and more I realize that you're making a drastic change in your life."

"Any more than you?"

"But you have everything just right," Pearl reminded him. "You're somebody, Nick and I'm a nobody and you know that and have known it ever since you've known me. You're pulling yourself downward. Think about it for a moment. Born a sharecropper, going into the mills, graduating into a waitress, and now the wife of a prominent Tennessean who has a brilliant future cut out for himself. Things like that don't happen once in a million years."

Nick picked up a handful of sand and rose suddenly, throwing it as far toward the water as he could "You make me angry Pearl," he said as he began walking toward the sea. He looked back as he moved farther away and said, "I don't know what in the hell I would have to do to make you understand that I love you more than life itself that I haven't already done.

I don't give a damn about "social standing" (he said it with a slur and a shrug of his shoulders) "or anything else that would cause me to feel differently about you. And I wasn't born with any kind of standing and wouldn't have a dime today if it weren't for my poor immigrant dad who slaved his life away just to make life easy for me. Don't you think for one minute they were paying any attention to Nick Staphyl until they learned I had acquired a lot of property in the Memphis area. That kind of crap makes me sick, Pearl, and you're making me sicker. Here we have all this beautiful weather, the entire Atlantic at our disposal, everything conducive to making love, and you come up with shit like that."

"I didn't mean to start anything," Pearl said as Nick returned to where she was lying on the beach towel. "It's just that you've taken on so much with me, Nick. But as God is my witness, I wasn't trying to snare you for your money, for I was head-over-heels in love with you before I knew you had vast property holdings. And then there's Hobby and all his problems. Can't you understand why I feel as I do? There are so many extremes between our ways of life I wonder whether we'll be able to bridge them."

Nick lay down beside her and took her into his arms. He squeezed her tightly and said, "Darling, if that's all you've got to worry about, your troubles are all over as of this moment. I'm your husband now and not something of the imagination. And I didn't come down here for such as this, so we're going to have fun for the rest of the week. You hear me you little old country hick?"

Pearl pinched Nick's thigh and he screamed. He reached down and tickled her toes and she screamed and they rolled off the towel onto the sand and Nick gathered it in his hands and rubbed it all over her body, and she did the same to him. And the sky was blue and a few people were running up and down the beach, for the most part they were isolated from the world and both reflected on life and it seemed to be a fairyland with all the magical elements in place to make it a perfect siesta. Only white specks of cirrus clouds formed over the Atlantic and seabirds pitched on a fishing wharf nearby, squawking their songs to the lovers.

When night fell they walked under the stars along the big waters and listened to the sound of the sea as the waves lashed the shore and one night they saw a sliver of a Carolina moon and it prompted a love song with Pearl singing soprano and Nick coming in with the bass. They embraced and laughed and Pearl thought about Hobby and what he was doing and about her parents and the people in Bear Grass and she wished they could only be as happy as she was at this very moment.

The next day they took a dip in the ocean and it was cool and Pearl had chill bumps on her and Nick pulled her down beside him on the beach towel and placed his arms around her and pulled her close to him to give her warmth from his body. She nestled there, content and happy to be in his embrace. He rubbed a toe over her thigh and tickled her and she frowned and he laughed and continued running his toe over her leg.

"Pest," she said and he said, "Little old hick hash-slinger, what you talking about girl?" laughing.

"Watch it," Pearl responded.

"Lem' me see them fingernails girl. Have you got all that "bacca" gum off of you from the summer?" And Pearl laughed because he didn't have the proper pronunciation for tobacco, that was called "backer" in Bear Grass.

"City dood," she said, "you can't even say backer." Then she went into a hysterical laugh and Nick laughed with her, not knowing what she was so demonstrative about. Between spasms of laughter she tried to tell him about the day she saw him running to a big hill of grass with a chicken dropping squashed between his toes and him trying to walk on the side of his foot. She reached down and pulled up one of his feet. "Lem' me see if you're still loaded with chicken shit," she said. Then they both became hysterical and acted silly and finally got up and ran for half a mile down the beach and then back to the cottage. It was exactly what they needed.

Then the week was over and it was time to return to Tennessee.

"What are we going to do now?" Pearl asked as they were dressing to begin the trip back home.

"I thought we'd go to your place for a day or so and get things ready for moving," Nick said. "Then, we're going to Memphis and you're going to be a part of the Memphis scene. I'm going to settle down to being the husband of the only woman in the world and you can do anything on earth you want to except to pay any attention whatsoever to any other man in the world. Do your thing, whatever it may be. But we've got to find out first whether you like my little place."

"I'll like it, don't worry about that," Pearl replied.

Then it was time to prepare to leave the coast and return inland. And fall was in the air and life became a fairyland for the two lovers as they traveled along the Carolina highways that would take them back to Tennessee. A man was raking hay in one field. He would gather the hay in the rake for a distance of about twenty five feet, then lift the rake to leave the hay in a straight pile across the field. Cows were standing contentedly in a pasture that came up to the edge of the highway. A fence with barbed wire at the top kept the cattle from getting out. Some men were breaking corn and throwing the ears into a pile to be picked up later with a mule-driven wagon and hauled to the barn. And everywhere there was color, reflected in little ponds alongside the highway and on hillsides and in marshy places and the bluest of skies added to the color.

"This is really a beautiful state," Nick said as he gazed out over the landscape. "You'd think that this region, being generally flat, would be a dull and dreary background. But that's not the case at all. It is so serene looking and everything looks in order and it's just a lovely setting. I wouldn't mind living in this area at all."

"It's no wonder Hobby loves it so much," Pearl said. "That boy loves everything about this section and nothing on this earth will ever change that."

"Yeah, you've mentioned something about wanting Hobby to become a doctor, and I've been thinking a lot about it, and I sort of question whether that's a good decision Pearl. You can keep Hobby out of Bear Grass, but you can't get Bear Grass out of him. He loves you enough that I know he will abide by your wishes, but I believe it might be better if he majored in the field of agriculture. He loves plants and animals and terrain and trees and everything about nature. Have you thought about all of that?"

"I sure have, Nick, and I want Hobby to be happy more than anything in this world. However, I believe that once he becomes acclimated to something new he will feel differently. God knows I'm not ashamed of his rural background, but I want that boy to really be somebody, and I'm afraid he will limit his potential if he goes into the agriculture field. He will be limited as to what he can do because of his leg, despite surgery, and with the benefits he will receive from surgery, I am hoping he will have a desire to become an orthopedist. I'm going to try that approach first, and if it doesn't work, then he can choose on his own. Okay?"

A sign ahead said breakfast, and Nick slowed down. It was an old, dillapidated building that had once been a country store.

"Want something to eat?" Nick asked. "The place looks pretty run down but that's not saying the food might not be good."

"Let's try it," Pearl said.

They went in and took the only available seats in front of the window. The waitress brought a menu and two cups of coffee.

"What's the best you've got?" Pearl asked.

"Country ham, scrambled eggs, grits, homemade grape preserves and buttermilk biscuits, of course."

"I'll take it," Nick said, remembering Viola's ham from the summer.

"Best food on God's green earth," he said, and Pearl indicated she would take the same.

A calf was pulling on its mother's teats in a lot across the road. The little animal would nudge its mother's udder with its head, jabbing into her side in an effort to make the milk come down.

"Gosh, it looks like that would hurt," Nick said, and Pearl said yes, it probably did hurt, but it brought the milk down also and allowed as how she was glad human mothers didn't have to be exposed to such nudging.

As they relished the home-cooked food they observed a group of convicts cleaning up along the highway. Most were in shackles and all wore the black and white stripe uniforms. Through the open window they could hear some of the group singing and humming as they labored. A trusty was bringing a bucket of water from a nearby well. A guard with a shotgun in his hand hollered at the men at the end of the line. "All right, down there, don't lie down on the job. And don't get too thick. Looks like three of you are awfully close together. Don't start anything funny, you bastards, or I'll shoot your balls off."

"It must be awful to live like that," Pearl said.

"Yeah, but it's awful what they did too," Nick replied. "I don't know what crimes they committed, but they broke the laws of society and they're having to pay for it."

"But do you suppose that kind of punishment gets them straightened out?" Pearl asked.

"It might not, but if they are put on the chain gang enough times they will get the message eventually," Nick said. "Look at 'em. They're as tough as nails. Look at their faces. They look like they could kill a person without any thought of guilt. They're mean bastards, Pearl."

"I was thinking how we kids used to watch them on the opposite side of the road when they came through Bear Grass," Pearl said. "It was the most exciting thing in the world to see the chain gang come by. And of course the minute Mama or Papa saw me along that road they'd get me to the house immediately. 'That ain't no place for a girl to be,' they'd say and I'd wonder why, and they'd say 'if one of them men was to git loose no telling what they'd do to a little girl.' I wondered why they wouldn't do the same thing with little boys."

They could do the same thing to boys," Nick replied. "There are all kinds of people in this world - queers and weirdos and things like that, but society just doesn't tolerate such actions and if men did those things openly they'd be candidates for lynching squads."

"This is depressing," Pearl said. "Let's talk about something else."

"Let's pay our bill and get back on the highway," Nick said. He noticed a gasoline pump out front and had the attendant fill up the car and check the oil.

"I wonder what Hobby is doing?" Pearl asked.

"Having some kind of fun," Nick replied. "I sure wish we could get him out to Memphis when we have our "sheebang". He'd love that and he should be there."

"And just when are you planning your "coming out" party for me, Mr. Staphal? You would think that with the woman receiving the honors she would have at least some input into the festivities."

"Well, there wouldn't be any festivities if it were left up to her," Nick said. "But I was hoping, and I was planning to confer with you as to when and all that Mrs. Staphal. But I was thinking of the Christmas season. What would you say to that?"

"The ideal time," Pearl replied. "Maybe Hobby will have had surgery again by then and will have a less grotesque cast on his leg. If that is the case we should be able to get him out to this magical city of Memphis, Tennessee that I've heard a good bit about, but know nothing about."

Nick looked at Pearl and she was staring out the window at the distant forests with their shades of gold, pink, yellow and red.

"Look at me," Nick said. Pearl turned toward him. "Why?"

"I've forgotten how your eyes looked, and I don't want to get that vision out of my mind. You've put some kind of spell over me, Pearl Staphal, and you've got me just where you want me. A man is not supposed to be like that. He's supposed to stand up for himself, to make decisions and expect the woman to conform. But no, you've gone way beyond that. You've got me to where all I want to do is all the things you want to do and try to think of others you haven't even mentioned. You know that I adore you and you keep using your wiles on me and I'm lapping it all up like a little puppy."

"What do you mean"? Pearl asked with a grin.

"Last night, for instance."

"Silly."

"And what about clothes and all that, getting back to the great "coming out" party?"

"Oh, just leave that to me," Nick said. "Not a stone will be left unturned when it comes to your introduction to Memphis society. As a matter of fact, a seamstress of great renown is a personal friend of mine, and I know I can finaggle her into getting you fixed up properly."

"One of your lovers?" Pearl asked.

"No. In fact, she's a colored woman. Used to have her shop next door when we were in the restaurant business. She would come in every day to get something to eat. It might be just coffee, or a full meal, or whatever, and we would laugh and pass the time and talk about things in general. She is really a swell person, Pearl. Her name is Mavis. And the first thing I'm going to do when we get to Memphis is go see her, tell her the situation, take you along to introduce you to her and tell her to give you the works. She will really carry on about you."

"What do you mean?" Pearl asked.

"Conceited," Nick replied. "Your beauty, of course. You've got it all, woman. You just don't know it."

They passed the Lenoir County line and Pearl realized they would soon be in Waynesborough County. Nothing had been said about her parents while they were gone, but she knew they would go by and see them before they went on to Tennessee. It would be unthinkable to come this near home and not see them.

"We're going by to see Mama and Papa," she said and Nick replied, "Of course."

"Maybe we'll stay a few days," Pearl said. "And this time we'll have Hobby's bed."

"Fine," Nick replied, "but how are the springs?" He looked at Pearl with a boyish grin on his face.

"Squeaky," Pearl said.

"I've been thinking, and I think it would be nice to have Mama and Papa at the "shindig" too. And I want to explain that I don't say this in an effort to embarrass you Nick. I don't want to be embarrassed either. But if we invite them, I'll see to it that they go to Memphis in style. It'll take a little doing, but I think I can pull it off. There's a fine store in Hallsborough that sells the best merchandise that can be bought. And my gosh! I've never worn a rag from there. But just walking past their show windows taught me about style and what there was out there for those who could afford it. Well, we'll visit them now and "put on the dog." Nick had arranged for a joint bank account immediately after they were married and Pearl had been flabbergasted. She had never had money deposited in a bank and couldn't imagine what it would be to make purchases, sign her name and walk away with the loot.

"Fine with me," Nick replied. "As a matter of fact, I had entertained the idea myself, but I wanted you to be the one to make the decision."

"Mama and Papa are fine looking people still. Oh, they're like the typical sharecropper and their manner of dress is the same as the general population in the area, but they could be groomed and dressed and made to really look good. But God! I've got a job on my hands. And Mama and Papa will almost have a fit. They'll give a thousand excuses why they shouldn't be there and they'll tell all about how crude they are and that we should go on and have all the fun we can but just leave them in Bear Grass. And I won't listen to a word they say."

"You're a bossy little gal, I'll say that," Nick said, laughing.

"With people like my parents, you just have to put your foot down and keep arguing the point until you get it across Nick."

"They'll be surprised to see us but I'll be happy to see them. I love them Nick, and I know you already know that."

They were now in Hallsborough County and Pearl took a deep breath and said, "even the air smells better here than anywhere else. It's just home, Nick and no matter how long you've been away it's the same every time you return. That says a lot about our heritage, doesn't it, and about who and what we are?"

"Yeah," Nick replied. "But I think you people down here have a greater sense of heritage than people that I know. I love Memphis and I've lived there all my life, but I've never been as attached to it as you and Hobby are to Bear Grass. And I think it's great that you feel that way. It's roots, Pearl, that give our lives some sort of special meaning. If I had been brought up an All-American boy and had had brothers and sisters and we had formed roots in Memphis I know I'd feel the same way. But despite the fact that I was born in Memphis and went to the same school with all those who were born there, I didn't feel all that All-American if you know what I mean. There are many different cultures in Memphis, like all large cities, whereas in rural areas such as Bear Grass, the same families have planted their roots here and there is a continuity to it that I find missing in my own culture. In that respect, I envy you people down here."

On the outskirts of Hallsborough Pearl noted that the county fair was holding its annual event.

"Whooopee! The fair is running," she said. "We've got to go to the fair, Nick. I haven't been to the fair since I went to Tennessee. You don't mind do you?"

"No, that should be fun," Nick said.

"We'll go tonight," Pearl said. "That really ought to be something we can enjoy. And I'll be just like a young'un again Mr. Staphal, and to hell with your grandiose plans for my "coming out" party."

"My, you're using big words, Mrs. Staphal," Nick said, shaking his head. "For one of these country hicks with little book learning, you do have quite a vocabulary." Pearl stuck her tongue out at him.

Viola was wringing out shirts to hang on the line when Pearl and Nick arrived and she was taken aback. After kissing her mother, Pearl said, "Mama, let me take one end of that sheet and you take the other and we'll wring it easier."

"I'm about through," Viola said. "Just one more sheet and Craven's work shirts and overhalls. They're boiling in the pot now."

"How have you and Papa been Mama?"

"Fine," Viola said. "And how is Hobby? I've never missed anything in my life like I have that boy. Sometimes it seems like I can't hardly stand it. And Craven's the same way. I write to him near 'bout every day, but there's not much to tell for you know how dull things are in Bear Grass."

"Not as far as Hobby is concerned," Pearl said. "That boy hangs on every word from Bear Grass. And he's doing fine."

"I even think Wilbert Lee misses him," Viola said. "He comes by pretty often and asks about Hobby. I don't know what else Wilbert Lee is into, but I'm afraid it's not so good. Wilbert Lee is gitting wilder it seems like and I heard him and Philip Stroud talking sassy the other day. I just acted like I didn't even hear. But it might be good that Hobby's away from that."

Craven came up and greeted them and he and Nick had a long handshake.

"What brings youall back to Bear Grass?" Craven asked.

"Been down to the coast for a few days," Nick replied. "It seemed like we needed a little time to sort things out and I thought the beach would be a good place to do that. And it was."

"I hope all that hard work last summer didn't git you down," Craven said.

"Oh no," Nick said. "I'll admit I was sort of sore for a while, but the work was good for me."

"I couldn't hardly believe it when I found out what Pearl had done to you and putting you out in the hot fields to work. I thought she went a pretty fer ways in that."

"She knew what she was doing," Nick told him. "I had asked Pearl to marry me and she knew I didn't know anything about her background, and she wouldn't even consider marriage until I agreed to come down here and work in the fields and see how people live here. It was a great experience and I think more of her for what she did."

Pearl and Viola hung out the clothes and Pearl told her mother they wanted an early supper; that they planned to go to the fair that night.

"Lord child," Viola said, "they's plenty cooked. I boiled a big pot of collards today. Figured this would be the last boiling before the frost struck the collards and I love them better before they're frost-bitten. There's plenty of good meat boiled with the collards and a pot of ish taters already boiled in the iron pot. And I had a right smart of cold biscuits lying around so I made a biscuit pudding. You know how your daddy loves biscuit pudding. They was a little dry coconut in the safe and I added some cocoa and it's good if I do say so. And I think about how skeered I was to cook for Nick when he came in the summer. But now I know he'll love all my "plain" country cooking."

"He never stops raving about it," Pearl said, and Viola smiled. "He'd give anything if you'd go to Tennessee and cook for us, but he said he couldn't let you even if you wanted to because he'd feel like he was making some kind of slave out of you."

"I'd be happy to cook for Nick every day in Bear Grass," Viola said, "but I know Craven and me wouldn't never be satisfied way out there. Our roots is too strong here, honey."

"Why Mama, we were talking about asking you and Papa to move to Tennessee. We'd get you a nice little place out there and you'd be nearby and we could be a real close family again."

"Me and Craven have done talked about all that, honey. We know a big change is coming up for you and Hobby, but we've decided that whatever comes, we will face it here in Bear Grass. We're known and respected here Perline, and friends are mighty good in these parts. You have your life to live and we have ourn. We can't live in a world we don't know nothing about."

"Well, that's what I'll be doing," Pearl said.

"But that was your choice honey. Women follow their men, wherever it may be, and that's the way it's supposed to be. That's God's plan for he said a man and woman were supposed to leave their parents and become one flesh in marriage."

"Okay, we won't argue about that," Pearl said, "but there's something else I want to talk to you about. I want you and Papa to go to Memphis for whatever doings Nick has planned for me."

"Lord have mercy Perline. Ain't they no end to this? You know just as good as me that we'd stick out like a sore thumb in such a gathering. We're the plainest folks you ever seen and you know all about that. I don't see why in the world you'd want to git us out there to be made a laughing stock of as well as embarrassing you half to death and gitting you off to the worst start you could git. No honey, don't plan on nothing like that." She was wringing her hands with a dishrag."I knew you'd be like that," Pearl said and Viola noted tears in her eyes.

"I knew there would be fussing and carrying on and giving excuses and all that. But Mama, I know that you know I wouldn't take youall out there to be laughed at and to embarrass me. I've thought it all out, and many things are possible now that couldn't have been before I married Nick. There's something involved that we never knew anything about and that's money. You can do almost anything with money except buy your way to heaven. Even in these hard times, a very few people are living good. We can fix you and Papa up so you'll be like everybody else." She took Viola's apron and wiped her eyes.

"Well, we'll talk about that," Viola said.

"Mama," Pearl said firmly, "I've never asked very much from you and Papa, and there's no way you can say I don't love you, but I'm asking you to do this and I'm not going to take no for an answer. You can cry and wring your hands and try to put me off all you want to, but I plan for both of you to be in Memphis when that ever-loving shindig comes off. And if there's any way possible Hobby will be there also."

"Oh, I want to see that boy," Viola said, "and if he's going to be there that makes it all the more enticing. When is this "thing" coming off, Pearl?"

Sometime around Christmas, Nick says. That gives us almost two months to plan for this so we've got plenty of time. And don't say a word against going Mama, or I swear I'll really get angry with you."

"Don't swear Perline. You've always been worldly, and I declare you are getting worse."

. . . .

They heard the blare of the horns, the beat of the drums, the hawkers yelling above the crowds, telling about the monstrosities, the freaks of nature, the Hoochee Koochee show, the trapeze artists, the half-man-half-woman, the hermaphrodite that was perfectly proportioned on each side and the fattest woman on earth, an eight-hundred-fifty-pound glob of human fat. They smelled the odor of roasted peanuts and hotdogs and onions and the wild smell of confined animals.

"I used to think the fair was the grandest thing on earth," Pearl told Nick as they walked arm-in-arm toward the midway. The ferris wheel was carrying a load of laughing, screaming people. The swings were circling round and round and people were holding tightly to the chains. Clowns were walking around the grounds doing their antics.

"Throw the balls and win the lovely lady a fine teddy bear," the man with greasy hair shouted as Nick and Pearl passed by. "Six throws for ten cents." They ignored the man as he caught the attention of another couple.

"Guess the man's weight and win a fine prize of your choice," the woman told Nick. "This pretty lady with you deserves one of our fine prizes. Come on, take a gamble."

"Hoochee Koochee show," the barker chanted. "See the most beautiful ladies in the world in a different light than they're seen on the streets, men. Your ladies will wait outside while you go inside for a few minutes. They could prove the greatest blessing to your marriage you've ever known about."

Nick stood erect and stuck his thumbs in his waistband. "I'm going woman," he slurred and Pearl pinched him sharply on his arm. He yelled, "Ouch" and they moved on, laughing.

"We're going to ride the ferris wheel," Pearl said and Nick pinched Pearl lightly. "No Pearl, anything but that," he pleaded sincerely. "I've been scared to death of those things all my life. Always felt like I was going to fall out and land on my head."

"Sissy," Pearl replied. "I love the ferris wheel, way up there where it seems like you're as free as a bird."

"I always feel like my stomach's going to fall out when the wheel starts down," Nick said, "and I don't have anything that I want to lose that way. Let's do something else," he pleaded.

"Okay, if you don't want to ride I'll go by myself," Pearl said.

"I'd be just as worried with you up there and and me down here," Nick replied.

"I swear Nick, I never saw the beat of this," Pearl said disgustedly. "The ferris wheel is a young folks thing, and here you are a man in his forties making a big deal out of it."

"All right, I'll ride," Nick said, and Pearl stood on her tiptoes and rubbed her nose against his and patted him on his shoulder. "Now now," she mimicked, "that's mama's good boy." Nick stepped lightly on her foot and she pushed him and then he added pressure and Pearl said, "Please," and Nick released her foot.

"And since you're a boy I'll get you some cotton candy," Pearl said as they came up to the stand where the sugar was spun into tiny threads. She paid for two and pulled off a hunk and stuffed it into Nick's mouth, or around it, rather. She put a wad in her mouth also and they laughed and Nick said the mess was all between his fingers and Pearl told him to pull out his shirt and wipe his fingers in his shirttail. "When we girls used to get cotton candy we'd stoop over and wipe our hands in our petticoats."

"Washing is what they need," Nick said, "not wiping."

"Sorry 'bout that," Pearl said, laughing. "And I just thought about something else too. We've got to wash in the wash basin tonight or either a tub. I sure hope Mama has hot water in the reservoir. She ought to have though, after boiling a big dinner. The longer she cooks the hotter the water gets."

They bought tickets and got a seat on the ferris wheel. And Pearl was so mischievious she was determined that she'd scare Nick further. Nick was as still as he could be, and Pearl was at first, but after they crested the top and Nick looked out over the fairgrounds and felt squeamish in his stomach, they began descending and Pearl deliberately tipped the swing forward and Nick screamed, "Pearl, in the name of God don't do this to me!" Pearl was laughing hilariously. She reached over and kissed Nick, then shook the swing again and Nick didn't say a word. He just closed his eyes and gritted his teeth. But as they were climbing out after the ride, he said, "Perline Staphal, you're a mean woman. Some old ladies would get beat up for such carryings on."

"Just try it, buster," Pearl said as they made their way around the fairgrounds.

"Next thing I'm going to ride on are the swings," Pearl told her man.

"Well, you'll ride them by your lonesome. I'm done trying to protect you agin yourself, woman. You're one of these red-necks that can't nobody do nothing with so you go right on, you hear, woman." He had picked up a good bit of Bear Grass slang.

The swings whirled around and Pearl was out a good ten feet from where the swings were attached. Each time she passed Nick she hollered, "Whoopee" and Nick just shook his head. "Crazy woman," he said to himself as a smile came over his face. She's the greatest thing that ever lived, he thought. If she only knew what she means to me she couldn't believe it.

They just walked over the grounds after the swing ride and Pearl told Nick she'd love to go to the livestock barn and see the hogs and cows and sheep and goats and rabbits, the geese and ducks and turkeys and chickens and all those things but that it would take her a day if she got into all that.

Nick looked up and that Carolina moon had grown since they observed it a few days earlier over the Atlantic. "Sing me your song," he said to Pearl and she crooned, "Carolina moon keeps shining....." They kissed with throngs of people milling about them and they might have been on the beach again for all that it mattered to them.

"I'll remember this night forever," Pearl said as they were driving home. "It was so simple, but I felt like a teen-ager again and there didn't seem to be a care in the world. It was sheer fun, wasn't it?"

"All but that ferris wheel," Nick replied. "But I forgive you if it means anything to you."

"Thanks," Pearl said.

And there was warm water in the reservoir for their baths and Viola had placed a tub in the kitchen and the room was still warm from a fire in the cookstove. Their bedroom was chilly and they snuggled close and just as Pearl had told Nick, the springs squeaked and Nick felt himself blushing, although all that had happened was that he had turned over to face Pearl. "Sorry 'bout that," he whispered to Pearl and she placed her hands on his face and pulled his lips to hers.

"Stinker," he whispered. "Beautiful, lovely little stinker. The girl with the shiny hair and the sky-blue eyes. The little temptress with the golden skin that appears to have been covered with honey, then smoothed to perfection and a mouth that defies description with those lips sweeter than wine and oh, that bosom of love and the whole of you." He kissed her passionately and she was warm in his arms that embraced her and they fell asleep in that position.

Viola called them when it was still dark outside. "Mama, what in the world are you getting us out of bed so early for?" Pearl asked, yawning.

"Honey, you won't be here long and we want to be with you every minute we can while you're here. Breakfast is already on the table."

Nick turned over and held the covers close about him. "Yeah, I already smell it and I'm ready to crawl out."

All the ham was gone from the smokehouse now, so Viola had fried pure fatback after letting it boil for a moment to get the salt out before frying it crisp. Then she scrambled the eggs to perfection while the buttermilk biscuits were browning.

"Don't reckon you ever had fatback before Nick," Viola said apologetically. "But I love it and Craven does too. It's just the best I can do this time."

"If you cooked it, it's good Mrs. Turnage," Nick said. He took a piece of the meat and bit into it and bit off a mouthful of biscuit, then forked up a portion of his eggs and savored it for a moment. "It's absolutely delicious," he told Viola. "I swear Mrs. Turnage, you're the best cook on earth I know. Tell me, did you teach your beautiful daughter to cook?"

"Nah," Viola said with a shrug. "Perline was always doing something else when I was cooking. She'd rather work in the field than cook, and Craven needed her too, so Perline didn't learn the art of cooking."

"I'm sorry Nick," Pearl said with a pout. "I'd give anything if I could cook like Mama. But then, I know that not a whole lot of women can and that makes me feel a little better."

They ate in silence for a while, the only sound being Craven and Viola sucking coffee from the saucers into their mouths. They still poured their coffee in the saucer and drank it as it cooled. They'd blow on the liquid if it was still steaming after it was poured from the cup.

It all seemed wonderful to Pearl. It had been so long since she had been able to be at home and enjoy it. Visits had been few and far between during the years at the mill, and money had been so scarce just managing bus fare to Carolina and back to Tennessee had been a near-impossibility. Pearl was a family-oriented person and being away had made the closeness of the family setting even more dear to her.

"It would be just perfect if Hobby could only be here," she said as she smeared butter over a biscuit hot from the oven. "If he could see the closeness we are sharing right now he'd cry his heart out, and I'm about to. She wiped a tear from her eyes with the back of her hand.

"Nick, I had meant to ask you something, "Craven said, "and I don't know where it's the right thing to do or not. Anyhow, if you don't want to answer it'll be all right. But you know everything is turned bottom-upwards and they don't seem to be no money nowhere. So I was wondering how you managed to hold on to something during these hard times. You seem to be a very rich man and all that."

"Glad you asked, Mr. Turnage," Nick replied. "And I'm not a very rich man in any sense of the word. But the way things are now anybody with a few thousand dollars could be considered rich. But most of my holdings are in property that won't do me any good until the Depression is over and property values begin to rise again. All I'm doing right now is to keep the taxes paid on the farms and buildings and homes I have bought in the Memphis area.

"As to how I got it, that's another story, and I can't be credited with anything about that. You see, my parents were both born and raised in Athens, Greece. It was very bad in Greece and their greatest desire was to sail to America where they could make their own way. And that was made possible soon after they were married by one of Dad's brothers who had managed to save a little money. He loaned Dad enough to get them to New York. And they realized when they were sailing that a baby was on the way. It was their hope to have a houseful of children, but I was the only one they ever had.

"Dad got started in the restaurant business after deciding to go to Memphis. A cousin of Dad's had lived in Memphis and he had convinced Dad it was a good place to begin a new life."

"Pass the biscuits," Pearl," Craven said. Pearl passed the plate and took a swallow of coffee and as she tilted her head back it went down her windpipe and she became strangled. She farted and everybody at the table realized it was a time to hold a straight face. And they did try. Then Nick looked at Pearl and he became hysterical with laughter. He lay his head on the table and shook, while Pearl got down on the floor and rolled in spasms of laughter. Craven and Viola cackled with laughter also.

"I'm so ashamed," Pearl said and her face was crimson. "But you know something? That's not all I did," and she was again in spasms of laughter with tears streaming from her eyes. Nick looked at her and cackled. "You what?"

"I shit in my britches, dummy. Mama, you come and help me. I can't get to the privy." She rose and went to the bedroom with Viola following her.

The laughter finally ceased and Nick said, "Now where were we? Oh, I was talking about Dad getting started in the restaurant business. He managed to rent a little hole-in-the-wall in Memphis and started out as small as is possible. It took time to get going and Dad dedicated himself to making a go of the restaurant business. It wasn't easy for my parents in America. They spoke no English and never did master the English language, although they did speak well enough to get by. Dad felt self-conscious because of the language barrier. He loved America and all that it stood for, and after I was born he had a new goal - to make an All-American boy out of me. I would be and do all the things he could not do. And he saved every penny he could after paying his bills. He never put a dime in a bank either, and that's the secret of me having anything today. During all the years Dad worked he stashed his savings away at the house we lived in. He had a small iron safe in a large closet and the back room upstairs on the right of the hall was Dad's office, as he called it. Neither Mom or I ever went into the room.

"Well, World War I came and with it high prices. Dad did real well during those years. And his savings grew. Then hard times struck but the restaurant still did very well, until Dad died. It was a sudden thing. And when Mom and I got into the safe there was a small fortune there. So we decided to leave things just as they were for a while. I didn't want to put the money in a bank with economic conditions such as they were. We continued to run the restaurant for a year and Mom died suddenly. But I think she died from a broken heart. She and Dad were inseparable in life and after his death she didn't seem interested in life. So that's the whole story. There was no will, no records except the invoices and things where Dad had paid the bills. That's when I decided it was time for me to get out of the restaurant business since I didn't know enough about it to run it on my own. I also reasoned that I should invest in some of the give-away property in and around Memphis. It was nothing that I did on my own ingenuity. All the credit goes to those two dear immigrants who had a bright vision of America and who dedicated their lives to trying to make me what they would have wanted to be."

Viola ran out on the porch and brought the wash basin to the reservoir on the stove, opened the lid and stuck her finger in the water. "Not warm enough to dent the chill hardly," she said. "Stove's not been burning long enough. Perline will just have to shiver for a little while."

Craven and Nick walked down to the hogpen. Nick went to the opposite side of the boarded-up pen from the house, let out a deluge, shook off and joined Craven who was calling up the hogs. "Pig, pig, pig," and the shoats and old sow came hurriedly from the far end of the pasture. He had taken a basket of corn to them. "Right pretty shoats," he told Nick. "They'll make good meat in the smokehouse later on. They've got the frame on them to make good-sized hogs and they'll really put on the weight after running out in the fields and picking up the stray ears of corn left when the corn is housed and the cut sweet taters left in the fields as well as the "soja" beans on the ground left from the bean picker. Let them run out a few weeks after everybody in the neighborhood gits through housing corn and then put them in that floored pen there and you can see them fattening."

"You like to mess with hogs, don't you Mr. Turnage?"

"Oh yeah, I love my hogs. In fact, I love everything around me, even to the old lady's chickens. You see Nick, poor folks like us got to have something to love and look after. We ain't got nothing and I don't even have to tell you that. We don't know too much about what's going on in the world and if we knowed, wouldn't be nothing we could do about it. But it looks like they ain't nothing nobody else can do about it either, don't it? But with our nothing near about we can look over the little things we have around us and get a lot of satisfaction out of them. If you're little enough, you think little, about like the level of our education. I tell you Nick, about the only hope for poor folks like us is education. These young'uns around here need to go to school and stay there until they finish high school. Raise 'em up ignorant and just let them have this to look forward to, and you're raising up another crop of ignorant people. And it ain't because we ain't got no sense, Nick. They's some brilliant minds right here in Bear Grass, but they ain't developed, and that's pitiful."

"You're one of them Mr. Turnage," Nick said.

"Yeah, but I'm just like the rest of 'em," Craven replied. "And I'll tell you something else. We're about as opinionated as you can git. And as stubborn as a bull. Just let us make up our minds about something and ain't nothing on earth can shake us."

"What do you think about President Hoover?" Nick asked.

"God a-mighty! Craven exclaimed. "He's the worst thing that ever happened to the United States. I'm thankful he hain't got but one more year cause I know nobody would vote for him agin if he was to run. Republicans don't do nothing for this country Nick, and I don't even know what your politics is. But we couldn't stand another Republican right now. I was bred and born a Democrat and I'll die a Democrat and whenever I go to vote, I make just one mark and that is the straight Democrat ticket. My daddy would turn over in his grave if he thought I'd ever vote for a Republican. What party do you belong to, Nick?"

"I'm a registered Republican," Nick replied, "but that doesn't mean that I always vote for a Republican. I vote for the man and what he stands for if I am able to judge. And I voted for old Herbert, but I've lived to regret it."

"They's all this talk about Franklin D. Roosevelt from New York running, and I can see a hope for the future in him, but I'm going by what old Teddy Roosevelt did when he was president. And I hear tell they's a man called Al Smith that might run on the Republican ticket. And that's where I draw the line cause they've already said he's a Roman Catholic. That would be asking for the Pope in Rome to dictate the presidency of the United States. Now you know that if they's one thing most folks in the South ain't it's Roman Catholics. Why, we'd be having to have all them graven images in our churches and all that if such a thing was to happen Nick. When it comes down to the Lord God Almighty, we ain't going to worship no image but His image."

"Wait a minute Mr. Turnage," Nick said. "I beg to disagree with you about that. I respect your right to your opinion, but I don't think if Al Smith were to become president it would have one bit of effect on your religion. Everbody except atheists, who have religious beliefs, place their faith in a higher being. But other religions don't impose themselves on the presidency and I think that in this case you're thinking in terms of what you yourself termed "opinionated."

"Maybe so," Craven replied, "but you just try to git that across to a sharecropper like me and you'll run up against a stone wall."

"Yeah, education would help," Nick said with a shrug.

"Ain't them pretty shoats Nick?"

"They sure are. Let's see, there are nine of them. It won't take nine hogs for you and Mrs. Turnage. What are you going to do with all that meat?"

"I've got to look out for you and Perline, Nick. Some of this meat's going to Memphis, Tennessee to grace your table. I've toted slops to them all this year, bought wheat middlings and fed it to them when food was scace in the pasture, trimmed them little boars and got them in good shape for fattening. Now it's gitting time to reap the rewards."

"We'll remember what you've done Mr. Turnage," Nick said.

Pecans were falling and hitting the tin top of the house as they returned to the barn. Walnuts covered the ground under the tree near stables. Acorns were thick on the ground under the big oak.

"That tobacco sure smells good in the shed room," Nick said. "Smells mellow."

"Yeah, it's our last barn," Craven said, "Pretty backer too. Good color with good body, a good lemon color with little trash. Me and the old lady's going to start grading and tying it next week. But it's pitiful Nick. It won't bring nothing - maybe a eight or nine-cent average. That ain't nothing for a year's work. It's the same old story every year. If one thing don't git you another will. One year it's the dry weather; another too much rain; one year the boll-weevil; another the backer worms. I've seen a good crap of backer ruined almost overnight when the worms took over in light nights in July. You could pure hear them eating on the backer. We'd git out there and spray as hard as we could with Paris Green but a lot of times they had already stripped most of the leaves. I've seen the leaves pure white with Paris Green and often wondered whether the mess was fit to smoke with all that "pison" on it. Must have been though, for I never heard no complaints about it. But farming's a mess, any way you look at it."

"I'll tell you what, Mr. Turnage," Nick said. "We're going to do something about this. Pearl and I have already discussed it, and we want to build a nice little place for you and Mrs. Turnage, somewhere that you would be comfortable so you wouldn't have to worry about farming at your age."

"Oh, I don't 'spect nothing like that, Nick. You can't take us on just cause you married our daughter."

"It was my idea, Mr. Turnage."

"Well, that's mighty nice of you, but I don't want you to do anything like that. We'll make our own way somehow. We always have."

Craven took off his hat and began scratching his head. He seemed to be in deep thought for a minute or so before speaking. He looked directly at Nick. "I can't hardly figger it out," he said with a puzzled look on his face.

"It's one of the strangest things I've ever run up aginst. Here you are, a Greek, and Lord knows I ain't casting any reflection on you for that, for you're as good as anybody, and a lot better than me, down here among a bunch of sharecroppers as far removed from what your life has been like as a person can be, staying in this old rundown house with no conveniences and acting like you enjoy it. And I can't believe you're putting on Nick. What does it all mean?"

"Simple enough," Nick said. "I happen to love your daughter more than I love my own life. She is the greatest thing that ever happened to me and I am as sincere as I can be when I tell you that I enjoy your company and Mrs. Turnage's as much as anybody I've ever been around. You're genuine, Mr. Craven. You're for real. You've got values, and others that I've met in the community appear to be the same way. I don't give a damn about social status and all that shit. I like people for what they are."

"Let's go over yonder and see if there ain't some scuppernongs left," Craven said. "They're as sweet as sugar this time of the year, what few are left. But you've got to watch out for the "wasts" and yaller jackets. Them rascals are all up among the grapevines and they'll pop you 'fore you know it if you git your hands on them. You know, I planted this vine Nick, after me 'n Viola moved here with Wilbur. That's been a long time ago but we've shore enjoyed the grapes."

As they went under the vine, Viola and Pearl came out into the yard. "I got something I want to show you," Viola told Pearl. "Come on with me to the barn and I'll call the chickens up. Did Hobby ever tell you about his little blue bantam rooster? Well, that boy was crazy about that rooster. He was a pretty thing too. Hobby got him so he'd come up and jump on his shoulder and flap his wings and crow and he was pure jealous. If another chicken came up to Hobby that little old rooster would get pure ornery and walk around Hobby with his wings down near 'bout to the ground and his hackles up. Anyhow, the little fellow got the limberneck and died soon after youall were here in the summer. There won't no time to show you chickens or nothing else at that busy time. A kitten died out in the woods near the hogpen and the rooster got the maggots there and you know that kills a chicken every time.

"But there is another young rooster just like him on the yard, and another not just like him but I'm going to keep both of them." She took an ear of corn and shelled off some of the kernels from the end. "Chicky, chicky, chicky," she called and they began running toward the barn from all around the place. She threw several kernels of corn and told Pearl to look. "I don't believe

Hobby could tell the difference in them by the time the young rooster is grown," Viola said.

"Ain't he a pretty color slate blue? And look at them breast feathers, red and white spangled and the orange hackles coming out. And there are two pullets too Perline. I'm going to keep them all and carry on with them so that if Hobby ever comes back to Bear Grass the same line that he loved so much will be waiting for him. I've already wrote him about them."

"They are beautiful," Perline said, "but Mama, I don't want you to encourage Hobby about coming back to Bear Grass. I really want him to become a doctor, and I hope he will pursue a medical career. I love Bear Grass too, but I don't see how Hobby could ever reach his potential here."

"Oh, I have no doubt but what Hobby will do whatever you want him to," Viola said. "He loves and respects you that much. But in his heart, Hobby Turnage will never be happy away from Bear Grass. And I know that there ain't nothing here for him. But Hobby's different Perline. You're his mama, but you know he's spent most of his life with me and Craven and we know that boy like nobody else does. He's what I'd call a nature boy, honey. He loves it all - the woods and the streams and the trees and the plants and the birds and the animals as well as the people."

"Look over there on the ridge Mama. Aren't the colors beautiful? They are as colorful as those in the mountains. There are just fewer of them. But this splash of color is especially pretty in Bear Grass, where the landscape is dull most the time."

"But it's all about to change for you Perline," her mother said. "It'll be such a big change you probably won't even be thinking about this place in no time."

"I'll never forget this place Mama," Pearl said as she surveyed the neighborhood about her. "And it has been just wonderful this time. I think I've enjoyed it more than any time I've been home since I left. I've been the Perline of old. I've done exactly as I've wanted to and been the farm girl that I was and really let my hair down. I guess it's because I'll be anything but that in a few days now."

"Do you dread it honey?" Viola asked.

"Not really. It will be something new, and I can't even visualize it all since I haven't been there either. But I'll conform and I don't think I'll feel all that uptight about it. You see, I've been totally fair with Nick about me and my background, so I don't have anything to worry about there, and he has enough confidence in me to believe that I can carry out my role in Memphis. And all I care about is pleasing Nick anyway. I certainly owe him that, for

God knows he took on something when he took on me and all my problems."

They sat down on the back porch and Pearl noted the morning glories shining on the brown cornstalks and the goldenrod along the road. A few zinnias were still in bloom and the coxcomb at one corner of the house and the cannas at the other corner were still colorful, "I'll keep all this in my heart," she said to herself in a whisper.

"Now, about getting you and Papa ready for Memphis, Mama. We didn't ever finish it when we were talking before. We're going to Hallsborough this afternoon and get you all fixed up."

"Where at?" Viola asked.

"The only place to go is H. Weil and Brothers" Pearl answered. "They've got as good clothes as you can buy and I've never had a rag from there as you know. But Lord, it wasn't because I didn't want them. I remember the only time I ever went inside was one Saturday when you were looking for a piece of cloth to make me a dress. I was holding your hand when we went in, and there was plenty of cloth displayed on the counters - fine materials and beautiful colors, but when you saw the price tag you walked out without saying a word."

"What have I got to have?" Viola asked.

"A whole lot of things Mama. First, you've got to have an evening gown and several dresses and suits. You'll be seen more than once. And underthings and all that. I'll bet that corset of yours is at least five years old." She reached over and patted Viola on the stomach. "It's not holding you in too good. You've let yourself get a little bit thick in there too. You need to lose a few pounds before Christmas, Mama."

"Lord Perline, you know I can't do that," Viola replied. "I love vittles too good and I'm at that age where you just spread out anyhow."

"You look good, Mama," Pearl assured her. "You're a good-looking woman for your age. You're not wrinkled and you've still got some shape to you. But it all needs a little help. And I'll bet you don't have a single slip except the ones you make out of nard homespun, then let them bleach as they age from washings. You've got to have new slips Mama, with lace on the bottom and square at the top with straps instead of the round-necked ones you're used to. Then there are hats and bags and shoes and hosiery. You'll need everything, Mama."

"You're trying to make something out of me I'm not," Viola said. "I'll feel totally out of place in such get-up."

"Oh, it'll feel good Mama, and you'll be so proud of yourself you won't hardly know what to think."

Nick and Craven came up to the house and Nick said they were going to the store to see what was going on up there. Nick cranked up his 1931 black Packard that some of the neighborhood folks had said looked like a hearse it was so long, and they drove smoothly with dust rising along the road.

"We'd better get started on getting you ready for trying on clothes," Pearl said. "Are you sure your best slip is clean? And have you got good bloomers to wear? You won't want to go up there and be embarrassed when the sales clerk is in the dressing room with you."

"None but what's got runs in them."

"You do wear bloomers don't you Mama?" Pearl asked as she looked into her mother's eyes.

"Sometimes," Viola said.

"Uh huh, I knew it," Pearl said, shaking her head. "I never understood how older women wanted to go without any drawers. Looks like as they get older they would want to hide what they've got."

"It's well hidden with our long dresses," Viola said. "I don't know. The "lasket" in the waist always bound me and they just always seemed to be a nuisance,"

"Why, so you can go out behind the barn and pee without squatting down or anything?" Pearl said with a sneer. "God, I've seen old women urinate standing up and it getting on their black patent leather shoes more times than I care to think about. And Mama, it's been twenty years if it's been a day since you wore a brassiere. You're a pretty filled out woman, but you just go unbound and it looks like it would be uncomfortable like that."

"Don't bother me," Viola said.

"Well, with the "new" Viola, you'll wear a bra and panties, not bloomers." Viola was wearing a short-sleeved dress and Pearl held up one of her arms. "Just look under your arms, Mama. Your arm pits look like a bird's nest with all that hair under there. I'm going in the house right now and get the scissors and cut that mess and if I can't shave under your arms with Nick or Papa's straight razors, I'll get Papa to shave them. You can't go to Weil's looking like that."

"I declare Perline, I don't know whether I can do all the things you want done. You know hair stubbles coming back under my arms will tickle and stick in me."

"Not if you keep them shaved," Pearl said. "So after the first time, you get you a safety razor and some blades and keep those hairs from under your arms."

"What in the world will Craven think of all this?" Viola said.

"I don't know Mama, but I guarantee you he'll notice, and you'd better be glad you've already gone through the change or you might get in trouble in your old age."

"You embarrass me Perline," Viola said, blushing.

The odor of new-mown hay drifted with the autumn breeze. Someone was burning leaves up toward Beston Road and a small circle of white smoke rose into the air. Pearl loved to smell burning leaves. A guinea cackled out in the field and there were thoughts of days when she had gone to the nests and removed the eggs. Viola treasured guinea eggs for cakes. They were yellower than hen eggs and made rich-colored layers. Pearl always asked her mother to make lemon cakes when she was a little girl. Viola would grate the rind, split open the lemons, squeeze the juice into the icing and add the rind and it was always a Sunday delicacy.

A cow bell jingled and Pearl remembered all the times she had recreated all these things in her mind when she was at the spindles performing a monotonous task that required little thought.

"And what will Craven need?" Viola asked just as he and Nick returned from the store.

"We're talking about what you'll need when we go to Tennessee Craven," Viola said as the two men sat down on the porch with them, all their feet hanging off the side.

"Have you ever seen a tuxedo Papa?" Pearl asked.

"Nope. What is it?"

"Formal wear. And the "coming out party" (she shrugged and held her head at a haughty angle) "will require tucks and tails." Pearl laughed. "Picture you, Papa, in a black or blue-black suit with satin collar, a coat with long tails, spats on your shoes and a fancy shirt that looks like something a woman would wear. You'll want to curse with all of it on I know. And there'll be studs in your shirt and cuff links and a bow tie. Now won't that be some get-up for the old man?"

"God a-mighty!" was all Craven said.

"How about your sleeve-holders Papa. Have you got any decent ones?"

"Naw. Had some pretty good ones but I had to use them in the backer patch a year or so ago when the old lady couldn't find no kind of shirt 'cept the one with the arms so long they hung over my whole hand. Got backer gum on them and they've looked nasty ever since."

"And how about your supporters?"

"Ain't no account either. Viola sewed them up for me a time or two. They don't hold up a sock like they ought to though."

"You've got to have a new suit too, and some new shoes. And Papa, you'll be wearing wing tipped slippers this time. I've never seen you with a pair of slippers on. It has always been those black, high-top shoes and I reckon you'll catch your death of cold with your ankles bare but you can just blow snot and you'll get over the cold. You'll need two or three new shirts and a couple of neckties even if I've never seen one on you. I've always wanted to and I'll finally get my chance. Nick will tie them for you. And I reckon that about does it for you except for a couple of pairs of pants and a few pairs of socks. Nick, will Papa need an overcoat?" Nick nodded his head in the affirmative. "All right then, an overcoat. There's no need to even try to get you to wear any kind of new underwear since you've never worn anything except those Mama made for you. So we've got you all planned out. But Papa, you be sure to cut your toenails before you go trying on shoes. I know you let them get half-an-inch long sometimes, and that would cause your foot to hurt in wing-tipped shoes and God, I'll bet you'll say they're killing you anyway."

"If they git to hurting bad I'll pull the durn things off right there amongst all them hotshots too," Craven said.

"You wouldn't do any such thing, Papa. You'd do anything to please Nick and me."

So they had an early dinner and left immediately for Hallsborough and Weil's.

A nice sales person came up to them as they entered the store. "May I help you?" she asked.

"We need a long list of things", Pearl said. "For both of my parents. There's a man in Men's wear. I believe they said his name is Melvin Jackson. I'd like for him to wait on my father, and you'll be fine for Mama."

The clerk took Craven over to where Melvin stood, with Nick following. "I'm Nick Staphal." He offered his hand and Melvin shook it heartily. "And this is my father-in-law, Craven Turnage. Perhaps you know him. He lives out at Bear Grass. "

"I'm sure I've seen him," Melvin said, "now what can I do for you?"

The lady returned to Pearl and Viola. "Now tell me what you need."

"Let's look at your evening wear first," Pearl said. The woman looked startled, for Viola was an average woman of the area with no outstanding features. "Yes Ma'am," she said. "Will you need an evening gown?"

"Yes, let's look at them first," Pearl said.

The clerk went to a rack where numerous evening dresses were hanging. She took a beige silk with high rounded neckline with the accent in the back which had a wide v-opening down to the waist. Viola liked the front but when she saw the treatment at the back she shook her head.

"That's not your color anyway Mama," Pearl said. "It's too somber and would make your complexion look sallow. Let us see another one," she said.

Next was a pink shantung with good lines, but Pearl didn't like the color for her mother either. Next was a white on white damask with a sequined, shirred waist with tight sleeves extending below the elbow with plunging neckline and slim skirt with side slash up to the knees.

"I like that Mama." Pearl said. "Try this one on."

"Just do look at how low the neck is," Viola said. "And that split in the skirt. You know that's not me Perline."

"Mama, there's nothing about the neck that a small safety pin can't fix, and with a form-fitting skirt you'll have to have a slit in the skirt in order to be able to walk comfortably. You're in pretty good shape and except for the little bulge in your tummy, I'll bet this gown will really look good on you. Just go to the dressing room and try it on." She turned to the clerk and said, "but get a brassiere for Mama before she tries on the gown. I'm ashamed to say it, but Mama's not used to wearing a bra. She doesn't even know what size it will take. And while you're at it, get a slip for her also. This homemade one she's wearing doesn't go with evening wear."

The clerk found the underwear and took Viola to the dressing room. In the meantime, word had already spread throughout the store that a customer was purchasing a lot of clothes, and business hadn't been all that good despite the fact that the tobacco markets had been open almost a month and people were already having cotton ginned. Besides, it wasn't the season yet for most of Weil's customers to buy. Weil's had a special clientele that valued quality merchandise with brand names. They shopped Weil's from towns a good distance from Hallsborough - Calypso, Wallace, Burgaw, Wilmington, LaGrange, Kinston, Faison, Greenville, Wilson, Rocky Mount and places even farther. Weil's sent out brochures on its wearing apparel in late October or early November, catering to women who were fashion-conscious.

Joe Rosenthal was one of the top managers at Weil's. He was a personable man and enjoyed a large acquaintance among the people in the area, both city dwellers and their country cousins. As well as offering top-quality wearing apparel, the store had a farm department in which a large variety of agricultural equipment was sold. Almost anything in the farm line was available at Weil's and landowners would often send their tenants there to purchase items needed in farming.

Rosenthal noted Nick and Craven in the men's department, as well as Pearl while she waited for her mother to dress, so he approached and told them his name and shook hands with them. "I believe I know you," he said to Craven.

"Yeah, I 'spect you do Mr. Rosenthal," Craven replied. "I go over to the farm side sometimes to pick up a few things. Of course Wilbur Stroud stands for it. I've farmed on his land some thirty years now." He motioned to Pearl. "This is my daughter, Perline, and her husband, Nick Staphal. Nick is from Tennessee."

Rosenthal extended his hand to Pearl. "Very pleased to meet you, Mrs. Staphal, and also you, Mr. Staphal," as he extended his hand to Nick.

Rosenthal was a little puzzled, and it showed in his face. Here was this everyday sharecropper telling him this most attractive woman was his daughter and the handsome man, obviously of foreign descent, his son-in-law. It didn't all go together.

"Did you grow up around here?" Rosenthal asked Pearl.

"I sure did, out in the Bear Grass community. Lived there until I was seventeen as a matter of fact. Helped farm, and then got a job right here in Borden Mills and worked there for a year before going to Tennessee to work."

"You never told me you had a beautiful daughter," Rosenthal said to Craven.

"Well, a man don't go around saying such things Mr. Rosenthal, and I didn't feel like I knowed you well enough to say a thing like that nohow."

"It sure is a small world, "Rosenthal said as the sales clerk called Pearl to see the gown on her mother.

"It looks beautiful on you Mama!" Pearl exclaimed. "Like I said, it's a little tight in the waist, but you've already promised me you'll lose a few pounds, and it will be perfect then. I can't hardly believe you're as well-preserved as you are Mama. Doesn't it look good on her?" she asked the clerk.

"Beautiful," the clerk agreed, but at the same time she thought that it would take other things to make Viola into the woman Pearl was hoping for. Her hair was certainly a problem but she had no doubt that the daughter would see to all that for whatever grand occasion they were planning.

"Perline," Viola said with a disgusted look in her eyes, "just look at me in this thing." She pointed to her breasts. "You can pure see them in this gown or whatever you call it and you know I'm not going to be seen in public like that. And this split on the side is sickening."

"Mama, I've tried to explain all of this to you and you know why you are getting these things. Now I'm not going to quarrel, and if you want to spoil the entire thing, that's up to you. Poor thing, you're like me in that you've never had anything decent to wear, but in your case you didn't even want it which is entirely different from me. The cleavage looks good on you, and with a proper brassiere I must say you're quite endowed and should be very proud of what you have instead of trying to hide it. We can close up the cleavage, but we can't sew up the split in the skirt or you won't be able to get around comfortably. I love the fit but you'll have to be the one to decide."

"Oh, all right," Viola said with a shrug. "I just hope God will forgive me and that the Bear Grass news-toters won't make a Jezebel out of me."

"You won't be in Bear Grass Mama. And I know you won't ever wear the gown here. You've always heard the saying, 'When in Rome, do as Rome does.' Well, we'll be in a "Rome" of sorts and we'll be doing what society dictates that we do. Okay?"

"Yes, Perline," and that ended Viola's complaints about her new wardrobe.

In dresses, the clerk first brought a beige silk with high rounded neckline with the accent on the back; the V-opening extending down to the waist and full skirt. "I don't like that Mama," Pearl offered. "It makes your face look sallow and the full skirt wouldn't work too well on you. What do you think?"

"Oh, I don't like it either," Viola said.

Next came a pink shantung with good lines but both women frowned on the color. But a lavender silk with a muted flower design, a V-neckline and a semi-straight skirt won their approval. A black was offered, but Pearl flatly refused to put her mother in black. They settled on a pale green silk shantung, shirtwaist style with half sleeves and matching jacket. Both Viola and Pearl were pleased with a navy suit in Botany wool in a soft weave with a silver fox fur collar. And a black loose-fitting wool coat with mink collar and cuffs won their nod.

While Viola was changing Pearl walked over to the men's department where Jackson was having Craven try on the tux and a navy pin-stripe suit they had chosen. Henry Weil came up and introduced himself. He had been talking with several customers in the store and Pearl noted that when a sale was made the ticket was made out and slipped into a metal cylinder with the money and placed in a chute where it went by a suction system to the main office for retabulation of the sale and change made.

"Henry Weil," he offered his hand to Pearl, then Nick. "We appreciate your patronizing Weil's and hope you're finding all the things you need."

"Fine, fine," Pearl said and Nick nodded assent also.

"Did you buy your clothes here when you lived in the area?" Weil asked Pearl.

"Lord no," Pearl replied. "The only time I ever came into this store was when I was little and came in with Mama when she was looking for a piece of material for a dress for me. And of course she didn't buy when she saw the price on the bolt of cloth. But I knew what kind of clothing you sell. The first "dummy" I ever saw was in your show window. I had never heard of the word "mannequin" at that time. The "dummy" was dressed in a tan tweed suit, fur-trimmed, and a skull hat in tan with orange, yellow and brown feathers, holding a beaded bag and wearing spike-heeled shoes and I almost had a fit I wanted the outfit so badly. I just went on by and bought a ticket to the Paramount and saw a motion picture starring Clara Bow. But I dreamed about that outfit for months."

Then Abram Weil came up and introduced himself also. They were all curious as to just what was going on, but knew better than pry into the affairs of other people. What was more disturbing was the fact that there would perhaps be no one else to provide any information. They were aware that some gala event was planned, and the couple was already married, so the situation provided for much thought. It was most unusual, and something the Weils' hadn't run into before.

Craven came out of the dressing room wearing the trousers to the tux. Pearl noted that the seat was a little baggy. She pointed to the seat and told Jackson to be careful. "Papa has been known to wear pants large enough in the seat to hold a hen and biddies. Please get the pants properly fitted and the coat sleeves the right length."

Viola was out of the dressing room again and was directed to the shoe department where they chose black suede shoes with medium heels and a strap across the ankle. In the millinery department they chose a navy skull hat with light blue and pink feathers and veil to wear with the navy suit and a black hat with narrow brim for general wear. A navy sequined bag was placed against the navy suit to see whether the colors clashed. They bought the bag, and a white one of the same design in keeping with the style of the day. Four pairs of silk stockings were purchased - two natural, one black and one navy; two white rayon slips with lace at the hems; three brassieres; six pairs of rayon panties; a pair of long white muslin gloves and a pair of short black gloves, also of muslin. "That completes it Mama," Pearl said.

"Lord, I'm glad," Viola replied. "I'm tarder than if I had been stringing backer." The sales clerk laughed.

"Will you have Papa's pants ready in the morning?" Pearl asked. "And Papa, did you get the supporters and the sleeve holders?"

"Naw, I had done forgot," Craven said. Jackson went to the drawer where they were kept and added them to the boxes. Nick had helped Craven select two white Arrow shirts, two foulards - one navy silk with tiny polka dots and one red silk with a tiny figured pattern; four pairs of lisle socks, two black and two navy; one pair of navy silk socks; one pair of Florsheim shoes, black with wing tips; a dark navy tuxedo (Nick told Craven it was the same color he would be wearing); the navy pin-stripe suit; a fancy, ruffled soft cotton white shirt to wear with the tuxedo; a cummerbund, spats, studs and a white boutonniere.

Joe Rosenthal walked by again and Craven said, "Can you believe this, Mr. Rosenthal for an old sharecropper like me? I feel like I'm a guinea pig in some kind of experiment (he emphasized the "ment". "But you know something. I'm enjoying it. I'm fixing to find out how the higher-ups live. Now won't that be something?"

Rosenthal laughed, wondering what it all meant.

The sun was getting low when they left Hallsborough for Bear Grass. A few clouds were forming and there were periods of shade when the clouds crossed the sun. They noted people at work in the yards and fields on the way home and there were a few fishermen on the creek banks. They smelled the sweet odor of cut hay when they passed freshly raked fields and a feeling of euphoria came over Pearl. It was all coming to an end. It would never be the same again. The biggest change she could ever imagine awaited her and she was filled with anticipation about what the future held, yet trying to hold on to her roots.

After their purchases at Weil's, Pearl had gone with the sales clerks to the main office and paid the bill by check. There had been too many items to tabulate on a sales slip. The office personnel had smiled as they stood at the window and she was aware there was a great curiosity about the entire transaction. She thought to herself: The poor farm girl has finally come into her own, but she also thought about the circuitous route that had brought her to this moment and she realized that all of us are in the hands of fate; that we never know the hand of the cards being dealt.

They had supper and the air was chilly. A mist was coming in and rain was in the air. Despite the chill, Pearl wanted to sit on the porch for a while. "Let's put on coats and go sit outside for a little while," she told her parents and Nick.

"Ain't it too cool outside?" Viola asked.

"Yes," Pearl said, "but this is the last time I'll be around for a while Mama. I just want to sit and reminisce for a little while."

There were no stars and the lightning bugs had gone with the summer. So much goes with the summer, Pearl thought. It offers so much, demands so much, promises so much, seems endless when the stifling heat becomes so oppressive it seems impossible to endure. So much is accomplished during the months when people are at their busiest. This had been the only really good summer she could ever recall, or any other season for that matter. She felt melancholy, yet happy and fulfilled.

"I'm very pleased with our purchases at Weil's," she said. "It's really nice to have a top-quality store like that out here in the sticks. And I was very careful about what we bought. I read every word in the latest issue of McCall's Magazine and thumbed through every fall and winter catalog I could find to be sure what is in style. I ran across Montgomery Ward's, Sears Roebuck, Spiegel, National Bellas Hess Co., and even Lane Bryant that sells clothing for the "fat" women, and Weil's selection was as good as anything I ran across."

The breeze blew cooler and a mosquito bit Pearl on the leg and she scratched the whelp and snuggled closer in Viola's heavy sweater. She heard the rumble of a train in the distance. "It's the train passing Miller's crossing," she said. She reached over and placed her hand on Nick's knee. "Honey, you have no idea how many times that train has put me to sleep. Listen to the cars running over the ties, and when it reaches Miller's crossing the whistle will blow and after it passes the rumble will go on for a little while and it sings a song to me and I'll never, never forget that sound. And on cloudy, rainy nights like this the sound is magnified.

"Papa, do you remember how you used to sit on the doorstep at night when I was small while I caught fireflies and put them in a jar? And how we'd walk down the road on moonlit nights and listen to people singing and children playing in the yards? And how we'd go to Hallsborough on Saturday and you'd buy me a cone of ice cream and I'd lick it as long as I could? Strawberry was my favorite flavor. Those are things I will carry with me to Memphis and I'll keep them in my heart."

Then they were silent. It seemed like a time to cry to Pearl. She wept silently and Viola said the rain was coming down faster and Craven said Claude Sauls' hay might be ruined for he'd seen it still curing when they drove by his place and Viola said she wondered what in the world Abie would have to say about all the things that had been happening the minute Pearl and Nick left and that whatever she said it would be broadcast all over Bear Grass in a day's time and would get back to her turned completely around.

It was an emotional time for Pearl. Everything coming together at one time was just too much. She wondered how she could have such a warm feeling for the neighborhood and the people and all that Bear Grass stood for. It had been where she had grown up, first learned about life, experienced her first love with Jimmy Exum who lived at Beston. Their romance had flourished when she was sixteen and he had asked her to marry him and she had said yes. But that was before his parents learned her low status in life. They were large landowners in Beston and like most people, they were struggling during the Depression, but they were of a different breed and had hopes for their boy. He was eighteen and handsome and they foresaw a future when the world would be brighter, and Amaziah Exum wasn't about to let his boy get tangled up with a sharecropper's girl, no matter how good-looking she was, according to what people had told him. He told Jimmy he couldn't marry Perline Turnage and he might as well forget it. He couldn't have his Ford to drive the distance of twelve miles to see her and he might as well nip the whole thing in the bud. She had cried for weeks and longed to see him for months. Then there had been the advent of her pregnancy and all the tales told about her and how she had left it all behind and gone to Tennessee, knowing nothing at all about what life was like. Still, she loved the place and the people and harbored no malice in her heart for them.

Tonight she had been avenged for everything. She had never seen Jimmy Exum since they broke up and she wondered what he was like now and what had happened to him.

Viola said she had to go in; that she was getting a chill to the bone. Craven said he had to move closer from the end of the porch; that rain was coming in on him. There was a lullaby of raindrops hitting the roof and Nick yawned.

And the central part of it all was Hobby, Pearl thought. All the anguish she had known; all the guilt. Here was a boy about to become an adult that she hardly knew - her own flesh and blood. Circumstances had dictated that he go away from her in order for both of them to live. That made the guilt harder to bear. And the distance between them had made her love grow stronger by the day. At last he would be the beneficiary of something in which she had made a contribution.

The smell of burnt leaves came in with the rain and Craven said cottonpicking would be held up; that it would take a week for the fields to dry out and the cotton to be fluffy again and Viola got up and moved quietly in front of the others to get inside, her teeth chattering as she passed. Craven allowed as how backer in the warehouses as well as in the packhouses would git in high order from the rain and might mold on the outside edges of the piles.

As Viola entered the hall door she said, "I wonder what little Hobby's doing tonight. He used to love rainy nights like this dearly." And Pearl thought that she didn't even know that about her own boy. She thought about her so-called "freedom" and her choice to live her life as she pleased. Yes, free to slave just to make ends meet and trying to save money for Hobby's surgery. Free to spend endless nights in the closeness and shabbiness of a room in a mill town, making starvation wages. There were no jobs for qualified people, to say nothing of a decent job for a person of her circumstances. Nobody with a seventh grade education was qualified for any job beyond menial labor such as working in a mill.

She knew nothing of freedom and she wondered, as she sat in the darkness and dampness of an October night, whether she would ever have real freedom. Would Nick make demands on her freedom? She loved him with all her heart but the real test hadn't come yet. That would all soon begin. You could never know a man until you lived with him, and it had been too short a time to make any judgment.

And as she thought she realized that all the others had gone inside, so she sat and cried softly to herself and a few wet leaves stuck to her face, brought in by the shifting winds and pecans were hitting the roof and the rain picked up and became a downpour. She went inside and stopped in her parents' bedroom door. "Mama, she said, "Nick and I will carry all the packages back with us so youall won't have to mess with them when you go to Memphis. We'll pick them up at Weil's and just keep them until you come. We'll be expecting you there at least a week before Nick's big bash. We'll let you know when, you hear?"

She sought the warmth of Nick's body when she slipped quickly into bed. Somehow the security she felt in his arms negated all her problems as if she had been touched by a magic wand. The storm increased and she thought about what her father had said out on the porch; that this must be the "equinoxical" storm that usually comes in September to separate the seasons; that it was unusual to be able to house the cane without it being blown down by the September "gust" which was another term he used to express the equinox storm.

She remembered how she had helped her father cut the heavy seeded tops from the cane stalks, then held up stalks that had been blown down by the wind or from the weight of the top-heavy seeds, and stripped the leaves as you did when pulling fodder. And going to the cane mill to have the stalks pressed and the juice going to the cooking vat to be made into syrup and how the old plug of a mule had walked round and round all day long, turning the grinders that pressed the juice out of the stalks.

It had been one of the delights of her childhood except for the yellow jackets that always swarmed around a cane mill, attracted by the cooking syrup. She visualized the large piles of stalks that were placed there after they had been flattened by the press.

Limbs from the big oak were scraping the tin roof as the wind picked up and played around the house.

"Penny for your thoughts," Nick whispered in her ear.

"Just thinking about a million little trivial things that make up so much of our lives," she replied.

"I love you," he said and she kissed him tenderly and they made love in the bed she had slept in as a child when she had become frightened sometimes from bad dreams, and as a teen-ager when her thoughts turned to other things, and the same bed her little boy had claimed as his own from his first remembrances of life. She was drifting off to sleep but there was a dream of a blond head and a boy's face smiling and she was trying to call his name and another voice said "Hobby" and there loomed over her a smiling face with flashing white teeth, with a large, muscular body, and she realized it was a Greek god, and she drifted into deep slumber.

Morning came soon and Nick went to Hallsborough to pick up the packages while Pearl packed their things for the trip back home. When he returned they took their things to the car and the back seat was filled with packages, but Nick opened the trunk compartment and stored their bags there. They kissed her parents goodby and Viola asked when they were going to see Hobby and Pearl said they were going right on up Highway 301 to Baltimore and from there to Memphis. As Nick was cranking the Packard, Pearl said, "Mama, you and Papa are going to fly out to Memphis." Viola's mouth flew open and Craven just stared.

"You're going to be the death of me," Viola said. "I'm scared half to death just to think about such a thing. No, we won't do that Perline. We'll catch a bus."

"You'll fly, Mama," Pearl replied and Nick pulled out of the yard and they were on their way to a new life.

It hadn't been an hour since they left when Viola spotted Abie coming up the back path toward the house. "I knew it," she said to herself.

"Howdy Viola," Abie said. "I saw them packing so I know they're on their way and I declare there has been a lot of going and coming since they've been here. What in the world is going on Viola?"

Viola had to be very careful what she told Abie, for she realized that whatever she said would be in the grapevine before sunset.

"Is that man rich?" Abie asked. "He shore must be driving that brand new car half-a-mile long it looks like. I've not seen nobody else with a fine car like that."

"I don't know what he owns," Viola said." More than us though, I'm sure."

"I tell you, that Perline has done good for herself," Abie said, standing a little spraddle-legged with her hands clasped, holding them over her prominent stomach. "Still, I reckon it seems a little funny, him being a foreigner and all."

"Abie, Nick Staphal was born right there in Memphis, Tennessee. He's as American as any of the the rest of us."

"Oh, that ain't what I mean, Viola. I imagine he smells different than us and things like that."

"Yeah, he smells a lot better than most of us," Viola replied.

"They going to live in Memphis?" Abie asked. "That's a fer piece from Bear Grass. And how about little Hobby? Is he going to live with them?" She felt a pang of jealously about Hobby and wishing something like that would happen to her Wilbert Lee.

"I reckon so," Viola replied. "They've not decided about that yet because he'll have more operations on his leg and all that's got to be finished before they make any kind of plans. They're on their way to Baltimore to see him now."

"I declare we're hearing about places we've hardly thought about out here since Pearl's courtship got started," Abie opined. "Memphis and Baltimore and all them places that we knowed about but never thought of them ever being associated with Bear Grass."

Viola realized that she might as well tell Abie about their planned trip. It would get out anyway eventually and Abie would spread the word without any effort on her part. She looked out the door as she said," Me'n Craven are going to Memphis in December."

"You don't mean!" Abie said, looking aghast. "Will you fit in out there Viola? I mean, we's such ordinary folks down here we've got our place to stay in. I mean, we're all one class and everything's fine that way. But we'd be as lost as a snowball in hell in that hifalutin crowd. I'm surprised Perline would ask you to go. I know I'd be ashamed to go sommers like that even if I was asked. But I don't have a thing to worry about for I'm not going to git invited nowhere nohow."

"They've taken care of all that," Viola said. "We went to Weil's the other day and got outfitted and all that."

"Weils!" Abie exclaimed. "You mean you've got clothes from Weil's to wear out there? Can I see them Viola?"

"They took them with them," Viola said. "There were half a dozen or more boxes." Viola wanted to emphasize what she was going to say next, although it brought on a shudder just to think about it. "And Craven and me will be flying out to Tennessee."

"Lord God," Abie said, "and I hope I ain't taking His name in vain in what I said, but I just can't take it all in. I'd pure wet my pants if I was flying way up there."

"I probably will too," Viola said. "But things are changing Abie, and we can't stay on in the same old way forever. And Pearl didn't give us a chance to say we would fly. She didn't even tell us until they were driving off."

"I'll tell you one thing," Abie said. "That Perline has shore changed things in Bear Grass. This will be something for folks around here to talk about for months."

"I'm sure it will," Viola said.

Chapter 16

They were on the outskirts of Memphis, and Pearl's heart was beating wildly. After all that had been talked about Memphis and the place she would call home, she would soon arrive at Nick's home. There was nothing outstanding to be seen. Mostly small homes and a lot of places that were definitely slums. People were walking up and down the streets in patched clothes and it could be any city in America, for the Depression was felt everywhere. Money was as scarce in one place as another. She saw people pulling boards off an old dilapidated house and realized that they would be used for firewood.

Then they passed through the central business district. She noted a lot of boarded up stores and a minimum of cars on the streets. But she was amazed at the largeness of the city. They had ridden miles and miles before reaching the business district. "I want to see where your restaurant was sometime when we have the chance," Pearl said and Nick told her they would get around to it in a few days. Then they were in a district where the homes were handsome and large and she knew this was the affluent part of Memphis. But she wasn't prepared for what she saw when Nick finally turned into a winding driveway that led to a house sitting far back from the street.

"This it?" Pearl asked and Nick said, "Uh, huh."

It looked like a mansion to Pearl. There were large columns in front of a veranda extending the width of the house and large windows with black shutters and tree-shaded lawns and mums in various colors blooming in plots along the driveway. She thought of it as a place George Washington would have lived.

Nick didn't say a word as they made the circle and stopped in the back. Then he said, "I always enter from the rear. It's more convenient and I just like the back entrance." Pearl noted that there were dozens of geraniums blooming at the edge of the entrance and a large weeping willow tree about fifty feet on the slope going down to the water with a swing underneath and a large building that she assumed was Nick's workshop.

"It's beautiful," she said.

"Glad you like it," Nick replied.

"We've got to unload the car," Pearl said.

"We'll wait for that a while," Nick said. "Let's go on inside."

He took his keys from his pocket and unlocked the door. After it was opened he gathered Pearl in his arms and took her across the threshold. There was a long hallway leading to the front of the house, and he carried her all the way to the front and pushed the swinging door with his foot and they entered the "great room" as he called it.

Pearl was aghast when she saw it. Her first thought was that this one room was larger than the house they had slept in last night. And she could not believe the furnishings. She had never seen anything even approaching what she saw. There was a fireplace at least ten feet wide and a stone mantelpiece with a large mirror, a chandelier at least six feet in width, draperies of damask in a soft shade of green with wide cornice boards, mahogany folding tables polished to the extent they mirrored everything around them. There were twin couches in bright colors and chairs in damask and others in leather and a baby grand piano as shiny as the tables and a plush rug that matched the shade of the draperies. There was a mahogany secretary that stood almost as tall as the high ceiling. There was polished crystal everywhere and vases with colorful fall flowers.

"Now let's see the other rooms," Nick said. They crossed the hall and entered the dining room through an arched doorway with another large chandelier. The dining table was eight feet long with Chippendale chairs at the ends and upholstered chairs at the other six places. An eight-foot highboy was on one wall filled with silver and fine china. White draperies allowed soft sunshine to come into the room. A large silver urn was the table's centerpiece, filled with bronze chrysanthemums. And there was an oriental rug in autumn colors. An antique serving table adorned another wall. The windows looked out on the wide expanse of lawn still with a carpet of green grass but upon trees already bare of leaves.

Next was an oversized kitchen furnished in the manner of modern kitchens with a large stove and sideboard, sink, drain board, overhead and lower cabinets, a table in the center overlaid with a red-checked cloth and beyond the kitchen area another large fireplace with logs burned down to embers and rocking chairs with fancy designs, on each side of the fireplace and a dough tray filled with magazines beside one of the chairs. An old loom sat against one wall and there were two calendars on the walls. A box filled with oak wood sat beside the fireplace.

Beyond the kitchen was Nick's study, furnished in leather furniture with a large roll-top desk in front of one window and Nick's swivel chair. This room was smaller than the others.

"Now for our bedroom," Nick said as they re-entered the "great room" and opened the door beyond.

There were heavy white curtains criss-crossed adorning the windows that had small panes typical of the Reconstruction era, pictures on each wall that showed they were original paintings and between two smaller windows on the back wall was a tester bed, giant in size, with six-foot posts and a heavily ruffled tester above. A plush Martha Washington spread adorned the bed. There was an eight-foot-wide dresser with sparkling mirror and a six-foot chest of drawers. A luxuriously furnished bathroom adjoined the bedroom.

"Let's go upstairs now," Nick said, taking Pearl by the arm. They re-entered the "great room" and ascended a spiraling staircase with paintings on the wall at various levels as they ascended. The steps were heavily carpeted.

"There are six bedrooms upstairs," Nick said, "so that when we have guests from Bear Grass, or any other place, there will be adequate room for them." Pearl noted that each room had a large bed with full suites of furniture in several designs with the same color carpeting on the entire floor.

"Now, this is our kingdom, Mrs. Staphal. And what do you think?"

"I think I'm in the wrong place," Pearl said with tears in her eyes.

"I'm more ashamed than I've ever been in my life that I put you through what you endured in Bear Grass. I put you on a mattress on the floor to sleep! I had you bathing in a wash tub. I put you in the fields to crop tobacco and subjected you to all manner of torture, never realizing that you were some kind of god! I feel as small as a grain of sand and I want to go back to Bear Grass, Nick." She was crying openly now.

Nick took her into his arms and her hair was golden and it fell around his shoulder and he smelled the sweetness of her body and tried to think of a way to fully explain to her what she really meant to him. He gently pushed her away so he could look into her eyes. He held her hands in his own and said, "Pearl, you really don't understand, and maybe I don't understand myself. Anyway, I feel worse than you, for I've learned more about the reality of life since I've known you than I ever knew in all the other years of my life. And I feel like the worst kind of heel. I look at this house and think about the unfortunate masses who can hardly exist during these crucial times, and I want to go out and give it all to the poor. The only problem is that if I did that it wouldn't even make a dent in all the poverty around us, and I know that is a selfish attitude to assume, but it's true and you know it.

"I also have to make another confession. This is the result of an ego trip for me. You see, I grew up in Memphis and knew a lot of the boys and girls I was in school with, and while I was helping Dad in the restaurant they were rising in their careers and many became very successful before the Great Depression struck. And Nick Staphal was forgotten for the most part. After a while those whom I knew seemed to forget our association in school as well as college. They were becoming the upper crust while I seemed to be the forgotten one.

"This bothered me, Pearl. Call it ego or whatever you wish, but I felt badly toward them. I thought to myself that I'd pay them back if the occasion ever arose. This was childish thinking I know, and I was thinking as a child.

"I became sort of a recluse from society and I was very unhappy. I went out with women occasionally, and met with a few boys I knew who hadn't made it in the bigtime, and passed the time that way. I had a chip on my shoulder, so to speak, and I wasn't at all happy with myself. Then it all happened. Suddenly, I was in possession of money, big money, during the greatest Depression this country has ever known. I had at my disposal money that would purchase almost anything my heart could desire, not that It was all that much but, rather, because of the times when property that had been confiscated was selling for a pittance.

"I was able to capitalize on that, and so I began investing in property, and that's how I came to own this home. It was up for sale and I went to look the place over, and it was magnificent, although it needed work to make it what it is today. So the transformation began, and I was obsessed with the idea of making it the best I could make it. I knew of a man in Boston who was an expert on antiques as well as interior design. I contacted him and he came to Memphis to see what the situation was, and he immediately began his work. I always liked antiques and I told him I wanted the best he could find, and that I wanted this house furnished so it would be the envy of Memphis.

"Boy, did they wake up once they realized Nick Staphal had entered the society scene. It's unbelievable how many of those who had forgotten suddenly remembered. Those "society" dames were calling me constantly and the boys who had risen high but had come down the ladder with a jolt suddenly became my best friends. I became the most eligible bachelor in Memphis. And I must say that it pleased me very much to entertain the "wolves" in my luxurious home. They ooed and ahhd and came on stronger than you can believe. They cajoled me into holding balls in the "great room" and sometimes there were twenty five to thirty in attendance. There was plenty of whisky and hors d'oeuvres were plentiful and I was the talk of the town. And it was totally boring!

"Then I started going with Tina. She was pretty and young and I thought she would fill the great void in my life. She made her debut and all that and she went in the top circles in Memphis. I tried to believe that I loved her and finally proposed and she accepted instantly. So I brought her here and we didn't hit it off from the start. Only after I married her did I realize that she was a real gold-digger, bent on becoming the socialite of Memphis.

"It disgusted me and I wasn't long in realizing that this was the most fictitious life a person could live. I suddenly hated this place and all that it stood for. After only one year and many, many fights and screaming and hollering and Tina trying to make me over and making impossible demands, we called it quits. It had never been love in the first place.

"Since that time my home has been a shambles, meaningless and with no attraction for me. You've always heard that a house doesn't make a home, Pearl, and no truer words were ever spoken. This has been the coldest place I ever remember and I've often wished I had never acquired it. And I didn't really know how meaningless it was until I met you. If you only knew, my darling, that the little place you had near Joe's Restaurant was the greatest haven I've ever known, you wouldn't be talking like this.

"I remember how happy I was when I was cutting and stacking wood for the fireplace and how cozy it was inside and how really wonderful you were and when we sat by the fire I was in my seventh heaven. Then you took me to Bear Grass, and that did it for me. It never bothered me one iota that I slept on a mattress and bathed in a washtub. That was living, Pearl. Really living! I learned then what life is all about. I learned what real people were, with no apologies and with complete sincerity. Nothing has ever touched me liked the experience I have had with you and your family.

"Now, you say you want to return to Bear Grass. Well, I won't let you, not until you've given this a chance to succeed. Then if you wish to go, that will be up to you. But you won't do that, Pearl, for you know beyond any shadow of doubt that I truly and sincerely love you. You can make of this place whatever you wish. It can become a place of love and understanding and you can bring the warmth of your apartment near Joe's to this big place. Or it can become a total shambles with no redemption. You will make it whatever it becomes, Pearl, and if you fail I will get rid of it as fast as I can. Nobody else on earth could make of this what the potential holds. You have a great responsibility, yet it is so simple. Just be Pearl. Don't ever change. Don't apologize to anybody and just love me. Nothing else on earth matters Pearl. You're my wife and I am more proud of you than all the property I may own or whatever I may become. My life will be over and will have no meaning if you renege on the vows we made."

Chapter 17

It was a sunshiny day in June. All the children large enough to work were in the fields, for grass was growing furiously after a recent rain, and folks were chopping and plowing to keep the grass from getting the upper hand. There were cirrus clouds floating across the sky, portending no danger. Butterflies were flitting about, pitching on foliage and showing their rainbow of colors. Birds were singing and bees were busy gathering nectar for their hives. A cow would low occasionally in the pasture and younger children were in the yards; the girls playing hopscotch or making playhouses and jumping rope and the boys rolling wheels with a stick or pretending they were cowboys with an old belt around their waists and homemade guns by their sides or bean shooters or slingshots.

If their mothers were at home they were in the kitchen preparing dinner. For the most part, the children were left unattended. And the children usually stayed in their yards, for they knew better than to roam over the neighborhood without asking. But a teen-ager that had come from Hallsborough told one of the children that the chain gang was cleaning up the woods in the area of Pineknoll school, which was a good mile away, and when the news got to all the children they went crazy. They loved to watch the convicts at work. They knew better than to ask their mothers for they wouldn't let them go where convicts were working, although the children always stayed on the opposite side of the road from the convicts. But the guards carried shotguns and they always feared something might happen.

There were Jimmy Joe Smith, LaBeth Sims, Lisker Johnson and Wilbert Lee Turner who was plenty large enough to work but whose mother, Abie, saw to it that he didn't do field work to any extent.

Wilbert Lee went to each house and said, "Let's go see the convicts. Our mamas won't even know it, and we'll be back home before they even miss us," and the children were afraid to go, but they wanted to see the convicts at work. The woods were thick from Pineknoll school almost to Wilbur Stroud's store on one side of the road.

The highway department always dreaded to clean this stretch of highway along Beston Road. The undergrowth was thick, almost jungle-like, and they were very careful with the convicts. Most of the group wore shackles, for they were dangerous, although a few were unshackled. And on this morning there seemed to be a tenseness that was more evident than on most days. The men seemed to be stirred up somehow, and their songs were more plaintive. The trusty brought them water from a nearby well after getting permission from the tenant to draw water. The men would drink from the dipper and let the water run down their neck to cool them off. When Cap'n Hinnant saw the children coming he shook his head. He called to them as soon as they were in sight and told them to go back home, that it was no place for children. Men in shackles could not resort to the woods to relieve themselves. They would stand and urinate when nobody was coming and men in chains just pulled down their breeches, squatted and defecated as if they were in a secluded place. Children had no business seeing this.

The children stopped fifty feet or so before getting to the convicts. They squatted and searched the area for colored glass and bottles and anything else that drew their attention. Still, Cap'n Hinnant was not satisfied. He told them to leave again and said he'd tell their parents if they didn't go on back to the house.

Wilbert Lee said, "Shit, they don't even know who our parents are. How can they tell if they don't know who to tell?" But LaBeth Sims and Lisker returned home, leaving Wilbert Lee and Jimmy Joe Smith behind.

The men assumed the same place on the chain gang every day. Each convict knew his place. At the end of the line was Earl Ward, a colored man who had been convicted of armed robbery and was serving a twenty-year sentence. He had served eight years of his term. Second from the end was "Bad Boy" Sims, a very dark colored man of two hundred and fifty pounds at least, six feet, six inches tall. His distinguishing feature was an angry-looking scar on the left side of his face, extending from just below the eye to his chin. He was inky black and when he sweated, and he always sweated, he glistened in the light. There were twenty eight men on the chain gang, and when they moved the shackles made a great noise.

A week or so earlier when the convicts had been cleaning the side of the road on the other side of Hallsborough, "Bad Boy" had found an old, rusty hacksaw blade in the debris, and Earl had seen the blade. "Bad Boy" shook his head and winked his eye for Earl to keep silent. He casually slipped the blade in the heel of one of his shoes and they continued working as usual. Bill Petty, the convict next in line to "Bad Boy" didn't speak to "Bad Boy." They had had trouble at the camp and Bill had knocked "Bad Boy" down during an argument and "Bad Boy" had threatened to kill Bill. So Bill never looked back at "Bad Boy" when they were working. In fact, he helped to shield "Bad Boy" and Earl from the men at the front of the line.

"Bad Boy" had a file in his cell that was well-hidden under a window sill. He could slide it under the sill and nobody would ever see it unless they felt under the window sill and looked at the narrow hole in which it was hidden. He filed the hacksaw blade until it glistened, then meticulously filed the narrow teeth until it was sharper than when it was new. He had planned his escape for a long time. He was convicted of arson and attempted rape. He was given a thirty-year sentence for arson and ten years for the attempted rape, the sentences to be served concurrently. He had been a convict for ten years. He had been waiting for the right time to make his getaway. Everything had to be just right. He didn't want any blunders, for he was itching to get out of that place and be long-gone from North Carolina.

When he learned they would be cleaning out the edge of the woods on Beston Road he determined that that would be the time to make his break. In muffled tones, he told Earl about his plans. "This is the day," he said to

Earl as they were cutting undergrowth in the thick woods. "I'm going to break the blade half in two and give you one end, and I'll show you how we will git these shackles off and make our break."

Wilbert Lee and Jimmy Joe were watching it all beyond where the convicts were working. Cap'n Hinnant saw the trusty bringing water to the men and there would be a brief rest period while the convicts drank from the cup that was passed from man to man. But the rest period would not do "Bad Boy" any good. He had to be able to squat. He called to Cap'n Hinnant, "Hey boss, I got to do number Two, please sir."

"Don't you ever shit before you come on the job "Bad Boy?" Git them britches down in a hurry and get it over with while we're drinking water."

"Bad Boy" slipped his britches down and took the hacksaw blade out of his shoe, bent it half in two, handed Earl one half, doing it all in a sleight of hand motion, and quickly began cutting through the chain that held him to the main chain. He applied pressure to the hacksaw blade, and it cut quickly through the chain. He had both chains cut through before all the men had swilled the water.

Earl had squatted down with "Bad Boy" and began working on the chains and he finished about the same time as "Bad Boy." But they rose and started back to work with the other men. They faked being chained to the Chain Gang for a while. The convicts were cleaning a twelve-foot swath at the edge of the woods, cutting down overhanging limbs and vines and clearing the undergrowth. Cap'n Hinnant had placed three guards in the woods to lessen the risk of an uprising. The captain was the only one guarding the chain gang.

They were now working at the very edge of the woods. Two convicts were cutting down a fairly small dead tree and all the men were alerted that a tree would be falling and to get out of the path of the tree. "Bad Boy" whispered to Earl that the tree falling would be the time to make their break. Everybody's attention was focused on the tree anyway and at the moment when they heard it begin to fall was the time to go.

Cap'n Hinnant was nervous. He felt that there was something in the air because the men seemed restless. He had a premonition and he wanted the men to remember that he was carrying a loaded gun. He cocked the shotgun and shot in the air one time as a reminder.

Wilbert Lee was really excited when he heard the shotgun. Jimmy Joe said it was time for him to go. He told Wilbert Lee he'd better leave too, but Wilbert Lee said it was just getting exciting; that he couldn't leave.

Then there was the sound of the tree beginning to fall and Earl broke away and ran toward Hallsborough while "Bad Boy" went straight into the woods.

"Halt," Cap'n Hinnant yelled to Earl, who was still in the clearing, but Earl continued to run. Cap'n Hinnant drew the gun on him and fired a shot that seemed to pick Earl up off the ground, and he fell instantly.

Now the excitement reached a climax for Wilbert Lee. He had seen the convict bolt and stop dead in his tracks, then fall. He was nervous but he felt like he was having an orgasm the sensation was so exciting.

"Where's "Bad Boy?" Cap'n Hinnant hollered to the guards in the woods.

"We've not seen him," they hollered back. The woods were so dense anybody could hide within five feet of a guard and not be detected.

"Bad Boy" was inching his way flat on the ground, careful not to shake the bushes and give himself away. He wanted to get out of range of the gunshots.

Cap'n Hinnant hollered to Wilbert Lee, "Hey boy, do something for me. Go to Wilbur Stroud's store and tell whoever is there to contact the Sheriff's Department and tell them to send all their deputies to the store. Tell them there's a dangerous convict on the loose and for everybody to take all precautions. Tell 'em to hurry."

He hollered to the guards in the woods, "Come on out boys. We've got to get these convicts back to camp. We'll have to deal with "Bad Boy" later."

The guards came out of the woods and held their guns on the shackled men. They were nervous now and showing it in their actions. Cap'n Hinnant was really worried about "Bad Boy." He knew he was named properly and his fear was that the convict would harm somebody before he was apprehended.

Wilbert Lee ran all the way to Stroud's store. Wilbur was there and Wilbert Lee told him what the captain said. Wilbur got in his truck immediately and headed for Hallsborough. He told Wilbert Lee and Barney Steele who was a clerk at the store to warn everybody about the escape. Barney closed the store and he went one way and Wilbert lee the other and told everybody they saw to be on the lookout for the escapee.

"Bad Boy" crawled farther and farther in the thick growth. When he felt that he was out of shotgun reach he stood and took off the convict suit. He had on a pair of shorts that were so dingy they were gray, but he told himself he'd stand a better chance with them than with the striped convict suit. He made his way toward Greene County Road. He knew that was where the colored folks lived, and if he had to come in contact with people he'd fare better among his own color.

A sense of freedom came over him and he felt like he was almost in a trance. He'd hide out and beat them at their own game and when the coast was clear he'd be on his way, on top of some freight train leaving behind North Carolina and Hallsborough forever.

There were plenty of ripe huckleberries in the woods, and he filled up on them. He found holes with water in them. Pine straw was thick at the bottom of the holes but the water was clear. He lay down beside the hole and drank his fill. He pondered his moves as he rested. He reasoned the best thing to do was cross Greene County Road and find some dilapidated building and hide. If he had to he could go up in the loft at somebody's house on Greene County Road and just wait.

He was getting nearer to Greene County Road and the undergrowth was not as thick as it had been farther back.

Before Cap'n Hinnant set out to Hallsborough he went over to where Earl lay, took his foot and rolled him on his back. A trickle of blood oozed from his mouth and he noted that the blood and foam had made a little puddle on the grass. Earl's eyes were open and he stared as if he were looking beyond the skies. He called two of the guards to get the body in the truck. The convicts sat silently as the body was placed at their feet.

People in Bear Grass were rounding up their children and trying to find ways to lock their houses. Many houses had no locks at all.

Abie Turner was in a tizzy. She had stood in the yard and yelled to the top of her voice, "Wilbert Lee, you come home right now. Your life is in danger." But her words went on deaf ears. There was no sign of Wilbert Lee anywhere.

"Bad Boy" made his way slowly. He was still pondering what to do. He had heard the shot from Cap'n Hinnant and he wondered whether Earl had been shot. He had no intention of being shot. He would evade them. He felt lucky.

Stephen Sauls, a landowner who lived some three miles from Wilbur Stroud's store, heard about the escape sometime before dinner and went into panic. His wife, Sallie, and their thirteen-year-old daughter, Nervy, had gone huckleberrying in the woods across from Wilbur Stroud's store. He had taken them there about nine o'clock. He knew they were in the area of the escape and his heart went into his throat, or it felt like it anyway. His knees became limp and he had to exert all his strength to get in his truck and drive to Wilbur's store.

Wilbur was there when he arrived and Stephen said, "I hear there's been a convict escape around here."

"Yeah," Wilbur said. Stephen noted that a crowd was gathering outside the store.

"All the sheriff's deputies are combing the woods now," Wilbur said.

"God Wilbur," Stephen said, "Sallie and Nervy are out there huckleberrying."

"God almighty," Wilbur said.

"I'm scared Wilbur," Stephen said, and Wilbur noted that his whole body was shaking, "They're all I've got Wilbur."

His daughter, Nervy, was his eyeball. Her real name was Minerva but Stephen started calling her Nervy when she was a baby, so everyone knew her by her shortened name, or her nickname. She was a pretty child with black hair and brown eyes, with dimples in her cheeks. She didn't live close enough to associate with the children around Wilbur's store, although all of them knew her.

Nervy was outgoing at thirteen. She would be entering Hallsborough High in the fall.

When they entered the woods and found bushes loaded with huckleberries, Sallie told Nervy they could spread out and find the fullest bushes, for some had already been picked. The colored folks and many whites went huckleberrying every chance they got.

So Sallie and Nervy were some fifty feet apart when "Bad Boy" spotted Nervy picking berries. His heart began to race and a feeling in his groins went all the way up his spine. He went wild. In the confinement of the camp he hadn't seen a woman at close range for years, except those that came to visit their kin on Sunday. Suddenly he wanted to feel woman flesh.

He remembered how it had been when he was charged with attempted rape. It was at a house in Hallsborough. She was a married woman and her "old man" had gone to a bootleg house to get a bottle of whisky. "Bad Boy" and Aaron were both about drunk. And Aaron had a good-looking "old lady" and a house full of young'uns. But she hadn't given "Bad Boy" any cause to want to rape her. "Bad Boy" said her big tits got to him and while Aaron was away he took hold of her arm and the soft skin got to him. She pulled away but "Bad Boy" tried again and got a hand on one of her breasts.

"You black son-of-a-bitch," she said, "leave me alone. I don't want nothing you've got." But "Bad Boy" was too wild to be put off now. He yanked up her dress and she raked a fingernail across his face but it didn't faze him. He was fumbling at his pants when Aaron walked into the room, and she was wearing pointed-toed shoes and she gave him a kick in his crotch and he doubled up in pain. Aaron went for his shotgun that hung over the door in the bedroom and while he was gone "Bad Boy" got himself together and got out of there. As he left the house he took a piece of wadded-up newspaper and set some tow sacks afire that were thrown into a corner of the kitchen and as he ran to the woods he looked back and the shanty was ablaze.

He slipped up behind Nervy for he was too near the road to risk her screaming. He put his large hand on her mouth and turned her toward him. He ripped her dress and placed the other hand on her budding breasts. He lost all his control and realized that the only thing to do was to choke her first to quieten her, for she was making an effort to scream. He felt for her jugular vein and tightened his grip. He watched her face as she became unconscious and her eyes gaped open.

When she was dead he removed his dirty shorts and raped her viciously. He was spent when it was over with and he wanted to lie down and sleep, but he knew it was time to move on, and fast. Sheriff's deputies would be in the area soon, he knew. So he slipped on the shorts again and prepared to cross Greene County Road. He had to have some clothes to wear and he had to figure out how to get them.

He looked at his body and it was covered with scratches. Blood had oozed from some of them and appeared darker than his skin. He knew his eyes were puffy for they felt swollen. They had filled with sweat for it was hot in the woods.

When he reached the edge of the woods he went farther down Greene County Road before crossing. He heard noises at Wilbur Stroud's store and saw men milling around the place. He knew then the word had gotten out and that he was the object of a manhunt. This excited him.

He looked up and down the road to see if anybody was on the road. He wasn't near a house. There was another stretch of woods across the road and he ran as fast as he could across the road and jumped a side ditch. He just kept on running for time was of the essence now. He had to get situated and hole up some place.

After going several miles up into the woods, he saw a pile of old rusty tin that had been dumped at some time. It looked like somebody might have put a new roof on a building and just hauled the tin up in the woods to get it out of the way. But he didn't see any buildings through the woods. There was an old path beside the tin that hadn't been used in years for there were no tracks and bushes had grown in the path.

The tin was thrown on each side of a tree and there was sort of a wigwam effect. He peeped under the tin and there was space enough for him to get under it. He decided this was his best bet for the moment. Only one thing really worried him. He knew that bloodhounds would be put on his trail and he would have to face them. But he'd tackle that when he had to. There were a lot of things to face before reaching his freedom.

There were large spider webs under the tin and he found a dead brush and ran it all around, accumulating a web, and some large spiders. He went under the tin and a lizard jumped out. He saw a snake on the ground, or half a snake. It was the tail end and it slid into the open as he entered. He cleaned out from under the tin and pulled up a few hills of grass. Then he took a piece of the tin and placed it over the opening.

He crawled under the tin to begin his long wait. It was hot inside even though the tin was shaded from the sun. He didn't have any choice now. He was so far up in the woods he didn't hear a sound.

Meanwhile, after Stephen Sauls let it be known that his wife and daughter were huckleberrying in the woods across the road, the sheriff's deputies entered the woods searching for them. None of the people in Bear Grass wanted the task. They were only hoping that Sallie and Nervy would be found safe. They didn't even want to anticipate the worst.

The deputies were not in the woods thirty minutes before they found them. Sallie's head was resting on Nervy's legs and she was incoherent. Uncontrollable sobs racked her body.

Nervy was peaceful looking, with her head resting on pine straw. When they removed Sallie they saw that her dress was ripped apart and that blood and semen were all over her stomach. And there were bruises on each side of her throat accentuated in purple where "Bad Boy" had gotten huckleberry stain on his hands.

The deputies stood silent for a moment, too shocked to speak. Some of them had daughters and they made a self-case of what they were witnessing. One of them sobbed. Another was too angry to express himself. He just said, "God damn, what a world." Another shook his head. None had ever been on a case where a rape-murder had been committed.

"Toughest thing I ever had to do," the head deputy said. "Going back and telling that man that his daughter has been momicked up in any such a way. I swear I believe it'll kill him. And this lady has got to be sent to the hospital immediately."

"Not only that," another said, "these people around here will go crazy. No telling what they'll do."

"I know what they'll do," the head deputy said. "They'll go hunting for the bastard. And I don't blame them. But that's a dangerous situation when a group of men take the law into their own hands. Still, how much can people take without cracking? And there ain't no way of handling a large group of men under such circumstances. Anyhow, one of you boys stay with Miss Sallie and the corpse and the rest of you come with me. We've got to break the bad news."

Sheriff Brown was standing at the edge of the store when the deputies came out of the woods. Head deputy Taylor motioned to the sheriff. Brown was a distinguished looking man, clad in his khaki uniform, portly, with thick gray hair and a mustache. His shoes were shined and his holster was polished to a fine luster and the automatic sticking out of the holster was pearl-finished. He spat as he started toward Taylor.

"It's bad," Taylor said. "The girl has been raped and strangled to death."

"My God!" Sheriff Brown exclaimed. "I hate for these men to find out about it."

Stephen Sauls spotted the men talking and he came up to them, breaking into the conversation. "What's the news?" he asked. He was pale and short of breath.

"Let's sit down here beside the road," Sheriff Brown said. Stephen and the deputy joined him.

"It's not good news Stephen," Brown said and Stephen began sobbing.

"Are they dead?" he asked.

"I'm so sorry Stephen," Sheriff Brown said. "But your wife's not dead. Little Nervy is though."

Stephen fell back on the ground and held his hand over his heart. "Oh God, he said, "Why have you forsaken me? I've always tried to lead a good life. I've lived by your principles. And I loved my little girl so much. Only you know how much God. Why? Why? Why?" Everybody had gathered round to hear what happened. The word spread like wildfire across Bear Grass.

"My God, nobody's called the undertaker," Sheriff Brown said. He called to Wilbur Stroud who stood nearby, "Hey, Wilbur, call the undertaker. We might need an ambulance too, but don't call just yet. Have you got any ammonia in the store?"

"I don't think so," Wilbur said, "but I think my wife has some at the house." He motioned to the clerk who stood in the door, for nobody was inside, and said, "Run to the house and tell Callie to fix a dose of ammonia. Tell her to hurry."

"Make that two," Sheriff Brown said. "We'll give Miss Sallie and Stephen both a dose." Stephen was still lying in the yard. "And let's fix a place inside for Stephen to lie. We've got to get out there and get Miss Sallie too."

Wilbur had a cot with a heavy ducking bottom and they carried it to the woods to place Miss Sallie on. Two of the deputies handled the cot. Miss Sallie was still lying as they left her. The deputies who had stayed with her said she didn't appear to be conscious. When the sheriff got the ammonia he rushed to the woods, held Miss Sallie's head up and got it into her and she came to in a minute or so. "Where am I?" she asked. Then she saw Nervy's body and gasped.

"Look after Stephen," she said. "I'll be all right. Just look after Stephen. He's got a bad heart, you know." She looked again at the body of her daughter and said, "Poor baby. It was my fault for I was not with you when it happened. Who was it?" she asked the sheriff.

"A convict cut his chains and escaped," the sheriff explained. He was a big man, two hundred and fifty pounds or so. He'd have gotten both of you if he had known you were nearby."

"Black or white?" Miss Sallie asked as she looked directly into the sheriff's eyes.

"You already know don't you Miss Sallie?" was the sheriff's only reply.

"Yeah, I know," Miss Sallie sighed.

"We're ready to take you out Miss Sallie," the sheriff said. "We've brought a cot from Wilbur's store to carry you on."

"I can walk out sheriff," Sallie said. "A man can get on each side of me to give me something to hold on to. I'd rather walk than be toted out."

The crowd had thickened when Miss Sallie came out of the woods with a man on each side supporting her. The sheriff noted a look of anger on the men's faces. This frightened him.

"How's Stephen?" she asked.

"They got a dose of ammonia in him and he's come to," Wilbur said. "But he's pale and worried about you. You go on inside and that will help him a lot."

The sheriff asked Miss Sallie if she or Stephen wanted to be taken to the hospital.

"I shore don't," Miss Sallie said. She went up to Stephen and put a hand on his forehead. "How are you feeling?" she asked.

"Don't even ask that," Stephen replied.

"I'm trying to find out if you need to go to the hospital," Miss Sallie said.

"Naw" Stephen said. "Let them just take us home and we'll be all right there. We'll call Dr. Miller and get him to come out and check us over."

Wilbur took them home in his truck and Miss Nancy Mewborn, who lived directly across the road from them, went over to stay with them.

Sheriff Brown was becoming more anxious by the moment. He knew what the men were going to do and there wasn't a thing he could do about it. The group had grown to at least a hundred by now and they were mumbling among themselves. The sheriff paused and then said, "Gentlemen, let me have your attention for a moment. Please don't take the law into your own hands. That's not a democracy. That's not the way to do things. I guarantee you that we will deal with the convict if he is caught. He'll get the punishment he deserves. I ask you to go back to your homes and let the law handle it."

The men were not paying him any attention. They had come with axes, knives, pitchforks, shrubbing blades, and a few men were carrying pistols. You could see their shape in the men's pockets. And the area around Wilbur Stroud's store and even the road became clogged. All the white men took out their mules and put them in the stables. Every able-bodied man in Bear Grass was there. The colored folks were still plowing in the fields but they would gather in little groups and talk. They had heard that a colored man had raped and killed a white girl and it put fear in their hearts. They didn't want any Ku Klux Klansmen in Bear Grass.

The Negroes were trying to find out who it was. Somebody said they thought he was called "Bad Boy" and another said, "Naw, you don't mean "Bad Boy". "I used to know that nigger when he lived in Hallsborough. We's ought to join the white folks to git him if'n they'd let us. But you know they wouldn't have no nigger in a manhunt for a black man."

"Bad Boy" needs to die just on general principal," another said. "He's a mean nigger and he was mean to his own color too, just as mean as he'd be to a white man. But what I'm skeered of is that he'll want to hole up with some of us and you might as well chop ours heads off if that happened. They'd 'cuse us of harboring a hunted man."

"What are you going to do Wilbur?" the sheriff asked.

"I wish you hadn't asked me that sheriff," Wilbur replied. "You know what I'm going to do, but that's off the record."

"I was afraid of that," Sheriff Brown said.

Just then a truck drove up with the two bloodhounds the sheriff's department owned, and the men who trained them.

"Hurry and get them out there," the sheriff said. "I wouldn't take them where he entered the woods. They'll find tracks too easily and will stay in a small place too long. I understand he stripped off his stripes and is running around with a dirty pair of drawers on. If we need the suit to get the dogs on the right track we'll find it. Go on down Greene County Road and I believe you'll find where he crossed the road. That ought to give them the scent."

The two deputies set off with the dogs and the other deputies started to follow, but Wilbur got the deputy aside and told him he might as well go on into town, that the men were not listening to anybody and it would be an embarrassment if the sheriff's department and the men in the neighborhood were part of the same posse.

"I can't go home Wilbur," the sheriff said. "It's my duty to be here. People in the county would never understand if I didn't make any attempt to catch the man."

"All right, you stay in the store and if you want your deputies to stay in there they can too. You can lock the door and nobody will know it except those who see you go in. But it's best for you to stay out of this Sheriff. Those men are as mad as hell and there's no reasoning among them right now. They're good men too. Honest men. God-fearing. But they want revenge for this great injustice."

"All right," Sheriff Brown said. "We'll go into the store. But the men with the dogs will follow his trail."

Gant Turner and Craven Turnage arrived about the same time. They spoke to each other and Gant said, "This is a mighty bad thing that's happened in our community Craven."

"Yeah," Craven replied, "you wouldn't think something like this would happen right at home. It's always somewhere else."

Gant turned his head and saw Wilbert Lee and Philip up near the store. He stepped over to where they were standing and said, "Wilbert Lee, you go home right now. You've got no business here and your mama has hollered your name so much she's lost her voice. She's been calling since she heard about the escape. I heard her way down in the mash. Where on earth have you been?"

"I saw him when he run into the woods" Wilbert Lee said. "I saw the sheriff when he shot that nigger."

"You had no business there either. You've been told to stay away when convicts are working along the road. Now go on home, right now."

"Philip is going." Wilbert Lee said.

Gant called to Wilbur, "Hey Wilbur, you're not letting Philip go up in the woods are you?"

"No sir ree," Wilbur said. "I didn't know he was in the group. You, Philip, get to the house with your mama right now. She'll be afraid at best and she'll be scared to death if nobody is with her."

A worried look came over Wilbert Lee's face, for he was determined to go on that manhunt, and his daddy had never been one to challenge him. He looked at Gant and said, "I'm going."

"Listen to me, Wilbert Lee," Gant said. "If you don't go to the house like

I told you to do I'm going to straighten you out."

"And what are you going to do?" Wilbert Lee said insolently.

Gant Turner realized that people were staring at them, and he could tell they were expecting him to get the young upstart straightened out. People in the neighborhood had a loathing for Wilbert Lee and were itching to see him put in his place. And they blamed Gant a lot for what was happening to the boy although they realized that he was up against it with a neurotic wife like Abie.

There was a peach tree at the back of the store, and Gant pulled off a good-size switch and stripped the leaves off.

"Don't you hit me with that thing," Wilbert Lee said about the time Gant wrapped it around his legs. Wilbert Lee felt the piercing sting and Gant was holding him by his overalls bib. He reached down and tried to bite his father, and Gant slapped his face, causing his head to go backward.

"I won't cry," Wilbert Lee declared. But there were tears in his eyes.

"Are you ready to go home now?" Gant asked

"No," Wilbert Lee said.

Gant spotted a paddle used in making soap standing at the back of the store. He motioned for one of the men to hand it to him. He took the paddle about half way down and gave him half a dozen licks and Wilbert Lee screamed out in pain.

"Are you ready to go home now Wilbert Lee?" Gant asked. He was red-faced from the exertion and the boy's obstinance.

"Yeah, I'm ready," Wilbert Lee said, screaming.

Gant turned him loose and Wilbert Lee went off running and sobbing. But after he was far enough away that Gant couldn't catch him he looked back and yelled, "I hate you." Gant just shook his head. By then most of the men had entered the woods, except for those who wanted to see Wilbert Lee get what he deserved. They joined the other men who were already well into the woods.

The deputies were still waiting in the woods for the coroner and the undertaker. They didn't want the body removed from its position. They finally heard them entering the woods. Deputy Davis, who had remained with the body, would remember later how peaceful it seemed in the woods that day. In a tall oak nearby he had listened to a woodpecker far up in the tree as he pecked at the wood and how it sounded so loud at the foot of the tree. He wondered how anything so tiny could work his bill so fast. He had watched a pretty butterfly pitch on a bush nearby and how it opened and closed its wings showing its colors of purple and yellow.

There was a late-blooming violet at the foot of a pine tree with a cluster of lavender blossoms and a bee was gathering nectar. He watched the movement of the insect's wings. And a caterpillar moved slowly across the floor of the forest. A bluejay was in a huckleberry bush, pecking away at the fruit. A fly swarmed around the mouth of the body where the blood had stained the face. An ant came from the body's hair and ran down the face and onto the blanket that covered the body. It was quiet and the sun coming through the trees made a pattern of shadows. It seemed so peaceful in the turmoil that swirled around the setting.

The dogs were on to the escapee's scent and they barked far up in the woods. The deputies were unable to keep up with them. "Bad Boy" could hear them in the distance and he knew they would be on him before long. He was waiting for them.

The men were searching through bushes and behind fallen trees and in holes for the killer. One hollered out, "We got to have his codsack boys. We got to hang him in a tree with just enough stand-up space to keep him from breaking his neck. We want him to hurt and to think about what he's done before letting him die. Yes sir, we got to cut off his codsack and hold it in his face."

The bloodhounds were nearing "Bad Boy" and he stood up in anticipation. Their barks were stronger as they approached. Then they were in sight. They came up to him as if he were a bear or a lion and they were in a frenzy with saliva running from their mouths and their long ears getting in the way of their sight sometimes. They grabbed at his legs and he felt the teeth of one. He grabbed his head with his large hands and the dog pulled away and tackled his legs again. He grabbed the head again and got a firm hold on it. It was massive and he was strong, but so was "Bad Boy." His big hand worked around the dog's throat and he applied all the pressure he had. The dog was gagging and his tongue was completely out of his mouth and "Bad Boy" felt urine on his leg and the dog became limp and fell to the ground.

But the other dog was jumping into his face and got hold of an ear one time, bringing a stream of blood. He got hold of the other dog's neck and made swift work of him too. He knew the deputies were running as fast as they could since they heard the unusual barking that signaled they had found their prey. Quickly "Bad Boy" pushed the dogs to the back of his wigwam and set about arranging the tin so it would appear as a heap rather than a wigwam. He took the tin on the other side of the tree and placed it on the main pile. Then he closed the wigwam with another piece of tin and slipped himself carefully under the heap. There wasn't an ounce of space left and his head had to rest on one of the dogs' bodies. He shook the tin and it came down on him and he felt like he was smothering. A nail was piercing his body and he reached up and pushed it through the tin. It appeared as a pile of rubbish with no room for anything underneath. He was stifling for there was room for little air to penetrate the space. He waited.

He heard the sound of the men as they approached. His heart was beating furiously and he knew the men were puzzled by not hearing the dogs. Then they were upon him. He heard a stick pounding on the tin and somebody stepped on it and his stomach felt like his guts were being pushed out of him. Then they were gone and he breathed a sigh of relief and he lay prone and urinated. He lay thus for a long time. He didn't want to risk exposing himself to anybody that might be in the area.

He was sweating profusely and the cuts and scratches over his body were burning, made worse by the perspiration that filled them. But a smile was on his face. By God, he had outdone them, he told himself.

He finally got the courage to push the tin off him. He took his arms and lifted it enough that he could get his feet above him, and he pushed as hard as he could and the piece of tin fell forward and he felt the cooling breeze and just lay there for a while, getting himself together.

The deputies were puzzled. They knew something had happened to the dogs and they assumed he had destroyed them. But they weren't found and the men had combed the woods thoroughly. They admitted that he had outdone them and that apparently he had left the woods. The men gathered in groups with long faces and a look of defeat.

The shadows were beginning to lengthen and the men realized that they could do nothing at night, so they began walking toward Greene County Road.

The sun had already set and a few stars were in the sky when they reached the clearing. But everybody was in a state of restlessness. A fugitive was on the loose somewhere in the area. What his next move would be was uppermost in their thoughts.

"Bad Boy" saw a dilapidated old tobacco barn when he reached the clearing and he knew that it would have already been searched, and he made his way there. There was a sagging door that he didn't even try to close. It was a log barn and had given way on one side and looked like it was just waiting for the elements to ease it of the strain of standing up. He had already decided what he was going to do.

When Wilbert Lee reached the house Abie hugged him and asked what on earth was wrong with his face. It was pited and she could tell he had been crying.

"What on earth is wrong Wilbert Lee?" She asked with concern. "And why didn't you come home long ago? I know you heard me hollering."

"I hate him, I hate him, I hate him," Wilbert Lee said and he began sobbing again.

"I hate him too, the way they say he did that girl," Abie said. "He's not even a human being."

"You don't even know what I'm talking about," Wilbert Lee said. "It's that son-of-a-bitch they call my daddy that I hate."

"Watch your mouth Wilbert Lee," Abie said, "and tell me why you hate him."

"He whipped my ass at the store, right before a whole gang of men."

"What on earth for?" Abie asked.

"Just to show off," Wilbert Lee said. "And I was as nice as I could be. I said, Pa, can I go with youall up in the woods? That's all I said and he pulled off a peach tree switch and lay in on me, and he got a soap paddle and beat me with it before he was through."

Abie's face was frozen in a look of terror. "You mean to say Gant Turner did you like that, for no reason?"

"Yes Mama."

"Well, he'll pay for this," Abie said. "He's the poorest excuse for a father and a husband I ever seen. Are you sure that's all you said Wilbert Lee?"

"And where were you this morning when I was hollering so loud?"

"I went down where the convicts were working."

"Wilbert Lee, do you mean to tell me you were down there when they were shooting guns and that nigger got killed? Lord have mercy! I ought to whip you myself. I'd have died if I had known you were around them convicts. And they mess with boys too, you know. Some of them quares rather mess with a boy than a girl."

Abie saw Gant coming down the path and she was set for him. He looked like he was bone tired but that didn't make no difference. He had done something that he knew better than to do and that was to whip her boy. She didn't even think about him being the boy's father. She caught him as he entered the door. "What's this about beating Wilbert Lee and causing red streaks on his leg and a bruise on his bottom?" she shrieked.

Gant pushed her aside. "Leave me alone Abie and I mean it." His tone was different than it had been in the past.

"Well what's got you so riled up?" Abie said in a loud voice.

"That boy embarrassed me to death before them men," Gant said. "He acted so ugly and them men looked at me with such a disgusted look I wanted to turn around and go home. That won't no place for a young'un and

I told him to go home, and you never saw such carryings on."

"Not according to what Wilbert Lee said. He talked as nice to you as he could. And I believe him."

"I don't care what you believe and I'm through listening to your whining and griping. I was wrong all the time. I pitied you when you went wild about him living when all the others had died. I tried to understand and I let you go on spoiling him and taking control. I should have put my foot down and straightened you out and made the boy go to the fields and work. I should have teached him to respect grown folks. God. I'm to blame more than you. But I'm through Abie. I ain't going to listen to your whimpering and his sass no more. I'm saying it to you too boy."

"I'd tell you to git out if it won't for having somebody to tend the crops," Abie said. "You've not been any good as a husband in God knows when. You don't do nothing for Wilbert Lee. You've turned yourself against him. He would have loved you if you had given him a chance. You're an outsider Gant and you can take the other bedroom. My bed is closed to you now."

"Thank you," Gant said. "Nothing could please me more."

"Ain't it a shame that it had to come to a head on such a tragic day as this, when a young girl has been murdered and messed up like that?" Abie said.

"Wilbert Lee, tell me one more time that you acted like you ought to when your daddy showed hisself." Wilbert Lee didn't answer.

"Watch out," Gant said. "The seed have been sowed. Watch out for the harvest."

People were going by the Sauls' to see how they were doing. They were quiet but showed the strain on their faces. They had turned over the funeral arrangements to Stephen's brother who lived in Johnston County. Miss Sallie had made Nervy a white Sunday dress a few weeks earlier, and she said it would be all right to bury her in that. It was voile and had a large, round collar. Stephen told his brother to pick out the cheapest coffin he could find, but he wanted it to look good if he had to pay a few more dollars.

People that didn't have locks on their doors were nailing them shut with twenty-penny nails and they were putting nails into the windows also. They would have to stay closed up even if it was warm inside.

Some of the Negroes along Beston Road were nailing their doors shut also. They were about as afraid as the whites.

"Bad Boy" waited until about 10 o'clock to make his move. He didn't want to risk getting out and finding himself surrounded by a gang of angry men. For one thing, he had to have clothes to wear. For all practical purposes he was naked. The old shorts that he was wearing had been picked by bushes until they were in shreds. He had to have a drink of water and he had to doctor the cuts and scratches. And dogs were going to be a problem. Practically every family had a dog, and there were strays in the area too, waiting to pounce on anything that moved. And he could find himself with a shotgun staring him in the face. Tonight called for all his cunning to survive.

He carefully made his way toward Greene County Road. Did he remember the house? He thought so, but he wasn't sure. He wanted to go to the right house for he could handle the situation if he went there. That wouldn't be the case if he went somewhere where he was unknown.

He felt the hacksaw blade striking his heel every step he took. But he might need it as a weapon. When he reached the clearing he stopped to get his bearings. There was no moon and it was hard to pick out buildings in the distance. There was a field between him and Greene County Road. A piercing screech near him caused him to jump. Two cats were playing a rutting game in the field and their cries caused an old hound at one of the houses to let out a slow bark and that awakened other dogs and several got into the game.

"Son of a bitch," "Bad Boy" growled.

As best he remembered there was a chicken house close up to the house. There had been a tin tub hanging just outside the kitchen door. If it were still there and there was a chicken house nearby, he could be sure that was the place. It must have been seven or eight houses past the curve on Greene County road.

He walked close to the row of houses but he still couldn't tell which house was the one he was looking for. Then he was at the edge of the back yard and he saw a house with a tin tub hanging outside the door and there was a chicken house nearby. He felt reasonably sure he was at the right place. The dogs had stopped barking and all that he heard was the chirping of the crickets and the croak of rainfrogs in a pond nearby.

He knew where the bed had sat and there was a window on that side of the room. He stuck his face to the window and wrapped his hands around his mouth and called, "Blossom."

There was that voice that brought fear to her heart. She had already thought about the possibility of him coming to her door. There was terror in her heart. She would about as soon die as turn him in, yet she knew that she would open the door, for he held complete dominion over her after all these years.

"Open that door," he said in that same commanding voice.

"Roscoe, open the door," she called.

Roscoe had heard the voice and he was already shaking inside. He had been little then, a boy of eight or nine, when "Bad Boy" had been abusive to him and his mother also. He remembered the beatings, the cursings, the times he made Roscoe sit in hot weather and fan him with a newspaper. He remembered how he abused Blossom; how he'd hold her and rape her right in his presence. He was worse than hellfire, he thought. And they had been spared only when he found another woman and other children to abuse. That had been when they lived in Hallsborough. He had often wondered since those days how Blossom ever saw anything in him.

"Bad Boy" entered the door and told Roscoe to get him some cool water, and Roscoe hurried to the well and drew up a bucket.

"That ain't cool much," he said.

"It's straight from the well," Roscoe said through chattering teeth.

"I got a job for you to do boy, and I hain't got long to wait. I've got to have some clothes to put on. You got to find me some. I imagine somebody has washed and there are clothes still hanging on the line. And they've got to be big. I don't want to call attention to myself by wearing something too small. Got to have pants or overalls and a shirt, a dark shirt. Need some drawers and that reminds me. I've got to wash my nasty ass and body. Blossom you git that tub outside and youall draw up some water real easy like. I don't want anybody to hear you and get suspicious." They went outside in a hurry and got the water and brought it into the kitchen.

Roscoe was older now, but he was just as afraid as he had been a long time ago. He was stuttering, as he always did when he was upset. "It...'s goo-ing to be hhh...ard to fififififind the cloo...th...es in the dark "Bad Boy.""

"I said find 'em boy, "Bad Boy" said. "Dey find me here dey'll 'cuse you of harboring a killer and it'll be bad on you two."

"Y-es sir," Roscoe said as he went out into the darkness.

Blossom knew what was coming. He was in the kitchen washing off and after that he would have his way with her, one way or the other. If she resisted he would tear her apart. She knew "Bad Boy" in the bed and out. She might as well do whatever he wanted and make no outcries.

He came into the room naked, his black body glistening in the lamplight. "Do just what I say," he told Blossom," and I won't hurt you." He told her just what he wanted her to do and she obeyed. Blossom had had her share of men, but she had never run up with anybody like "Bad Boy." He wanted everything that man could do to a woman. He was insatiable and he was like a crazy man. She remembered the old days when he left her feeling less than a human being with her body torn and bruised.

When he was through he lay back on the pillow and told Blossom to fan him and she obeyed. "Dat nigger boy better bring me some clothes," he said, "or I'll use that hacksaw blade around his neck. I ought to of killed that boy a long time ago. I imagine that boy's got hatred for me in his heart. He might try to do something to me one of these days. Maybe I'll do just that when he gits back here."

"No "Bad Boy," please don't do nothing to Roscoe. He don't hate you. I don't even ever hear him call your name. Roscoe's a good boy and he helps me out and he'll find the clothes for you. He's risking being shot right now for somebody might mistake him for you and put a bullet through his body." She was holding back the tears for "Bad Boy" didn't want to see no woman crying.

"You got any likker?" he asked.

"No money to buy none." Blosson said.

Roscoe had found some clothes hanging on a line at Remus Edmundson's house, and he was a large man. But he had a bulldog that he kept to catch hogs. And he was tough where hogs were concerned. When he got his teeth into a hog's ear or nose he had to be beaten on the head to release his grip. Remus carried a hickory stick for that purpose.

Roscoe heard the dog growl and he lay down between two rows of cotton. He heard the dog coming toward him, growling as he drew near. Roscoe began calling to him as softly as he could, drawing in his breath and making a sound that denoted friendliness and the big dog cuddled up to him and lay down and Roscoe scratched him under his belly. He was more afraid than he'd ever been in his life. He was "Bad Boy" out there, or he thought of himself as being. He was the fugitive. He was expecting to hear a gun go off any minute. He stood up and Boss followed him toward the clothesline. Not a sound was heard. Not a light burned in any window down Greene County Road. Time was of the essence for if he were gone too long "Bad Boy" might kill him when he arrived home. Either way, he was at the worst point in his life. He wondered what "Bad Boy" had done to his mother. He knew he had done something. He had been gone at least an hour, he knew.

He took a pair of pants off the line and went on farther down toward the end nearest the house and found a dark shirt. He found some drawers in the middle of the line. Anybody would know that the clothes had been taken down for "Bad Boy" no matter who had taken them.

He felt like somebody was at his back every step he made. But he made a hasty getaway once he had the clothes. Old Boss followed him a little way, then turned around and went back to his own yard.

Roscoe moved swiftly at the edge of the fields. He didn't want to risk being on the road. He was thankful for a moonless sky but millions of stars shone and he wondered if any poor boy had ever been in his position. He thought about how it had been with him all his life. He had been afraid of everything; his own people, white folks, white boys in particular. They sometimes beat his ass and called him nigger and his body had grown so accustomed to pain it was a part of his being. He had had a tooth knocked out in a fight with white boys. They had hit him with a stick. But he had asked for it. He'd put his mouth into their business and had said things that he knew would upset them.

He wanted to play with white children more than black. He didn't understand that himself. And neither did he understand why he felt as he did about "Bad Boy." He was the meanest man he had ever known. Everything about him was violent. He had had no male role model except "Bad Boy" for he was there as far back as he could remember, slapping him around and taking his big fist sometimes and slamming it into him. He was always knocking his mother around and she had learned to take his knocks without crying out for if she screamed he would knock her completely out.

Poor thing. She hadn't ever been right after the years with "Bad Boy." He had done something to her senses. It was perhaps all those knocks to the side of her head. And he hated the big man who had caused so much terror in his life. Yet, he saw in himself some of the same qualities "Bad Boy" possessed. He had a violent streak in himself also. He wanted power like "Bad Boy" possessed. He wanted dominion over people. Something about physical power intrigued him. He was big and tall and he thought of "Bad Boy" as a real man.

He realized at an early age that there was something powerful between men and women. In the closeness of their three-room rabbit-box type house in Hallsborough he had seen it all and heard it all. "Bad Boy" would get quiet for a while and he heard him talking baby talk to his mother. Then he would hear the creaking of the bedsprings for a long period of time and there would be long breaths and sighing and then "Bad Boy" would go crazy and moan and groan and all would be quiet for a little while.

Sometimes "Bad Boy" would go right to sleep and his snores would fill the house. But those snores were a welcome relief, for he and his mother were safe when he was snoring. He would climb in bed sometimes when "Bad Boy" and his mother had gone to work and he'd get all gommed up in something sticky and he'd take his hands and wipe it off on the sheets and move to another place on the bed. And he knew that there was something exciting about it. He could never forget how "Bad Boy" would carry on so and he knew that it took something powerful to calm him down for a spell.

He hated himself for feeling as he did, but there was something in that big man that made him want to be like him.

He was nearing the house and he thought about what a dangerous mission he had been on on this quiet June night. He began shaking as he got into the yard, for he still didn't know what awaited him when he got inside.

"God damn boy, where you been so long?" "Bad Boy" said as he snatched the clothes from Roscoe's hands. He held them up and looked at the pants. "They'll work," he said as he held them up to his waist. He pulled them on and felt a little dampness from the night air. "They feel good," he said as he pulled the shirt on. "It's tight in the belly, but I'll let the button stay undone. Did you fix me something to eat woman?" he asked.

"They's some meat and collards in the sack, and some biscuit pudding," Blossom said.

"I got to hurry," "Bad Boy" said. "Got a long ways to travel and not long to git there. I be lucky, I'll be a long way from this place twenty four hours from now. I be unlucky I'll be burning in hell soon. Don't know as it matters though. It's always been hell with me. He walked out the door into the night. He didn't even thank Blossom for harboring him. Nor Roscoe for stealing the clothes. When he was gone Blossom sighed and said "Lordy, Lordy. I hopes they git him 'fore morning and skin him alive."

"Bad Boy" started off at a trot. He moved on the edge of the forests where there were forests, and far back in the fields when he was in open places. He was oblivious to the night noises. He wasn't thinking of anything except escape. There was nothing beyond tonight if he failed. He didn't allow himself to think about the young girl he had killed. He knew there would be hell to pay if he were caught.

He had to get to the trestle before them. He had to prepare to jump fast when the train came through. He knew it always slowed down before it crossed the trestle. That was his only hope. And he knew they would stake out men at the trestle. He knew he would be more vulnerable there than most any other place, and he'd like to catch the train at some other point, but it would be traveling too fast to board anywhere else in the area. He had looked at Blossom's alarm clock at the house and he knew it was about one o'clock when he left. He gave himself three hours to get to the trestle.

Meanwhile, Gant Turner retired to the bedroom across the hall, glad to be there without having to make any excuses. He resolved to never go into Abie's bedroom again. He thought that sometimes out of sorrow and catastrophe, came something good. It had been so long playing a game that had no meaning. When he was young and Abie was a young girl, she had been pretty and likeable. He had been proud of her and was happy that she was his wife. He didn't think of her as being the same woman today. Everything about her had changed. He knew that people called her a gossiper, and he knew what they were talking about. She saw everybody negatively and thought the worst of even good people. He wondered whether Wilbert Lee living had caused something to snap in her brain. He had heard that sometimes women went into some kind of shock or something after having a baby. Maybe there was a weakness in her family for going off the deep end. Some of her people were a little touched in the head, he told himself.

He peeped out the window and wondered where the convict was and he felt sad in thinking about little Nervy.

"Bad Boy" was in the area of the trestle. He had run most of the time since he left Blossom's. He was nervous. He told himself it didn't matter which end of the trestle he took, the sheriff would have deputies there. He would rather face them than the men who were on his trail yesterday. He was aware that they would have killed him on the spot if they had caught him. In a tree no doubt.

It must be about four o'clock now, he guessed. He saw a few lights in windows along a dirt road near the trestle. All that he could do now was wait till he heard the train whistle as it approached the trestle. A rooster crowed in the distance. A truck passed along the road. He heard someone drawing water. The tackle made a sound as the rope passed over it. He heard the cars crossing the ties and felt the movement of the crossties before he heard the whistle. There was a rumble of the cars on the track and then he heard the shrill cry of the train whistle and he knew it was time to make his move.

He stepped from the shadows onto the road and as he did they came at him in a wave, several men tackling him all at once. He said, "I give up boss," holding his hands over his head and they were brought down instantly and handcuffs slipped on. Shackles were placed around his legs also.

As they were getting him ready to be taken to Raleigh for safe-keeping he heard the train going on down the track, blowing its whistle at another crossing and the sound of the cars rumbling over the tracks and in his mind he was on his way to the far reaches of the South. He thought he was on top of the freight train smelling the turpentine from the pine trees as the train sped through the Carolinas and Georgia; smelling fish as they crossed rivers; seeing boats cruising through the waters.

All the shackles were gone in his crazed mind. He was free forever more. Goin' on down where the citrus fruits grow. I work in the orchards in the daytime when the sun is hot, bringing the sweat and warmth over the body, smelling the orange blossoms and free of things that bother the mind.

Goin' to find me a shanty by the sea like them I remember, way down past all the beaches where the seaweed is thick and my shanty looks like all the others. I go down to the water, parting the seaweeds and looking as far as I can into them blue skies that meet the water way out there. I put my footprints in the sand and walk back to my shanty and I find something I never had before. I find peace of mind. Always weary before. Troubled mind. Troubled body. The headaches all gone. The headaches that penetrate the skull and make a man blind. And all them strange feelings. No use to tell nobody though. They just wouldn't understand. The big hands. I can't tell nobody about the big hands. They think one thing. I know another. It's the hands pressing on bones and feeling the leaders and glands and the crack of the adams apple and the little bits of bone in there and taking the thumb and the next finger and rubbing the neck so them little shivers of bone run a thrill through me I can't describe to nobody. Felt the same way with the dogs as it did the girl. And that woman in Alabama and that boy in Texas.

The warm days and the nights by the sea will clear the mind. Won't be no more of them strange feelings. I'll save my money. Won't be no more women pestering me. They don't know my needs nohow.

"Where's my mama? Never saw my mama. All I know 'bout my early days is from old woman that lived beside my mama when I was born. She say my mama cut the cord and left me right there on the floor with blood everywhere. Didn't tie off the cord and I was still bleeding when they found me. Women in the neighborhood took me but when I got my senses I was too bad for them. I was shoved around and beat by all the men. One of 'em bashed my head on a stone and the little black boy growed up with no friends and no home. But I growed big. I had my body to protect me. They had done it to me and I done it to others. An eye for an eye and a tooth for a tooth. One big ole nigger tried to choke me and I felt his grip tightening. I was going under but I kicked him in the balls and he cried out and let me go and I was so far gone by then he couldn't catch me. That was my real start on the wrong track.

Dere bees Savannah. Oh, the memories of Savannah. Not happy though. Got tangled up with white folks for the first time. Invaded their neighborhood but they said I was a peeping Tom and threw my ass in the can. I learned to hate whites then. Got out of that town fast after I served my time.

Old train moving down the track, smoke rising and left behind in its wake. All the shackles gone and my mind at ease. No more hurting and walking with them things dangling around my ankles.

Somebody said, "We are in Raleigh," but it was only an echo. They said, "We've arrived" and he saw the cabin by the seaside and felt the cooling breezes and there were his footprints in the sand. And there was an old chair on the porch and he was rocking away and the sun was bright and he watched the gulls winging over the water and he went to the back porch where a hatchet sat in a corner and there was a chopping block at the back door.

"I'll cut off my thumbs and there won't be no temptation then. It will be like a trimmed man. I won't be able to feel crushed bone and get them feelings. I'll pull the fruit with four fingers and smell the blossoms and my legs will be free and I won't ever wear shackles agin and I won't be hated no mo. "Bad Boy's" done running.

These were his thoughts as he was being taken into Central Prison to await trial and sentenced to death in the electric chair.

A new day dawned as bright as yesterday had been, but there was a pall over the community. People were still dazed. The white folks planned to plow and chop till dinner time and then take off and go to the funeral, which would be held at the holiness church on the way to Hallsborough, where the Sauls' were members. The burial would be in the family cemetery back in the field.

A group of children sang "Jesus Loves Me."

The minister preached a long sermon, eulogizing young Nervy. There was a large crowd, some standing in the yard. The church was overflowing. There were a lot of handkerchiefs seen in men's and women's hands, as well as children's. It took more than an hour for viewers to pass by the casket. Some mourned silently. Heavy sobs would rack others. The saddest sight was to see a man look down with a handkerchief wiping his eyes. Some just looked as if they were seeing their own daughter in the casket.

Nervy looked like she was asleep. There was a red rose in her hand and her white Bible, a prize for perfect attendance at Sunday school, was placed beside her in the casket.

Hobby Turnage thought about how beautiful yesterday had been and how he had looked upon his world and thought it was a very special day. He thought about all that had happened in one day's time, and it came to him that we never know when it will all end. You can be young but that doesn't mean you'll be around to see the sun rise tomorrow. To him, life was a big puzzle. It was made more of a puzzle by Nervy's death. She was so young, and he had seen her only a few days earlier. And she was smiling and they were telling jokes and carrying on. It happended in June before he left for Tennessee.

Wilbert Lee was moved by Nervy's death also. Things didn't usually get to him and he didn't think much about dying. He was usually tougher than that. And to think that he had seen the man who did it and another man's life snuffed out in a second put him to thinking.

Chapter 18

N ick beamed with pride as he escorted Pearl across Memphis. Nick loved his hometown and carried many happy memories of his life in the city. He wanted Pearl to feel a part of what Memphis meant to him, just as she wanted him to feel a part of the place she called home. And he was so proud to show Pearl off to his acquaintances. He thought a lot about why he felt such fierce pride in the woman who had agreed to share his life.

He would never have dreamed that he would be fatally attracted to a woman whose background spoke of the lowest level of society. He even asked himself sometimes whether it was because of a physical beauty that appealed to the prurient instincts of man. This would frighten him, for he was aware that such an attraction was not the basis for a lasting relationship. She caught the attention of all men although it was evident this was not something which Pearl did to get such attention.

Was it because of her sparkling personality? What magical attraction had captivated him and placed him forever at her disposal? With the worship he felt for her, she could crush him if that were her choice.

Then he would feel guilt for having such thoughts. In reality, Pearl was the personification of all the qualities he had been looking for in womanhood. She was as lovely and feminine as a fragile orchid; as bold as a vixen; as proud of her heritage as the women of society he had mingled with (and far more interesting). And she had mellowed him completely. There had been a hard edge somewhere in his character that had been softened and brought under control.

Things that had bothered him no longer mattered. She had no breeding, no background to flaunt before others, no accomplishments in which to take pride. She was all the things people of breeding usually shied away from. Yet, she possessed all those qualities and they came out spontaneously without any conscious effort on her part. She was an enigma within an enigma and he found her near-perfect in everything she did.

"And what do you think of our fine city?" he asked as they rode over Memphis.

"It's simply beautiful," Pearl replied. "It's like a dream almost. It's so different from anything I've known Nick. I marvel at its size and I think about how far removed it is from the way of life I've known. And even with the Depression having such an impact on the world, people here are managing very well it seems to me. We're fifty years behind in Bear Grass, Nick. And every time I think about it I'm ashamed that I exposed you to the rural life as it is lived back home. And it's a good thing I didn't come to Memphis before I decided on such a drastic course. If I had come to your place before you went home with me, it never would have happened. Of course, our relationship would have fallen apart also."

"You brought me to life Pearl," Nick said as he motioned to her to look at the river scene below. "You made me alive and aware of what life is all about, my dear. Now you just think what my life would be like today if it were not for you. I'd be wandering around, pretending to be enjoying the scenery as I was doing the first time I saw you. I was a lonely man that day, Pearl. I saw the beauty but it didn't sink in. I was trying to determine what to do with my life. I was as miserable as a fish out of water. I had no sense of direction. I considered going abroad but then I asked myself what in the hell that would accomplish. What would seeing the Mediterranean mean to a guy with no real focus on life? You changed all that Pearl."

He had never imagined that another man's son would have any appeal for him. Why should he be bothered with the responsibility because of other people's mistakes? The last thing he had considered was playing father to a child who carried none of his chromosomes. And now he felt as much a part of Pearl's son as if he were the real father. And it wasn't imaginary. That boy had captivated him the first time he saw him. He wanted to protect him, to help plan for his future, to portray a father image to him and to do all in his power to help him succeed in life.

"It's a large place," Pearl said. It was the first time Nick had taken her across the width and breadth of the city.

"We've covered the city," Nick said as he turned into their driveway.

They had been in Memphis three days now. "But we've got things to do Pearl, and the most important one right now is to get you to Mavis so she can be planning a wardrobe for you. I can't wait for you to meet Mavis. She is quite a gal, Pearl." But Pearl was apprehensive about meeting Mavis. Pearl knew that Mavis was a black woman, and that didn't bother her, for she had associated with Negroes all her life. But she didn't know whether they'd be able to talk the same language. Of course, she was aware that just the name Mavis was instantly recognized in Memphis as being the very elite in women's circles.

"Have you called her?" she asked Nick.

"Not since we came back, but I talked with her just after we were married and told her what I wanted, and she said for us to get in touch with her as soon as we got to Memphis and she would arrange to meet you and go over what you wanted. I'm going to call her now and see when it will be convenient for her." He picked up the phone and got her immediately. Mavis said the next day would be fine and Nick consulted with Pearl and she said that was fine. So they arranged the meeting for the next morning at nine o'clock.

"There's one other thing I've been thinking about," Nick said. "I haven't done any ballroom dancing in so long I think I should brush up on my step."

"And I don't mind saying that I'm intimidated by Mavis," Pearl confided. "I fear that I will feel inadequate when I talk with her. If a personality can become a legend using one name only, then I may show an inferiority that I don't want to impart. And there's no doubt but that part of it is because she is black and I am white. And God knows that I'm not a racist."

"Put every worry that you have aside this very moment," Nick said. "You will never meet a finer, more down-to-earth person than Mavis. She's as warm as the morning sunshine. She has an unbelievable sense of humor and if it'll make you feel any better, she grew up in the cotton patches of Arkansas."

"Really!" Pearl said.

"What did you think of Beale Street?" Nick asked.

"I was intrigued," Pearl said. "I felt right at home for the blues ain't nothing new to the South. I could see myself out in the fields working and the colored people singing such tunes as they were playing there."

"And Parkway Drive and the estates?"

"Beautiful," Pearl replied.

"I want you to be happy here Pearl," he said and she saw in his eyes that he was perfectly sincere in what he was saying. "I want you to feel as much a part of Memphis as you felt a part of Bear Grass if that is possible. I want you to be happy Pearl and I only wish I knew just what you are looking for in life. It would give me a goal to strive for."

Pearl looked him directly in the eyes. "Nick, I'm not reaching for the moon. I'm not out to chart new courses to change the world. I'm not of that mentality or inclination. I wish I were the kind of woman who was willing to attempt to change the world. If I had had proper training I might have felt differently. As it is, I only want to be the best wife possible for Nick Staphal, to stand behind him in whatever his goals may be and to be the best possible mother to Hobby. Is that simple enough Nick?"

"I couldn't ask for more," he replied.

There was a call for supper from the kitchen and Nick and Pearl ate by candlelight as the shades of darkness settled over Memphis.

Pearl was still apprehensive as they waited outside the door of Mavis, the designer. A young woman answered the bell and Nick told her they had an appointment with Mavis.

"Please be seated," the woman said. "I'll tell Mavis."

It was only a moment before Mavis entered the room with a broad smile on her face as she went up to Nick and shook his hand. "How in the world are you Nick," she asked, shaking his hand briskly.

"Fine Mavis," Nick replied, thinking about all the times they had conversed over the years and how that friendship had grown with the passing of time. "But I want you to meet Pearl, my wife, Mavis."

"My my," Mavis said. "Now you told me you had married a very pretty girl, and I knew that would be the case. But you didn't emphasize it enough Nick. And how are you Pearl?" she said.

"Fine," Pearl said, "and it's a pleasure to meet you. I've heard so much about you."

"Don't you listen to everything you hear," Mavis said.

"It had been a long time since I'd heard from you Nick," Mavis said. "I was beginning to wonder about you. You know we used to talk for hours sometimes when things were at rock bottom and there just wasn't much to do but talk. I've missed all that Nick."

"Me too," Nick replied. "But I'd better be running along. I have a lot of things to attend to and you and Pearl need to get at your task."

"Don't worry Nick," Mavis said. "Pearl and I will get along fine and I'll do everything possible to please her."

"I know you will," Nick said as he closed the door behind them.

"Come on over and sit down," Mavis told Pearl as she gathered up several books of sketches. "I've been doing some preliminary sketches for you indicated that you needed an entire wardrobe. That's a big order and will require a lot of work over the next month or so. I have plenty of orders, but none that are of an emergency nature. I can put some of the other girls on those orders and I can concentrate totally on your wardrobe."

"I appreciate that," Pearl said. "And I really do need an entire wardrobe. You see Mavis, I am just entering this kind of life and I'm green in the gills about it all. Not that I don't know something about fashion but because I have not been privileged to indulge in the fashion world. I am from a very poor background and there's no need in trying to present any other image before you. I was as open with Nick as I'm being with you and I make no apologies for being poor and rural with a sharecropper-mill-worker background."

"All that doesn't mean beans to me Pearl," Mavis said. "And if it will make you feel any better, I am a product of the Arkansas cottonfields. Lord, I've toted a cotton sack till I felt like my back would break and had cockleburs sticking in my knees from crawling that felt like wires sticking to the bone. I've had stinging worms to bite me when a dip of snuff or a chew of tobacco was the only thing that would give any relief. You know, take a mouthful of snuff juice and plaster it on the sting, or a good spit of juice from tobacco on the injured place. And hangnails. Did you ever get any of them from cotton burs Pearl?"

"You know I did," Pearl said, and wasp stings and all other kinds of stings from hornets, yellow jackets, honeybees, you name it."

"Well, it just lets you know that it doesn't matter the background," Mavis said, "It's what you do with what you've got. And you sure picked a winner with Nick Staphal. I don't know how you could have done better. But I think Nick is the big winner for choosing you. I declare you're something else Pearl. You know, in my job I'm expected to try to hide the things that are wrong with the female figure. But what a relief! All I've got to do with you is to emphasize your natural endowments. I don't hesitate to tell you you're right at the top of the list of the most beautiful women I've worked with."

"Please don't overdo it Mavis," Pearl said, "although I'm grateful for your remarks."

"I'm as sincere as I can be," Mavis said. "It's going to be a real pleasure working with you. And I want you to look over these drawings. They are originals and came entirely from my mind. I just want to get a feeling of what it is you are looking for. I won't know how to become your exclusive designer unless I can know the real Pearl." She handed the drawings to

Pearl. Then she rose and left the room. "I have some things to do and I'll be back in about half an hour, Pearl."

There were a number of drawings of evening gowns, some with large, flaring skirts, others with more trim, narrower skirts; those with sequined bodices and sleeves of various designs; deep V necklines as well as rounded ones and deep slashes in the back. but they were all different from styles shown in current stylebooks. Pearl was impressed.

There were suits with fitted coats with extended waistlines; others with unusual skirt effects with long waists and cutoff bottoms sewn on the bias. There was plenty of fur trim as well as those with fabric collars and cuffs. There were certainly plenty to choose from.

Dresses ranged from the simple to the extreme, offering a large variety from which to choose. Pearl was amazed at Mavis' expertise as a designer. It didn't take her long to realize why Mavis was held in such high regard.

She thought about the attractiveness of this black woman who had made a mark for herself in a man's world and an image greater than most white women. A black woman's place was still in the kitchen or the cottonfields. There was no image of a black woman competing in the commercial world. And Mavis was as natural acting as if she had been born into the world she knew now, rather than coming from that world and making a name for herself through her own ingenuity. She thought about her earlier apprehensions and how quickly they had been overcome. She felt that she had grown up with Mavis and that they had worked together in the fields.

"Well, what do you think?" Mavis asked as she re-entered the room.

"I'm impressed." Pearl said. "You have some beautiful designs."

"Do you think I'll be able to please you Pearl?"

"No trouble at all," Pearl said. "And I can see why your name stands so tall among fashion designers. It's a pity you were not recognized nationally."

"I don't ask for anything like that," Mavis said. "I'm happy to be recognized in Memphis and I have all in the world I can do anyway. But I got to tell you something girl," she said in a tone she had heard colored people use many times. "I'se pleased to be black and command the respect of the white race."

"I see so many women of my race still plaiting their hair with all those little parts showing in the scalp and the long plaits standing out on their heads, and when they take it down having it saturated in pomade and standing out from their heads. They don't seem to care Pearl, and that bothers me. There are many beautiful colored women who refuse to bring out their beauty by really trying to improve.

"And I can say as much for many white women also. You know when I was in my teens in Arkansas, I'd take the scissors and cut out some of my thick hair. But I did it from the underside so it didn't show. My hair lay close to my head and I didn't grease it to the extent that it glistened in the light."

"I like you Mavis," Pearl said. "I feel that I've struck up my first real friendship in Memphis and I hope we can be friends forever. I will look forward to you visiting with Nick and me at any time and I will consider it an honor."

"Well, I don't want to be an imposition," Mavis said, "but I hope you will invite me out soon. I always wanted to see that fabulous house of yours that I've heard so much about."

"Well, what do we do next?" Pearl asked.

"I think color is vitally important in choosing a wardrobe," Mavis said. "We have to match complexion with colors that bring out our best features. But thank God, you have all the things necessary to allow a wide range of colors to accentuate your beautiful skin and radiant hair and deep blue eyes. You will be a joy to work with Pearl. You've got more going for you than you even know about. And ain't it good that something like you can come from them cornfields?" she said with a laugh.

"You too," Pearl said.

"Yeah, me too," Mavis said demurely.

"You've got all the good facial features and boy they sure fertilized you good "up there" she said, pointing to Pearl's breasts. "Still, when they got to your waist they starved out all the guano and just look how tiny you are there. But they put out a nice sprinkling of the good stuff when they got to your thighs and tapered off so that you've got beautiful calves and slender ankles. I can't wait to get started on you Pearl. But for today, I need to get all your measurements.

She called in one of the girls to get Pearl's measurements. "Then we will call it a day for now. You come back tomorrow and we'll start choosing the materials and the designs that please you and get started on your Memphis debut."

Pearl called the house and Nick had just returned from his business activities. He came for her immediately. Pearl knew how to drive but had been out of practice for many years, and Nick had been giving her lessons. But she didn't have a driver's license. As soon as she learned more about how to get around in Memphis, she was determined to get her license. She wanted to be independent of Nick for all the things she could do for herself.

"Well, how did it go?" Nick asked as they were driving home.

"You were right," Pearl said. "I never felt more at home with anyone than I felt with Mavis. I was awed by the beauty of her creations and she told me all about her background and I felt that we were sisters in a sense. Although we grew up hundreds of miles apart, her early life was not all that different from mine. She's certainly an attractive colored woman too. But I thought about her limitations also, simply because of the color of her skin. With all the success she can boast, she's still out of the mainstream of America, and it will be a long time before that will happen. She rubs noses with the higher echelon and converses with them and they can appreciate her talents, but it ends when Mavis has created something for them that satisfies their desires in fashions."

"Did she talk about that?" Nick asked.

"She didn't mention a thing about that, but I know how it is for I know how people are. You know about my own reservations even though I sincerely like her as a person. I know back home we got along well with the Negroes and some were highly regarded, but there was no socializing, and still isn't. And if there were, I'd feel uneasy about it. But I'm going to invite Mavis to our home Nick. In fact, I already have."

"Fine," Nick said.

The next morning Pearl and Mavis greeted each other warmly, and Pearl thought about how apprehensive she had been only a day earlier.

"Well, it's time to find out what you want," Mavis said and Pearl handed the drawings to her with each marked.

"Fine," Mavis said. "Now let's go to the room where the materials are displayed." They entered a back room that was fairly narrow but lengthy. Windows filled the outside wall to give a clear view of the colors of the many varieties of materials on display. Bolts of cloth were stacked on end with some of the material draped around the bolt. The material ran the gamut - from soft long-staple cotton, all wool, rayon, damask, velvet, luxurious silks in many colors.

Pearl was dazzled by the beautiful materials. She gasped and said to Mavis, "You know Mavis, this all seems like a dream to me when I remember that I went to the finest department store in my hometown with Mama. She was looking a piece of cloth to make me a dress to wear to a Sunday school convention, and the material was so expensive she didn't even wait for a clerk to help her. She took my hand and practically dragged me out of there. Now I find myself able to pick and choose without worrying about the cost when in reality the piece of cloth I saw at the store when I was a girl was more important to me then than this is at this point in life. It's like

I have touched Aladdin's lamp and am reliving the fairytales I read about in school."

"Well if anybody deserves it I think you do," Mavis said. "And I keep saying it, but it's true, you are such a pretty woman I'm just overjoyed. And if I flub up here, I'm going to get out of this business for you are the perfect model to work with." Pearl blushed.

"Now, let's get down to the nitty-gritty about your evening gown for the ball. It's the one most important item and the most urgent at this point. And I don't know what color you prefer, but blue would be the ideal color." She draped a piece of light blue silk over Pearl's shoulders. "This is perfect to bring out the blueness of your eyes and your hair looks beautiful placed over the fabric."

"I thought blue would be best," Pearl said. "But I'm depending on your expertise and I want you to have the final say."

"I feel like my career is on the line," Mavis said. "I'd feel terrible if I didn't outfit you in the latest fashions without fearing that they would be duplicated in the local department stores, or any other for that matter. And if I wanted to lose a friend, just let me flub up where Nick Staphal is concerned and I know he'd never speak to me again."

"Don't worry. None of that is going to happen," Pearl said.

"You're so unaffected by it all it surprises me," Mavis said.

"Oh, this was all Nick's idea Mavis. I can't quite figure out why he wants to go to all the trouble."

"Honey, he's proud of you, that's why. He wants to show you off to Memphis society to let them know his taste in women. And honey, you going to bowl 'em over. Some of them will hate you though, for a number of women have had their eyes on Nick Staphal for years. He's a catch as a man and whether they are frothy-mouthed over his masculinity, they're hogs about his money, especially at this time when it has almost gone down the drain."

And Nick's friends were becoming more inquisitive about his wife. He would meet them on the street and invariably they would ask when he was going to let them see his wife and he would tell them that they were getting adjusted and that Pearl was trying to get her bearings but that as soon as possible they would all be introduced to her.

"A North Carolina Girl?" Babs Broderick asked him as they ran into each other on Main Street. "I knew a girl from North Carolina one time and she was nice." Babs Broderick was one of the social set in Memphis. She was more attractive than most of the society crowd with ash blonde hair and dark brown eyes. She wore fashions created by Mavis also.

Babs looked up at Nick and smiled. "The only question I have is why you had to go all the way there to find a wife? Golly, there are a lot of us here in good old Memphis on the hunt for a good husband. And God knows you're a catch," Babs said with a smile.

"It's a long story," Nick replied. "As to the local gals, the chemistry just didn't work somehow."

"What is she like?" Babs asked.

"Pleasant, nice, good-looking, witty, unaffected, charming," Nick said. "But you'll get to meet her before year's end. I promise."

"I'll look forward to that," Babs said. "But I must hurry. I have some errands to run. Ta-ta."

"Ta ta yourself," Nick said as she was leaving.

And when Nick went into a popular local bar some of his male friends were always there and they hounded him about Pearl also. "Man, you can't keep her to yourself forever Nick," Peter North said. "Are you afraid we wolves will try to devour her?"

"Something like that," Nick replied.

"Well, you've got to entertain her a lot at home if you keep her hidden away like that. And I know Nick Staphal wouldn't marry a girl he was ashamed of."

"You'd better believe that," Nick told him. "I'm more proud of her than anything in my life."

And so it went during the weeks after they returned to Memphis and plans were made for the ball and Mavis was busy designing and making Pearl's wardrobe.

Chapter 19

It was time for the gathering of the family. After all the planning, the day had finally arrived. Viola and Craven stood by the road until the bus came by. They waved it down and with their new traveling cases in hand boarded the bus. Viola was fidgety and Craven might have been; however he kept his emotions hidden. The weather was cloudy and that made Viola more nervous. She leaned over and said almost in a whisper, "Do you reckon the man can see how to drive that plane Craven?"

"He knows what he's doing Viola," Craven said. "He wouldn't be doing it if he didn't know."

"Lord, I hope so," Viola said as she looked out the window and observed life in Bear Grass in the early morning. "I just wish we were there Craven."

"Viola, are you going to be like this until we arrive in Memphis?" Craven asked. "If you are you'll drive me crazy before this day is over."

"I can't help it," Viola said. "I've prayed about it and told myself everything would be all right. "But I don't see God in this at all. Going to Memphis is one thing we don't have to do, so if the plane falls it's not God's fault. I believe in asking God's help when you need an answer to a problem that you can't do anything about."

"Just calm down Viola," Craven told her. "Quit talking about it and try not to keep your thoughts on it, you hear?"

They were now on their way to Raleigh after changing buses in Hallsborough. Viola was silent during the trip to Raleigh but as they drew nearer and nearer to the airport she began to shake inside. Then she saw the planes at the airport.

"Don't say a word," Craven warned. "It won't do no good to fume and fuss, and for God's sake, don't show yourself when you get on that plane, Viola. If you cut a shine everybody will be looking at us and snickering and we'll be embarrassed to death."

"I ain't making no promises," Viola said. "Pearl's trying to put us way above our raising. I sometimes wonder if it wouldn't have been better if she hadn't met Nick. But I love both of them, God bless 'em. And poor Hobby's got the same thing to do and him in a cast. He'll have it worse than us. Pearl ought not to have put us through this nohow. Poor folks like us are supposed to stay in our places; not trying to show off at some fancy dance and all that mess. Well I tell you one thing, she may regret the day she thought this up. We're as red-necked as they come, and you can come up with some dillies too, Craven."

They were boarding the plane now and Viola looked down as she walked up the steps and almost got sick to her stomach.

Then the plane was taking off and she closed her eyes and held on tight to Craven's arm and once they were aloft she said, "What are we doing sitting still up here Craven? The plane ain't moving."

"Yes it is," Craven said. "Look out the window."

"Don't want to look," Viola said. Then they hit an air pocket and the plane dipped and Viola shrieked, "My God, what's happening. Father save us if it be your will." And everybody looked at her and laughed. Craven nudged her with his elbow and said, "For God's sake, quieten down Viola."

Viola soon adjusted to the movement of the plane, lay her head on the seat and relaxed the rest of the trip. Hardly before she knew it the pilot announced that they were approaching Memphis and Viola's mouth went agape. "You mean we're already here?" She asked Craven. "We just got started seems like."

"Planes fly faster than cars and buses travel," Craven reminded her.

Then the plane came to a stop and Pearl and Nick were running to greet them and they embraced and Pearl asked how their trip had been and Viola said, "Fine," and didn't mention anything about her carryings-on and Nick took their bags to the car and they were on their way home.

"It seems like a dream," Viola said, "with things happening so fast I can't keep up with it all."

"I know," Pearl said. "And what do you think about me?"

Then they were in a neighborhood with large houses and immaculate lawns and Viola remarked about how pretty it was. When they turned into the driveway Viola said, "Are we going to a hotel or something? People don't live in such houses."

The car stopped in the back driveway and Nick took their bags from the car and they were ushered inside.

"Is this where you live?" Viola asked Pearl.

"Uh huh," Pearl said as she took their coats and Nick took their bags upstairs.

"Lord have mercy at my ignorance," Viola said. "To think that I would put a man on the floor in the shed room of my shanty that's got a place like this is the worst thing I've ever done. It's a wonder he would even speak to a one of us."

"How do you think I felt when I saw all this and it was I that took him to Bear Grass in the first place? And it's a good thing I did it before I saw this place, or he'd never have gone down there," Pearl said.

Nick came into the room as they were talking and heard the conversation. "Miss Viola," he said, "I am honored to have you and Mr. Craven in my home. I have many things lacking in yours, but I never felt more at home, nor have I ever received as warm a welcome as when I visited you. I wouldn't have missed that trip for anything in the world. And I can only hope that you can feel as welcome in our home."

Viola looked about her at the spaciousness of the rooms, at the wide archway between the living room and the dining room and the glow of the furniture and the beauty of the setting. She noted that on the dining room table there was a large arrangement of beautiful red flowers. She had never seen such flowers. "What are they?" She asked Pearl.

"They're poinsettias Mama. I never saw them when I was living in Bear Grass. And this is something new to me too. You know that we never decorated for Christmas. We didn't have anything to decorate with. So I said to myself I'd brighten up Christmas this year and make it different." Viola noted the green linen tablecloth and the crystal already laid and the napkins that matched and the arrangements of holly and mistletoe, something that she could associate with, and the wide fireplace aglow with fire in the living room and she cried.

"It's prettier than anything I've ever seen in my life," she said as she took a handkerchief from her dress pocket and blew her nose. "I'll be ashamed to be poor after seeing all of this."

"Here now," Pearl said, "we're not gathering here to cry. It's a celebration so let's enjoy it. Come on Mama and let me show you the house. You want to come along Papa?" Craven had just sat and looked, unable to take it all in and feeling ill at ease. "And Papa," Pearl said, "you just forget hog pens and cow stables for a little while. You make yourself as much at home as Nick did when he visited you."

"I'm just afraid I'll mess up something," Craven said.

"Well if you do, we'll clean it up," Pearl said as she took them into the rooms on the second floor.

"I'll get lost up here," Viola said. "I'll be hollering down and calling you to get me straightened out."

"Oh, it's not that bad," Pearl said. "And we're going to talk to Hobby tonight."

"I can't wait, " Viola said. "I'm dying to see him. Can you really hear him good on the telephone Pearl?"

"Just like you were with him" Pearl said. "You haven't ever talked on the telephone have you Mama? Or Papa either."

"I called the doctor one time," Craven said. "I got somebody else to do whatever it is you do to get them on the line. But I thought of how far away he was and I hollered into the thing and they told me I'd have to stop hollering or they couldn't hear me. That was my only time trying to talk on the telephone."

"What have I got myself into?" Pearl asked, shaking her head.

"How in the world do you keep this place cleaned up Pearl?" Viola asked. "You must work at it every minute."

"Mama, I have help," Pearl answered. "They're all off this afternoon for I wanted us to have the house to ourselves when you arrived. I have a maid and a cook and Nick has a man that looks after the yards. A woman comes in on Thursday and does the laundry, both the washing and the ironing. So you see, I'm living the life of leisure."

"Well sir, Miss priss," Viola said. "You're going to get above your raising to be sure."

"No I'm not," Pearl said. "I'm going to fix supper tonight."

"I'll cook," Viola said. "I'll be tickled to death to cook, 'specially since Nick seems to like my cooking."

"He does," Pearl said, "but I want you to get a taste of the good life too, so I don't want you to turn your hands. Sit and let me wait on you for a change."

"Well I'll declare," Viola said.

"I need to relieve myself Perline," Craven said. "Where do I go?"

"There's a bathroom in your bedroom," Pearl said. " Do you remember which room it is?"

"I don't know," Craven said. "But I'll find it." He left the room hurriedly.

"It's almost too much for youall, isn't it Mama?" Pearl asked.

"It's just new to them," Nick said. "It's something they've got to get used to. They'll be all right. Don't worry about them Pearl."

After supper they sat in the living room with a bright fire going and the table lamps shedding a warm glow over the room and talked about things that had happened since they saw each other and Viola asked when they were going to call Hobby, and she said they were to call at 8:30; that Hobby would be at a telephone at that time. It was now 7:30.

"I want youall to see downtown Memphis," Pearl said. "They have it all decorated for Christmas. I know they have some decorations in Hallsborough, but they have a lot more here. The downtown store windows are decorated too."

"The way they do some things you'd never think it was hard times everywhere," Craven said. "They shore God must have more money than we've got down in Carolina."

"No, it's just as bad here," Nick said, "and I don't know that Memphis should be doing this either. You're seeing the good side of it Mr. Craven. But it's a sad picture out there. You ought to see the slums and how they're living if you want to get an eyeful. And I don't mind telling you that I get a guilty feeling myself when I think of all the things we have and I think about the people in need. It almost wants you to take what you have and give it to the poor. But there are so many of them it would be gone without doing anybody any real good. But I console myself that I am providing a soup kitchen for some of the poor in the slums. They can go there and get a bowl of soup and a cup of coffee."

"That's mighty nice of you Nick," Viola said. "I tell you it's a bad time for folks that don't have nothing at home like farmers have. It ain't nothing to see folks from town, 'specially the coloreds, walking the roads and asking for something to do to get something to eat."

"This is getting me in the dumps," Pearl said. "Let's quit talking about unpleasant things. It's about time to call Hobby anyway." She looked up at the clock on the mantel and it was 8:20. "I'm going to place the call. By the time they get him and transfer the call it will be 8:30."

Almost immediately she got the hospital and in a moment she was connected with Hobby.

"Hi sweetheart," she said and Hobby said, "Hi Mom, and merry Christmas. Have Grandma and Grandpa got there yet?" He knew this was the day they were to arrive.

"Yeah, they're here and anxious to speak to you. But I'm going to say a few words to you first. How are you doing?"

"Oh, I'm fine. It seems good to have that awkward cast off and one I can manage."

"Do you have any pain now?" Pearl asked and he told her he didn't.

"We've got the house all decorated for you honey. It's different from anything you've seen."

"I'm dying to get there," Hobby said. "Now can I speak to Grandma and Grandpa?"

"Mama, come and speak to Hobby," Pearl said as she handed her the receiver. "Just put the receiver to your ear and talk into the mouthpiece."

"Hey there Hobby," Viola said and when she heard his voice she began to cry. "I'm tickled to death to hear your voice son and you sound good."

"I'm fine Grandma. But I miss youall and Bear Grass so much. I'd give anything if I could see you right now."

"Me too" Viola replied. "Why wouldn't they let you come on now son?"

"I was just operated on last week Grandma. It's too early for me to get out after an operation. Two days before Christmas is the earliest they will let me go."

"Well you be good now, and I'll be thinking about you. I see Craven is dying to talk so I'll say goodbye for now."

"Hey there boy," Craven said and Hobby said, "Grandpa!"

"How are you doing son?" Craven asked. "It seems mighty good hearing your voice and I've sure missed you helping me feed up and things like that."

"And I've missed being there Grandpa," Hobby said. "Hey, what do you think of Pearl and Nick's Place?"

"It's mighty fine son. Course you know it's all new to Viola and me." He lowered his voice and said, "I keep looking at the bottom of my shoes. I'm scared I've got a chicken tird on them." He laughed and Hobby joined in.

"I got in a tight this evening," Craven said. "I had to go to the bathroom and you know it has always been the stables with me, and lo and behold the durn thing was in the room Pearl put us in. I was scared to stand on the white seat and squat down. Then I was scared the hole was not in line with me and I tell you I had me a time, but I got through it." Hobby was in fits of laughter.

"And I hain't never wanted a corncob as bad as I did until I realized there won't nowhere to throw it. Folks like us are too ignorant to be at places like this Hobby, but Perline is determined to make us human beings. I imagine she'll regret ever trying before it's all over with."

No, you'll do fine," Hobby said, "and Grandma will too."

Then Nick talked and there was laughter and Pearl talked again and then it was time for Hobby to return to his room.

"We'll call again Sunday night," Pearl said. "And you be a good boy Hobby and before you know it it will be time for you to join us."

Viola and Craven retired to their bedroom and Craven said he dreaded to go to bed for fear he'd mess up the sheets and Viola said he was not nasty and there won't no reason to feel that way, but when she slid between the sheets and felt the firmness of the mattress she knew she was a long way from Bear Grass. But they slept well.

Nick had to go to his office the next morning and Pearl took her parents to the large kitchen with a fire going in the fireplace and the sun coming in through the windows. There was a bird feeder outside the window and Craven watched the birds as they flew to the feeder and vied for the seeds.

Pearl said, "I'm tickled to death that both of you are here. I feel like I'd be doing it all wrong if you stayed in Bear Grass when Nick is making such a big thing out of this. And I'll admit the whole thing is ridiculous and about as far-fetched as you can get. I don't know why Nick wanted to go to such extremes. Maybe it is because of what I made him do. They're both extremes - something you would read in novels - that doesn't fit into normal patterns. Rich and poor go together about like salt and sugar. But since we're into it good and there is no backing out, I'll be damned if I'll make Nick the laughing stock of Memphis."

"Pearl you watch your mouth," Viola said. "You've been raised better than that."

"I've already heard what they're saying around Memphis," Pearl said.

"What?" Viola asked.

"That he went down to the cotton patches of North Carolina and picked him a little old farmer's daughter for a wife when he had all of the bluebloods in Memphis to choose from. They're saying it's a slam on Memphis society. They're laughing out loud at me and they say that proves that Nick is a simple-minded man. They can't wait for the ball in January to get an eyeful of me. And that makes me mad. Mad as hell."

"There you go again," Viola said.

"Oh mama, I've got to get this out of my system or I'll bust open. When you're in my position you have to try harder. And I'm well aware of all my disadvantages. And I could endure embarrassment for myself, but if I were to let Nick down I'd never forgive myself. And that's why we've got to carry this thing out right."

"Well you'll have to tell us and show us what to do," Viola said.

"That's just what I'm going to do. That's why I wanted you to come early, besides having you through Christmas. There really won't be a lot to do. You won't be expected to be the leaders. You'll be there to shake people's hands, smile, and answer politely when you're asked a question. You'll get on the dance floor and go through the motions of dancing. But I'm going to take you to the school of dance and give you a few lessons. Nick and I have been going already, and they'll teach you how to be at ease and get by without calling attention to yourselves. The clothes that we bought you have already been pressed and are in your closet . I had them inspected by the fashion experts and they gave their approval. You can start feeling at ease right now."

"What kind of affair is this Pearl?" Viola asked.

"It's to introduce me to Memphis society," Pearl said. "I haven't been introduced to any of Nick's friends and he wants it to be a big affair. There'll be hundreds there and he'll be using a national radio show to introduce me. It's a big, big thing and think about what I have confronting me. But do you know something. I am fool enough to think I can carry it off and come out the winner. Is that a sign of ignorance?"

"All I can say is you've got more gall than me," Viola said. "Of course you've always been crazy about style and I reckon you've studied it more than girls who were brought up with it. You always stood out from all the girls in Bear Grass. And you didn't try to be above them either. Seems like it came perfectly natural with you."

"Oh, I cared," Pearl said. "The only thing was that I couldn't carry it out for the wolf was always at the door. But that is true in many cases. Many things could have been accomplished by others too if it hadn't been for that infernal wolf."

"It seems like this is right down your alley," Craven said. "And with your looks you will be the prettiest thing there. And I know you'll have the best that can be bought to wear."

"But it all has to be carried out in a natural manner," Pearl said. "There can be no air of cocquettishness and there must be no hint of put-on. It calls for naturalness and sincerity. I must not make any blunders. And all of this is my thinking only. Dear old Nick thinks I can do anything, which of course I can't. But when he trusts me so much I must make sure I don't let him down. And I couldn't care less about the group I'll be expected to impress. Somehow or other I think that Nick may be trying to get even for some snub he's had in the past, although Nick has never told me of such an incident."

"Well, we'll do the best we can," Viola said.

"After the ball, I'll settle down to being Nick's wife and I will make my own friends in Memphis. As to our future, we'll stay in Memphis until Hobby finishes high school and is enrolled in a university. Beyond that, we have no plans at the present. He's said something about a world tour later on. But our first thought is of Hobby. We want the very best for him if we know what the very best is."

"I'm so glad we won't have to worry about his education," Viola said. "There wouldn't be no way he could go to college without Nick's help."

"Don't you worry one minute about Hobby Mama," Pearl said. "Or yourselves either. Nick is getting started on your new house sometime in January. He's getting somebody in Bear Grass to build it."

"He ought not to do that Perline," Craven said. They had never been able to get him to call Pearl by the name she had chosen.

"I couldn't rest easy here if we left you in the house I grew up in," Pearl said. "It was fine when we couldn't do any better, but we can do better now and it's time that you had it a little easier and a better house to live in. You're even going to have three bedrooms so that when all of us visit you there will be room enough for all of us. And you'll have a bathroom inside Mama. Nick's putting in a septic tank to take care of the sewage. And Papa, there'll be five acres of land for you to tend. You can grow all the sweet corn you need and I wish I had some right now. You can have a large garden and your cow and chickens. You just won't have all the hard work of tending tobacco and cotton and all the responsibility."

"You've still got to have some money in order to survive," Craven said. "Nick's not supposed to take me on as a free rider."

"Mama, Pearl said, "let's you and me go to the hairdresser's today. I want you to get your hair fixed and I need mine washed. Have you ever been to a hairdresser's?" "You know I've not," Viola said. And it sure could stand some fixing but I never gave such a thing a thought. There was never no money for anything like that you know." "Yeah, I know, Pearl said. They are finger waving hair now and I'll bet a finger wave at the top of your head and extending to where you ball it up would look good on you, especially if you combed the waves out instead of leaving the heavy set wave like a lot of women do. Have you ever seen one?" "You know I've not Pearl. They don't do them things in Bear Grass."

"You go up and choose something to wear downtown Mama," Pearl said. "Women dress when they go downtown. Any of the street clothes that you bought will be all right, with your new coat."

"You come on and help me," her mother said. "I don't trust myself to do anything right."

"You look real nice," Pearl said after Viola was dressed in one of her new outfits. "Don't feel self-conscious now. Go look at yourself in the mirror."

"I'll have to say it looks better than the plain Viola," Viola said.

"You're almost pretty Mama," Pearl said. "And when they get through with your hair you will be pretty. Turn around and let me see if you've got the seam of your stockings straight." She examined the seams and had Viola to undo one stocking and straighten it.

When they returned home Craven said, "Is that you Viola? I declare I didn't hardly know you."

"Isn't she pretty?" Pearl said as she took Viola's hand and ran it through the finger wave. "I'm real proud of her." Viola smiled.

"Pity but what they could do something for a man," Craven said. "Plain old ugly men don't have nothing going for them."

"Oh hush Papa," Pearl said. "A man's not supposed to be pretty. You look as good as any man your age. If an older man hasn't got shaggy hair, and it's clean, and he keeps his body clean, that's all that matters."

Nick came home and Craven said he wanted to walk over the grounds, and Viola said she wanted to go too. So all of them walked over the back grounds and Nick pointed out the different shrubs in the yard and the various trees and they stopped where there were chairs and outdoor furniture. "This is where we recline in summer," he said. "That is before it gets too hot and the bugs and mosquitoes become a problem. We have parties out here sometimes." Then they went to the front and Craven and Viola noted that they were on a high hill.

"Let's take a drive." Pearl said, and Nick took them all over downtown Memphis. They saw Beale Street and Pearl told them this was where the blues originated.

"The blues - what are you talking about Pearl?" Viola said.

"Blues music Mama. I thought sure you knew what the blues is."

"You mean like the niggers sing in the fields that sounds so pitiful?"

"Yeah, that blues," Pearl said.

"They've even got a place here called Raleigh," Craven said when he saw the sign.

Nick told them about Mud Island and about the steamboats that came by sometimes. He took them to the Memphis zoo and they walked over it and Viola declared she didn't know there were so many kinds of animals in the world. "Hobby'll have a fit when he sees this," Craven said. "They ain't an animal in the world that boy don't love."

"Yeah, even a snake," Viola said.

"Oh Mama, you know not," Pearl said.

"Pearl, Hobby's your boy, but you don't know him as good as Craven and me. He's had snakes in jars and he'd punch a hole in the lid so they could get air. He's even caught mice and put in the jar for the snake to eat. He hated to do that but he knew the snakes would eat some of them anyway. He knew that one animal eats another in nature and that it was planned that way."

"Yeah, I've got a lot to learn about my boy," Pearl said.

Nick took them to some of the museums and they enjoyed all the places they visited for they were so different from anything they'd seen.

"I always thought of mountains when I thought of Tennessee," Viola said.

"There are mountains," Pearl said. "When I was working in the mills I was in the Great Smoky mountains. Beautiful too, but this section of the state is far from the mountains just as Bear Grass is far from the North Carolina mountains. When you think of Asheville and Boone you think of mountains, don't you?"

"Cotton's big here," Nick said and he directed his remarks to Craven. "This is cotton country and Memphis is a big cotton center."

They visited the school of dance and Viola and Craven watched the couple on the floor. Viola looked at Craven and he saw her face was troubled. "This is against the rules of the church," she said. "What are we going to do Craven?"

"We're going to do just like we're doing, "Craven said. "If God sends us to hell for what we will be doing here he's not much of a God. And if it gets back to Whispering Pines church and anybody calls us to the carpet on account of it I'm going to change churches."

"You know you wouldn't do that," Viola said as they motioned for them to go on the dance floor.

Their dancing lessons began and they learned to waltz about on the dance floor and that broke the ice and they were not as shy as the lessons progressed. Pearl coached them about their manners and reminded them that being good listeners rather than trying to dominate a conversation and show their ignorance would be the course to follow.

The days passed swiftly and finally it was two days before Christmas. Nick and Pearl conferred with the hospital and then talked with Hobby, and everything was set for him to arrive in mid afternoon. Everybody in the house was in a state of excitement as they awaited his arrival.

They met him at the airport and Nick took along a wheelchair and he was smiling as they took Hobby off the plane. They all embraced him and looked at the cast on his leg.

"It looks mighty straight to me," Viola said. "There ain't no crookedness to it now Hobby and I am so glad."

"I'm so happy to see all of you," Hobby said as he kissed each of them.

When they entered the house Hobby said, "This is the prettiest sight I've ever seen. I never saw any decorations like these. Mother, you outdid yourself didn't you?"

"I just wanted everything to be pretty for once," she said. "That's taking nothing away from how it has always been, but it's different."

"And how is everything in Bear Grass?" he asked his grandparents.

"The same as when you left," Craven said.

"I'm so homesick for home I can't hardly stand it," Hobby said. "I dream about it almost every night. Have you seen Wilbert Lee or any of the other boys lately?"

"I see Wilbert Lee out in the yard occasionally," Viola said, "but he never comes by anymore."

"Say, can I ride over Memphis?" Hobby asked.

"We have strict orders for you," Pearl said. "You are to stay in your wheelchair with your leg elevated, so we can't let you do all the things we'd like to Hobby. I wish we could take you all over town and let you visit all the places of interest, especially the zoo, but that will have to wait until your surgery is all over with. I'm just glad you could come home in a wheelchair to spend Christmas with us."

"I know," Hobby said, blushing.

"The tree is beautiful," Hobby said. Then he looked toward his grandparents. "Remember the little tree we had last Christmas? It was so small and there were no lights on it, but I thought it was beautiful too."

"It was pretty," Viola said.

"There are a lot of gifts under the tree," Hobby said. He thought about the little tree back home with a sheet around the bottom to hide the homemade stand to hold it up, and no presents underneath.

"Nick and I bought gifts for all of us," Pearl said.

"They're all pretty and fancy too," Hobby said as he observed the brightly colored paper. "I reckon a few people in Bear Grass have such things, but it's funny that we didn't think anything about it."

"That's another world," Craven said.

Christmas morning all of them gathered around the tree and opened their gifts and Hobby was delighted with the clothes, including brightly colored sweaters and a radio. He couldn't imagine himself owning his own radio. He also got games and a science outfit and a magnifying telescope.

Craven got a heavy work coat made of denim and leather work gloves and a pair of corduroy pants. "I knew you wouldn't like anything else I might get you," Pearl said.

Viola got the first wrist watch she had ever owned. She cried when Pearl put it around her arm.

Nick gave Pearl a pin with a diamond in it and she gave him a tie pin, also with a diamond.

All of them had been introduced to the servants and Viola enjoyed talking with them, especially the cook. She found out that people in Memphis cooked different from the way food was prepared at home. She was looking forward to Christmas dinner. "I can't believe that I'll be eating Christmas dinner I didn't prepare," she told the cook.

"Well I sure hope you'll enjoy it," Carrie, the cook, replied.

Hobby said, "Look at all the fruit in that bowl. My gosh I got an apple and orange and sometimes a tangerine in my stocking, and I thought that was a lot." He picked up a large banana and peeled it.

Carrie did a good job with Christmas dinner. The turkey was tender and moist. The gravy was brown, the dressing tasted good, made with cornbread and biscuit crumbs, with celery and sage and onion seasoning. They had turnips and turnip salad cooked together, but it was too watery to suit Viola and Craven. They were used to having greens mashed to remove most of the water. They didn't particularly like the potato salad. There was some kind of herb in it that didn't suit their taste buds. But the pecan pie was delicious as was the chocolate cake and there were mashed sweet potatoes with marshmallows over them that Viola had never tried and which she found delicious. And the ambrosia was good.

It was cozy inside and after all the presents were unwrapped they spread out over the room, Nick and Craven in one corner and Hobby and his grandmother in the other, while Pearl took all the presents to the rooms upstairs.

"It's the prettiest Christmas I've ever seen," Viola said. "Still, it seems different don't it?"

"It's so pretty I want to cry," Hobby said. "It's like something we would imagine, never expecting it to come true. It's like a fairy tale, Grandma."

Then he leaned over in his wheelchair and lowered his voice. "I feel really guilty about it Grandma. I love Pearl and Nick more than I can say and I know they'd do anything in the world for me. And I'm glad we're here enjoying the season together, but I'd be happier if we were back home."

"I know," Viola said.

"Nothing will ever take those memories from me," Hobby said. "I can see the big fire and the tree and the little mounds of holly on the mantelpiece and the mistletoe over the door and the sun shining on a frosty field and the bright quilt on the bed and the picture of Jesus over the mantel and I get all homesick and there's something missing that nothing else on earth will satisfy. But it would hurt Pearl and Nick's feelings if I told them that. You understand but they could not and I'm all torn up inside. Do you reckon I'll ever get straightened out Grandma?"

"Maybe one day son," Viola replied.

"I want you to do something for me Grandma," Hobby said. "I want you to keep everything in my room just like it was. Keep all the furniture and even the old curtains. I want to keep it forever and I will always treasure it even when I am a man. And if I ever have a home I'll want to place all the things I have in a special room. Will you do it Grandma?"

"You know I will Hobby," Viola said.

"What's really sad is that those days are coming to an end," Hobby said. "I will be away from Bear Grass and it'll change and I'll grow up with nothing but a lot of memories about such a happy time."

"Son, them years don't last for nobody," Viola said. "You look back upon them and it seems like they never happened. You think of it like it was a dream. You won't be different from other people in that respect."

"But Grandma I appreciated those days while they were happening. I saw every day as a paradise and I always knew that they would end. But I held on and got everything I could out of them."

After everything was put away they settled down to a quiet Christmas afternoon. Pearl read a book for a while and Nick and Craven drove out to the Mississippi river.

"A mighty river," Craven said. "I've always heard of the Mississippi as the great muddy Mississippi."

"She's mighty all right," Nick said. "Do you know how long she is Mr. Craven?"

"I know she's long but I don't know how long. I never studied things like that in school."

"Three thousand seven hundred and ten miles," Nick said.

"Whew, that's long," Craven said. "But you know Nick I never thought too much about big waters on account of there won't no river near Bear Grass. The river's on the other side of Bear Grass and I know when the rains came people over there had to leave their homes sometimes and I was always glad that I didn't have that to contend with. But I bet that old river has played a pretty big part in your life."

"Oh yeah," Nick said. "Especially when I was a boy. But it's something you learn early to respect. I used to love to go down and watch the river and the passing boats and Dad used to take Mom and me on an excursion down the river occasionally. That's a pleasant memory."

"I guess we'd better get back to the house or they'll accuse us of spoiling Christmas," Nick said. He replenished the wood in the fireplace as they entered the house.

"I'll bet youall have been to the river," Hobby said. "That's not fair for I want to go so bad I don't know what to do."

"That's about like you Hobby," Craven said. "Remember when we used to get a stick of blow gum and divide it between Viola, you and me, and after you'd swallowed yours, and you always did eventually, you'd want us to spit ours out? And the worst thing about it is that we did what you wanted us to do just to please you."

"My, how little I know about my own boy," Pearl said. "That's the result of not being with them when their character and all the things they will be is developing." She wiped a tear from her eyes in thinking about what she had missed and which she would never be able to recapture.

"Now," Nick said, "we're going to tell you about the party we're having for Pearl."

"Yeah, I've been anxious to know about that," Hobby said.

"And I shore have too," Viola chirped in.

"First, I want all of you to know this was Nick's idea from start to finish," Pearl said. "The only reason I'm going through with it is because he wants it."

Hobby thought about how kind that man was and what an impact he had already had on all their lives. He couldn't understand how he could take an entire family under his wing, a family so far removed from the world he knew.

"It's going to be a big one," Nick said. "There will be about two hundred invited guests. And it's to acquaint Pearl with Memphis society. And I'll admit that there is an ulterior motive in this. Pearl is prettier than any of the society dames in Memphis and I'm as proud of her as any man could be. And I want Pearl to form her own circle of friends, and they may not be the society set, and that doesn't matter in the least. She can choose the friends of her choice."

"So I heard this band would be playing at the Peabody in early January and I thought that would be the best way to carry out the ball if I could arrange it, so I got to inquiring and it worked out so it could be done."

"Whose band is it?" Hobby asked.

"Kay Kyser's" Nick replied.

"Kay Kyser's!" Hobby said. "Gollee! He's from our area. Right on down the road north from Hallsborough. He's bound to have passed through Bear Grass at some time."

"Maybe that helped," Nick said. "When I talked to him I told him that Pearl was from Bear Grass, about fifty miles from Rocky Mount, his hometown. He said he knew where Bear Grass was and that he'd be happy to focus national attention on her for a moment."

"It's beginning to be a small world," Viola said. "But I don't know nothing about bands and such. The only thing I know about music is the country songs sung along with banjo, guitar and mandolins. Lord, I love mandolin music."

"This is different," Hobby said. "It's popular music and they use horns and saxophones and clarinets and things like that."

"How about your wardrobe?" Viola asked. "You've bought all this stuff for me and Craven but you've not said a thing about what you'll wear."

"I had mine made," Pearl said. "By a black woman."

"You know not," Viola said. "The niggers around home are about the sorriest sewers I ever saw. They'll take a needle and thread it with any color thread they've got and sew up anything and make big, crooked stitches and make a pure mess out of it."

"I remember," Pearl said, "and some white folks too, but wait until you've seen Mavis' sewing. She's the most popular designer in Memphis and is one of the nicest people you ever saw. I want you to meet her, Mama."

"Have you got everything you need?" Viola asked.

"Everything," Pearl replied.

"I think I mainly want this to prove that because a person is poor and has missed all the advantages is no reason he or she can't be a winner," Nick said. "Pearl's story should be a big boost to many young women who want a different lifestyle but have been held back by poverty. You can have all that and still make something out of your life."

"But every girl can't marry a rich man," Viola said. "This is as far from Bear Grass as you can get and a girl could wish forever to amount to something and if Mr. right don't come along you can forget it."

"I'm well aware of that," Nick said, "but Pearl captivated me without any of those advantages. She was as charming in that dining room as she is now. So it wasn't anything that I did to make her that way. She had already learned those lessons while she was in Bear Grass and the mill."

"Aren't you afraid she'll flub up and embarrass you?" Hobby asked.

"I haven't given it a thought," Nick said. "And if she did it wouldn't be worse than I've seen some of these society dames do. I have complete faith in Pearl."

"That's what scares me so much," Pearl said. But she looked at Nick and patted his arm. "I promise I won't let you down dearie."

So Christmas came and went and Pearl and Nick were busy planning for the ball and Hobby sat by the window and watched life through his window and dreamed about life in Bear Grass and took a yardstick and ran it down his cast to try to relieve the itching of his leg. It itched so badly he sometimes cringed and held his leg up with his hands and tried to shake it.

"I wonder if anybody back home knows that Pearl will be on national radio Tuesday night?" Hobby asked.

"A notice has been sent to the Argus," Nick said. "I know people in the whole area will be interested. The Raleigh paper has been notified also."

"You didn't leave out a thing did you Nick?" Hobby said.

"I tried not to."

Then it was Tuesday and the entire household was in a stir. After all the talking and planning, the day had finally arrived.

Nobody wanted breakfast. Everybody said their stomachs were sort of squeamish. "But we ought to eat something," Viola said. "It'll help to settle them," as she got up and poured coffee.

Pearl helped Viola get out the clothes they would wear and Craven was fidgety. "I'll be glad when this thing is over," he said. "I want to get back to Bear Grass now and see how things are going around home. I imagine Gant is getting tired of feeding up and all that by now."

"Hush. Don't mention Bear Grass right now. We've got other things to think about," Viola said.

The sunset was golden and the rays coming into the house cast a red glow over the furniture and Viola stood and watched. She was already dressed. Pearl had taken her to the hairdresser's in the afternoon and they both had their hair fixed. She felt a little bit nervous but not nearly as much as she had feared. Craven came in all dressed up too. "I declare you look right good Craven," Viola said. "That tuxedo looks good and I never saw such a fancy shirt. And they did a good job on your hair at the barber shop. Nick must have taken you to his barber."

"He did," Craven said, "and dared him to cut it so I'd look like I had been skint. He told him to just edge it up and think nothing about I'd need one next week. Told him this was special."

"Are your fingernails clean?" Pearl asked as she came through the room. "And Mama and Papa, when you shake people's hands don't just lay your hand in theirs, you don't want to hurt them, but grasp their hands firmly like you've got some life in you. Papa you say, I'm Craven Turnage, Pearl's father, and this is my wife, Viola. And when they say It's nice to have met you you say, It's nice meeting you too. That's all you have to say."

Hobby wore a suit with a coat and white shirt. He wasn't coached in what to say.

Pearl's things had been taken to the dressing room they had rented for her at the hotel. Not even Nick had seen the gown. There was a diamond necklace and a diamond brooch and a watch whose band sparkled with jewels. There were also diamond earrings.

Then the stars studded the skies over Memphis and it was Pearls' night.

The ball was scheduled for eight o'clock and people began arriving by seven thirty. The women came in capes of various furs and evening gowns in a rainbow of colors and all the men were in dark suits and top coats. It was evident that this was the cream of the crop in Memphis society.

Craven, Viola and Hobby waited in Pearl's dressing room until quarter of eight when Nick took them to the main floor where the ball would be held.

Viola and Craven stood in awe when they saw the great ballroom with the huge chandelier and waxed furnishings and the mellow glow of the lights and the shadows as they played over the faces of hotel employees who were busy getting everything in order.

Beyond the ballroom was the large dining area with tables set diagonally and guests, after depositing their coats at the hat-check booth, seated themselves and an air of expectancy filled the room. It was not unusual to have a ball in Memphis, but the circumstances were usually different. People were waiting to meet the newest arrival of the society set - a farm girl. They had no earthly idea what to expect. It was rather comical to many of the group and they made all manner of light talk, adding a joke occasionally and there would be muted laughter from a table sometimes.

Nick was walking among the guests, shaking hands and making them feel at home. A number of women were rather piqued at Nick for going out of their circle to choose a wife. Nick Staphal was a catch in Memphis. Charming and handsome, he played upon quite a number of feminine hearts. Such a man was worth fighting for. But he had spurned their advances and more or less ignored them. They were seeking retribution and were secretly hoping that something would go amiss that would put the flamboyant Nick Staphal in his place.

The dining area was filled and the spotlight focused on the band area where the announcer stood behind a microphone.

"Ladies and gentlemen. It's the Kay Kyser show sponsored by the Ligget and Meyers Tobacco Company." And the Kay Kyser theme song filled the airwaves and the ballroom of the Peabody Hotel. The young bespectacled bandleader, who had reached national prominence and was an up-and-coming musician with his College of Musical Knowledge format had formed his band while attending the University of North Carolina. "It was a pure coincidence that this was all planned without my knowledge. When the man who planned this honor found out that I would be playing in Memphis in January, he contacted me and asked if the ball could be held and the honoree could be introduced on my show. And I was a little reluctant to do this until I learned that she was a native of eastern North Carolina, within fifty miles of my beginnings in Rocky Mount, and an area of which I was familiar. I changed my mind and told him I would do it. I assure you you won't be disappointed."

"Ladies and gentlemen, I present to you Pearl Staphal."

The band played the introduction and there was a moment of quiet. The spotlight focused on a gold dais and there she was!

There was an "ah" from the audience.

She was an image in blue with sparkles in her hair that caught the light and accentuated her shoulder-length blonde hair that lay on her shoulder in gentle waves. Her eyes were aglow and a smile was on her face and she stood tall and slender in a gown with a full circular skirt of ice blue silk with a net embroidered with blue sequins and a blue satin underdress.

She was poised and confident and her voice was clear and perfectly modulated as she said, "Ladies and gentlemen, I am pleased to be in Memphis and I look forward to meeting all of you."

Then Nick came up to the dais, knelt and then rose and offered his arm and he escorted her to the dance floor.

"Ladies and gentlemen," the announcer said, "to Pearl Staphal we offer as our contribution, a song that puts her into her proper setting and for the dancing audience to enjoy. Here is the very popular song, "Carolina Moon," with the lovely Miss Ginny Simms as vocalist."

The spotlight focused on Nick and Pearl as they swayed smoothly over the dance floor. They were joined by many couples while others remained at their tables and reflected on what they had just seen.

"Well well," Candy Suggs said, "I'm all of a sudden seeing magnolia trees and stately houses and mint julep being served. All this talk about a farmer's daughter is hogwash. No wonder Nick went to the farm for a wife. My god! She's beautiful."

Her date, Kent Staton, said, "She's the nicest thing to happen to Memphis in some time. She's as fresh as a daisy and as unassuming as I've seen in a long time." He leaned over to the table where Babs Angley and Bob Sutton were seated. "What do you think about that Bob?" Bob raised his hand and made a figure 0 and nodded approval. "Nick Staphal knew what he was doing. I know there are plenty of jealous dames here tonight with fallen feathers."

Next came a foxtrot and Nick, resplendent in tails, drew Pearl unto the dance floor and they twisted and turned and swung around the floor as he looked lovingly into Pearl's eyes and held her bare back as they danced. They saw Viola and Craven among the dancers as they came in close proximity to each other and all of them smiled. Pearl managed to whisper, "Are you all right?" And they nodded their heads.

They danced a rhumba, the Big Apple and ended up with the Lindy Hop, or jitterbug, and Nick and Pearl set the pace and all eyes were upon them as they gyrated, turning, twisting, going far apart and coming close together. Both were laughing and obviously enjoying themselves and men and women admired the slim figure of the girl in blue.

Diners were treated with rare wines, tasty hors' d oeuvres, smoked salmon, stuffed mountain trout, shrimp salad, oyster cocktails and other seafood tidbits. Even Craven and Viola enjoyed the fare.

After dining, Pearl returned to the dais and Hobby was rolled before her. Craven and Viola stood by his side and Nick stood on the dais with Pearl.

"Ladies and gentlemen," Nick said. "Standing with us are my wife's family. Pearl will introduce them to you at this time."

"Below me is my son, Hobby, who has recently undergone surgery for a leg injury. Hobby, will you say hello to the folks?" Hobby waved and said a loud hello.

"Next is my mother, Viola Turnage, and my father, Craven Turnage." Viola and Craven waved at the group.

"Now we will resume dancing," Nick said as the band returned to the bandstand. Pearl and Nick did not dance; instead stopping and talking with guests. Nick was obviously elated and proud of his wife, as well he might have been, for she was the queen of the ball and conducted herself in a manner befitting a queen. She was charming with white teeth flashing, laughing, light, jovial, without any pretense, mixing with the group as if she had always known them.

Hobby rolled his chair to the table where Craven and Viola sat, "She must be the most beautiful woman in all the world," he said. "Have you ever seen such beauty Grandma?"

"That's saying a lot son," Viola said. "But I'll admit she is a very pretty woman."

"Aren't both of you proud to have such a daughter?" Hobby asked.

"Yes, we're proud," Viola said. "But we're more proud that she's pretty inside as well as outside."

"I know," Hobby said. "She's in the setting she deserves right now. But the good part about mother is that she shines through no matter what the setting. I'm so happy for her I can't even express myself. Like so many others, she has had her share of knocks, but she never let that get her down. She's a happy person, and whatever the circumstances, she will make the best of them. She's a remarkable woman."

Finally the line was formed and Pearl, Nick, Hobby, Viola and Craven were shaking hands as people came by.

Over in a far corner Ginger Lafarro, Penny Osmond, Rex Tyndall and Mo Streaker were discussing Pearl.

"I heard the boy is illegitimate," Ginny said, "and that she is responsible for his leg defect."

"Shit! It doesn't matter about any of that when she's already captured the most eligible bachelor in Memphis. It's not even worth mentioning," Penny replied. "As far as that goes, I heard she was a sharecropper and plowed the fields just as we've seen Tennessee farmers doing. But all of it doesn't mean a thing. It's too late, no matter what the circumstances. She's a clear winner." She sighed. "And to think that I threw myself at Nick Staphal like a cheap whore and he wouldn't even have me. And I get goose pimples, just thinking about him. He's the sexiest man I know. A woman that could lay in his arms at night could reach ecstasies few women know, and spend his money in the daytime."

"Is sex all you think about?" Mo asked.

"Well goddammit, you won't do anything," Penny said. "What's a girl supposed to do? Without?"

"If you had what that lady's got, you could interest me," Mo said with a grin. "You act as if you think you've got all that it takes to win any man when you don't know how goddamn pitiful you are. Wake up woman. Being listed among society doesn't mean a damn thing if you can't be warm and pleasant and cater to a man's whims."

"Hey, hey, don't get so carried away," Rex said. "And it ain't all the woman's fault. Some of we male sons of bitches are like leeches, hanging on to these society misfits trying to get every penny out of them we can in these hard times. I tell you, this Depression has changed lifestyles by the million. I'll admit I'm lazy, but no matter how smart I might be, the reality is there ain't no jobs out there. So I figure a little screwing, a little leeching, an occasional party, I'll weather it until things perk up and I'll be my own man again."

"At least he's honest," Ginger said.

"But as for talk, the least that is said about Nick Staphal and his country wife, the better," Mo said. "She's got what it takes and Staphal is one of the very few who has profited during the Depression. Think what you will, but stop any rumors you hear right now." They decided to go to the receiving line to see Pearl close-up.

"Hi, I'm Ginger Lafarro," she held out a slender hand to Pearl.

"Pearl Staphal," she replied and Ginger noted the huge rock on her finger. But Ginger noted that she was sincere and very beautiful.

"Penny Osmond."

"Hi Penny."

"Rex Tyndall,"

"Pearl Staphal." Pearl smiled approval.

"Mo Streaker."

"Hi." She smiled again.

"Hot damn," Mo said as they returned to their table. "Really first class, I'd say."

"Some get everything," Penny said. "She got it all with Nick Staphal. Looks. Money. Prestige. Breeding. Nick has all these assets and no matter what her background as long as she has that to fall back on she has nothing to lose. And with her looks, she has nothing to worry about."

"Do you think she will dominate the society scene in Memphis?" Ginger asked.

"If she wants to," Ginger said. "But frankly, I doubt that she will go that route. Judging by appearances I'd say she's pretty independent and you'll have to admit we're a boring bunch of bitches. She may not find us interesting at all."

"At least we can stop hoping for Nick to fall victim to our charms," Ginger said. "We can concentrate on new conquests, although the field seems to have dried up. And we certainly haven't got what it takes to pull him away from that beautiful young thing. Want to get married Rex?"

"Mo, do you want to marry Ginger?" Rex said. "I've just got a proposal and I'm a committed bachelor."

"Me too," Rex said.

Viola and Craven's hands were getting tired from shaking hands, and Viola's feet were aching from standing so much. It was nearing midnight and they were waiting for the ball to end.

Hobby was sleeping away in his wheelchair and Pearl was thinking that in a few short moments the night she had feared most would be history.

Goodbyes were finally said and they were on their way home with many things to talk about the next day. Hobby had to return to Baltimore and Craven and Viola had to return to Bear Grass.

Nick placed a hand over Pearl's and felt the diamond that represented a token of his love. "You were absolutely perfect darling," he said as he squeezed the fragile fingers.

"I did the best I could for you Nick," Pearl said as she lay her head on his shoulder. "I tried to do as well as you did when you went to Bear Grass with me." She laughed and looked up into his face. "And now we've come full circle in deception. I was your queen of the ball and you were my farmer incarnate and we've been as extreme as you can be. And I was happy to do this for you Nick. I think I proved something to myself also. I learned that we can do whatever we set out to do if it's important enough. I will be more confident of myself in the future. But I am fully aware Nick that behind all the show I'm still the simple-minded farm girl; that I am lacking the intellectual touch; that I could never be an equal where important issues are discussed; that I will be limited in expressing myself because of my education."

"Pearl, let me tell you something," Nick said. "I've observed a lot of people including the so-called intellectuals. And on a specific topic they can talk with authority and make people believe they are real scholars but you can talk with them about topics in general and when they get out of their specific fields they are lost. Some of them can't even talk about life in general. So don't feel that you are lost in a world about which you know nothing. You have a general knowledge of life. You have experienced many very valuable things. All that you have to do is to continue observing life as a whole and you have nothing to worry about."

"Thank you for your confidence in me." She yawned and said she was very tired as they drove into the garage.

Nick got Hobby out of the car and carried him into the house. Craven and Viola put on their shoes and walked stiffly into the house with both of them yawning, for it was way past their bedtime. Nick thought about the night and smiled.

When they were in bed and the lights were out and Pearl was in Nick's arms, she pulled his mouth to hers and kissed him passionately and said, "Thanks for giving Cinderella the ball she will always remember, Prince Charming."

Chapter 20

Wilbert Lee Turner was not an "average" child. It was a time of "spare the rod and spoil the child" philosophy, and although children were defiant and often misbehaved, they could surely look forward to a whipping, with a switch, a paddle, a razor strap or a rope. It wasn't that children wanted to obey. They just knew better than not to. It was different with Wilbert Lee.

Being the only child of Gant and Abie Turner to live longer than a few weeks, it had become his mother's obsession to protect him. She had seen nine others, five boys and four girls, fade away and die within a few days after birth. But Wilbert Lee thrived from the start. Abie considered this no less than a miracle. On bended knees, she thanked God every day for him and she devoted her whole life to his care. Gant often complained that she wasn't even cooking meals for him, and Abie would have some excuse concerning Wilbert Lee as being the reason he was left with scraps to eat sometimes.

She'd hold him on her ample lap and talk baby talk to him. She would hold him up in her arms until she got a smile out of him, then shower kisses on him. "Mama's itty bitty boy," she'd say, "Mama's darling itta baby. All Mama's to love and hold. You'll always be a Mama's boy, itta angel. Nobody else in all the world compares with my itty bitty darling." She'd open a breast to him and as he suckled, she felt that she was in seventh heaven. It was the most satisfying feeling she had ever known. Whatever other mothers thought, Abie knew in her heart that Wilbert Lee was a blessing from God and that he was meant for larger things than other children in the area.

Occasionally Gant would try to hold the boy, but it always made Abie miserable. She wanted the baby to know Gant was his father, but she didn't want him to exert a great deal of influence over the boy. Gant was too worldy, too much like all other men to trust her baby with. "You're going to ruin that young'un" Gant was saying before Wilbert Lee was six months old.

Gant would gather up the boy and hold his hands above his head, turning Wilbert Lee upside down, and Abie would scream, "Gant Turner you're going to turn his liver over!" She'd run and take the baby from Gant's arms.

Abie had put Gant in the other bedroom to sleep after Wilbert Lee's birth. "I can't help it," she'd told Gant. "It's gitting time to stop thinking about lustful things anyhow, and with God's blessings, I'm going to raise this baby up to become something big in this world." This lasted for two years.

She nursed Wilbert Lee the first six months without any additives. Then she began masticating every mouthful of food from the table that went into his mouth before placing it on his tongue. If it were ham, she'd chew it until it was a mush, and only old, dried out irish potatoes were fed to him. She could mash these up without having to chew them. No cabbage until they were old enough for all the soda put to the plants had had time to grow out. If the food didn't go down in a moment she would run her finger into his mouth and pull the food out and start over. If he cried when she was doing the things that simply had to be done, like washing his diapers and the other clothes, or making the beds at least three times a week, she would fix him a sugar teat (a rag about three inches square with a spoonful of sugar placed inside and tied together) and place it in his mouth.

"Precious, precious itta boy," she'd croon. "The best itta boy in all the world. Momsie's little darling. My king! My darling."

One time after she'd nursed the baby, she noticed that his tongue was covered in white and she became alarmed. She opened the baby's mouth wider and his entire mouth looked white and Abie almost panicked. Gant was out in the field behind the smokehouse plowing corn and she ran and waited for him to get near the end of the row. She cupped her hands around her mouth and hollered, "Gant, come here right quick. Something's wrong with the baby."

"What in the world?" Gant asked. "He was all right when I was at the house eating cold ish taters and flourbread."

"It's his mouth," Abie said, and Gant noted she was shaking.

They ran to the house and Gant picked the boy up to look into his mouth, noting that he was pretty contended if he was sick. He was playing with the side of the spread that hung off the bed. He opened Wilbert Lee's mouth and began to laugh. "I declare, you're the craziest woman I ever seen Abie. That boy hain't got nothing on his tongue or in his mouth but your own milk. When did you nurse him?"

"Just before I called you," Abie replied. "But I want you to git him to the doctor Gant."

"I'll do no such a thing," Gant replied. "Look at him, he's playing and acting perfectly natural."

"I can't stand it when you act like this Gant. You don't know that it's just milk on his tongue, and that's just another of the things that make me disgusted with you. You know e-v-e-r-y-t-h-i-n-g."

Gant walked out and went back to his plowing. And Abie fumed.

The months passed and Wilbert Lee began walking and talking. "Say Mommie darling," Abie would say. "Talk to Mommie little one. Say M-a-m-a." And Wilbert Lee would ignore her. Abie sensed that there was something about him that resented her from the time he first began to take notice of life about him. As soon as he was able to speak full sentences he was talking ugly to his parents. He would say "no" when Abie pleaded with him to do something and he'd become angry and stomp his foot. It was funny to Abie, for she saw no wrong in her child. "He will change when he gets older," she told herself.

Wilbert Lee didn't change. His vocabulary grew and he began saying no-no words and openly sassing his parents.

"Whip that boy," Gant would say after such outbursts, and Abie would take the baby in her arms and go into another room.

Abie nursed the boy long enough that he remembered it when he was older. He'd scream, "I want ninny," and would run his hand into Abie's dress and pull out one of her breasts. He'd cuddle his head low in her lap and take a nipple into his mouth and place his hand on the breast that showed purple veins and if milk wasn't there in a very short time he'd bite Abie's nipple and she would cry out and remove the breast from his mouth, and there was often blood there. Wilbert Lee would rake his tongue on Abie's dress to remove the blood.

But no matter how abusive the boy was, Abie never scolded him or disciplined him more than saying, "Now, now, that's a bad boy," and Wilbert Lee took full advantage of the situation. Gant Turner was completely removed from the picture as far as discipline went. "You leave the correcting to me," she told Gant. "You're too rough and you just don't understand," and Gant would shake his head and think to himself that the woman had a problem in the head that nobody but God could correct.

Wilbert Lee was given to temper tantrums from birth. He'd flail out at his mother and she would try to gather him in her arms and the boy would scream and bite and kick and lie on the floor and scream.

"He ain't right," Gant would say, and Abie would defend the baby and tell Gant he would grow out of it. She reminded Gant that God had given her the boy as an answer to a prayer; that he was destined for something big and it was her hope that he would become a preacher of the word of God. Gant would sigh and look off into the distance and think: She has already sown the seeds of destruction by the way she is treating him and letting him get away with the things he does.

Abie tried taking the boy to church, but he would upset the entire congregation with his mischief. He'd place his feet on the back of the bench in front of him and stomp with his feet. He would get up and run up and down an aisle or speak out while services were being conducted and Abie would have to take him outside. If Gant had tried to take him out the boy would have screamed to the top of his voice.

One Sunday Abie invited the preacher and his wife home for dinner. She had prepared a good meal and enjoyed the company of Reverend and Mrs. Pell. But Wilbert Lee spoiled the day. After filling up on smothered chicken, butterbeans, rosen ears, beans, tomatoes and apple pie, preacher Otto allowed as how he was so full he was uncomfortable and they all rose from the table and Reverend Pell stooped down to lift Wilbert Lee into his arms and play with him a bit but Wilbert Lee caught him on the shin with his shoe and the preacher released his grip and showed pain on his face. "What's wrong with the boy?" he asked Gant. This placed Gant in an untenable position, so he pointed to Abie. "She has taken on the responsibility of correcting the child," Gant said after which Reverend Pell directed his attention to Abie.

"Sister," he said, "this boy is too large to carry on like this." (The boy was five). "I'd advise you to take stronger measures with your little boy, or you'll face trouble ahead." And Abie's face turned red and it was evident the preacher's words had angered her.

"Reverend Pell," she said, "you don't have any children and I don't know that you are any authority on telling me how I should correct my child. I was luckier than you and Vicey. You lost all of your children but God was good to me and gave me this boy as an answer to my prayers.

"My boy is a fine child. You can tell that just by looking at him. Look how pretty he is." She took her hand and placed it on the boy's head where burnished gold hair was thick and shone in the sunlight coming through the window. "Look at his eyes - soft brown with a sparkle that everybody notices. Look at the shape of his head." (Abie was giving Gant no credit for his contribution to what the boy looked like.) As a matter of fact, he looked very much like Gant Turner, still a handsome man with a bearing that bespoke a higher heritage than was evident.

"He is the picture of health with a fine body and a good mind, and time will take care of his outbursts of temper. And I'd appreciate it, Reverend Pell, if you would leave his training to me."

"I didn't mean to upset you Sister Abie," the minister said. "I apologize for butting in."

The afternoon went fairly well and nothing else was said about the boy, but Abie Turner never felt the same about Otto Pell again, and she took every opportunity to find flaws in his character.

And so went the early years of Wilbert Lee Turner.

But there was also another side to Wilbert Lee. He could be charming and graceful and he learned to use those characteristics to his advantage. He was popular with the other neighborhood children, and perhaps brighter than most. He could cause laughter among the group and whatever he wanted to do he could persuade the others to go along and he was the undisputed leader among the children. He was even more popular than Philip Stroud, whose father owned about all the land for a mile or two around his large country store.

Wilbert Lee would dare to do things other children in the neighborhood were afraid to do. He was using curse words strong by the age of ten. Vulgarity was his specialty and every child was educated as to the use of the wrong words. Wilbert Lee knew them all. This made him even more popular in school than the other children. Girls were swooning over him by the age of thirteen. He was a handsome boy and looked older than his age.

Wilbert Lee's power base was dampened somewhat after Hobby Turnage and the Tobey Finch family moved away from Bear Grass. If Wilbert Lee had, in a sense detested Hobby, the boy had been a great ego booster, for Hobby attempted to do anything Wilbert Lee suggested, whereas Tom and Billy Earl Finch often challenged Wilbert Lee during some of their games. Of course, Wilbert Lee stepped all over the Finch girls, Robyn and Arlene.

But Wilbert Lee was undaunted as his world began to expand. "What the hell," he said to himself, "life's just beginning. I'm finishing school at Bear Grass Elementary this year, and it will be on to Hallsborough high next fall. Philip Stroud will be going to Hallsborough High also, and together we will make a team, and if those smart-asses in town try anything they'll have both of us to contend with."

But Wilbert Lee was too smart to try to intimidate the town boys. He and Philip would join them and they would become integrated into Hallsborough

High and each would become one of the boys and he could more or less forget about the "hicks" in Bear Grass.

And so it was that in the fall of 1932 Wilbert Lee, Philip Stroud, Buddy Stone and Lisker Johnson boarded the school bus in Bear Grass every school morning and made the six-mile trip to Hallsborough High morning and afternoon. Wilbert Lee and Philip were friendly enough to the other Bear Grass boys, but they set themselves apart from them from the very beginning. The other boys didn't share the same visions as Wilbert Lee and Philip.

Learning had not really been a part of Wilbert Lee's thoughts in anticipating attending Hallsborough High. At Bear Grass Elementary he had not been required to study at night in order to make passing grades. He had received mostly A's during the school years. It wasn't that easy at Hallsborough High. For the most part, he liked his teachers, but he was assigned to Mrs. Eliza Cox's algebra class, and she proved to be a holy terror for him. They disliked each other from the beginning. Mrs. Cox was old, sharp-witted, white-haired with a pinched nose and bespectacled. She was tall and thin and foolishness was not one of her games.

Wilbert Lee began wisecracking from the first day and Mrs. Cox gave the class a lesson in deportment. In a shrill voice she said, "Let me tell you one thing, every one of you in this class. I will not put up with sass in any form. I will send you out of this class if you try your smart-alecky antics in my room and if that doesn't work I'll send you to the principal's office. I cannot tolerate a smart-aleck, and I see I already have detected one in this class." She looked directly at Wilbert Lee, pointed her finger at him and said, "Come in front of this class, young man."

Wilbert Lee stifled a grin and went to the front of the class.

"Tell the class your name, young man."

"W.L. Turner."

"That's your initials," Mrs. Cox said. "What is your full name?"

"They call me W.L.," Wilbert Lee said, determined to remove the full name that he had always hated. "Just call me W.L. Turner."

Lisker Johnson, who was in the same class, could not stifle a snicker. Mrs. Cox could hear a pin drop and she heard the snicker and looked over to the outer edge of the room. "Who was that snickering?" she said. Nobody spoke. "All right," Mrs. Cox said, "if the culprit doesn't come clean the entire class can sit in after school until somebody admits to being the culprit."

A girl near Lisker's desk pointed at him. "He's the one," she said.

"And what's your name?" Mrs. Cox asked. "Did you snicker?"

"Yes ma'am."

"Why?"

"Because his name is Wilbert Lee Turner." The entire class burst out in laughter, and Wilbert Lee's face turned red. Bastard, he thought, I'll get even with Lisker Johnson, although realizing that Lisker was a two-hundred-pounder and could trample Wilbert Lee to the ground in a minute.

"Okay, I'm Wilbert Lee Turner," he said with a smile. "So what, I thought it would be easier saying initials than a full name, especially when it's one like mine."

"All right young man," Mrs. Cox said. "You are an example of a smart upstart planning to carry on in my class, but I won't tolerate it, even if it means having you expelled. Now you act like a gentleman in this class and it's none of my business what you do elsewhere. But I do hope you'll learn better manners than you are showing. Where are you from, Wilbert Lee?"

"Bear Grass," he replied, and the class laughed again.

But soon Wilbert Lee became indoctrinated into the city high school and he was quick in adjusting to the new routine. He learned to apply himself and to get his homework regularly and still have plenty of time to fool around in Bear Grass. Wilbert Lee was perhaps the only boy in Bear Grass who did hardly no field work, with the exception of Philip Stroud. The no-work ethic had been established by his mother when he was a very young boy and his father had long-since written Wilbert Lee off as to being any help to him. And with his mother, Abie, doing everything in her power to supply the boy with spending money and buying a piece of clothes for him occasionally Wilbert Lee did as well or better than many who toiled in the fields after school and stayed home at times to help in harvesting the crops.

Wilbert Lee and Philip made friends with the boys from Hallsborough and they hung around together during recess and the dinner hour. They'd go over to a large oak tree on the school grounds, sit down and smoke and tell jokes.

"Hey, what is it you've got Wilbert Lee?" Bill Savage asked one day. "Have you boys noticed how the girls are hanging around Wilbert Lee in the halls all the time? They tease him and he smiles at them and I swear I believe he could get any one of them he wants, and he's only an eighth-grade freshman. Hell, he's not even on the ball team. But I swear he's right up there with them and he ain't even wearing a jock and a uniform."

"Charm," Wilbert Lee said with a shrug and taking his hand and smoothing down the sides of his hair. He thought for a moment, then said,

"Nah, it's not that. Mostly I don't pay 'em any mind and I don't think anything special about them. Maybe I just don't respect girls. And they seem to like that. I reckon I'm some sort of roughneck and I know what they've got and that's all I'm studying."

"Yeah, that's the kind they fall over for every time," Winslow Proctor, son of the chief of police, said. "I've done everything but kiss Samantha Fox's ass, and she treats me like dirt." Wilbert Lee understood this, for Winslow was a wimp.

Wilbert Lee was obsessed with sex. He was masturbating by the time he was eight and pinching neighborhood girls on their fannies whenever he could. Some would threaten to tell on him, but others enjoyed it. So Wilbert Lee began thinking about womanizing in his pre-teen years.

He was fifteen when he entered Hallsborough High and by then he had a beard and had shot up during puberty and stood five feet, eight inches tall and was athletically built. Mr. Poof, the football coach, had tried to get Wilbert Lee to sign up for football. But Wilbert Lee was too clever for him. He was well aware that he had never done enough exercising to go through the rigors of practice, so he gave the excuse that he had a tendon problem in his left ankle. The coach said that was too bad, because he had the build to be a good football player. Besides, he'd rather fool around with some of the other "cool cats" who didn't make the team either.

One day at lunchtime several of the boys on the football squad came by and sat down with Wilbert Lee and his group under the oak tree. "Hi, you're new here aren't you?" Mitch Miller, one of the tackles who weighed a good two hundred and twenty five pounds, said.

"Yeah," Wilbert Lee said nonchalantly.

"Where from?"

"Out at Bear Grass."

"You're trying to act like a city boy, ain't you fella?" Mitch asked.

"And the reason I'm saying that is that I've seen the girls all around you in the halls and out on the grounds. What have you got to attract them like syrup attracts flies? I thought all of that was reserved for the guys on the squad."

"It's nothing that I do especially," Wilbert Lee said. "Just born like that, I guess."

"Well more power to you," Rick Thorne said. "A football uniform will get you into a girl's panties sometimes, but I say there's more to it than that."

"Same way with my friend Philip," Wilbert Lee said, motioning toward his buddy. "The girls like him too."

"Yeah, but I've seen them paying more attention to you than to him."

"Say, maybe you could get me a date with some of them sometime," Wilbert Lee said.

"Hell," Ike Perlson, a running back, said, "you've got the pick of the litter looks to me like already."

"But I don't have a car," Wilbert Lee said. "Neither does Phil. That makes all the difference."

"Man, we ain't got cars either," Mitch said. "We just have to find the best ways we can, like under the stadium after the games are over or things like that. You ought to stick to the Bear Grass girls and leave ours alone."

"You mean they actually meet you down there?" Wilbert Lee asked. "And do they really put out?"

"Well, not all the time," Mitch said, "unless they're so ugly you have to put a sack over their heads. I mean, the really pretty ones are more teasers, but they can drive you crazy if you know what I mean."

"I understand," Wilbert Lee said, and Phil said, "Me too." Wilbert Lee thought for a moment, then said, "But in the dark, what difference does it make whether they're pretty or not?"

"Yeah, you've got a point," Rick said.

After another round of cigarettes the football players headed for the practice field and the other boys returned to the school rooms and Wilbert Lee and Phil talked about ways to get to Hallsborough and play the girl field.

And that was the philosophy of Wilbert Lee Turner during the earliest years of growing up. And this philosophy was no different than that of many other youths; however, most of them were less outspoken about it. It was a perfectly normal reaction to adolescence when every bodily process was changing; when a young person's sexuality manifest itself in an explosion of hormones that caused them to dominate the minds of most youths.

But it would be erroneous to assume that Wilbert Lee and Phil went around the community showing all the things they felt inside. They acted like all the other youths, often throwing balls to each other and young people who sometimes gathered in the yard at Bear Grass Elementary and played games and sat around chewing the fat. They often talked about things in Bear Grass and discussed their earlier childhood.

"I wonder how Hobby is doing out in Tennessee?" Wilbert Lee asked.

"Me too," Phil said.

"I swear that boy almost drove me crazy," Wilbert Lee said. "Sometimes I felt really sorry for him because of the way I treated him when he was my greatest supporter. But it actually made me feel inferior because I was looked up to by a cripple, rather than the he-man type like you. Hobby just got under my skin and I felt like he was a total drawback for me. I remember when all we kids were playing and Hobby was always looking up to me for everything, I was so ashamed I didn't know what to do. I wanted to choke that little rascal sometimes, and that was wrong Phil, and I knew it even then. And now that he's away I feel even worse about it."

"He was a pitiful little rascal," Phil said, "and I wonder what will become of him in Tennessee? He was the absolute craziest about Bear Grass of anybody I know of here. Hell, a lot of us would love to leave and never return. I mean the young folks. There ain't no way you'd ever get our parents and the other old folks who have lived here through the years to leave. I guarantee you one thing. I sure as hell won't spend the rest of my life in this God-forsaken place with all the hard work that accompanies it. Of course, you and I have escaped most of that because of your mama and my papa. Papa has tried to tell me that I should learn all about the land and that I should prepare to follow in his footsteps and take over the plantation when he's gone. But I don't want that Wilbert Lee."

"I know what you mean," Wilbert Lee replied. "My folks don't have any footsteps for me to follow except that of a sharecropper and I'll be damned if I'll do that."

"I've missed the Finches too," Phil said. "I used to like Tom and Billy Earl. But I got disgusted sometimes with Robyn and Arlene always following us around, and boy, you could tear them out of frame when you upset their playhouses and tripped them and tormented them in every way possible."

"Those girls were pure pests," Wilbert Lee said. It was now October and the Finches had moved away in December of the preceding year. "I wonder how they are liking it down in Jones County though?"

Wilbert Lee remembered the day they had loaded all their things on two big-bodied trucks piled high with furniture and other household furnishings. There was a mental picture of the washpot sitting at the back of one of the trucks, filled with broom sage, and high atop the truck feather beds in striped ticking with brown places where urine had gotten on the ticking. He remembered that as the truck started down the road feathers were coming out of the ticking, merging with a few flakes of snow that were falling and you couldn't tell which was snow and which feathers. He had noticed when they got the cow on a smaller truck they had dug a trench and backed the tires into it so the cow could walk up the incline. They had tied a tow sack around her head and led her up into the body of the truck without any problem. And the night before he had heard them out in the yard catching the chickens and occasionally one would give a squawk as they were being caught. He could even hear the flap of wings when one would fly from its perch in a tree. And after they were gone there were two or three chickens and a lone guinea that had escaped and would be left behind for anybody who moved there.

So went Wilbert Lee's first year at Hallsborough High. But he claimed one very important victory that year. When he told "Miss Liza" as she was called by all the students, to call him W.L. and she had insisted on him announcing his full name, over a period of time those who knew him became tired of pronouncing his full name because of its length. So they began calling him W.L., and even "Miss Liza" was calling him that before the school year ended. Afterward, only those in Bear Grass who had called him Wilbert Lee all his life continued this practice.

Meanwhile, life in Bear Grass went on as usual. It was a never-ending ritual, depending on the season of the year. Now the fields were white with cotton and people were out picking from sunup to sundown, filling the sheets with the fluffy lint. Some whites picked, but more Negroes were in the fields than whites, for they were better pickers than whites and when they hired out to landowners the money they received for their labors was something they looked forward to.

Wilbert Lee and Roscoe Gooch had remained friends even though they saw each other less after Wilbert Lee entered high school. Somehow, they spoke the same language and shared similar interests. When they were together they talked about girls and Wilbert Lee was convinced that Roscoe was really an experienced male among the black population. Wilbert Lee asked Roscoe whether he did it much, and Roscoe said, "Man, what you'se talking 'bout? Ever night and I swear it on a stack of Bibles. You'se white foks don't know nothing. Y'all thinks you got it all, but looks to me lak you missing out on the best things in life."

"You're jiving me, Roscoe," W.L. replied. "I'm not saying you ain't had none, but not this every night stuff."

"Wilbert Lee, from the way you'se talking boy, sounds to me lak you ain't never had none. Now you tell me the truth, so help you God. You ever really had any Wilbert Lee?"

"Well, not really," W.L. said hesitantly.

"You want some black meat Wilbert Lee?" Roscoe asked. "If you do, I'll fix you up any time."

W.L. thought for a moment before answering. There was a puzzled look on his face. "I don't know about that Roscoe. You know how most people feel about that."

"Well, I won't argue with you," Roscoe said, "but all you got to do is look around if you think it ain't happening. My gosh, they's four or five near 'bout white babies out on Greene County road right now. So somebody's messing around wid dem black girls."

"Do you reckon it's the young men doing this?" W.L. asked.

"Naw, it's them old men that don't git satisfied at home," Roscoe said.

"Fix me up," W.L. told Roscoe, and Roscoe told W.L. to be at the backer barn sitting off to itself past Ed Suggs' house that night and just wait there. "But you got to give her something Wilbert Lee, so don't go and just do it and leave. Give her at least a quarter."

So W.L. went home and told his mother he needed a quarter and Abie told him she didn't have a quarter but that there might be enough eggs to take to the store to get a quarter for them.

Thus, W.L.'s mother supplied the money, his black friend, Roscoe, supplied the girl, and in that manner Wilbert Lee was indoctrinated into his sexual exploits.

Wilbert Lee told Philip about this, and Philip followed suit and the three youths formed a close friendship. But even W.L. and Philip were troubled at times about this alliance. They noticed that Roscoe was becoming bolder, enough so that he even brought white girls into their conversations. They had never experienced anything like this before, not even in all their talks with other youths at the store and throughout the community. That's where the line was usually drawn. Hell, everybody knew that white men were accommodated by colored women. There were plenty of high-yellows in the community, some of the women actually beautiful, and strapping men, light-complexioned and arrogant. But it was all between white men and colored women; never the reverse. W.L. and Philip talked with Roscoe about this.

"We know where you're coming from," W.L. said. "And I reckon if we were judged by God almighty, he'd say it was no different which it was, it was all wrong, but that one was as bad as another. But you just don't hear tell of anything like that around here Roscoe. It's one of them unwritten laws I reckon. If you keep such thoughts in your mind, you're liable to get in big trouble, Roscoe."

"I ain't talking about actually doing it," Roscoe said. "I'm just saying it's something I thinks about all the time."

"Hey look, we're friends," Phil said, "but you just get them thoughts out of your mind Roscoe. I shudder to think what would happen if such a thing came about. Not only that. We'd have to stop being friends with you. Everybody would be suspicious of me and W.L. You just play this thing cool Roscoe and don't get yourself into a pack of trouble that you can't get out of."

That ended the conversation but W.L. and Philip left scared and wished they had not taken Roscoe up on his offer.

"He's crazy," W.L. said. "I never heard a nigger talk any such mess before. That boy's going to get hisself killed if he's not careful."

"Yeah, we'd better lay low with Roscoe," Philip said. "I wouldn't put it past one of them mullatos Roscoe was talking about being sired by my own father but I swear this mess Roscoe's talking is as crazy as hell. I tell you what W.L., we'd better stop being so close to Roscoe. People are going to start noticing and if he should do something like messing with a white girl, you and me would be mud and probably get our asses beat besides."

"He wouldn't really do it, would he Phil? W.L. asked. "Now I know we talk a lot of junk with him, but he's not crazy. Roscoe is plain mean if you ask me. And another thing bothers me. You don't see him all that much with the other niggers. A lot of times you see him traveling down the roads alone. There's something sneaky about him. And I don't know how he gets by working no more than he does.

"I reckon he expects his mammy to make enough money in the fields to buy something to eat for them, and she ain't got no more sense than to do it. Sometimes you pass the house and there's old Roscoe, beating on that old guitar with his feet propped on a post, and his mother out in the field chopping or picking cotton or suckering backer. But who in the hell am I talking about being sorry? That's my middle name around Bear Grass."

"Mine too," Phil said.

"Yeah, but you can afford it," W.L. said. "And if it won't for the old lady I'd have my ass in the fields too. I guarn-dam-tee you that the old man wouldn't give me any handouts. That old fogey hates my guts, and I hate his. But Ma's a sucker and I'm willing to admit I've got her twisted around my little finger. Always have had, just by living. And man, I've squeezed her out of every dime I ever could. She's a stupid old lady and I knew that before I was five. Hell, I ain't never loved nobody Phil. I mean nobody. I'm strictly for old W.L., and my buddy Phil, of course.

"And I know that the old lady's measly handouts won't take care of me from now on, for I've got higher ideas than this shitty place. So I've got to figure out a way for me, and I don't know how to do it unless I can get tangled up with some girl whose old man has got a little something or is in a position to help me climb up a little. It's hard to climb out of dirt, Phil."

"Shit Wilbert Lee, you can be somebody if you want to," Phil said.

"That's easy for you to say when you're already somebody," W.L. replied. "Look at these hundreds of acres of land Wilbur Stroud owns and the big store and all that. You've got something to look forward to whether you stay on in Bear Grass or not."

"But the old man tells me that he's just holding on to the plantation," Phil said. "He says he's not even paid the taxes on the land for the past three years and he's afraid they're going to foreclose on him. The only consolation he's got is that the land ain't worth nothing to nobody else either during these days. Nobody's got the money to buy land with. And he talks like some of the people he runs through the year and others that beg for credit sometimes don't pay and that there's not much left from running the store."

"This talk is making me sick," W.L. said. "We ain't settling nothing, not even about Roscoe. I wish I could think up something to do to make a name for myself, like old Lindy for instance. Who else would have thought about flying across the Atlantic ocean without stopping, and landing in France?"

"You wouldn't have had the nerve to do it even if you had had a plane and knew how to fly," Phil said.

"Who says I wouldn't? W.L. asked. "I'd dare almost anything Phil. A person like me who has no conscience would do almost anything. Ma has begged me to go to church and become a Christian and to look at life in a different way. But I don't place no faith in a church, or its pastor, or its members, Phil. I don't believe in nothing. I reckon I'm just a lost cause."

"You said that, I didn't," Phil said. "And I'm bad enough, but you're worse than me W.L. You scare me sometimes."

"That ain't nothing, I scare myself too," W.L. said. "And they say you're born with them traits, but I don't believe it. I believe the old lady did this to me. She made a little god out of me and stood between me and the old man or I wouldn't have been like I am. What ought to have happened is the old man should have beat the shit out of me a few times and put me in my place and I knew that long before I went to school. But I saw that I had it made with the old lady sticking up for me all the time. And that's the reason I'm the mess I am today. But it's too late to care now. All the patterns have already been cast and there ain't no turning back."

"I'm going home," Phil said. "I'm tired of all this talk. It has depressed me." They were approaching W.L.'s house and it was time for supper.

Chapter 21

J iley and Lany Moore had raised five boys to be grown, with the youngest seventeen when their only girl, Minnie Mae, was born. They were shocked when Lany found out she was carrying a baby at the age of forty-six, but they consoled themselves and said maybe God was preparing for their old age by providing someone to care for them when they couldn't look after themselves.

But Minnie Mae was a problem by the time she was five years old. She was head strung and strong-willed and refused to obey. They would whip her and she would cry, but she continued in the same way. They wondered sometimes whether she had all of her buttons up there. She learned well in school and made good grades. She got along well with the neighborhood children and her school mates. But Minnie Mae's thoughts went beyond her years. By the time she was ten she was always dreaming about men. She thought every man was sexy - young, old, middle-aged. She had hidden in the bushes and watched boys strip naked and swim in the creek and she was fascinated by their bodies. And she started having periods at the age of ten.

Her mother never bothered to tell her the facts of life. Nobody bothered. She observed herself bleeding and became frightened. She asked an older classmate and learned what the monthly cycle meant. Then she was proud to bleed and wanted it to be copious.

Minnie Mae roamed all over the neighborhood. She'd walk a mile or more to a plum orchard when the wild fruit was ripe. She'd climb mulberry trees and eat on the purple fruit. She'd roam the back fields and pick maypops and burst them and watch the birds flying, and revel in her little world about her, always dreaming about a man.

By the time she was thirteen, Minnie Mae was slipping into tobacco barns or up in haylofts, or in the woods with men and boys of the community. She liked married men even better, for they were experienced. The entire community knew about Minnie Mae's escapades.

Jiley and Lany were in a constant uproar about Minnie Mae. They knew trouble lay ahead for her and there was nothing they could do to control her. They thought about trying to get her into reformatory school but didn't know the proper procedures to take. They were amazed that she hadn't become pregnant and Jiley actually went to their doctor in Hallsborough and talked with him about it. He was red-faced in talking to Dr. Miller, but he had to confide in somebody and Dr. Miller was the only physician they had had in twenty-five years.

"What am I going to do with Minnie Mae, Doc?" Jiley asked. "She's driving me and Lany crazy."

"What's this all about Jiley?" Dr. Miller asked.

"She's wild, doc. I mean as wild as a rabbit. Won't listen to a word we say and she's carrying on with men like a dog in heat. And I'm ashamed to tell you this, for you know that ain't the kind of life Lany and me's lived. We are respected in Bear Grass, but I know tongues have been wagging day and night about Minnie Mae's carrying-ons."

"Sounds like you do have a problem," Dr. Miller said. "How long has this been going on, Jiley?"

"Oh, a year or more," Jiley replied. "And I don't know why she ain't bigged long before now. I been 'specting her to turn up with a baby for I don't know how long."

"Must be some obstruction in her reproductive organs," Dr. Miller said. "Under such circumstances a girl her age - how old is she now? gets caught immediately after she becomes sexually active. Sometimes her tubes are twisted and that prevents the sperm from entering the tubes. That could be the case with Minnie Mae. If that's the case it is a blessing. But if she ever has to be operated on for appendicitis or anything else they would probably rectify the situation, and she could become pregnant after that."

"That is one question I'm glad you answered, Doc. Something like that would have to be the only reason that girl ain't already bigged."

"Sounds like she is a nymphomaniac," Dr. Miller said.

"What's that?" Jiley asked.

"It's when a woman can't be satisfied, no matter how many men she screws."

"Yep, that's what she's got to be, Doc. Write that word down so I can tell what it is. I know Lany will want to know. I tell you, Doc, nothing in my life ain't never got to me like this. And that girl hain't got no shame."

"Yeah, you've got a problem, Jiley," Dr. Miller said, "and Minnie Mae does too. And I'd never have thought it the day that young'un was born. I remember taking her and slinging her around to get her breathing and telling you and Lany you had a girl at last, and how happy you were. But we never know, Jiley. Whatever has happened though, it wasn't yours or Lany's fault. You know we are all born with our own sexuality and there's nothing we can do about it. Minnie Mae's just a highly-sexed girl and it is just as natural with her as an old maid that never craved a man is natural for her, but I'm not saying all of them didn't crave men. But it spells trouble for Minnie Mae in the long run. She'll get a venereal disease or eventually get pregnant and she could never be satisfied in one man's bed."

"I 'preciate this advice, Doc," Jiley said. "It ain't the answer to the problem, but at least maybe it will help us to understand a little better. And don't say nothing about it to nobody that don't know Doc. Our heads are already drooping, and we feel like we're the trashiest people in the world."

"Don't feel like that Jiley," the doctor said as Jiley was leaving. "Maybe things will get better." But he didn't say it very convincingly.

And it was only a week later that all the mess with Roscoe came up and Jiley couldn't feel the sympathy for Minnie Mae a father should have. He knew too much of the story, and he regretted later that he even mentioned the fact that Roscoe had stripped naked and paraded in front of Minnie Mae. In his heart, he knew it was as much, or more Minnie Mae's fault as Roscoe's. But he felt that he had to do something.

Jiley considered Wilbur Stroud to be a friend. He didn't live on Wilbur's land, but Stroud's General Store ran him through the summer months and he paid up when the cotton and tobacco were sold. And he and Wilbur talked at length sometimes when he went to the store. Of course Wilbur was not always there, for he had other interests besides the store. With his large land holdings, he went into the fields often to see what the sharecroppers were doing, and during harvest season, kept up with cotton-picking and getting the tobacco out of the fields. Wilbur was a busy man.

And whatever Minnie Mae didn't tell about the men she played around with, she made it her business to inform Jiley and Lany that Roscoe had stripped naked in front of her and acted like he wanted to mess around.

"Minnie Mae, you were tempting that nigger, and you know it," Lany said. "I know just as good as anything they was some reason why Roscoe done that. Now you tell me just what happened."

"Nothing Ma," Minnie Mae said. "I was squatting down peeing behind some weeds and I didn't know nothing about Roscoe being anywhere around. If you've got to pee, you've got to pee."

"And he saw you squatting right there in the open daylight with nothing hardly keeping you from being seen all the way to the road."

"Oh Ma, you sound like I do everything wrong," Minnie Mae whined.

"You do," Lany replied. "If anybody on God's green earth does everything wrong it's you. Still, I don't want no nigger tangling up with you. But Lord. If one ever does it will be as much your fault as his."

"Who else have you told?" Jiley asked.

"Nobody yet," Minnie Mae said. "But I'm not going to let no black nigger get away with this. I'll get on the courthouse doorsteps and tell it if I have to."

"God help us," Jiley said. "Now we've got a bigger scandal over our heads than we had before. But you just keep quiet Minnie Mae, and let me see what I can do about it. You hain't got no business spreading the news all over the neighborhood. Anything you said would just make it worse. Let me handle this, you hear?"

"Oh, all right Pa," Minnie Mae said, passing it off as if nothing had happened.

The next day Jiley walked down to Wilbur's store, and Wilbur was there, although he was not behind the counter working. He was busy talking with other farmers for half an hour after Jiley arrived, but he sat there until nobody was waiting to talk with Wilbur.

"Howdy Jiley," Wilbur said as he came up and shook Jiley's hand. "Ain't seen you around in a while."

"No, I've been busy," Jiley said, not bothering to tell Wilbur that he was ashamed to be seen in public these days.

"What can we do for you?" Wilbur asked.

"I need to talk with you Wilbur," Jiley said, "but I'd rather talk on the outside."

"No problem," Wilbur said, and they went out the door and entered the front of the premises.

"I hate to mention it Wilbur," Jiley said and a lump came in Wilbur's throat for he was afraid Jiley was going to say something about him hanging around with Minnie Mae. Lord! what a piece, he thought as he waited for Jiley to speak. Wilbur Stroud felt like a new man since his romps in the hay with that tender teen-ager, although his actions bore heavily on his conscience. Nothing on this earth made an older man feel like a young sapling as much as tangling up with a young thing like Minnie Mae.

"It's about Minnie Mae," Jiley said, and Wilbur felt like a stroke was coming on.

"I'm ashamed to even broach the subject," Jiley said, "and I wouldn't if I didn't feel like I had to. But something's happened that I've got to have advice on, and I thought you might be able to tell me what I ought to do."

"I'll do whatever I can," Wilbur said.

"You know that nigger Roscoe, don't you Wilbur?"

"Yeah, I know him. Sort of uppity if you ask me. That nigger's waiting to get into trouble sooner or later."

"Well, that Roscoe saw Minnie Mae squatting in the weeds to piss yisdiddy, and he stripped off and come out of a backer barn and paraded his nakedness in front of her. What do you think about that, Wilbur?"

"Awful, awful," Wilbur said. "Something's got to be done Jiley. God! that's awful. You mean he stripped down to nothing and had his black pecker out dangling before her?"

"That's what she said," Jiley replied. "God knows she does everything she ought not to do, and I wouldn't put it past her to lie about anything, but I don't know why she would make up anything like this. From what I know about my own young'un, she'd take them black or white, brown or yellow."

"Now Minnie Mae can't be all that bad," Wilbur said. "She's like a whole lot of young folks - you know - hot blooded and raring to go. Of course it's usually boys instead of girls, but they can have the same urges as boys."

"Do you reckon I could git her in a 'formatory school Wilbur?"

"Lord no, don't do that Jiley," Wilbur said, realizing that that would upset his apple-cart completely. "Don't even think about that Jiley. We'll find some way out of this. But that Roscoe's got to be taught a lesson. We can't have nigger men messing with white women in Bear Grass and no other place in these parts. You let me think about this and I'll come up with something, and I'll get in contact with you after I talk it over with other people and we decide what course of action to take."

"All right," Jiley said. "I just had to git it off of my mind and I know we can't allow such things, but in my heart I know that Minnie Mae was partly to blame Wilbur. You just don't know what it's like to be in this position. On one hand, you want to git a shotgun and blow his brains out, and on the other you know that Roscoe is a man like every other man, 'cept he's black. I hate to say it Wilbur, but I wish Minnie Mae had never been born. Still don't know why she was. The old lady hadn't bled in over five years and we never thought about another young'un. But you just don't never know, do you?"

"Nope, we never know," Wilbur said as Jiley started down the road.

"Thank you for listening," Jiley said, and Wilbur walked back in to the store.

Chapter 22

The late September sun bore down on the community, causing mature bolls of cotton to pop open, dotting the fields with white. Corn stalks were brown with pea vines encircling the plants, using them as a solid structure on which to produce their late crop of peas. Morning glories vied with the pea vines for running space to open their blossoms to early-morning dews.

Tobacco fields were stripped of their leaves and suckers were green at the top of the plants. Grass was beginning to turn brown in the middles.

Along Greene County road children played in the yards and along the road; chickens ran over the premises and old hens with naked backs pecked at seeded-out grass, waiting for another old rooster to top them to add to the nakedness of their backs where they clawed them as they sent their sperm into their cloacas.

Dogs lay on doorsteps, scratching themselves and fighting gnats that plagued them and children rolled wheels and made mud pies and walked in old shoes discarded by adults.

Trees were beginning to acquire a yellowish tint and some leaves were already falling. The song of the Junebugs was muted in the waning days of September but birds were still singing in the trees. Blue Jays were shedding and their feathers accumulated in the yards.

Every family on Greene County Road was black, but not every black family in the Bear Grass community lived on Greene County Road. Blacks loved their own neighborhood where white people seldom penetrated and where they could live their lives in their own style. Though their houses were mostly shanties, they were not concerned about aesthetic values where dwellings were concerned. It had never been different with them, nor with most whites, and other factors were more important to them than nice homes and fine furnishings.

They hung clothes on the line en masse, particularly on Saturday when most women took time off to catch up on housekeeping. There was a woman at just about every wash bench rubbing clothes on a wash board with a diaper or some other article of wearing apparel tied around her head. On Saturday afternoon, some of them would go to Hallsborough and stand on the streets with the other Negroes from the area and laugh and talk and drink soda pops (and white lightning if they could get it) and return home to partake in Saturday night festivities in their own community, while others would take down their hair, comb and pomade it and re-plait it, dress and go to Stroud's General Store and congregate with the other black people in the community who didn't make it to Hallsborough. They would buy scoops of vanilla ice cream and lick the cones as black teen-age boys courted the laughing girls and mamas watched their daughters to see what was going on.

But this was a Tuesday afternoon, with several days of field work before another Saturday fest.

Two cars turned right at Stroud's General Store and headed down Greene County Road, driving leisurely as they came around the curve, observing the community. Children watched as they passed, for all the grown-ups were still in the fields or in packhouses grading tobacco for early sales when the markets opened. A few adults saw the cars as they passed and wondered who would be going so slowly along the road.

The cars apparently went on into Greene County, for they returned about an hour later, when the sun was beginning to get an orange hue and people were leaving the fields.

As twilight approached the yards were filled with people. Men were taking the mules to the stables after their swill of water at the troughs. Last year's corn was gone from the cribs and new corn was pulled, shucked and fed to the mules and hogs.

As the sun began to set, smoke from kitchen wood stoves settled above the treetops and appeared as a cirrus cloud in the skies. Fat back or streak-of-lean was frying in pans and the aroma spread over the community. Some people were hollering at others to communicate between houses. There was usually a distance of several hundred feet between dwellings, allowing for barns and shelters, privies and stables on the premises. It was an average night, like thousands spent in the Bear Grass area.

As darkness descended, people flocked to their front porches to seek a cooling breeze. Some lay flat on the porch. Some sat with straight-backed chairs resting on the weatherboarding of the porch. Some sat on doorsteps and children were going in and out of the houses. Kerosene lamps provided dull light inside the shanties.

Fireflies performed their nightly ritual, becoming little specks of light in the night and a far-away thunderhead produced distant flashes of lightning. From the woods came occasional cries from owls and other wildlife and mosquitoes swarmed in droves. Pots with burning rags were set in some yards to ward off the insects and the stench permeated the atmosphere.

Roscoe Gooch sat on his front porch with his old guitar, trying to get it tuned. There were only five strings on the guitar. The first, or "E" string had been broken months before and Roscoe had twisted the metal together since it was broken beyond the keyboard, and by tuning the instrument lower he had been able to play it in a chord suitable to his voice by improvising a capodaster with a lead pencil and a piece of heavy cord. He placed the pencil several frets down the keyboard, tied the string tightly to the pencil and wrapped it securely around the neck of the guitar. He was chording the guitar as if it had six strings.

Roscoe would run his fingers up and down the keyboard, picking out the tune of the blues songs that he either composed or sang bars from popular blues songs of the day. "I got the blues so bad I don't know what to do," Lawd, I got the Blues," ".......... can lead a man around, by de apron strings, oh Lawd".... and such phrases were his specialty. Blossom, his mother, was piddling around in the house.

A teen-age girl from up the road came by. "What you'se doin Roscoe?" she asked teasingly.

"You knows what I'se doin girl," Roscoe teased back. "What you want, girl?"

"Nothin," the girl replied. "Just stopped by. You ain't been around lately Roscoe. I been missin you, boy."

"I reckon I just been busy," Roscoe said.

"Yeah," the girl replied. "And I be messed up, Roscoe."

"What you mean, messed up, girl?"

"I bees knocked up Roscoe,"

"Don't you start no such talk to me," Roscoe said. "I knows you been messin around wid dem other niggers. You can't do no such talk to me, girl."

"It bees your baby, Roscoe."

"You don't know whose baby it is," Roscoe replied. "You just go on down de road girl. You done barked at the wrong dog dis time."

"I'll see you later about this," the girl said as she rose from the porch and started down the road. "And I'se goin to tell Pa it's your baby, Roscoe."

"I don't care who in the hell you tell what," Roscoe said. "I ain't 'bout to marry you girl, wid your swelling belly from some nigger you don't even know who. You can't hand me that kind of jive."

Blossom came out on the porch. "Who you been talkin to, Roscoe?"

"Some little old girl," Roscoe replied, not bothering to tell her what the conversation was about. Blossom retreated into the house with the light from the lamp casting her shadow over the porch as she entered the doorway.

"My mama done tole me........." Roscoe's finger ran down the fret of the "B" or second string and he felt the sting as the metal bit into his finger to give the desired effect, picking out the melody as he patted his bare foot.

He fought at the mosquitoes, still plaguing him despite the burning rag. "Go way, dam skeeters. Pick on somethin yo size.."

Two cars came around the curve, their headlights lighting up the gravel road. They were moving fairly slowly, and Roscoe saw they were stopping as they approached his house. Who could they be? he thought. His porch was only eight or ten feet from the road.

The cars stopped and cut off their headlights and two men jumped hastily from the cars. They were by Roscoe's side before he had time to take any kind of action.

"Are you Roscoe Gooch?" one of the men asked.

"Y--y—es suh."

"Come with us," the man said as both men took Roscoe by an arm.

"Wh-h-h-a-a-t for?" Roscoe asked. His heart was beating rapidly.

""Don't make any outcry," the man who had been silent told Roscoe.

"Wh—a-e- we goin?" Roscoe asked.

They were behind the rear car by now. One of the men took a rope from the boot of the car and tied it around Roscoe's waist.

"The cars are full of people," one of the men said, "and there's not room for another rider, so we'll let you tag along behind the car for a little while. We won't be traveling too far and we'll try to go slow enough so you can keep up."

A quarter moon shone down on the community and provided enough light for Roscoe to see men clad in white inside the automobiles. He was stricken with fear. The "Klu" Klux Klan!

People from other houses had seen the cars stop at Roscoe's place and they listened for anything unusual, but all had been quiet. But they were restless. Something unusual was happening. As soon as the cars left the house, neighbors ran to ask Blossom what had happened, and Blossom said she didn't know anything had happened; that she was inside with a hot comb trying to straighten her hair.

"They come and got Roscoe," Hubbard Bryant said.

"Who got Roscoe?" Blossom asked, her voice becoming hysterical.

"We don't know, but it looks lak them men in white robes and wearing something over dees faces is working on Roscoe."

"Lawd have mercy!" Blossom shrieked in a shrill voice.

"Less follow them," some of the men said. Some said they were going home and lock themselves in and cover the windows with quilts.

"If we's follows we got to stay far enough away they won't git us too," one of the men said. "We ain't got nothing to fight the Klan with."

The cars were moving at a fast enough pace that Roscoe soon became tired. He was breathing deeply and the cars seemed to be picking up speed. He managed to run fast enough to stand on his feet until they turned off the main road into a narrow path that led to the creek. Then the path became filled with roots and debris from the wooded area and his body was dragged by the rope. Roscoe attempted to grasp the rope to lift his body from the ground, but was unable to keep a firm grip. Rocks and limbs and roots nibbled at his flesh, piercing it in places. He would lie on his back for a while until it became sore and then he'd grasp the rope and lie on his stomach. His knees were burning where the skin was rubbed off. His feet were sore with small pieces of wood penetrating the flesh.

"They's goin to kill me, Lord!" Roscoe said softly. "Please God, please save me. I don't want to die Lord. Ain't but seventeen years old. Ain't even had a taste of life. You spare me Lord, and I'll live a different life from now on. I didn't know they was anything like what I'm goin thu right now, Lord. I heard about the Klan, but they was way sommers I didn't know nothing about. I never thought they would be in Bear Grass."

The cars finally reached the banks of the creek and came to a standstill. The lights were left on while the men took a dozen or so kerosene lanterns from the boots of the cars and placed them in a circle on the river bank. The site chosen was where Negroes came sometimes on picnics and where they baptized new converts. It was a place of semi-tropical foliage with tall trees growing near the banks. Their heavy branches overlapped the water and shaded it during daylight hours. Frogs croaked and a few fireflies cast their tiny metallic glow in the night. A sliver of moon gave just enough light to keep the night from being midnight black.

A man untied the rope from around Roscoe's waist and shoved him into the ring. The car lights were cut off, and the lanterns were flickering and casting shadows as he stepped into the ring.

"Your name's Roscoe Gooch, right?" one of the men said.

"Yas—su-h."

"What you think you're up to, nigger boy?"

Roscoe didn't answer.

"Haven't you been messing around white women, nigger boy?"

"Please, Mister, I didn't hurt her."

"You want white pussy, don't you nigger boy?"

"Nah—s—uh."

"Then how come you stripped as naked as a picked bird and walked around in front of that girl with that black pecker of yours dangling? Everybody knows niggers' got ten inch pricks and you just felt your manhood didn't you nigger boy?"

"Nah—s—uh."

"Do you want to mess with any other white women, nigger boy?"

"Nah-s—uh, never no mo." Roscoe's teeth were chattering.

"Haven't you done and wet your britches, nigger boy?"

"I—don't know suh, I so scared." He felt the wetness when it was called to his attention.

"We're here to teach you a lesson tonight, nigger boy," the leader of the group said. "And you can take it for what it's worth, black boy, but this is the only chance you are going to get. There won't be a next time."

Two of the men took lanterns and held them up so Roscoe could see a rope dangling from one of the limbs in a nearby tree.

"See that rope up there, black boy?"

"Yas-s-u-h."

"If we ever come back for you, they'll find you dangling from that rope up there and there won't be anything around to console you but the screech owls and the 'possums and skunks. Your soul will done be gone to hell, nigger boy."

The woods were filled with people hiding under the cover of darkness. They came as close up as they dared to try to determine what was going on, but not close enough to draw attention to them. Not a human sound was heard except for the exchange between the klansman and Roscoe.

"Take him to that tree over there," the leader said, motioning to a tree nearest the circle of light. "Place his hands and arms around the tree and tie them so the nigger boy will be restrained."

Roscoe almost cried out in pain as he was shoved toward the trees.

"We're going to be kind to you, nigger boy," the spokesman said. "Just eight lashes on your bare back with this rawhide whip." He took the shining new whip and held it before Roscoe's eyes. "Plaited cowhide, with a keen, sharp end to tickle your flesh, black boy. Isn't that little enough to do to you for what you did?"

"Yes-s-u-h."

"Now we have an expert with the rope," the klansman said. He motioned to one of the men to step forward. "Yes sir, this gentleman knows all about whips." The man took the handle of the whip in his hand and lashed out in the night, causing a swishing sound as the rope spent its fury in the wind.

"Now give this nigger boy a sample of what a real whip is like."

The man lashed out in the night one more time, then directed the whip toward Roscoe's back.

A scream pierced the night; wild, inhuman, as if it were some beast being tortured in the wild. "O-o-o-U-a-ha-ahh!" Guttural, penetrating, tortuous.

"O-o-o-U-a-ha-ahh!"

Roscoe was vomiting. "Ur-arp-urr!" All the food he had eaten at supper was in a puddle beside the tree, he could feel large whelps rising on his back and the flow of blood as it trickled down his spine and seeped into his pants at his waist.

"O-oo-U-a-ha-ahh!" Roscoe was becoming glassy-eyed. He lay his head against the tree and hot water came up into his mouth. Saliva ran down the sides of his face.

The whip struck for the fourth time, and Roscoe felt himself going under. His knees buckled and mucous was running from his nose, suffocating him and seeping into his mouth. He felt soft feces running from him, sliding down his legs. His breath was coming in gasps and he fought to revive himself. He had to live through it. He was strong, only seventeen, and he had to be able to take punishment and live to tell about it.

Roscoe didn't make an outcry when the whip lashed around his back for the fifth time, although he had lost count of the number of lashes. It had been a lifetime since he felt the first lash. Things were moving at such a slow pace he thought it would never end. The soreness in his back became a living hell and he felt like pitchforks were being pushed into his back. He didn't know whether it was reality or a tortured dream.

The sixth, seventh and eighth lashes came in quick succession. Whish! Whish! Whish! And it was ended. Roscoe made no outcries.

One of the men untied Roscoe's wrists and he sank slowly to the ground in a state of semi-consciousness. He was in a sitting position and he raised his head for a moment, then let it drop.

The men took the lanterns from the circle, lifted the shades and extinguished the fire. There was a kerosene smell as the wet wicks cooled. The cars' headlights were turned on, the men entered the cars swiftly and made their exit from the creek moving slowly over the crude path that led to the gravel road.

As they entered the road, the cars stopped and two men alighted. There was a right-of-way kept up by the state where brush and undergrowth were cut regularly to give a better view of the road. One of the men struck a match and tossed it a foot or two in front of him, and a blaze rose quickly, lighting up the night. A ten-foot cross had been placed there and the shape of the cross could be seen all over the neighborhood as the flames leapt toward the sky. While the cross was still burning brightly, the men got into the car and drove in the direction of Hallsborough. They had a long journey ahead of them down Highway 301, heading for Georgia.

The black people who had been petrified while the Ku Klux Klan whipped Roscoe came to life after the automobiles left the scene. No one had thought to bring a lantern, and they found him in the darkness. They struck matches in order to be able to see him.

"You'se awright Roscoe?" one of the men asked.

"That boy's 'bout dead," another said. "We got to do something to git Roscoe out of here."

"His back's in a mess," another said. "Looks lak a piece of raw beef."

"Speak to me Roscoe," another said. "Can you talk Roscoe?"

Roscoe answered in a voice almost too weak to be heard. "I be awright."

"You bees 'bout dead if you ask me," another man said.

By then somebody had accompanied Blossom, Roscoe's mother, to the river and they were carrying a lantern.

"Lawd Chile, what dey done to my boy?" Blossom said as she knelt and put Roscoe's head on her shoulder. "Let me see his back." Her companion held the lantern so Blossom could see the condition of Roscoe's back. She screamed and fainted.

Lem Stewart spoke to the group gathered around. "We got to git Roscoe out of here as quick as we can. But we can't tote him cause we hain't got nothing to tote him in. Somebody's got to go git a backer truck and hitch a mule to it and bring it here. We can place Roscoe on the truck on his stomach and git him out. But somebody's got to go git the truck right quick."

"Who's got a mule and truck we can borrow?" Big Boy Speight asked.

Blossom had come to by then and she spoke up. "Mr. John Henry that lives next to me's got a mule and backer truck. He'll lend it to us, but whoever goes to ask him better holler out 'fo they steps up on the porch else they might find a shotgun in they faces. Mr. John Henry's a good man but he's scared to death of them white robes and doe faces. And if he lets you use one of the mules, git old Jim cause he's gentle and easy. That old Jimbo is mean as hell."

"Is they anything we can doos to ease you off Roscoe?" one of the men asked.

"Ain't nothin nobody can do," Roscoe replied weakly. "Just git me home so Ma can melt a pound of lard and soak it in rags and lay it on my poor back. Seems lak dat might help."

"Lawd" I hain't even got no lard," Blossom replied. "Nothin but fried meat grease. That would burn my boy's back wusser than it's burning. Maybe somebody's got a pound of lard though."

"Sons 'a bitches," one of the group said.

"Careful there brother," another man replied. "Whites might be listenin'," he said almost in a whisper.

"Lawd, please help me," Roscoe pleaded.

There were night cries from the woods. Frogs croaked and the night became black after the moon set. But the skies were filled with a million stars and the Milky Way and the Big Dipper stood out in the heavens.

Crickets chirped around the group and mosquitoes still hummed around their ears.

"What time it be?" a teen-ager asked.

"Don't knows what time it be," was the reply. "Ain't nobody got no watch. But it's way past midnight. And a hard day in the fields. We'll be dragging in them fields this day."

After an hour or more lantern light could be seen far down the path and soon the squealing of the tobacco truck wheels rubbing against axles that needed greasing could be heard. When the truck arrived, two of the men assisted Roscoe and got him on his feet, but the youth was unable to stand and walk on his own. They brought the truck by his side and twisted him so he was able to sit on the side. A quilt had been placed on the truck and the men helped Roscoe lie down on his stomach. They noted blood trickling down his sides and puddling on the quilts.

A group of men walked beside the truck and kept Roscoe from falling off. It was a slow process getting down the path that led from the creek.

When they finally reached Greene County Road all signs of the cross that had burned were gone. But there was the odor of burned wood.

As they headed for home, the first signs of dawn were appearing. In the East, there was a hint of light. The stars were becoming dim in the heavens. The first roosters crowed to signal a new day. A few birds were singing in the trees. Lights were appearing in windows.

Roscoe was removed from the tobacco truck and taken into the house where he cried openly and Blossom was becoming hysterical. Other women came to help and to console Blossom, while Roscoe sank into a troubled sleep.

Chapter 23

EIGHT ELECTROCUTED AT CENTRAL PRISON was the banner headline in the Argus. It was an Associated Press story with a Raleigh dateline.

One white, and eight Negro men were electrocuted at Central Prison early today. Starting soon after midnight, each man was taken to the Electric Chair and strapped at the arms and waist. Each was asked whether he had a last statement to make.

Gus Best said he didn't rape the little girl he had been convicted of raping and then strangling to death. "I'se done made my peace with God and I ask forgiveness for the trouble I'se caused."

As the current coursed through his body, Gus Best's arms flexed and he appeared to be trying to break the straps that bound him. His head jerked forward and his tongue protruded from his mouth with saliva running down his face. Then he slumped in the chair and there was a wail, "Lord have mercy" from a woman in the audience.

Abram Hill was a massive man, weighing more than 250 pounds. His body filled the Electric Chair. He was led in with his eyes closed, wearing prison garb and white socks. When asked whether he had a statement to make, Hill shook his head and chose to remain silent. He had been convicted of killing his landlord, a white man, in Yancey County.

Hill's eyes stared and appeared to be popping out of his head as the current claimed his life. His muscles contorted and he appeared to be in convulsions before losing consciousness. No one was there from his family or the white family to witness his execution.

Woody Spell was a thin, light-skinned Negro in his late twenties. His hair was almost straight with deep waves that glistened in the diffused light in the chamber. He had been convicted in the arson deaths of two elderly people after robbing them and setting their frame house afire.

Spell was crying as he entered the death chamber. "I've done made my peace with God," he said between sobs. "I don't want to die. I had everything to live for. I don't knows why I done it. God's forgiven me. I asks all the rest of you to forgive me. I asks all young folks to learn a lesson from my life. I knows now that money don't mean a thing. I got a good mama that taught me better than I've lived. I ask God to have mercy on her."

Spell's head jerked backward the instant the switch was pulled and his eyes rolled and his eyelids twitched as his life ebbed away. He vomited and it ran from his mouth and puddled on the floor back of him.

"Scoop" Jenkins had been convicted of murdering two other Negroes in a brawl at his house a year earlier. He had taken a sharp ax and split the head of one of the victims in two, and slashed through the stomach of the other, leaving his intestines hanging on the outside of his body with feces running from the entrails and puddling on the floor.

Jenkins showed no remorse as he was strapped into the Electric Chair. He appeared nonchalant and paid little attention to those witnessing the executions.

As the electricity flooded his body, a heavy sweat broke out on his face and he heaved and appeared to be choking. His hands opened and closed and for a moment fire from the electrodes flickered around his face.

One person viewing the execution was heard saying, "God, he's burning to death."

"Poor Boy" Toms had been convicted on circumstantial evidence of taking a monkey wrench and beating a white man, Joe Letchworth, to death in a tobacco field. Letchworth's body had been found between two rows of tobacco with the wrench lying nearby and Toms had been seen in the area of the field the afternoon of his death. Toms had maintained throughout his trial that he had been cat-fishing down at the creek and was only on his way home when he was seen walking along the path near the tobacco field.

"Sometimes we pays for things we didn't do," Toms said when asked whether he had a statement. "Ain't no way to ever be sure that what you do might not be taken in the wrong way. Seems like some people is made to be at the wrong place at the wrong time. I swears befo' God I didn't kill that man, or no other man."

Toms died quietly with fewer convulsive movements than any of the others put to death.

"Nubbin" Rountree was so named because of his right hand with only the thumb left intact. His fingers had been severed at a saw mill when he was a teen-ager. He also had a glass eye that didn't focus and a long scar from his cheek bone to his throat.

Rountree walked slowly and had to be nudged by the guards who accompanied him on his last walk. He had been convicted of killing Eli Porter, his partner in a liquor still, in the woods of Greene County. Porter's body had been found burning over a wood fire that had been set near the still.

Under the eerie lights of the prison, Rountree spent his last moments in convulsive twists and body contortions with phlegm rising up in his throat and running from his mouth reminiscent of a dog having a running fit. Some family members wept as his life ebbed away.

Lee Aswell was the last man executed. He was white. Aswell had been convicted of killing his pregnant wife in cold blood. His trial had caused a sensation in Lenoir County. He had been a respected man in the community and "Miss Pearl" his wife, held the respect of all the people. There had been a number of witnesses attesting to the good character of Lee Aswell, but there had also been damaging testimony from a woman on "Sugar Hill" that told of Aswell's escapades with her and other women she named in her testimony. And at the autopsy, sperm had been found on Aswell's clothing, which medical authorities sought to discredit, saying that semen was often discharged when a man was dying.

Aswell walked calmly to the Electric Chair and appeared unconcerned as he was strapped to the chair. He was leaving behind five children, ages fifteen to three, as wards of the state. He made no outcries as the electrical surge entered his body, only showing the convulsive movements of his muscles as testimony to the power surge that claimed his life.

After the executions, those who had viewed them walked silently from the death chamber as the first signs of dawn appeared over the city. Everything was quiet around Central Prison and roosters were heard crowing in the Raleigh suburbs.

In the same edition of the Argus was a brief story about a young Negro being brutally beaten up by members of the Ku Klux Klan in the Bear Grass community. The story read:

Roscoe Gooch, seventeen, a young Negro from the Bear Grass community, was brutally beaten by members of the Ku Klux Klan last night. This is a first as far as Klan activity goes, in this area, and the men participating are believed to be from the Knights of the Ku Klux Klan from Georgia.

Gooch had been accused of parading naked before a young white girl from the same community.

Details of the incident are not known at this time.

That afternoon Abie Turner went to Stroud's store to get a spool of thread. Miss Callie was tending store while the regular clerk was eating dinner.

"Shore was a mess around here last night," Abie allowed as Miss Callie searched for the thread.

"Scares me," Miss Callie said, shaking her head. "We've never had anything like this in this neighborhood before. But we'll be criticized everywhere after what the Klan did I reckon."

"It really put Bear Grass on the map," Abie laughed, wiping her mouth, "but I'd rather we stayed hid than to have such a thing happen around here."

"It was uncalled-for," Miss Callie said. "Everybody knows there's not a thing to that Minnie Mae Moore. She hikes her tail up to every man that passes, and I don't believe in no nigger-white mixing, but that girl could tempt a nigger as good as she could a white man. And I got to admit that that Roscoe is a biggety nigger. But they won't no need of the Ku Klux Klan coming into our neighborhood and destroying the peace in the community. That mess with Minnie Mae would have blowed over in no time, and she'll be getting out of here in a little while anyway. Why I've not seen a black person around the store all day, Abie."

"They're scared half to death," Abie said. "I know I'd be if I was one of them."

"And to make matters worse, they came out with that story about all them people being electrocuted, and seven of the eight niggers."

"Yeah, and why in the name of God do they have to tell about all the gory details when they're in the Electric Chair, Miss Callie?"

"I reckon the people that write the stories think it'll scare them and make them stop killing and raping and all that mess."

"But niggers don't read, Miss Callie."

"Other folks tell them about it," Miss Callie replied. "Still, they're going to keep on killing. Seems like it's born in some of them and there ain't no stopping 'em."

"Do you reckon somebody around here notified the Klan?" Abie asked.

"You know somebody had to or they wouldn't have known about what Roscoe did," Miss Callie said. "I'm keeping my eyes and ears open Abie, and if I find out who did this I'll deal with them." Miss Callie exerted a lot of influence in the community.

"You're going to be called a nigger-lover if you ain't careful," Abie said.

"I like a Negro in his place," Miss Callie replied, "but I don't like to see injustice done to anybody, and this was a case of injustice if I ever saw one."

"Well, I hope you find out," Abie said as she left the store.

Rumors were spreading as to who might have tipped off the Klan. Several men's names were mentioned. Some blacks who were close up enough in the woods to see what was going on while Roscoe was being beaten had said they saw a pair of shoes mighty familiar to them, but they wouldn't call names, and what they said was only to other blacks, and their lips were sealed. Still, some blacks said enough that the white people of the community became suspicious.

Chapter 24

S aints Delight Church was crowded with people and the heat was oppressive. They were fanning with fans donated by a funeral home, and some used folded newspapers. Women mopped their faces with their sponges and declared they were 'mite near' sweating to death.

The small windows of the church were open, but there was no wind. Leaves on the oak trees that surrounded the yard were still and the temperature was well in the 90s.

Crowds milled on the outside of the church also. It was evident that something was on the minds of the people other than the usual Sunday sermon and the singing and shouting and praying that went on well into the afternoon.

The choir sang "Jesus Save Me" and "I Shall Not Be Moved" and sister Annie B. Speight led the congregation in prayer. Then the Rev. "Skint" Bowden took the podium.

"Brothers and sisters we are gathered here today with more trouble heaped on our people."

"Lord, how can we take it much longer?"

"One of our brothers has been hurt bad by the Ku Klux Klan and we are asking you for our deliverance this day, mighty Father."

"Lord, help us now if you're ever goin' to do anything."

"They done beat up our brother and made his back bloody and drug him behind a mobile that mangled up his poor body."

"Like a piece of beef I cooked yisdiddy."

"They done told our brother to mend his ways or face a rope around his neck if they have to git him agin!"

"Kill 'em, Lord, for what they done."

"They've got us shuddering in our boots, almighty God. They've struck fear in our hearts."

"We can't even stick ours heads out the do' no mo'."

"We been gitting along good wid the white folks, Lord, till all this come about because of Roscoe."

"They's as much to blame as Roscoe, Lord."

"Now Roscoe is a little different from most of us black folks. We mostly stay in our places and if we see things that ain't right, just play shut-mouth and go on singing and smilin' and acting lak nothing ain't wrong. And I don't know if it's because Roscoe's got more gumption than most of us or if it's plain meanness. But Roscoe is different."

"Ain't no wusser than the whites."

"All of us knows what Roscoe done. And it won't right. Wouldn't have been right if it was a black girl. But a white girl saw what he done, and that meant hell was to pay."

"Ain't no wusser than the whites."

"Roscoe shouldn't ought to of done what he done, and I don't rightly know why stripping necked and strutting out in front of a girl give him some kind of pleasure. But it takes all kinds."

"Roscoe was tempted, Lord."

"And we knowed about them hooded men all along, but ain't never been nothing lak dat in this community befo'."

"Saying white soda crackers to them don't mean a thing, Lord. We call dem white soda crackers and dey jus laff, cause it gives 'em a chance to call us niggers."

"Lord God Almighty, please look down on us po black foks. We done carried a big burden, Lord, and something like this gits our poor spirits so low down makes us feel lak snakes crawlin' on the ground."

"Lord Jesus, have mercy."

"What the white man doos is one thing, but what the black man doos is another."

"Lawd, don't you know it."

"The white man tempted our black women, Lord, and we got a race all mixed up with dem high-yaller skins that the white man won't accept and the black man may envy, but he knows the white man done been there."

"They was tempted, Lord."

"The white man got a little change dangling in his britches and the poor black woman ain't got nothing, and she hear that change dangling around and she needs that change, Lord. That old white man take the black woman somewhere in the bushes and gits to messing around and first thing you know he's done put his white seed in her. Maybe for a box of snuff. Lord, you know dem black women love that snuff, and the white women do too."

"Lord, I knows temptation, for I was tempted too."

"But it ain't that way with the black man. Uh, uh, he can't do nothing like that. He ain't even supposed to think about the white woman."

"Lord, why would they want to mess with a white man wid all that sickly white skin?"

"We are scared, Lord. We don't want to feel lak we can't even move about freely and that every move we make somebody's looking over our shoulders. We wants to be good people and git along good with everybody. But we ain't never had no crosses burned in this community befo and no visit from them men wid the white robes on and the hoods over dees faces."

"Lord, it makes us want to run. And you give us swift feet, Lord. Help us sweet Jesus."

"We got to find a way to keep peace in the community. We got to tell every black person to mind his business and walk the straight-and-narrow. We got to tell all the black men to stay away from white women and stick to dey own kind. Else we'll be running on them swift feet, and You know we ain't too good to run, Lord."

"Lord, if dem white women would look after dey men wouldn't be all this messing around lak dey is. It's nature to the black woman. But dem white women is cold, lak a piece of ice."

"One thing about it. The black race got rhythm, we give our women what dey want and we got passions the white man don't know nothing about. In that respect we are blessed. We just got to keep all that between blacks."

"Our black chillun plays wid the white chillun and dey git along pretty good. But dey's a difference. When dey gits through playing the white chillun goes dey way and the black chillun goes theirs. All 'cept one. Dat little crippled white boy they call Hobby loves to visit the black chillun just as good as he does the white. I seen him stay right on at the house and when dinner time come he is asked to eat with the blacks and he just sits down and acts lak dey ain't no difference. He looks pure funny wid his honey-colored hair and dem blue eyes, lak a albino or something. But all he do is smile and laugh and talk and enjoy eating at the black houses and dat is one boy dat don't see no color.

"If all our folks was lak dat, it would be a better world. I mean black and white. We'se got our faults too, youall. And too, we feels sorry for the little white boy, but I don't knows why. He don't feel sorry for hisself. Seems lak dey is something special 'bout that child that I can't put a finger on.

"But he's done left us too. Gone on out to Tennessee and he might could of done us a lot of good in the bye and bye when he gits older. We got some good white folks but none of dem don't act lak that little Hobby.

"We got good black folks too, and the whites recognize them. They calls them "uncle" and "aunt" And they's always the old folks that done made they mark on the community. But dey don't call dem "Mr. and Mrs." Who ever heard of a white person putting such a handle on a black person in these parts?

"Us black folks, we's humble lak our ancestors. We's men going to pull off them hats when we goes inside a building where dey's white folks. That's a sign of reverence and in our hearts we don't want to do it, but we knows it's expected of us. We got a problem, brothers and sisters. We just got to struggle along till a day when maybe won't be all this hassle 'tween black and whites.

"Yes sir, we going to miss that little Hobby. He was a fine white boy and he thinks everybody is God's chillun. Ain't many Hobbys black or white. Most of us got prejudices and biases inside us and I reckon it's lak Abraham and his descendants. Don't look lak it will ever be settled. God made all of us and I don't know why we can't all live together in peace and love one another without thinking 'bout the color of his skin or the things the different races doos that's different from what they is used to.

"Now less all of us pray for our brother, Roscoe. I went by to have prayer with Roscoe, and that po boy is scared to death. Didn't act right. Had to lie on his belly cause his back is beat to a pulp. Roscoe was fidgety with his head sort of jerking and his eyes gitting a wild look in 'em sometimes. I said, 'Roscoe, what you going to do? 'and he shook his head and said won't nothing he could do, and Roscoe said for us to pray for him, cause nobody but God could help him."

"Hallelujah!"

"Less pray for Roscoe and all us downtrodden black folks. Less make our cry heard in heaven this day."

Prayers rang out in the church. There was hollering and crying and singing and testimonies and people were milling about on the church grounds.

Ham Bone Artis was half-drunk already, and he pulled a pint bottle from his hip pocket, pulled out the cork stopper and held it toward his open lips. Some of the stump-hole whisky spilled on his shirt and he laughed, trying to steady his hand. Ham Bone was a friend of Roscoe's. And a dozen or more young men were gathered around Ham Bone.

"Ro—s-coe wan— wan—wan—ted that white pussy," Ham Bone said. "And she wanted him too."

"Shut yo mouth nigger," one of the men said. "Don't you knows some white man passing along the road might hear you and you'd be in the same fix as Roscoe?"

Ham Bone's eyes were glassy looking, but he still wanted to talk. "I—'ll whis—per then," he said. Then his voice was barely audible. "R—r-r-oscoe said that white girl what's 'er name? Minnie Mae? was squatting pissing in a bun-n-n-n-ch of we-e-e-ds when h—e slip-p-ed off his br—r-r-it-ches and ste-p-ped out of t-t-t-he backer barn an she saw him and just squ-a-tted dere and let 'em see h-i-s eyes full and giving him the come-on with her finger, wid dat pat—ch of black hair just a shining and that split r-r-r-e-d and juicy look—in-g. Roscoe went cr-r-r-azy."

"Ham bone, you'se drunk as a hoot owl," Roosevelt Best said. "You better go home and git some sleep boy. And you better not tell this mess to nobody else."

"White folks wouldn't believe it nohow," Hoot Amos said. "They ain't going to listen to no nigger telling white folks that a white girl wanted no black dick stove up in 'er. Them men in the white robes would be back here 'fore you could turn around. But according to what Roscoe said, he could have had it that day if he had tried. But he said he got so skeered he couldn't git it up and finally the white girl pulled up her drawers and sashayed on up the road."

"Lawd, Lawd! Ain't it a mess?" Noah Smith said. "I tell you, men willing to risk they lives just for a little old piece. What wrong wid men, anyhow? Dey is crazy. But I just lak dem. It just something that gits in the mind, travels down the spine, settles in the balls and make a man go crazy."

"Nothin else don't satisfy him," Shorty Spell said. "Hit just as natural as breathin'."

Ham Bone had quietly passed out and the men took him to the edge of the church yard and lay him under the shade of a tree. Inside, the worshippers became quieter and the movement on the grounds increased. People were getting hungry.

At about 2 o'clock the wire table that stretched between two large oak trees was spread with the food the women had prepared and everyone gathered around and waited for a glass of lemonade dipped from a wooden wash tub and plates of food.

Some of the women said they couldn't eat at such a time of trouble. Didn't have no appetite and didn't see how nobody could stuff a gut when so much trouble was around. But most of the people had their hands full of food - chicken thighs and biscuits and cucumber pickles and boiled potatoes and cake and pie.

A black cloud was forming during the time the group was eating. The heat had been oppressive and the humidity had been high. There was everything essential to creating a severe storm with heavy thunder and sharp lightning, high winds and hail.

The crowd had begun to disperse with many going home before the storm struck. The lightning flashed and struck a tree in the church yard. Thunder was deafening and the wind had the trees in the church yard bent. Rain fell in sheets and those caught in the storm took refuge inside the church.

Water filled the side ditches along the road and overflowed fields and people hurried home to get shovels and cut trenches in the fields to let the water drain off. It seemed to be a bad omen to a troubled people.

Chapter 25

Rev. Otto Pell entered Vicey's room quietly, not knowing whether she was asleep. If so, he didn't want to disturb her. But she was awake and he came up to her bed and took her thin hand into his. "How are you feeling this morning?" he asked.

"About the same," Vicey said in a weak voice. "I slept some and that helps. And Mama brought me some coffee and an egg and I managed to get it down and a biscuit too."

"Good," Otto said. "I'm praying for you every day, Vicey."

"I appreciate that so much," Vicey said as she looked into his eyes. It was evident that she adored him.

"I hadn't mentioned it to you, for I didn't want to worry you," Otto said. "But I've got to go off for a couple of days to a business meeting. I'll be leaving Wednesday morning." It was now Monday. He felt a choking sensation after uttering the lie.

"Where to?" Vicey asked with concern.

"Winston-Salem."

"That's a long ways," Vicey said.

"Not so far" Otto replied.

"Something concerning the church?" Vicey asked.

"Not really," Otto said. "There's an insurance meeting up there and I wanted to confer with the company that handles my insurance. And you know how important insurance is, Vicey, especially since you are poorly so much."

"I sure do," Vicey said. "When a man has a wife that is in my condition he knows anything can happen and he's got to do the best he can to have everything in order if something should happen. How much insurance do you have on me Otto?"

"Five hundred dollars," Otto said. "That's enough to provide a nice funeral, although I don't want you to feel like I'm thinking about you dying or anything like that. I hope you'll live fifty more years."

"I know," Vicey replied. "And how much insurance do you have on yourself?"

"Five hundred dollars, just like you."

"And how many days will you be gone?"

"I'll be back Friday so I can be at Quarterly Meeting on Saturday."

"I sure wish I could go to Quarterly Meeting," Vicey said. "But I try not to think a lot about things like that anymore. I reckon I'm on my death bed, Otto."

"Oh, don't talk like that."

"I'll miss you," Vicey said.

"I'll miss you too, Pet."

"Going by train or bus?"

"Greyhound."

"Well, I'll be there with you in my thoughts," Vicey said. This bothered Otto. He bent and kissed her lightly on the forehead.

Otto flagged Seashore in front of the house, carrying his one suitcase. He rode Seashore to Hallsborough where he connected with Greyhound for the trip to Winston-Salem. He was fidgety.

Otto and Maybell Aswell had corresponded since he held the revival in her community. She addressed her letters to him on a typewriter with no return address, and Otto was the only person who opened Whispering Pines Church mail.

Maybell had boarded Greyhound in Lenoir County and Otto spotted her the moment he boarded the bus, looking around to see whether there was anyone else he knew. She was looking good, dressed in a royal blue dress and a string of pearls. Her long hair was in a becoming bun with the sides puffed out and bejeweled combs in her hair. His heart skipped a beat.

"How have you been?" he asked as he reached overhead to place his luggage on the rack. The seat beside Maybell was empty.

"Fine," she replied. "How about you?"

"Everything's been okay I guess," he said. "There has been the usual problem with Vicey, like any family with a sick member experiences. A little disharmony at the church, which I'm sure you know happens everywhere. It seems that that is the case at all churches from what I hear. And no matter what the denomination either."

"Is your wife any better?" Maybell asked.

"No, Vicey's no better, and unless a miracle from God occurs, she never will be. And somehow I feel like Vicey has willed herself to be this way. The doctors never have found out what's wrong with her. I believe if Vicey had had a stronger will she would be up and around now. But it seems like that losing all those babies just did her in. The doctors said mine and her blood didn't match and that poisoned the babies. But that wasn't any consolation for Vicey."

"Such a shame," Maybell said as she took Otto's hand in her own.

They rode in silence for a while, watching the countryside as the bus made its way westward. Both had feelings of guilt they were unwilling to express to each other, made stronger by a force greater than guilt that somehow lessened the feeling.

"Do you have reservations for us?" Maybell asked.

"Yes," he replied.

"Separate rooms?"

"No, we'll be registered as Rev. and Mrs. Otto Pell."

"Won't you be taking a big chance Otto? Suppose the people in Bear Grass were to find out."

"It's something I'll have to risk," Otto replied. "To tell you the truth Maybell, I didn't have the money to pay for two rooms."

"Oh, it's all right Otto," she said with a smile. "I've looked at it from every angle and I know we stand to be ruined for what we're doing, but I love you enough to take that chance."

"God forgive me," Otto said. "He doesn't approve of what we're doing and I don't ask that he approve; just that he understand. Is that a silly way to put it?"

"It's the best you can do, or me for that matter," Maybell said. "If any holier-than-thou could only understand my feelings they wouldn't be so ready to criticize. And I know all people are individuals with different views and tastes, and that there are untold thousands of women who couldn't care less about the maleness of a man. They don't know the deep emotions that lie within women like me."

"And I don't know whether the way I feel is the worst thing in the world for a woman without a husband, or one of the greatest pleasures any woman can have to want a man as much as I want you. But it's so tied up in religion and God's word it's as controversial as anything can be. I think about my son and how he would feel if he knew I was playing the harlot when he doesn't appear to be interested in women at all. How can people be so different Otto?"

"It goes right back to what we were born with," he replied. "Some people have sluggish sexual drives and I've heard men say once a month was enough for them. My God, once a day is too little for me. So you can imagine my frustration with a sickly wife. I'm about ready to blow up like a balloon. But I know one thing: It's one of the greatest temptations of the human race and the one thing that gets men and women into more trouble than anything else.

"It seems like those who were given high sex drives are the devil's playthings. He'll tempt them with lust and make them feel they're doing nothing wrong until he gets them just like he wants them - like he's got us now - but I swear that I can't help it Maybell."

"I think we'd better change the subject," Maybell said, "or we'll feel too guilty to enjoy our tryst later on."

They were within a few miles of their destination. Otto took Maybell's hand and smiled at her. "You're as pretty as a doll." he said.

"You're just teasing Otto."

"No, seriously, I think you're a fine-looking woman and about as sexy as they come. I'll bet your husband was the happiest man in the world."

"Not really," she said. "He wasn't like me at all, and he thought I was pretty brazen. He always accused me of having a wild streak in me."

"Have you?" Otto asked. He wondered whether other passengers had taken note of their conversation, although they had been talking in semi-whispers.

The bus rolled into the station and Otto hailed a taxi to the hotel. He was getting more and more nervous. Few people from Hallsborough or other points east came to Winston-Salem. Still, there was always the possibility someone they knew could be there. He found it almost impossible to register them as Mr. and Mrs. Maybell stood by his side, unperturbed by what was going on. The bell hop took their key and luggage and took them to the fifth floor. Otto gazed up and down the halls to see whether he might spot anyone he knew. He tipped the bell hop a quarter and locked the door. Then he took Maybell into his arms and they kissed hungrily.

"Otto," Maybell asked, "is this just a roll in the hay or is it something deeper? Is this all it is?"

"No," he replied. "I'm crazy about you Maybell. I've had you on my mind almost constantly since the revival. The devil has worked on me stronger than he's ever done in my life, and he has won, for I really don't feel all that guilty even if I know it is all wrong. It's not the first wrong thing that's ever been done."

"I'm glad you said that," Maybell replied. "I want you just as much as you do me, but there's more to life than just 'that'."

"But despite our feelings," Otto said, "that doesn't change the fact that I've got a sick wife back home."

"I know," she said, "but we just can't dwell on that now Otto. We'll have to deal with that later on." She kissed him again and ran a finger into his shirt and felt the mass of hair on his chest.

"It's driving me crazy," Otto said. "Let's pull off our clothes and lie down for a while."

"My, you're all fired up," Maybell said. "Are we going to stay in bed all the time we're here? I think we ought to go down in the lobby and sit for a while and then walk around. It's a beautiful section of the city."

"It's just that I'm afraid to be so bold," Otto said. "Somebody could see us that knows who we are and the news could get back home before we do. We have to be very careful, Maybell."

"I know that," she replied. "But you know women don't see things in the same way as men. Their thoughts are dictated by their hearts, and my every thought is consumed with you."

"It's hot in here," Otto said as he began unbuttoning his shirt. "I'll call down and have some ice sent up." He stood before her stripped to his waist and she ran her hands over his chest and felt his hard muscles. "You look like a man that exercises a lot," she said.

"Not as much as I should," he replied. "Don't you want to get comfortable too, Maybell? Why don't you take off your dress and we'll relax on the bed."

"I want to get naked," she said, "and I want you to also. We didn't come here for a church conference. We're here to fornicate, Otto." She undid his belt, unbuttoned his pants and pulled them down. She placed her hand on his crotch where the swelling was already evident. "This is what I want," she said as she undid his shorts and they fell to the floor, leaving him stark naked. She hastily got her slip off and rid herself of her panties. Then they fell on the bed and embraced.

"I'm a hussy in bed," she confided. "Can I do anything I want to with you Otto?"

"You couldn't do anything that wouldn't please me," he replied. She placed her hand on his penis, amazed at its size, and felt it throb with his heartbeat. She raised his leg and placed her hand on his huge testicles and felt the wad of hair surrounding his pubic region. Otto felt like he was going to ejaculate even before they began making love.

Maybell raised up and placed her face on his stomach, rubbing his penis with the end of her finger. The man smell drove her wild and she opened her mouth and took the glans inside, tickling it with her tongue. Otto shivered and moved his hips. "I can't stand it Maybell," he moaned. "Just lie still for a moment until I cool down a bit." Both his hands were cupping her voluptuous breasts. He reached up and took a nipple into his mouth and created a suction that drew it deeper inside.

"Are you sure you want to do that?" Otto asked. "I've never had anything like that before. Isn't that getting a little on the perverse side?"

"It is if it offends the other partner," Maybell said. "Does it offend you Otto?"

"No, no, no," Otto said as visions of Sodom and Gomorrah entered his mind. He could also better understand how temptations of the flesh could cause a people to bow to such practices.

"Do you love me?" Maybell asked as she held him closely in her arms. She felt his perspiration wetting her body.

"Oh my darling," he cried, "you know I love you. Why else would I be here? After all, I'm a minister of God, but somehow he feels far, far away right now and I can even accept that."

"Did you bring any protection?" Maybell asked.

"I didn't give it a thought," Otto said. He didn't tell her he had never purchased anything for protection in his life.

"It doesn't matter," she said. "We'll just run the risk."

Suddenly he was inside her, and almost as suddenly there was an explosion within himself and he could feel Maybell's orgasm as they lay completely immersed in each other.

Otto groaned with his breath coming in gasps and Maybell was showering kisses on him, running her tongue deep into his mouth. She was insatiable in her desire.

The moment of passion finally passed and they lay side by side, completely apart now and reflecting on the aftermath of their indiscretion.

"Why does it have to be this way?" Otto asked. "Why couldn't it be like this in a normal relationship? Why do I have to feel that I've committed an unpardonable sin just because I'm a man with a normal man's desires?"

"You know Otto, I feel totally reponsible for what has happened. I've cheapened myself before you and God. I'm no less than a whore and I've been a respectable woman all my life."

"Please don't feel that way," Otto replied. "I'm a lot more at fault than you. It was in my mind long before I met you. I knew that sooner or later it would happen. I just didn't know with whom. If I know my own heart I love God and I have a desire to do His will. But where sexuality is concerned I just haven't been able to keep that under control. I don't think a man should always be at odds with himself because he's given all the ingredients that the world respects in man.

"We are supposed to be strong and truthful and to uplift mankind. We're supposed to marry and beget children, and that involves sex. And it's true the Bible says marriage is for better or for worse which I presume means that if a man marries a woman that isn't able to have sex with him on a regular basis he is supposed to acquiesce and accept a non-sex role and not dwell on those aspects of his manhood.

"But it is those aspects that make a man a man in the first place. If he has none of those traits, then he's less than a man. Look at everything in nature. The male is the hunter, the conqueror, the one that ensures the procreation of all forms of life. The biblical account of sexuality goes against all the male instincts."

"The same could be said for women," Maybell said. "Of course there are millions of women who have such a low sex drive they consider it a duty rather than a pleasure. You know how they are. The old man has got to be taken care of every once in a while. They're supposed to open up themselves to satisfy his desires, with so few ever reaching the heights of sexual fulfillment. They submit without any thought of their own personal fulfillment. They allow the old men to plant their seed inside themselves, spend years of their lives with growing babies inside them, going through the rigors of pregnancy and slaving away all the while they are carrying the babies, then going through labor at home with nothing to soothe the pain, straining and trying to bear the pain without complaining, when they have received no personal rewards for it all. Since they do all those things anyway, if they could only feel the sheer joy and ecstasy of orgasm they could at least feel they had gained something out of submission.

"But it's no wonder our generation of women feel as they do. They've been taught from birth that sex is the worst thing a woman can participate in before she is married. It's nasty. It's against the rules of society. It's a dirty word that shouldn't even be spoken. But they're told that marriage rectifies

all that and that once they are married, sex is the thing to do. And they sure
do it too. Just look at all the babies women have, one right after the other with
those sex-hungry men poking it into them every chance they get. Boy, men
with healthy wives sure ought to feel superior. They'll have almost grown
children with the old lady's belly sticking out like there's a watermelon
inside them.

"All this while healthy young women are supposed to think of it as
something people just aren't supposed to do. And of course everybody
accepts the fact that a grown man is supposed to try to deflower them and
they're supposed to resist while the unmarried men run around hassling all
the time with their tongues hung out with froth running from their mouths."

Otto took his arm and wiped the sweat from his brow. "It's hot in here,"
he said. "We could get up and take a bath and dress and go down and get
something to eat. Or we could call down and have something sent up. They
had hung a DO NOT DISTURB sign on their outside doorknob when they
entered.

"We ought to do something," Maybell said. "I bought a pretty dress just
to wear while we are here."

"Or we could just stay as we are and continue to wallow in sin," Otto said.
He was becoming rested now and the same old urges were tugging at his
groins.

Maybell had gotten a filmy gown from her suitcase and put it on after their
first encounter. It was short, coming midway up her thighs and her dark
aureolas showed through. Otto took his mouth and touched one of her
breasts through the thin fabric. Maybell shuddered and removed the top of
the gown and he took her breast into his mouth. She was suddenly on top of
him and their tryst lasted much longer than the first, with both of them
panting and exploring every crevice of their bodies.

Spent, sated with sex, lethargic, reflective, they lay in bed for a while, then
Otto ordered breaded veal cutlets and vegetables and they dressed and
waited for the food.

They looked down where pedestrians crowded the streets with cars and
buses shrieking their tires and horns blowing, something entirely new for
people accustomed to country living.

"Can I put on my new dress so we can go out after dinner?" Maybell asked.

"I'd love to," Otto said, "but I'm afraid we'd be recognized honey. We're
in a position that makes us have to feel like wanted people now. We can't
take the risk, and I'm just as concerned about what it would mean to you as
for myself. We're on the outer fringes of society now Maybell."

"Oh, please, Otto, don't make me have that guilty feeling at this time. It will settle on me soon enough and I'll sink into depression so deep I won't feel like living. Let's pretend that we're just two unencumbered people out to have a good time. I can't stand the thoughts of guilt just now."

"Okay," Otto said. "But we still can't afford to go out Bell. Do you mind if I call you that?"

"I love it," she replied. "I'll just let that be your pet name for me."

The food was brought and they munched over the veal cutlets, neither showing hunger, and dabbled at the chocolate ice cream they had ordered for dessert.

"I'm just not hungry somehow," Otto said. He was usually a big eater. "I guess I'm living on love." He reached over and kissed Bell on the mouth.

"Me too," Maybell said. "I'm usually crazy about chocolate ice cream."

The shadows lengthened and the street lights came on. It was growing dark in the room and they went to the window and looked across the city at the thousands of lights flickering in the distance. "Pretty," Maybell said, and Otto agreed.

"How are you feeling?" Maybell asked.

"Fulfilled," Otto replied. "All the pent-up emotions are gone. I feel like I've been deflated. My internal tensions are relieved. I feel in my body the way people feel when their overloaded bladders are emptied.

"Poor man, you've been denied your male needs for too long," Maybell said. "How long have you been without sex Otto?"

"Gosh, too long," he replied. "Vicey has been sick for years, but in the early years of her illness we had fairly regular relations. But Vicey and I haven't lived together as man and wife for two years."

"Well, there are other ways of relieving yourself," Maybell said.

"Yeah, but it isn't the same, Maybell."

"Shall we turn on a light Otto?"

"No, let's undress and get back into bed."

They made love again and both were exhausted. They turned their backs to each other and went to sleep. But it was a troubled sleep for Otto.

Voices were hollering from the cotton patches and tobacco fields and corn patches in Bear Grass. "Otto Pell is a backslider. Otto Pell is a fornicator. Otto Pell has turned his back on his poor sick wife. He has brought shame on the community. He has violated the trust placed in him by the congregation at Whispering Pines Church. Otto Pell is the satan we read about in the Bible. He has preached hell and damnation and he has warned all the people against all the things he is doing.

"Otto Pell ought to be run out of the community," a shrill voice cried out. It came from Abie Turner. "Otto Pell has committed a cardinal sin and he deserves to die." Abie's face was deep red and anger showed in her eyes. "The very likes of a man of the cloth stooping so low as to bed up with a slut to satisfy his male whims is so disgusting he ought to be stoned by every person in Bear Grass, whether they belong to Whispering Pines Church or not."

Otto was holding his hands over his ears in an attempt to distort the sound so he wouldn't hear all the venom poured out against him. He knew all about Abie's sharp tongue and had often associated it with a snake's tongue. But the voice became even more shrill.

"If a man stoops so low as to whore around with other women with a wife on her death bed, he has sinned against God and man. And God help such a woman. How can she consider herself a woman when she opens up her body to such a man? She don't deserve to be called a woman. A female dog is a bitch, and that's the best name to give to such a woman, BITCH." The word reverberated over the community.

Abie was coming closer to him and she carried a lightwood knot in her hand. He saw the stray strands of hair hanging down the sides of her face where it had come loose from the tight ball on top of her head. She looked like something inhuman and he flinched.

"She's going to hit me right in the face," he said and tried to move out of her path, but found himself paralyzed. That was when he realized he had no one to call on for help. There was no God there to sustain him in his time of need anymore. And over in another corner the devil was laughing and toying with his long tail. "I gave you what you wanted," he said. "What more could you ask for? Whatever else Eve did, she gave Adam sex, and what more could any man want than that? You've chosen your own path, Otto. You're filled up with woman. What more could you ask? You thought God was all there was; that if you believed in Him your every wish would be granted.

"But you now know that all the things that you read about the Holy Bible were written two thousand years ago and have no bearing on today's world. You've been practicing a religion so far outdated it doesn't even relate to what is happening in the world today."

Then they were shouting at him at Wilbur Stroud's store. "Whoremonger!" one of the teen-age boys shouted. "You tell us to keep it in our britches, to stay clean and pure and all that shit. But we didn't pay no attention to you nohow, not if we got the chance. But you, you son of a bitch, have broken the laws of God and man. At least we don't have a sick wife at home waiting for us like you've got."

Abie Turner caught up with him, still carrying the lightwood knot. She was riled up even more, now that she had the crowd at the store in on what was going on. She ran at him with the piece of wood and raised it over his head.

"Please Abie, don't kill me!" he screamed and tried to duck his head. He heard someone speaking and felt an arm on his shoulder. "What in the world is the matter Otto?" Maybell asked. "You were hollering and screaming and carrying on like a mad man."

Otto rubbed his eyes and shifted on the bed. "My God, I had a nightmare," he said.

"Tell me about it," Maybell said.

"No, I'll just keep it to myself." He realized that if he went into details Maybell would become disgusted with him.

She leaned over and kissed him and he felt the warmth and softness of her bare breasts on his bosom and he was instantly crazy for her again. They were consumed with desire and Maybell was eager to please him in any manner he chose. "You're the sweetest woman I've ever known," he said.

"Is it just lust Otto?" Maybell asked. "Sex is fine but it's not enough to base a relationship on. It supplies one need, but not all needs. The heart is involved more than any one thing."

"I know," Otto replied. "And it does go beyond sex Bell. But I'm in a position where I don't know what to do. So long as Vicey is alive she's a millstone around my neck. I just can't cast her aside. As we were just saying, there's more to it than sex, and I did take Vicey for better or worse, just as I'd do you if I were marrying you. And I'd have the same obligation to you that I have for her if that were the case."

"I don't know the answer Otto," Maybell said. "I don't know what will happen as a result of our trip. I certainly stand a good chance of being pregnant and if that is the case I have no idea what I will do. Just stay at home and take the rap I reckon. If my son disowns me, I can't help it now. And the community would crucify me. But we can't think about those things just now my love. We'll just have to wait and see what develops."

"You know something Bell," Otto said as he raised on an elbow and looked into her eyes. The window gave off enough light in the room for him to see the sparkle in her eyes.

"I'm beginning to have doubts about all the stuff written in the Bible. How could all of it be true? It was written so long ago by a few men who were not known for their scholarly prowess. How could they dictate what mankind should do forevermore? And I know some of the words were Christ's. But

Bell, Christ never knew a woman. The Good Book doesn't say he was ever tempted by a woman. It makes you wonder whether he had all those hormones that clog men's bodies and make them feel and do as they do. Do you reckon he really did, Bell?"

"Well, I don't think Christ was tempted," Maybell said, "because he was without sin and was not begotten by mortal man. There had to be an egg in Mary's womb, but there were no semen swimming around that egg. So maybe since his was the Immaculate Conception, He didn't inherit the male characteristics other men inherit. That could account for his purity."

"Yet Christ himself preached against the sins man commits because of his sexual makeup. If he only knew how it feels to a man when he knows that in one more second he is going to spurt his semen and the exact second of his orgasm, he might see it differently."

"It doesn't matter what our philosophy may be," Maybell said, "people's attitudes about that will never change. And a woman just isn't supposed to have the consuming urges that I have. My inclinations are equally as strong as yours, Otto."

"Let's turn over and go back to sleep," Otto said. "What time is it anyway?" Maybell held her watch toward the light. "Eleven thirty. And what are we going to do tomorrow Otto?"

"The same as we did today, of course," he replied.

Then it was dawn and traffic was beginning to move on the streets. They heard people walking up and down the halls. "Hungry?" he asked.

"Starving," Maybell said. "I want grits and eggs and sausage and biscuits and jelly and coffee."

"Me too," Otto said. "But first, let's do something else, and they were continuing their tryst as it had begun.

"I love you," he said as he rose over her "I've got to have you and I don't know what I'll do when it's over."

"You really are a hog about it aren't you my love?" Maybell replied as she placed her legs around his thighs.

This continued for the entire time they were in Winston-Salem. Not once did they dress and mingle with other people at the hotel. And Otto was worried about the money he was spending. A country preacher that often received poundings of food rather than money had very little cash on hand.

Preaching was more of a dedication to humanity than monetary reward. Room service was much more expensive than going down to the dining room for food. He checked his wallet in the privacy of the bathroom and shook his head. He didn't know what the bill would be and he only had fifty dollars to his name. Vicey would need medicine in a few days.

He admitted to himself that he was playing the fool, although in his present state of mind he was able to defend his actions. And parting would be so hard. When they returned to Hallsborough he would alight from the bus, leaving Maybell alone to return to Lenoir County and with no hope of seeing her any time soon.

He was unable to see anything clearly and his future was a big blur in his mind. He didn't want to think. Rather, he was content to drift in a dreamland in which all his fantasies had become realities. He was consumed, body and soul, with the beautiful woman who had made all this possible and he wanted her by his side forever.

It was morning and the day of their return home. They awakened at dawn and went through their last ritual of love-making. They were both in tears and thinking more from the heart than the physical.

"I love you so much," Maybell said as she ran her hand over his face, rough with beard. "You are so handsome and so manly and I worship you. I never before had as much satisfaction from a man as I've had from you. You consume my soul and my body. And I will cry every day away from you. But I came into this with my eyes wide open and I am aware that your first duty is to your wife. I have no idea what will happen to me, especially if I am pregnant. But you have made my life complete, my darling. Please keep that in mind when you think about me." Otto felt her tears dripping on his face.

"Please don't talk like that Bell," Otto said. "I can't stand to think that we will be separated. My life will be empty without you. Whatever I do and wherever I go, my thoughts will all be on you."

"What are you going to do about the church?" Maybell asked. "I would think you could continue on as you are and ministering to the people of Whispering Pines Church."

"I've been thinking about that," Otto said, "and I think I'm going to resign. I feel that to do otherwise would be doing an injustice to myself and the church. I feel like I'd be a hypocrite to continue in the pulpit. But I'm not all that worried about it Bell. I have a different perspective on life now, and I'm not as Godly a man as I was. I'm having a lot of doubts about many things I've preached over the years. I can find fulfillment without being a country preacher.

"I see no need of making a confession of what I have done. I can just ask for my resignation and say it is because of personal reasons. I don't know of anything I can do so long as Vicey is alive. I could walk out on her but

I would be ostracized by the community and frankly, I think my conscience would kill me if I did that."

"No, whatever you do, don't walk out on Vicey," Maybell said. "I'd feel badly toward you if you did that. It would lessen my opinion of you."

"We'd better get up and get dressed," Otto said. "Our bus leaves at ten o'clock and it's already eight."

"I'm going to wear my new dress home," Maybell said. "I bought it just for you and I'm not going to let it go to waste. It will be a reminder of you whenever I wear it."

"It's beautiful," Otto said after Maybell had taken a bath and dressed. It was red with small multi-colored figures in the modern style.

"That's the thing about you," Otto said. "So many mature women just let themselves go and pay little attention to their personal appearance. But you shine like a diamond the way you dress and carry yourself. No wonder men admire you so much. If women only realized that by making themselves more attractive they would ensure holding on to their husbands."

"You look handsome yourself even if your suit isn't new," Maybell said. Otto was wearing the same suit he had worn at revival at her church.

Otto checked the halls carefully as they left their room and took the elevator to the first floor. He was nervous as they entered the dining room and scanned the diners to see whether there was anyone there he knew. Maybell did the same and they didn't see any acquaintances.

They sat an hour over breakfast and Otto bought a morning paper and they scanned the news. Then Otto went to the front office to settle his bill. After paying, he had a dollar and eleven cents left. He had purchased a round-trip ticket. When he returned to the table Maybell had her purse open, feeling inside for the money she had placed in a small billfold. She pulled out a twenty dollar bill and when Otto sat down she held it out to him. "I want you to have this Otto. I didn't intend for you to pay the entire bill. I know how it is with preachers. They just don't have much money. And I don't have any money to speak of. Who in the world does these days? Anyway, with my little farm I am able to lay aside a dollar or two occasionally. I want you to have it."

"Oh, I can't do that Maybell," Otto said, blushing. "I can't take your money when you have given me so much pleasure."

"Don't be silly Otto," Maybell said. "You need the money and I'd rather spend it this way than any way I know."

It's a Godsend, Otto thought to himself.

"I'll bet it took all you had to pay the hotel bill," Maybell said. "Didn't it?"

"No, I had a dollar and eleven cents left. But I feel like a heel taking money from you Bell."

She placed the money beside his plate and he took it sheepishly and put it in his wallet.

They were silent for the most part on their way back home. They held hands and observed the countryside through the bus windows. Each was deep in thought. Otto was aware of a man sitting in front of him, almost at the front of the bus. He had seen the face somewhere although it was no one he connected with Bear Grass. He passed it off as a chance acquaintance at some time.

It was late afternoon when the bus pulled into the bus station at Hallsborough. Otto stood and took his suitcase from the overhead rack, then lingered for a moment looking down at Maybell. There was nothing left to say except goodby, and he wanted to prolong the moment but realized that to stand in the aisle for an extended period of time would call attention to them. He placed his hand on Maybell's and said, "Goodbye, my dear." Maybell smiled and Otto noted tears in her eyes.

"Goodbye," she said, squeezing his hand.

It was a dismal ride from Hallsborough to Bear Grass. The sun was going down and he noted people feeding up and smoke rising from kitchen chimneys. Because of his low spirits, the surroundings looked strange, somehow. It almost seemed like a different country. He dreaded to return to his own home. What would the circumstances be? He dreaded to face Vicey, not that he expected her to complain; rather because of his own guilty conscience and he associated her with being responsible in a sense. His own wife had become the enemy in his heart.

He alighted from the bus in front of the house and Ma Price, his mother-in-law, met him at the door. "Hi Ma," he said, "and how is Vicey?"

"I can't tell much difference, Otto," she replied. "Vicey just gets weaker and weaker. If something don't happen soon Vicey's not going to be with us long Otto. She don't seem to have a will to live anymore. She just lies and looks like she's in a faraway land and nothing seems to interest her anymore."

Otto entered Vicey's room and she perked up at seeing him.

"How are you Vicey?" he asked and she said, "Pretty good Otto." But her voice was so weak he could barely hear her. He stooped and brushed his lips against her forehead.

"I feel better now that you're here," Vicey said with an effort to strengthen her voice. "I've missed you so much, Otto. I hope your insurance meeting went well."

"Yeah, yeah it went fine," Otto said. He had a sinking feeling inside.

"I hope you got my insurance straightened out," Vicey said, raising on her elbows. "I've worried about that ever since you've been gone. I thought about how hard it would be on you if I were to die and the policy on me was not in order."

"Yeah, that's all taken care of," Otto said. There was smell of sickness in the room and Otto wanted to get out in the open air, away from the stench. Ma Price had sprayed spirits of camphor over the room with a spray can used to kill flies and the slop jar Vicey used had been washed thoroughly and lye soap placed in the pail in an effort to kill the scent of urine. Still the odor persisted.

"I'm so glad you're back home," Vicey said again. Mrs. Price came in with a hard-stemmed match, lifted the chimney from the oil lamp and held the lighted match to the wick. A small, yellow flame flickered, casting shadows over the room and Otto thought about how poorly they lived with not even the convenience of electricity. His visit to the hotel had brought this into closer focus.

"Quarterly Meeting is tomorrow," Vicey said as Otto was leaving the room.

"Yes, I know," Otto replied. "I made sure to be back in order to be at church tomorrow."

"Supper is ready," Ma Price announced as Otto entered the kitchen. "I've just cooked turnips and there's plenty of good pot liquor. I've got cornbread to break up and put in the liquor too." She knew that Otto loved pot liquor with greens. But Otto's stomach felt squeamish. Food was the least thing on his mind.

"I'm not hungry," he told Ma Price. "I reckon it's all the travel. But I hope Vicey will eat something. She's mighty weak, Ma Price. Did she have any company while I was away?"

"Yeah, Abie Turner came one day, yesterday I think, and Lany Moore came today."

"What was Abie running off at the mouth about?"

"Oh, the usual mess about Bear Grass. She was mighty concerned about your trip too. Wanted to know everything about it, but me and Vicey didn't tell her much."

"I hate to feel about a member of my flock like I feel about Abie Turner," Otto said, "but that woman gets to me."

"Don't worry about that," Ma Price said. "She does that to everybody."

Otto walked out into the yard. Everything was crowding in on him. He noted the yellow lights in the windows along the road. There were the usual smells of evening with smoke hanging in the air and wifts of odors from hogpens, chicken houses and stables, coming in with the breeze. But it was an unfamiliar odor now. What had seemed as much a part of him as breathing had taken on a different meaning and he felt that he was in enemy territory. His thoughts were troubled.

He wished there were some place else where he could spend the night. He felt violated in having to return to the closeness of his small house. But he felt even more that he was violating his wife than being violated himself. She was the woman who had upheld him every day of their marriage, who had worked in every way possible to help him in his ministry; who had been a wife in every sense of the word so long as she was physically able.

And hadn't he taken her for better or for worse, in sickness and in health, so long as the two of them should live? He simply could not let his thoughts bear on those things now. He'd go out of his mind if he did.

The night was warm and he sat on the edge of the porch for a while and listened to people going up and down the road. Then he lay down and cupped his hands under his head to rest his back. He decided to get up, go to his room and retire. He needed sleep. He hadn't slept much during the past two nights. He stretched as he rose and gazed into the heavens where millions of stars blinked and he felt a sense of relief. A good night's sleep might restore his spirits and he might be able to recapture some of his former optimism.

He went to Vicey's room to say goodnight but he wasn't prepared for what Vicey said to him. Her mother had given her a bath, changed her gown, brushed her hair and changed the bed. He stooped to kiss her forehead and said, "Goodnight Vicey."

She placed her hand on his arm and said, "Otto, I have a favor to ask of you" in such a weak voice he found it hard to understand her.

"What is it?" he asked.

"I want to talk with you Otto. I want to have a long talk. I want you to sleep with me tonight sweetheart. It has been so long since we slept together. And it's not what you think, Otto." She was out of breath by the time she had spoken those few words.

"I don't think it would be wise for you to try to exert yourself like that, my dear. You're already out of breath. I think I should go to my bed and let you rest." My God, it's already catching up with me, he thought.

"It's so cold, Otto. I'm chilled all through my body. I need your warmth beside me. It would seem almost like heaven to have your healthy body beside me. And if we don't talk tonight it may be too late. If you will just agree to lie beside me I can place my mouth near your ear and you can hear me without me having to exert myself. Please, Otto."

There was no escape for him. As unpleasant as the thought was to him, he could simply ignore Vicey and go to his room and feel guilt for the rest of his life, or he could bear the ordeal and come through it somehow.

"All right," he said as he unbuckled his belt, slipped his pants and shirt off, sat by the bed and took off his shoes and slid carefully into bed beside his wife.

"Place another pillow under your head," Vicey said. "I feel like I'm smothering and a little more height for my head would help that." Otto took Vicey's pillow and placed it above his own.

"I'm so glad you agreed to sleep with me," Vicey said. "My heart is overflowing with things I want to say to you. I've prayed about how I would be able to do this. And I'm very sick, Otto. It's near the end with me.

"First, I want to tell you what a wonderful man you have been to me; how your life has been a shining example for me to follow, what a wonderful person you have been; what an inspiration you have been to the Bear Grass community and to all others who have known you. No other person knows you as well as I do and I am your greatest follower."

"Vicey, there's no need of heaping such praise on me," Otto said. "I am only a mortal man with my flaws just as all of us have."

"No one is perfect," Vicey whispered in his ear, "but you are as near perfection as any man I ever knew. Despite temptations and trials and me to contend with in my weakened condition you have kept the faith. You have looked to God for your strength and He has given it to you. You stand for all the ideals men try to live up to. Many fail, but you have met the test Otto.

"I have tried so hard to be all the things you would have me be, and I feel that I've come up short. But it wasn't because I didn't try, sweetheart. I wanted to be all the things that you are. But I need to rest Otto. Let me turn my back to you for a while. Just hold me close and let me lie on your arm."

Despite all the efforts of concealment, there was the stench of the sickroom, a feverish body, stale air. Vicey's body felt hot against Otto's stomach. Her backbone felt like he imagined a skeleton would feel against him. There seemed to be nothing but skin and bones. He felt the sharpness of Vicey's hip bone and a great compassion came over him along with revulsion at the awareness of a human body consumed by disease. "God help me," he said in a whisper.

After an interval of rest, Vicey slowly turned toward Otto again. "I'm going home soon," she said. "I mean my heavenly home Otto. And do you know something. I'm looking forward to that with all my heart. I'm no good to the world anymore. There is nothing left here for me. And I will be opening a new world for you, my love. A new world in which you will be free to marry a good woman and still have healthy children that will make your life complete. You are entitled to all those things Otto.

"And I will be at home with all our lovely babies that never drew healthy breaths here and were called to God to add to his kingdom. Won't it be wonderful Otto, for me to be in Heaven with those beautiful blonde and red-haired little angels, and those with black, curly hair - little boys and girls - by my side and with no worries about the burden of raising them? I know there will be angel caretakers there to meet our every need. And you will be here with a lovely wife I hope, and with more little boys and girls to play with, to counsel and love and enjoy during their formative years and looking up to you as a real-life hero. This can all be yours after my body is laid in the cemetery at Whispering Pines Church."

It was time to rest again, to get air into her lungs in order to be able to finish saying the things that were heavy on her conscience. She placed her hand on Otto's face and there were tears there. They were running onto the pillow.

"Please don't cry my darling," she said. "I'm so sorry I am making you unhappy by what I am saying. It's not a time for grief Otto. It's a time for rejoicing. My faith has sustained me since I was a teen-age girl, and it all boiled down to this: the time when I know my life is ebbing away. But that's what it's all about Otto. If we have lived so that we have faith to sustain us when we are facing death, we have fought the good fight.

"With the great chill I feel in my body, I am as secure as if I were already in heaven. I feel God's hand on me and I have no more fear of death than if I were as healthy as a person can be with no thought of death entering my mind. That's true faith, Otto and I shudder to think what it would be like for me at this moment if I didn't have a Father that I know will protect me and wait for me as I walk through the valley of the shadow of death. It is appointed to every man to die, and after death the judgment. But we both have done the best we could, and I have no fears about your future Otto. You'll minister to the people for as long as you are able and God will bless you. Because of you I am what I am."

Otto had never felt as tormented as he did with the things Vicey was saying to him. If she only knew, he thought. But she would never know. She would go to her grave with his deep dark secret intact. He thought about the great faith she was showing while he had begun to doubt the reality of God and sobs shook his body.

"Just hold on to what you have," Vicey whispered into his ear. "Keep the faith and God will be with you."

"Vicey, you should try to get some sleep," Otto said. "You're wearing yourself out and you are carrying a high fever. Your body is hot beside me"

"If you don't mind, would you get me two of my pills?" Vicey said. "If you will I won't have to wake Mama. Bless her, she's been so good to me, and you be sure to take care of her, Otto."

"Oh, I will," he replied.

Vicey placed her lips on Otto's face in a loving gesture. Otto felt repulsed and her breath smelled bad. He felt that he was at the end of his endurance, but Vicey wasn't through yet.

"And Otto," she whispered, "when it's all over, I don't want any kind of eulogy said over me. Let my life in Bear Grass be my testimony. Those who know me know what I have been like. And don't have any long sermon. Let the congregation say the Lord's Prayer and the twenty-third Psalm in unison. That's all I want said. And honey, tell them not to grieve over me for one minute. I'd hate to think there were tears shed for me when I've already made my journey, for you see, I'm the one being treated.

"My bags were packed long ago with finery fit for a bride. And tell them not to worry about flowers, for I've already seen them and they are strewn from here to heaven, in colors never seen on this earth. I've seen it all Otto and I wish I could adequately describe it to you, but that's impossible. I've seen waterfalls with water as clear as crystals that catch the glow of the Heavenly Father and radiate every color in the rainbow.

"I've seen thousands of miles of trees of magnificent height with foliage so beautiful the mountains in fall are dull by comparison! Fields of flowers beautiful beyond imagination and birds and animals that defy description. And I've already seen our babies, Otto. Oh, how I wish you could see them too. Their little faces look like angels and their bodies are plump and they're all almost the same size, just as they were on earth."

The pills were beginning to take effect and Vicey was becoming drowsy. She yawned and Otto was tense, waiting for her to drift off to sleep.

"I'm about finished," Vicey said, "but I want to tell you a few other things. You know that I've never made any kind of show in Bear Grass Otto. I've only been a wife and tried to help you in any way I could. But I've stayed in the background and just because I am a preacher's wife has made me no different than anybody else.

"Some people may think you have to make a big show to have the faith and love in your heart that I have, but it's not like that at all. It's simply what you have in your own heart and what is between you and your maker. And every person can have the same things that I have in my heart. It's the simplest thing in the world. Don't worry about what others do or say. Keep on a straight path. Pray unceasingly, try to see the good in others rather than backbiting and love your fellowman. That's what will take you to heaven.

"And my darling, thank you from the bottom of my heart for lying here and listening to me tonight. I believe this was my last chance to tell you, for I think the end is near. I feel that God gave me this strength tonight to say what I felt compelled to tell you. Thank you for being willing to lie by my side when I am so repulsive with nothing but skin and bones and unpleasant odors about me that I haven't been able to hide. Only a man of your calliber would have done such a thing."

Then Vicey was silent and Otto noted that she had finally fallen asleep. He carefully lifted her head from his arm, slid himself out of bed and left her resting on the twin pillows. He went to the back porch and poured water from the bucket into the washpan, found the soap in the semi-darkness, for signs of dawn were in the skies, and washed off. This night had been the greatest ordeal of his life and he felt it would be impossible to attend Quarterly Meeting in a few hours. But he was expected to conduct the business meeting and the Lord's Supper. He would have to wash feet with the other men and do the preaching. He wasn't up to it and he knew that his resignation from the church was only a matter of days away.

Within a few days of Vicey's talk with Otto, her condition deteriorated rapidly. She became semi-conscious and it was necessary for someone to be with her at all times. The women of the community organized and took turns sitting up with her at night. Two women would sit with her, attending to her needs.

Rev. Otto Pell went around in a daze, unable to concentrate on Vicey or anything else. He was a completely changed man from the caring, understanding pastor he had been, and the public took notice, although they were unaware of the mental torture he was experiencing. He couldn't even concentrate on Maybell Aswell who had helped to bring about his change in attitude.

It was late summer and the fodder was ready for pulling. He watched as the men entered the cornfield in front of his house and began pulling the blades of corn and fashioning them into bundles. Several of the men were black and they became engaged in singing Negro spirituals as they went about their work to take their minds off the menial task. He heard one of them give the key in a hum and then there was the harmony and the words,

"Planted by the water, I shall not be moved, planted by the water, I shall not be moved just like a tree, planted by the water, I shall not be moved."

Otto noticed the bundles of fodder placed on broken-down stalks. And the cowwitch vines that grew along the road and overspread the little ditch alongside the road were filled with their red blossoms. There was a loneliness about the surroundings that he hadn't observed before. There was the premonition of death in the air. The woods beyond the fields looked forlorn and there was a yellowish cast over the land because of the slant of the sun's rays. It was a strange land to him. He would sit on the porch for hours, going inside occasionally to check on Vicey and trying to show a concern he didn't feel in his heart. The uppermost question in his mind was whether the people of the community could see this. Passers-by would stop sometimes to inquire about Vicey and a few men from the church visited him and asked whether there was anything they could do.

Then came the end on a morning when the sun was just breaking over the treetops and Otto breathed a sigh of relief. It had seemed so long and so hopeless and then he realized that if he had only waited a few more weeks the burden he carried in his heart would have been greatly lessened. Being untrue to the church was one thing, but being untrue to a sick wife was another entirely, and one that he could not forget, no matter how hard he tried.

As preparations were made for Vicey's burial, Otto told the members of the church what Vicey had told him about her wishes. They had wanted a long funeral extolling Vicey's virtues and having special singing, when Vicey hadn't said a word about any singing. They found it hard to believe that so simple a service would be held, although they acceded to Otto's wishes. And Otto wondered whether they even believed what he had told them. And as a matter of fact, there was some disbelief.

Abie Turner was the first to voice her complaint.

"I tell you right now," she told Mrs. Ada Creech, a member of the board of Whispering Pines Church, and one of the most respected citizens of the community, "they's something fishy about all this Miss Ada. And I don't mean no disrespect toward Reverend Pell, but did you know that he was away for two days when Vicey was beginning to go downhill? Yes sir, he went on the bus to Winston-Salem on a Wednesday and didn't come back until late Friday. Told Vicey that it was something about his insurance. That sounds like a poor excuse to me."

"Now Abie, don't go thinking the worst," Miss Ada said. "Reverend Pell has served Whispering Pines Church well and about everybody in Bear

Grass likes him. And when he says Vicey told him what she wanted as far as her burial is concerned I believe that. Why would he want anything different if that was not the case?"

And down at Wilbur Stroud's store it was discussed further. "It's going to be a strange funeral, 'specially for a preacher's wife," Lloyd Smith said. "We ain't used to no kind of burying like that around here. I'm afraid Otto Pell has got something to do with that. And the tales going around that he went out of town for two days without saying anything to the church members about it is shore strange."

"Give him the benefit of the doubt," Wilbur Stroud said. "All of us have known Otto for a long time and I shore think he's a fine man and I'll have to know different before I think any other way."

So the burial service was carried out exactly like Vicey had asked Otto to do. People flooded the church and stood on the grounds. The entire service was over in ten minutes and they watched as dirt was spaded over Vicey's grave and went back home, changed clothes and got in the fields by two o'clock. The funeral was held at one o'clock.

. . . . .

Three days after the funeral Pell called a meeting of the Board in which he told them he was resigning as pastor. He knew that he would be called before the Board and he acted first in order to escape the searing questions that would be put before him. He admitted nothing and said it would be in his best interest and that of the church if he left immediately. His every move implied guilt. The church accepted his resignation and he hurried home to pack his belongings and made a hasty exit. The only thing he said to his mother-in-law was that he was leaving for good; not offering to help her overcome the grief of Vicey's death or financially.

In his haste to leave he left behind one of Maybell's love letters that was stuck in the back of a drawer in his desk at the church. Anything that the people had wondered about was disclosed in that letter. He headed for Lenoir County and rented a room in a little community near Maybell.

Chapter 26

People were plowing in the fields and a few women with fishing poles were heading for the creek. An old dog in heat had attracted a gang of he-dogs and the bitch was teasing them to her heart's content and causing fights among the dogs. Clara Bell said, "Lawd, lawd!"

Clara Bell was on her way to Miss Callie's to help her with the house chores. She went on Wednesday every week. It was a fun day for Clara Bell - much easier than slinging a hoe or doing other farm chores.

Clara Bell liked Miss Callie. Clara Bell was a talker and she teased Miss Callie into telling her a lot of things going on in the community. Miss Callie liked to talk too. Miss Callie was a fine woman, and Clara Bell recognized that just from being around her.

Clara Bell was squatty, standing no more than five-foot-two and slightly on the plump side. She had a mass of hair that she plaited every week and her eyes were large and expressive. Her mouth was large, with full lips and her round face was smooth.

Clara Bell always entered the house through the back door. She had never entered the front door. The benches on the front porch intrigued her. She wanted to sit on a bench and look out over the countryside and watch the other "niggers" working their tails off in them fields. Clara Bell said to herself that she wanted to be "Miss Priss." But except for the times when she swept off the porch or scoured, she didn't even get to the front of the house, and when she was working there was no time to sit and dream.

Sometimes Miss Callie put her to scrubbing clothes on the wash board under the trees where the chaney ball blooms smelled like lilac perfume. Clara Bell would take the soiled clothes out to the wash bench and put them in the hot water that had been heated in the wash pot. There was a big hunk of lye soap to run over the clothes to make suds and help wash out the dirt. And Clara Bell did something she was ashamed to admit even to herself.

When she got ready to put Philip's underwear in the water she'd look to see if anybody was watching, and hold them up to her nose and smell them. Philip was handsome, large, tall and muscular. Clara Bell had her man, and she never entertained the thought of having anything "like that" to do with no white man. But she'd think about her Leroy and say, "Mm, mm."

Sometimes after the clothes dried on the line Miss Callie would put Clara Bell to ironing with the flat irons that were heated on the wood stove. There was a gas iron in the pantry, but Miss Callie didn't trust Clara Bell to work it, and Clara Bell was dying to iron with that gas contraption.

They'd strike up a conversation as soon as Clara Bell entered the house. "Mawning Miss Callie," she'd say, "how's you?" and Miss Callie would say, "Fine Clara Bell. I hope everything is all right with you."

"I bees fine Miss Callie. I hope everybody else be awright too. How is the family?"

"Everybody is all right, Clara Bell."

"What been happening since I was here last week?"

"Nothing new."

"Everything be awright at the Church Miss Callie? I been hearing that yo preacher done jumped the coop and gone the way of the sinner."

"Who told you?" Miss Callie asked.

"You know how news travels in Bear Grass Miss Callie. Colored folks hears all the things the whites be doing, more than the whites learn about the coloreds, cause they don't care that much."

"Yeah, Reverend Pell has resigned and left Bear Grass, Clara Bell."

"Shame, shame, shame!" Clara Bell replied. "Everybody thought he was a good man too, even the colored folks. He sho fooled me. Course, you never knows about folks when it comes down to "that." Miss Callie wouldn't have stood for her saying the word "sex."

"Ever hear anything from Hobby, Miss Callie? He was a fine little boy and us black folks loved that young'un, looking like an albino with that white hair and them blue eyes."

"No, I never hear from Hobby anymore," Miss Callie said. "But I understand Hobby had an operation, or maybe more than one, on his crippled leg. They're living in Tennessee now, you know."

"How far that be, Miss Callie? Seems lak dat on the other side of the world."

"Oh, several hundred miles away. But I reckon a fast car could drive there in a day, and I mean a long day."

"That too far away for me," Clara Bell said as she twisted her mouth with a dreamy look in her eyes.

"Lawd, I remember Hobby's mama," Clara Bell said. "I was 'bout eight I reckon when she left Bear Grass, but I remembers how purty that girl was. She didn't look lak the rest of the foks round here. I thought she was like a movie star." Clara Bell wanted to go into the details about Perline Turnage leaving the community. She wanted to find out who Hobby's father was, but she knew better than to try to get into a conversation with Miss Callie about that. Miss Callie was straight-laced and didn't do a lot of "foolish" talking. She was not a gossiper.

After finishing the ironing Miss Callie put Clara Bell to dusting the furniture, and Clara Bell liked that. She liked to scrape the varnish off of furniture and eat it. This was perhaps due to some chemical imbalance in her body. Clara Bell would take a case knife and put in her apron pocket, and while dusting raise the cloth from small tables and scrape the varnish from hidden places that couldn't be seen from the outside. Miss Callie would have a fit if she caught Clara Bell scraping her furniture.

Clara Bell did venture to ask Miss Callie about Minnie Mae Moore, realizing that she would probably get nowhere with that one.

"I ain't seen Minnie Mae lately, Miss Callie. I wonder where she is. She was flouncing around everywhere a little while back. Now nobody don't see her."

"Huh," Miss Callie said, shrugging, "She's not even worth talking about. Bear Grass will be better off if she has left for good."

"Yeah, I reckon so," Clara Bell said, smiling.

But Clara Bell passed along a little gossip that gave Miss Callie plenty to think about. "I'll tell you what I heard Miss Callie. And it's all over Bear Grass. I hear tell that Minnie Mae caught a disease and passed it on to all the men she was messin around with in Bear Grass. The colored boys are telling what they hear at Mr. Wilbur's store. They says that half or more of the men is skeered half to death."

"What in the world do you mean Clara Bell?" Miss Callie asked. Her face was flushed and she seemed almost too embarrassed to pursue the subject further.

"All I heard it called is clap, Miss Callie. And from what I been told the white men talks about it at the store all the time. Some of the colored boys say they've heard names called by the white men when they didn't know no colored boy was anywhere nearby. My Leroy say he's heard groups of white boys talking about it behind the store and all of 'em were asking the others if they had seen any signs and some of 'em had and the others was just waitin'. They say the menfolks is going to the doctor and filling up his office."

"Did anybody hear Philip's name mentioned?" Miss Callie asked. She felt her heartbeat in her throat.

"No'm Miss Callie, he don't say nothing about Mr. Philip." Clara Bell didn't tell Miss Callie that the boys had heard Mr. Wilbur's name mentioned. Clara Bell would have died before telling that to Miss Callie. And for all she knew it was just a bunch of men talking.

"Thank God," Miss Callie said. "I think Philip is a fine young man but he's a man, and you know how they are. And he messes around with that Wilbert Lee Turner, and I've always had my eyes on that boy. He was ruined the day he was born and his mother has tried to shield him from everything and make him think he's above the other neighborhood boys. And I'm told he's dangerous where girls are concerned. You can even see it in that boy's eyes. And I declare Philip seems to like him better than any other boy in the neighborhood. I'm very upset about what you told me Clara Bell and I'll worry about this until I know my boy was not involved with that Minnie Mae."

"And that Roscoe, what has become of him Clara Bell?"

"Roscoe done gone up de road Miss Callie. The white folks was skeered of him and the colored folks too. The colored folks that liked him was skeered to be seen with him. So Roscoe just trucked on up the road one day to Lawd knows where. But he'll be back one of these days."

"I'll tell you who I miss Clara Bell. That's the Finches. They were fine folks and good neighbors. Cora and Tobey were always neighborly. Whispering Pines Church has certainly missed them since they left. But that's another family the community has lost contact with. They didn't have any other relatives around here and they just don't get back this way anymore. I think about them a lot."

"Lawd, I used to play hopscotch with the girls even if I was older than them. I'd play with them in they play house sometimes too. Robyn and Arlene were friendly little girls and all the chillun in the neighborhood like them."

Miss Callie had a walnut-finished refrigerator in which ice was kept to cool milk and foods. There was a pail under the refrigerator to catch the water as the ice melted, and Clara Bell always emptied the pail when she was working at the house. And she always opened the refrigerator to see what was stored on the shelves. Today there was a jar of lemonade, with slices of lemon in the jar and it set Clara Bell's mouth to watering.

"Miss Callie, I clare I'se thirsty. I wonders if I could have a glass of that good-looking lemonade?"

"Sure Clara Bell. Chip you off a little ice in a glass and enjoy the lemonade."

"Thank you, Miss Callie and I do declare that stuff cooking on the stove makes me as hongry as a she-wolf."

"You can have dinner too, Clara Bell. You know you always eat with us when you are working." Miss Callie always sat a plate on the side table in the kitchen for the colored folks who ate at her table.

"You'se too good to me, Miss Callie. You done got me spoiled. I wish you could keep me all the time. I'd really feel like somebody if I worked at your house every day. Wouldn't I be something if I could wear some kind of uniform and stuff like dat? I'd really show them niggers something if I could." Clara Bell didn't mind calling other people of her race niggers, so long as she felt she was lording something over them, especially those who thought they were "high and mighty" as she called it.

When all the work was finished Miss Callie reached into her apron and pulled out a one-dollar bill and handed it to Clara Bell. She was paid a dollar each week, and Clara Bell always made something big out of it and thanked Miss Callie and said she'd be back next Wednesday and began her journey back home.

Folks were still working in the fields and she waved to them near the road and thought to herself that she was a mite higher up the ladder than them. Tomorrow she'd be out in the fields too, but for today she had been in the "big" house working. The only thing that bothered her about white folks'es houses was that they had a funny smell. They just didn't smell like colored folks.

Clara Bell watched the buzzards soaring in the skies and heard the June bugs singing in the trees and smelled honeysuckle somewhere and Bear Grass seemed like the most wonderful place on earth. A snake crossed the road and Clara Bell crimped up her face and drew a deep breath. The sight of a snake mortified her. She waited until the serpent crossed the road and slithered into the bushes.

When she came to the clay hill, she went to the spot where she always scraped the clay until she found some several inches below the surface. She took out the case knife and scraped the clay as she always did. Clara Bell had a craving for clay. It smelled good and tasted good. It hit the spot sometimes where nothing else on earth could. If there were a choice between the two she'd take clay even over varnish.

"They just ain't lak us," she said to herself as she walked leisurely home after getting her fill of clay. "They don't know what we is like. They just don't have as much fun as we do. They don't open up and laugh and holler

"Give him the benefit of the doubt," Wilbur Stroud said. "All of us have known Otto for a long time and I shore think he's a fine man and I'll have to know different before I think any other way."

So the burial service was carried out exactly like Vicey had asked Otto to do. People flooded the church and stood on the grounds. The entire service was over in ten minutes and they watched as dirt was spaded over Vicey's grave and went back home, changed clothes and got in the fields by two o'clock. The funeral was held at one o'clock.

. . . . .

Three days after the funeral Pell called a meeting of the Board in which he told them he was resigning as pastor. He knew that he would be called before the Board and he acted first in order to escape the searing questions that would be put before him. He admitted nothing and said it would be in his best interest and that of the church if he left immediately. His every move implied guilt. The church accepted his resignation and he hurried home to pack his belongings and made a hasty exit. The only thing he said to his mother-in-law was that he was leaving for good; not offering to help her overcome the grief of Vicey's death or financially.

In his haste to leave he left behind one of Maybell's love letters that was stuck in the back of a drawer in his desk at the church. Anything that the people had wondered about was disclosed in that letter. He headed for Lenoir County and rented a room in a little community near Maybell.

Chapter 27

Whispering Pines Church was without a leader for several months following Rev. Otto Pell's resignation. Lay preachers filled the pulpit when church officials could get them. Several men in the community spoke at Sunday morning worship services. Some people stopped attending. Some lost confidence in the church. Most of the people who attended Whispering Pines had had great confidence in Rev. Pell and placed him on sort of a pedestal. They expected more of him than other people in the community.

A committee was appointed to conduct a search for a pastor. They labored long and faithful. A candidate would receive a nod from the committee and he would preach on two Sundays in succession, and the membership would find something wrong - his deliverance was poor or he didn't seem to be spirit-filled, or he didn't appeal to them as a person - and they would turn him down.. And with limited resources to search for a pastor, they had to search in the local area, mostly in Hallsborough. It seemed almost hopeless when they were told about a minister in Hallsborough who had pastored two churches on the coast for a number of years, but because officials were unable to pay him enough to keep his car running and to buy gasoline for travel from Hallsborough to the little coastal towns to hold services, they let him go with regret. His pay was mostly from their gardens and the livestock they grew on the farm which was their only resources.

Rev. Willis Newcomb was a humble man who had had more than his share of problems. With a large family, he sometimes found himself facing foodless days. He often wondered whether another profession might not have been his best course in life, until he realized that he was called by God to minister to the people. That fact sustained him and God had always provided, although he often wondered whether his Master were coming through.

His blue serge suit was as shiny as a new penny. He had worn it longer than he cared to remember and as his abdomen grew with age his good wife had let out the waist as far as it would go, then added a "V" from another pair of blue serge pants that were of a slightly different color. The hem of the coat was frayed and his shirts were threadbare from wear. The collars had been turned but they showed the results of wear. His shoes were stuffed with soles made of cardboard to keep his feet from touching the ground. His socks had been darned so many times there was no longer anything to darn. He wasn't an educated preacher, but his study of the Bible and his sense of reasoning resulted in a man of learning.

Now seventy years old, his years of raising a family were behind him and he was possessed with good health. He and his wife required little in life. Yet, dollar weddings and funerals where there was no money to pay the preacher, left the good minister with little enough to depend on.

When the committee from Whispering Pines Church contacted him he was elated. Although he had never visited the church, it was widely known in the community for it boasted a large membership and that had a great bearing on a church's prestige.

He had heard about the Rev. Otto Pell scandal, but the subject was not mentioned in the interview except when he was told why there was a vacancy at the church. He was invited to preach at the church for two Sundays, and he told the committee he would be happy to oblige.

Of a portly stature with a cherubic face and snow white hair and warm brown eyes, he looked the part of the kindly minister.

There were no complaints and the committee was cheered. The church voted on him the first Sunday after his appearances, and he was chosen pastor unanimously.

Willis Newcomb realized that he had to get the Otto Pell scandal behind him at the outset, and he pondered long at what he would say. Rather than crucifying the fallen minister, he would use it as a lesson for the entire church and give them all something to think about.

So after the prayers and singing and testimonies he stood before the full house with a pitcher of water and a glass at his disposal and his handkerchief in his hand.

"We are in perilous times," he began.

"Look around you and see all the signs of the Bible coming to pass. But God said it would be like that in the days before his coming. He said there would be a great falling away, that people would become lovers of men rather than lovers of God. He said there would be blasphemers and His Holy Word said except time be shortened there would be no flesh saved.

"My friends, we are living in those days now. But do not be afraid. It is nothing new. I preach a God of love and mercy and compassion rather than a God to be feared. I don't mean by that that we should not know God's power, for He is above all things. But we shouldn't stand before Him shaking and fearful. We should stand before Him with thanksgiving and praise and adoration."

"Hallelujah," came from a woman in the audience.

"Whispering Pines Church is in shambles. A leader stands in disgrace, scorned by those who loved him. He has been stomped in the ground and has been called a Judas. But I would ask you to have mercy. And you shouldn't be too surprised at his downfall. He isn't the first minister to fall by the wayside and he won't be the last. Why? Simply because he's human.

"Sure, Christ was human but he was perfect and had the ability to cast aside temptation. Man - no man - has that ability. Man is tempted from the time he reaches the age of accountability and I believe men of the cloth must have more temptations than other men simply because they attempt to live exemplary lives and hold up a pattern for men to go by. Have mercy on this man.

"Make a self case of him. He actually succumbed to the desires of his heart whereas most of us think about those things but refrain from carrying them out. Does that free us if we think about carnal things but let it end there? No. Go back to the Holy Bible. And what does the Bible say about that? It says if a man look upon a woman to lust after her he has already committed adultery in his heart.

"And that could be reversed to apply to womankind as well. So if you can say with a clear conscience that you have never had that thought then you can condemn Otto Pell. If, on the other hand, you have looked upon the other sex with lust in your hearts you'd better be careful what you say for you're as guilty as Reverend Pell who let his desires dictate his heart.

"This church is in a time of crisis but it's not the time to bow down and give up. It's a time to be reborn, to work harder than ever for God and to think about godly things rather than wallowing in the pits of human failures.

"There have been other negative things happening in the Bear Grass community, not the least of which was the Ku Klux Klan making an appearance and calling a young colored man to the carpet. And what was involved? It goes right back to human flesh and bowing down to the lower instincts of man. The devil can always get you with the human body. He knows just what it takes to set a man's heart aflame. He tempts a man with a woman. He sees he's weak where the flesh is concerned.

"What happened to the young Negro was a great pity. Not that he may not have deserved punishment for this act, but because the woman involved was as much to blame as the colored boy. And the Klan was not a court of law and had no right to set itself up as being the group to mete out justice.

"I have read of the moonshine raids in Bear Grass. Right here among us there are men making whisky and selling it to bootleggers who supply these little stores and who keep it in their own homes and sell it to fathers who desperately need the money for their families. They sell it to teen-age boys who defy their parents' wishes and play the fool and take risks with their own lives. Boys under the influence of whisky have no scruples and will do things they'd never think about if they were sober. These things cause children to rise up against their parents and brother against brother. They cause other people to become angry and sometimes a young boy loses his life all because of whisky. What a pity.

"But Bear Grass is no worse than other communities. Don't you ever think that it's worse here. We're alike everywhere so being at some other place doesn't make it any different. It's a sign of the times.

"God set a pattern for our lives in His Holy Word. But we must remember that every human being is a unique individual, governed by the components that make up each person. All of us don't receive the same amount of genetic components. The human body is such a complicated structure and man knows so little about himself we remain a mystery as to our own inheritances. But the medical community is seeking to unravel the mystery.

"We do know that those minute chemicals that certain glands in our bodies produce have a tremendous impact on what we are and how we react to our environment. Certain glands may produce more chemicals in some people than others, causing them to react in different ways. So different behavior in some people may be due to the interaction of those chemicals. Thus, although God gave us an example to go by, those minute amounts of chemicals may not fit the pattern for all people. What I'm trying to say is that although the pattern is established, chemicals control how we react and it may not be in the traditional manner.

"That, however, doesn't excuse us as members of society who are expected to follow the traditional pattern when we err, despite their effect on the human body.

"How are we to know what motivated Reverend Pell to act as he did? Was there something in his make-up that overshadowed his sound reasoning? I'm not attempting to vindicate him. I am asking each of you to question your own hearts to see whether you have a problem you find hard to control. If that is the case, you should pray that God, in his all-wise judgment, will right some chemical imbalance in you that causes your problem.

"If all men are created equal then why is it that some people are born so deformed and brain-deficient they can never function normally? We see them almost on a daily basis. Somewhere along the way the development process went awry and Mother Nature failed to fulfill her purpose. The result was a human being that had no control over his destiny. God didn't cause this to happen. The pattern of inheritance was set at the beginning of time and that pattern follows the lines of nature. Therefore, all living things are subject to mishaps in nature.

"Have mercy on these unfortunate people. If you feel among the norm in your inheritances, give thanks to God. It would be well for you to say 'but for the grace of God, it could just as well be me.' It would be well also for us to overlook the failings of our fellowman and pray for him instead of criticizing. We never know what we would do if we were in the other man's shoes.

"We allow for man's animal nature in society. And the church is not immune either. What do we tell our young women? Dress modestly. Don't expose any part of your womanhood to the male gender. You know what his nature is. Don't tempt him. Gird yourselves to ensure that he will not defile you. That very admission says that men are supposed to be endowed with the nature to conquer, to defile, to ruin a maiden. Why? Because of those chemicals that are flowing through his body that make him a man. And what does society say to him? Nothing. But they say nothing about those chemicals that make women female also. Is that a fair way to judge? Isn't a woman entitled to her nature as much as a male? Who knows what her chemical imbalance may be that she cannot resist the urge for male companionship that might be judged inappropriate?

"We've got to be realistic brothers and sisters. We cannot pull the wool over our heads and pretend ignorance. Ignorance will not excuse us if we have the knowledge to know.

"And above everything I would not have you think that I condone improper behavior. I do not condone what Reverend Otto Pell did. But I am asking you to judge only after taking into account the entire picture. You may be sure that man will be judged by the only fair judge - Jesus Christ. And aren't you glad it will not be any man with all his prejudices and opinions? God will know the very heart of each individual. He will see the pluses and minuses and he will mete out his punishment accordingly.

"You have noticed, I'm sure, that I haven't taken a topic for my sermon today. I have quoted at random scripture in the Bible. But any Bible scholar would tell you that what I have said is true, and if you aren't a Bible scholar you can find each passage if you will read the Bible through this year.

"In closing I would say to you that Whispering Pines Church has had its share of dissent. You have been troubled and it's time to turn it around. Let's start building from here and let bygones be bygones. Let us not be narrow minded and backbiters. Let us pray diligently that we shall do good works, strive to help our fellowman, lift him up if we can, and if we see those who have fallen by the wayside, let us stop and try to help. If we do the best we can I assure you that God will hear and understand and answer prayers.

"May God bless you."

Chapter 28

Hobby was nearing sixteen. He had grown tall and his voice had become deeper. Thick down covered his face until he had to resort to the razor, which was embarrassing at first. Pearl had to look up to him now and that was a source of great pride to her when she remembered how she had had to look down to him for so long.

It was time to set him straight about the advent of his birth. He was able to understand now and there was no use in putting it off any longer. Nick was away on business in Alabama and looking afar, she saw the Mississippi from her window, noting a lot of activity on the water.

"Let's go to the river," she said to Hobby as he came into the room, stretching and yawning.

"All right. I don't know anything better to do. You ready?"

"Yeah, as soon as I get us a towel to sit on and fix some sandwiches."

"Going to be there a good while, I reckon."

"Maybe," Pearl said as she came into the room with two folded towels. "Here, you carry the bag of food."

They found a spot to their liking, spread their blankets in an isolated area and sat down to observe the traffic along the waterway. A riverboat was moving slowly upstream, its paddles churning up the water and barges loaded with cargo moving slowly.

"Strange how people are so fascinated by water isn't it," Hobby said. "I remember our fascination for just a creek back home. Heck, we didn't even have a river on our side of the county."

"Yeah, people are crazy about water," Pearl said. "And we don't even stop to think about its value. We like to wallow in it, drink it, sail on it and all manner of things. And we can only see its true value in places like this. Just think what it has done for Memphis. And Nick feels about the river like you do about Bear Grass. It's something he grew up with and that is a part of him."

"The only difference is it's not threatened Mom," Hobby replied. "It will just keep on moving along with the passing of time."

"Have you grown accustomed to Tennessee?" Pearl asked as Hobby lay facing her while resting on an elbow.

"Ah, I guess so," he answered with a shrug.

"I kind of like it," Pearl said. "People can get accustomed to about anything. It seemed like a foreign country at first, but it has grown on me. And Nick has helped a lot. He has told me everything he knows about Memphis, its customs, its ways, how people think and it has brought me much closer to the people."

Hobby stared down the river and didn't comment.

"I sure hope you can learn to like it here, hon," Pearl said. "I'd be very happy if you could adopt Tennessee and make it your home." Hobby didn't reply to that either.

"You're getting to be a really big boy," Pearl teased and Hobby flexed his muscles and laughed at her. "A real he-man," he teased.

"Seriously, you're a big boy," Pearl said. "And I'm so proud of you Hobby. I was just thinking that it's time to start calling you Hob. I don't know why mamas are always naming their little darlings Hobby and Bobby and Billy and names that always sound babyish when they know that the name will be shortened when they are men. So you're Hob Turnage now and getting all grown up."

"Are you trying to make a man out of me before I'm sixteen?" Hobby asked.

"No, but it's time to do something I promised you I would do when you were old enough to understand. And that time has come, sonny. It's time to tell you about your father, so prepare yourself for a shock."

"You're really going to tell me?" he asked. "All right, go ahead and shoot. I'm prepared for the worst."

"Gant Turner!"

Hobby rose with a start. A look of complete shock came over his face. He had thought about several men in the community but Gant Turner had never been one of them. Then he realized that that made Wilbert Lee his half-brother.

"Really?" he asked.

"That's right," Pearl said.

"I can't believe it. Of all people, I'd never have thought about him. But I must say he's a nice person. But Mom, why have you been silent all these years?"

"It was my fault more than his," Pearl said with a blush. "I never blamed him for what happened. I thrust myself on him at a time when I was very vulnerable. And I knew that he wasn't getting any attention from Abie. I actually took advantage of him, and I know that sounds like I was a real hussy, but it was just one of those things Hobby - an interlude when passion seems to take precedence over everything else. Then when I found out I was pregnant and moved away to Tennessee, I thought that there was no need of ruining his life by naming him the father when it would have done me no good anyway. So I decided to just let everyone think what they wanted to and say nothing. And just look what I have as a result. I'm just as proud of you as I would be if President Roosevelt was your father."

"Wilbert Lee is my half brother," Hobby said. "I find that hardest to believe of anything else. Do you reckon that is why I worshipped him when I was small?"

"No, that's not the reason," Pearl said.

"But we're so different," Hobby said. "He must have gotten some of it from Miss Abie."

"He got an awful lot of it from Miss Abie," Pearl said.

"Gosh, what a puzzle life is," Hobby said with a sigh.

"And I'm sorry for any embarrassment I have caused you," Pearl said as she reached over and touched a leg. "I know there is a certain cheapness about it that you can't overlook. That's the way the rules of society work. And it's good to have those laws. In general, it has worked but of course there are always those who go beyond what society sanctions, and that's when the participants are relegated to the seamy side of life."

"Mother, I never thought of you in that light," Hobby said. "I knew that I was different because I couldn't claim anybody as my father. But I never thought of you as being responsible. And if I had known and had told people that my father was Gant Turner it would have been worse than it was. It's no big issue, so forget about it. Sometime I'll tell Mr. Gant that I know he's my father and I'll mention to Wilbert Lee that I'm his half brother. But I'm not half as proud of it now as I'd have been when we were little boys. Are you going to tell the people in Bear Grass?"

"Yes, I'm going to tell Gant Turner next time I'm home and I think that will be soon. I'll tell Nick as soon as he returns from Alabama. Then I'll tell Mama and Papa and I don't care who else knows about it. Once a person knows about it in Bear Grass the news will spread with the wind. But that is no concern of mine Hobby. I still feel like a human being despite my indiscretion."

"Did you meet with him a lot of times?" Hobby asked.

"Just once my dear. And he was the only man I knew until I met Nick. So you can see the extent of my "running around.""

"Thanks for telling me Mom," Hobby said as he rose and began brushing off his pants. He noticed a river boat with many people on deck going for a cruise and a whistle blew as Pearl rose, dusted off her skirt and yelled over the noise, "You're welcome."

Chapter 29

Oh, the joy of being eighteen; the pain and trauma of growing up rapidly receding, the visions of manhood more clearly defined: A world to conquer and a future to look forward to.

Hobby stood on the threshold of life, thinking about all the changes that had occurred since he was a child; changes that few people could associate with. By a twist of fate he had been transformed from a sharecropper shanty in North Carolina to a shining white mansion in Tennessee. Unbelievable. Even a body transformation, going from a stooped cripple to a normal-proportioned body that gave a new perception to life.

Because of major surgery that kept him hospitalized for a good part of a year and a half, and the tutoring he received while hospitalized, his time had been taken up without too much time for thought. And then four years in high school.

During the intervals between surgery he had been allowed to go to his mother's home in Memphis to relax, to be wheeled about to the many places of interest in the city; trying to adjust to a new way of life.

Because of the circumstances and a carefully-designed plan by an over-solitious, but loving mother, he had been kept from the haunts of his childhood for six years. Six years! He had not been once to Bear Grass. He had not seen the people he grew up with and the older generation that he respected and liked. Some had died. Some had moved away. Change had occurred in Bear Grass also. People had changed. Nothing stands still, he told himself. Change is like a fast-moving weather front that affects everything in its passage.

Rather than coming to visit his grandparents, they had come to visit him once or twice a year, sometimes by bus, several times by plane, and once via train, although the route was so circuitous they refrained from railroad travel after their first experience.

He had been apprised to a certain extent as to what was going on in Bear Grass but that was far short of being there to see the whole picture. He was about to enter his freshman year at Tennessee State and he was going home for a visit before beginning the school year. He was going home!

Absence had not diminished his love for the place and the people. It had only accentuated it.

A million questions were on his mind as he made plans for the visit. What would his buddies be like as grown-ups? Would they accept him as he had been accepted as a child? Would he be regarded in a different light? Because of the rise in his position, would he be shunned and thought of as an oddity? He couldn't resume old ties in the same way it had been when he was a child. When you are a child you think as a child, act as a child, do as a child. But when you become a man you put away childish things. At heart he still thought of the boy who had left Bear Grass with misty eyes, giving up everything in a boy's world; now wanting to pick up where he had left off, although realizing that was an impossibility.

Had the landscape changed? Would all the beauty still be there that he had carried in his heart every day since he had been away?

He was overjoyed to see his grandparents, but he greeted them with a feeling of strangeness. The new house was nice and Craven had already planted fruit trees that were beginning to grow. Most of the things he remembered best had been left at the old house. Nick had bought it from Wilbur Stroud who had promised to leave it just as it was until a time when the family might want to move it.

Soon after his arrival he visited Stroud's store just to see who might be there that he knew. But being a work day, all the young folks were in the fields and most of the older ones. Wilbur greeted him with a hug and held him off a distance to look at.

"I swear I can't believe it," he said as he patted Hobby on the back. "They've made you over. I watched you as you approached the store and I couldn't tell who in the world it was. Then I saw your face and I knowed that you had to be Hobby Turnage. Here, have a drink on me," he opened the box and pulled a Coca Cola from shivers of ice. "How have you been son?"

"Fine Mr. Wilbur. But I missed you folks more than you'll ever know."

"I would have thought that being in that mansion and everything would have changed you so you'd forget all about down here."

"This is just about the happiest day of my life," Hobby said. "It seemed like I wouldn't ever return to the place I love best in all the world."

Several men came into the store and all were shocked when they saw Hobby.

"I reckon all the boys are in the fields," Hobby said, remembering all too well what farm life was like.

"Yeah, they're working as usual," Jasper Parker said. "You come back tonight and a lot of 'em will be here. Everybody will want to see you."

"How are Philip and Wilbert Lee doing?" he asked Wilbur.

"Anybody'd have to have a search warrant to find them two," Wilbur replied. "They're not doing like they ought to, Hobby. Since they got grown seems like they're trying to show theirselves."

"I still want to see them," Hobby said.

"Well, I'll pass the word along that you're home and they'll probably look you up while you're here. How long will you be down?"

"A couple of weeks," Hobby replied.

On the way back to the house he noticed Gant Turner working under the shelter. Might as well break the ice, he thought. He felt a little ill at ease as he approached Gant. Gant looked at him without appearing to recognize him.

"Hobby Turnage, Mr. Gant," he said as he extended his hand.

"Well I'll be damned," Gant said as his face reddened and while he scrutinized the boy. "When did you get here? And my, my, what a change in you." It was hard for him to realize this was the little crippled boy that used to limp over Bear Grass.

"I haven't been here long," Hobby told him. "I feel like I'm in heaven just to be on this soil. And so much has happened Mr. Gant."

"Yeah, I know, and all of it good for you Hobby. I'm so glad for you I don't know what to do."

As they talked Abie watched through the kitchen curtains. She didn't want to face Hobby Turnage after all she'd said. She shook her head as she looked at him. "I wouldn't admit it to a soul," she said to herself, "but he's got everything. And he looks like a man but you can see something about that pretty Perline in him." Then she became angry when she realized Gant was his father.

"I don't know how to say this," Hobby said with a sort of stutter. "I reckon maybe you think I ought to jump all over you and raise hell and say all the bad things I can think of because you're my pa, but I'm not like that Mr. Gant. I always respected you and I still do. You've always been nice to me, and I appreciated that, even when I was a little boy. And I thank you for the gift of life Mr. Gant. I love life as good as anybody on earth. Wouldn't change places with anybody. Wouldn't change a thing if I could. I wanted to say those things to you. Mother explained everything to me very simply when I was old enough to understand."

"They's some things people just can't say, Hobby," Gant said. "This is one time when I find I'm completely tongue-tied. There's nothing I can say. I'm glad your ma explained it to you so you could understand. But I think mighty highly of you. And I know you can't never think of me as your father and I shore don't blame you for that. I'm just glad that you can still look upon me as a man with a little common decency. Thank you Hobby."

"When will Wilbert Lee be home?" Hobby asked.

"You know as good as me," Gant replied. "It's a shame about that boy Hobby. He's as different from you as black and white. I don't even try to keep up with him no more. You know how it's always been and now Wilbert Lee just runs wild. Is that enough said?"

"Yes sir," Hobby said as he started up the road. "Tell him I want to see him if you get the chance Mr. Gant."

"Oh, I will," Gant said in a louder voice as Hobby was going down the road.

Hobby stopped at the old house filled with a million memories. His grandfather had given him the key when he started to the store. He opened the door and thick cobwebs went all the way across the room. He ducked his head and went inside. Everything was covered with dust, but he made a visit to each room, stopping in the room that had been his. He longed to spend the night in the old house but realized immediately that that would be impossible. He knelt by the bed and put his face on the dusty quilt. He promised himself that one day the old place would sparkle again and would be preserved forever so that he could go there for solace when things in the everyday world were turned upside down.

He returned to the store after supper and saw several of the boys. They didn't seem the same somehow, although they were all friendly. All were young men now with a different look about them. He saw both blacks and whites that he remembered, and a few whom he had not seen before. People were moving in and out of Bear Grass just as in any other place.

Viola cooked all the foods that he liked and every meal was a veritable feast. Her knack for cooking had not changed at all with the years. His grandparents' love was as strong as it had been the day he left when they cried all day and for several days afterward, as he had done.

His only worry was that he'd so soon have to leave his backwoods paradise and return to Tennessee and enter college.

He actually kissed the ground in his grandparents' yard. He stood and looked all about him for familiar sights, and they were there along the roads and in the woods and the silhouette that composed the horizon. He laughed aloud.

He waved his hand at everybody that passed, whether he knew them or they knew him. All of them were a part of home.

Down Greene County road, where the Negroes lived, he walked leisurely and talked to the hands in the fields. All that knew him were glad to see him, and he was even gladder to see them. He asked about Roscoe and was told he stayed up North most of the time. Circling back on another route, he stopped and saw La Beth Sims who happened to be working at the house.

"Hobby!" she exclaimed. "I can't believe it! Just look at you."

"And you've grown so pretty," Hobby complimented her. "How's life been and how are things in Bear Grass?"

"The same old Bear Grass," she laughed. "It never changes Hobby."

"Yes, it changes," Hobby said, "and I'm aware of it more than you for I've been away so long."

"How long has it been?" La Beth asked.

"Six years, and it seems ten times that long."

"I'm so glad to see you," La Beth said. "Have you seen many of the boys and girls we used to play with?"

"Quite a few, but not all of them. I've been trying to get up with Wilbert Lee and Philip but it seems that they are steering clear of me somehow."

"You haven't missed too much Hobby," La Beth said. "No nice girls around here will go out with them and if they would their parents wouldn't let them. They've got a reputation a mile long."

"And I heard a lot of things about Minnie Mae Moore," Hobby said.

"Lord! Don't even mention her name, Hobby. She turned out to be lower than a dog and I'm not trying to be critical in what I've said about Wilbert Lee, Philip and her. But you know all the other boys and girls that we knew turned out pretty good. We've got a right decent set of young folks around here."

"Is Minnie Mae still around La Beth?"

"They say she stays in Hallsborough most of the time. I never see her anymore. She's one person people seldom mention anymore."

"Poor Mr. Jiley and Miss Lany," Hobby said.

"I'm so sorry for them," La Beth said. "They've tried twice as hard to keep their heads up since all the scandal about Minnie Mae."

"Well I admire them for that," Hobby said.

"You look so good Hobby. I can't believe what they've done for your leg. You're really a handsome young man."

"Thank you," Hobby said, blushing. "And I know the Finches have moved away but do you ever hear from them?"

"I sure don't," La Beth said, "and I loved them girls like I would my own sisters, I used to play a half a day at the time with Robyn and Arlene. We made enough playhouses to have a city, crushed enough poke berries to supply the county and mixed them with mud and had the best looking pies you ever saw. And the juice got all over us." She laughed.

"I liked them too," Hobby said. "The whole family - Miss Cora, Mr. Tobey and all the boys and the girls too. I've been thinking about going down to Jones County to visit them while I'm down."

"Oh, I know they'd be tickled to death to see you," La Beth said. "I wish I could go. And if you see them, tell them I said hello, you hear?"

"I will," Hobby said as he stood to leave. "I really want to see them, and I may just go tomorrow."

When he told Craven and Viola they were pleased. "Remembering how you used to stay around them so much, I know you'll enjoy it," Viola said. "And they'll be glad to see you Hobby. They were mighty good to you when you were little."

Hobby boarded the bus early next morning, carrying a small bag with him, for he expected them to ask him to stay for a day or two.

He took in all the sights along the way and appreciated every one of them. Every tree, every creek, every pasture, every building spoke of home. "Beautiful, beautiful homeland," he said to himself.

Cora and Tobey were delighted to see him. They were the only ones at home.

"That's not really you is it Hobby?" Cora said as she hugged him soundly. "I can hardly believe it, can you Tobey?"

"It's hard to believe," Tobey said. "But my, how you've changed. You always had a handsome face but there was always that bum leg to contend with. Manly too," he said as he felt the muscle that showed in Hobby's arm.

"Oh, this is so nice," Cora said as she primped her hair. "I've thought about you a thousand times, especially since you left for Tennessee, for I know that you loved Bear Grass enough to almost give your life for it. Was it hard Hobby?"

"You'll never know, Miss Cora. The hardest thing I ever did in my life."

"And I'm so happy about your mother. I heard she married a wealthy man and was living the good life in Memphis."

"Yes, that's right," Hobby replied. "Life has been real good to Pearl. She married a Greek, but he's about the most wonderful person you ever saw."

"Well, didn't the good life rub off on you?" Tobe asked.

"Not enough to make me want to stay out there. Everything's fine and it's luxury for anybody, and so far removed from what I was used to it can't even be compared. But I'd rather be in that little shanty I grew up in Mr. Tobey. But that's just my nature, you know."

They spent the day reminiscing. Cora cooked a good meal. Cora Finch was a topnotch cook and she liked to see people enjoy their food. She remembered the many times Hobby had eaten with them when he was playing with the children and meal time came. He acted like he always relished his food, and she knew it was not because he didn't get good food at home, for Viola Turnage set as good a table as anybody in Bear Grass. And he ate with the same relish and told Cora how good it was, and she felt a glow inside.

They sat on the shaded front porch in the afternoon and Hobby felt completely relaxed. It almost seemed as if he had never been away. The shadows lengthened and the sun made patterns on the ground where it slanted through the trees. Tobey said he had a little work to do in the field and around the barn, so he told Hobby to sit and enjoy himself; that the children would be coming home soon.

Karen and Clyburn returned from school first. Cora introduced them and told them Hobby had been a good friend of her children when they lived in Bear Grass. They had been born after they moved to Jones County. And Hobby made over them and said they favored the others and he'd know they were Finches wherever he saw them.

Arlene returned next. Hobby noticed her coming up the lane and asked Cora which one that was.

"That's Arlene," Cora told him. "When she gets close enough you'll know her all right. She looks like she did as a child."

Arlene stared when she saw Hobby sitting on the porch. She couldn't quite make out who he was. Then she saw his face and began running. "Hobby Turnage," she said as she grabbed him around the neck and hugged him. "I heard your leg had been fixed but nobody told me that you were a girl-killer also. My, you're handsome."

"Don't be too nice," Hobby said with a blush. "And you're quite a killer yourself. Stand off and let me look at you. Yeah, you look the same in the face as you did when you were little. But you didn't have all this then," he made the figure of a voluptuous woman with his hands.

"Teaser," she said. "God, I'm glad to see you. Just seeing you brings back a thousand memories of Bear Grass and childhood."

"The boys would be glad to see you too," Cora said, but Billy Earl is in service and Tom is in the CCC. Tobe got a tractor a couple of years ago and he didn't need the boys to farm so they did what they wanted to do."

The sun was about to set. The setting had turned golden, accentuating the color about them. White clouds had taken on a pink hue as they floated low on the western horizon. The cows were in the pasture and had come up to the watering trough. Tobey was drawing water and the well tackle was making a squealing sound as the rope slipped through. The guineas came across the field and scratched about in the barnyard.

Hobby saw a figure coming up the path and he knew it was Robyn, but he had no premonition of what was about to happen. She was indistinguishable from any young woman as she walked leisurely, returning home from work in the dime store. She noticed someone sitting alone on the porch and wondered who in the world it could be. She knew it couldn't be one of her brothers. She was almost hesitant to approach the porch.

Hobby stood as she approached and she saw his face and knew instantly that it was Hobby Turnage.

His heart almost stopped beating when he recognized her. In an instant, he said a prayer in his mind. Oh God, I wasn't prepared for this. I am so young, Father and my life is just beginning. Is it time for this?

"Hobby!" she screamed as she reached him and they embraced. He looked into the two most beautiful eyes he'd ever seen, dark pools showing shades of violet, completely impenetrable, with a lovely body, warm and soft. It happened in an instant and another burden was thrust upon his shoulders. So young, with so much to be accomplished. He was hopelessly in love.

Chapter 30

Hobby's thoughts had been consumed with Robyn since he visited the Finches in Jones County. He could not make reality out of what he had experienced. Nothing in his young life had ever affected him in the way Robyn had the moment he saw her close-up, realizing that she was the same girl he had played with so many times along with the other neighborhood children. He had never given a thought about falling in love with any person from Bear Grass. He just didn't think in terms of love about those with whom he had grown up. And he knew that he was fatally stricken the moment he placed his arm around her in their greeting. He couldn't concentrate on his classes and she was so far away from him it left a longing inside that nothing would assuage. He wrote her a letter a few days after returning to Tennessee.

Dear Robyn:

I should be studying but I can't concentrate on books. I can think only of you and wondering what you are doing.

I can't begin to tell you how happy I was to visit you and your family and I'm not going to beat around the bush. I fell madly in love with you the moment I saw you and I know that it will be that way with me for as long as I live. I don't know how you felt, but I hope that the feeling I have for you can be reciprocated. I don't feel like I could bear it if you just cast my love aside. And I know that you have been going steady with a boy down there, but God, I hope you're not serious about him. I've never felt jealously before in my life but I'm jealous of him. You said he was a handsome boy as well as nice, and that his father was the head of the Lenoir County school system, and that makes everything going his way.

Another thing against me is that I can't be there to date you, in case you would consider it. Long-distance love has many disadvantages. There are

the football games between rival schools, and young people love to attend
the games and boys and girls who go steady are always looking for places
to go that the parents will approve of. So you'll go to the games with the boys
in your community while I will have to go with the people here. I get scared
inside when I think about all the things going against me.

I hope I do have one thing going for me Robyn. And that is the fact that
you know me from birth almost. You know my sincerity and my love for life
and my happy-go-lucky nature. You can remember all the years that we
played together and how we had such good times. There is no way I could
deceive you if I tried. Of course I know there has to be a picture in your mind
of how crippled I was as well as being unable to participate in all the goings-
on when we were kids. You know my background just as I know yours. We're
just simple, honorable people and I don't know of a better basis for judging
people, although I know the best families can have "niggers in the
woodpile."

You perhaps think this is a very silly letter, Robyn, but I hope not.

I'd give anything if I could be down in Jones County tonight and could
hold your hand in mine. I don't want anything else.

And as to dating, I've been dating a girl here. She is nice and I enjoy being
with her. But it's nothing serious Robyn. That is why I am hoping that you
have that same feeling about the boy you're dating. I have a number of
friends on campus, both boys and girls, and I have no trouble in finding a
date. But it's all in fun. But I'm very grateful Robyn, for I know if my leg had
not been made almost whole it would be a different case. I don't care what
anybody says, to be different is the worst thing a young person can go
through. Girls just simply don't like to go out with a boy whose condition
calls attention to his body and it would be the same if the reverse were true.

I always heard that a person's life pattern was formed by the age of five
or six, and I feel sure that that is the case with me. Here I am in a large
Tennessee university setting out on a medical career. And I sincerely wish
my heart was in it. But it's not Robyn. I was fatally smitten by Bear Grass
and the domain we shared when we were younger. I don't know why it is that
way but I don't regret it. And my mother has my interest at heart one
hundred percent, but she can't seem to understand that my life is tied up with
the area in which I grew up. Mother thinks that in time I will see that I have
chosen the best course. But as a matter of fact, I didn't choose this course.
Mother chose it for me.

But time changes many things and I know that we have to wait for the
passing of the years to look back and see all the crooks and curves that make

our lives what they are. I can't say at this moment what the future will hold. But I know that mine will be somehow associated with Bear Grass.

Why is it that I have to feel this way Robyn? Why can't I adjust to a new way of life that is as different from the life I knew back home as day and night? Not one in a million youths would view it as I do. You wouldn't believe the magnificence of Nick and Mother's home in Memphis. Compared with Bear Grass, I would think I was in heaven. Yet, I think about my little room at Grandpa's and Grandma's, and that is still where my heart is.

Why is it that a boy that grew up with pain every day and had to overcome the obstacles a rural environment imposed upon me sees it all with beauty still? My life was pure pain in Bear Grass, Robyn. You will never know the challenge life presented me when all of us played together along the roads, in the fields, along the creek banks and in the woods and thickets and swamps. Everything was an obstacle for me.

The tall growth along the ditches and in the fields and forests; the crawling vines and briers and crossing the ditches was so hard for me and I would sometimes be so tired after accomplishing those feats I wanted to just lie there and rest. But I was determined to be a participant in all the things the others did. There were deep scratches on my arms and legs that would burn and there was the ache in my leg, always an ache from the time I arose in the morning till the time I fell asleep at night. Grandma would take the salve box and soothe the cuts and scratches and bruises, but nothing soothed the ache in my leg, extending to my hip. I was a young child and I felt like I had the body of an old man.

And knowing all those things, why did I still feel that I was in some kind of paradise and that life in Bear Grass was the grandest adventure in all the world?

I ask myself these questions and I wish you could provide me with some insight as to my feelings, since you were also a part of those days back home.

I guess it was my naivete. But I thought of the morning mists as rain from heaven. And I was selfish in my thinking for I thought of the trees and the streams and the little secret places I explored as being mine alone. I thought of it as my world and I never imagined that anybody else would see it as I saw it in my heart then and still carry the image as vividly in my thoughts as if I were there today. I felt then, and I feel now that I was trying to protect something that would pass from the scene one day in the future and that there would be some of all this beauty to share with the world, even in my lifetime.

I never heard other people proclaim the beauty of Bear Grass, neither children nor grownups. Oh, when the leaves were in color they'd mention that beauty, or the climbing roses on fences or outhouses when they were nourished with spring rains that brought out their blooms. But when all had wilted and the leaves had fallen from the trees and the earth looked bare, I was still seeing the beauty of the naked land. I cannot get those thoughts out of my mind Robyn.

But seeing you again has brought a new meaning to my life. A million thoughts are swirling through my mind - thoughts that I won't express at this time. I feel that I've been reborn and my life is no longer painful. I will be forever indebted to Dr. Robards at Johns Hopkins for performing the miracle of my life. Through rehabilitation I have become for all practical purposes a "normal" American youth. You cannot imagine what that means to me. I find myself popular on campus and I certainly don't feel that I'm the object of pity from those who know me. And I wish so much that I could be down in Jones County so that I could see you often. It might not be dating, as such, for I am aware that you do have a boyfriend that you like very much. For that matter, I have a girlfriend that I like very much but it's far from love. But I am missing out because of my absence and I know I'd have to sell myself to you. And the distance between us makes me very despondent sometimes. At any rate, I would love to fly down to visit you some weekend if that is possible. I won't have time to stay any length of time, and I know that such visits would have to be very limited. In fact, if I went to Jones County I wouldn't even have time to stop by and see Grandma and Grandpa. And even flying, I'd have to take a bus from Raleigh to Jones County and that would take up a good bit of the time I had off.

Please write to me Robyn. A letter from you would be worth more than I can tell you.

Sincerely,
Hobby

· · · · ·

Ten days later Hobby found Robyn's letter in his dormitory mailbox. His heart leapt in his throat. It had seemed like a month since he had mailed his letter to her and he was beginning to worry that she might not bother to reply. He held the envelope up to the light to see where to tear it without ruining the contents of the letter. He threw his books on the bed and sat down in his easy chair, one leg sprawled across an arm.

Dear Hobby:

What memories your letter brought back! I could see it all again. I had no idea you carried such vivid memories of those days.

Needless to say, it was nice hearing from you. I have thought about you many times since those days. I have thought of all the others also and wondered what turns their lives had taken. In a way it seems in another world, not that mine has changed to that extent. I'm still the rural girl and I still love the country and can't quite visualize any other kind of life.

I was shocked when I saw you Hobby. But it was a good shock. I felt like a charge of electricity was flowing through my body and I couldn't hardly believe it. I don't have to tell you that when I visualized you I always saw the little tow-headed boy with the sincere smile and a leg badly out of shape. To have that image shattered in a split-second is a pretty big order. And there I was confronted with a really handsome young man who had grown tall and had matured and whose white hair had turned into a golden blond with flashing white teeth and the same smile I remembered was really something. I was flabbergasted and I found it very hard to realize that you were indeed Hobby Turnage. And you had the same impact on all the rest of the family too. We were tickled to death to have you visit us and you would have been thrilled to hear Mama's praise of you.

Your life has taken a three hundred and sixty degree turn Hobby, and I'm happy for you, although you say it isn't as satisfying as one might believe. But I'm inclined to agree with your mother that in time you will come to appreciate the way of life you know now. You've got a bright future ahead of you Hobby.

Well, quite a bit has happened since you visited us, particularly with me. Chip proposed less than two weeks after you were here. He was really concerned when I told him about your visit and how you had changed so much. I had never even mentioned you to him for you were only a part of all the people I had known in Bear Grass and of course I had told him about my days there.

Chip is a fine young man, Hobby, and he is majoring in engineering at N.C. State College. He thinks that we could live all right with me working while he is going to college. But I haven't accepted as yet. I just want to be sure Hobby, and at this time I'm not really sure. I don't want to make a mistake and forevermore regret it. I want marriage to be a lifetime thing. And I will have to say that I think Chip is more committed than me. He gives me the impression that he worships me, and I can change his moods almost instantly.

I sometimes think that people our age are far too young to take on the responsibility of marriage. I know that the trend today is to marry young and fill the nest with babies and grow up with them. But I may be a little unorthodox in that category.

It would be nice if you came to visit again, although I don't see how I could date you since I am going steady with Chip. You would be welcome at the house and everybody would be glad to see you. But I'd go with Chip to the Friday night game. Arlene isn't going steady and she might consider dating you for the game. Arlene doesn't care about spending all her time with one boy. She's one of these happy-go-lucky gals that wants to get the most out of life possible.

I love all the things that you wrote about Bear Grass and I will have to say you do see it differently from the others I know there. I loved Bear Grass but you had a deeper perception of what it means than I have.

I have to get ready for work and I want to get this letter mailed today so I'll say so long and thanks for writing. Write again any time. All the family sends their love.

Sincerely,
Robyn

Chapter 31

What a combination! Chip Wilson was class president at Jonesboro High. Robyn Finch was valedictorian. Cindy Cole was top cheerleader and Mark Smith the popular quarterback on the football team. Just their positions at school gave them a popularity envied by most of the students. They were the top of the list.

And all this was new to Robyn Finch. She had never dreamed that in her senior year she would be valedictorian. Not the simple Robyn Finch who lived at the end of a lane six miles in the country in a five-room sharecropper's home. She was studious and made excellent grades. And it didn't come all that easily with her. But she applied herself. She had a desire to learn. But her distinct advantage was her looks. She was a beautiful girl, clean-cut, not flapperish or pretentious, but an All-American type with a healthy look including a pretty face with dimples and eyes that always had the look of dreaminess with unfathomable pools of mystique lurking beneath.

Cindy Cole had jet-black hair and dark brown eyes and was shapely in a way that drove boys up the wall. She commanded cheers when the cheerleaders were out on the field supporting the team and urging them on to victory. Most students considered her a bit conceited, although it was not her intention to be that way. But as top cheerleader she wielded a power over the other cheerleaders that they sometimes resented. But the boys at Jonesboro saw her in an entirely different light. She was a sex symbol to them and they raved over her, causing jealously among other girls of the student body.

Chip Wilson was the idol of the female student body. He had all the attributes to make girls' hearts beat faster. He was charming and good-looking. His dark-brown hair was wavy and girls would sometimes go up to him and place their fingers in the waves to set them deeper, and of course such adulation pleased Chip. He had a captivating smile and teeth that would do justice to any toothpaste commercial. He had a full mouth and sensuous lips with an athletic figure. He had the best of all worlds.

Mark Smith could have gone with almost any girl on the school campus. He had a ruggedness about him with a large body towering six feet five inches that made him appear as a giant among the more petite girls. Mark was not handsome. Rather, he gave the appearance of being completely dominant where girls were concerned and they thought of submission when they dreamed about him.

They were a foursome. Everybody at school knew that Robyn Finch was Chip Wilson's girl. They also knew that Cindy Cole and Mark Smith were inseparable. They double-dated regularly. And when games were played on Friday night Cindy sat with Robyn and Chip and flirted with other boys while Mark was on the field.

Weekends were no different. Chip owned a new Model-A Ford and they made the rounds every weekend, riding into Jonesboro and drinking Cokes and eating sundaes at the corner drugstore, the most popular meeting place for the teen-age set. And after taking in the scene they would get in the Model-A and ride around town and out into the country with Cindy and Mark in the rumble seat and Robyn sitting close to Chip in the front. Sometimes they would park and talk seriously and speak words of love to each other. The boys would become amorous and attempt to have their way with the girls, but Robyn and Cindy were wise to their advances and they put them in their place in short order. They had had good teaching at home and premarital sex was taboo with them.

Sunday afternoons were fun times. With few boys able to afford an automobile, it was a distinct advantage to have a car to ride over the countryside, with their hair flying in the breeze and the top of the Model-A down. There was much laughter and joking and they'd stop by a lake sometimes when young people were swimming, although they never had swim suits with them at such times.

Chip owned a Kodak camera that had been a Christmas present from his parents when he was fourteen. He always kept film in the camera and during their Sunday afternoon jaunts they would take pictures. They numbered in the hundreds and the four of them shared the prints when the film was developed.

There were shots of Robyn and Cindy standing in the rumble seat with their hair blowing as well as their skirts, with their mouths open from laughter. There were Robyn and Chip sitting on the hood of the Model-A with Chip's arm resting on Robyn's shoulder. There was Robyn standing on the running board with the door open as if she were fixing to enter the car, with Chip's hat set at a jaunty angle on her head.

There were Mark and Cindy kissing (which they never showed to their parents). There was Chip standing beside the car with his arms resting on the top and a very special smile on his face. Robyn liked this better than any picture she had seen of Chip. There was Mark in all his masculinity standing tall above the automobile dwarfing it with his height. Cindy would kiss the picture sometimes when they were going through the collection. They determined to keep them always as a testimony to their youth.

Everybody at Jonesboro High assumed the two couples would wed. In fact Chip had spoken many times about what he planned to do after he and Robyn were married, and Mark was always saying, "My woman forever," in referring to Cindy.

Robyn had done a lot of thinking about her high school years since her reunion with Hobby. There were so many memories of her days at Jonesboro High and she treasured them all. They would be ending in late May when she graduated. She had hoped to enter EcTc (East Carolina Teachers College) with emphasis on the E and T with no apparent reason for saying it in such a manner except that it was the way it was spoken. But her father had not had a good crop year and despite his and her mother's efforts, there would not be money for tuition. She accepted that, however, being the practical girl that she was. She would find some kind of job in Jonesboro.

The real question in her mind was whether she really loved Chip. It had been that way since the outset of their courtship. Chip had declared his love early and although he didn't show it to a great extent, there was jealously that he manifested that bothered her. If she spoke to another boy when they were together he became upset. He was always watching to see whether she smiled at other boys and there was a possessiveness about him that didn't set well with her. And she really wanted to love Chip and to be all the things he expected of her.

But somehow there was a bridge between them she could not cross. It was generally expected from those who knew her that she would marry Chip. This was assumed by her family as well as her friends. She had come to expect this and whatever reserve there was in her mind she shoved it into the background until she received the letter from Hobby. She had done a lot of thinking since then.

First, she was made fully aware that she didn't love Chip in the sense that a girl should love the boy she intended to marry. That is why she had refused the beautiful diamond he had tried to give her a year earlier. She had told him that they were a little too young to go that far; that a diamond meant total commitment and she wasn't sure they should go quite that far. But Chip still had the diamond and he was always trying to get her to place it on her finger as a token of their love.

They attended church on Sunday night after she received Hobby's letter and after the service ended they rode to Jonesboro for a little while, cruising up and down the streets, and Chip showed a nervousness that wasn't a usual part of his actions. She had mentioned in church that she had received another letter from Hobby.

"What's wrong Chip?" she asked.

"Oh, nothing," he replied. "I was thinking about this new boy that has come into your life and I am all shook up. I believe you have a feeling for this boy, Robyn, and it bothers me."

"Jealously showing again," Robyn said and Chip admitted that he was in turmoil. There was a hint of a sob in his voice. They parked on deserted court square. Chip took her chin and pulled her face toward him. "I love you too much to lose you, Robyn." She noted a tear in each eye. "I can't stand the thought of it and I love you so much my life will end if you refuse to marry me. Why did he have to come back into your life? We were doing so well and I was looking forward to marriage and starting a family. And you seemed to be happy with me even if you haven't agreed to marry me as yet. I gathered it was only a matter of time."

"Why does life have to become so complicated at such an early age?" Robyn asked. "These are the years to be happy and carefree and they are so short-lived. Childhood and youth should be the two really great periods in our lives. But the problems begin early, don't they Chip?"

"I have been the happiest boy that ever lived," Chip answered. "There wasn't a cloud in the sky until the day that Hobby" (he said the name with a sneer) "came back into your life. Since then I feel I have been in the path of a tornado. My world has gone to pieces." He was sobbing now.

Robyn felt awful at causing Chip so much grief. She placed an arm around him and tried to console him. "Please Chip," she said, "don't be like this. I haven't committed myself to Hobby Turnage. We have a lot going for us. We've been sweethearts for three years. We both have had many opportunities to date others. I've seen girls pawing over you and I've been jealous also. You've seen other boys paying attention to me and you have become enraged. But we have remained true to each other. It isn't over Chip."

"Then will you marry me?" he asked as he pulled her face to him and kissed her passionately. She smelled his breath edged with the odor of Dentyne chewing gum and she felt the sensation that she always felt when Chip became amorous but she tried to push the feeling into the background.

"Oh, maybe," Robyn replied.

"Does that mean we are engaged then?" Chip asked.

"I didn't say that Chip. I just said maybe."

"Then please accept my ring Robyn. That's all I ask. Just let everyone know that we are engaged and I will wait as long as you wish to marry you."

Robyn felt that she was at the crisis of her life. She had a feeling for Chip she had never experienced with any other person and she realized that she had not had the opportunity to experience that feeling before for she had become involved with Chip as soon as she was old enough to date and that had excluded all others from her life. And she had to tell Chip that Hobby Turnage was coming the next weekend and she knew that that would only increase Chip's worries.

After a long silence Chip said, "If you only knew the extent of my love for you you would marry me right now Robyn. We could elope and drive to Dillon, South Carolina within a couple of hours and get married by the justice of the peace tonight. Mother and Daddy think very highly of you. They think you are a fine young woman as well as beautiful. I'll admit they've said several times that I should play the field to be sure I know what

I'm doing. But they said that to try to get me to be sure I was doing the right thing. They love you, Robyn and they want the very best for us."

"I know what you mean," Robyn said. "Mama and Papa have also told me I should date other boys just to be sure I was truly in love with you before entering into marriage that might not work out like I expected."

"I don't need any of that," Chip replied. "I know my feelings and I want only you, Robyn."

"But there is something I must tell you," Robyn said as they sat in the dim light of the street lights on Court Square. A few pedestrians were walking casually down the streets, oblivious to them in the shadows of the trees.

"Hobby is coming to visit the family weekend after this, Chip, and I don't want you to go all to pieces about it. It's no big deal since Hobby is a friend of the entire family and he can be at home with any one of us. It won't be a dating weekend and I will attend the game with you at New Hanover High."

"He's coming to see you Robyn. I know it. What other reason would he have to leave Tennessee to come way down here for a weekend?" Robyn noted anger in his voice and he turned away from her. She knew him well enough to know that he was red-faced and at such moments there was a look in his eyes that disturbed her.

· · · · ·

Hobby's heart sank after reading the letter. He sat staring into space for a long time, his leg still thrown across the arm of the chair. He heard the clock ticking and a cricket was chirping somewhere in the room. The ticking of the clock reminded him that he was working against time and that the odds were all against him.

He pondered the letter he had written Robyn again, assimilating all the words he had written for a meaning as to why Robyn could not see how sincere he was and the seriousness of the situation. Then he realized he had written as if he were the main character, not she. He had told her his deepest thoughts about his view of his little kingdom without really considering whether she would think of it in the same way. What had he really offered her, he asked?

He had said nothing about becoming a doctor and what that pursuit offered. He had discounted that completely, allowing his heart to rule his head. Robyn would have an opportunity to enter an entirely different way of life if she married this Chip fellow that he disliked very much despite Robyn's high opinion of him. He was consumed with jealousy.

From what he had written, Robyn would have to consider him an eccentric who had some weird conception of life totally removed from the mainstream. Few people on earth would be able to view it all as he did.

He had played on her sympathies in describing his life of pain as a child and he hadn't been asking for sympathy; only stating that despite the pain and suffering during those years, he was still able to regard his kingdom as the greatest place in the world.

Robyn could not know the pain he was experiencing at this moment. It was greater than the physical pain he had experienced in getting about his domain. He knew that he loved her fully and completely and that whatever happened Robyn Finch would always be the most important person in his life. It was so poignant, so tender and protective, so all-consuming and he wanted to impart that feeling to her for all that it meant to him.

But he was fully aware that if his life was ever to be complete, it would have to be with a girl from a rural background that would love the things in nature that were so important to him. Despite his great love for his princess, if she were to be unhappy in the environment he loved it would never work. He could not blame Robyn if she felt differently than he. She had the right to choose the way of life she loved. With him it would be a continuation of the lifestyles of the poor and unknown. Oh, they wouldn't live as he had lived. They would have all the good things in life although shielded and protected from the eyes of the world. But it would be far different from handsome houses and manicured lawns on windswept hills with walkways sloping down to streams, he thought.

But you just didn't see a girl for one time and fall hopelessly in love with her, he tried to reason. Yet, he had read of this and he knew that it could happen.

What course of action should he take? There would be plenty of time to scheme and plan to work his strategy on Robyn if she were not already deeply involved with this Chip something or other. Every moment that he waited would be putting her farther from him. And he didn't blame the youth for trying. He just wanted to prevent Robyn from accepting his proposal of marriage. No doubt he had been urged by Hobby's interest in the girl.

Hobby had to see Robyn as soon as possible. It wasn't important that she go to the game with him. What was important was declaring his love for her without any beating around the bush and trying to get her to delay marriage until he and Robyn could really get reacquainted again. At this moment, to think of a week seemed like a lifetime when so much was on the line. It was the most critical point in his life.

While he was sinking deeper and deeper into depression the telephone rang and it was Pearl. "Hi son," she said, "and how is my young collegian today?"

"Okay," Hobby replied.

"Well, you're not very convincing. Something's wrong Hobby. Tell me what it is."

"Nothing really Pearl, just one of those days. You know what I mean." He didn't want to go into any discussion about Robyn at this time.

"Well, I would hope so," Pearl said. "Whatever affects you affects me son and if there is anything I can do let me know, Hear?"

"Nothing's wrong Pearl. I've got a heavy work load and it requires a lot of study and you just feel burned out sometimes. That's all." He didn't even intend to tell his mother what he was planning to do. "And how is Nick?" he asked.

"The same old good boy that you know, Hobby. He is the nicest fellow in the world. But I will hang up now and let you work yourself out of this mood. Call me soon for I'll worry about you until I know everything is okay. Bye now, and take care."

"Bye Pearl."

The shadows were lengthening but Hobby had no desire for food, so he didn't go to the dining room. He just sat, still staring and was oblivious to what was going on on campus. He thought about how lucky he was, despite his present feelings. All because of Nick Staphal. He had just thought about boarding a plane and flying to North Carolina, thanks to the generosity of old Nick. He had a wardrobe of clothes comparable to the upper echelon of students. He didn't have to stint to have money for Cokes and movies. All these things would be an impossibility without the help of the man who had come into his family's lives. And he was so sincere in wanting to help and went out of his way to keep you from feeling you were an imposition on his life. There was only one Nick Staphal.

He would rather wait and say all the things he needed to convey to Robyn in person, but he wasn't at all sure she would talk with him or whether there was time before she might accept the youth's proposal. His mind was tormented. If she only had a telephone and he could talk with her it would mean so much to him. He smiled when he thought about the telephone when not a person in the Bear Grass community had a telephone nor had he ever talked on one until he came to Tennessee. He realized that modern conveniences meant as much to him as they did to all those who were fortunate enough to have them available to them.

There was only typing paper in the room and he took out several sheets and placed them on the table. He filled his pen with ink and found a blotter and put it beside the paper. He rubbed his hands together and cracked the knuckles in each hand as he tried to think how to begin. It was so important and yet he felt inadequate in trying to express himself.

Dear Robyn. He knew that was the beginning. But what should he say next? Dear Robyn seemed inappropriate for the occasion. He tore up the paper and threw it in the wastebasket and took another sheet. He decided to say the entire body of the letter with the first three words.

Dear Robyn:

I love you!-Sincerely, hopelessly, for as long as I shall live.

I had to say this Robyn for I fear I may lose you and I just want you to let that settle for a while before you make your final decision about marrying the young fellow you are going with.

I don't know how it came about that just seeing you after growing from a child into a man brought about this revelation, but the moment I saw you and we embraced on your front porch, everything about my world changed. I have lived in a cloud since that time. It was the most magnificent feeling I have ever experienced and although my world was bright and beautiful, because of you additional colors were added that gave it an almost ethereal effect. I will never be the same again Robyn.

But there are other things I must say to you. Things from the heart and the bright hopes and plans I have for the future.

As you know, I am in pre-med school and will major in orthopedic surgery.

I will take great pride in being a bone surgeon Robyn, and I will devote my time and energies toward reaching the goal I have set for myself in that field.

But there is a very sad fact I have to admit about being a surgeon. It will be an interim profession. It will not last forever. I hate to admit that even to myself, but that is the way it will have to be.

You know Robyn, some men are governed by their heads rather than their hearts. They go through life, never looking below and listening to the things the heart tells them. To do otherwise would be admitting a weakness they don't want to associate with manhood. You've seen so many of them. Nothing in life appears to appeal to them - not their wives nor their children who are the greatest assets they will ever have - never stopping to relax and look about them for things that could bring smiles to their weary faces.

My life is dictated by what the heart tells me. Maybe that is impractical and maybe I look upon life from a slanted angle. But I have to listen to those things that speak peace to my soul and a fulfillment not possible in any other manner.

I know I sound like a sentimentalist who has no real goals and who expects to go leisurely through life without work and expecting the world to provide a living for me. That isn't true my dear. I have a giant goal to achieve and it will require much work and planning and many obstacles to overcome. And the clock is ticking Robyn. There isn't the time to experiment and lay out strategy and work leisurely. The time clock is already set and within ten years it will be too late. I will tell you all about it when I see you.

I hope you will let me come down next weekend, ten days from now. If you will, write to me immediately and I will arrange to leave here on Friday and will return on Sunday. I look forward to hearing from you.

Love,
Hobby

Chapter 32

Hobby was in a state of excitement as he prepared to travel to North Carolina. He decided not to tell his mother of his plans since she probably wouldn't call during the weekend, and if she did he could say he was on a date or give some plausible excuse.

As he boarded the plane, he was in the depths of depression. Everything in his young life was going wrong and there didn't seem to be anything he could do about it. He hoped the stability of the Finch family would restore his confidence in life.

He rode a Seashore Transportation bus from Raleigh to the little Jones County town of Jonesboro where Tobe, Cora and Robyn met him. Tobe had owned a Model A Ford for a couple of years now. They were all smiling and welcomed him and he was suddenly at ease. He embraced all of them and looked deeply into Robyn's eyes for some sign of endearment, but they were elusive, as they always were.

He felt the same warmth in the Finch home that he remembered from the past. Tobey placed two or three oak saplings on the fireplace upon their arrival and the smell of burning wood and the accompanying smoke brought on a peaceful feeling. When he went into the kitchen a brightly-colored tablecloth that still had the smell of newness and the jar of hot pepper, the vinegar cruet and the salt and pepper shakers took him back in memory to his grandparents' home in Bear Grass.

He felt close to these people. They were one of the best memories he had of his early years.

"It seems just like home," He told Cora.

"I'm glad Hobby," Cora said. "You always seemed like one of the family anyway."

Robyn came in and said, "Hobby, I will be going to the game with Chip and Arlene had told a boy she would go with him when I suggested that you ask her, so I don't have anything for you to do except sit around the fire and talk to Mama and Papa."

"Oh, don't worry about me." Hobby said. "I can be comfortable with Miss Cora and Mr. Tobey."

"Yeah, we can catch up on the old days," Cora said. "They have already become history no longer than it has been. I declare time passes so fast there's no keeping up with it."

"I am aware of time passing also," Hobby said. "I suppose when you're young you aren't supposed to notice the passing of time, but I feel there won't be time enough to do all the things I want to do."

"I know you have ambitious plans Hobby," Cora said. "I'd like to hear about them sometime when you feel comfortable about telling them."

"I'll just do that one day," Hobby said.

Arlene came by and joked and carried on with Hobby for a while and they laughed as they recalled events from their days in Bear Grass, but the girls had to hurry for their dates and soon Hobby reclined in a rocker beside the fireplace and he was joined by Tobye and Cora. The younger children, whom he had never known, were in another room studying. Tobey built a fire in their bedroom at night so they could be comfortable and do their lessons without interruption.

It seemed strange to Hobby. At the Finch's there had always been a large group of children, but with Tom now in the Army and Billy Earl in the CCC, there were no boys his age around, and with Robyn and Arlene away there was a quietness he could not associate with the Finch household. He looked into the fire and spun a dream of Bear Grass and a smile came upon his face and Tobey said, "You must be dreaming a pleasant dream Hobby, judging by the look on your face."

"Yeah, I guess so Mr. Tobey," Hobby replied. "I've dreamed so much that seems to be part of my nature these days."

"Say, tell me about your home in Tennessee," Tobey said. "What's it like and do you like it out there?"

"The home is beautiful and so different from what I've been used to I pinch myself sometimes to be sure it's reality," Hobby replied. "Tennessee is beautiful and all that, but I'm not happy out there, Mr. Tobey. I am one of those unfortunate creatures who can't seem to accept change. And too, I was fatally stricken with Bear Grass in my formulative years and my visions of the area won't go away."

"Bear Grass was a good place to live," Tobey said, "but I just couldn't make it there. I have done better farming with my uncle. Of course he has given me every break possible because I'm looking after his farm now that he's not able to take care of it himself. I've learned to like it down here in Jones County just as well."

"Yeah, it's fine here," Hobby said. "But I got my start in Bear Grass and I studied my terrain, knew it and learned to love it, and I don't believe anything will ever change that."

"There's just one thing about it," Tobey said, "and that is the fact that it's just farmland with a lot of very poor people and it's more or less isolated and I don't know what you could hope to accomplish out there."

"I know what you mean Mr. Tobey," Hobby said. "And I can't tell you my plans right now, but I believe everything will come out fine in the final analysis if things work out according to my plans."

"I'm sort of in the dark about the whole thing," Tobey said. "You are planning a medical career, instead of studying about farming when your goal is out in the rural areas. I'm confused."

"The medical career is my mother's idea," Hobby said. "She has insisted on me studying to be an orthopedic surgeon. So I gave in to please her."

"Orthopedics deals with bones doesn't it?" Tobey asked.

"Yes," Hobby replied. "Mother became obsessed with bones because of my crippled leg and she had in the back of her mind all along that if I could be made whole with surgery she would insist that I become an orthopedic surgeon to repay society for what I had received. And I accept that as a noble idea, but I feel that I'm trying to hide something by studying, or I will be at least, when I should be pursuing my own dream."

Tobey replenished the fire and Hobby wondered what was going on between Robyn and Chip. He wondered whether he was placing Robyn in an almost impossible situation by being here and he suddenly felt guilty about coming down. It seemed that everything he did was wrong.

Then Cora came in and asked him about Miss Viola and Mr. Craven and Pearl and Nick and whether he had to take any special care of his leg now and he told her all the folks were fine and that he didn't have to take any special care of his leg.

"Well, it's a modern miracle." Cora said. "You had a bad leg Hobby, and to see you so normal is almost unbelievable."

"I'm most grateful Miss Cora," Hobby said. And so the conversation went until Robyn returned about eleven o'clock, when Tobey and Cora said they would retire and allow them time to talk for a while.

Hobby noted that Robyn had been crying when she came in, and he felt more guilty than ever for he knew that he was involved, whatever emotions had caused her to cry. This put them both ill at ease and they sat silently for a while and stared into the dying fire.

Finally Hobby said, "Did you have fun Robyn?" and she just shook her head.

"I notice you have been crying and I'm sorry and I feel guilty for I know I am a part of it all. I'm so sorry Robyn."

She stared into the fire for a long time without speaking, then said. "You know something Hobby. I wish I were ten years old again. Life was so easy then, so carefree and I didn't have to make any decisions. I could play with my baby dolls under the oak trees and I lived in a world all my own. But maturity brings on problems and I feel that I'm too young to assume them. I feel like there's a heavy weight on my shoulders. We never know how to appreciate childhood until it's past do we?"

"We sure don't," Hobby said. "I will go along with everything you said Robyn, and maybe we're still children at heart. Don't you think?"

"I think we're trying to evade the responsibilities of life," Robyn said. "But I think we're trying to assume responsibilities we're not prepared for."

"You wish I hadn't come, don't you Robyn?"

"I didn't say that," Robyn replied.

"I intruded," Hobby said as he took the fire poke and turned the piece of wood that was still burning. "I shouldn't have come, but I felt that I had to. I felt it was the most important thing in my life; that everything hinged on this visit. And I didn't come to hurt you. The last thing I want to do is to hurt you Robyn. I had to plead my case. I wanted to be sure you knew what you wanted. This is life or death with me and I feel that I need some kind of answer so I can get on with my life. I have been miserable Robyn. My grades in school are suffering. I have lost weight. I can't sleep and I don't seem to ever be hungry anymore. Maybe I'm just being a fool Robyn. I feel like sometimes that whatever I do is wrong. I can't explain it to you, but since the moment I saw you when I was here before I have been affected that way. That's why coming here was so very important."

"I understand," Robyn said. "My life has been in turmoil too. I haven't known which way to turn. Chip is insisting on getting married, and if I have learned anything from this it is that I'm not at all sure that's what I want to do."

Hobby's heart skipped a beat when he heard those words.

"I'm not sure that I love Chip, Hobby, but I'm not sure that I love you either. Somebody is always getting hurt in love it seems, and I don't want to hurt anybody. Anyway, I broke my half-way engagement to Chip tonight. I told him we would be friends and I said that I wasn't committing myself to you either. I told Chip to let up and give me a little room to breathe and do some thinking for myself."

"I'm glad you made that decision," Hobby said. He felt a load lifted from his shoulders. He couldn't ask for more.

"And there's something else Hobby. Your lifestyle is so far different from mine now I don't know how you can even associate with me."

"Do you mean because my mother married Nick?" Hobby asked. "If that is the case, they have a beautiful life and all the things that go with it. But that is their life but it doesn't apply to me. Oh, it could if that were what I wanted. But that's not like me, Robyn. I guess the song "Home On The Range" would describe me as well as anything could. You know about 'giving me a home where the buffalo roam and all that and where never is heard a discouraging word and the skies are not clouded all day,' that's me Robyn, a sense of freedom under the skies of Carolina, a sense of space and nature and you could find those conditions in a thousand different places. I have already chosen mine and it's a dream I have to follow and maybe you consider all that I am saying silly and the pursuit of an elusive dream rather than getting down to the practical things in life. But to me it's a serious business."

"And just what is this dream you are pursuing Hobby?" Robyn asked and he noted those impenetrable eyes who might be envisioning some pursuit he could not know about her.

"I will only be preserving what is already there Robyn," Hobby replied. "All the things that are in evidence now will be gone one day, only memories of a time that was. I already see it beginning. Aren't we seeing tractors taking the place of mules on the farms? The age of the mule to till the land will be gone before we know it. The tools and the farm implements will go by the wayside, forever forgotten and lying in the rubble of yesterday. All those things must be collected, for they will no longer be available. There must be a 'gathering of the sheaves' so to speak. Only a few years are left to begin the process and I have a compelling urge to begin now even though my hands are tied at this point and there's nothing I can do about it."

"And how do your mother and her husband feel about it?" Robyn asked.

"Mother can't quite understand it, and that's something hard for me to understand for Mother is my greatest ally in all other endeavors. And her background is as rural as mine, as you know. It's only where my becoming an orthopedic surgeon is concerned that she differs from me.

"And Nick Staphal is the greatest guy in the whole world Robyn. He has taken me under his wing as if I were his real son. I don't believe there's anything he wouldn't do for me. As a matter of fact, it is only because of Nick that I can pursue my dream with a reasonable expectation that it might come true. It couldn't be without Nick. And he understands my position thoroughly but he loves my mother so much he wouldn't hurt her for anything in the world.

"So while he encourages me to keep working on my plans he also encourages me to become the best bone doctor in the country. If Nick had a choice without hurting anyone he'd tell me to go for it now, for he knows I mean business. So you see I am caught in the middle and I feel like I'm being pushed from every angle. And maybe you can't see it from my point of view and I don't blame you if you can't but I think you should know where I'm coming from."

"Oh Hobby," she said as she looked straight into his eyes, "who would ever have thought the little Hobby Turnage who was so carefree, so happy, so smiling and exuberant about life would have carried such thoughts inside?

"You are amazing Hobby. Do you know that? I don't know what I thought about you back in Bear Grass, but in my wildest imaginings I would never have guessed that you would have grown up to be what you are today - handsome and tall with broad shoulders and a seriousness that I didn't know you possessed. It all seems like a dream. I ask myself whether we are the same girl and boy that played together a long time ago."

"I ask myself the same thing," Hobby said. "Those were such wonderful days Robyn, when all the children in the neighborhood played together and there wasn't one care in the world."

"Yeah, I remember Wilbert Lee and Philip Stroud, and Tom and Billy Earl and the colored boy - what was his name? Roscoe? And all the others. Have you seen any of them since you left Bear Grass Hobby?"

"No, I've not seen any of them," Hobby said. "I'm sorry about that too. I loved all of them. And do you remember how I worshipped Wilbert Lee in those days? How I pestered him and how he treated me? I reckon if he had known in those days I was his half-brother he would have killed me." He laughed as he recalled those days.

"That's something else I need to know about Hobby. When you found out that Mr. Gant Turner was your real father, how did it affect you?" She had heard about Hobby learning who his father was through a friend in Bear Grass whom she saw at a church conference.

"It didn't affect me in any way that I know of. I always had respect for Mr. Gant," Hobby said. "He lived close by and I had a chance to observe him closely and I'd take him over Miss Abie any day of the week. Miss Abie was all right I suppose, but you know how she was. Always ready to criticize everybody except Wilbert Lee and always ready to defend him, whatever the circumstances. She was Wilbert Lee's worst enemy Robyn. And that's hard to say about a boy's mother.

"If it's possible Miss Abie poisoned Wilbert Lee. She didn't even teach him to respect her or his father. They had no more control over Wilbert Lee than if he were not even their son. He is a good example of what happens when there is no parental control over a child. I always felt sorry for Wilbert Lee although he went around presenting an image of the community leader among the children. I knew what his life was like at home and I always felt that he was covering up for what he was missing at home."

"It's midnight, and time for us to be in bed," Robyn said with a yawn. "You'll sleep in Tom and Billy Earl's room." They stood before the fireplace and Hobby stooped and kissed Robyn lightly on the face and they said goodnight.

"We'll take a walk at the edge of the woods tomorrow," Robyn said as she entered her bedroom door. "You always liked to roam the woods, I remember."

Hobby drifted off to sleep immediately and slept all night, the first time he had done this in weeks. He only woke up when Cora Finch knocked on the door and told him to get ready for breakfast. He felt at a loss for a moment, for he had to go to the back porch to wash his face and brush his teeth. He thought: how soon we forget things that are commonplace once we are used to modern conveniences.

They laughed and joked over breakfast and little incidents of the past were shared and Hobby was calm and there was a sense of peace inside himself that brought a smile to his face. And Robyn appeared more cheerful also.

"Hobby, I'd like to fix something for dinner that you especially want if I can," Cora said. "Have you had any chicken stew lately?"

"No mam," Hobby said. "I've thought about chicken stew a hundred times when I went for chow and there was nothing on the menu that I liked. They have what they call chicken and dumplings but it's nothing like you fix, and I think I've tried most of them. Chicken stew would be as good as anything I know of."

"And chocolate pie?" Cora asked. "I remember that you used to relish that."

"You haven't forgotten a thing Miss Cora," Hobby said.

It was warm outside and the sun was shining. There was a gentle breeze and it was a typical late fall day. The color was gone from the forest which was a subtle brown now, mixed with the tans of autumn. As they walked at the edge of the forest Hobby heard a sound he hadn't heard in six years - the crackle of the leaves as his and Robyn's shoes touched the coating of leaves on the ground. It sounded as if it had only been yesterday that he had been there and he could see the birds as he remembered them, perched in the trees and chirping for attention. He remembered his little blue bantam rooster and the little blue-spangled hens that roamed with him in the fields and into the forests and he was the boy again.

"It's beautiful," he said to Robyn. "Take all the high places and all the cities and suburbs and just give me the open spaces and the forests and I'll be happy." He gazed into the skies and Robyn thought he was seeing something beyond. After a while he said, "But there is always the loneliness," more to himself than to her and his words startled her, for on so many occasions she had felt the same way. "In the largest crowds, on busy streets, any place, there is always the loneliness. There is always something crying in the soul, unknown that seeks expression, something that will set a mortal free and release him from all burdens. Is that my lot in life? To search forever for that which will fill my soul and make me a whole man?"

He then looked down at Robyn who was sitting on a tree stump.

"I guess I got carried away," he said. "But in all the flood of memories and having you here with me I felt like I was coming alive after lying dead, waiting for a miracle to breathe life into me. Forgive me Robyn," he said as he sat down on the carpet of leaves.

They sat silent for a few moments, listening to the sounds about them. It was quiet except for the wind in the trees and an occasional chirp of a bird.

Then he resumed the conversation. "I am calmer than I've been in a long time Robyn. And now that I've upset your life I feel guilty about coming. But I won't do this again I promise you."

"Now wait a minute Hobby," Robyn replied. "It was good that you came. It helped to open my eyes. I think this has been a good meeting so please don't make any apologies for coming."

"Do you sincerely mean that?" he asked and she reassured him that she did. "It takes the pressure off me Hobby and gives me time to think. My mind was in a jumble and I couldn't see my way clear. This has helped me a lot and I feel like I can relax now and be a teen-ager for a while."

"And I can go back to Tennessee and get down to my studies. I feel like I can get a grip on my life at last. So many things have happened it doesn't seem real anyway," Hobby said.

"I can imagine," Robyn replied.

They stood and headed for the house, but Hobby lingered for a moment. He turned to Robyn and took her into his arms, "I won't show my real feelings," He said, "for to do so would be pressuring you again. I have already told you that I love you. But I want you to have time to think things out. It will be such a great distance between us and I won't be able to come down often, so ahead of us stretches a great distance and a long period of time. And if there is any consolation in it for me, they say absence makes the heart grow fonder and I will have to believe that in order to survive."

"I won't forget you Hobby," Robyn assured him.

They walked hand in hand to the house to the chicken pastry and chocolate pie that awaited them, and it seemed like old times as Hobby ate two large plates of pastry and a sweet potato with the gravy from the stew. "Pass the dishrag" he said, laughing, remembering how they had used a dishrag as a napkin at his grandmother's.

Arlene got up from the table and went to the stove and got the rag, and Hobby wiped his hands and they all laughed again. It seemed perfectly natural to Hobby for it was something he had always done before going to Tennessee. And it had been common practice for the Finches as well.

These were such fine people, Hobby thought as they sat and laughed and discussed life in general on Saturday afternoon. Nobody had any plans for the weekend. After learning Hobby was coming, they planned the weekend around him. Tobey took him over the farm and to his uncle's house, and introduced him and they had a long talk with the old man, who told him stories about the "old days" and they roamed over the barnyard and the chickens were running about the yard and the mules were in the lots and Hobby felt a real sense of home.

Sunday morning was the same way. Cora had one old country ham left and she cut it and Hobby knew long before breakfast was ready that there would be ham and gravy and scrambled eggs for breakfast along with the buttermilk biscuits and he'd bet anybody there would be grape preserves too.

It was such an important day in his life, yet it was carried out so casually and normally there seemed to be nothing to mark the occasion. In later years when he recalled that day, it seemed to be the most important day of his life.

The Finches took him to the bus station Sunday morning for the long trip to Raleigh to catch the plane that would take him to Tennessee. He felt sad at leaving Robyn behind, yet there was a feeling of hope in his heart. There were many obstacles to overcome and theirs would be a long-distance courtship, if there were to be a courtship, at best.

He said goodbye to the family and stood for a moment alone with Robyn and little was said. He wanted to gather her in his arms and tell her all the things he felt, but the family was nearby and it was an awkward moment and he kissed her cheeks lightly and told her he loved her. The bus was ready to leave and he sat at the window and waved goodbye and there was a lump in his throat and he couldn't see too well. He realized that was because there was a tear in each eye.

By the time the bus reached Hallsborough the blues had set in and he became depressed. Just a few miles away was his beloved Bear Grass and there were remembrances of happy times when he had gone to town on Saturday. And his grandparents were nearby but he didn't have time to visit them. There were no telephones out that way and he was unable to contact them. Nostalgia swept over him and he felt completely alone in a big world. He felt that he was too young to accept all the responsibilities of an adult.

The plane trip to Tennessee was uneventful and he was soon back on campus at the university. He had to think of it as a new beginning. It would be a long time before he could take off for a weekend with Robyn again. He had to really get down to his studies, so he settled down to campus life and applied himself, and his grades improved greatly.

Chapter 33

I t had been three weeks since Hobby's return from his visit with Robyn. He had not heard a word from her. He was discouraged, yet heartened because she wasn't engaged to Chip Wilson. She said she'd think about the situation and he wanted her to have ample time. Let her make comparisons and she would be better able to make her decision. He dreamed of her day and night, seeing in her the answer to everything he could want in life. She was radiant and beautiful, yet it was a subtle thing and not all-encompassing. She looked like the All American girl with a healthy skin and chestnut hair that flew in the breeze. An All-American bobby-soxer with a face that looked like it had just been washed, a good figure made for sweaters and legs that only really showed their loveliness when she wore heels. But she was pretty beneath that front. She was kind and considerate and understanding and she always smiled. That brought out the dimples in her face and her smile brought out the beauty of her teeth.

He had gone so far as to visualize their children. They would have many to make up for his loss of brothers and sisters. He could see little girls as carbon copies of Robyn and maybe boys that resembled them both.

In thinking of her his mind seemed to cross every valley, every hill, every highway and artery that separated them in distance. It was a broad expanse that enhanced his longing for her. She was the only thing that could complete his life and make his existence worthwhile. The fact that it would be a long time, if ever, that they could be one added to his solitude. It didn't seem normal to him. People in Bear Grass fell in love, married and settled down without distance being involved. It was like the rest of his life in that there was always something that kept him out of the mainstream; always something a little different, leaving him on the outside.

He wanted to blame his present situation on his mother, for he was acceding to her will rather than his own choosing. Yet, he admired and loved his mother so much he found it impossible to blame her. He knew she was doing only what she thought was best for him. He always had to live for tomorrow, knowing that nobody even had a promise of that elusive word; that tomorrow never comes.

And he realized that the young years were so important; that they would never return and if you couldn't look back upon youth with nostalgia there would always be something missing in your life. It had been so happy in childhood and the world appeared as a rainbow with all the colors blazing and the beauty ready to pluck, like gathering grapes. It had ended so sudden. He knew it would be wrong to write to Robyn in such a state of mind. Then he received her letter.

Dear Hobby:

I've been doing a lot of thinking since you were here. And it seems like a fantasy world. I've walked in the woods a lot, for I can think clearer there and I get a touch of nature also. I am always able to find something that interests me. Sometimes it's a cocoon hanging on a bush and I think of its homeliness and what lies within its silken shield. I think of the lovely moth that will emerge one day and I always wish I could be there at the moment it makes its appearance. Sometimes I see the squirrels gathering acorns and I watch their furry tails as they work and how beautiful they are. Sometimes I look through the trees and see patches of blue sky and I think I must like nature as much as you.

And I think about you Hobby. I find it hard to associate you with the little boy I played with. You were handsome and likeable then, but there has been such a transformation in you I see you as a different person. I see your broad shoulders and slender hips and your shock of thick, blond hair and your flashing smile, which is your trademark. And the smile is the same as always. You smile the happiest smile I ever saw. It lights up your whole face and your eyes become bluer and you show such a sincerity there is no reason for me to doubt you.

I think it must have been predestined that you would re-enter my life, for I see something in you that I haven't seen in any other person, even Chip.

I have fallen in love with you Hobby. You seem to be a part of me. I don't quite understand it but I guess I'm not supposed to. We don't know what the future holds, but nobody does. Look what's happened to you. And your mother. Nothing is impossible. I'd never have dreamed that you would ever be in Tennessee when we roamed over the fields in Bear Grass. Nor that I would be down in Jones County.

But I am committed Hobby. I didn't write earlier for I wanted to be absolutely sure. This is serious Hobby. The most serious step we will ever take. I learned that lesson well with Chip. I didn't want to make the same mistake again. Distance will be a problem for us, but it's something we have to contend with. You have to prepare yourself for life and becoming a doctor is good preparation I believe. That requires dedication and much study. I know it won't be easy for either of us. But we're adults now and we have to act as adults. And one day, one fine day, we'll be together forever I hope, and that all these things that seem such huge obstacles now will be overcome and we can live in that world that we visualize.

Love,
Robyn

Hobby almost jumped to the ceiling when he read the letter. She was his! There was no longer any doubt. They would share life together one day! He hadn't proposed to her but he would as quickly as possible. He would write to her and tell her to call him collect from a telephone booth in town and he would get on his knees and ask her to marry him. He would call her darling and all the endearing things and then he would go and visit his mother and Nick and tell them. He hadn't even told them about Robyn. That would explain his indifference and his problems with his studies.

Things were finally beginning to change for Hobby Turnage. It seemed as if he had been wading through a jungle that was choking him off from life, overtaking him with its untamed growth despite all his efforts. But there was a clearing in the distance and he could see the sunshine. He was emerging and he was the winner.

What a life! he thought. So much was happening in the world. Life was whirling by and each person had to grasp whatever he could and hold on to it, for life is for the living and it's an individual thing with each person savoring whatever he can which holds the most meaning for him.

He hadn't told Robyn about his plans for the future beyond his medical career. He always thought about that as a secondary career despite his admiration for the medical profession. That always brought a feeling of guilt, for he was aware that medicine was one of the most respected professions. There were degrees in agriculture, but he was not pursuing such a degree. To his knowledge, there were no degrees awarded in what he was planning to accomplish.

But he would take Robyn there and show her and explain. He would show her the exact location and try to make her understand that what he was doing was for mankind; to capture a time and a place and a way of life for future generations to see and know how the world was in the 1930s and 1940s. Not so much for this generation, for they knew. They saw. They lived it. But signs were everywhere that it would all end and it would be like animals that become extinct. Once gone, it could never be recaptured.

As he thought, he felt time closing in on him. He felt such an urgency to get started he couldn't concentrate on anything else. And he couldn't fit the actual world into the world he visioned, for a lot of bad things were happening in the real world and he thought of the world about which he dreamed as being a paradise in which there was nothing to detract from the paradise. But he knew that that was only a daydream; something he would have to look beyond, for nothing in life is perfect.

They would visit all the old haunts of childhood. He would take her to his secret places and they would find the wild fern and the little creek way up in the woods where the scrawny pines grew. They would see the tall trees where the wild grapes grew and he remembered where the wild flowers had covered the ground in spring and where the wild animals came out and scampered before him. It was a world far removed from his world of today.

Hobby didn't associate his world with that of his mother's and Nick's. As much as he loved them, he couldn't fit himself into such a society. He felt out of place in that setting, and that was of his own making, for they had gone out of their way to welcome him. He just wasn't built for that kind of world.

But now wasn't the time to dwell on those things. It was a time to be amorous, to be filled with thoughts of love; to be young and impetuous and to think of himself as a young lover, a role entirely new to him.

He wrote to Robyn and told her how happy he was to receive her letter and that what she had written meant more to him than anything in the world. And he promised again that he would not push her; that she could take her time and get all of her priorities in order. He expressed his undying love and said he'd give anything if he could be with her this very moment. He did tell her to call him from a public telephone collect and gave her the time and day to call; that it was very important. And Robyn called at the appointed time.

After telling the operator he would accept the charges he said, "Hi Robyn."

"Hi Hobby."

"I'm so glad you called Robyn. Of all the times that I've wanted to be somewhere else at the moment, this one has got to top the stack. I'm overjoyed that you said you loved me. I've waited for those words since I saw you that day when I went down to Jones County."

"Oh, I think it was just meant to be Hobby. It dawned on me like a ton of bricks. I hadn't planned it at all. I didn't know what was happening to me when you embraced me that day. It seemed comforting to have your arms around me. I think I must have known at that moment that yours and my future were tied together. In a way, it's scary the way things developed. Maybe there really is an angel watching over us."

"Bless that angel Robyn. I'm the happiest man that ever lived." He got down on his knees and told Robyn so, and said, "Will you marry me one day when everything is right and we can become man and wife with no strings attached? I'll wait as long as you like, and it will have to be after I graduate. I would hope we could wed when I enter medical school, but that isn't a must. Will you Robyn?"

"You know I will Hobby."

"Then I must plan another trip to Jones County. I want to give you your engagement ring. Tell me, do you like yellow gold or white best?"

"I'll accept your choice. You decide. I haven't worn enough jewelry to be prejudiced. It's the meaning that counts anyway. But don't spend beyond your means."

"Are your eyes as pretty as the last time I saw them?"

"They're the same, but I don't know what you mean."

"Like they're filled with violets and the purple is so dark they're impenetrable."

"Oh."

"I don't think it would do for me to be near you right now Robyn. You have a tremendous effect on me even this far away."

"I must be on my way Hobby. Someone is waiting to use the booth."

Chapter 34

A mysterious petition began circulating in the Bear Grass area that caused a commotion and much talk for quite a while. The mystery was that no one could pinpoint the originator of the petition. It concerned Abie Turner, of all people.

The petition read: We, the undersigned, do hereby petition Whispering Pines Church to take immediate action against one of your members, namely, Abie Turner, for the following reasons:

(1) This woman has caused more disharmony in the Bear Grass community than all the other citizens combined, and this has been allowed by the church who has turned its back on her gossip, allowing her to remain a member in good standing, despite her tongue that has the sting and venom of a snake, to ply her trade throughout the community, breaking up homes, turning wives against husbands and husbands against wives, causing hatred among children and disharmony in general.

(2) It has been stated over and over that when Abie Turner "totes" news around there are always additions and omissions that distort the facts. Abie Turner has never been known to have a high opinion of any other person, no matter what the circumstances. She calls herself a Christian and says she's out to save the world. In reality, it is her desire to destroy the world. Christianity to her is contained within herself.

(3) The people of the Bear Grass community are turning to other churches for their spiritual needs in the light of Abie Turner's crusades. The originators of this petition have a list of fourteen people who had a leaning towards joining Whispering Pines Church who turned elsewhere, but have a genuine concern for the Bear Grass area and recognize Whispering Pines to be the dominant church for the white community. And we realize that this petition in itself cannot be made to bear on the Official Board of Whispering Pines Church as to any action that might be taken. However, this petition can have great bearing on the membership of said church. It also gives a

community a perspective on the woman named in this petition.

- - - - - - - -

One hundred seventy nine names were attached to the petition.

For once, Abie Turner was not made aware of the news that was being circulated in Bear Grass.

The populace began hearing about the petition and everyone that heard about it wanted to read it. It was more than a month after the petition began to be circulated before it was presented to Whispering Pines Church, and excitement grew every day it was being circulated. Those who read it checked the names of those who had signed and placed it in the hands of someone who had not added a signature on the paper. Most everyone signed the petition.

Imagine the excitement when it finally reached Wilbur Stroud's store. It was brought in on a rainy afternoon when men flocked to the store to get away from the house. One group was playing penny poker and another setback when Wilbur said in a loud voice, "Hear this men. The petition about Abie Turner has finally arrived. But there are so many of you it will take a long time to pass it around so I'll read it to you if you'll be quiet."

"Hot damn, we've finally got something juicy," Jasper Parker said. "Hell, I'll sign it sight unseen. Go ahead Wilbur. Read it. But let us finish the game we've started first."

Wilbur went back over every name while the men finished their card games. Practically everybody in Bear Grass had signed it, he noted, and he pondered whether he should put his name on the list. After the games were finished, all the men turned toward him on their bottle crates and he read the charges against Abie.

Adam Pridgen rolled a golden grain cigarette, twisted up the end to keep the tobacco from falling out, took a wooden match and struck it on his rump. He shook the match until it stopped smoking and took his thumb and thumped it toward the heater. "Tell you one thing," he said, "if she was the last woman on earth I'd take to the water if I couldn't even swim."

"Amen," Enos Butts said. "I hain't never had nobody to git on my nerves as bad as that woman does. When I see her coming I look the other way cause it makes me not want none for a whole week, and I don't like to be like that." Everyone laughed.

"She has caused more young'uns to git whupped, more men to slap their old ladies, more women to hate their old men and more moonshiners to hate her guts than anything that's happened in Bear Grass this century. Not for what she said herself, but she got the news strewed and others picked it up and added something to it and God, it's been a mess. I shore hope they will do something at the church to shut her mouth."

"I hain't never heard of a thing like this before," Walter Finch said as he spat a mouthful of tobacco juice toward the spittoon, "but it's the best idea I've heard tell of around here. And by God, I can see why people are turning away from Whispering Pines Church. Now ain't she somebody to point to as a member of the church?"

"She was bad enough before it came out that Gant Turner was the daddy of Perline Turnage's boy," Enos said. "But Lord God! That just set her on far and she pure run that in the ground."

"I been thinking about it fellows," Jasper Parker said, "and I don't know how Gant Turner ever put up with that shit-face. But they's something else you got to think about too. Gant Turner has suffered the tortures of hell with that woman, but they's one thing that he's done that nary one of us hain't. And I don't mean no disrespect in what I'm going to say, for Perline Turnage has done something that few women ever do. But as you know, they hain't never been a girl in these parts that could half compare with her. So old Gant has had the worst and the best of womanhood."

"Ain't it the damn truth," Nelson Willoughby said, stretching his legs to get to an itching place. "Ain't nothing wrong with a little bit on the side if you can git away with it. 'Course, it's kind of sad what happened when the girl got knocked up."

"I don't believe she'd change it if she could," Wilbur said. "She loves that boy of hers like a hog loves slops. Acts like he is the greatest thing that ever lived."

"Pass that paper around," Enos Butts said. "Let all of us that hain't put our names on it write it down. I can't wait until the Church Board gets on her and she acts like she's got a corncob stove up in her."

"You ever heard of anybody hated that bad?" Nelson Willoughby asked.

"Naw," Enos Butts said, "and you know the women feel the same way. My old lady says whenever a woman sees Abie coming up the path to her house and Abie hain't seen her she runs and hides and don't come to the door."

"I really believe she was the cause of preacher Pell's downfall. If she'd kept quiet I believe everything would have blowed over and he'd have settled down. But naw, she got a far started and she just kept adding fat lidard to it," Jasper Parker said.

Everyone in the store signed it, even Wilbur Stroud. The pencil lead wore down and the pencil had to be trimmed and when it got dull the men would wet the lead by sticking the pencil in their mouths.

- - - - - - - -

Callie Stroud saw Abie coming up the road and went out on the porch. She had been delegated to get Abie to the meeting of the Church Board. "Howdy Abie," she said as Abie approached. "Come up on the porch and blow a minute. There's a little breeze out here."

"I hain't hardly got time Callie," Abie said. "I'm on my way to the store to git a box of lye. I've got all these meat skins saved up and my soap is gitting low and it's full moon you know, or near about, and I want to git a pot of soap made."

"I made a pot a few days ago," Callie said. "And how have you been getting along Abie?" She looked bad to Callie.

"Sort of low cotton," Abie said. "It's got so I hurt somewhere about all the time. And how is everything going in Bear Grass? Seems like I don't hear much no more."

"You know more than me," Callie replied.

"I did hear that somebody moved in the house on the other side of Luby Sauls that had been empty for some time."

"I didn't know about that," Callie said. "But I don't pay any attention to such things."

"I heard the family came from beyond Hallsborough and that he's a bootlegger and Lord knows we don't need no more of that kind in our midst. And they say he's got a daughter eighteen or nineteen that's throwing herself at the menfolks if you know what I mean."

Callie thought: She's up to her same old tricks. But she said, "You've saved me a trip Abie. If I hadn't seen you I was going to your house in a little while."

"Well, that would have been nice," Abie replied. "I don't know when you ever darkened my door."

"There's a meeting of the Church Board tonight Abie, and it's important that you attend."

"Callie, you know I'm not a member of the Church Board. I don't have no say in it but I will say that if I did there'd shore be some changes made. Besides, I've got apples picked and ready to be peeled and canned. I was going to peel them tonight. I've already washed the jars and wrenched them. I don't see how I can go."

"The Board appointed me as the one to see that you are at the meeting," Callie said.

Abie looked at Callie and it was evident there was a question on her mind.

"What's that?" she said as she looked directly into Callie's eyes.

"Because it concerns you," Callie said. "That's all I will say about it."

"Well I can't for the life of me imagine why," Abie said as she took her apron and wiped her sweating brow.

Callie noticed how fat Abie had become. She was stuffed into a corset that just pushed the fat in other places. She noted swollen ankles, a pited face and cloudy-looking eyes. She realized then that Abie was far from well.

"What time are they meeting?" Abie asked as she rose to leave.

"Seven o'clock at the church," Callie said. "And try to be on time Abie."

"Oh, I will," Abie said. "I'm curious to know what this is all about."

- - - - - - - -

The entire Board was at the church when Abie arrived. Board members included Ada Creech, considered the voice of fair play with a broad vision and the ability to sort out rumor from truth; Callie Stroud, Kenneth Tyndall, Joseline Hill, Hub Henderson and John Blount. Every member was on edge. They were confronting a situation different from anything they had encountered. They were, in effect, being judged by a community.

"I liked not to have made it on time," Abie said as she took her fan and began swishing it about her face.

"Well we're glad you're here," Miss Ada Creech said. "And this is not a happy occasion Abie. We've got a petition here that we want you to read in its entirety before any business transpires." She took the petition and handed it to Abie. "The overhead light ought to give enough light for you to see it."

The Board members walked into another room and left Abie in the sanctuary.

Abie began to read and sweat was pouring off her face. She was fumbling at her clothes and tears were in her eyes. Her name was on the paper but it was not Abie Turner at all. She was reading about somebody else. It had been her calling to save the Bear Grass community from the very things she was being accused of. Couldn't anybody look at her and what she had preached and know that she was against all such things? There is a straight and narrow path to heaven, she reasoned, and it is so easy for people to take the wrong path and end up in hell.

She thought about the charges again, and all the names that were on the petition and for the first time realized that she had been all the things she was charged with. She had been the first to criticize everybody else without taking a single look at herself. She had been the best Christian in Bear Grass in her own estimation. She had valued no opinions except her own. She had not gotten the moat out of her own eye as the Bible taught, before looking

at other people to criticize. She was about to be turned out of Whispering
Pines Church and that was the worst thing that could happen to her. She was
the most hated person in the community.

Abie was crying openly when the members of the Board re-entered the
sanctuary.

"What do you have to say for yourself?" Mrs. Ada Creech asked.

"Guilty," Abie replied meekly.

"Do we have any choice as to what to do?" Kenneth Tyndall asked.

"There's nothing to do but turn me out for the good of the Church," Abie
replied. "I can't stand it when I think that I have caused people to go to other
churches."

"I want you to know that we sympathize with you Abie," Miss Ada Creech
said. "We really do. But this petition has pointed out that we have not been
the governing board that we should be. We are guilty too, Abie, and our
heads are hanging in shame. We are criticized equally as much as you. We
knew that you were a person that carried news over the community and that
you caused a lot of problems, but you were a long-time member and we just
swept it under the rug, not even stopping to realize the effect it was having
on the community."

"God knows I'm sorry," Abie said with a sob. "But it's too late now.
There's nothing left for me. I'll admit I'm too open-mouthed. And for the
first time I see that I've ruined my own boy. I've ruined myself with Gant,
I may have played a part in what Otto Pell did and I've said enough about
Perline Turnage to send my soul to hell ten times. And I can't take none of
that back now. It's already been said. And I'm a sick woman folks. I don't
feel good in my body no more. I'm really poorly. But I'm not asking for your
pity because of that. It's each person on his own, you know. They's a time
for everything. A time to be born and a time to die. A time to be young and
a time to be old. A time of good health and to sow your good deeds."

Sobs racked her body and she sat with her head bowed as the Board looked
on this broken person with pity in their hearts.

"It's not too late Abie," Hob Henderson said. "God will forgive you for
everything you've done. You can still be the woman you want to be."

"But this community would never forget," Abie said. "And I'd have to go
to another church and I don't even know what it would feel like to sit in
another church and think of it as mine. Besides, all the churches in this area
already know about me if this many people know that are on that paper. No,
I'll just have to stay home and keep my face hid. I don't feel like ever getting
out in the public agin."

"Well, at least you have a husband that understands," Joseline Hill said. "Gant seems to be a fine man."

"People just never know," Abie said. "I've turned Gant against me too, Joseline. Ours is not a real home. We keep up a front like a lot of people do. But Gant has no pity for me, and I'm the cause of it. But you know, I never knowed it before tonight. I blamed everything on Gant. Even to all the things that Wilbert Lee did that I caused. I tell you right now, I've been made to see that I'm about the meanest woman living. These people that I've run in the ground are head and shoulders above me. And these things are hard to say. I've never been through nothing like this in my life before.

"I won't never be the same agin and I tell you one thing: You won't hear no tell of me toting news around. You just wait and see. But my life is over anyway. And you can't imagine what it is to know you're hated like I am. I'm sure Gant and Wilbert Lee both have either seen this paper or heard about it. But do you think they mentioned it to me? And why should they? They hate me too."

"We have talked it over," Miss Ada Creech said, "and the only thing we can do is to take your membership off the church rolls. We know that you understand why. And you know as well as me that we are a forgiving church. But we've got to take a look at others too Abie. We're going to purge our rolls of a few others. We don't want members that are a bad influence on the community. We need people who show Christianity by living it seven days a week. We are truly sorry that we had to purge you first Abie. But this petition named you specifically. And if any of us can do anything to help you feel free to call on us."

"Thank you," Abie said as she rose to leave.

"I'll take you home," Callie said. "You don't seem to be in any shape to walk. And it won't be out of my way."

They rode home in complete silence.

- - - - - - - -

Abie thanked Callie for taking her home and Callie said she would be checking in on Abie in a few days. "You take care of yourself now Abie," she cautioned as she left. "I think you ought to see a doctor. I can tell you're not well."

Abie entered her room but it was stifling inside. The windows were open but no breeze was stirring. She sat down and began to fan herself but she had a stifling feeling. Sweat was pouring off her. She felt faint but was afraid to go to the kitchen for something to take. She hadn't entered Gant's room when he was home since Nervy Sauls' murder. But she went to his room and called his name.

"What is it?" Gant said. She startled him for he had drifted off to sleep and woke up with the sheet wet where he had perspired.

"I feel sick," Abie said. "They's some ammonia in the safe on the top shelf. Would you mind fixing me a dose in a little bit of water?"

"Naw, I don't mind," Gant said. "What's the matter Abie?"

"I can't tell you now Gant. Just fix the ammonia and I'll tell you when I feel better."

Gant found the ammonia and brought it to Abie, stirring it in the glass as he entered the room. Abie was fanning and had undone the twists in her stockings, and they were hanging down her legs. She had pulled off her shoes and he noticed that her ankles were twice as large as they should be. She had large legs anyway and they were swollen up to her knee.

She drank the medicine and thanked Gant and told him to go on back to bed; that she'd be all right. Gant left the room. He had felt like an intruder for he had steered clear of her room for years. But he knew he would be back to check on her. He lay down in the hall where there was a little breeze stirring, with the door open.

Meanwhile, Abie was still uncomfortable although the ammonia had helped the shortness of breath. She managed to get out of the corset and her stomach dropped low and that gave her some relief. Her hair felt too tight and she undid it and it draped around her and she just lay her head on the back of the chair and rocked. Gant came back in the room and found her in that state of undress. It was a sickening sight and he didn't even see her as a woman.

"Look at me Gant," Abie said. "This is the true Abie Turner. This is what I am. And I was turned out of the church tonight."

"What?" Gant said in a surprised voice.

"Had you seen whatever it is they call that paper Gant."

"Naw, but I had heard about it."

"I know Wilbert Lee has heard about it too," Abie said. "But there won't nothing either of you could have done about it nohow. And I woke up tonight Gant. I want you to know that. But I'm not asking for your pity either."

"What do you mean you woke up?" Gant asked.

"I know what I am now Gant. I am bound to be consumed by a demon. And you know something, he had so much power over me I didn't even know about how I was. It was the easiest thing in the world to lay the blame for everything on you. You hain't got no idea how bad I've hated you. I thought you corrupted Wilbert Lee. There ain't one good thing I've seen in you since we were first married. But I don't feel that way no more Gant. And I know it's too late so I'm not blaming you for anything now. Look at me and see the real Abie Turner. I feel like some kind of witch. And I know I look like one. But it's too late Gant. I've neglected myself and nobody else cared and I have gone for a long time knowing that something bad was wrong.

"I have to prop up to sleep any at night. I know I've got fluid around my heart. I expect I've got sugar diabetes, and I know I've got some kind of heart trouble. And they ain't no cure for me and I see no need of running to the doctor now. I'll soon take to my bed and just lay there and die." She began crying.

"I hain't got no church to be buried at. You'll have to take me to the public burial ground. I doubt that there'll even be anybody to sing at my funeral and that won't seem right. It always seemed funny at Hardshell funerals when not a word was sung over the corpse.

"But I've got the biggest job before me that I ever had. I've got to pray until I reach the feet of Jesus. I don't know how He could ever forgive me for all the sins I have committed and I don't even remember some of them. But you know what consoles me Gant? I have felt guilty all my life for hating that little Hobby when he didn't have nary thing to do with it. I hated him because he was Perline's boy. And I'll tell you something else Gant, I hated Perline 'cause she was all the things I wanted to be. I wanted to be pretty worse'n anything in the world. And even at my best you know that that won't to be. I had them heavy set shoulders and I walked funny and ever time I tried to wear heels the shoes always turned sideways. Then after we got married right next door was a young'un that was like a gold penny. And as she growed she got prettier and prettier and it pure poisoned my mind."

"All this talk ain't necessary Abie," Gant said. It was obvious that her carrying on was getting to him. "Do you feel any better yet?"

"A little bit. And what has happened tonight has made what ails me a lot worse. And they ain't no need of going running to a doctor now. If I was going to do that I ort to have gone a long time ago. But I thought I could fight it off. I was strong and what happened to most people wouldn't happen to me. I'm crazy Gant."

"You ain't no different than you've been for years," Gant said. "It was just that you didn't listen to nobody. You acted like you was God himself. Just went on your way."

"I don't reckon they's any need of even letting Wilbert Lee know nothing about it," Abie said with a sigh. "He's like everybody else and I don't mean no more to him than if I was a dog."

Gant was puzzled. He sat and looked at this woman when she stopped talking for a little while and put spirits of camphor to her nose in an attempt to help her breathing. He could not associate her with himself. She had cooked his meals, washed and ironed his clothes while remaining completely mute in his presence. She had borne their children in the days when she was complaining about something constantly. The criticism had become even worse as Wilbert Lee developed. And as he watched her in the room that he hadn't been in in years he could not think of her as ever having been a part of his life.

Too many things had happened and too many angry words uttered. She was a total stranger and except for the pity that he felt for any human suffering he felt no closeness to her. He had ignored her to the extent that he hadn't noticed her swollen legs or her labored breathing. He stood and backed out of the room and retired to his own bedroom, the only place in his home where he felt comfortable.

The news about Abie being turned out of the church spread like wildfire across Bear Grass. Even the colored folks were laughing about it as they toiled in the fields. Abie Turner's reputation was known by everybody who had lived in Bear Grass for any length of time. The few people who had been closely associated with Abie - those who lived near her - received the news with mixed emotions, but even they understood why she would be turned out of the church. Their only question was why they had waited until such a late date to do it.

Abie drug around for a while and tried to cook a mouthful and wash out a few pieces of clothes, but she went downhill fast after the ordeal at the church. When people missed seeing her making her rounds over the community they began asking questions.

Viola Turnage went to Abie's house and found her in bed. She inquired as to what the matter was, already having assumed that being turned out of the church had had a big impact on her. "Why you look pure sick Abie," she said as she went over to the side of the bed Abie was facing. "They's something wrong besides what happened at Whispering Pines. Have you been to a doctor?"

"No," Abie said feebly. "I've known they was something bad wrong for a long time but I thought my body would fight it off."

"Well why don't you have Doctor Miller to come out? He might be able to help you."

"It's too late," Abie said. "And besides, I don't care anymore. I'm a woman without a country. I just want to go on."

Viola thought about what a burden it would be for the few women who would help look after Abie at this time of the year. Tobacco was coming off and all the women would be needed at the tobacco shelters. There would be hands to cook for and people wouldn't even have time to do their own washing.

But the Bear Grass community couldn't let its sick suffer. Some way would have to be found to do the best by Abie they could. Viola figured that she could count on Callie Stroud, maybe Lany Moore although she had to come some distance. But Lany had been through so much with Minnie Mae she had sympathy for every other sufferer. And a few people from Whispering Pines Church would help despite what had happened. She couldn't remember a case like this before. Usually everybody in the community pitched in and looked after the sick and the family. But Abie had set such a bad example in the community most people would let her suffer before they'd help out. She had asked for it, they would reason.

In sweltering heat, a few women went to Abie's every day. They fanned her with folded newspapers, bathed her and changed her sheets daily and washed them out. One woman would stay at night. But Abie got worse and worse, despite Dr. Miller's visit. He found her too far gone for medical help.

Gant was seldom seen when the women came. He either sat on the porch or tended the tobacco barns at night. He was on foreign soil in Abie's room and he couldn't tell people why he felt that way.

Abie died just before sundown on a day when dark clouds were on the horizon, obscuring the sun at times, with lightning flashing in the western sky and the heavy rumble of thunder.

She died as she had lived, with few, if any, real friends.

Gant said he didn't have the money to have the body embalmed, so he decided to bury her the next day. Viola laid out the body and they awaited the undertaker to bring the casket. The body would remain at home.

As Viola washed Abie's face, combed her hair and closed her eyes and placed a penny over each eye, she thought about how Abie had been such an enemy to her daughter and little grandson. Tears came to her eyes when she thought about the tragedy of Abie's life.

The same women came to the "sitting up" that had ministered to Abie during her sickness. Craven Turnage came with Viola and Jiley Moore came with Lany. The women sat in the room with the corpse and the men sat on the front porch.

"When are you going to bury her?" Craven asked.

"Tomorrow sometime," Gant replied. "I'm going to get in contact with the man from the Salvation Army in Hallsborough as early in the morning as I can. I hope he can come no later than dinnertime. Bodies spoil in a hurry this kind of weather."

"Yeah, they shore do," Jiley said. "And how about the grave. You got anybody to dig it?"

"I've already talked with Nub Hill," Gant said. Nub was the grave-digger for the community. "He'll be there right after sunrise, he said."

A car stopped in front and the men recognized Wilbert Lee. His cigarette gave off a tiny speck of light as he came up to the porch.

"Howdy," he said.

They all recognized him and he went on into the room where the body lay. He spoke to the women and they spoke to him. He stood at the casket and looked down at his mother. "She looks better than I've ever seen her in my life," he said. "She don't look like she's carrying any hatred in her heart anymore. She looks peaceful and rested. And her hair is combed so that ball doesn't show on the top of her head. And there's some pinkness to her cheeks. That's not my mama there," he said as he left the room.

"Wonder why he didn't bring his wife and children?" Lany asked.

"He never brings them," Viola said. "He has distanced himself from his mama and daddy ever since he's been married."

"I declare," Lany said. "What strange people."

Gant got Wilbur Stroud to take him to the Salvation Army early the next morning. He talked with the Chaplain who said he could be there at twelve o'clock.

"Good," Gant said. "Just read some scripture and whatever else you want to. Ain't no need of trying to say anything special about her."

At the house, Viola chased a blow fly around the room. It had pitched on Abie's lips several times. Others were on the outside of the screen door. Abie had brought a quart jar filled with cape jasmine that she sat on the sewing machine. The flowers were in bloom on the south side of her house. Callie sprayed camphor around the room and all of it together smelled exactly like death.

Gant had not taken the slops out to the hogs and they smelled. Lany took the bucket in the yard and chickens immediately jumped on the edges of the bucket and began pecking at sour biscuits that had risen to the top of the pail. People were cropping tobacco in the field in front of the house. The workers were singing and talking to each other as if there were no corpse across the road.

Viola stepped out on the porch and a dominecker rooster flapped his wings and flew onto the porch. He dropped manure on the floor and stood and crowed in the doorway. "Now ain't that something," Viola said to herself. "I don't know why it is that roosters have to crow on porches when somebody dies. But they'll do it as shore as the world. It's pure quare." She went and got a pan of water and a broom and cleaned the floor.

The chaplain arrived at the house about a quarter to twelve and a few people were already there. Some six people from Whispering Pines Church came and the faithful ones who had looked after Abie during her illness. The chaplain read the twenty third psalm and offered a prayer. Abie's name was not mentioned. The casket was removed from the house and placed in the hearse. On the sides of the casket there were signs of body deterioration. A few wet places could be seen at the bottom edge of the casket and green flies flew close by.

Abie was laid to rest at the public burial ground. She was placed on the outer edge of the cemetery where few bodies lay. The heat was sweltering. The few in attendance wiped their brows as the dirt was spaded into the grave. Then it was all over. Abie Turner had paid the supreme sacrifice. And a community breathed a sigh of relief.

Chapter 35

Wilbur Stroud sat with a group of neighborhood men around the coal-burning stove in his country store. It was cold outside and clouds swept across the sun sometimes, creating a shadow for a moment, then allowing the sun to shine through again outlining the cobwebs in the barred windows. He removed his knife from his pocket, took a plug of Brown Mule tobacco from his breast pocket, cut off a slice at the corner and placed it in his mouth. He chewed down on the tobacco, then allowed it to soften up before masticating it thoroughly. After juice accumulated in his mouth, he picked up the spittoon that sat beside the stove and spat a mouthful of the juice, taking his left hand and removing the excess from his chin. Then he wallowed the tobacco around in his mouth.

"What's been going on in these parts?" he asked Jethro Harris. "I don't hear tell of anything going on much. Seems like most folks are staying inside and waiting for the weather to break so they can start farming."

"I don't know of nothing to tell," Jethro replied. Then he smiled. "But you know how folks around here is. If nothing ain't happening they'll find something to talk about anyhow. And the latest thing I heard was about Viola and Craven Turnage."

"Don't start that mess Jethro," "Nub" Brown said. "I swear they ain't no end to what people will talk about around here."

"I was expecting something about Viola and Craven," Wilbur said, "after their trip to Memphis. Now what on God's earth have they come up with?"

"Oh, it's in the church so I hear," Jethro said. "And I wouldn't doubt it. It seems to me like we're about the most ignorant bunch of folks they is according to the things we git so riled up about."

"But you've not told me anything," Wilbur said. "Go ahead and spread the word so it'll go all over Bear Grass before dark."

"Well, from what I hear the church is at odds with them because when Viola and Craven were in Tennessee they attended a big party and got out on the dance floor and swayed around with the other dancers, and you know that's against the rules of the church. They could turn them out of the church for dancing, you know."

"And just about anything else they might do," Nub said. "I know that all churches have rules but some of them seem to be so far out ain't hardly nobody going to abide by all of them. If I ever join a church it sure won't be Whispering Pines Free Will Holiness Church."

"Well, I'm a member of the church," Wilbur said, "although I'll be the first to admit I sure don't follow all their rules. But don't quote me on that or they might turn me out too. But there ain't no way they'll turn Viola and Craven out for that. They may argue about it and hem and haw for a while, but it'll die down and they'll stay on in the church."

"Lord God," Jethro Harris said, "if they turned out everybody that broke the rules they wouldn't be enough left to hold services. They think even screwing is wrong 'less it's a holy wedded man and his wife and then they've got to go straight up and down and it has to be totally dark and they just have to feel the goodness of life without witnessing it with the naked eye. They're a bunch of extremists and they ain't no way around it."

Sally Cox's boy entered the store with a gallon kerosene can. He went up to Wilbur and said, "Ma said send her a gallon of "careseen," a box of lye, a ten-cent box of Sweet Society and a can of fish roes and she'll pay you Saddy." Wilbur thought that the boy was the spitting image of his drunkard daddy, "Red" Cox. He had the same heavy coating of large brown freckles and deep red hair, and squinted his eyes the same as "Red." Wilbur knew that he could count on Sally to pay her bills. He had long ago stopped extending any kind of credit to "Red." Not only was he a drunk, but a liar as well. He told the clerk to get the items for the boy and to put them down on Sally's account.

"I wonder how the church got into it about something that happened in Tennessee?" Wilbur asked.

"Don't you know Wilbur?" Jethro replied. "Who starts everything around here? You know as good as me. And how it come about was that Viola was talking with her one day and without even giving any thought to what she was saying and especially to who mentioned that they'd be going to a big what they call a "Ball" while they were out there and that Perline had bought them evening clothes and they'd probably be out tipping their toes a little on the dance floor. And Abie Turner almost had a fit. Within five minutes after she talked with Viola she was heading for Miss Ada Creech's, pausing just long enough to put on a clean dress and touch up the ball of hair on the top of her head. And Miss Mabel Sutton was visiting Miss Ada, so she heard all that was said. This was the way Miss Mable told it: "Miss Ada," she began, "something is going to happen that I feel I have to talk with you about, since you're one of the officials of the church and I know that you uphold what is right."

"Yes, I do that to the best of my knowledge," Miss Ada said.

"Well, I was talking with Viola a little while ago and she was talking about their big trip to Memphis, Tennessee and talking about all the new clothes Perline had bought for them and she said they'd be out on the dance floor out there and it tore me all to pieces. To think of a church member getting out on the dance floor disgusts me and I knew you'd want to know what's going to happen and can maybe warn Viola and Craven before it takes place so they'll know they're likely to be turned out of the church if they go through with it."

Miss Ada was silent for a moment while the three women just rocked in their chairs. Then Miss Ada said, "Well, I don't know what to say Abie. It is a little unusual, but I don't know that it fits into the general rules of the church. You know the Bible says if the ox gets in the ditch on Sunday you are supposed to get him out, although the sabbath is set aside for rest. And although this is not the same situation, Viola and Craven will be in a position where they will feel obligated to go along with what most people consider to be a normal function. I think our church rules apply to people going to these speakeasys and shady places and dancing and carrying on like that. But I'll take it up with the Board, but not before Viola and Craven go to Tennessee. I doubt that they will be turned out of the church." And Abie's feathers fell with a bang.

"It just seems like Bear Grass can't stay on an even keel," Wilbur said, spitting into the spittoon again, and repeating the wipe under his chin. "But I reckon it's the same everywhere in the sticks. Folks don't have much to occupy their time so they harp on either the church or the things men and women do. They're the big things out here, and may be the same in bigger places for all I know. But Abie won't be the guilty one no more.

"And talking about bootleggers and moonshiners and mess like that," Nub said, "I reckon youall heard about the big still raid in Greene County yisdiddy, didn't you?"

"No, Jethro said, "what happened? Was it Paul and Saul again?"

"You got it," Nub said. "The sheriff's department raided the still and poured out a hundred gallons of mash and took all the sugar. Course, Paul and Saul got away, like they always do. And everybody knows who it is and everybody says the brothers pay off the Greene County sheriff and they ain't no doubt about that."

"Well, who can blame them to deal in a little stump-hole whisky," Nub said, "as hard as times are?"

"Where are your boys today," Wilbur asked Jethro. "They're usually hanging around in the evening on cold days like this." Jethro had four teen-age boys.

"Lord, ever one of 'em's gone to town I reckon. they were talking at the dinnertable and Ike told the other boys if they had a quarter they could hitch a ride to town like he planned to do and see Buck Jones. They hadn't gotten to town on Saturday but the feature was still playing. "And you know how a pack of boys is. Whatever one wants to do, the others are hell-bent to do the same thing. Course I had to run my hand deep in my overhalls pocket to find a quarter apiece for the other boys. But they've got to have something to do and I've already had them shucking so much corn I'm ashamed to put 'em out there when it's cold enough to be uncomfortable."

"I don't never know what that upstart of mine is into," Wilbur said. "We have spoiled him since he's the youngest and he and that Wilbert Lee Turner mess around together all the time and they ain't no telling what they're getting into. But like they say, boys will be boys."

"And something else about them moving pictures," Jethro said. "To hear this crowd around here, or the church crowd that is. The way they tell it anybody that habitates them places is on his way to hell in a basket. It's sinful and against God's teachings, they'll tell you. And I don't go to the show much. Now once in a while when I got a little likker in me and I've got the time when I'm in town, I'll go to the show and I really enjoy them. I hain't never seen nothing wrong with them less you want to call a boy and girl kissing or cowboys trying to git even with wild people who have done others wrong. Seems like they teach a good lesson to me. It's things like that that really bother me with Whispering Pines Church and some of the church members."

"I'll tell you something else," Jethro continued. "The holy-rollers can condemn all they want to and in doing so they keep something stirred up in the community all the time, but if folks don't do nothing worse than Viola and Craven shaking a leg and a girl having a bastard baby once in a while, they stand as good a chance of going to heaven as the news-toters, the back-biters and them that instid of wanting to help people who have strayed away a little want to turn them out of the church and they don't have nothing else to turn to. I dare say they ain't a man in Bear Grass that wouldn't git a bastard baby if he had the chance. Men just ain't like what most people and 'specially women try to make them be."

"You're all riled up ain't you Jethro? Nub said.

"Naw, fed up," Jethro answered. "But I'd better git home. It's gitting late and cloudy too. This is the time of year for snow but maybe the one we got Thanksgiving will hold us this winter. I promised them upstarts of mine I'd feed up for them since they won't be back before dark. I started to tell 'em no, but then I thought if a daddy can't never do nothing to please his young'uns, he's a pretty sorry man. Now I wouldn't take it as a everyday thing for I believe in making young'uns work. But if you give 'em a little leeway they'll respect you for it and bye and bye it'll pay off when you're too old to cut the mustard. Give 'em hell when they need it, I say, but for God's sake, pat 'em on the head once in a while too."

"You're a good man," Wilbur said as Jethro stuck his head out the door to test the coldness. "Yep, it's shore going to be cold tonight," Jethro said. "This is a good night to lay so close together no telling what a man and wife might do," laughing.

While the door was still open with some of the other men taking a look over the countryside Jethro looked back and said, "But don't worry boys. We'll never get Bear Grass straightened out, but we'll have a hell of a good time talking about it." All the men laughed.

Amos Allgood, who was older than the other men and had been nodding during the conversation, suddenly raised up and stretched. "What time is it?" he asked and Wilbur took his watch from his pocket, having to pull in his stomach to retrieve it. "Four thirty Amos. You got anything pressing to do?"

"Naw, Amos said. "All I got to do is just pass the time. And it's gitting sad when a man reaches the age that that's the only thing to look forward to."

The store door reopened and Jethro Harris came in. "I swear I plumb forgot what I come for," he told Wilbur. "The old lady sent me here to pick up a bottle of vanilla extract. Got some cold biscuits and I don't know how that come about, seeing as how many them four boys eat. But I reckon if they's one biscuit left and then another she just keeps 'em till they's enough to make a biscuit pudding."

"Yeah, you'd better get that vanilla extract," Nub Brown said. "You was talking about sleeping close together and all that, but if you don't do what Miss Mary tells you, you may be sleeping in the shed room, Jethro."

"Ain't it the God's truth," Jethro said with a smile. "And I was near 'bout home when I thought of it too."

While Jethro was waiting for the vanilla extract and fumbling around in his pocket for a dime, Amos Allgood said," Jethro, your boys catching any rabbits these days?"

"Yeah, Wayne and Jimmy's got boxes set and they git quite a few rabbits and a 'possum once in a while."

"I don't want no 'possum," Amos said, "but I'd love to have a rabbit. I used to set rabbit boxes as long as I was able to make the rounds in the morning and I love a good rabbit. The old lady can really cook good smothered rabbit and I can sop that gravy with biscuit. You tell them boys I want a rabbit and I'll pay them a quarter for a nice one."

"I'll tell 'em," Jethro said as he left. "It's going to git dark on me 'fore I git the feeding up done if I don't really high-tail it."

A group of neighborhood youths entered the store and the older men soon went home and Wilbur got in his Ford and rode over his plantation, leaving the activities to the young folks of Bear Grass.

Book 2

Chapter 36

Wilbur Stroud was a man with many responsibilities. To look at him you'd think he was able to shoulder every one of them, judging by his girth. He was a large man, weighing in at slightly over two hundred and fifty pounds, a lot of it around his waist. He was six feet tall. The buttons on his shirt always puckered, straining to keep his large stomach inside his clothing. He had a ruddy complexion, a round, pleasant face, hair still dark as he approached the age of sixty.

His father, Abe Stroud, had been a miser and instead of spending his money on "foolish" things as he called them, he invested in land. As the years passed whenever crops did well and he made a little money, he bought land in close proximity to his own holdings in Bear Grass, and in time had a large plantation. And Wilbur was the only child, so he inherited the land at Abe's death. Wilbur had disappointed the old man for there was a wild streak in him that Abe couldn't tame, but as his only heir, there was no one else to give it to. There were times when he threatened to give everything he owned to the Salvation Army, hoping it would cause the boy to straighten up. But death caught up with him before he got the chance to do anything about the will.

Perhaps Wilbur's worst decision was in building the store, which had proved a millstone around his neck. It had required more than diligence to keep up with all the accounts where credit was extended. None of the sharecroppers had a dime of their own and they looked to him like some kind of god to put food on their tables if they were hungry, tobacco in their mouths, lye in their pots for washing clothes, kerosene in their lamps in order to see at night, molasses to sop with the flour he furnished them for biscuits, even pomade to straighten their hair.

Wilbur Stroud was the best-known man in the community. He was known far and wide, by judges, lawyers, law enforcement officers, bankers and church officials. He was the official spokesman for anything that happened in the Bear Grass community. His word was valued.

Wilbur had long ago realized that he needed a place to get away from all the things that preyed upon his conscience. There was just so much a human being could endure and keep his sensibilities together. And he had planned such a place a quarter century ago.

A creek ran through the back of one of his farms and there was always a flow of water there no matter how dry it became. He had the hands on the farm to dam up the creek and create a pond, taking in many acres of swampland that was no good for growing crops.

Wilbur called it his hideaway and he guarded it jealously. Sometimes when he met with important men he would entertain them down at the pond. There were tables under the trees and a lean-to in which he kept utensils for cooking. After fishing on the pond there would sometimes be fish fries and the men would imbibe in good stump-hole whisky. But such occasions were rare and for the most part, Wilbur visited the pond alone.

The pond was far back from the beaten path. There was a road going a mile and a half through woods to gain access to the water. Beyond the woods there were fields of corn, soybeans and cotton. It required crossing those fields to get to the pond and the sharecroppers just plowed across the path and when Wilbur visited the pond he created another path, going slowly over the rows in his Chevrolet truck. He tried to leave everything behind and get down to his retreat once a week.

It was like heaven there in all seasons, but on this late October day it was like having entered the pearly gates and being given a foretaste of what awaited in the beyond. It was mid-afternoon and the sun glittered on the water. Fish were jumping out of the water occasionally; the lilies were swaying. A gentle breeze was blowing. The master painter had taken all the left-over colors and splashed them on the trees surrounding the pond. There were gums, sourwoods, maples and water oaks growing near the edges and their reflections in the water that moved gently gave a ripple effect of the landscape. So colorful was the display it obscured the view of mallard ducks floating on the far edges of the pond.

Wilbur had brought several fishing poles and plenty of juicy worms that one of the Negro boys on the place had dug for him at a mule lot where the rich manure nurtured them and allowed them to grow several inches long. But the scene got the better of him and he decided not to cast the poles. He wanted to grasp this moment and just think. The breeze was cool and except for a yellow fly plaguing him around his feet and an occasional mosquito that hummed around his ears and the gnats that apparently were after the matter in his eyes, everything was peaceful.

Near the picnic tables was a heavy-duty swing that Wilbur often sat in and unbuttoned the top button of his pants to relieve his stomach and just relax. From his vantage point under the trees a lot of the pond was in view. And the breeze was cooling. He especially appreciated that, for he had sweated through a sweltering summer and looked forward to the first frost. So crisp was the air he reasoned that frost might be early this year.

What was happening to time? He was a man growing old and it wasn't possible to keep up with its passage. The years had passed so swiftly, gradually chipping away at the human body, until its toll was showing.

In a sense, it seemed only yesterday that the British ship, the Titanic, sank in 1912, taking more than fourteen hundred people to their watery graves. He remembered it being the topic of conversation for months, even years. And people in Bear Grass said it was because the British claimed that it was unsinkable and that God was getting even with them for making such a claim. How could anyone expect a ship to survive an iceberg if you ran into it deliberately?

There had been the total eclipse of the sun before he was old enough to remember and people were not aware of its coming. The earth began to turn dark and people became afraid and thought it was Judgment Day. Chickens went to their roosts. People took out their mules right in the fields. Many fell on their knees and prayed for God to forgive them of their sins. It was a time of turmoil until the sun began to appear again although everything was in a shadowy haze until the shadow of the moon cleared the sun.

The Zeppelin Hindenburg burned at its mooring in Lakehurst, New Jersey on May 6, 1937, killing thirty six people. What a story that was!

The dust bowls of Texas and Oklahoma; the soup kitchens across America, the faces of starving people with the saddest look Wilbur could remember; the great Depression that was still not over. But out on the farm, the people were more or less forgotten as they maintained some semblance of order in their lives.

So many things over the years that caught the eyes and ears of the poor ignorant people out in the sticks.

He noticed a splash in the water where a large fish had come near the surface. Golden leaves fell around him, adding their beauty to the scene.

He had a twinge of conscience sometimes. He dealt with the poorest class of people on earth it seemed - sharecroppers. Both black and white, they were always there, especially since he ran the general store. And they were forever in his debt. They didn't think about debt as long as they got the items they were seeking. And if the scales were off a little, it was the only way he had of hoping to come out even. A pound of sugar that weighed only fourteen ounces allowed him to make a penny on the sale if they ever paid. Few of them could read, and when the sheets of cotton were weighed at night, five pounds could be deducted from the weight to take care of the wet cotton they covered in early morning when the dew was on.

Negroes in general all looked alike to him, but they had a way of wrapping themselves around your heartstrings with their pleas. He sometimes wondered whether they really were human but realized that if a Negro and a white man were skinned you couldn't tell the difference between them except for a broader nose on the Negro, thicker lips and a larger "tool."

"Missah Wilbur," the nigger women would say, looking into his eyes as if he were the greatest thing that ever lived, although he realized that they cursed him when they were out of his presence, "I declare I ain't got nary thing to put on my table. Please, Missa Wilbur, lets me have just a pound of fatback and five pounds of flour. I can make flourbread to go with the fatback and make gravy to pour over rice and my eleven children can have a full stomach to sleep on."

"Missa Wilbur, I want a jar of Sweet Georgia Brown pomade to put on my hair. I knows it ain't something to eat, but just look at this mess of plaits. I believe they's pure lice in there. And I ain't got no man you know. I'se going to a church meeting Sunday on the other side of Hallsborough. Please, Missa Wilbur, let me have that pomade and I'll pay you the fifteen cent next week I declare."

Black faces all looking alike, glistening in their covering of sweat.

A black man with shaky hands and breath reeking of wine. "Boss man, you got a bottle of alcohol I's can git hold of? I got a sore on my behind that I need to doctor. The old lady said alcohol would cure it."

Pleas that often got to him, depending on his mood. If he were in a bad mood he could turn them down without any feeling of guilt. He was spoiled to an extent for he enjoyed privileges that no other person in Bear Grass could lay claim to.

With the large number of Negroes in Bear Grass, many of them on his plantation, there would be Saturday night nigger fights. Maybe one would shoot another or a knife would be involved. Occasionally one was killed. On such occasions he'd say to himself, "Hell, so what, they'll git another one Sad'dy night." If it were a Negro on his place, he'd move another family in, for there were always Negroes looking somewhere to live and something to do. If it were just a regular "Sad'dy night fight," the law enforcement officials would contact him for his counsel. In most cases, the man who lived on his place was favored. If both farmed with him it was a draw. But Wilbur Stroud had a conscience. That's what bothered him.

There were plenty of sorry whites as well as Negroes. In those cases, he had no more respect for them than the Negroes. But after all, they did have white skins and he'd come nearer letting them have merchandise than the niggers.

It was enough to worry the living life out of a man. He had to have time for himself to collect his thoughts and put his life into proper perspective.

He worried about signing the petition condemning Abie Turner for the things she did in the Bear Grass community. Sure, what she did was wrong, but was Wilbur Stroud without blemish? He remained a member in good standing at Whispering Pines Church. But he knew that was because of his position, not his conviction. The sly cheating at his store preyed on his conscience. He was not a man without faults.

He felt that he had been a good husband to Callie. He recalled how pretty she had been as a young girl and how she had swept him off his feet when he was eighteen. But even in marriage, she was unwilling to give of herself wholly. He was amorous and craved the flesh, and she did yield at proper intervals for her. But "that" had never been more than animal lust for men.

Two boys were born to them in the first three years of their marriage. They were James and Wilbur Jr. They grew up in Bear Grass and never liked it. They hated the farm and moved far away when they reached the age of eighteen. He didn't hear from them once in five years and had almost forgotten they were his sons.

Then Philip came along just as Callie was going through the change of life. Callie had raked him over the coals for messing around at a time like that. But when Philip was born all the maternal instincts came into play once again.

The Minnie Mae Moore thing pissed him off worst of all. There she was, a luscious young thing, getting herself a case of clap that infected most of the men in the community who were desirous of her charms. He hated giving the disease to Callie about the most of any one thing he'd ever done. And he wouldn't have done it if he'd known he was infected at the time they had relations. And what would Whispering Pines Church think if they knew such a thing? But he'd paid every day since. He had walked the chalk line with Callie Stroud.

But there were the good moments too. Like now when he was in the splendor of nature and could savor the good things along with thinking about the bad. A mockingbird went through its repertoire in an oak tree with blood red leaves. On either side of the oak was a maple with bright yellow foliage and a dark green magnolia that he had planted years earlier. A movement in the distance caught his eye and a doe on the farther side of the pond drank from the cool water. The mallards were near the middle of the pond now with the slant of the sun casting long shadows of the painted trees in the tranquil waters.

There were plenty of good people in Bear Grass. As fine a people as you could find anywhere. People whose word was their bond; people who lived by the principles laid down in the Good Book. And other people sometimes talked about them. Craven Turnage and Viola were fine people. Gant Turner was a good man. He couldn't think of all of them for the moment but they stood out when he thought about the good deeds performed in the community.

And he had always been proud of Perline Turnage and how she had conducted herself despite the gossip that went around periodically. Whatever the gossip may have been she'd shown them a thing or two. And that little old Hobby had the winningest ways you ever saw for a boy.

A million thoughts ran through his mind as he enjoyed the coolness and the beauty of the day. Maybe it was getting time to close up the store, permanently. That was one way to ensure a certain amount of peace and contentment. He couldn't imagine what it would be like to be free of that responsibility. Nor did he know where the people who depended on him for supplies would turn, but that would be their burden. If times were better he'd think about selling off some of the farms. But land prices were too low to anticipate that. He'd have to wait until there was an upturn in the economy to do any planning on that. But one thing was for sure. He had to let up.

He sat a while without thinking, just admiring the scene about him. The sun filtered through the trees, highlighting the color of the leaves around him. He closed his eyes for a moment. It was peaceful and he drifted into sleep in the quietness of his paradise.

He awakened with a start. He had the feeling that he was being watched. He rubbed his eyes and looked about him. It was growing late. The sun was low on the horizon. He'd better get started back home before darkness caught him. It wouldn't be easy following the path through the woods after dark. He glanced toward the pond and there was someone there. It angered him. The land around the pond was posted. And he wasn't so naive as to believe that no one ever invaded his private property when he wasn't around. He knew the Negroes living nearby would come to the pond and set nets occasionally or cast poles into the water. Sometimes they needed fish for a meal and loving catfish stew as many of them did, they could take several fish, peel potatoes and put them in the washpot to cooking, add onions and boiled eggs, put a little parsley in the pot if they had it, thicken the mixture with flour, add the fish and have enough stew to fill a dozen people's bellies.

But he knew that when they did that there were people watching the path so that if he were en route to his hideaway they would get the word out ahead of him and the pond would be cleared of all evidence before he arrived.

"Who's that?" he called, but got no answer. The figure began moving a little closer to him until he saw it was a black man.

"What in the hell are you doing here nigger?" he called. "You know damn well this land is posted. So you get your black ass off my land right now or I'll beat the hell out of you." He was shaking with anger. Negroes around Bear Grass always listened to what he had to say. They didn't buck Wilbur Stroud.

When the Negro came a little closer he saw it was Roscoe Gooch. This angered him even more. He was one uppity nigger that didn't follow the traditional pattern of his race. And he had been up North and learned a lot of things around Harlem and how people differed there from those in Bear Grass. He ought to have stayed in Harlem or somewhere away from Bear Grass, Wilbur thought. He was too sorry to work in the fields like the other hands. Always had been. His mama, Blossom, had had a time with that boy.

"Roscoe, you get away from here right now," Wilbur said with emphasis.

"I d-oo-n't wants to leave, Missa Wilbur," Roscoe replied as he came nearer. "I'se got somethin to s-s-ay to y-o-u."

"I don't want to hear it," Wilbur said. "There ain't nothing you can tell me that will have any meaning. And I'm tired of telling you to leave. How did you know I was here in the first place?"

"I been check-i-ng on y-ou for a month, Missa Wilbur. I b-e-en stalk-ing you whenever you left the store. I even seen what you put in your truck. If you happened to put your shotgun in the truck I didn't follow you. And I knows tha-t y-o-u hain't got it today."

"You damn right," Wilbur said. "If I did have it I'd blow your brains out right now and leave another dead nigger for them to bury tomorrow."

Roscoe laughed, exposing his blue gums and white teeth. "I'se the one with the gun today, Missa W-i-lbur." He pulled a twenty-two caliber pearl-handled pistol from his pants pocket. He had stolen it the last time he was in Harlem and smuggled it home on a Greyhound bus.

Wilbur felt like his heart was in his throat. He was afraid. It was the first time he could ever remember being afraid of a Negro. He had done too much for the ones in the community to fear them. They depended on him for their very lives. He changed his tone of conversation.

"Now Roscoe, I know you must be upset or something. So let's just talk this over, whatever it is bothering you. I'm a reasonable man and I'm willing to listen to what you have to say. Okay?" He felt a tightening in his chest.

Roscoe toyed with the gun, rubbing his fingers over it and pointing it toward Wilbur, who closed his eyes and breathed a prayer in the interval, but somehow God seemed far away. "Roscoe, don't point that thing at me," he pleaded. "I've never shot a man in my life and I've carried a gun for twenty five years."

"I'se got a score to settle with you Mi-s-sa Wilbur. A r-e-al big score. I sees all of the bad 'stid of any good right now. It's eat at me for so long it's the onl-y th-i-ng I thinks about."

"Lord, I've helped you and your mama so many times I can't even think of them all," Wilbur said with quickened breath. "You've both been hungry when I let Blossom have things in the store, not knowing whether I'd ever get paid. But she always paid Roscoe. And don't you ever forget that."

"I knows dat, Mis-sa Wilbur," Roscoe said as he pointed the muzzle of the gun at Wilbur's stomach. "But what I r-r-e-e-member most is when you d-d-i-dn't let her have them. The worst time of all was one Christ-mas Eve when I was 'bout seven years old. I believed in Santa Claus then, Mis-sa Wilbur, and I didn't get nary thing for Christmas. And it w-as y-o-ur fault. Ma had had a few drinks and was feeling all r-i-ght and she wan-ted somethin for her boy. She went to you. Who else was there to go to? You were God, weren't you? She asked you f-o-r a box of spark-lers that cost ten cen-t and a nickle's worth of suckers that had candy on both ends. She begged you for them, Mis-sa Wilbur, cause she told me so Christmas morning when I was crying 'cause I didn't have nothing. But you smelt likker on her breath and y-ou was afraid you wouldn't git your fifteen cent, never thinking 'bout the little nigger boy at the house. That's the w-orst thing you ever done to me, Mis-sa Wilbur, cause a boy never forgits somethin lak dat.

"But dat ain't all." He took the gun and actually put the muzzle on Wilbur's stomach. He noticed Wilbur's belt was undone. "What you been doin? Playin' with yoself? You'se gittin too old for dat, Mis-sa Wilbur. You knows dat. Oh, I knows that several years ago you got your ass burned up by that Minnie Mae Moore. Y-ou didn't fool nobody Mis-sa W-Wilbur. Every nigger in Bear Grass knowed a-bout it. You hears everything right there at yo store. Everybody knowed it. They just didn't say nothing cause they were skeered. You was too big for us to go tongue-wagging.

"But I wants to tell you somethin else Mis-sa Wil-bur. Minnie Mae Moore rubbed it all over me after she got the clap. Tried her best to git me inside of her. And I walked off.

"And I knows you were the one that got the "Klu" Klux Klan on my ass, Missa Wilbur. Ain't nobody else in Bear Grass could have done it. And I thinks it's time to do something I got all planned out. You go out to that tree there by the bank, the one that's shed most of its leaves. I'se goin to tie you to that tree, Mis-sa Wilbur."

Wilbur's head was swimming as he rose and walked toward the tree. "Please don't do this Roscoe," he pleaded. "I'll do anything you want."

Roscoe took a rope from one of his hip pockets. "You stand aginst that tree facing me," he ordered. "Now I got to tie you up and I'll have to lay the gun down for a minute, but I'll put it so I can git to it in a second. And if you tries to break away I'll blow your head off. Do you'se hear?" Wilbur nodded his head.

Roscoe wrapped the rope securely around Wilbur's wrists, enough so that it was uncomfortable for Wilbur.

"Do you'se deny it was you, Mis-sa Wilbur? Well you needn't to, cause your shoes was seen in that group of men that strung me around that tree. You seen what they done Mis-sa Wilbur."

"Have you thought about what this will mean to you Roscoe?" Wilbur asked. "They'll kill you for what you're doing. So what will you gain by killing me?" There were tears in his eyes. The sun had disappeared and black clouds were floating on the horizon near the sunset. It was beginning to grow dark.

"I don't care what dey doos Mis-sa Wilbur. I don't care 'bout nothing. I don't fit in nowhere, not even with my own race. You 'member "Bad Boy" that killed that white girl a few years ago? But I'll bet you didn't know that I stole clothes off of a clothesline for him to make his getaway with. He made me, Mis-sa Wilbur. That was the meanest nigger that ever lived and he was the first man I ever had any dealings with. He used to be Ma's man when I was little and we lived in Hallsborough. He done everything to me but kill me. My britches stayed wet with piss all the time I was so skeered of him. He beat the living hell out of me and my Ma so many times I couldn't keep up with them. He butted our heads aginst the walls or the doors till I don't know how we had the sense of a billy goat. And I hated him wusser than I ever hated anybody.

"But the more I hated him the more I wanted to be like him. He got anything he wanted. He was big and tough and he just took what he wanted. He had power and I wanted that same power. And I got that power right now for the first time, old man."

He pulled a rope from a pocket and lashed out at Wilbur, striking him on the face and drawing blood. He then hit him across his large stomach and blood came through his shirt.

"Now does you know how it feels Mis-sa Wil-l-bur to be in somebody else's power and ain't nothin in God's world you can do about it? I'se got to kill you, Mis-sa Wilbur. And I hain't got long to do it in. Darkness done caught me and I was goin to string it out longer than this. I was going to blow yo balls off and see you cringe. Why ain't you hollering Mis-sa Wil-b-ur? I was screaming to the top of my voice whe-n th-e-y did it to me." He glanced at Wilbur's face and his head was drooping.

"You wake up here old man," he said as he took hold of Wilbur's hair and raised his head. He saw that the man was out cold. Then lightning streaked the sky over the pond and thunder rumbled. Drops of rain began to fall.

"I better cut him down," he said to himself. "Dey'll soon be looking for him and dey knows he come to de po-nd. Maybe he'll come to in a minute. At lease I hain't killed him. But dey'll see his wrists where I tied 'em up. If he's dead I'll be blamed as much as if I had blowed his brains out."

When he cut the rope around Wilbur's wrist he fell to the ground a dead weight. Roscoe got on his knees and listened for a heartbeat. He couldn't find one. Then it dawned on him that the trauma of what had happened to Wilbur took its toll on the man's heart. The great Wilbur Stroud was dead. Then Roscoe became frightened. He had killed the mightiest man in all of Bear Grass.

A sharp flash of lightning, accompanied by a deafening clap of thunder, came down near him and he realized that lightning had struck a nearby tree. It had come so close by he felt his wiry hair straightening and goose bumps came over his body. Rain began falling in sheets and when the lightning flashed the pond gave the appearance of an angry sea. Roscoe began running through the fields toward a safe haven. He felt safer when he reached the woods.

But he knew his days were numbered. They'd soon be looking for him. He had not escaped everyone's notice on his journeys to the woods. He'd be the first suspect.

- - - - - - - -

Wilbur's body was found two or three hours later. Callie knew he had gone to the pond and she told the search party to go there.

His body was seen as soon as the automobile lights shone on the pond. It was still raining hard and the men were shocked at what they were viewing. His body was covered with sand and debris where the water spattered as it hit the soil. A little blood had trickled from his mouth and nose and at first the men reasoned that he must have had some kind of attack and died suddenly until they saw his wrists where he had been tied up. Then they knew foul play was involved.

His heavy body was loaded in the back of an old truck and a tarpaulin used to cover tobacco in wet weather was thrown over him.

"My God! It's like hauling a dead hog to be scalded," Marvin Sullivan said as they were leaving.

"And you ain't never seen nothing like what this will cause in Bear Grass," Jasper Parker said. "I don't know what folks'll do, not even me. Wilbur Stroud helped so many people and especially the niggers, they'll be worst off of all."

They stopped and told Callie about Wilbur. She came out to the truck, they removed the tarpaulin and she saw the body. Rain was steadily falling and lightning flashed occasionally, revealing the corpse's half-open eyes and faint blood splotches on his shirt and around his mouth. She placed her hand on his forehead without speaking and went back into the house.

Inside, she told the men to take him to the funeral parlor in Hallsborough and asked the men who they thought might have done such a thing. They did not incriminate anybody. Everything had happened so suddenly they were in a state of shock.

Few people learned about Wilbur's death that night. But it spread like wildfire the next morning. Most people didn't even go to the fields. None of those who lived on Wilbur's farms went to work. People were standing in their yards in groups. Some were even wailing. Women sat on front porches and suckled their babies and cried openly. They had lost the best friend they ever had. Missa Wilbur had put food in their mouths when their old men had used the little bit of money for whisky.

The main thought on people's minds was who did such a thing. Who would tie up a good man like Wilbur Stroud? There were plenty of men in Bear Grass that needed tying up and beaten to death. Sorry men who didn't look after their families. And everybody thought about Roscoe Gooch. They remembered that he had been tied up and beaten by the Klan. And a lot of people said Wilbur was the one who got the Klan out there.

"Any nigger that'd do such a thing has got to be crazy," Nab Hester said. "I knows I'se black but I knows my place. You don't cut off the hand that feeds you. We might as well take our rags and go on up de road. Ain't no other white man goin to do us as good as Missa Wilbur did."

"Well, who's gwine take over?" Annie Battle said. "Miss Callie can't handle that sto and Missa Philip done moved to town. They other young'uns might as well not even be theirs. Don't never come around or nothin. It's the wust thing I ever heard tell of."

Wilbur looked good, dressed in a blue serge suit with a pin-striped red and blue tie. There appeared to be a hint of a smile on his face. Hundreds of people passed by his casket at Neville's Funeral Parlor. He was as well-known in Hallsborough as the townspeople. He remained at the funeral parlor until the day of the funeral, when he was taken to Whispering Pines Church.

Callie had taken pastor Willis Newcomb aside and talked to him the morning of the funeral.

"I don't know how to say this pastor Newcomb," she began. "And I want you to do justice by Wilbur. He was a well-known man and did a lot for many people and that's well and good. But brother Newcomb, Wilbur was not the spiritual man some people believe.

"So I don't want you to preach him into heaven by saying things that I know not to be true. Wilbur ought to have been turned out of the church like a lot of others. And he stayed in because of his position. And I felt as guilty as anybody.

"But you know a wife is not supposed to speak against her husband. A wife is supposed to stay in the background and do whatever she can to help him."

"Well, what has he done you're ashamed of?" Reverend Newcomb asked.

"We won't go into that Pastor," Callie said. "I hope Wilbur was forgiven for every misdeed and I forgave him long ago. But for years Wilbur and I were husband and wife in name only. And that's all I'll say."

People from far and wide came to the funeral. Craven drove his wagon to the store that had a telephone and called Pearl and Nick.

"My God, papa, what's going on down there?" Pearl asked. "I can't believe it. When anybody thinks of Bear Grass Wilbur Stroud always comes to mind. We'll have to go down for the funeral."

"What about Hobby?" Craven asked, knowing that Hobby had thought a lot of Wilbur.

After conferring with Nick, Pearl said, "He's very busy with his classes, so let's just wait till later to tell him. He'll hear soon enough anyway and it will bring on a spell of depression. He already thinks about everybody in

Bear Grass is dying out and there won't be anybody he knows there in a little while. You know how Hobby is."

Whispering Pines Church was overflowing and the grounds were filled. There were as many blacks as whites on the grounds and they were wailing and crying.

Reverend Willis Newcomb preached a good sermon, although as his wife had requested, he didn't go into his religious experience. Callie had a black quartette to sing at the service. She had heard them at the tobacco shelter one day and they did very well harmonizing. They were dressed in white, two men and two women, and sweat was rolling off their faces and tears were in their eyes as they sang the Negro spiritual.

The body was taken to the Stroud cemetery about a quarter of a mile directly behind the house. On an incline was a cedar grove and it was in this grove that the cemetery was started. Wilbur's parents and three of his uncles and aunts were buried there.

The large crowd gathered around the grave and Pearl thought that she had never seen as many dignitaries at any funeral as were there. Even the lieutenant governor was in attendance, with his bodyguard overshadowing him. The sheriff and most of his deputies were there, standing in one body. The city aldermen and the Hallsborough mayor were there. The county commissioners also stood in a body.

After the funeral was over people gathered under the cedars where shade was plentiful and talked. Pearl saw Faison Thompson, a prominent Hallsborough lawyer whom she knew just as an acquaintance. Passing him, she offered her hand. "Pearl Staphal," she said. "Meet my husband, Nick Staphal. I used to be called Perline Turnage."

"It's so nice seeing you again," the lawyer said. "Pleased to meet you Mr. Staphal."

They passed Reverend Newcomb and Pearl introduced herself and Nick to him.

"I've heard so much about you," the pastor said, "and every bit of it good. And they always bring your looks and demeanor into it, but even then they shortchanged you."

"Ah, preacher, don't tease me," Pearl said with a smile. "I used to attend Whispering Pines church but that was a long time ago. I was acquainted with Reverend Pell but Mr. Jackson pastored the church when I was in Bear Grass."

"It would be nice if we could have you on our rolls now," the minister said.

"It's a little too far for that. But I am certainly saddened at Wilbur Stroud's death. He did so much for so many and this gathering today attests to the kind of man he was."

"Yes, it is a great loss," Reverend Newcomb said as others came up to converse with him.

Nick got into a conversation with the lieutenant governor, causing his bodyguard some concern for a while, and Pearl continued to mingle with the people. A group came up to her and she was not aware of having seen them before. The man removed his hat and said, "I'm Waldo Spence with the Hallsborough National Bank." She offered her hand. "And this is my wife," and Pearl shook her gloved hand warmly.

"And this is our daughter, Anne." Pearl hugged her and pressed her arm. "You're so pretty," she said.

"I'm Wilbert Lee Turner's wife," Anne said, and Pearl noted pain in Waldo Spence's face, as well as a blush.

"Really," Pearl said. "There's a connection there as I'm sure you know. My son, Hobby, is Wilbert Lee's half brother. And I'm so glad to meet you Anne."

She hardly moved from where she was standing when she recognized the men from Weil's - Joe Rosenthal and Henry and Abram Weil.

"Well hi," she said as she turned. "Remember me?"

"How could we ever forget?" Rosenthal asked. "We still talk about the day you were there. I've been with Weil's for many years and there has never been anything like what happened on your visit since I've had dealings with the company."

"Terrible about Wilbur's death," Pearl commented. "Such a tragedy."

"Awful," Henry Weil said. "And by the way, what designer's clothes do you wear now, if I may be so bold as to ask?"

"Mavis of Memphis is my designer, Mr. Weil. She's a colored woman who is regarded as the best in Memphis."

"How interesting," Abram Weil said as Pearl was leaving. "So nice to see you, even under such circumstances."

Nick rejoined Pearl and the crowd was beginning to thin out. As the vehicles entered the dirt road dust rose about them. Pearl wanted to speak with Callie but realized it would be best to visit her at home. She'd like to have a conversation with her alone if possible, but realized that would be hard to do, for others would be stopping by the house also.

"Tell you what," she said to Nick. "Let me take you to Papa's house and you can rest. I want to talk with Miss Callie alone if I can. I'll go on to her house and park. Maybe I will get to see her a few moments and people will know our car and will wait to drop by until after I leave."

It wasn't long before Philip brought his mother home. He had planned to stay a little while but noted that Pearl was in front of the house. Both of them got out of the car and approached Pearl. "Come on in," Callie said as Philip shook Pearl's hand and told her how glad he was to see her. They exchanged pleasantries as they walked toward the porch.

"I'm so glad you could come," Callie said. "Come on in and we can talk a while." Philip told his mother he would be running on to Hallsborough but would be back after supper.

While they were standing in the parlor Pearl gathered Callie in her arms and hugged her warmly, sobbing at the same time. "I'm so sorry Miss Callie. It was such a tragedy. I was very fond of your husband and recognized all the good things he did for the people around here."

"I appreciate that Pearl," Callie said. "I hope he is being rewarded for his good deeds now." But a troubled look was on her face that Pearl didn't see when she thought about the other side of Wilbur Stroud. "Life is such a mystery and we are always asking "why" when there is no answer. We shouldn't even ask. Just accept until one day everything will be cleared up when we enter another realm."

They were seated and Callie found some Japanese fans, offered one to Pearl and took one herself. "But I want to know about Pearl. Your life fascinates everybody around Bear Grass. Catch me up on how you're living and what it's like in Memphis."

"Everything is fine, Miss Callie," Pearl replied. "And yes, I like Memphis, although there will never be a place like home to me."

"And I heard you were in high society there," Callie said. "That's something completely unknown in Bear Grass. Tell me about it."

"It's not what you think Miss Callie. I guess I could have been a member of what is called "society" in Memphis because of Nick. Of course I'm no blueblood, and not every member of that particular group is bluebloods either. Now the real McCoys are genuinely fine people and as plain as an old shoe. It's those who are social climbers who are a pain in the butt. But I wasn't one of them, Miss Callie. What I did was strictly for Nick. He wanted me to crash that circle, and I think I did a credible job for him. But I'm not a member of that high-flying circle.

"I have chosen the things I will do and they are voluntary. I don't want to sit and fold my hands. There are too many good causes to work for and spend my time constructively. And Nick doesn't want me to be one of those society dames either. He just wanted to prove that a backwoods girl like me could do such a thing."

"That sounds like you Pearl," Callie said. "You're too genteel for such a thing. But I'm glad you crashed that circle anyway."

"And I'm certainly glad the church didn't get after Mama and Papa for getting on the dance floor in Memphis. I heard about all the commotion around here but I couldn't imagine having a big to-do over it under the circumstances."

"Oh, it was nothing but Abie's doings," Callie said. "Everybody saw through that right quick."

"Changing the subject," Pearl said, "but who do you think tied up Wilbur?"

"It had to be Roscoe Gooch," Callie said. "Everybody knows Roscoe was tied up by the Klan and they know that nobody but Wilbur could have gotten them down here. And Wilbur was done about like what Roscoe had experienced. I expect they're already looking for Roscoe. But tell me something Pearl, how is Hobby?"

"He's fine Miss Callie. And he'll be very disappointed when he finds out that I've been down and he didn't get to come."

"Well, it would have been nice if he had come," Callie said. "Wilbur always thought a lot of him and he and Wilbur were always teasing when he was at the store."

"I thought about it," Pearl said, "but Hobby's real busy with his studies and I felt that it would put him behind if he were out several days. And I'm ashamed to say this Miss Callie, but I've carried so much guilt ever since the day he was born I put him before everything and everybody. But I don't know if I'm doing the right thing. I'd love to talk with you at length about that but I know this isn't the time to do it."

Callie leaned back in her chair and fanned for a moment with the Japanese fan that had a flower design in it. "Listen Pearl, I'm all right and I see you so seldom you just go ahead and say whatever you want to."

"Hobby is a dreamer, Miss Callie. Hobby has always made his little world like he wanted it. He chases butterflies and looks for the pot of gold at the end of the rainbow. But that's not reality. And he talks nothing but Bear Grass. And do you know something. It worked out for me to get him away from Bear Grass and I've done everything in my power to keep him away."

"What's so wrong with Bear Grass?" Miss Callie asked.

"Oh, Bear Grass is fine and I love it still above all other places. But I believe that if Hobby were here all the time he would waste his time on some elusive dream."

Callie placed her hand on Pearl's arm. "You've worried needlessly Pearl. You have done it for so long you have convinced yourself that it's the only way you can atone for everything that's gone wrong with Hobby. The really sad part, Pearl, is that when Hobby was a little boy and you had to be in Tennessee making a living, we saw him every day around here and he was the happiest child you ever saw. I've never seen a sweeter smile on a child's face than his. And he talked with everybody without any signs of shyness."

"It's my whole idea about him studying to be a doctor," Pearl admitted. "I never really asked him whether he wanted to go in the medical field. I talked to him and just kept on suggesting it until he agreed."

"Oh, I hope he makes a fine doctor," Callie said. "Hobby can be anything he wants to be. But mark my word, whatever he becomes he will put it to use somewhere near this very place. And you can be sure that one of these days Hobby will pursue his dream and nobody is going to stop him. And he will succeed Pearl. Hobby is no quitter. And something else. However you and I may see it, Hobby is going straight for the heart. That's what rules his head, Pearl. He isn't thinking about money or prestige or how high he can climb. He's thinking about things that bring peace of mind; a clear conscience, laughter throughout the day. Hobby has already made his mark in Bear Grass Pearl."

"I don't know whether it was the right thing to do," Pearl said. "You know how mothers are - wanting the very best for their children."

"Yes, I know Callie replied. "I thought I knew what was best for Philip too. I advised him all the time but I might have been saving my breath to cool a hot sweet potato for the good it did. Philip and Wilbert Lee Turner were the terror of the community. I've concluded Pearl, that a mother serves best by setting an example before her children rather than telling them what to do."

"I'm sure you're right Miss Callie," Pearl said as she mopped her brow. "But Hobby is deeply involved in university life now, although he hasn't actually begun medical training yet. He could soon graduate without that. But I've talked so much about it I don't know how to change the subject now. I've just flubbed up all around," she said as she wiped a tear from her eyes.

"We worry needlessly," Callie said. "We so often fail to take God into account. If we stop to realize that he takes care of the birds of the air, knows the number of hairs on our head, sees into our very hearts and knows what is contained there, surely he takes care of his children. I sometimes think we try to make gods of ourselves."

Pearl rose to leave. "You don't know how much I appreciate your talking to me, Miss Callie." She put her arms around Callie and held her close.

"You're one of the good ones Miss Callie. Whenever I hear of all the bad things that happen in Bear Grass I get afraid until I think about the people like you who are holding everything together. Then I know that the good will always outshine the bad. You have had a tremendous influence on my life and I just wanted you to know ."

Callie walked with Pearl out to the car. Pearl stopped for a moment and said, "What are you going to do Miss Callie? I mean about the store and the farms and everything. You have such a load on your shoulder."

"Philip said he'd give up his job in town and come out and look after the store for a while. There's a lot owing for Wilbur always ran the hands on the farm and many others. But Philip won't stay at the store but a few months, no more than a year at the most. Then it will be closed. I'm hoping Philip will take over looking after the farms."

"It sure will be the end of an era when that store closes," Pearl said. "I don't know what on earth the men around here will do when it's gone. I don't know what the people will do who depended on Wilbur. And I'm so sorry Miss Callie. If there is ever anything I can do, you know where I am and I'd do anything I could for you. God bless you," she said as she got into the car.

- - - - - - - - -

Roscoe was taken into custody without incident at his mother's house. He had been seen in the area of the pond on several occasions. Negroes living in the back fields told of seeing Roscoe around. They said he sometimes rode an old bicycle.

Roscoe admitted to tying up Wilbur but he was emphatic in denying that he killed him. "Now I ain't saying I won't going to kill him," he told the sheriff. "I wuz go-o-in to k-ill him, Sheriff. I had a debt t-o-o settle wid him. But he died 'fore I had a ch-a-a-nce."

Roscoe was tried at the next term of Superior Court.

After the selection of the jury of thirteen white men, including one alternate, the judge charged the jury thus:

"Gentlemen of the jury, this is rather an unusual murder case in that the man charged did not actually kill Wilbur Stroud, the outstanding citizen of Waynesboro County. Instead, he went about preparing for his death and Wilbur Stroud died before he got to carry out his plan.

"So it is up to this jury to decide whether, as a matter of fact, the things Roscoe Gooch did to Wilbur Stroud actually caused his death. Or, realizing that all of us are subject to death under normal conditions, if he died of natural causes the Negro would not be found guilty of a murder offense, but rather guilty of the lesser crime.

"That is your responsibility, gentlemen of the jury, and after hearing the evidence it will be up to you to determine Roscoe Gooch's fate. May God help you in your decision."

The jury brought in a guilty verdict in less than thirty minutes of deliberation, with a recommendation that he be spared the death penalty. Judge Simmons sentenced him to life in prison at hard labor.

Chapter 37

Philip Stroud reluctantly took over his father's place at Stroud's store.

He instituted a tough policy from the day he took over. He was not going to continue allowing the hands on the place to get further in debt. Credit would be drastically limited and only absolutely essential items would be charged.

Philip was very concerned with the burden that had been placed upon him by circumstance. He was not qualified for the job and only wanted to get through it as best he could and close the store within a year. He knew nothing about what his father's association with the sharecroppers had been. He had never once gone with him over the farm and didn't know how much acreage was involved.

He was completely intolerant of the Negroes who came in pleading for assistance. They'd come in hot from the fields, stinking and sweaty, and get up close and he felt a repugnance he was unable to disguise. And he would turn them down flat. And sometimes they even cried, especially the women.

There were rumblings in the community. It was something that could be felt, as much as seen. There was a restlessness that could not be overlooked. It seemed like a changed place since Wilbur Stroud's death. Everyone had known that he was an important man but they had not known the extent to which he had ministered to the needs of the poor people who worked on his land.

Down on Greene County Road it was more than rumblings. The Negroes were angry as well as destitute. They gathered in groups in people's yards and planned their strategy.

"We ain't got nobody to turn to," was a general complaint. "We might as well try to find work on other folks'es farms," they said as the November sunshine and gentle breezes whitened cotton patches, making the cotton soft and fluffy.

"We can find work until cotton is housed," they said. "If we can make a few dollars we can git by a little while. We's going to starve if we's stay on here with that Mr. Philip running the show. They's other old shanties as good as the ones we lives in."

Cletus Brown was sort of a leader among the Negroes on Greene County Road. They listened to him and he was better versed than the others. He could read and write well and had a reasoning power about him that the others didn't possess.

"We can't git to Mr. Philip," he said. "Everybody that knows that boy knows that he don't know nothin about the sto nor the farm. He was not teached about them things. Mr. Wilbur must a thought he was goin to live forever. He didn't leave nobody to take his place.

"But Miss Callie bees a good woman. As white as a lily. Never heard nothin bad about her. We's got to let Miss Callie know that we's can't stand it no mo lak it is now."

"Amen," was the response from all that heard.

"This bees Wednesday," Cletus said. "But we got to spread the word that we goin to Miss Callie's house Friday morning. And I wants every person that's ready to leave to be there. I'll talk to Miss Callie and you'ens will be there to back me up. And I mean be ready to leave if Miss Callie don't listen to us."

Friday morning dawned with an overcast sky and it looked like rain. But the clouds floated away soon after daylight. And the Negroes congregated at Cletus' house. "They's some white folks goin too," Ben Swift said. "Some of them's ready to walk too."

"Fine," Cletus said. "Now less begin our march to Miss Callie's."

The neighborhood watched the procession moving up the road and they knew something was afoot, although they didn't know what. When the group stopped at the Stroud place they knew it had something to do with the store.

Callie Stroud was shocked when she saw the large gathering filling her yard. Why there must be a hundred at least. She knew trouble loomed and she was not prepared to cope with it. Wilbur had always handled everything about business.

She opened the door and came out on the porch, putting her hair in place in an effort to improve her appearance at such an early hour. She could tell the group was angry because they were muttering among themselves and moving about.

"What can I do for you?" she managed to say, although she was shaking inside.

Cletus separated himself from the crowd and came nearer to the porch. He removed his old hat and bowed before Callie.

"Miss Callie," he began, "We's got a complaint to make and they ain't nobody that can settle it but you.

"Some of us is hongry Miss Callie, and none of us ain't got nothing as you knows. And Mr. Philip ain't doing us right at the sto. He won't let us have things to git by with until we's can pay him. And we's hain't got nobody else to turn to Miss Callie. Mr. Wilbur saw to our needs for so long and he was a reasonable man, Miss Callie. Nobody else on earth will let us have a dime's worth of credit. And we's got to do something."

The ghost of Wilbur Stroud stood before Callie. He was more real in death than he had been in life. She had been like Philip in that she had not considered the role the sharecroppers played in the community, nor the extent of Wilbur's involvement. She didn't have an answer since there was no one else to take Philip's place, and she also wanted the responsibility of the store off her shoulders. Wilbur had gone his own way, never bothering her with details about his responsibilities. And she had tolerated him, although ignoring him for the most part.

"We's ready to walk off, Miss Callie. Every person in this yard is ready to leave the plantation today. We's can find work until the crops are harvested and we'll just have to take our chances when all the work's done for the winter. But we won't git nothing here so we'll be just as well off.

"They's hundreds of acres of cotton to be picked Miss Callie. And hundreds of acres of corn to be housed. And hay to bale and taters to dig. We hates to leave but we got to do something. So we come to you cause if anybody can do anything it's you. And we wants a answer now. We'll be packing up and leaving Monday less you give us a answer."

Callie had never thought before what it meant to harvest a crop. But she knew it involved an awful lot of work. And if the crops weren't housed it would mean a total loss. She didn't hesitate to answer.

She brushed her hair back and said, "Give me until Monday and I will make some kind of arrangements. And don't a one of you leave. I promise that things will be worked out."

Wilbur Stroud's ghost was coming home to roost in Callie's heart.

She went into the house in a state of shock. She couldn't think clearly. Everything had happened so quickly, yet she realized that the Negroes and the few whites who were in the yard was of great magnitude. She took two aspirins and lay down on her bed. An all-day meeting was planned at Whispering Pines Church Sunday with dinner on the grounds, but she suddenly knew that she wouldn't be there. It would be one of only a few Sundays when she didn't attend church.

She could not rest. Her mind was in turmoil. She had to come up with someone that would be willing to take over the store; someone who was reasonable and intelligent enough to carry out the responsibilities that went along with the job. It was a big order and she couldn't think of anyone in Bear Grass who would fit the bill.

Oh, why had Philip grown up without knowing any responsibility? But she had been as guilty as Wilbur. She had allowed Philip to choose his own course. Was it because he was the baby of her later years? But that was no consolation, for her older children had gone their own way also, doing mostly as they pleased with no firm hand to guide them. She hardly knew them. There was a time when she hoped they would return to the nest and take an interest in the plantation. But she had stopped hoping over the years and didn't hear from them for years at a time.

Suddenly her world was turned upside down and she wondered why and gave herself a critical look.

Absolutely above reproach. A leading woman in the community. Of proper decorum, she conducted herself in a Christian manner. She set an example for others to follow. Her duties at the church were numerous. She spoke at circle meetings, chaired boards, took a keen interest in the young people and instituted programs that would involve them in church activities. She helped out in the choir, visited the sick and did all the things a person of her character would be expected to do. Yet she was troubled. Her eyes had suddenly been opened.

"I have directed my efforts in the wrong channels," she said to herself. "I have accepted that which was good as being the right thing to do. But those who chose to follow a different path I have shrugged off and said it was because of their sinful nature. Take Wilbur for instance, I gave up on him years ago, realizing that he would never see life from my point of view. And there was no other view. I was right and because of his sinful nature he was going to go on in the same way. I never looked to see whether I might be able to influence him by listening to him and learning about those things that bothered him. I taught myself to detest him for all his sinfulness. Oh, I thought I loved him when I was a young girl, but because he was a man and his nature was so different from mine, I learned to tolerate him. But there is one passage of scripture that somehow never registered with me - the part that says a man and woman become one flesh in marriage. She had made them entirely separate entities in her and Wilbur's marriage.

But she couldn't dwell on all that right now. There was a greater urgency at hand. She racked her brain to come up with someone. Such a task would normally require months of search and checking out, and she had only two days. Did she know anyone in Hallsborough who might be willing to give it a try? There were plenty of people available but few of the caliber she sought. She could think of no one.

She finally drew up a list, writing down all the men she could think of in Bear Grass, and all came up short. Then she came to Gant Turner's name and something rang a bell.

Gant Turner was unencumbered. He had kept batch since Abie died. Had even given up on raising a crop. He worked out by the day and she had seen him at work on the farm. Yes, Gant Turner might fill the bill. He was intelligent enough, knew most of the people in the community, both black and white, had no enemies that she knew of, was well spoken of and was known as a hard worker.

A little colored boy passed Callie's house and she ran to the door and called to him, "Son, come here a minute." The boy turned around and came toward her. "What's your name she asked?"

"I'se Hoobert Sims, Jim's boy." The name meant nothing to Callie.

"Do you know Mr. Gant Turner?" she asked. "He lives on down the road a piece, on the left side."

"I knows Mr. Gant," the boy said. He must have meant his name was Hubert. You never could tell, the way they talked.

"Well, I've got a dime in my pocket and I'll give it to you if you'll go to Mr. Gant's and tell him I need to see him right away. And if he's working out in the fields, find him."

The boy was thinking about all the things a dime would buy. He said, "Yes ma'am, I'll go right now," and he went on up the road, trotting.

Callie sat down on the porch, for the air was warm and the sunshine bright. She noted that the mob had trampled some of her chrysanthemums and a plant of coxcomb was actually broken off. The fields across the road were white with cotton and cockleburs grew thick at the end of the rows. She was able to relax for a little while.

It wasn't long until she saw Gant coming down the road, walking at a brisk pace. She thought that he was well-preserved for a man his age. No signs of flabbiness and straight in stature. The last time she had seen him she was thinking how lucky he was to be robust and healthy when so many of the older men were ailing.

"Howdy Gant," she said as he approached the porch. "Come in and have a chair."

"I got here as fast as I could," Gant said. "I was just fixing to get a sack and go see how much cotton I could pick before dark. I hope nothing bad ain't wrong."

"Something bad is wrong Gant," Callie said. "I reckon you saw all the people in my yard early this morning or heard about it anyway. And they're ready to walk off the place Gant. Just look at all that cotton in the fields. If they walk off the crop is ruined for the year. And I reckon it's my fault Gant. You know that I don't know a thing about Wilbur's business and nobody else does either. So I got Philip to take over the store for a while, thinking we would soon close it and everything would be all right.

"I had no more idea how deeply Wilbur was involved in the lives of the people around here than anything in the world. They're telling me how wonderful he was, how compassionate. One woman told me this morning that "Missa Wilbur," as she called him, took her to the doctor in Hallsborough when her last baby was born. She had had all the others without any problem, but this one just wouldn't ripen and come out like the others. She said she'd been jumping ditches and doing everything she could to break it loose, but it didn't budge. She saw Missa Wilbur driving by on his truck and she ran out to the yard and begged him to take her to the doctor.

"I don't understand Lissi Bell," he had told her and she said, 'but Missa Wilbur my water broke yisdiddy and I have a little pain every once in a while. I needs to git down to business and have dis baby.'"

"So Wilbur had driven her to town and the doctor had given her a shot and told Wilbur to get her home as soon as possible. And that woman bent double while Wilbur was breaking the speed limit to get her back to Bear Grass. She screamed and said, Blessed Jesus helps me now, straining as hard as she could,' lawd, Missa Wilbur, I'se goin have this baby right here in your truck.' and Wilbur saw signs of the baby being born - a large baby with a big head encased in a bluish membrane and twisting about in its fluids.

"Wilbur stopped the truck and tended to the baby, getting his hands all gommed up in the fluid with blood all over him and nothing to wipe with. He took a handful of dirt and rubbed it over his hands to get the wetness off.

Now who would have thought that Wilbur Stroud would do a thing like that? I sure wouldn't.

"And Philip has clamped down on them Gant. He won't let them have hardly anything on credit and most of them never have a dime, as you know. They want a good man to run the store; a man who understands them and who is willing to trust them to pay whenever they get paid. They say it won't do for the store to close because they have nobody else to turn to.

"But Gant, I've been so blind I saw none of this. I was busy with what I thought was doing good in the community. But I failed to look in my own household to find something to really do good.

"What I'm saying Gant is that I want you to take over running the store and when you get the chance look over the plantation. And I know it's a big order, but I want to pay you a good salary because I believe you are capable of carrying out such a big order."

"Well, thank you, Callie," Gant said as he gazed out over the fields. "But I don't feel up to the task. I could no more fill Wilbur's shoes than I could fly. It's not in me Callie. I'm just a simple man and Wilbur was not like that at all."

"I don't expect you to take Wilbur's place," Callie said. "There won't be another Wilbur. But he's gone and I'm left with all this responsibility."

Gant scratched his head and looked out toward the store where people were entering and leaving at regular intervals. He stretched and placed his clasped hands on the back of his neck.

"I don't know if my figuring is good enough for that," he said as much to himself as to Callie. Most of the figuring he did was in his head. He wasn't used to putting down figures in a row and adding them, or multiplying or dividing or subtracting.

"Gant Turner, you've got a good head on you," Callie said. "You've got to give a better excuse than that."

"Let me think about it, Callie," Gant said.

"There's not long to think Gant," Callie told him. "Just until Monday."

"I'll have you an answer tomorrow morning," Gant said. "I won't plan to go to the homecoming at the church. I'll shore miss all that good something to eat, but this is important. I'll be at your house by mid-morning."

"Thank you Gant," Callie said as he rose to leave. She shook his hand soundly and said, "I'll be depending on you."

She walked to the store where Philip was busy with customers. She could see a look of disgust on his face. "What was that stir all about earlier?" he asked. "I was so busy I couldn't leave the store. You have to watch every minute or somebody'll try to take something, especially at a time like that when people's attention is on something else."

"The sharecroppers are mad Philip. They don't like the way you're running the store. They came up to complain about it."

"Well I don't give a damn how they feel," Philip said. "And I'm not changing my plans because of them."

"But there's something we hadn't thought about," his mother said. "There's a great big plantation out there that the sharecroppers tend. And they're ready to quit Philip."

"Well, let them quit," he replied. "The quicker they quit the better off we'll be."

"Now you wait just a minute, Philip. They're ready to walk off Monday, three days from now. That means there'll be nobody to pick the cotton or get up the corn or dig sweet potatoes. It's not as easy as planning it out."

"Ah, they've not got anywhere to go," Philip said. "But if they did walk off we'd be in a mess. That makes the cheese more binding."

"I've been thinking about something," Callie said. She had to wait for Philip to draw a gallon of kerosene. He got some of it on his hands and grimaced. "That Heber is never around when you need him." Heber was a black boy that hung around the store who had gained Wilbur's trust over a long period of time. He wasn't paid a salary but got small items from the store at no charge. Sardines, Vienna sausages, pork and beans and soda crackers were his favorites. And when he got a pack of Avalon cigarettes he was especially pleased.

"It's not going to work out with you running the store," Callie said. "You don't have the patience to deal with the public Philip. And you're too close-minded to deal fairly with the people. We've got to find somebody to take over the store. And I have seen right quick that closing the store is not the thing to do.

"I've thought of a man that might work out if I can persuade him to try it. And I want you to give it some thought. I think Gant Turner would do a good job."

"Gant Turner!" Philip exclaimed. "Wilbert Lee's daddy. Boy, have we given that old man a fit in our day. But I've got to admit he's okay by me. He's a decent man and I can't say I've ever heard people down on him for anything he did. But do you think he has enough education to do the job Mother?"

"I think so," Callie said. "Gant has a good head on him and I don't know why he's not addle-brained as much aggravation as Abie caused him. And

I've asked him to take over the store and he will give me an answer tomorrow. If he does agree, you can go back to Hallsborough and take over your old job."

"Well, I'm ready to go any time," Philip said, relieved at the possibility of being able to dump the responsibility of the store in someone else's hands.

Callie had a fairly restful night and it didn't seem like Sunday morning. She always prepared for Sunday school and church early and cooker her dinner and had it on the back of the stove when she returned from church. And people would surely wonder why she was not at church. But the matter of the store was too important and the issue too pressing to put off.

She took a seat on the front porch and waited for Gant to arrive. And it wasn't long until she saw him striding down the road. The first thing she noticed when he arrived was that he had gotten a haircut. Not too short to give the appearance of his head having been shaved. Rather, it was neatly trimmed and he was clean-shaven. He was a rather handsome man, she thought.

"Well, what's the verdict?" Callie asked right off the bat. She couldn't bear the suspense.

"I'll do it," Gant said.

"Thank God!" Callie said with emphasis. "Thank God I can tell Cletus to put the hands in the fields to picking cotton Monday instead of having them walk off and leaving a disaster on my hands."

"You're having it tough Callie," Gant said. "And I thought about it a long time and I saw that you were in such a bind I felt like I ought to do anything I could do to help you as well as keeping the store open. It would be a mess if this store were closed Callie. It means too much to the community to close its doors."

"Yes, I've learned that," Callie said. "I've learned many things I was blinded to in a mighty short time. But with your help we'll lick this thing. But we haven't said a word about salary. And I want to pay you well for your services Gant. Would you accept for twenty five dollars a week? No, that sounds too little. Make it thirty dollars."

"Well, that's mighty generous of you Callie," Gant said. That would mean more money in his pocket than he'd ever had. He could start saving some on such a fine salary. "I'll do the very best I can Callie and I hope I won't disappoint you. And I'll really try to be fair with the folks I deal with at the store."

"We'll go over the books Monday," Callie said. "And you will get together with Fred and Clee and have an understanding about issuing credit." Fred and Clee were clerks that Wilbur had hired years before to work in the store.

- - - - - - - -

Gant had bought him a pair of Chino khaki pants while he was in town Saturday. He wouldn't feel right going to work in the faded overalls and blue chambray shirt he wore in the fields. He wanted to present a little better image than that. He walked with an air of confidence as he went to Stroud's store.

Philip met him at the door. "Howdy Mr. Gant," he said, shaking his hand. "I've not seen Wilbert Lee lately. How has he been doing?"

"You know as good as me," Gant said. "How have you been?"

"Oh, all right I reckon. Say, I'm glad you're taking over the store. It's set me free to go back to Hallsborough. This shit's not for me."

"I know," Gant said. He had learned more about Philip than he cared to know from his association with Wilbert Lee.

"Come on and let's look over the credit book," Philip said. He took the rather large ledger from beside the cash register. Nothing fancy, rather crudely inscribed with some names marked through where they were spelled wrong and the correct name added. There were lots of accounts, Gant noted.

Philip smoked Gant over while he was looking over the book. "Hey, you're kind of dressed up aren't you? Wearing that white shirt and khaki pants. It seems odd to see you dressed like that, I've been so used to seeing you in overalls and all that."

"I felt like I ought to look a little different behind the counter than I do when I come to the store for things," Gant said. "And when do you want me to take over?"

"Right now," Philip said. "I'm ready to go to town and you know the people around here as well as I do. And there's one thing for sure. We can't close this store like I planned to do. It just wouldn't work out with so many people depending on it."

Cletus Brown had already met with Callie and he stopped at the store on the way back to Greene County Road. He removed his hat and paused for a moment to show proper respect. "Everything's set," he said. "Everybody's goin to pick cotton today and folks'll be at the store after weighing up time, cause they ain't got hardly nothing in the house to eat. And I'se mighty glad you'se taking over Mr. Gant. All the folks will be glad when they hear it. You're a good man Mr. Gant. Now I'll be on my way for there's work to do."

- - - - - - - -

Gant liked the work from the start. And he was kept busy from sunup to sundown at the store. And he extended credit to most of the sharecroppers and day hands. Once in a while a drunk person would try to buy items that were not really needed, and Gant would stand pat and refuse them. But where the basic necessities were concerned, he saw to it that families were fed.

In due time all the cotton was picked, the corn housed and the potatotes dug and hilled. Then there was a period when there just wasn't much work to do. People would be in the woods cutting next year's wood for kitchen stoves, fireplaces and the tobacco barns when warm spells came in January and February. So the sharecroppers loafed a lot and those without any money bought things on credit as they had always done.

Callie came out to the store occasionally to see how things were going. She was pleased with the job Gant was doing and she noted that he was respected by those who made purchases. They'd often talk and joke with him and it had an effect on Gant. He had no look of forlornness on his face. And he laughed a lot. She was so glad she had thought about him in her hour of deepest crisis.

- - - - - - - -

The Christmas season was approaching and there was a feeling of Christmas in the air. It had been an average year and most sharecroppers had enough to take them through the holidays, after which they would start charging again on next year's crop. Those who worked by the day fared worse than the others.

Gant was learning more about the operation of the store every day. He busied himself studying the records and the bank statements and learning the financial condition of the store. He was pleased that the store was in the black, despite all the credit extended.

The men and boys continued to habitate Stroud's store during the winter as had been the case for many years. When talk had surfaced that the store might be closing, it was like some great disaster had been forecast. Wilbur's place was as much a part of the community as Whispering Pines Church.

Gant was doing a good job with the store and learning more about its operation all the time.

During cold spells in January and February it was a common sight to see several hogs hanging on the gallows to be salted down for the year's meat. A lot of wagons and carts were going in and out of the woods hauling firewood for the fireplaces.

Children would get their hopes up for snow when the weather was cold, a whistling wind would cut around the corners of the houses and a few flakes would come down for a little while. Deep freezes would leave thick ice on watering troughs and it would have to be broken with an ax or anvil and water added for the livestock. It was a time when it was easy to tell every time the fire in the fireplaces was replenished for puffs of smoke would rise quickly from the chimneys and if the wind were blowing it would lie low to the chimney and give the appearance of the roof of the house being on fire.

And then came spring with its rejuvenating power, making the countryside colorful with its wildflowers and flowering bushes in people's yards. And the fruit trees were a spectacle in their coats of pastels or white, decorated in their lacy blossoms.

People were busy in the fields again with activities reaching a fever pitch as planting time came.

People opined that time passed so swiftly. At the store men would say, "Just think, it's already been half a year since Wilbur died, and it seems like yisdiddy. And summer'll come and go just as fast. No wonder we're gitting old."

Callie continued to take an active part in the church, although her activities had been curtailed considerably. Miss Ada Spence assumed some of the responsibilities Callie had carried. Callie was taking more interest in the store and the poorer people in the community. She would spend days driving the truck and stopping by houses and seeing how things were going. She was a fair woman to say the least, but she began taking even more interest in her appearance. She changed her hairdo. She set the waves in her hair and had done so for years. But she made them even deeper and combed her hair becomingly on the sides. She was not a stout woman but had worn a corset many years due to a slightly protruding stomach. She reasoned that she was eating too much and decided to cut down. She left off sweets and limited her intake of bread. Over a period of a few months she lost seven pounds.

She gave an excuse that Gant might need her to assist with some of the business, fully aware that she knew nothing about the business. At least it kept her from feeling guilty about going to the store far more often than she had when Wilbur was alive. She knew that the main interest was Gant Turner.

She could not explain that, even to herself. She had determined long ago that men were all alike. She judged every man by Wilbur, whose habits and idiosyncrasies she found disgusting. Yet she was thinking about Gant in an entirely different light. She blushed to herself when she realized that if Gant possessed those qualities, she would find them exciting.

"Growing up is such a slow process," she said aloud as she made the bed one morning. "We go through life with our minds set against so many things we poison them to any view except our own. And I'm just now growing up and I'm fifty-eight years old."

She had never thought of Gant Turner in that light. He was a neighbor who worked hard, never accustomed to an easy life and made harder by a nagging wife as well as a gossiper. He was always dressed in overalls and a work shirt and she had seldom seen him without a hat. He could be termed drab in his appearance, even on Sunday when he was in church. He had an old blue serge suit and the pants had worn out before the coat and he had worn that with grayish looking pants and with his shirt collar buttoned but without a necktie. She remembered distinctly how he looked, now that she had him on her mind.

But he looked different now. She could understand that because he hadn't been able to afford anything better until he came to the store to work. But as his savings grew, he added a little to his wardrobe occasionally and she noticed that he was having his white shirts starched stiff and was wearing a clean one to work every day. He had told her one of the colored women nearby was doing his laundry for him.

And he had ceased wearing a hat. His hair was still dark, mixed with a sprinkling of white, particularly around the temples. There was a slight wave that hadn't shown when he wore a hat. And his hair was still thick and well groomed. His beard was dark and there was a dimple in his chin. And no matter how close he shaved there was the tell-tale dark sign of a heavy beard that showed on his face.

Put all that on a six-foot frame and a thirty-six inch waist and he was a handsome man as far as Callie was concerned. She worried that some other widow would have her eyes on him. (Gant had told her his measurements one day when they were talking).

She laughed at the things he said and noted that there was an air of mischievousness about him and a certain way he smiled that especially appealed to her. She was unaccustomed to looking for any such nuances in men. He talked interestingly about things in general. He talked positively about life and she wondered how in the name of God he could do that, realizing what he had been through.

Callie had not gone into black mourning after Wilbur's death. The practice was becoming old hat everywhere, even out in the country. She felt, too, that to dress as if she were in mourning would be sacrilegious, after the way she had felt about him.

But time would pass. She simply could not let any person, not even Gant, know that she was interested in a man, until a respectable length of time had passed. But Gant Turner loomed large in her thoughts.

- - - - - - - -

The infinitesimal seeds that were planted in spring sprouted, some hardly discernible when they were placed in the ground. Warmth from the sun, tended with care, nourished with rains that sometimes beat the tiny plants to the ground, in due course of time they gained stature and began showing up across the fields. With fertilizer to give them advantage over the weeds and grasses, the seeds became plants and took over the fields, in due time reproducing their own kind, and crops were maturing.

Prospects for a good crop cheered landowners and sharecroppers and gave them new hope.

Farmers had little time to habitate the store. Only those too old to work in the fields could afford the luxury of sitting idle when there was so much work to do. And it was at those times that Callie and Gant had long talks and learned more about each other. Each told things about themselves that had been locked in their hearts and had never been uttered before.

"I don't know what we're going to do about all this," Gant said one day as he observed the violet-colored dress Callie was wearing and smelled the sweetness of perfume.

"I don't understand," Callie said, pretending not to notice his implication of endearment.

"Yes you do," Gant teased. "Things are beginning to get serious between us, Callie. You've got me thinking all sorts of things I hain't got no business thinking about. But so help me God, I can't help it. And I thought such thoughts had passed me by years ago."

"Well, it's nice of you to think about me like that," Callie said as she placed her hand over his.

"It's not right Callie," Gant replied. "Oh, I don't mean they's anything wrong with me liking you or you liking me and all that, but I'm not good enough for you Callie. You're a woman of means and here I am a nobody and I wouldn't have anything to offer you and I've got my pride and wouldn't feel like I was getting the best of the deal. Do you understand what I mean?"

"Oh, that's foolish Gant," Callie said. "What people have or don't have has nothing to do with how they feel about each other. If you think I feel above you, then you start thinking again. I have the highest opinion of you of any man in Bear Grass. And I wouldn't be ashamed to be seen with you any place, any time. Now, does that ease your mind?"

"That sounds mighty good Callie," Gant said. "So do you mean you'd sit on your front porch with me on Sunday evening with people passing and feel all right about it?"

"I sure would," Callie said. "I'd be happy to be seen with you at church or any other place."

"And just supposing you and I was to get married. And suppose you had to move to my house 'stid of living in your fine place. What about that?"

"Gant, I'm not above living in your house and if circumstances made it necessary I would do it in a minute. And I know how you feel. But I hope you'll stop thinking like that. Oh, I smell the sweet corn silking across the road and a honeysuckle plant is blooming nearby, and it's a beautiful summer morning."

They were like young lovers, dreaming all the dreams as if youth had been reborn.

"Let's ride around Sunday," Callie said after Gant brushed her lips with a kiss.

"Fine, where are we going?" Gant asked. Callie had a Buick Wilbur had left her. He had purchased it only the year before.

"Oh, over to Hallsborough, maybe over to the Cliffs, down by the river. Just sightseeing."

"That's fine with me, Gant said, realizing that he was entering a world about which he knew nothing; a world in which there were things besides just trying to make ends meet, never able to indulge in anything like sightseeing.

So after church, they began their journey. Callie had packed a picnic lunch and they laughed at each other and life in general, and that was the outset of their real courting.

Sunday afternoons would often find Callie and Gant on Callie's front porch and if the weather wasn't good they'd sit in the sitting room. But Gant was always uncomfortable for the furniture was formal and stiff and the mohair pricked him through his pants and there was a thick rug on the floor and he was always afraid he might carry chicken manure inside. And he loved her food but the dining table was formal with a china plate and silverware arranged properly and napkins beside the plate. He didn't know what to do with the spoons and forks, so he watched what she did and followed suit. But he didn't enjoy the meals.

Callie was not all that concerned with his manners, but she did try to get him into the habit of good table manners and to build up his image of himself. Her main concern was the man himself. The more she was around him the more she realized what a fine person he really was, and she wondered sometimes how he could ever have sired a child like Wilbert Lee. But then she had to take a critical look at herself, for Philip had developed in her own body and he wasn't anything to boast about.

And he was so different from Wilbur. He showed concern; was tender and loving and observant and made a woman feel she was something special. She tried to keep thoughts of his and Abie's life out of her mind, for she almost knew that that wasn't the case with them.

She tried to keep thoughts of Wilbur out of her mind. Nothing had worked right for them. And Wilbur hadn't observed good table manners or good bedroom manners and he had walked all over her feelings. Yet, she had been made to realize since his death that it wasn't all his fault by any means.

Whatever she and Gant could salvage from a bad life was her major goal. What was past was over and could not be recalled or relived. But it might be possible to live out their lives in contentment and with love the dominant factor. The future looked bright.

And so the midst of the harvest season was at hand. The July flies sang in the trees, the blue jays squawked and shed their feathers and became sassy in their ugliness. Scorching days caused the crops to wilt when the sun was at its highest point. A haze would be over the fields at such times and it was easy to spot "lazy lawrences" when specks floated before the eyes when gazing into the skies.

And the young men flocked to the store at night to catch up on what was going on in the community. The store boasted electric lights, now that the light company had extended service to Bear Grass. But it was too hot inside, so the boys would gather outside to fight the millions of insects that flocked to the lights. They were constantly fighting them with their hands while they told lies and joked.

It was a time of good spirits in Bear Grass. Everyone expected a bumper crop and that in itself brought an air of optimism to the people.

One night when Gant was about to close, having let Fred and Clee off early, Callie walked out to the store to say goodnight and to tell him about an idea she had.

"Have you ever been to Wilbur's pond?" she asked as he locked the back door.

"Once or twice," Gant said. "But it's been a long time. He had the land

posted and I didn't think I had any business down there. Didn't even look
it over good but I did see that it was a pretty place. Why?"

"I've never been down there," Callie confided.

"What!" Gant said as if he were flabbergasted.

"Wilbur invited me a few times. But I never thought he meant it and I
thought I'd feel out of place there. But you know something Gant. I want to
see it."

"Well, we'll sure go sometime if you want to," Gant answered.

During the middle of the next week, a time when things were slow at the
store, Callie and Gant made a trip to the pond. Gant drove the truck, since
it was a rough path through woods and rough terrain.

"I don't see why Wilbur didn't have a good road down there," Callie said.

"I do," Gant answered. "He didn't intend it for the public. He wanted it
quiet and a place where he could go just to be hisself."

"Well, it's sure rough," Callie said as she held on to the dashboard as the
truck moved over bumps and mudholes.

"How far?" Callie asked.

"Oh, two or three miles I reckon."

Callie noticed houses where sharecroppers lived this far back from the
road.

"Wilbur had men to keep the place cleaned up," Callie said. "I've known
him to talk with the darkies that looked after the pond and grounds. I wonder
if they're doing the same thing now?"

"I speck so," Gant said. "They may have made a special effort to make it
look good in remembrance of Wilbur."

They were approaching the pond and there was an air of expectancy for
both of them. Then they saw the sparkling water and they were in Wilbur's
haven.

Neither spoke at first; instead looking about them at the expanse of the
pond and the trails that wound about under the trees. Everything was in
order for the men had indeed taken a special interest in the place now that
Wilbur was gone, perhaps anticipating a visit by his wife at some time.

Callie had no idea what Wilbur's vision had been. He had a veritable
paradise hidden from the world. She didn't know he had long since had
crepe myrtles set along the farther bank of the pond that now glowed in
raspberry and watermelon-colored blossoms that reflected in the pond. And
he had had cannas planted in beds, yellow in one, red in another, and beds
of summer flowers that added beauty to the landscape. And the trails were
clean with all underbrush kept trimmed and even accumulations of leaves

were swept and the chairs were inviting under the trees.

"It's absolutely beautiful," Callie gasped after taking it all in. "I would never have believed it." They sat down in the swing Wilbur had had built. Callie noticed that there was even a well under the trees and a tackle and chain attached.

Tears filled Callie's eyes. "He was a man I never knew," she sighed. "But I didn't try to find what was hidden behind his cruel exterior Gant. Maybe if I'd come with him to this place sometimes I would have learned about the real man that was there."

"No need to grieve over all that Callie," Gant said. "Think about the good things that make you happy."

"I'm so glad to be here with you," Callie said. "If anybody should know how to appreciate such beauty it should be you and me."

"Amen," Gant answered.

"It's so pretty looking across the pond," Callie said, pointing toward the bank in the distance.

"It's pretty everywhere Callie. And I'm as shore as anything in the world that Wilbur had a make-believe world back here where he lived a lot of his life in dreams. We're all hunting for something Callie. Something that we never find. But we can think about a world where everything is all right and it makes life a little more livable. God knows I lived a dream most of my life. But I didn't have any of this around me. I had to dream from a shelter or a shed room or a stable or in the field. Couldn't have stood it if I had to live a nightmare all the time in my personal life. No woman to love me. No son to care, to look up to me as daddy with bright eyes shining. Always criticizing from Abie, criticizing from the young'un. Never able to make ends meet and no cooperation. I felt less than a man and I had to go into that world of dreams to make my life have any kind of meaning. Know what I mean, Callie?"

"You poor man," she replied. "Oh, what is life all about?" she asked as they strolled along the trail by the lake where they ran into a rose garden that had been hidden from view. "What beautiful roses," Callie said as she gathered a large purple bud between her fingers and stooped to smell its fragrance. "This is the most unbelievable thing I even ran into Gant. Who would have thought that Wilbur Stroud would have placed a rose garden in his private world? Yellow, rose, pink, white, red, so beautiful blooming back here where they go mostly unobserved."

They passed where Wilbur had moored his paddle boat. It swayed gently with the movement of the water, the paddles resting on its seat.

They returned to the swing where Wilbur had sat and observed his private world.

"What are we going to do about us?" Gant asked, taking Callie's hand into his. "I love you Callie, and I want to marry you, but you have every right to say no. I'm not the high-type man that you are a woman."

"Nonsense Gant," she replied. "I will be happy to marry you and don't even think of yourself as being unequal. I will feel honored to be your wife. And I will try to be all the things you say Abie wasn't. And no one shall be above you Gant. And I will try so hard to minister to all your needs and you will finally know a woman's love, for I have learned from life too. I've missed so much too, but I must confess that I was to Wilbur what Abie was to you. It's late Gant, and we have to take what is real now rather than looking back at our mistakes. I now know what it takes to be a real wife and a lot of it is recognizing that each of us is different. We may not always see things alike, and maybe each of us will have ways that irritate the other. But we have to look beyond them, Gant, and give each other the right to be individuals. I won't hem you in and expect you to forever be at my beck and call. But I will be there and there will be love in my heart and I'll respect you Gant, for you're a good man."

"I don't even know how to think about what you're saying," Gant said as he watched a fish jump out of the water for a moment. "Did you see that fish Callie? I'll bet it was a foot long. My God, I wish I had a fishing pole to put in that water."

Then he paused for a moment as he looked into the distance. "I always wanted a loving woman. I felt like it took that to make life complete. Even under bad circumstances I thought if you had a woman that you could lay your head on her bosom and she'd understand and give you her love in return you could overcome about anything. But I never knowed that Callie. I've missed about everything it seems like."

"I love you so much," Callie said, "and it will be the happiest time of my life to be what you want me to be Gant. You will be as much a part of my estate as I am. You will share in all that has been left to me during our lifetime. After we are gone, most of the estate will go to Philip. That's the way Wilbur had the will set up. In the meantime you will be the boss of all that's mine. You will look after the plantation and Fred and Clee will run the store. You need to know all about the plantation and to see that the farm is run well."

"I'm the happiest I've ever been," Gant said. "It's like being reborn and starting all over. I feel like a silly boy Callie."

"I was thinking that our marriage will unite us with several others that I had never thought about being associated with my life. There are Pearl and Nick, Hobby and Wilbert Lee."

Gant blushed at the mention of Pearl and Hobby. He knew that Callie would think of him as being a central character and he hoped she would not ask about any details. Not that he was ashamed of what he had done except for the fact he had been a married man and she a teen-age girl.

"Nick and Pearl and Hobby are three of the finest people I've ever known," Callie said. "And I'm not even going to go into Wilbert Lee and I'm sure you understand why. I'm not trying to deliberately put him down and I want you to know that. But he's nothing like the other three."

"Oh, I know," Gant replied. "If there ever was a black sheep he's one of them. I've not even laid eyes on him in several months. I wrote him off a long time ago Callie. I had to. He was a millstone around my neck and I had to let him go his own way and try to not even see the boy. They's a limit to what anybody can stand."

Callie spotted a fawn with head bent down to the water. She smiled and said, "If I will ever remember a perfect day, this is it Gant. Of all the days of my life this has to be the best. Look at the little fawn over yonder. Did you ever see a prettier sight?"

"It seems like everything is favoring us today," Gant said. "That's because this is right Callie. Nothing to hide. No shame. Nothing backhanded. And I believe the good Lord is looking down upon us. Giving us a second chance to find peace and happiness in life. When are we going to be married Callie?"

"Let's make it the second Sunday in October. Let's have a very simple wedding at Whispering Pines Church. Let's just have two or three people there. If we invited the members of the church and the public in general the church would be overflowing. But I don't want that. I want the marriage sanctioned by God but I don't want any show or anything like that. Is that all right with you?"

"Just what I'd like best," Gant replied.

And so they became man and wife and a community gave their blessings.

On the Christmas morning after she and Gant were married, Callie made a wreath of holly and took it down to Wilbur's grave. She smelled the cedars before she reached the graveyard and upon arrival broke off a small bough, bruised it slightly and placed it to her nose and smelled its freshness.

Placing the wreath at the newly erected head stone, she stood for a moment in silence. She was aware that nothing she might say would be heard by Wilbur, yet she felt that she should say something, to satisfy herself at least.

"You'd have been pleased, Wilbur," she began. "Something good has come out of tragedy.

"But I'm not here to proclaim any kind of victory for myself Wilbur. I was so blind I couldn't see, and I'm sorry but I know it's forever too late to say that to you now.

"You were a kind man Wilbur, and as God is my witness I never knew it. You have been praised as highly as any man I ever heard of. But I only saw the other side of you. And it's because I didn't look beyond your failings. And I was your wife, Wilbur.

"There's no need to ask your forgiveness now. But I have spent countless hours since you left us in prayer to God. I know he can forgive me, and that he has already done so. But your life is ended Wilbur.

"May your soul rest in peace and I know that one who can see far beyond the realm of man saw every good deed you did, and I know you'll be rewarded for them. I miss you Wilbur."

Chapter 38

W.L. Turner sat in his office in Hallsborough National bank. His secretary, Dorothy Smith, stood at her desk across the room with her back to him, filing papers. He admired the scene. She wore a cool blue dress and it draped snugly across her hips. Her high heels showed off shapely legs and the seams of her silk stockings were straight. He unclothed her in his mind and was filled with thoughts of lust.

Anne had called and said Will and Beth were at her mother's and that she and a girlfriend were going out to eat and then take in a movie. The Spences loved for Will and Beth to visit them. They lavished all their love on their grandchildren and it was easy for Anne to have some free time.

W.L. pushed back the lock of hair that hung down his forehead and sometimes blocked his vision for a moment. He was aware that Dorothy felt something for him. He had caught her watching him when he would turn suddenly and she looked as if she had unclothed him in her mind. Too, there were times when they were in close proximity and she would brush up against him when it wasn't really necessary. He had casually placed a hand on one of her breasts when they were in close quarters one day and she had sighed and her eyes looked dreamy. He felt that there was more there for him if he pursued it.

"What are you doing tonight Dorothy?" he asked.

"This is the night to wash my hair," she replied. "I'll do that and listen to the radio I guess. Any good programs on tonight? And why do you ask?"

"Oh, no reason. Anne just called and said she was going out tonight with a girlfriend. I thought it would be nice if we drove out to Catch Me Eye Inn and had dinner. I want some seafood and they have good shrimp and oysters there."

"You're a married man W.L. And I have a reputation to protect. Suppose we were seen. That's a public place and a lot of people go there."

"I have some pull with the owner," W.L. said. "I instigated a loan for him a while back. He has some secluded booths and I'm sure he would arrange a table for us where we wouldn't be seen by the public."

"You know something W.L. You're a bad boy, but you're so handsome I can't resist. I accept."

"Don't leave the office then," W.L. said. Dorothy lived about a mile from the bank and he decided they'd drive around till about seven o'clock.

He went to the drug store so he would be prepared. He couldn't run the risk of just doing nothing. He thought fleetingly about Anne and the children. But there was no feeling of guilt. W.L. didn't harbor guilty feelings. He didn't have a code of ethics to go by. Least of all where sex was concerned. It was the driving force in his life.

They left Hallsborough via the back entry to the bank. Dorothy was crouched over in the seat so no one would see her. W.L. drove down by the river and Dorothy was sitting up now and the top of the roadster was down and her hair was flying about her face and they were laughing and giggling. W.L. told her to reach in the glove compartment and get out the bottle of whisky hidden there. There were also cups and she took out two. She poured two small drinks. "We don't want to get tight to begin with W.L. It's early and if we start out with big ones we'll be out of shape."

"Right," W.L. said.

"It's really secluded here by the river," W.L. said. "Nobody would ever see us here. Let's walk down close to the water."

"Who said I was going to do anything like that W.L.?"

"Nobody. I just assumed."

"Besides I have a boyfriend. Had you forgotten?"

"And I have a wife."

"Well obviously that doesn't matter to you."

"Not really."

Dorothy looked up the river where the water was white with foam and where overgrowth hung heavy, even dipping into the water in places. "Edgar would kill me if he knew I was riding with a married man," she said. "Edgar's a good man but he's a farmer and he has been taught that a man should respect a woman and make no attempt to shame her before marriage."

"Do you mean he hasn't laid a hand on you?" W.L. said.

"No sir ree. He's gone no further than kissing. He's never placed a hand on my breast even. I'm a lot more pent up than he seems to be. If I were a man I'd be trying to get into every girl's pants I was around."

"I know what you're talking about," W.L. said. "I know a boy or two at Bear Grass who don't know the first thing about a girl. My half-brother is the first that comes to mind. I swear I don't believe he's ever even seen a naked person. He's no more had a piece than a five-year-old boy. I don't know how in the world two brothers could be so different."

"Are you talking about Hobby Turnage?" Dorothy asked.

"Yeah, how did you know?"

"I heard about him, and I knew he was a bastard."

"He's that all right, in more than one way. If I'd known that he was any kin to me when we were little I'd have killed him. He tortured my life and looked up to me like he thought I was some kind of god. He was under my feet wherever I was. I couldn't even piss without some of it getting on him. But he's out of my hair now. He finally moved away to Tennessee when he was twelve or so and I've not seen him since, and don't want to. But knowing him, he's keeping it in his britches until his "true love" comes along. And I can't imagine what on earth she will look like."

"Go to the car and get us another drink," Dorothy said. "I'll need one to get up my courage if we're going to have a roll in the hay." W.L. quickly obliged.

"I know I shouldn't be doing this," Dorothy said when he returned. "Edgar loves me and there's no telling what he would do if he knew I was down by the river messing around with a married man. Does upbringing mean all that much W.L.? I know Mama and Papa tried to bring me up right but that didn't stop these feelings in me."

"Me either," W.L. said. "Ma talked to me till she was blue in the face and said it was sinful to even touch it, but I could go in the yard and see a rooster jump on a hen and go crazy. Naw, it's not how we're taught. It's how we are that counts."

It was warm by the river and there was little wind. W.L. unbuttoned his shirt, revealing a hairy chest. The liquor was taking effect too. He was perspiring on his forehead. Dorothy reached up and undid his belt and unbuttoned his pants. He was straddling her now and she unbuttoned his shorts and he stood above her naked. She gasped and pulled him down on her.

Afterward when she was lying in his arms, she said, "I've wanted this so long W.L. I thought you would never notice me. I could just look at you sometimes and my flesh would crawl. It was pure animal lust. You really know what to do with a woman."

"I'm thinking about my half brother again," W.L. said. "I just wonder what he would do with something like this? I'd love to be standing in the bushes and watching him with a girl."

"Why are you so concerned about him W.L.? He's never lived with you and you never see him. Why does he matter at all?"

"There's always been something about him that bothered me," W.L. said. "I don't mind telling you that I'm jealous of the bastard. He was always the goody-goody and I was always the son of a bitch. But not with Mama. She must have hated him too, for she was always taking up for me and not paying him much attention. She thought he was tainted because his mama wasn't married. If she had known it was the old man's sperm that gave him life there's no telling what she would have done. I reckon I got my taste for wild oats from the old man. That was the only thing that surprised me when I found out he was the daddy of Hobby. I didn't even know my daddy had a dick. But I tell you one thing. That woman would have brought up a dead man's prick. Prettiest woman you ever saw. Out of this world pretty I mean. And just think, she was a teen-ager then. Let's do it again."

After the second time when he had gotten his breath he laughed. "I just wonder what a girl would look like that would take up time with my half-brother? I wouldn't touch her with a ten-foot pole. You're pretty too Dorothy," he said as he pulled her mouth to his. "We can do this a lot if we're careful. I can work it out with Anne and keep her in the dark. But you'll have to be careful too."

"Do you care for me W.L.?" she asked.

"Of course I do."

"Do you love me?"

"That's a strong word to use right now Dorothy."

"Did I please you?"

"God, yes."

"Is there any hope that you might fall in love with me and leave your wife?"

"Oh, I don't know."

"I was in love with you before today, and I'd do anything to have you. I'd slave for you and have your children and I'd take your two children if it came down to that."

"I think you're a little bit ahead of yourself Dorothy. A piece of ass doesn't necessarily mean marriage. That's lust, and I think you know what I mean. You think about Edgar for a little while, and what he really means to you."

She got up and straightened her clothes. "Now we can enjoy our supper at Catch Me Eye and not have other things on our minds," she said.

"We'll see about that," W.L. replied.

The seafood was good and they had a table in a corner that looked out on the lake where a few people were fishing in boats and late bathers were in the water near the shore. Dorothy looked out over the lake and said, "I wish I had my bathing suit. I'd love to go swimming. Maybe that would wash away the scum I feel all over my body."

"Guilty conscience?" W.L. asked.

"You're damn right I do. You think about doing these things and they take over your mind. Then when you do them you feel defiled. But I'll bet you don't feel that way W.L."

"Not especially. But then, men see differently than women."

"Just another conquest huh?"

"You just don't understand Dorothy. Men and women are poles apart where that is concerned."

"I hadn't thought about it before, but now I wonder how you can do this to your wife and children. How do you do it W.L.?"

"Now you're trying to make me feel bad. Women are always trying to make men feel bad about running around. And what harm is it really doing them? I'm a good father and husband."

"Yeah, when you're there."

"Well, I don't go off every night."

"How would you feel if it were your wife running around?"

"She'd better not do that."

"Then you think standards for men and women are different?"

"You're damn right I do."

"W.L. Turner, I've learned more about you in two hours than I had learned from working with you a full year in the office. You have really opened my eyes. Not that I expected you to forsake your family and run off with me, even if I did sound that way in what I asked you. I never saw anybody so conceited in my life. You sound like you're God's gift to women."

"Something like that," W.L. smiled.

"And I suppose you have other buddies who go out woman hunting with you."

"No, I'm more of a loner Dorothy. Always have been except for Philip. He was my best friend when I was a boy. We ran around together and learned about life together. We were two of a kind I guess, for we dared to do what most boys our age apparently didn't even think about. But Philip got married and he's the most dedicated husband and father you ever saw. I don't even like to be around him now. He's so different and we can't even discuss the things we did a long time ago."

"I want to go home W.L.," Dorothy said. "I've got a headache."

"Will you go out with me again?" They were riding under the stars with the top still down.

"I don't know W.L. Probably not, although I still have a feeling for you. I only wish Edgar had your nature but not your attitude. You know the way people act has a lot to do with how they are accepted. Most any woman would be turned off by your superior attitude and your bigotry. I feel like you could put me out on the road and never give it a thought. I'm not sure I can continue working with you in the same office. I wish you'd get me a transfer to another department. You know how scarce jobs are."

"As you wish," W.L. said with not the slightest concern.

They rode in silence and Dorothy looked at the lighted windows along the road. She thought that that was where the real life was. That was where families lived the good life in a simple way. But it was genuine, not a fictitious world filled with fantasy. She wished that one of those windows were reserved for her. There was sex behind those lighted windows - not in the bright lights of reality - but behind closed doors in the darkness of anonymity and blessed by God. Not down beside a river where the waters flowed and sunshine exposed the lusts of human flesh and dehumanized the participants. She wanted to disclaim her part in what happened and blame it all on W.L.'s domination of the situation. But she knew that was wrong. She had wanted to see and know everything about W.L. beneath his clothing to satisfy a lust in her that she wanted to deny. In thinking about him she wanted him again. It was something beyond her control. Yet, she was angry that he was so casual about it all. She had to force herself out of his grip.

To W.L. it was just another conquest which he thought of as a case filled with trophies. But W.L. loathed himself inside. He saw other men who appeared happy in a monogamus relationship who were doing something with their lives. They appeared to be happy with their mates and their children while he floated along with no sense of being situated in life and no real goals. He knew he should be proud of Anne and his children. They represented the best of Hallsborough's society. Anne was an attractive woman as well as responsive. She was a good mother and kept a spotlessly clean house. Will and Beth were handsome children and they showed much love for him.

There were times when W.L. appreciated the house on the hill on a good street in Hallsborough. Sometimes it would give him a sense of belonging for a little while. He'd even get out in the yard and work occasionally, planting shrubs and flowers in places designated by Anne. He even had a workshop at the back of the garage and he'd tinker with furniture to put to use the lathe Anne had given him on some special occasion. But then the old hankering would come over him and he'd resort to the old life.

He knew there was something amiss in his life and he wondered sometimes whether he was mentally disturbed. If he were, he blamed it on his parents - Abie for indulging him in everything possible, and Gant for not bypassing Abie and putting his foot down and standing up as a father. He hadn't been brought up properly.

After taking Dorothy home he went to his own home and saw the lights were still on. But it was only ten thirty. Anne and the children were in their pajamas and W.L. asked the children why they weren't in bed and they told him they wanted to see him before retiring. Both the children climbed up in his lap and he kissed them.

"How was the show and dinner? W.L. asked Anne.

"Fine. The movie was good, an old Gloria Swanson love story, and the meal was average. How was your night?"

"I worked late," W.L. said. "Then I went out and had something to eat."

"You must have already left when I called," Anne said.

"Yeah, there's a lot to do at the bank after working hours."

"I heard something today that might interest you," Anne said. "I was talking with Penny Speight who lives in Bear Grass, and she said your half-brother was getting married."

"Well la de da and hallelujah," W.L. replied. "Did she say to whom?"

"I didn't pay much attention. Something like Spence or Lynch or Finch or something. Anyway she said the girl used to live in Bear Grass. I had never heard of her."

"My gosh, who could she be talking about?" W.L. said. "But it would be about like him to pick out a plain Jane from Bear Grass." He tried to think who she might be talking about. He knew people with all three names.

"Do you know anybody you could call tonight to find out?" Anne said.

"No, Joe Jones lives out there and works in Hallsborough. I guess he'd know. I'll call him tomorrow."

"Well, I don't know why it should matter to you W.L. You certainly don't hold any love for him and you take no pride in being his half-brother."

"It's for the opposite reasons that I'm interested," W.L. said. "I detest him so much everything that he does affects me in a negative way."

"You sure are an odd one," Anne said.

"None of your goddamn wisecracks," W.L. said angrily.

"I'm going to bed," Anne said with a yawn. The children had gone upstairs soon after W.L. came home.

W.L. slept poorly. He dreamed something about Hobby. They were playing somewhere but he couldn't bring the dream into focus. He turned over, disgusted that he would dream about something so trivial.

Anne turned toward him and placed a hand on his shoulder. "I love you," she said close to his ear.

"Uh, huh," he replied.

"Let's make love W.L."

"No, not tonight. I'm tired and that's the farthest thought from my mind."

"All right, I just asked," Anne said as she turned to his back.

W.L. woke with the thought of Hobby's forthcoming marriage. He'd be glad when Joe went to work. He'd call him right after nine o'clock. Then he was upset with himself for giving a damn about who he married. But he called Joe's ice company when he thought he'd be there.

"Hi Joe," he began. "W.L. Turner."

"You mean Wilbert Lee? I've heard you referred to as W.L. But it was always Wilbert Lee in Bear Grass."

"Yeah, I shortened my name when I came to the bank. The name was so long and cumbersome I thought it would help my image to be known as W.L."

Joe thought that the man needed something to change his image, but he put all those thoughts aside. "What can I do for you?" he asked.

"I heard yesterday that Hobby Turnage was marrying some girl that used to live in Bear Grass. I was curious as to who she is. Do you happen to know?"

"Yeah, her name is Robyn Finch. Moved down to Jones County when she was ten or so. You probably remember Tobey Finch. His daughter."

"My God," W.L. said. "I used to play with her. She lived right near me. Well I'll be damned."

There were visions of a stringy-haired girl always making playhouses. Half the time her dress was raveled at the waist, causing the hem to dip. He smiled.

"Thanks Joe. You already know that he's my half-brother. That's the reason I'm curious."

"See you W.L. I have a customer waiting for ice. Got to be going."

W.L.'s mind was suddenly at ease. Since Hobby had moved up in the world by the advent of his mother marrying a wealthy man, W.L. had feared that Hobby would show him up again by marrying some Tennessee socialite. He could not bear the idea of Hobby getting ahead of him, not that that seemed possible for Hobby was an odd one. And he'd heard that Hobby no longer walked lamely or was misshapen because of his bum leg. But there had to be something that called attention to him.

His mind was more at ease than it had been for a long time. He hated to admit to himself that Hobby Turnage had a big impact on his life, made doubly so because of their kinship. He thought that he ought to go to Tennessee and visit Hobby. But then he told himself that Hobby would take that as meaning W.L. was interested in his welfare, and he didn't want to give that impression.

But there was something confronting him that he dreaded more than anything in life. It was the morning he went to the office of Waldo Spence for the shakedown, as he thought of it. Sometimes it would be very pleasant and they would go over the past week's activities and Mr. Spence would be very cordial. On those occasions he would settle down and his heart would resume its normal beat. The perspiration on his forehead would disappear and he'd feel almost like a man. He always expected the worst and when the hour-long ordeal was pleasant he could resume his superior attitude for another week.

Waldo Spence was a large man in stature as well as a respected leader in Hallsborough and the community. He was a no-nonsense banker and valued each person as a human being and expected the best from the human race. He believed in decency and principle and didn't judge a man by his appearance. Some of his best friends were sharecroppers who came to the bank for help. He judged a man by his character and he knew a lot of the people in the county and something about their background.

He knew W.L.'s parents and heard all the rumors about his mother's emotional problems and about her gossiping and about Gant Turner being the father of a son out of wedlock. He had heard about Abie Turner indulging W.L. in things that were not good for his own welfare. He was disturbed about what he heard, especially since this no-good young man was a part of his family. The only redeeming feature was that he found Gant Turner to be a likeable man, moderate in his reasoning, and fairly well-read. But because of that wild streak in W.L. he had to be firm in his dealings with him. He often wondered how it could be possible that a man of his caliber was the father of his two precious grandchildren. Or the husband of his only daughter. He had to instill fear in the dunce to hold some control over him. He'd still be out in the cotton patches if he hadn't given in to Anne's pleas and taken him into the bank. He had no other choice if his daughter and family were to maintain a fairly decent standard of living.

He'd heard all about his carousing, not from Anne but from others who were all too eager to tell him about W.L.'s indiscretions. He would burn with anger after hearing about his whoring around. Someone had seen him yesterday down by the river. They were not close enough to see him clearly, but had recognized W.L.'s car, and there were two of them. He had the urge to kill. He thought about the possibility of W.L. taking a venereal disease home to Anne and his blood boiled.

As always, W.L. entered Waldo Spence's chambers with apprehension. He took his usual seat and he could tell that the boss' eyes were boring into him. Waldo Spence looked you directly in the eye.

"This is not about business today Turner," he said. He slowly twisted a pencil through his fingers and looked out the window to the street below. "I'm as mad as hell Turner and I'm not asking for an explanation and I won't put up with your lies. So you just say nothing and listen to me. Do you hear?"

"Yes sir."

"You were seen out on the river yesterday. Need I say more?"

"No sir." The sweat was already beginning to form on his forehead. He wanted to jump out the window. He had a notion that Waldo Spence never thought about sex, much less practiced it. He hated this man who held such dominion over him, although it was because of his generosity that he was anything at all.

"You are a whorehopper from the word go. Is that all you ever think about Turner?" he asked and there was such a look of disgust on his face W.L. turned away.

"A fine wife and two of the nicest children any man could wish for. Sitting in the Vice President's office with your name on the door. You remind me of a dog when a bitch is in heat. You're sniffing all the time, watching, looking for some sign that she will accept you. You're scum Turner, that's what you are. You're lower than a dog.

"I've done my best to teach you the banking business. And you have the ability to learn, despite your lack of education. It's been six years now and I can't see where you've advanced very far. Got your mind on something but it's only women. You act like you think you're the only man that had such urges. Well, you're wrong. We all have those urges, Turner, but a real man puts those urges behind him and does as a man should. You know the marriage bed is sacred. You also know that your way is wrong. But you're going to keep messing around until one day you're going to find your ass out on the street. I'll be damned if I'll sit by and see my daughter and her children's lives destroyed. And if you ever use this bank as an excuse for being away from home and I find it out, I'll throw you out for that too.

"But there's one thing I want you to know. I've neither told my wife nor Anne what I've heard about you, now nor in the past. I couldn't fix my mouth to say the words to describe your extracurricular activities. And I'm about through giving you another chance Turner. I see it's getting worse instead of better and I'm risking the health of my daughter, even aiding and abetting it by not coming down on you."

W.L. was sweating all over. He felt it running down his shirt. He cringed in the chair and he knew better than to try to defend himself. Knowing it was true made it all the harder to bear. He wouldn't have been surprised if Waldo Spence had risen from his chair and reached over and struck him. He was shaking all over. His father-in-law did stand and straighten his pants and W.L. actually flinched. No other man had ever affected him this way. And he knew about all his indiscretions. He shuddered.

"Times are hard out there Turner," Spence continued. "Just a few short years ago the banks were shut down. You seem to fail to understand that we're struggling to come through this Depression. I mean it's a fight to the finish. Think about how hard it is for farmers to make it now. You should be able to appreciate that for you were among them, although I've heard you were one of the favored ones who didn't even do your share of the work. I pity you for that and you should have been horse-whipped to get you in line. You had the worst upbringing of anybody I ever heard of and you're not to blame for that, and I won't pass judgment on those who raised you, but I know that your daddy can look at you today and see the mistakes.

"I'm laying down the rules for you today, Turner, and you'll follow them by the book or I'll see to it that you get out of my daughter's life, at least as far as living in the home I provided for you. Knowing Anne, she wouldn't have the nerve to do it. And as God is my witness, and I don't know why, but she still loves you. What a pity.

"You are going to settle down and make a contribution to this bank. You're going to stop your running around and become a father to your children and a husband to your wife. Last chance Turner. Do you get me?"

"Yes sir."

"I think I'll even put in that you are to start going to church with your family. Anne and the children are there every Sunday - without you. You're setting a bad example for Will and Beth. You're setting a bad example for the community. It causes the public to question why the man of the family is always absent.

"You're going to become a family man by staying at home with your family and finding something constructive to do there. I would suggest gardening, but you wouldn't even know how to do that. Anyway, there are many ways to make yourself useful at home.

"You are going to do all these things or you're through W.L. If you choose not to do them you can say so and I'll pay you off and you can go now. What is your answer?"

"I will abide by your rules," W.L. said in a weak voice.

"Then go back and hide behind your Vice President's door and think about the man that you really are and the man you can become." Waldo Spence stood and motioned for W.L. to precede him.

W.L. returned to his office, beaten and in shame. He couldn't hardly take it all in but he knew things had reached a climax and that this really was his last chance. Waldo Spence held one hundred percent control over his life - job, family, everything. He thought of himself as less than scum.

Dorothy Smith came into the office soon after his return.

"Did you get a chance to mention a transfer?" she asked.

"Lord no, and I can't ever ask for one," W.L. said. "He knew about me being at the river yesterday. He didn't see us, or the person who saw him didn't. But he saw my car and two people. If I even suggested a transfer to another department he would become suspicious. I don't want your name dragged into this, so you will have to do whatever you think best. But you don't have to worry about me Dorothy. I guarantee you that I'll never bother you again. I'll be a different man from now on. You won't know me as the same man in the future."

"My gosh, he must have really let you have it," Dorothy said in a whisper.

All their conversation had been in a whisper.

"I had it coming," W.L. said. "But you'll see. I've got to change or I won't have a job or a family."

Chapter 39

W.L. Turner was leaning on a hoe at the back of his fenced-in yard. He had had the rear of the lot plowed up and clods of soil lay drying in the morning sun. Bill Ferrell, his neighbor, was working in his garden also.

"Hi Bill," W.L. said as they met where Bill's rows ended.

"Well, hi W.L.," Bill replied. "This is quite a treat. It has been a long time since I've even seen you."

"Yeah," W.L. said. "We have arranged my schedule so I'll have more time at home. I tell you, the way I've been working left no time for family life. And I've got a fine family and I told the boss I just needed more time at home, and since he's my father-in-law he understood and so you'll be seeing a man of the neighborhood now. I really want to get to know the boys in the neighborhood. Although I know most of you on speaking terms anyway, I don't know what makes you tick. I'll be joining you in some of the things you do."

"Well, we'll look forward to that," Bill said. "We've often wondered why you never took part in anything. Like our baseball team, sponsored by the Baptist church. We need all the manpower we can get and you look like you've got plenty of that. But you're a little pale from working inside all the time. Boy, that sun will put a tan on you in short order."

"Yeah, I'm looking forward to that," W.L. said but he wasn't thinking that. He remembered how hot the sun had been when he was in Bear Grass, and how he hated to get out when the sun's rays beat down on the fields. He remembered how he'd feign sickness and retreat to the shade by ten in the morning. He really didn't know how to go about fixing a garden and it was already June and things should be planted.

Anne came out of the house with a smile on her face. This domesticity was something entirely new to her. "Hi Bill," she said. "This is something new to have W.L. around the house in his time off." It was late afternoon and she noticed the tomatoes and beans and corn growing in neat rows in his garden. "I'm so glad W.L.'s schedule has been changed, or that he's been relieved of some of his duties."

Will and Beth came running across the clods of dirt with their dog, Smut, trailing after them. Will stooped to pick up a clod of dirt and Smut grabbed his leg with his paws and began riding it like it was a female dog. Will said, "Daddy, why does Smut do that?"

"Will, just go on and play," Anne said."

"How about joining the team," Bill said and W.L. said he would.

"Let's take rakes and break up these clods," Anne said. "We've got to have the soil soft before we can plant a garden." She went to the garage and brought out rakes.

"Better get to work," W.L. told Bill. "I'll be seeing you boys around, hear?"

"Okay," Bill said as he resumed dusting the bean vines.

W.L. took one hoe and Anne the other, and Will and Beth took hoes and they began breaking up the clods. But W.L. became winded right off the bat and wanted to resort to the shade while Anne seemed to be enjoying the work. W.L. would stand and lean on the rake for a while and he wondered whether he'd ever be able to carry out all the demands made upon him by his tough father-in-law.

Anne looked up at W.L. while he was getting his breath. "It seems so good to have you here," she said.

"It seems good to be here," W.L. answered with a sigh.

And when Sunday came eyebrows were raised when Anne and the children entered the First Presbyterian Church with W.L. leading the way. Several women held fans over their faces and remarked that a miracle must have happened, for there was W.L. Turner with his family. Men noticed too, for although Anne was a faithful member and attended church regularly with her little boy and girl, they never saw anything of her husband.

W.L. fidgeted throughout the sermon, for church had been one place he hadn't had any use for. He remembered how his mother had pleaded with him to attend Whispering Pines Church after he reached the age of accountability. She had taken him when he was younger, and he recalled how he would make scenes in the church and she would have to take him outside.

Many members of the congregation came up and shook hands after the service and welcomed him to the church. Waldo Spence and Mrs. Spence stood on the sidelines and watched and only Waldo Spence knew why this was. He watched W.L. carefully and saw that he was tense and nervous. He had no sympathy for him and would never relax the rules he had set down. And W.L. averted Spence's gaze, although he was very much aware of his presence.

Night would find W.L. in his chair near an open window, reading the Argus and having the children climbing all over him and Anne dropping by sometimes and kissing him on his forehead in a gesture of love. All these things were foreign to W.L. as well as boring, and he'd often engage in sexual fantasies to make it all possible. He was in a straitjacket from which there was no escape.

And Bill told the boys in the neighborhood about seeing and talking to W.L. The boys had done a lot of speculating about W.L. They didn't know about his escapades but they suspected something. "He seems cordial enough," Russell Hill said, "but we never see him. These are people mostly our age, with families, but he doesn't fit the mold somehow. Anne and the children fit into the neighborhood fine and all the kids like Will and Beth, but he's an outsider somehow and he acts like he intends it that way."

"If you ask me," Harper Mewborn said, "he thinks he's better than the rest of us, or at least he acts that way. There's something about him I don't trust. Look at his eyes if you ever get close enough. They look like they hold secrets that he doesn't want the world to know about. I'd be afraid for my wife or children to be around him with nobody else there."

"Oh, I don't think that," Johnny Spence said. "Sure, he's different, but ain't we all got our peculiarities? I believe he'll come around with time."

And W.L. did come around as best he knew how. He was in the world of reality now and was aware for the first time that the family was the backbone of society; that it was what held the world together. He had never thought about it that way in the old days. He never thought of his family in that sense. He knew far too late that despite their efforts, they had been lax enough to allow him to escape that realism. He hated his upbringing and there was a softer feeling for his father, for he remembered all too well the venom his mother could spit out of her mouth.

His parents had never been to his home, for he had warned them at the outset of his marriage that they didn't fit into the kind of people he associated with. He was ashamed of them; their dress and their mannerisms, especially his mother's. Abie Turner had dipped snuff and it would embarrass Anne for her to be there carrying a can around with her to use as a spittoon. His mother had worn an apron except when she was at church; she had a large stomach and didn't wear a corset and her hair was piled high on her head in a tight ball and he thought of her in terms of a washwoman. But Anne had never mentioned their country customs to W.L. She had often wondered why they never came around.

W.L. would see several of the neighborhood men together and he'd join them. There was a large oak tree at the corner of the street back of him with benches underneath, and the boys sometimes gathered there to fan the breeze and just talk about anything in general. Since women always saw the men gathered there, they never used the benches, unless it was an older woman who had walked uptown and rested on her way home. The boys called it their girl-watching station, and their wives accused them of undressing every woman that came by, but they did this laughingly, for they had faith in their men and were glad if they were going to try to do anything on the sly it was in thought only.

They'd see a woman coming way down the street, and most of the time one of the men knew who she was. Bill would say, "Watch this sweet thing shake it around," or something like that if he knew her. And, "Don't you know her old man stays in a hassle all the time."

Such conversation would get W.L. all excited and he'd watch and whistle and say, "Hot dog, that's right down my alley."

And another one would say, "Mine too," and W.L. decided the men were regular after all.

"Wouldn't do for me to be single now," Russell would say. "If I wasn't tied by the balls it would be hard to deal with me."

"Dream on," Harper said. "A married man always has an excuse for not going over the deep end. He blames it on family and then he can tell you what a real he-man he would be if—."

"Let's quit talking this shit," Russell said. "W.L. have you practiced enough that you feel like pitching Thursday night?"

"I'll try," W.L. said. "But my arm is still kind of stiff. Maybe if I get a good warm-up before the game I can at least start."

And so it went with W.L. after his "transformation." Anne became attractive to him again for a while. He also noticed that when they were in mixed company men were always staring at Anne. This surprised him, although if he had thought about it he would have known that it was her charms that had won him over in the first place. But his dallying around had closed his eyes to her as a woman. Somehow motherhood had taken away her sexiness. He thought of her in a different light than in the past. She was busy with the babies and didn't seem to have time for him anymore. He noticed the stretch places on her stomach from pregnancy and it repulsed him.

What bothered him more than anything else was that he was forbidden to stray. If it had happened in any other way he could have accepted it better. But to be told like a child that he couldn't do something made the forbidden all the more attractive. And it took very unusual circumstances for that to be possible. But he knew in his heart that what Waldo Spence did was the only way he would have given in and taken his medicine. He hated his father-in-law.

He decided that Waldo Spence was not a real man. He had no mercy on him for acting out the male role. But then he reasoned that Waldo was not forbidding him playing out his male role, but rather with whom.

During this time he wasn't able to concentrate on Hobby and his fiancee as he would have been able to do if it were not for his own predicament. But somehow, after he found out who it was Hobby was marrying, he was less troubled than he might have been otherwise. After all, she was of their own background, a plain poor girl from the fields just as they were. He was bothered more by Hobby's rise in stature by virtue of his mother marrying a wealthy man. It seemed strange that he would be mixed up in this triangle and he, W.L. Turner, was on the short end of the stick. He could imagine that Hobby was living the life about which they had known nothing in their childhood. But the wedding was a year away and he'd have plenty of time to concentrate on it.

It seemed preposterous to him that Hobby could be a man with even thoughts of matrimony. He had such a low opinion of the crippled boy he kept him at ground level in his mind. He didn't have the same kind of chromosomes as the average person. He shook his head sometimes when he thought about it.

Everything was working against W.L. During the days when he and Philip Stroud had been sowing their wild oats he never thought about how some people were learning about life from a different point of view. He went to school but learning was the least of his thoughts. He depended on the brighter students for help - looking at their test papers and turning to those who sat close to him for answers - cheating by looking up the answers in the back of the book, any way to get by without absorbing the knowledge that was there for him. He had reaped the payoff all right. He was a product of his own folly and the pathetic person he had become repulsed him. Was it too late?

But despite everything he could muster to pull himself up, the old grudges filled his heart. He felt that life was unfair. He didn't want to change his attitudes. He was pleased with what he felt in his heart. He was entitled to happiness in any way that he chose. And society should accept him for what he was. He couldn't change, and he admitted that to himself.

He might be chained by circumstances, but by golly, they couldn't change his feelings.

He wondered what Hobby looked like today. He had thought of him as a little dwarf stooped low and looking up with that stupid smile on his face. Always smiling, even when a few of his classmates were mocking him about the way he walked. But Hobby had plenty of friends and there were those who stood up for him, and were even willing to fight when some of the bullies got on Hobby's case.

W.L. was devastated by the confinements of his life. He wanted to remember the good things when he was a child and before his mind became tangled up with grown-up things. He recalled his playmates and how they explored everything about Bear Grass. But somehow he had missed the bloom on the rose. He hadn't looked for the beauty and consequently only saw the thorns. That was when he knew that something was wrong with his way of thinking and that he couldn't blame that on his mother or father or his environment.

Others he knew were exposed to the same things. The people in his neighborhood had lived the same kind of early life as he. Oh, maybe there were a few exceptions: those who had grown up in the city like Anne, and whose upbringing had been different than his, but even then, they were exposed to the same way of life that he knew and were aware of how things were out in the country. The Depression escaped no one - wiping clean with its fine tooth comb.

He felt the need to change, to refocus his thinking. He needed someone to talk to but no one would sympathize with his distorted view of life. He sank deeper within himself although trying to put on an exterior show of normalcy. He sought excuses for his actions. He was obsessed. He would be irritable with Anne and the children, even striking them sometimes for all the wrong things. When they needed correcting he laughed at their misdeeds. He wondered what it would have been like if he had married one of the girls he had grown up with and moved into a sharecropper house like so many in Bear Grass. At least he would not have been made to feel inferior by a family whose life had been lived differently.

He could have gone around with rolled-up overalls and barefoot, with half-a-week's growth of beard and an old lady with stringy hair and pregnant, and felt like a part of the community. Not many people rose above their raising. But then again, it had happened right in his own family. Look at Perline Turnage, who bore his half-brother. God knows her life had changed. And he knew why. Not only was she pretty but she had also been smart. Beauty alone wouldn't have taken her to a mansion in Tennessee. It took more than that. He envied his old man for his participation in the whole thing and it never ceased to amaze him that Perline Turnage would turn to him, of all people.

He thought about "Bad Boy" Sims and the day of the great manhunt in Bear Grass. That was the day he saw himself for what he was. He remembered more about his participation than about the murder of Nervy Sauls. He would always remember the look on the men's faces at Wilbur Stroud's store when he challenged his father to whip him and the men's repulsive gestures as they gazed at him.

He could see their tobacco-stained teeth and their heavy growth of beard, showing dust and particles of trash. They looked at him with such revulsion he knew that he was the most hated child in Bear Grass. They had a murderous look in their eyes. They were not used to a child standing up to a parent.

A father was the head of the house. His word was gospel. You didn't defy him for he was king. And by him standing up to his father as he did, they knew that everything they had been told was true. He saw some of that scorn directed at his father also. But he knew that they blamed his mother more than Gant Turner. It was common knowledge that she was off the rocker and that she had to have her way or there was no living with her. They often mentioned "poor Gant Turner."

Sometimes he thought of Minnie Mae Moore and the days of his adolescence. He remembered her voluptuousness and how he and Philip Stroud had used her and how she had loved their game. He'd smile when he remembered such incidents.

But he never saw the things that Hobby would point out to him when he was being pestered by the boy. They would be some place playing and Hobby would suddenly look up and say, "Look Wilbert Lee. See that place in the sky? Look at the clouds floating and the colors they get from the sun." Such things had no meaning for W.L.

He laughed. Just as he had shortened his name, Hobby would be shortened to Hob. With something added. Dr. Hob Turnage.

Sometimes his mind seemed to be whirling in space. He'd feel disoriented and it would cause him to walk awkwardly and he would have to sit down for a short while. Sometimes he thought he was going crazy. At such times he would go to his room and absent himself from the family, pretending to have a headache.

A big shot of whisky might relieve the pain but he had been warned not to bring whisky home before his children. Waldo Spence had seen the bottles in the cabinet in the old days, and Waldo was a teetotaler. He could understand a man taking a drink if that were his choice, but he couldn't understand him doing it before his family. The family was sacred to the banker. Nothing came before it, not even church. He reasoned that the whole basis of life was founded on the family and from the family church life evolved, laying_down principles for man to go by. He considered the home the place for those rules to be instilled in children. But inside, he was the same old Wilbert Lee Turner.

Chapter 40

P aralysis gripped the nation throughout the 1930s. An unhealthy economy poisoned the atmosphere. There were dry years when crops failed and the harvest was slim. There were the dust storms in Oklahoma and the grass died on the ranches in the west where cattle roamed and were a large part of the economy. With no pasture lands for grazing, cattle were starving to death. Arrangements were made to ship them across the country where there were grazing lands, but they were sick from malnutrition and when they were unloaded from the trains they stood on wobbly legs with their backbones prominent and hip bones that appeared to have nothing over them but skin.

Some were sent to Hallsborough and they must have been the poorest of the lot, for they began dying and their carcasses were burned. The stench of leather and meat and bones lay heavy over the surroundings.

But life went on in Bear Grass. Life goes on despite catastrophes. There were years when nobody paid out of debt. Knee-high cotton and waist-high tobacco and corn, with only nubbins due to drought, are a sure sign of failure. When there is no water from general rains there is nothing to hope for. There is a saying that dry weather will scare you to death, but wet weather will kill you. But farmers turned their heads negatively. They needed water.

But not every year was that bad. There were years of adequate rains and crops flourished. But that only helped catch up from the bad years. There never seemed to be any money left over for the farmer.

Cholera broke out among the hogs one year, and people lost most of the meat, leaving few for the smokehouse. Sow belly became the main meat diet for the farmers the next year.

Years when it was hardest to make ends meet took their toll on chickens. With little corn in the barn, and what there was shipped in from other places and doled out to the sharecroppers in minute amounts, the chickens had to forage for their food, catching insects that flew low to the ground. Their breasts were peaked and their feathers dull, with pale combs and hackles.

And hogs were unhealthy because of a lack of a sufficient food. Sows would have their babies and have empty udders. The pigs would develop scours and go off in the weeds and die. Chickens would eat the dead carcasses, filled with maggots, and they in turn would die from limberneck. The live things in their crops would result in their inability to hold up their necks. And the odor of dead things would permeate the premises and children would be sent into the weeds to find the dead animals and they would heave and vomit as they brought them out to be buried.

People tried to help each other as best they could. Tom Best's house burned and people were quick to help. There was little to give from their homes, for there was not a surplus of any item. Some people gave a quilt, for there were twelve children in Tom's family. Some women made sheets from 98-pound flour sacks and gave them. Some people had old bedsteads and dressers stored in cribs that they drug out and donated to the Bests.

The men in the community got enough timber together to make a table for the family. They also made benches to go at the table.

But there were no cries of defeat. Nobody in Bear Grass cried wolf. They shook their heads and went on with life, and even had hope. They had been defeated for most of their lives and added hardships made them all the more determined to weather the storm and to hope for tomorrow. There was always that silver lining behind the cloud they could not penetrate. Always tomorrow was their motto.

Enough things were happening across the nation to consume people's thoughts, and were the topics of conversation daily. Many very poor people managed somehow to get a radio. Nothing had ever affected the people as had the advent of radio. It put them in touch, even on isolated farms and in remote areas. Radios put them in touch with what people on the "other side of the mountain" were doing. It forever obliterated total ignorance from the masses.

Radios were hard to come by for poor farmers who had no resources. And they made sacrifices to get them. They'd save up eggs and sell them. They'd sell a chicken if they had to. The radios required batteries, for there was no electricity in many parts of the rural area, certainly not in Bear Grass. People soon learned programs that appealed to them. They liked all the shows that were liked nationally.

They'd pull their chairs as close to the radio as possible when the batteries were weak in order to hear the programs. And sometimes static prevented the program from coming through, with foreign stations taking over, usually from Mexico, and in a voice not understandable. If a battery went dead many boys gave up their ten or fifteen-cent allowances each week for a ticket to the Saturday movies for a battery.

"Lum and Abner" kept many boys at home as did "Amos and Andy," and they would return from the store early to hear "The Shadow." They could forgo some popular shows, for they had their activities with their friends in the community.

And when the World Series came most people were grading tobacco and they would move the grading bench where the radio was, or unhook it and tote it to the packhouse and lug the batteries along. They cut pine saplings and ran a wire up the poles to hook to the radio to bring in a strong signal. Everybody that could listened to "The Grand Ol Opry" on Saturday night.

First Lady Eleanor Roosevelt came down to Wallace to attend the Strawberry festival. She was dressed in cotton stockings and flat-heeled shoes and she was laughed at by the penniless sharecroppers. Poor folks are proud and women even on the farm usually wore silk stockings when they went out in public. Yes sir, they'd sport silk stockings and high heels with legs covered with hair.

They called Eleanor a "nigger-lover" and you'd have thought she was nothing the way ignorant people in North Carolina ranted and raved about her. That made big news in the state and people resorted to the newspapers rather than radio for that story.

Chancy Smith's boy, Claude, was charged with bastardy and that caused a commotion in the neighborhood for a little while. Chancy hired a lawyer for Claude, who said he wouldn't marry the girl even if he had to go to jail. He told Chancy she was turning it up to other boys and he knew it to be a fact. He didn't deny that he'd had anything to do with her. You'd have thought it was a murder trial the way men flocked to the courthouse to hear all the details. They were disappointed when the judge cleared the courtroom and held the trial in secret.

During the course of the trial, the Press reported Chancy's wife called the girl a strumpet and the girl's father, Kencheon Williams, got into a shouting match with her, and both were cited for contempt. But Claude was sentenced to prison for two years, and he served every day of it, but he didn't marry the girl.

Several whisky stills were blown up by the sheriff's department. The calmness of the night would be interrupted by the loud explosions and people would say, "There goes another whisky still."

School buses were transporting students to Hallsborough High School and many more students were attending. And the Negroes had a high school too that the white folks called "The Academy." But the real name was Pineknoll and professor Rinehart was the principal.

Charles Lindbergh, who made the first solo non-stop flight over the Atlantic, was a hero to all Americans, and when his son, Charles Jr., was kidnapped people went into a frenzy. They listened for any information about the baby. They tuned in to every news broadcast to hear about the kidnapping and to get the weather reports. After going for a lifetime without knowing what to expect from the weather until after it occurred, they listened to weather reports religiously. Then when it didn't develop like it was forecast, and it didn't on many occasions, they said weather reports didn't mean a damned thing.

When the Lindbergh baby was found men cursed and swore vengeance. Women cried.

Now the search was on for the kidnapper. When Bruno Hauptmann was arrested and charged with the crime, there was a sense of relief for a time, although reports surfaced that he wasn't the real killer. But Hauptmann paid with his life for the crime. On the day of his execution, there was a long wait until the execution was carried out. A young reporter was at the prison to describe the scene and the delay resulted in a long ad lib to fill the air waves. But this young reporter met the challenge and won his right to become a commentator when World War II came along. He was listened to by millions who hung on his every word. He was their consolation. No matter how dark the war news, he was somehow able to inspire mothers who had sons in the war zone. His name was Gabriel Heatter.

We didn't know much about our neighbors in Canada and we didn't give them much thought. But a story in the 1930s captured the attention of the world. Quintuplets were born to a poor family, the Dionnes. And you wouldn't have wanted to be at Stroud's store after the news broke. You never heard so much carrying-on as those men did.

Those tobacco-chewing, crotch-scratching farmers thought it was superhuman efforts of the man that put five babies in the woman's uterus. Lem Coor put it down to the level of dogs. "My God, what was he doing?" Lem said. "He must have put it there all night long."

Connie Coor said he thought he was pretty good, but he'd be damned if he could come up with any such a record.

"Hell, one dog can get a dozen puppies," Lem said, "and a boar can get enough pigs to fill a sow's belly to the brim."

"We're looking at it in the wrong way," Connie said. "We ought to be thinking about what a miracle it is that all five babies are living."

Thomas King, a student at Hallsborough High who was taking a biology course, listened to the men carrying on. "What happened was not anything unusual as far as the man is concerned," he said. "One man that is healthy produces enough sperm every time to fertilize every woman in the world. He will fertilize ever how many ripe eggs the woman has."

"How do you know what you're talking about young'un?" Lem asked. "These upstarts have got all the answers. What in the hell do you know about such things?"

"I am taking biology," Thomas said. "We have taken sperm from animals and studied them under the microscope. You'd be surprised to see how many sperm are wiggling around in just one drop of semen."

"Can you imagine them teaching such things as that?" Lem said. "They'll get them from their own selves first thing you know and see them under the magnifying glass. And they'll go wild when they learn what they possess. I believe it's better to keep them behind the plow and let them find out about such things when they're grown up and they get all hot and bothered and have to find out about such things or climb a wall."

"Lem,"Connie said, "you're so far behind the times it's pitiful. Show me any fifteen-year-old boy and I'll show you a boy that's already found out about all that. Were you so backward that you were a man before finding out Lem?"

"Naw, I won't that far behind," Lem said. "But I was smarter than most boys my age."

"Sounds to me like you were the most bass-ackards boy in the neighborhood," Connie Coor said.

The Dionne Quintuplets made news for years. They were photographed in magazines and displayed through windows in which they could not see the throng of visitors they had daily but the viewers could see them. All such news was read around the nation, and even in the out-of-the way places such as Bear Grass, although it may have been interpreted differently by the uneducated.

In 1936 King Edward of England abdicated his throne to marry the American divorcee Wallis Warfield Simpson and that made everybody in Bear Grass mad. Now divorce was unheard of in the area almost. There had been a very few cases of divorce. And that is not saying a lot of people wouldn't rather have been divorced than living like they were. The trouble was there was no way but to stay together for there was nowhere else to go. Everybody needed each member of the family as a prop (All propping together to make it work).

But at Wilbur Stroud's store they said by God an American, even one divorced, was as good as the bloody British who stuck their nose up like somebody had farted in their faces, and that the Simpson woman was as good as anything they had to offer.

They called all the British sons of bitches. A lot of folks called the woman a beauty, but the men at Wilbur's store said they'd be damned if they could see all that much in her. They said she looked sort of like she was underfed and didn't have no meat on her bones and they said they liked a woman with a little meat on her. Said it gave them something to feel of. But they said they'd be damned if they'd give up a throne for no woman and didn't know what kind of man the king could be when he could have the pick of the women. But somebody said no he couldn't; that he couldn't have no "common" woman cause they'd heard it on the radio and there was plenty of them. They said he was expected to pick one of them high and mighty dames that held their head a certain way and looked down on everybody. The boys concluded that they'd rather be plain old sharecroppers and live like a dog than to be up there with royalty.

Unemployment stood at 12 million in 1932 but that was no problem in Bear Grass where everybody tilled the soil. Black and white, young and old, farmers looked to the soil for their livelihood. Through weather extremes and normal periods it was six-days-a-week trying to survive as well as to get some satisfaction out of living.

When spring came and the world turned green, farmers were out in the fields observing the beauty of nature. They saw tiny buds burst forth with leaves forming on the trees and then the blooms that followed on flowering shrubs and trees.

They smelled the fragrance of spring blooms and observed the petals that were the leftovers of fragile flowers and they marveled, as they always did, at the beauty of nature. It was the same with all the seasons.

Wilbert Lee Turner and Philip Stroud were the neighborhood hell cats and they were beginning to feel their sprouting manhood. They were pestering all the girls in Bear Grass, grabbing them in inappropriate places when they got the chance, and although the girls resisted, some of them were affected by the boys' brashness and Wilbert Lee and Philip got their share of thrills.

They had a special place they used to lure girls. There was a bridge on the way to school and the land sloped down beside the bridge and underneath there was a clean place to sit, unobserved by the public.

They'd invite a girl to go under the bridge to watch the water as it trickled by, clear and with a sandy bottom, where they waded sometimes when the weather was warm. If a girl went under the bridge with them she was anticipating a thrill, although she was often afraid of the boys.

They had quite a reputation in Bear Grass. And Wilbert Lee and Philip would start off slow. One would casually put an arm around her shoulder and like most teen-age girls, she would giggle and when the boy looked into her eyes she would feel chill bumps over her body.

Next, the boy would lay a hand on her breast and she would feign pushing it away, while all the time feeling a scorching heat from the hand. And when one would take a nipple in his hand and the other boy taking the other, the girl would breathe deeply and wriggle free of the hot hands.

Then Wilbert Lee especially, would run a hand up her dress and fumble at her panties, while unbuttoning his pants. This would really frighten the girl and she'd scramble free most of the time and run out from under the bridge and get herself together. But there was a thrill as she remembered the touch of a finger on a hard nipple or the sliding of a hand toward her womanhood. But sometimes Wilbert Lee and Philip were luckier, and went all the way. They kept rubbers in their pants pockets and at least they practiced protection. They didn't want to be teen-age fathers.

Several things happened in 1933 that had a bearing on Bear Grass. President Franklin D. Roosevelt ordered all banks in the U.S. closed. This affected the Hallsborough bank, although very few people in the area had a penny in the bank. Landowners who did have a small amount of money in the bank could not touch it, and that in turn made it harder for the sharecroppers and tenants to get supplies. If it hadn't been for a few store owners like Wilbur Stroud and Pope Smith, some of them would have gone hungry. Of course, Wilbur and Pope were the beneficiaries eventually for the farmers had nowhere else to go and the merchants extended credit to them in small amounts and the farmers paid dearly when they settled up.

Roosevelt called for a special session of Congress on March 9 and it lasted until June 16, in which his New Deal program was fashioned. This started the nation on its slow climb from the Great Depression. NRA signs were everywhere and they were in Bear Grass too. They were tacked on store doors, placed in store windows, and became a part of the scene nationwide. In blue lettering and with the picture of a spread-wing eagle, people learned to recognize them as a symbol of a new America and they were associated with the man that became a god to Americans - Franklin Delano Roosevelt. But the seven points of the eagle's wing were associated with the seven seals of the Bible by some.

That was the year the gold standard was dropped by the U.S. also. It was also the year prohibition ended.

In 1935 a beloved American, Will Rogers, was killed in an Alaskan plane crash. Everybody could identify with Will Rogers. His witty comments were read in the Argus as well as across the nation.

Side by side, Negroes and whites toiled the fields. The Negroes sang spirituals, harmonizing as they chopped or plowed, and waited for water from the children who brought it to them in jars. It was lukewarm by the time it reached them and there were beads in it. Sometimes they'd spit it out and whip the children for being so long in getting it to the fields. The white people did the same as the Negroes.

When it was warm, people gathered on their front porches at night to get the southern breezes. Laughter could be heard all over the neighborhood. And the sweet smell of honeysuckle and cape jasmine filled the air. And the fireflies appeared en masse. The nights were dotted with the yellow glow of the lighted lamps in windows and the brighter glow of the fireflies with their tiny specks of light. Mosquitos also swarmed and people fought them off or retreated inside, where some also waited for their victims. On those beautiful nights the populace felt snug in its little world.

Things changed little. Some people moved away each year and others moved in. The light lines finally came through Bear Grass and a few people hooked on. Wilbur Stroud's store became the brightest place in the community. Most people, however, were not affected by the power lines. There was no money to pay the two-or-three-dollar charge each month. The light line extended to the Greene County line.

Whenever possible, boys thronged to town on Saturday to see the show. Westerns were the only kinds of movies they cared about. And the movie industry knew just what it was doing, for there was a serial every weekend that left the viewers hanging as to what was going to happen next. Boys had to know what happened in the next episode and when they couldn't attend they'd get a boy who did attend to give them all the details so they could pick up the story when they did return. Few girls got this opportunity.

Sometimes, especially in March and April, great whirlwinds would play over the land, gathering up soil from freshly-plowed fields, scattering it everywhere and partially shading the sun. Dust would get into the homes and even foods would be gritty. Looking glasses in the bureaus were covered with dust and children would spell out words on the glass.

In summer there came heavy storms. With the openness of the surroundings, people could see the black cloud making up. Many people were afraid of the storms for they often spawned tornadic winds and brought hail and torrential rains, as well as sharp lightning and heavy thunder that seemed to roll all across the heavens. When people were in the fields while the skies were darkening they would take out the mules and head homeward. They would run as hard as they could when the lightning began flashing. If there was a yellow cast to the cloud they believed there would be hail.

Once inside the houses, if there was a hall, the family would congregate there and shut all the doors. They were in the dark then, but the flashes of lightning would lighten up the hall as it showed in the door cracks. The tin roofs seemed to be just above their heads.

The old man would go to the windows and look out and he often saw the old trees in the yards that had weathered countless storms, with their boughs being battered by the fierce winds. Sometimes a tree would succumb to the storm when the force of the wind was just right. He would see his fields overflowing with water and he feared drowning of the crops. Drowned plants of any kind meant their ruination. As soon as the rains slacked up the men and boys took shovels and opened trenches for the water to run off.

And hens and biddies were always caught when the summer storms came. They foraged far into the fields hunting for worms and insects. The biddies would be beaten down by the rains as if they were dead. The women would roam the fields in search of the wayward hens, while the men opened trenches. The biddies that were beaten down were gathered up and taken to the house, dried off and placed in a warm place to come to. A few didn't survive, but most did.

In the fall sometimes, and at other seasons occasionally, there would come gentle rains when the water hitting the tin roofs would provide a lullaby for people to sleep by. The only thing families had to worry about when the rains came were the holes in the roof. They knew just where to put the buckets and pots to catch the water. And on those rainy nights they would often hear the refrain of the frogs in the pond.

Then there were balmy days during all seasons when everything in the world seemed right. The sun would warm the earth but without the heat that parched everything and caused the people to be miserable. The birds would sing their sweetest and even the sight of buzzards soaring over the woods was pleasing. There was a lot of beauty to compensate for the sordidness of their lives. They were not unhappy.

A new baby was added to the younger households about every two years or so. Men wore the pants and every wife had learned all she needed to know about men. All the pleading and all the humoring failed where that was concerned. They nursed their babies for as long as they could, thinking that nursing would keep them from ovulating, only to find in many cases they were carrying another baby while nursing a little one. The men were kidded at the store when their wives' bellies were seen growing. They really didn't mind the kidding, for they were proud of their manhood, but they'd have an answer for the kidders. There was always the one about just hanging the overalls on a bedpost would cause pregnancy to swearing he never left it in to finish; that she must have gotten the seed off the sheets and such mess.

In every season, there were certain rituals observed annually. In Bear Grass there were more rituals observed in spring than any season, because on the farm it is the season for new life. Take the guineas, for instance. When the weather has turned warm and ditch-bank growth is rank, they can be seen making their way to the reed beds and lush growth along ditch banks as the morning progresses. Their songs are heard all over the neighborhood. They cackle and roam together, unusual looking in their coats of black and white specks with their tails down and with unusual head decorations. It is the time of mating and they lay nestfuls of eggs, several laying in one nest sometimes. People look for their nesting places and go and rob the nests of their eggs, using a spoon to gather the eggs to keep the human scent from the nest. If they smell the human scent they will go to other places to nest.

They follow the geese to their nesting places also, usually always in a reed bed. The old geese prefer staying in the barnyard and picking up a few kernels of corn. They are lazy and nasty and their refuse covers the ground. Geese are kept to rid the cotton fields of grass. When the cotton is a few inches high they close the gate where the field is fenced in and they have to eat the hills of grass to survive. Still, the fields have to be chopped.

It isn't hard to see a goose nest for they are large and built up. Many reed blades are used in fashioning their nests. They lay eight to ten eggs usually and the mothers are very attentive to their nests. So are the ganders in protecting them. They'll fight anything that comes near with their wings. And those wings punch a real wallop. They also get a hold on whatever they are fighting with their strong bills. They'll almost flay a young'un half to death if he invades their territory.

The goose sits four weeks on the eggs and the goslings are pretty things, a fluffy yellow, and mama and papa goose are very proud of them and you'd better stay out of their way when they're parading them around the barnyard. If there's a pond nearby they'll spend much of their time there. But they'll get by in the barnyard.

The purple martins came every year. On time. Children watched as they refurbished the gourds with new grasses and strings, making last year's quarters habitable again. They would pitch outside the gourds sometimes and their purple sheen appeared to have been shellacked. They glistened in the sun and seemed as much a part of the premises as if they lived in the gourds year-round.

In the orchards the bluebirds built their nests and flew over the neighborhood, pitching in yards to bathe in the mudholes and preening their feathers. Many species of birds chose Bear Grass as their home.

Many animals were born in spring on the farm. The sows would have large litters of pigs of all colors. Beds were prepared for them under little shelters with tin tops to protect them from the elements. Plenty of pine straw was used for bedding. The sow would fashion the straw to suit her as labor approached. She would talk sow talk when the babies began arriving and got near her face. The pigs would nuzzle at a teat and were soon nursing, but many were mashed by the great weight of the mother who couldn't know that she was lying on them.

The cows usually drop their calves in the pasture in warm weather. In winter, their stables provide a place of birth. Large animals have painful births, although they usually weather the storm and little attention is given to their births. But once in a while something goes wrong, and this calls for immediate action. Then the farmer calls in the veterinarian. A calf or horse may be coming the wrong way or instead of both of the front feet presenting themselves first in the birth process, one may be turned backward, and this causes grave problems. The veterinarian may have to resort to fastening a trace chain attached to a mule around the part of the calf that has emerged, fastening it very carefully around the already-dead calf in an effort to get it expelled from the suffering cow.

And the children are explorers. The fields and forests are their domain. From the time the wisteria, which has climbed high in the trees and sheds its lavender blossoms overhead, until the lightning bugs have dwindled away, they see everything that is going on and are participants. They go wild when the brierberries are ripe. They risk hands, arms and face to reach the ripe berries with their protection of briers. They get nasty scratches on their hands.

Nothing hurts worse than to get a strong thorn at the end of a thumb. It feels like the brier has touched the bone and a sharp pain goes half way to the elbow. And the bloody scratches hurt just to bend the fingers.

They eat their fill first and their faces become purple from the berries. Their clothes become stained. And when they have eaten their fill they pick the berries to take home to be made into jelly. While the scratches are healing they take to the fields to find maypops. They gather all they can carry and take them to the house and put them under a shade tree and steal a knife from the kitchen and cut them into shapes to fit their fancy and take the purple blooms and shape them into playthings also.

The wild cherries begin to turn red and the children beat the birds to the trees and pit them as they eat and spit the seeds on the ground, often with grins on their faces, for cherries are bitter, especially when they're just beginning to ripen. They find toad frogs and lizards and baby rabbits and birds that have fallen from their nests and have a veritable circus under the trees. And nothing on earth pleases them more than when the road scraper comes by, cleaning out the side ditches and putting the dirt on the road, to be spread over the road later and which eventually will clog the side ditches again. They follow the scraper as far as they can.

They go to the ditchbanks where the wild bullises have climbed into the tall trees. They aren't concerned with the grapes now for they are hard and green. Instead, they cut one or two of the climbers and use them to swing over the ditch and land back among the thick foliage.

The children sometimes walk across the piles of old boards on the woodpile during some of their games. They step on boards that have rusty nails in them and for a moment their feet are impaled on the board. They have to literally pull their feet free of the nails, screaming and crying and having the mother run to see what is happening. The child is walking on one side of his foot with the dirt covered with blood. The mother rushes and brings the kerosene can and washes off the foot. A child is sent to bring a pine bough and she puts it into an old bucket and sets it afire and the foot is placed over the smoke and the turpentine goes into the wound. Finally, the foot is bound in a white rag and the child has to cease playing and nurse the foot.

This goes on all summer long and the children's feet aren't fully well until about the last of October, long after school has started. Sometimes a shoe is worn without being laced up and this causes the heel to rub against the shoe and blisters are added to punctures and they get little pleasure from new school shoes when they are their newest. All this the children suffer just to go barefoot. It's freedom, it's pleasure until the mishaps and they wouldn't wear the shoes anyway, for during the summer there are no shoes except the worn out ones with floppy soles and if they had a new pair of "tennises" they still would not wear them.

Then there is the ritual of late summer. When all the tobacco has been stripped from the stalks and all that's left are the suckers that have taken over the top of the plants and the tobacco worms are busy eating the refuse, when the last barn of tobacco is curing and the fields are taking on a yellow hue and the bullbats dive straight from the skies and dip down with their daring acrobatics and fly into the sky again, there is the barbecue to celebrate the end of another barning season with all its sacrifices, everything being devoted to harvesting the leaf for about eight weeks.

There have been weeks of rough-dried clothes and the men wearing the gum-covered overalls and hanging them on a nail on the porch when not in use, to searching for something to wear from the large pile in the old cradle and each member of the family ironing his own; to boys searching through the clothes to find a pair of underwear that's in one piece and often finding none and end up wearing a pair with half the seat gone.

There's plenty to celebrate. So the women cook all manner of good things, from eight-layer chocolate cakes with the layers no more than half an inch thick and saturated with chocolate, chocolate pies and lemon pies and apple jacks, butterbeans and peas and collards and corn, plus the barbecue that one of the men has cooked with oak wood for eight hours or so, and a wood tub filled with lemonade and tea in jars and homemade ice cream, drained of the water and salt and ice added and packed to harden and tow sacks put over the freezers to hold in the cold.

Meanwhile, everybody is clean. The men go down to the pond and bathe, washing their hair and getting the feel of tobacco off of them. They have gone through the clothes and taken out their one pair of overalls that are dark blue but are soft from several washings, and a white shirt that also has to be ironed. They dress at the pond and it seems like Saturday, although it isn't, for the clothes they are wearing are their Sad'dy evening garb. And the girls iron their voile dresses or whatever the material might be. They also wash their hair and everybody is looking good. And the very thought of being through green tobacco for a whole year puts everybody in good spirits. And a good time is had by all.

The ritual of the watermelons is a happy time. Show me a farmer that doesn't love watermelon and I'll show you a person that ain't got no business in the country.

They always use the largest. The farmers carry them to the house on the shoulders, often weighing fifty pounds or more. The melons are stored in the coolest places. Tobacco trucks are taken to the looping shelter that has been cleaned and swept as tidy as a yard for the weekend. Sometimes the watermelon cutting is at night, with lanterns furnishing the light and a canopy of stars overhead. And nothing is served but watermelon. Who wants to mess up the taste of a good, solid ripe watermelon with any other taste? The melons are split lengthwise, with each piece carrying about three inches of rind. The grown-ups enjoy them, but the children are ecstatic. They mire their faces in the melon, spitting out as many seeds as they can while they are eating, but swallowing some as well. They eat right down to the rind, then go for more, for there is an ample supply. A few of the grown-ups share a half of melon, digging it out with a fork and leaving the seeds in the rind. And there is an accumulation of juice and children love the juice. So when the grown-ups finish with the melon some of the children take over and cut V's in the rind and squat down and drink the juice from the melon.

They are fun times and the only thing the parents worry about is the possibility of a child's wet bed in the morning, for watermelons do act on the kidneys.

And there are the chicken fries at the tobacco barns sometimes. Tobacco barns serve other purposes besides curing tobacco. Quite a few social events are carried out at the barns. When the girls hold chicken fries it is a time for courting. Tobacco trucks at such occasions always serve as tables. They are covered with white tablecloths that adorn the tables on Sunday.

The rituals of childhood. Memories that will go with them as long as they live. A memory of happy times to sort out in adulthood and to reflect on as being too beautiful to describe; too fleeting to recapture; too nostalgic to forget.

Chapter 41

The years crept by at a snail's pace. There were times when both Hobby and Robyn felt that the sacrifice was too great. Each had given up so much during the years of their youth that both felt cheated. Many of their friends married and had already started families. Both had been tempted to break their promise to each other because of all that was happening where each was, and the other far away in some dream-like world that seemed like a fairy tale.

Robyn had borne the brunt of Chip's scorn after she broke their engagement by flaunting other girls before her, ignoring her for the most part. He seemed to have a sneer on his face when he saw that what he was doing was an embarrassment. She would go to the Saturday night dances just to get away from home and to mingle with the other young people who were there. She told Hobby about this and he suggested that she stop habitating the places she knew Chip would be, and Robyn detected a tone of jealousy in his voice. So she started staying home more and listening to the radio.

She also asked Hobby what he was doing to pass the time and he said he had about forgotten about time, concentrating most of his energy on his studies. He admitted that he had been tempted so long as he took part in student activities outside the classroom. "But let's be true Robyn. Let's beat the odds and we'll reap the rewards one day." And they had cried over the telephone. They cried often when Hobby called and there were times when both were melancholy and when words didn't seem to have much meaning.

They talked about the many things that were happening in the world and how everything was changing very swiftly. And Bear Grass was always prominent in such conversations.

Hobby would fly down from Tennessee about every three months and he and Robyn would have a reunion for a day or two. But such meetings proved to be agony in the final analysis for parting was worse on every occasion of their meeting.

Finally it was the fourth year of college and they actually celebrated with champagne. Hobby took Robyn to a restaurant in Jacksonville where drinks were served. Robyn had never tasted champagne before and the beads in the drink and the strength of the champagne made her sneeze and she almost became strangled. They laughed and danced and it again seemed like a dream world - a world in which all their dreams came true.

"One more year, my love," Hobby said, "and it will be over. One year Robyn!"

"I can't believe it," Robyn said. "The past three years have been long enough for a child to grow into adulthood it seems like. And this will be the longest year of all."

"I know," Hobby consoled her. "But the worst is over my darling. Start making plans for our wedding. You have a lot to do in the next year. And we're too near our goal to give up now."

Chip had married a girl from the western part of the state in the past year. He met her at N.C. State. And Hobby breathed a sigh of relief when Robyn told him. The girl Hobby had dated at the university also married a man from Arkansas who was a medical student. But Hobby had never considered her seriously and she was aware that theirs was only a friendship and each used the other when occasions demanded that both sexes be involved in special events.

Finally it was May. And their wedding was only a month away.

Cora was busy putting the finishing touches to Robyn's wedding gown. All the fine lace, all the sequins, all the snaps were sewn on. She was thrilled at her handiwork and when Robyn stood before her in all her loveliness it was her happiest moment. Arlene said it wasn't fair for Robyn to be so pretty and her so plain. But Arlene was exaggerating for she was a pretty girl also, yet in a different way than Robyn.

Hobby called and said he was going home two weeks before the wedding; that he'd need that much time to get everything in order. He told Robyn to go to his grandfather's then also, for both of them would have plenty to do. So everything was taking shape for the big event.

Chapter 42

Robyn came up from Jones County and met Hobby at Craven and Viola Turnage's home in Bear Grass. Hobby's grandparents were all smiles as they greeted Robyn. Hobby had arrived a day earlier. Viola had cooked one of her melt-in-your-mouth chocolate cakes that Hobby had already sampled. Viola took Robyn right to the table and offered her a piece of cake and coffee and Hobby and Craven joined them.

"Now you two are as much at home here as Craven and me," Viola said. "Go about your life just as if you lived here. It seems hard for Hobby to adjust to the new house and he seems a little bit lost not being at the old place although it's way above what we had and I know how to 'preciate it if any poor woman ever did. Not even an extra bedroom in the old place and staying cold unless you were before the fireplace or around the cookstove. But I do miss the old place."

"It's real nice," Robyn said.

"I'll show you around after you eat," Viola said. "I'm mighty proud of it."

"Hobby, you ought to be mighty proud of this nice place," Robyn said.

"Oh, I am," Hobby said. "Youall just don't understand. It's not at all that I'm not proud that Grandpa and Grandma have a good place to stay and life is easier for them. It's not that at all. But I've been away since I was a boy and when I left the old place was so real in my mind every day I was gone I can't think of this place as home. I guess in my heart I wanted it to stay the same, never changing, never keeping up with the times. But I'm glad they're having it easier as they grow older."

"Yeah, some of it seems good," Craven said. "But I miss some of the things at the old place. But I tell you son, when a man gets older it becomes harder to do all the things that have to be done when you've got a lot of things to tend to and the legs and back beginning to feel weak. It makes a difference."

"Yeah, I know Grandpa," Hobby said. "I'm the young one and I'm the one that thinks the oldest. But it ought not to be that way when we're here to get ready for our wedding."

"That's true," Viola said, "so stop thinking old and think about all the things young people think of when they're fixing to start life together."

"Two weeks from today," Robyn said with a smile. "I can hardly wait. Don't you think I've picked the handsomest man in the world for my husband?" She placed her hand on Hobby's arm and smiled.

"Of course he's the handsomest man in the world," Viola said. "But I tell you something Robyn, he can be just as proud of you as you are him. You're as pretty as a peach and kind and good and I don't see no way your future can't be good. Of course, we never know how the future will be." She rose from the table and told Robyn she'd show her over the house and Hobby took her bags to the front guest bedroom.

Afterward Hobby and Robyn took a walk toward Whispering Pines Church. People were busy in the fields and it looked like a good crop in the making, if the season was good and enough rain fell. Corn was shoulder high and showed no sign of firing up at the bottom for lack of rain. The blades were flat and green. In dry weather the blades rolled up and there was a wilted look about the plant.

Cotton was beginning to blossom. They stopped and watched people going up and down the rows, carrying a soda bucket to place the last fertilizer to the plants.

"I just had an idea," Robyn said as she admired a pink blossom that was rolled up now like a morning glory after the sun becomes hot. "I wish we could use cotton blossoms in our wedding Hobby" She looked up into his eyes to see his response.

"Nice thought," he said, "but if there's one thing a farmer won't do it's to let people pull his cotton blossoms. Now the boll weevil may get them, but not his children. He wants every boll to open. He wants to make a bale an acre and it takes many bolls of fluffy cotton to make a five hundred pound bale."

"I know," Robyn said. "It was just a nice thought. I know Daddy wouldn't let us pull cotton blossoms. He didn't care how many tobacco blossoms we pulled and put in our playhouse, for they were no good and not pretty either. Arlene and I got a whipping one time for pulling cotton blossoms. Daddy came home to dinner and we were playing under the oak tree and had our playhouse decorated with cotton blossoms. He looked at us hard, and right there he took his belt off and we had streaks on our legs and behinds too. We never pulled another cotton blossom. But I still think they're beautiful."

"Tell you what," Hobby said. "I'll talk to Mr. Gant Turner about selling me one acre of cotton in the field. He may not do it, but I'll pay him as much as he'd get for it at the gin. If he'll do it we'll have plenty of cotton blossoms I reckon. How many do you think it would take?"

"A lot," Robyn said. "Maybe a hundred dozen."

"That's twelve hundred cotton blossoms," Hobby said. "That's a lot of cotton blossoms but I reckon an acre would yield that many."

"Ask him," Robyn said with excitement. "And it would be unique. I never heard of anything like that."

"Me neither," Hobby agreed. "And we'll need fern, lots of it. But I've got the answer to that. I still remember where the tall fern grows around here. I'm sure it's still there, bright green with healthy foliage. Remember Robyn?"

"Of course I remember," Robyn said. "I remember how Wilbert Lee and Philip would pull it up and just leave it there to die. I never understood why they did things like that."

"Just to aggravate the other kids," Hobby said.

Hobby looked off to the horizon that still spelled home to him. At least that hadn't changed. Everything was in its proper place and even the buzzards were still patrolling their territory. He saw two soaring over the woods in the distance.

The cowwitch vines had taken over the ditchbanks by the side of the road just as they always did in summer; their branches overspreading the bank and hanging over the edge of the road, filled with their long, red blossoms. "Those blossoms would be pretty too," Hobby said as he pointed toward one where a bee was collecting nectar.

"Who in the world ever thought about that?" Robyn said. "No one would except you Hobby. But it's a great idea. We'll have a bowl of cowwitch vine blossoms gracing the entry to the church."

Hobby sat down beside the road and Robyn joined him. They began to laugh raucously. "We're the silliest two that ever lived," he said. "Here we are planning the most unorthodox wedding that ever was. People will think we're absolutely crazy."

"Maybe so," Robyn said, "but it will also be one of the most novel."

"But we don't want to be the brunt of a joke," Hobby said. "We want it to be in good taste, but different."

"Well, there aren't enough weddings at Whispering Pines Church, or in Bear Grass for that matter, for people to judge by. And you know something Hobby: I don't care. We'll do it like we want to and I believe we'll carry it out in good taste too. We've got to talk to a florist about this. It may be novel to him also, but he will know how it should be done. Do you know any florists in Hallsborough?"

"Heavens no. When I lived here I wasn't in town enough to know anybody in the commercial world. But we can find one."

"I'm so happy," Robyn said as she reached and kissed him.

"Me too," Hobby replied. "And even the heavens are smiling down on us. Look up there. There's not a cloud in the sky, not even those white fluffy ones. Everything is as bright as a daisy." He stood and threw a clod of dirt as far into the field as he could. "After all my worries it seems like a paradise to be here today, in the land of my dreams. I feel like I've crossed every bridge that separated me from you." He took her in his arms, right there on the road, and kissed her hungrily.

"People will see us," Robyn said, sighing.

"I don't care," Hobby said. Several people had ridden by since they had been on the road, but they didn't show any signs of knowing them. They had been away too long if there were any that knew them. They had been a girl and a boy, the boy very crippled and the girl just another among the many children in Bear Grass. But neither recognized any of the passers-by.

"I want to take you somewhere," Hobby said. "Somewhere I've wanted to take you a long time."

"Well, let's go," she said. "I want to see whatever it is." They started back toward the house. "What is it you want me to see honey?"

"A place," Hobby said.

"Anything unusual about it?" Robyn asked.

"Very unusual," Hobby said. "The most unusual place I've ever seen. It's ours Robyn."

"Ours?"

"Yes, but it's a secret. You can't tell anybody about it. Not your father or mother nor your brothers and sisters. Not even my mother or my grandparents. Promise?"

"Sure, you know I wouldn't do anything that was against your wishes. But why all the secrecy?"

"Well, as you know I'll be entering medical school next fall, and all my time will be devoted to study. But it will be here that I'll fulfill my mission in life. I'm doing the doctor bit strictly for my mother Robyn. And I really regret that I'm so much into becoming a doctor when it's not my life calling."

"Well how did this come about?" Robyn asked.

"Through Nick," Hobby said. "He's the best man that I ever knew Robyn. The most generous and understanding. Nick loves my mother so much he wouldn't do anything against her. And he knew it was her goal for me to become a doctor. But he also knew my dream, for I detailed it to him and I sold him completely. I showed him the plantation. Did you hear what I said Robyn? Plantation! It stretches seven miles toward Hallsborough and is three miles wide in some places. And it's ours sweetheart."

"I don't believe it," Robyn said. "And what will you do with it when you're several hundred miles away?"

"I won't do anything," Hobby said, "except dream about it. But Nick will act as my manager, although he won't be doing anything himself. He didn't even buy it in his name. It's in the name of a holding company. It's one of those things where secrecy is required. I don't want people to know it's ours now. But there's a lot of preparation before the dream becomes a reality. And I'll tell you about that dream after our marriage. It's too long to tell now. And we'll talk with Nick about it when we see him, but not around mother."

"But is it right to have a secret that your mother knows nothing about?"

"I know Nick must have had some misgivings about it, but without boasting, I can tell you that Nick loves me as much as if I were his son. And he saw what I was talking about. So we entered into an agreement and Nick said one day Mother would see it as we do."

They were on their way for Hobby to show Robyn their kingdom. They stopped where a stab was driven into the ground in a patch of woods near the road. "This begins it," he said." For the next seven miles whatever you see will be ours Robyn. You'll be the mistress of it all and I will be master. That make you feel important?"

"I can't even imagine it," Robyn said. She was looking at the rolling fields and the crops growing. "My daddy's never owned anything but a house full of children, to say nothing of a home and land. But Uncle Lester has promised to leave his farm to Daddy if he'll stay on with him as long as he lives."

"Good," Hobby said. "And you know this could only happen through very unusual circumstances. I never stop pinching myself to see whether I'm dreaming."

"But it seems like wasting your time studying to become a doctor when you obviously plan to be right here in Bear Grass doing other things," Robyn lamented.

"Not really," Hobby said. "They use orthopedic surgeons around here, too. And I'll be glad of the knowledge. It's just the price I'll pay for having all my dreams come true."

"Yeah, that's one way of looking at it," Robyn said.

They stopped under the shade of an overhanging tree. Hobby's arm rested on the car door and he looked into Robyn's eyes. "Did anybody ever tell you you had the most beautiful eyes in the world?"

"No, I don't recall that they ever did," she replied with a grin.

"Not even Chip?"

"No, I don't think so."

"Maybe that's why he didn't win you over."

"I appreciate the compliment anyway."

"They're the deepest violet I've ever seen. You must wear a lot of purple and violet sweetheart. That will bring out their color to perfection."

"I'll remember that Hobby."

He reached over and took hold of one of her breasts, firm and prominent. She blushed but didn't push his hand away. After all, they were engaged to be married very soon. The hand felt hot through her blouse. She took his other hand and placed it over hers and there was a tremor in her body. She wanted him, but she knew that that would never do. Nice girls didn't do that until they were married. She gently removed her hand and he took his away.

"It's too long until our wedding day," he said, and she could tell he was shaken.

They rode until they reached another stab just past the old church. "This is where it ends," Hobby said as he pointed to the stab. "Do you want to go on to Hallsborough and find a florist? I really like the idea of decorating with cotton blossoms."

"And cowwitch vine blossoms," Robyn added.

They rode until they found a florist sign and went in. A rather young effeminate-looking man was making a wreath as they entered. Robyn noted the delicate touch he gave to the flowers and his obvious love for them. His hands were slender and thin, and he looked as if he felt the delicate petals as if he were feeling skin.

He came up and introduced himself, his arms bent at the elbow and holding his hands out from his body in a rather awkward way. "May I help you?" he asked.

"We've got this crazy idea," Robyn said with a big smile. "And I'm sure it is very unusual and you probably have never had such a request. You see, we are being married in two weeks and we're in Bear Grass planning what we want. And we want a first-class wedding, now, so you must be honest with us. Have you ever heard of using cotton blossoms in a wedding?"

"Never," he said, shaking his head. "I never thought of them as being beautiful. I used to have to work in the mess and I didn't see anything pretty about cotton."

"Even the plants are pretty to me," Hobby said. "I love their wide leaves with their good shape and purple skin on the stalks."

"Well, do you think they could be arranged so they would show their beauty?" Robyn asked.

"Oh, a good florist can do wonders with flowers," he said, realizing that he would be missing the sale of flowers if they chose to do business with him. "How many do you need?"

"About twelve hundred," Hobby said.

The florist's head jerked upward. "Twelve hundred! You must be planning a very large wedding. And you'd never get that many cotton blossoms around here."

"We will if I buy an acre of green cotton," Hobby said.

Rich people, the florist thought to himself.

"We don't want it overdone," Robyn said. "We were thinking of having a bouquet at the end of every pew, and there must be about forty pews."

"It will take a lot of flowers for that," the florist said. "And I'll be happy to arrange them for you. Come to think of it, I remember that cotton blossoms look sort of like crepe paper when they are just opening and if they were stripped of the foliage they might show up very well in a bouquet, interspersed with fern. They might be similar to roses. Artificial stems would have to be created. And I have another idea. Ice could be chipped up over them until time for them to be placed in the church and they would be fresh and it would appear that they had been pulled while the dew was on. I'm excited about it, now that you've called them to my attention. I'd love to try it."

They didn't mention the cowwitch vine blossoms. Robyn said they'd talk about that nearer the time for the wedding.

They went to the creek in the afternoon. It was the same place they had played as children, except they went farther upstream than where they had played in the old days. Hobby lay back on his elbows and surveyed the scene. He thought that this was perhaps his happiest moment ever. He had the girl of his dreams beside him. He was at the place he loved best in all the world. His future seemed secure. There were no unfulfilled longings in his heart; no sense of wanting to be elsewhere.

"This is my magical moment," he said as he rested his head on Robyn's lap. He pulled a blade of grass that had seeded out and took the end in his mouth. Robyn caressed his forehead, happy to see him completely relaxed and all signs of worry erased from his face.

"I love you with all my heart," Robyn said. "You are all that I could ever want in a husband and a lover. You bring out the best in me and I am happy just to be near you."

"I would be nothing without you," he said. "You are my inspiration and my hope for the future. You have no idea what you mean to me. I want to climb mountains, to sail the seas, to conquer the world and I feel like I have the strength to do all those things because of you."

They laughed aloud. They were just a girl and boy saying endearing things at this very special time in their lives.

"Do you want children Hobby?" she asked.

"Sure I want children."

"How many?"

"A dozen would be fine with me, but people would accuse me of keeping you barefoot and pregnant all the time."

"Who cares what people think?" Robyn said. "I want children running around the place like rabbits. The more, the merrier. I wouldn't take anything for growing up in a large family. I feel sorry for you in that respect. You grew up without brothers and sisters. You've missed so much, Hobby. No matter how happy you've been, you would have been happier with brothers and sisters."

"I know," Hobby said. "I always knew that. Look about you. There's a large family in just about every house. They may feel crowded in, and no matter what they want they know it's impossible, for there are others to consider. And they have a greater appreciation for everything good, but they learn a great lesson in life in that they're sharing and caring and there's a bond so strong that it draws them together in a way nothing else could. I've always noticed that."

They were quiet for a while. The moment seemed to be etched in time, there by the creek, isolated from the world. A squirrel ran up an oak tree, jumping through its branches, another following in playful mimicry.

"Do you think they're lovers?" Robyn asked.

"I hope so," Hobby replied. "I hope they're as happy in their animal world as we are at this moment."

"Let's pull the curtain of time Hobby, and live this day forever."

"Wouldn't it be nice if we could?" he said. "We always dream of the ideal. And precious moments like this are such a fleeting thing, never to be recaptured; just a speck on the sands of time. We'll remember this forever but it is only now that it's a reality. Perfect in every way, nothing bad lingering over our conscience; nothing detracting from this moment. Let's savor it, Robyn, to its fullest."

They embraced and the world stood still. They consummated their love there on the banks of the gently-flowing creek on a lazy June day while field hands in a nearby field seemed to be blessing their union by singing songs that at this magical moment sounded like a chorus playing for a royal gathering.

"I'm sorry," Hobby said. "I got carried away. Forgive me Robyn."

"There's nothing to forgive," she said as she kissed him again.

"This is my first time," Hobby confessed.

"Mine too," Robyn said.

"Let's say our vows to each other here," Hobby said. "We have one witness who knows what is in our hearts - God. Human witnesses can never know our hearts, what we feel, see into our souls."

"Let's do," Robyn said.

They were on their knees facing each other. Hobby said his vows first.

"I Hobby, take thee Robyn for my lawful wedded wife, forsaking all others forevermore. I vow to love you, to honor you and to place you above all others. To protect you and revere you and to be by your side always, for better or worse, whether rich or poor, whatever the circumstances may be, in the storms of life and in the happy moments such as this in the quietness of this day and with God's love shining down on us. I will worship you as a queen and I will strive always to measure up to the kind of man you deserve, knowing that I will fall far short, yet, always striving for that goal. The Bible says that if a man thinks he has acted uncomely toward his beloved, let them marry. I don't think I have acted uncomely toward you my love, for in my heart I was already married to you. Now, in His presence, who can look into my heart and know what is there, I wed thee, Robyn, before God above who sees all, hears all, knows all."

Tears flowing down Robyn's face were captured by the sun and she had never looked more beautiful. She looked into Hobby's eyes and her face showed the love she felt for him. She held both his hands.

"Hobby, I take you to be my lawful wedded husband. I promise that I will be all the things I can be for you. I will help you in whatever you choose to do. I will follow you anywhere, trusting you implicitly to guide us in our chosen endeavors. I will put you before all others, make any sacrifice necessary to keep us together, thinking always of you first above myself, expecting you to lead me for I trust your insight far above mine. I may not always agree with you and I may speak my opinion when I choose to disagree, but in the final analysis you will be the winner for you are my man and I look upon you as my hero. I love you more than life itself. No woman ever loved a man more than I love you. You had to show me, Hobby, for I was mixed up and couldn't see my way clear. But you were patient. You opened your heart to me. You didn't press me. You were just there, the knight in shining armor that I couldn't see at first. Looking back, I think that I must have loved you always, as a child when we played together and you taught me to appreciate the things about me that you saw with such beauty and which I had not even looked for. Thank you for being there my love, to point the way for me.

"You are a man now, handsome and upstanding, about to enter the mainstream of life as an adult. You have all the qualities any woman would want. I'm so thankful you're mine. You deserve the best, Hobby, and I feel inadequate to the task, but I'll really try. Thank you for entrusting that task to me. This is the most beautiful setting for a wedding I can imagine. It's so peaceful and quiet. We can look about us and know the presence of God. Could any man make anything this beautiful? We will walk down an aisle in two weeks, before the world to pledge our vows. We will make a public show and it will be beautiful. But this day will be our real wedding sweetheart, for we have said the things that mean most to us. And we have said them before God. I feel sure that he has already recorded our marriage in heaven. And those are my vows to you Hobby."

They rose from their knees and embraced again and sobbed on each other's shoulder while a bird sang in a nearby tree and a frog jumped into the creek with a splash and a Negro spiritual came in on a gentle breeze. The day was waning and the sun's rays had become golden. Another day would soon end. It was a day for their memory file, indelibly imprinted in their minds; a day they would recall thousands of times.

Chapter 43

Apredawn thunderstorm swept over Bear Grass with heavy thunder and lightning, giving new life to crops that had been thirsty for water. No appreciable rain had fallen in three weeks. Thunder rumbled in the heavens and sharp flashes of lightning lit up the sky. The downpour lasted about half an hour and moved on toward Greene County, leaving a calm, and far-off thunder and dull flashes of lightning.

The storm awakened Hobby. He went to a window and watched its fury and the calm that settled after its passage. He noticed it was four o'clock, and his and Robyn's wedding day. He wondered whether the storm was a bad omen, but discounted that, for he remembered that usually after a storm came fair skies and low humidity.

Their wedding day! And everything was in readiness. His mother and Nick had arrived yesterday, excited about the event. They had held a reunion at his grandparents' home last night, Robyn had taken Pearl into her bedroom, along with Viola, and shown them her wedding gown. Both women oohed and aahed about it. The gown itself had been Robyn's mother's, but she had almost redone it completely. Pearl was surprised that Cora Finch would have been married in a wedding gown, being a poor sharecropper as she had been herself. But Robyn told her that her mother had an awful lot of pride and she had pleaded with her mother to fashion the gown. The material hadn't cost but a little over a dollar and Cora had worked out the money when she wasn't busy at home.

It was a soft silk material and she had used all her ingenuity in making it, never having made a wedding gown before. It had a fitted bodice and a flowing skirt. She had sewn tiny tucks in the bodice, and daring for the time, had fashioned a plunging neckline. The gown flowed behind her and she had made a veil also. So Cora had the ideal garment to work with. It was a perfect fit for Robyn. Cora said Robyn could use it, and when her other girls were married, they could use it too.

She had been planning for such a time for years. In her spare time she crocheted tiny lace, using sewing thread, and put it away as she accumulated a sewing basket full. There were hundreds of hours spent making the lace alone. She sewed the lace on all the little tucks and between the tucks she added sequins, thousands of them. She had had to repair a tiny tear in the gown. The material was very thin and dry rot over the years had had an effect on it.

Pearl was overcome by its loveliness, and Viola liked it also.

"You're going to be the prettiest bride that ever was," Pearl said as she reached and kissed Robyn. "My boy is so lucky to get you," she patted Robyn's shoulder. And Robyn was carried away by Pearl's beauty. She had only seen her a few times, and didn't know much about her. She wanted to fear her, to feel a jealousy toward her, but she was so warm and friendly she only admired her. She sensed a great power in the woman. She was so sure of herself, so natural, and had a very pretty smile. No wonder Hobby was going to medical school. How could he defy her wishes? Still, she wasn't completely at ease in Pearl's presence. And she didn't feel that way at all about Nick. He came across as an easy-going person trying to please everybody, and she had liked him from the start.

"Tell me about the church decorations," Pearl said after they returned to the sitting room.

"They're lovely," Robyn replied, almost afraid to tell her about the cotton blossoms. "But they're a little unusual. It was Hobby's and my idea though. And we consulted with a florist who is decorating the church."

"What's so unusual?" Pearl asked, showing a great curiosity.

"Cotton blossoms are the flowers we're using, along with fern," Robyn said.

"Cotton Blossoms! Pearl said. "My, that is unusual but I remember how pretty cotton blossoms are." She laughed. "My, that's a novel idea. And I'll bet the church will be beautiful." She tried to picture the cotton blossoms but the stalks got in the way. The blossoms were partially hidden among the foliage on the stalks. But she reasoned that if they were Hobby and Robyn's choice, surely they would be all right. She reminded herself that she hadn't gotten above her raising. People didn't do things in Bear Grass like they did in big cities. She felt guilty for even thinking that the blossoms might not be in good taste. "You'd better watch yourself Perline," she said under her breath. But she wanted everything just perfect for this wedding. She had offered to help in any way she could, but Hobby had declined, telling her that this was one time he and Robyn were going to do the job alone.

When Robyn and Hobby were alone, she acted ill at ease and Hobby asked her what was wrong.

"I guess it's wedding day jitters," she said. "Somehow I feel so inadequate and I thought I was so brave."

Hobby attempted to console her. "It's not unusual to feel like this, Robyn. I'm tense also. It's a natural thing. You have nothing at all to fear."

"I'm so afraid something might go wrong," Robyn said with a tear in her eyes.

"There must be more to it than that," Hobby said. "Tell me what it is Robyn."

"It's your mother," she said. "I'm afraid of her Hobby."

"Afraid of mother? That's preposterous Robyn. You'll find mother to be one of the best friends you ever had."

"I feel so inadequate in her presence," Robyn said. "She's so beautiful and poised and polished, I just don't feel like coping with her."

"You're forgetting something," Hobby said. "Mother worked in the fields around here just like all the rest of us. She plowed, just like a man. She climbed the tiers in tobacco barns and hung green tobacco and took out the cured weed. She hasn't forgotten her heritage and she feels no shame for that. You're all wrong Robyn. Sure, she's all the things you said, but she earned the right to be all the things that she is. She kept up with the times and she learned by observation and study. But she's as plain as an old shoe. She could get out there right now and wash clothes on a washboard, and might do it while she's here. For God's sake, give Mother a try before you condemn her Robyn."

"All right, all right," Robyn said as she reached around his waist and embraced him. "I'll remember what you said."

"This is our wedding day, remember?" Hobby said, "and there's a lot to do. Is there anything else we need to attend to?"

"I think everything is in order," Robyn said. "Quinton is bringing the flowers to the church at eleven o'clock. He's waiting till the last minute so they will be fresh. He has ice on them so they'll look garden-fresh. And you looked after the soloist and the organist didn't you?"

"Yeah," Hobby said. "I hope Miss Effie won't be offended at me for getting Rob Tyner to play the organ. Bless her, Miss Effie has played the organ at Whispering Pines more years than I can recall, but she still misses a note once in a while. And Eva Ward's solos are good, but she gets a little off key sometimes."

There had been a notice in the Argus, inviting the public to attend the wedding and an official invitation was issued from the pulpit.

"Do you reckon a lot of people will attend?" Robyn asked.

"Oh, I'm sure there'll be a crowd. They'll come out of curiosity if nothing else."

"It's time Mama and Papa and the family were arriving," Robyn said. "Do you reckon Wilbert Lee will attend?" His children, Will and Beth, were ring bearers.

"I don't know. He's invited like everyone else, but knowing him, he might decide to pass it up. But I'm not going to worry about it either way."

"How about Mr. Gant?"

"I expect he'll be there," Hobby said. "Mr. Turner may feel obligated to go."

Hobby walked out into the yard, where the sun had broken through, promising a fair day. The corn was silking and he noted half-grown cucumbers on the vine. The rain had rejuvenated the squash vines and they were blooming overnight. A cardinal darted from a sweet gum tree and pitched nearby, followed by its mate. A pigeon flew over and went to its nest on the eaves of the shelter. He took these as good omens: nature blessing his union with Robyn. He felt lighthearted and happy.

Pigs were barbecuing on the coals at the back of Whispering Pines Church, for there would be a feast after the wedding. The aroma of the cooking meat wafted over the community. Chairs were there in abundance, furnished by the local undertaker. Wooden tubs were filled with lemonade with slices of lemon showing among the ice. Freezers of homemade ice cream were packed tight with ice.

Trees shaded Whispering Pines Church and wedding guests could find comfort from the sun and eat and talk and enjoy the day. Hobby thought about it all and he could not imagine the wedding being held at any other place. Although Robyn attended church in Jones County, she also wanted to be married at Whispering Pines, which she still considered her home church due to her association there as a child.

Returning to the house, he found Viola and Pearl in the kitchen. Viola was taking cake layers out of the stove and Pearl was preparing to beat the eggs to be used in the icing. Hobby said, "Let's go for a walk Ma. Got something to talk to you about." Robyn was in her room laying out her wedding outfit, touching up wrinkled places with the iron.

"What do you want to talk about?" she said as they headed down the road toward Gant Turner's store.

"Something's worrying me," he said, "and it's not your fault at all. But somehow Robyn is afraid of you. I don't know whether it's jealousy because you're my mother, or nervous reaction. But somehow she stands in awe of you."

"Oh, I'm so sorry Hobby," Pearl said. "She doesn't know how much I admire her. I love her for being the girl that she is and because she's yours I love her even more. She just can't feel that way about me. And don't you worry son, after the wedding I'll get it all straightened out. She's confused in her mind about me."

"Just take care of it Mom," Hobby said. "I can't stand any jealousy among the family and of all people, I expect you, Nick and Robyn to be my greatest supporters."

Pearl placed a hand on Hobby's arm as they walked leisurely down the road. "Make this the happiest day of your life," she said. "Don't worry one minute about Robyn's fears. Have a honeymoon of your dreams and after a little while we'll straighten everything out. Okay?"

"Sure," Hobby said. "And Ma, I'm really happy today. I feel like I'm floating on air. Every bird in the trees is singing for us. Those white clouds above are sailing swiftly with the upper-level winds. "No muddy ones foreboding rain. And it's time for us to get dressed. It's eleven o'clock and in one hour we'll stand at the altar."

When they reached the house Tobey Finch's family had arrived and had already gone into the house to see Robyn.

It was almost time for the wedding.

- - - - - - - -

It was a hand-pedaled organ, but Hobby had had it inspected and tuned. Wedding music was being played as they arrived at the back of the church where they would enter from the rear door. The music swelled inside the church and floated out over the grounds. The church yard was overflowing with cars and people were parking on the side of the road. People were there in their Sunday best. A lot of new dresses were made for the special occasion, for people had had time to prepare for the day and sewing machines had been busy sewing voile and organdy and silk and eyelet as well as other fabrics into dresses. (No people are more proud that farmers).

Men were in coats and ties, even with warm temperatures. Men often went to church without coats or ties. Some had never attended a wedding before.

Tall fern decorated the pulpit, taken from the damp places in the nearby woods by Hobby and Robyn. On the lectern was a bowl of white cotton blossoms, interspersed with fern. They appeared as rose buds, shiny with dew, and every pew had a basket of cotton blossoms, each with the same color at each end. First, there were white blossoms on the front pews, all the way across the church. Next were baskets of pink, followed by a mixture of pink and white. Then there was a row of yellow blossoms. People at the end of the pews looked at the blossoms carefully, noting the crepe paper-like texture and the real beauty of the flowers which they had never fully observed before.

In the foyer of the church there was a large arrangement on the table. It was tall, perhaps three feet, and climbing on a tiny trellis was a vine with long, bell-like red blossoms except the blossoms were profuse, and a wide red ribbon was tied around the barrel-sized holder.

There was an air of expectancy in the church. The audience heard a mule neigh in a nearby lot and there was a dirt dauber's nest in a corner of the ceiling of the church and the insects became excited by the crowd and flew among the congregation, not bothering to sting them; just flying near enough that the people flinched and turned away from them. There was a gardenia bush beside the side entrance and it was in bloom and the sweet aroma of the flowers filled the sanctuary and a crowd gathered at the side entrance as well as the back; those who arrived too late to be seated, hoping for a glance of the bride and groom. White clouds crossed the sun intermittently, shading the grounds for a moment, then turning them into bright sunshine.

And there was the odor of barbecue filling the air. Everyone realized that it was Hobby and Robyn's day, and they had made the community a part of it. They were a part of the community by virtue of birth. Most everyone in Bear Grass had known Hobby, if not Robyn. They were waiting to see Hobby as a man, whom they had heard was no longer a cripple.

Then it was high noon and "The Wedding March" rang out on the organ and the processional began. The minister entered the pulpit, followed by Hobby and Nick Staphal, Tobey Finch, the four bridesmaids and the ring bearers.

"Here Comes The Bride" brought every eye to attention. Robyn entered from the back of the church with the long train of her gown following her and there was a gasp from the audience. This was not Bear Grass, they thought. This was city stuff. This girl was not bred and born in this area. But there she was, a vision of loveliness, clothed in white with dark, flowing hair and with a captivating smile. And that couldn't be the Hobby Turnage they knew. But then, there was the facial look; the same smile that showed all of his teeth; the same hairline but a deeper blond than when he was a boy and it was nearly white. And standing straight and handsome in formal wear.

Their hearts swelled with pride for what had happened to Hobby. And the loveliness of his bride made them all the more appreciative.

Hobby looked out into the audience and a thought flashed through his mind. It was all beautiful, but it was only a replay for the public. It couldn't match the beauty of their private ceremony on the banks of the creek when, on their knees, they had pledged their vows before God. It was so humble, so sincere, so poignant with no attempt at drama; rather two young lovers saying the things to each other that surpassed anything in a formal marriage ceremony.

A few tears filled Pearl's eyes during the ceremony. Why, she asked herself, had she worried that somehow things might not be carried out just right? It couldn't have been more beautiful. And she was carried away by the beauty of the cotton blossoms. And Hobby and Robyn had rehearsed their parts so well there was not a flaw.

The traditional wedding ceremony was carried out and the groom kissed the bride and the recessional began and Hobby, Robyn, Tobey Finch and Cora, Craven and Viola, Pearl and Nick formed a line in front of the church to greet guests.

The line was long but Hobby was thrilled to be renewing acquaintances from the past, most of whom he had not seen since he left Bear Grass. He shook their hands vigorously and they commented about how he had changed and those who had known Robyn did the same and it seemed like an old-fashioned homecoming as much as a wedding. There were a lot of smiles and occasionally an outburst of laughter.

Hobby had noted a large group of colored people at the edge of the yard. They were all dressed in white, and he was delighted to see them for he had had some very good friends among the colored people. They came after the line of whites had ceased, shaking hands and nodding their heads until they got to Hobby. Then their handshakes were filled with emotion and there was laughter and good wishes and praise for the handsome man he had become as well as recalling little incidents of the past. And Hobby remembered how he had played with some of them, rolling an old tire; how he had adjusted himself inside the tire and had been rolled over the yard, and how they had swung in a swing attached to a limb of an oak tree in the yard; how he had eaten poke sallet and fatback at dinnertime. Precious memories of a time when everything in life was a magical kingdom with nothing to detract from its beauty.

"Howdy Hobby," Amos Bowden said. "I just had to come by to wish you well, and I wanted to tell you that things are getting a little better. A few of us black boys' getting an education now. I'm going to Shaw in Raleigh. That don't sound like the black boys you grew up with does it?"

"It sure doesn't," Hobby said, "but I'm tickled to death to hear that. I'm real proud of you Amos."

"I thought you would be," Amos said. "And I wish you the very best Hobby."

Finally the line ended and Hobby, Robyn, Pearl, Nick, Viola, Craven, Cora and Tobey breathed a sigh of relief. They had greeted well-wishers for more than an hour.

People were taking plates piled high with food to the shade of the trees where seats were placed. They were talking about Hobby and Robyn and the fairytale-like setting. Most of the people who knew Hobby and Robyn were there, as well as some curiosity-seekers who did not know them.

Hobby had been overwhelmed when Wilbert Lee and Anne walked through the line. Hobby saw him before he approached and his heart beat faster. He had not expected him to greet them. And it was a last-minute thing for Wilbert Lee. He sat through the ceremony in a state of shock. His worst fears were realized. He had planned it all in his mind. It would be a very simple affair; the bride would be homely and Hobby would appear as the little boy he had been; lacking in the things that would give him distinction. He could go home and relax and start living a normal life without letting his old grudges fill his heart. He wasn't prepared for what he saw.

He was shaking inside as he told Anne he had decided to greet them. He was shaky in his knees as he took Robyn's soft hand into his. He greeted her and goose pimples ran all over him. He looked into those impenetrable eyes at close range and there was suddenly a vision before him of a destroyed playhouse and a very young girl in disarray and bloomers with a few specks of blood revealing a woman in body in a little girl setting. He knew at this instant that he fell in love with her at that moment; that she was the answer to all the problems of his troubled life. He remembered the look in her eyes that day. Why had he been so blind in his desire to anger her and to ignore his instincts? It had been there all these years, in his subconscious mind, waiting for expression.

He remembered the softness of her hands as he released them and looked into Hobby's eyes, taking his hand at the same time and shaking it vigorously.

It was an awkward moment for both of them. Hobby was no longer looking into the eyes of the god that had been his idol. There was something hard about him. He was disturbed by the look in his eyes. That was the same look he remembered the day Wilbert Lee had saved his life when they were swimming. He looked dissipated somehow even though he was still a nice-looking man. He saw immediately that he hadn't taken care of his body; that a pouch was building around his waist. He wondered how he could ever have been the hero that he worshipped so long ago.

"Glad to see you," Hobby said and Wilbert Lee said, "Likewise. How have you been?"

"Fine," Hobby said, "and you?"

"Oh, life goes on," Wilbert Lee said. "Not much to brag about. I see you've done well."

"Life has been very good to me, Wilbert Lee. I have no complaints, and I'm as happy today as a man can be. Funny, isn't it, that we all played together and it turns out that Robyn and I were the two in the group that fell in love. Who would have thought it?"

"I certainly wouldn't," Wilbert Lee said. "Funny thing about life, isn't it?"

"Stranger than fiction," Hobby told him.

Wilbert Lee felt an envy for this man who was his blood kin. He wanted him to be the Hobby that he was, looking up to him as he had done. Instead, he was forced to look up to Hobby. He hated him with a passion that was all-consuming. But he would not give up. He knew that Robyn liked him as a boy, and would have done anything for him if he hadn't been so mischievous and acted so much the boy. He would win her heart yet. Nothing else in life mattered. Anne and the children were the farthest from his mind at the moment. His forced act of domesticity made him feel less than a man. But this would all end once he had won the heart of this girl who stood so near him. And their brief encounter had left Hobby shaken. It was the only cloud over this beautiful day.

Waldo Spence and Mrs. Spence had observed the whole proceeding with interest.

"My God," Waldo said, "W.L. is not even in their league. You would expect some difference because of the woman's marriage to a man of wealth. But everything is different. And I can see why the woman won a man of means. She's absolutely beautiful."

"Don't get carried away," Mrs. Spence said as she placed a hand on Waldo's arm. "But I'll agree with you that she is lovely. Did she actually live around here?"

"Right in this area," Waldo said. "Worked in the fields around here."

"Well, you'd never guess it by her mannerisms. She looks first class to me, and acts that way too."

People swarmed around Pearl and Nick, wishing them well and

commenting about how beautiful the wedding was; how handsome Hobby was and that it was unbelievable how he had changed and how pretty Robyn was.

Gant Turner watched from the sidelines. He thought that this was incredible. Hobby was of his blood and his genetic makeup, and he couldn't see one thing about him and Wilbert Lee that was compatible. Evidently Hobby had none of his genetic components, or they didn't show anyway. And he found nothing in Wilbert Lee's nature that resembled him either. Maybe in looks somewhat, but nothing at all in disposition. He tried not to make comparisons, but it was evident that Hobby was by far the best of the two. He had always thought highly of Hobby, never dreaming that he was his father. And when he finally found out it had little effect. He felt guilt for what he had done. But he couldn't dwell on that at this stage. He was pleased that Pearl hadn't thought of him as a rascal. He just kept quiet about it, although once Pearl told who the father was, everybody in Bear Grass knew it. But nobody outside the family had ever brought it up to him. He was not shunned and many people said to each other that knowing Abie, they didn't blame him.

Neither had Hobby acted differently toward him. There were no declarations of love and no recriminations by Hobby. But once Gant knew he was his son, there was a tender feeling inside for the boy. He did give him a pocket knife one day when he was passing. It was a long switch-blade that his father had given him when he was a boy. He loved that knife, and often whittled with it. But he had other knives and his father's had dark brown horn on the handle and it was slender. He called Hobby to the yard and told him he wanted to give him something. He drew the knife from his pocket and told him it was a family heirloom; that his father had given it to him and he wanted to pass it on in the family. And Hobby had accepted it with a smile and said he was pleased and would always keep it. That had pleased Gant.

After mingling with the crowd under the trees, renewing old acquaintances and reminiscing, Robyn and Hobby partook of the feast and found chairs under a spreading oak near the edge of the yard.

Hobby said, "Are you enjoying the day?"

She squeezed his hand and said, "It's perfect."

"I wish time could stand still for a while," Hobby said. "I need a long time to reflect on it all, and it will be over so soon."

They sat in silence and Hobby became lost in the past. So much remembered; so much time lost. Time that could not be recalled. Years in which he and his friends had grown up, become men and women, growing from the gangly stage, through adolescence, finding their own places in society, while time marched on. But he reasoned that it wasn't vital that all of them be together to observe the changes in each other. Life wasn't meant to be that way. It was each person on his own, playing out what fate had destined. He told himself that he wasn't normal anyway; that he was only a sentimentalist and he placed too much value on this isolated place tucked away behind the pines in an unknown corner of the world. But he wasn't able to convince himself that this was his real conviction. It was in his blood. He was a part of it. And he had been away during the years it would have meant so much to be here, within hollering distance of Whispering Pines Church. Everything spoke the message of home, of closeness, of friends and families and a sense of belonging. That, to him, was what life was all about.

"Good barbecue," he said as he took Robyn's napkin and wiped the grease from his mouth.

"Hm Hm," Robyn said. "And I was starved. And this lemonade just sets it off."

"I'm about ready for some of that ice cream," Hobby said. "Miss Rachel has an early-bearing peach tree, and I know she's made some peach ice cream. I've got to sample it." Children were walking over the grounds with ice cream cones, licking the cream as it melted. The cones were getting soft and the children were biting off bits as the liquid seeped into them

"I guess I'm so sentimental today because we'll soon be gone from Bear Grass for years, youth will be all over and we'll be settling down to routine living," Hobby said. "But we have so much to look forward to Robyn. We'll be together and I won't be yearning to be with you. I can't imagine what it'll be like to come home to you every day, having my meals prepared, my clothes clean, a warm fire already lit. It'll be wonderful sweetheart."

"Oh, it'll be a dream," Robyn said.

"Do you think you can settle for a little cottage in a valley in the mountains?" Hobby said. "People would choose it ten to one over Bear Grass. You can look any way and see mountain peaks and there are little pools everywhere where cold water from the higher elevations feeds the streams and the water is as clear as a crystal. You see paths leading into the mountains for miles around you. I often wish I had something in common with the place; knew the people and when a name was called could associate it with a place as well as their place in society. But I'm an outsider Robyn. I don't know their customs, what they value most, how they see life. But it would be fair to assume that all of us are about alike in that respect. People usually have the same values."

"You're a dreamer Hobby," Robyn said. "And I respect that. Many people who dreamed saw them to their fulfillment. What would the world be like without visioning a better life and bringing it to fruition? Those dreams may pay off one day."

Nick and Pearl joined them.

"It's been beautiful," Pearl said. "About as perfect as a day can be. And I have seen so many people I haven't seen in years. It seems like a family reunion."

"When are you and Nick leaving?" Hobby said.

"Tomorrow," Pearl replied.

"We'll go out and visit you in a couple of months," Nick said. "In the meantime, savor all that life has to offer. But I still wish you'd let us send you some place for a few weeks so you won't have anything on your minds but each other."

"I think it's best to enter summer school," Hobby said. "I need the summer courses in order to start the fall semester with some advantage. And that's going against my heart for I'd be completely happy lying on some deserted beach with Robyn, watching the ships come in and the natives selling their wares and the excitement of a foreign shore. But we'll have all that one day, you'll see."

After Pearl and Nick left Hobby and Robyn lingered under the tree. Hobby was aware of the smell of corn silks in the air and the lingering fragrance of oak coals still burning in the barbecue pits and a feeling of Saturday afternoon coming down settled over him. It always felt different on Saturday afternoon. There was something in the air, as if it were electrified; an air of expectancy, of more fully participating in life. Those fortunate enough to be able to go to town could walk the streets, congregate on street corners and in the dime stores and enjoy the respite from farm chores.

He thought about his beloved homeland and how he had often wanted to make excuses for its shortcomings to the world. Some very unpleasant things had happened in Bear Grass; things that he wouldn't have thought would happen in this hidden little haven. He had thought the area was unique; that other places were better, that people acted differently elsewhere. He had only learned better after studying more about the world. Bear Grass was no different than any other place. People were alike everywhere, most of them law-abiding and decent, the good always outshining the bad, but with the bad always magnified and the good overlooked by the world. The murder of Nervy Sauls had brought national headlines, depicting a bad image of the people of the area, placing a lot of the blame on ignorance. The Klan incident involving Roscoe Gooch and Minnie Mae Moore was prominently played by the state press although it had been played down by the Argus in an attempt to spare the community as much shame as possible. There had even been a story about Rev. Otto Pell's downfall. These were all bad things that reflected on a community. But learning that such events were not just reserved for Bear Grass made him feel better. And Wilber Stroud's death had brought national headlines.

"A penny for your thoughts," Robyn said as she took his hand into hers.

"Just reminiscing," Hobby said. "Thinking about so many things that make this such a special place; thinking how it will end in a day or two and we'll be away for years. It's ending Robyn. We're man and woman now, not boy and girl. But we're just beginning together and I wouldn't have it any other way. Being together I mean."

"I'm anxious to get to Tennessee," Robyn said. "I'm dying to see our cottage and meet the people in the little town."

"Well, we'll be on our way very soon," Hobby said as he stood and embraced her.

The church grounds were deserted now, leaving Hobby and Robyn to their own thoughts for a while.

They returned to the Turnage home and continued their family reunion. Craven was cheerful as was Viola. The Finches said goodbyes, embraced Robyn tearfully, promising to write often and were off to Jones County. Pearl and Nick left the next day and Hobby and Robyn remained two more days. Then all was quiet in the Turnage home with lingering memories of the reunion and the wedding. But both Craven and Viola were happy, for Hobby had married a fine girl and Pearl and Nick were doing fine.

Chapter 44

I t was three months after Hobby and Robyn moved to their cottage at the medical school before Pearl and Nick got to visit them. The newlyweds had settled down to housekeeping and learning about each other, each new day bringing added insights. It was a time of adjustment, of learning as can only be done when people live together. It wasn't easy for either of them although their love had grown since their marriage. They learned about concessions. Both had to give ground to make marriage work.

Pearl and Nick felt that they were intruding even after three months, but Pearl was anxious to be with Robyn particularly, to let her know that she wasn't the woman she supposed her to be. She had worried since Hobby told her that Robyn feared her of all people. It was something she had never thought about. But it was understandable that a girl would stand in awe of the husband's mother. She had heard all the stories about mothers-in-law, and she didn't want to be regarded in the same light.

If Robyn only knew the heavy guilt she had borne all these years because of Hobby's condition she would know better about her as a woman. Whatever else she might accomplish in life, nothing could take away the shame she felt even if it were a time of youth and its irresponsibility, that had left her son a cripple. She could never do anything to repay him for that suffering .

Pearl was particularly pleased with Hobby and Robyn's little cottage, furnished in Early American maple furniture with chintz curtains at the windows where the sun came through brightening everything, indoor plants looking like they had been waxed and the whole place gleaming and cheerful. Their choice of furnishings showed good taste and she thought of her first apartment and its drabness; not that she wouldn't have done better if she could, but rather, the lack of money to do anything with.

Then she thought of the little house near the restaurant where she and Nick had found so much joy; perhaps the greatest joy both of them had ever known. That was the kind of place she liked to think about. Nothing fancy, nothing expensive, just comfortable and cozy and livable. The mansion in Memphis seemed awfully large when she thought about the little house in the mountains by the side of the road with a view of the hills about them..

He loomed larger than life, this easy-going, understanding, wonderful Greek she had married. There wasn't anything selfish about him. He thought the best of everybody; wasn't critical; bore no grudges, respected all people, yet stood tall among men and commanded respect just by his demeanor.

The world seemed turned upside down. There was upheaval in Europe and there was constant talk of war. Adolf Hitler's name became a byword. Pictures of the Swastika brought fear to people's hearts. Josef Stalin ruled Russia with an iron hand and his name brought fear to the hearts of Americans also. Mussolini's name was prominent in the news, as President of Italy. President Franklin Delano Roosevelt was regarded as a god in America and the masses looked to him to lead them into green pastures and to avert war. And times were still hard.

All these things bore on Pearl's mind as she stood at a window and observed the scenery about her. None of it really seemed real. She thought of herself as a Cinderella who wore the magic slipper and met her prince and courted him till midnight and that the clock was about to go off and she would again be in the Clyburn Mills among the spindles. It had been too much of a change. Years of living the good life had not changed her completely. Or had they?

Did she see life from a different point of view as a result of being lifted from poverty to a status she was unable to comprehend before she met Nick? Perhaps she had changed to an extent. But she had promised herself that there was a line drawn in her mind beyond which she would not go. She would not allow herself ever to become so sacrosanct as to believe she was above her heritage. She reasoned that plenty of others could have done as well, maybe better if given her opportunity.

She sought to ease Robyn's mind before talking to her about what Hobby had told her. She saw little to criticize and she would not offer any kind of advice. She would be warm and friendly and would show concern about anything Robyn said. She would spend most of her time with Robyn and that would give Nick and Hobby some time together after classes. Hobby was anxious to talk to Nick anyway. He wanted Nick to know why his plans were so urgent. So a day or two after their arrival Hobby's classes ended in early afternoon and Nick had seen a stable where they rented horses for riding and he wanted to go over some of the trails in the area. "Do you ride horseback?" he asked Hobby.

"I haven't been riding in Tennessee," Hobby replied. "In fact, I'm not really a horseback rider. But I remember so well how Grandpa used to put me on the mule's back when we were way down in the "mash" and it was hot and the bell had rung for dinner. 'You feel like riding boy?' he'd say and I was waiting for him to ask me. He'd take me and lay me on the mule's back and I'd grab the reins and hold on for dear life. I remember the mule's shoulders' moving as it made each step would jolt me but I felt like a real man riding that mule's back."

"Let's go rent a couple of horses from the stables on the edge of town and ride out on the mountain trails for a while. It's a beautiful day for riding."

"That would be fine," Hobby said as he headed to the house to tell Robyn and his mother where they were going. This would be the perfect time to tell Nick the details of his plans.

Nick chose a chestnut mare with a dark mane and Hobby a black with white blaze in its forehead and white feet. They were sleek and gentle. They rode about a mile down the road to where there was an incline and riding trails spread out, going into the mountains.

They rode for a while, getting the feeling of the saddle, smelling the polished leather and the closeness of beast and man, bringing the horses to a gentle gallop. Nick had his horse jump over a barrier that had been placed there for that purpose, but Hobby didn't try it.

Colorless leaves lay on the ground, causing a rustling noise when the horses ran through them. On the higher elevations color was already beginning to show, still subtle, more of a yellowish tint that would burst into rainbow colors as the temperatures dipped and the clorophyl dissipated. Chestnut trees were heavy with still-green nuts and squirrels darted through the leaves and ran up trees, playful with their furry tails held merrily. They were used to man so they were not alarmed, although they ran away when people approached too close to them.

"Beautiful country," Nick hollered to Hobby who was on another trail. There were other riders also and they would pass each other occasionally and nod.

They had ridden a good hour when they came to a clearing. It was sort of a park and there were tables for picnics and a deep well of cold mountain water and a stream that ran down a crevice. There were crude wooden seats made of various woods sitting under the trees. They had been made from small limbs of hardwood trees.

"Let's talk for a while," Hobby said, and Nick joined him under a tree laden with moss. Nick had drawn a bucket of water, drank from the heavy aluminum bucket and wiped off his chin with his hand.

"Okay buddy, what have you got on your mind?" Nick asked.

"A lot of things," Hobby replied.

"Well I hope they're good things," Nick said. "I'd be very worried if I thought anything was really wrong at this time in your life."

"Oh no, it's not anything like that," Hobby said. "But Nick, even though I'm here with the intentions of becoming a really good orthopedic surgeon, I cannot forget for the life of me what I plan to do back home. And I feel that I am defeating my own purpose in being so far away from it. I feel like it's almost dooms day and the clock is about to go off. I feel like every minute wasted will help to defeat me."

"I don't think it's that bad Hobby," Nick said. "I think you've got a little time to spare. But I realize there's a time limit. You've got Mr. Butler's place and that is a big start."

"And I'm so proud of it. You have no idea how humble I feel in your presence Nick. To think that you, a prosperous man of another nationality would do what you have done for me is mind-boggling. To think that you, of all people, would do so much for me is beyond belief. There I was, a mere boy, dreaming of a fantasy world and you come along to make that fantasy a reality."

"Knock it off Hobby," Nick said "I loved you the first time I saw you. I love you as much as if you were my own flesh and blood. I loved you for what I saw in you. You're lovable Hobby. You showed a simple faith in people and you didn't bear grudges. You and Pearl are my world. I never knew what living was until all of your family taught me. My contribution is small in comparison to what I have received."

"I know you've said that Nick and I believe you, but I never expected all the favors you have done for me. But I want to see if I can explain to you the urgency of action at the earliest possible moment.

"I know you have observed the changes all about us. We're leaving behind the old and taking on the new, in the cities, in the country, even in Bear Grass. That has never happened before Nick. We have gone for centuries without radical changes. Our forefathers lived basically the same lives we have lived. But there is a new order in the land now. We're all becoming modern. We want to shed the image of poorness and living second-class lives. That's what we have been working toward all these years. We don't want any reminders of that life.

"Look in the fields. What do you see? Tractors have about taken over where the mules left off. And where are the mules? I expect most of them have been sold to slaughter houses to be made into animal food and the old ones just left to die to make food for the buzzards. That means that farm implements are outdated and no more good. They'll end up as scrap iron or on the junk heap at the edge of some woods or a fill on a hillside to help keep the land from eroding.

"A place has opened in Hallsborough that they call a supermarket. They've got things there, I'm told, that we never would have imagined in a store before. Like chickens already dressed in refrigerated cases. Butter and milk and lard and eggs; things that we always grew on the farm. And you know what that will do to lifelong practices Nick. Every farmer in the county will manage to buy those things at the store. And what will that do to our way of life? It will go by the wayside. There isn't a man nor boy that doesn't hate the idea of feeding hogs and cows and mules and going out every morning and milking a cow. You didn't grow up on the farm so you wouldn't know about such things. And as soon as they can they'll stop cutting wood for the fireplace and the stove and the tobacco barn. They'll use oil or coal for those things.

"We're headed for the great roundup Nick. It's already on the horizon. That's making progress. But the things that will pass away are a way of life for all those my generation or older. It hasn't been bad Nick. It's been sort of backward and there have been many sacrifices as you know, but there isn't a one of us that doesn't have a special feeling about our way of life. They will miss it once it's gone Nick. There'll be many times when we'll want to go back and not only remember it, but see it as it was. It'll be as extinct as the dinosaurs that used to walk on the earth.

"Oh, there'll always be a few reminders of such a time. I doubt that all the tobacco barns will be torn down by the turn of the century. And some old houses will be left standing, but they will not show the era as it is at all, for they'll be neglected and bushes and trees and vines will take over and only show places with no soul, uncared for and forgotten. They will be worse than nothing to show for a way of life forever gone from the face of the earth."

Nick was perfectly content listening to Hobby pour out his soul. He found a piece of dead wood and used it for a pillow and lay down on the leaves. He looked at Hobby who seemed to be gazing through the trees into the sky. "This is really your heart and soul isn't it Hobby? I knew you were serious but I didn't think it was as all-consuming as it is."

"This is my calling Nick. The magnitude of it all becomes evident when you realize that we're talking about forever. All the things I'm talking about will pass away. We only have to project ourselves into the future to realize that. And if I'm to preserve I'll need all the things that are here now. It'll be gathering the eternal harvest, for all the things that are plentiful now won't be around in the future.

"I want to freeze time Nick. I want people to be able to see a way of life visually, as it is now. People of the next century can pass through this little community etched in time and there will be no question in their minds about it being a reality. It will be like visiting another planet almost. And it will be beautiful Nick. I will only be preserving what is, adding nothing and taking away nothing. But think what a job that will be. Not only do I have to have the things to project that reality, I have to have the tools and the supplies to last indefinitely. There must be great storehouses so that as things wear out there will be replacements."

Only then did Nick fully realize what Hobby hoped to accomplish. He felt a note of sadness for the young man not being able to devote all his time to this endeavor when it was evident his heart would never be in healing the sick. He was torn between Pearl's desires for him and his desire to help Hobby. And he realized that what the boy was saying was true. It was a matter of urgency.

"Tell you what Hobby," he said as the youth seemed engrossed in his own thoughts, "I can't tell you to drop out of medical school, for I know that would upset your mother terribly. And I doubt it could be explained to her at this time so she could accept your returning to Bear Grass. But there's something I can do. And I believe it will put your mind at rest and will allow you to devote your full time to your studies. I will hire a man who is knowledgeable about the things you are interested in. I don't know who or where he is, but such men are out there. I will take no part in it, for I wouldn't know what I was doing anyway. But when I find such a man I'll bring him to you and you can explain your plan and what you want. And he will start collecting just what you want. Would that make you happier?"

"Oh, Nick, that would be an answer to my prayers," Hobby said. "I could see much of what I need going away before I was able to begin my search. It seemed hopeless Nick, even with Mr. Butler's place. But knowing that someone will be doing something about what I have dreamed about so long will be more than I can hope for. Nick Staphal, you're the greatest man I ever knew and I love you more than you'll ever know."

"You're my son Hobby, and I have your interests at heart. And if you weren't my son and I knew you as you are, I'd still have those same interests.

And maybe we're doing wrong in keeping all this from Pearl, but somehow I don't feel guilty, and when the right time approaches I'll tell her what I've done, and I believe she'll understand."

The horses were tethered nearby, swishing their tails and occasionally pawing at the ground. "Aren't they beautiful," Hobby said. "There'll be plenty of horses in the pastures back home too. I can see it all come together Nick. I can feel the atmosphere and the feeling of peace that goes with such an environment."

"I know, Hobby. I look forward to seeing it all sometime in the future when change has come and what is now will be gone except for what you have preserved. What are you going to call it Hobby?"

"I really don't know," Hobby said. "I've thought and thought and haven't been able to come up with a name that suits me. Somehow "Echoes" rings in my ears but I don't know that that would convey the image that I'm looking for. That will probably be the last thing that I do."

Nick looked toward the west and the sun's rays were slanting through the trees. There were few riders on the trails now and it was one of the rare times when Hobby and Nick would be alone. Nick could not adequately convey to Hobby just how he felt about him; the pride he took in claiming him for a son; the joy it gave him to think of him as a man now, married and fulfilled as a man; the pleasure it gave him in knowing that he had a beautiful wife and had a helpmate that was as close to him as a person could be. The difference in them was that that knowledge came late in life for him whereas Hobby's came in his youth. In a flash he relived his courtship with Pearl and how it had changed his life, given it purpose, widened his horizons.

"It's great to be a man Hobby," he said as he looked into the handsome face and saw for the first time something that reminded him of Pearl. "I'm proud of my manhood as I know you are."

"Oh, I'm as proud of that as any man could be. Women should be proud of their womanhood and men should be proud of their manhood. I know there are great differences in the two besides physical. I know women think differently, have different outlooks, look upon men in some respects with pity as well as anger. But I know that men have their own feelings about women too. But it doesn't take long to learn that we can't get along without them. I've already learned that Nick, after being married only three months."

"You're a quick learner Hobby," Nick said. "And you have it figured out just right. But I love them for all their differences." He had an urge to tell Hobby the secret that Pearl was supposed to announce later. He wanted to say that Pearl was carrying a baby that would give Hobby a brother or sister that would unite them into one family by blood. And he, Nick Staphal, would also be united with the Turnage family by blood. He had wanted a child of his own for many years. He felt that the only way to be a complete person was through procreation. He had felt it wasn't to be since his first marriage turned out to be a disaster and he had never met a woman that he wanted to be the mother of his child until he met Pearl. And he knew Hobby would be proud to finally have a sibling, even if there would be a great difference in their ages.

"These are rare moments Hobby," he said as he rose and dusted off his clothes. "As close as we are, it seems that careers and geography will keep us apart. But I will always have your best interests at heart. You know that, and you can call upon me at any time."

"Yeah, it's a very special time, this afternoon on the trails," Hobby said. And he wanted so badly to tell Nick that he was going to be a father; that Robyn missed her first month; that they didn't have a honeymoon but they were overjoyed about the prospects of a baby. Each felt that they needed to express their views at this very special time. But out of respect for the women who were carrying the babies, each kept his thoughts to himself.

The sun was a large ball of orange on the horizon now. The treetops seemed to be an umbrella that was opening, obliterating the view of the sky above. They would have to leave the trails and head for open country below or darkness would catch them. Still, they lingered on for a few moments more.

It was calm and quiet. The other riders had already left and Nick was caught up in his own thoughts. He and Pearl would be leaving their estate in Memphis within a few years. Pearl's pregnancy had completely changed their trend of thought. They didn't want to bring up their child to be pampered and with a feeling of superiority that could be easily assumed in such a setting. They would move back to North Carolina; not to oversee Hobby and his estate. No, they would not be around to make Hobby feel he was being watched. That was the last thing they wanted. Instead, they wanted their child to be under his influence. Maybe he could convey his vision of the world to his sibling, make it see the beauty that he saw when so few even looked for it. Secretly, he wanted a boy to carry on the family name, but he'd never admit that to Pearl. And if it were a girl he would be absolutely wild about her and would still want her under Hobby's influence.

He had even thought about the name. He'd like him to be named Gustave after his grandfather whom he had never seen. But he'd want him to be called Gus just as his grandfather had been called. And Gus would roam over the land and learn Southern culture, so far removed from the lifestyle his grandfather had lived in far away Athens.

He would know the call of the wild and where the great stars hung in the heavens. And he would know the streams and the forests in his Carolina paradise and he would be a man of the land, lithe and fearless, taught by his brother who was a master of the art.

He could hear his name, "Gus," echoing across his domain and his life would be filled with happiness.

"We're late already," Hobby said. "Robyn and Pearl will be worried about us," as they headed down the trail, now almost in total darkness with the canopy of the forest cloaked in darkness. Nick rode first, with Hobby close behind. "We overstayed our time," Nick said, "but it was one of the most enjoyable times of my life. For the first time for us it was two men enjoying each others' company."

"And you fully understand why I feel as I do about Bear Grass?" Hobby asked.

"I think I always understood," Nick replied.

Robyn and Pearl made a fuss over them when they entered the house. "We thought something had happened to you," Robyn said as she kissed Hobby on the cheek.

"No, something good happened to us," Hobby said. "We got in one of our rare times together. And it was so pleasant out there on the trail. We'll have to go more often. You can just forget everything up there where it's quiet and a bird is always singing for you. It's like being in Bear Grass."

"Fancy, huh," Nick said as he observed candles on the dining table and the flicker as a breeze blew in from the windows.

"Not fancy," Robyn said. "Just cozy. And guess what we're having."

"Chicken stew," Hobby said, visualizing the thin pastry floating in chicken broth.

"Quail," Robyn said. "One of the doctors went hunting the other day, and he divided his kill with us. Now wasn't that nice? He said he knew that since we were rural we could appreciate the fine taste of quail. And it's dripping in its juices and we have rice and the drippings will taste wonderful poured over it."

"Sounds like a feast to me," Nick said.

"And there's chocolate meringue pie for dessert."

"Lordy!" Hobby said as he rubbed his stomach.

"Well, everybody gather around the table," Robyn said, designating the end chairs for Hobby and Nick. "Hobby, you ask the blessing."

"Dear Father, we are thankful to be together as a family. We thank You for all Your wonderful blessings. We are thankful to be together and we consider it a great honor to have my parents as our guests. I am what I am because of them. I feel humbled in their sight and I would gladly serve as their servant. Bless those members of our family who are not here. Bless the food to the nourishment of our bodies and bless this occasion when for the first time I entertain them in our humble home. We say these blessings for Your glory, amen."

There was a little apprehension as they ate. Nick knew that Pearl was going to announce her pregnancy and Hobby knew that Robyn was going to tell their secret. Nick noted when Pearl cleared her throat and looked around at the group. "I've got something to tell you," she said. "And all of you will be surprised." Then she was silent for a moment.

"Well come on," Hobby said, "Don't keep us in suspense."

"I'm in the family way," she said very casually. "So we'll be adding another member to the clan."

Both Hobby and Robyn looked aghast. Hobby rose from his chair and went over and kissed Pearl. "Well, at last I'm going to have that sister or brother I always wanted. Congratulations!" He went over and patted Nick on his shoulder. "This is absolutely great," he said.

"And I have a secret to tell you," Robyn said with a smile. "Your first grandchild is on the way. I missed my first month."

Nick and Pearl both rose and went over and kissed her warmly. "I'm so happy, Pearl said. "And you'll be a father Hobby. How great!"

"I wanted to discuss all this with you this afternoon," Nick said, "but I felt it was Pearl's right to tell you first."

"And I felt the same way," Hobby said. "I was just longing to tell you I was going to be a father. I felt that would place us closer together as men. But I knew Robyn should be the one to tell." But Hobby needed to talk to Nick further now, and he awaited his chance until Robyn took Pearl into their bedroom to show her what she was knitting for the baby already.

"But Nick," Hobby said in a hushed voice, "this changes things about the land. There'll be two of us now and we should both share in the Butler land."

Nick was shaking his head negatively. "It doesn't change a thing," he said. "The baby will be amply taken care of. You know I wouldn't give one more than the other. You just forget about that. The Butler place is yours."

"I would be happy if two of us owned the Butler Place," Hobby said.

"No, I want that for your very own," Nick assured him. "You and Robyn."

"You're the most generous man I ever knew," Hobby said.

Nick brushed his remark off with a shrug.

Nick and Pearl left for home the following day with everybody in a good mood.

Chapter 45

Pearl's water broke three days before her due date. Nick was at home for lunch and he suddenly became tense and nervous.

"Have you got your bag packed?" he asked, showing his excitement.

"They've been packed for weeks Nick."

"Well, let's rush to the hospital. Where is the bag? I'll get it."

"Now you just calm down Mr. Staphal," Pearl said. "It's not time to go to the hospital. This is just the beginning and it's a normal process but it does take time." Nick was chewing on a cigar and she took it from his mouth. "Just look," she said as she held the cigar before him. "You've chewed half way up that roll of tobacco like it was a piece of chewing gum. I see I'm going to have a time with you, old man, so let me say a few things right now. I don't want you filling up my room with flowers. You hear? One bouquet is fine and I'll appreciate it. But knowing you no telling what you would have delivered up there.

"And don't try to put on a show in the waiting room while I'm in labor."

"You tell me all these things Pearl when you know very well I've never been through anything like this before. There's no telling what I'll do before this is all over."

"We would be better off if you just stayed home Nick. Please stay here and get the doctor to come and give you something to make you rest."

"Nothing could keep me away from that hospital Pearl and you know it. I've got two to worry about now. Are you hurting anywhere yet?"

"I'm fine," Pearl tried to console him. She didn't say that her back felt like there was pressure low down.

"Well how will you know when to go?" Nick asked.

"When the pains begin they are far apart and you time the interval between pains, and when they come close together you're beginning to make progress. It's time to go to the hospital then."

The pains did become closer together around 6 o'clock, and she told Nick it was time to leave. "But if you don't feel like driving we'll get a cab. I don't want you to risk our lives on the streets."

"Oh, I'm fine sweetheart," he replied, leaning over and kissing her on the cheek.

Nick went up to the labor room with her for a little while but he couldn't sit down and relax. He paced around the room and looked out the windows at the traffic below.

"I'm going to ask the doctor to give you a shot," Pearl said. "You're already worse off than I am and you'll be completely out of it before the night is over the way you're going."

"No, no, I'll be all right," Nick said. "I'll be calm in the waiting room, I promise you."

"All right, but if I hear of any carrying-on down there I'll sure ask the doctors to intervene."

The obstetrician came into the room with rubber gloves in hand and with the smell of ether about him. He spoke to Nick and told him he would be better off in the waiting room, that he wanted to do a pelvic and see how much she was dilated. Nick stooped and kissed Pearl again and squeezed her hand. "I love you sweetheart."

"Me too," Pearl replied, not all that concerned about love at the moment.

Nick began pacing as soon as he was downstairs One young man was sitting in the waiting room, apparently at ease. Nick wondered whether he'd be like that if he were the man's age again.

"Your daughter expecting?" the young man asked.

"No, my wife is and I'm going crazy. This is my first."

"Well, congratulations," the young fellow said. "This is our third, only a year apart. We're getting to be old hats at this."

"I'll say," Nick said as he struck a match with his finger nail and lit another cigar. The man stirred the stale air with his hands as the smoke settled around him.

"Sit down," the young man said and Nick told him he couldn't. Felt like he had ants in his pants. Felt like he had the budges. Felt like the wild man from Borneo. "I'll just be a nervous wreck till it's over with."

Pearl asked Doctor Wong if he could get an intern to go down and give Nick a sedative. "I've already told him I might do this Doctor. And my husband is the sweetest man in the world, but when something very close to him is involved he just can't cope."

"Why yes, Mrs. Staphal, I can send an intern down but there's no assurance he will take the sedative. And if he is to take something that will be effective it should be via needle."

"Oh, he'll flinch like a baby but he'll take it," Pearl assured him.

So intern Wesley was soon in the sitting room where Nick was still pacing. He carried a hypodermic needle in his hand.

"What's that?" Nick asked. "I'm scared of those things."

"Your wife asked that we give this to you to make you rest."

"This just ain't my day," Nick sighed as he rolled up his sleeve and looked away from the doctor. "Ouch!" he said loudly as the needle penetrated his arm.

"Say doc, does it really hurt. I mean really hurt?"

"Oh, the sting will be over in just a minute."

"That's not what I mean. I mean actually having the baby?"

"You damn right it hurts. Women say if the men were the ones that had the babies there wouldn't be half as many as there are. And I expect that's right."

"Well I don't want her to hurt like that," Nick said louder than he should have in a public place. "I love that woman and I don't ever want to do anything to hurt her."

"Well, stay out of the bedroom, sir," the intern said.

By this time Nick was getting sleepy.

"Go lie down on that setee there," the doctor said. "You'll be asleep in a very short time." Nick pulled off his shoes and placed his head on an arm rest with his feet extending over the other and was snoring in seconds.

He slept six hours and was disoriented for a moment upon awakening. Then he thought about Pearl and the baby. He rose hastily and went to the nursing station to inquire.

"I'll ring Doctor Wong's office," the nurse said. The doctor answered the phone.

"Nick Staphal doctor. How's my wife?"

"She'll answer," Doctor Wong said.

"Hi," Pearl said, sort of groggy like.

"How are you my darling?"

"It's an eight and one half pound boy, the spitting image of you," she said.

"Oh my God!" Nick exclaimed. "A son! A Greek god! Can I see him Pearl?"

"Yes, he's already in the nursery. And he doesn't look like he's any kin to me. But I immediately saw something that I can associate with Hobby. Little babies do smile, you know, and as he yawned he smiled, and it was a Hobby smile."

"Oh, I'm so happy," Nick said. "And how about you sweetheart? Did everything go all right?"

"Better than with you I must say. But I'll admit it was the hardest work I've done since my sharecropping days. Heck, it was even harden than that. But I'm very happy Nick that we have a son."

Nick went up the stairs two steps at a time and rushed to the nursery. "Can I see the Staphal baby?" he asked the young nurse that was attending the babies. She pulled out a portable bassinette from among the babies and rolled it to the window.

"Oh God! He is like me. But he's all wrinkled. Is anything wrong nurse?"

"Mr. Staphal, haven't you ever been around just-born babies before? All babies are wrinkled at birth."

"No, this is my first experience." Nick admitted. "I never saw a just-born baby before. And I have so much planned for this little fellow I don't think I could take it if something was wrong right off the bat."

"He's got the best lungs in the nursery," the nurse said as the baby puckered up his face and attempted to put a fist in his mouth. "He came into the world screaming and searching for food. He's as healthy as can be. Don't you worry at all."

"Thank you," Nick said as he rushed to see Pearl. She was a little wan looking when he entered the room. There was a tired look on her face and he wanted to erase it right then and felt guilty for his involvement in the whole thing.

"What's wrong darling?" he said, placing his hands around her face and kissing her lips.

"Just tired," Pearl replied. "I need sleep now Nick so you go on home and let me sleep about all day and I'll be fine. We have a humdinger, don't we?"

"He's a Nick all right. And I'm so proud of him Pearl. I feel like I'm ten feet tall."

"Tell you what," Pearl said as she yawned. "I was going to call Hobby and Robyn but I'm too sleepy now. You call them when you get home. And call Mama and Papa."

"I'll spread the word all right," Nick said. "And I'll order the one bouquet you'll allow in here. If you hadn't given the order, people would think this room was a florist. I'd do that to show my pride in you and that little boy of ours."

"Bye now," Pearl said, for her eyes were closing and she wasn't hardly aware of Nick leaving.

Hobby and Robyn were ecstatic. "Everything go well?" Hobby asked. "Yeah, fine," Nick replied. "And what is he like," Robyn asked. "Wouldn't you know he is a Staphal from head to toe. But Pearl said he had Hobby's smile and that makes me mighty happy. And when are you due?"

"Most any time," Robyn said. "The doctor says I've already dropped, but the due date is two weeks."

"You tell Mother I love her," Hobby said, "as if she didn't already know. And I'm glad my sibling is a boy. And we'll be calling every day for a while just to keep in touch."

"Oh, thank God," Viola said when Nick called. "I was worried about Pearl, Nick. I don't know why. I just was." She held the phone while she told Craven about the boy. "What have you named him?"

"Haven't decided yet," Nick said. "But I've got something in mind now that I know it's a boy."

"Well, love the little thing for us and now we've got Robyn to worry about until that ordeal's over. I wish we could be with all of you. But it'll be a while before we can make it." Plans were already made for Craven and Viola to visit Memphis after both babies were born and after a few weeks passed until all the family could meet at Nick and Pearl's.

Pearl was in a private room the next day, having been moved from the maternity ward.

"Oh, you're looking good today," Nick said, reaching over and kissing Pearl. Her face was more rested and she appeared to be in good shape for what she had gone through.

"And how's the boy Mama?"

"Rambunctious," Pearl said. "They just brought him in to nurse and with swollen breasts and sore nipples he gave me a fit. I shudder to think what the little tyke will be like a little later on."

"Rambunctious, huh? Sounds like a Staphal to me. Wish I had been here to see it."

"They'll have him back in here in a few hours. Stick around and get in on the festivities."

"You have no idea how proud I am of you and our son, Pearl. And I've been thinking about a name, now that I know there's a boy to carry on the family name. I was the last, you know, until now."

Pearl noticed that there were actual tears in his eyes, the first time she had seen misty eyes in her man. She was touched.

"My grandfather was the man that made it all possible Pearl. He was brave enough to send his only son away from him for life, with a young wife, to seek a better life in America. He was Gustave Staphalopoulous, and his dream was for his son to reach these shores and to know the freedoms he had heard so much about. And just think what it has meant to me."

"To all of us," Pearl said.

"I know that Gustave is not a name heard around the Carolina countryside. But my grandfather wasn't called that in Greece either. He was called Gus, and that would have a good ring, even in Bear Grass. And if it's all right with you I'd like for us to officially name him my grandfather's name and just call him Gus."

"I love it," Pearl said.

Pearl left the hospital in one week, and their sleeping quarters were rearranged on the first floor and a nursery joined the bedroom.

"And let me caution you, Mr. Staphal, against bringing lavish toys in to fill the room. I can just see you bringing a teddy bear three times the size of Gus and everything that squeaks or squeals. I know you Nick Staphal. But we're not going to raise this boy in a luxurious atmosphere. So don't start off the wrong way."

"All right, Mrs. Staphal," Nick mocked.

And everything was in readiness for the blessed event in the little cottage near the university of Tennessee. Robyn was so large she had trouble getting up or down and she told Hobby she believed she was carrying a baby elephant.

"You're ugly," Hobby teased when he actually thought she was more beautiful than ever; that her mysterious eyes had a warmer glow.

"It's your fault," Robyn said, pulling at his ear lobe.

"It won't be long," Hobby reminded her. "And if I'm not here when the time comes you contact me just as soon as you know and I'll get you over to the hospital."

It was at breakfast when Robyn felt the first signs of labor. Hobby had fried bacon and scrambled eggs and they were eating.

"I feel something," Robyn said.

"You mean you're in labor?" Hobby asked.

"I think so," she answered as she was shaken with pain that felt like her stomach was being cramped.

Hobby almost turned over the chair when he got up to go over to her.

"There's nothing you can do Hobby," she said. "Go in the bedroom and get my bag and let's get on over to the hospital. I'm new at this, you know, and I'll feel better over there where I can be watched."

They were soon at the hospital and Robyn was immediately taken to the obstetrics department.

She was in labor for ten hours before the baby was born. Hobby was standing by in the room.

"It's a boy," the gynecologist said.

"Thank God it's over," Hobby said. Robyn was semi-conscious from the chloroform she had been given during the birth.

Hobby observed as the infant was cleaned up and he took a good look at his son, finding it hard to believe that this tiny bundle of humanity was a part of himself. "There doesn't seem to be any favor at this stage," he told the nurse. "Just a wriggling bit of humanity all red and wrinkled waiting for time to transform him into something of beauty and distinguishing himself from all others." But he was proud to be the baby's father.

Hobby stayed in the room until Robyn was fully conscious. All signs of birth had been dispensed with and Robyn was dressed in a gown she had taken with her. She had worn a hospital gown during delivery.

"We've got a boy," Hobby said as he sat beside Robyn's bed.

"What did you really want?" Robyn asked.

"It didn't matter an iota with me," he said. "Just so it was all right. And I noticed our baby had ten fingers and ten toes, so I figure everything else is all right. And I'm proud of you Robyn. You came through this like a Trojan and I want you to know I love you very much."

"I'm a mother!" Robyn exclaimed. "And I can't hardly believe it. But I ought to be able to believe, now that I know what a woman goes through from conception to birth that changes her forever from the girl she was."

"We called him John before he was born," Hobby said. "And now that we know he's a boy we'll just name him that if you want to. It's a good old American name that any man accepts as being masculine and without calling attention."

"Fine with me," Robyn said. "Now you go and call everybody and tell them the good news. They're all concerned, you know."

Hobby called Cora Finch first. "Your daughter is the mother of a seven pound boy," he said before anything else.

"And how is she?" Cora asked.

"She's fine," Hobby told her.

"I was so worried," Cora said. "You know Hobby, it's a woman's place to have the babies, but we somehow think our daughters aren't quite up to the task. We don't think they're tough like we were. And it's so foolish, but that's a mother for you. And have you named him?"

"John," Hobby said.

"Good, I like that. And hug Robyn for me and tell her I'll be writing her a long letter right away. I love all of you Hobby. But you already knew that."

"So long," Hobby said. "I've got to call the others, but I thought you should know first."

"Thank you," Cora said. "Be good."

"A boy!" Pearl said. "And I hope Robyn came through all right."

"Like a champion," Hobby said. "We named him John. And don't ask me who he looks like. He's just an ugly little rascal right now. But I wouldn't take a million dollars for him. And how is my little brother?"

"We named him for Nick's grandfather," Pearl said. "But we call him Gus and he looks as near like Nick Staphal as anything I've ever seen. He's no kin to me at all. But he has your smile Hobby, and I don't know of one better trait he could have. Maybe my genes contributed that little bit at least. But we're absolutely crazy about him. And he's already beginning to grow. Oh, babies make so much difference. And I had never thought about becoming a mother again. But I'm glad I did. And don't even ask about how Nick is. He's a fool Hobby. The very biggest fool about the people he loves I ever knew. And of course this baby is something very special. It means the continuation of the Staphal name."

"Yeah, I know," Hobby said. "I'll just be glad when we can all get together at your house. And I must be going. I've got to call Grandma and Grandpa."

"I'll call tomorrow," Pearl said. "Bye now."

"Oh Hobby, I'm the happiest person in the world," Viola said. "And just as soon as I tell Craven he'll be just as happy as I am. Just think! Our little boy has become a father. Don't hardly seem possible son."

Craven took the phone. "A real man now, huh?"

"A real man," Hobby said. "I'll bet you used to wonder if I'd ever fill a man's shoes."

"Never son," Craven said. "I knowed that one day you'd be everything any man is."

"His name's John," Hobby told Viola. "And I can't see much favor in him. But you know something Grandma. I couldn't be happier if he was the spitting image of Craven Turnage."

"Bless your heart," Viola said.

"You kiss Robyn for us and tell her we're mighty proud of her."

"I will Grandma. And I must be getting back to Robyn. I'll call again soon."

"Bye."

- - - - - - - -

What a change in the lives of the Staphals and the Turnages! With the addition of babies it turned their worlds upside down. There were so many things to do for the newborns, and although Pearl had a nurse for Gus, Robyn did all her work.

And the babies were growing so fast. Pearl would go into a tailspin sometimes thinking about it all.

Little pink gums showing when he smiled. Little fat hands with rings around the wrist, appearing as if they were corded off with a string. Little fists that gnawed and always went to the mouth, as if they had the necessary nutrients to survival. Yawns and stretches and always wetting his diapers.

She had not known the joy of motherhood with Hobby and she felt guilty somehow that she could lavish all the love and affection on this little bit of life that had been given to her in her later childbearing years. She could give him all the things she hadn't been able to give Hobby. Yet, because of Hobby's attitude, they were withholding the luxuries that could be provided, hoping that Gus would be able to see life from her oldest's point of view.

Oh, the joy of domesticity. When it boiled down to it, that was the very essence of life. Look what it had done for Nick Staphal, a man whose very name spoke of power and influence. A man with large holdings that would grow when the economy was full-blown again, promising great wealth in the future. And nothing like it had ever happened to him. He was as silly as a little boy, getting down on his all-fours in stockinged feet, crawling around a baby who wasn't aware of his presence at this stage. Begging for a smile, kissing soft cheeks and drooling all over his face.

His diaper was being changed and Nick was right there. "Hey, wait," he said. "I've not seen my little man in his birthday suit yet."

"Well have a look," Pearl said. The nurse was busy at something else at the moment.

"Look down there," Nick said as he chuckled. "Another Nick there too, I see."

"Braggart," Pearl said.

"Youall be very careful," Papa offered. "No pin pricks in the little Gus."

"Silly man," Pearl said. "Women don't stick pins in their babies. And you're going to learn to change him too. There'll be plenty of times when we won't have a nurse to change him."

"Oh, but I might stick a pin in him darling, and that would scare me to death."

"You stick a pin in my baby and I'll stick one in you Nick Staphal."

And he was so wise about some things, yet so ignorant in others. He was overcome with desire, yet he had thought there would be no relations between them during pregnancy.

"What am I going to do?" he had asked. "We can't do anything to hurt the baby. And that would surely press on it. That's the only bad part."

And she had kissed him and lay his worst fears to rest and he had been the happiest man in Memphis.

And he stayed at home so much as the pregnancy developed, offering to help her out of chairs, going with her to the bed and holding her legs as she lay down, even cupping her back and lifting her legs with one hand.

"Darling," she had said, "you're spoiling me to death and I love every fiber in your body for it, but women don't have all this attention you're giving me. Most of them work right up until the time of delivery, then go in and get the pot boiling and have the husband get the midwife. And they lie down and labor without the benefit of chloroform, feeling the baby as it makes its way down and experiencing all the pangs of labor. You just can't do all this for me. You'll drive yourself crazy."

"I'm already crazy," he admitted. "And I want to protect you at all costs, for without you life would mean nothing."

Oh, the vanity of men, she thought. She and Robyn had died with laughter when Robyn told her Hobby's reaction after the baby was born. He'd said, "Robyn, I've got real live sperm in me! Isn't that incredible?" And she had said, "Well, what did you think you had all the time my stomach was swelling?" And he had said, "But I couldn't hardly believe it that I had all the requirements to making a baby."

Just half of them," Robyn had said. "I have the egg, you know."

"Oh, but that egg has to be fertilized and that's where the real he- man comes in."

So proud of their manhood. So protective. Each man feeling that his sperm was the most special thing in the world; that it set him apart from all others. Never thinking that mother nature is so lavish in distributing the potential for procreation that any healthy man produces enough sperm at one time to fertilize millions of eggs. No special features are required, no special feat performed, only the meeting of the sperm and the egg. But try explaining all that to a man.

Skin as soft as a satiny rose petal kissed by a soft breeze. A little while when gender doesn't matter; when the endocrine system and the hormones that distinguish the sexes and give each their characteristics are dormant, giving the soft touch to little boys as well as girls.

Eyes as bright as stars. Eyes that explore the world about them. A time for kissing, for closeness, for bonding that will carry through eternity.

She laughed at Nick again. Pretending to show his male jealousy, over all things, his own baby. A soft mouth nursing a full breast. A pink tongue white with milk, having had its fill and toying with the nipple, pink gums and chubby hands attempting to get a grip on the source of its food supply.

"You've taken my place I see," he said with a smile.

"Oh, what a difference it makes when a man is in competition with his son." Silly man.

Holding him above her, she talked baby talk to this little bundle of joy.

"What will you be, little man? You could be anything in the world. Let me gaze into the crystal ball. I confess that you are so great I would indulge you in luxury just to see what my ita tiny boy would do in mansions with stock market trading as everyday as folks talk about tobacco and cotton in Carolina. But then you'd grow beyond wor waising and not even your rich papa lived like that.

"Oo will learn a language of the poor folks back home. Oo will speak a dialect city folks know nothing about.

"And your big brother can never think of you in that light. You're so near the age of his son he will regard you in the same light. But he's a good boy my ita prince and you will be mighty proud of him.

"Mama has brought two little princes from her body and both of you can make your mark upon the world.

"And part of my dream was shattered ita precious. My big boy is going to get his medical degree but Mama doesn't think it'll do him much good. Wor precious father told me last night what is in store for Hobby. And he at least made me understand. Mama used all her powers of persuasion on Hobby. Mama has a little bit of a guilty conscience. But wor father had the foresight to plan well for Hobby. Whatever his practice in orthopedics will be, it will be somewhere in the area of Bear Grass."

"Now what's wrong with my precious? Puckering up that little mouth and crying out. What is it precious? Don't you like me talking all this grown-up stuff? Are you hungry baby? Here, take your food." She nestled him to her bosom and removed a breast. As he nursed she shook him and he was asleep in moments.

Meanwhile, in the Tennessee hills, Robyn and Hobby were just as busy attending to little John's needs. All the people on the campus that knew them came by and sometimes the cottage was overflowing.

It became routine for Robyn and other young wives who had small babies to get together and talk about the domestic life. "I'm having to give Betty paregoric occasionally for colic and constipation." "Jimmy has a rash and the doctor said I must not use any lye when washing out diapers." "What kind of diapers do you use? Oh I don't know. They were given to him at a shower." "I use Birdseye, and that's a far cry from what I was used to. Mama had a lot of babies and we didn't have money for diapers and Mama would use the softest thing she could find. I've seen diapers made out of old shirts and things like that on my brothers and sisters. Heck, we used anything we could get and everybody got along fine."

The university was requiring more and more of Hobby's time, now that he was in medical school. But he found time every day to play with John. His time was so fully occupied he couldn't think about Bear Grass and his plans there, but he was consoled by the fact that Nick had planned well and his efforts were beginning to pay off.

When John was three months old they visited Nick and Pearl in Memphis. There simply was not enough room at their cottage for company, whereas in Memphis there was room to spare, no matter how much company came.

Viola and Craven met them in Memphis, and since it was the first time they had seen their grandson and great-grandson there was much merrymaking. Viola rocked both babies at one time and Craven was ready to carry them around when she would let him.

But Craven was not well and it was showing in his face. He was thin and pale and the least bit of exertion caused him to perspire.

"He's been getting poorly a long time," Viola said. "And he's been to Doctor Miller. He gave him a tonic but it didn't do nary bit of good. I really believe he thinks Craven's got cancer and he's scared to have him split open for fear it's already everywhere."

"Oh no," Hobby said. "Just when everything was becoming beautiful this has to happen."

"Mama, you and Papa just stay with us," Pearl said while Craven was out of the room.

"Pearl, Craven wouldn't be happy here. And our friends and neighbors will look after us. You know that."

Craven re-entered the room and Pearl said, "Papa, you're getting poorly and we'd be more satisfied about you if you stayed with us."

Craven shook his head. "Let me go back home Pearl. When a man feels like his life is about over he wants to be where everything is familiar; where there are friends and neighbors and the things that have always been close to you. And we'll miss youall and that precious little baby. But you are busy and you have him to consider first; not an old man that can't make anybody happy."

So Craven and Viola returned to Bear Grass; Hobby, Robyn and John returned to the university and Pearl and Nick were left alone with Gus.

But Craven's illness bore heavily on their minds. Hobby said to Robyn, "I was looking forward to little John really getting to know Grandpa and what a great person he is. And now I can't even look forward to that."

"There isn't any such thing as immortality." Robyn replied.

And Pearl was in tears. "It's coming to an end Nick," she said as she dried her eyes. "Nothing lasts forever and it's about the end for Papa. I can tell. It wouldn't surprise me to get a call any time. I just hope he won't suffer and have a long spell of agony."

"He's a good, good man," Nick said. "He's the kind of person few people can lay claim to. Just think, there are few people that you can sincerely say, he's a good, good person. I didn't know that man from Adam and he impressed me so much I'll never be the same again."

Nick and Pearl took Craven and Viola home and settled them down as best they could. Pearl talked to the women in the community about her parents and explained that she'd tried to get them to stay with her, but that they both wanted to return home. And the women understood and said the men and women of the community would attend to their needs when the time came.

Pearl and Hobby called practically every day to keep abreast of what was happening. And Craven became very ill and Viola told them it was time to come home, that Craven was about on the last.

He died before they arrived in Bear Grass.

Little was said while preparations were made for burial. The babies had been left in good hands in Tennessee so there was no worry about them.

When the body was brought from the funeral home to the house it was placed in the parlor and friends visited in the home. But the afternoon that Craven was placed in the living room each member of the family had a private eulogy for Craven.

Viola went first. She stayed in the room about half an hour and came out with tear-filled eyes. Pearl was next. She stayed about fifteen minutes. Hobby was third. He stood for a long time and just looked down at the body that had become a stranger to him. There was nothing that reminded him of the great man he had been except a corpse that had the likeness of him.

"What you were is gone, Grandpa. I now know what the soul means. Breath and life make up the soul. Without that we are nothing. You are so cold, so far away and all the things that I loved about you have left, even before your burial. I never thought about how final death is before. I've read somewhere a poem that says ... "Give me the roses while I live...." and it is priceless. Nobody can give you anything now. The whole world at your feet would mean nothing to you. But I gave you roses while you lived Grandpa."

Tears filled his eyes and he was quiet for a moment. "I didn't wait until you were gone and try to make up for all I have failed to do. I haven't been perfect, but you knew that I loved you very much and I told you the caliber man I thought you were.

"You were larger than life Grandpa. I saw no wrong in you although I realized that you had your eccentricities and I called you curious sometimes. But you have not died in vain dear one. The things you upheld live in my heart and I think that if a person can influence just one other in a positive way the whole journey through life is well worth it. Rest in peace Grandpa. You couldn't live to influence my children, and that was a dream of mine. But they might not have seen in you what I saw since I was with you in your best years. But I will tell them about you and the imprint you have stamped on my life.

"It doesn't take riches Grandpa. It doesn't take education. It doesn't take great wisdom. You had none of those things. You were very poor. You had very little formal learning. Your horizon was limited. And I didn't see any of those things in you. I just lived in a boy's world and you represented the security that I needed to make life good and simple and complete. You and Grandma, of course, for I could make no distinction between you as to what you meant to me.

"Thanks for being my grandfather. Thanks for taking me under your wing of protection. And they say we will be judged in death according to the life we have lived. Now reap the rewards Grandpa! They're there by the score, just from what I know about you. And others saw good in you also.

"Our loss is your gain, Grandpa. I leave you now, knowing that you have joined the throng whose lives have been spent, waiting for that day of reckoning that will be only an interval. Rest in peace, dear one."

The circle was broken.

Pearl talked Viola into going to Tennessee to live with her and Nick. "We'll take care of you Mama," Pearl said. "You won't be happy with us but you won't be happy in Bear Grass either with Papa gone. Loneliness will creep in and you aren't able to be a real part of the community like you were in the past."

"And you'll have Gus to play with," Nick said. "And it won't be like having to take care of him whether you like it or not. When you tire of him, you can call the nurse and be rid of the burden. We just want you to be as content as you can be, knowing that you'll miss the people you've been accustomed to. But there comes a time in life when we have to look at things differently, Mama. As sad as that is, it's a reality."

So Viola returned to Tennessee with Pearl and Nick after the funeral; never to return home in life.

- - - - - - - -

"I never knew a baby would change people's lives so much," Nick said as he and Pearl sat and watched their teething boy with saliva dribbling from his mouth and his gums gnawing at the edges of a table. He would utter a growl, followed by a big smile and pat his chubby hands on the table.

"It has completely changed our lives," Pearl answered. "I have concluded that our purpose in life is to nurture this manchild and see him grown up to carry on a family name and to make his place in the sun. Anything else we might have visualized pales in comparison as far as I am concerned."

"Oh, this is what it's all about," Nick said as he picked up the boy and held him high, with his head hanging down close enough for him to kiss him on the cheek.

"There will be years of this," Pearl reminded Nick. "Growing is a slow process and people generally go on about their business while the child grows. We could do that."

"It's too important to do that way," Nick said. "It's too short a period and babyhood is over so swiftly I just want to savor it and pack it away in my memory file for all the remaining years. I know that Gus will be my only contribution to posterity and I know I think of it differently than most people."

"I know I am thinking wrong Nick, so you are at least aware that what I am going to say is against what we've already decided on. But I can't help but think about how nice it would be to bring Gus up in Memphis society; let him be exposed to the life of the rich; spoil him to death and let him be conceited and aloof with an ego about as large as a mountain. I guess I want that for him for all the things I missed by being as poor as you can get."

"I'll confess I've thought of that too," Nick replied. "I want to lavish everything on him because I love him so much. But I know that's not what's best for him. Also think about how he might feel about Hobby if we exposed him to that life and his brother living out his life in a remote farming area. It wouldn't be compatible Pearl, and I know you can understand that since Hobby is also your son, and just as important as Gus."

"Oh, I know that Nick, and I agree with you it will be better for Gus to learn about life in Bear Grass rather than Memphis. And I wouldn't hurt Hobby's feelings for anything."

"Yeah, right now it would be very easy for us to go off the deep end with Gus," Nick said. "We're very vulnerable now, but I can't forget the lessons I learned in Bear Grass. They were more valuable that what I've learned in Memphis. So we'll have to work out of this reverie and get back down to reality."

"I know," Pearl sighed. "We must not forget Hobby's attitude and what he can mean to Gus."

At the university, Hobby and Robyn were equally as busy looking after John, watching him develop and laughing at his antics. Between family and medical school, neither had free time to reflect on life. Hobby found himself so taken up with other things Bear Grass only lay at the surface of his mind; not the dominating force it had been when he had had more time to concentrate on his dream world.

One reason for this was that as Nick had promised, after a thorough search he came up with Leland Wentworth to fill the job of procuring all the necessary items he could to begin filling the storehouses for the future. Hobby and Leland had hit it off from the start. Leland grew up in Georgia and was as much a farm boy as Hobby had been. They talked via telephone several times a week, and as Leland acquired things that would be essential to run the plantation according to Hobby's wishes, Hobby was much relieved and worried less about his plans.

When John was eleven months old Robyn became pregnant again, and the domestic life took over and they were so deeply involved with Hobby's studies and the family time passed swiftly. Heidi added to their work and their joys.

Pearl, Nick and Gus visited Robyn and Hobby fairly often, and John and Gus became buddies, each looking forward to being with the other.

The years passed swiftly.

Chapter 46

"Good damn them Japs," Jasper Parker said as he spat a mouthful of tobacco juice in a tin can at Stroud's store. He looked out the window and saw clouds billowing in the west. The trees were naked in the distance except for the pines that always gave a green background.

Stroud's store was normally closed on Sunday out of respect for the religious community. But the radio was telling about a Sunday morning attack on Pearl Harbor in Hawaii and that many American lives had been lost. Not everyone in the Bear Grass community had a radio so Gant opened the store as sort of a public service so the citizens could hear the news bulletins to keep up with what was going on.

"I mean they sneaked in and caught everybody napping," Jasper added. "You'd think they'd have been on the alert out there, wouldn't you? They say they've got these warning systems, what's it called? Radar or something, that sweep across the skies and show images of approaching planes. My gosh, they've sunk all the ships in the harbor it sounds like. I shudder to think what it's like there right this minute."

"And it's a whole lot closer to home than way out there in the Pacific islands. Walter Finch's boy is stationed at Pearl Harbor and Adam Pridgen's boy, the one they couldn't ever do anything with - I forget his name - is there too," Gant said.

"They call him Goose," Jasper said. "I didn't never know his real name."

"Well just let me say right here," Gant said as he lit a cigar and watched the wooden match glow until it became hot to his fingers, "there are big changes coming. We've set around and waited for something to bring about change. Well, we'll see so much of it we won't believe it. Lord God, I think about all the scrap iron we drug up from everywhere and sold 'em, and now they're shooting it back at us. And some of the boys that hauled up the mess are watching a picture show right now with money they got for that scrap iron. I don't know if there'll be enough boys left around here to farm. They'll be wearing a uniform in no time and toting a gun."

"It'll be pitiful," Enos Butts said. "These boys hain't never been nowhere and don't know the first thing about life. Some of 'em hain't never spent a night away from home in their life. They'll be so lost they won't know how to shoot a gun. They'll even forget how they aimed at rabbits and birds when they git out there looking at them gun barrels pointed at them. It makes me want to cry when I think about how pitiful it is."

"What's so bad," Gant said, "is that it caught us with our britches down. We don't have any military buildup. We don't have anything to fight a war with. We've been lulled into thinking that Roosevelt was a god and that he wouldn't let anything happen to us so much we've just gone on in our everyday way, trying to make ends meet. God, what an awakening."

"Somebody laugh or something," Nelson Willoughby said. "This is the somberest crowd I've seen at this store since Nervy Sauls was murdered."

"It's about as sad," Jasper lamented. "There ain't been anything like what we'll see a little while ahead. Them son-of-a-bitch Japs know better than that. And I was reading in the Argus last week about some big-shot Japanese official being in Washington talking peace and all that shit."

"Shut up," Gant said as he held his hand out to the crowd. "Here comes another bulletin."

"Japanese submarine believed in the area of the California coast," the newscaster said. "Security officials fear there may be air raids on the west coast. Stay tuned for further details."

"My God!" Gant said. "Are they fixing to invade us?"

- - - - - - - -

Up on Harker's ridge, Patience Finch was lying with a pillow to her back and a slop jar beside the bed. The radio was going full blast and she was crying. The unborn baby was stirring in her stomach and she felt like she was on water without any bearings. Everything was spinning around her. Bud, her eighteen-year-old boy, was a medic at Pearl Harbor. He had joined the Army because there was no way to make any kind of life for himself in Bear Grass. He was the oldest of seven children and Walter hadn't been able to give him an acre of tobacco or anything to call his own. Not that he didn't want to. There just wasn't enough to go around as it was.

And when Bud mentioned going into service neither Walter nor Patience had tried to dissuade him. "Besides," Bud said, "I'll be able to send some of the twenty one dollars a month to youall to help out at home. A few dollars will help out a lot." And Walter had nodded in the affirmative. But there had been no thought of war when they made the decision. Hitler had been cutting up in Europe and Mussolini was showing himself in Italy and a few countries had been invaded by Hitler's forces, but all that was so far away people in Bear Grass thought little about it. How could anything so far away affect people hidden by piney woods in North Carolina?

Patience, (it was called "Pashey,") turned on her side and vomited. She felt like she was going to roll off the bed. She told Walter to either turn the radio off or move it to another room, that she couldn't bear to hear it; it was tearing her nerves all to pieces.

"I can't move it Pashey," Walter reminded her. "The wire is attached to the radio and if you move it it won't bring in anything. You'll have to go to one of the young'uns rooms. I'll tote you if you don't feel like walking."

"I'll make it," Patience said as she held her hand against a wall and staggered into the other room. She lay down and vomited again and closed her eyes, but she couldn't keep the thoughts away.

He would certainly be out helping to gather up the dead and wounded and with bombs falling they couldn't hardly miss him, even if he were in one of the vehicles. And he didn't even have a gun to defend himself and she was glad. She didn't want him killing nobody, those with slant eyes or anybody else for that matter. She loved her Bud. He had been a good boy. Of course he was high-spirited like all boys. A right good-looking boy too with a shock of hair that fell over his right eye and with a sheen that sparkled when the sun shone on it.

He had grown up so quickly. One day he had been a high-pitched gangly boy and all of a sudden he had grown into a man with broad shoulders and a deep voice. He was her first, and so much like Walter had been when they were married. He must have been conceived the night they were married. Anyway, he had been born nine months to the day after they were married and she had almost died. She had strained so much through a hard labor she couldn't strain anymore and Walter had finally gone for Dr. Miller and he had had to split her so the baby could come through and she remembered all the soreness later and how weak she had been. But her Bud was worth it all.

"What is it all about?" she asked herself. "We bring them into the world, hoping they will do something to make it all better; that they will have a better life than we've had. Make something of themselves. Be somebody. Laugh and smile and be happy. And what happens? We don't have anything to offer them to make life better. They have to go to Uncle Sam and ask for his help to live. And Lord, that ten dollars a month the government sends us helps out more than anybody would believe. But my Bud is going to die on the battlefield I know. I just have that feeling inside.

"I could tell he had them winning ways right off the bat. He reminded me of my Walter from the start. The same eyes that could look up at you and melt your soul. My Bud was special. But some girl would have stolen him from me anyhow. Life's like that. Out of your own self comes something you see is very precious; something that you want to protect; something that you can look up to and be proud of. But you know from the beginning it'll be a short-lived thing that you can't hold on to.

"But I never thought it would be war that would take him. Not the Japs. Why we were always ashamed to have things in our house that you could look on the bottom and see the words "made in Japan," cause that meant cheapness. Little china figurines and dolls and toys and things like that. Whenever I see pictures of Emperor Hirohito in the paper I don't think much about it because I never thought of Japan like I did the United States, not big anyway. And here they are killing our boys, and mine among them as sure as the world."

She felt the kick of the unborn baby and waves of nausea swept over her. She leaned over and vomited in the slop jar and lay back down, breathing heavily.

"Lord help him," she pleaded. "He didn't go off to fight no war. He just wanted to better hisself; make a little money he could call his own. Even help us out. He had dreams of being a little better off than us poor folks out in the country. Not biggety and feeling better than anybody else. Just wanting to make life a little bit better.

"And on a Sunday, the Lord's day. Why in God's name would they pick a day like that? I reckon they thought the Americans would be a little off guard that day. I know how we feel on Sunday. After working hard all week it's mighty comforting to come up with a day when you can be a little bit lazy. Gives you a chance to stretch and yawn all you want to and just forget about all the cooking and washing and ironing and mending you've got to do next week. I reckon the Japs knowed us that well. But it will never be the same agin. They'll never catch us off guard no more. They've already teached us a lesson. We don't seem as big no more. Or powerful.

"I may be carrying another one in my womb to furnish for another war some day too. Lord, I wish I knowed the meaning of it all. It's always for us to wonder about the plan of life. It seems so wasteful to go through nurturing them in your own body, then laboring to bring them in the world and raising them from infancy for God knows what. 'Specially boys."

- - - - - - - -

A shock settled over the community. The day was cloudy and warm; not typical of winter weather and Christmas only two and a half weeks away. Hogs were fattening in pens and farmers were waiting for seasonal weather for hog-killing. Families were surviving on white side and rusty meat left in the smokehouse. People were longing for fresh meat. But those things were farthest from their minds as the magnitude of what the attack on Pearl Harbor meant. Everyone knew that on Monday Roosevelt would declare war against Japan. Nobody's life could be lived as it had been in the past. Christmas was ruined. Oh, there would be the same rituals, perhaps emphasized more for many boys would be on the battlefields when Christmas rolled around again. Nobody expected the war would be over soon.

- - - - - - - -

After hearing the news bulletin for hours, Pearl and Nick walked down to the mighty Mississippi River and gazed at the few ships sailing, their thoughts consumed by the tragic news. Pearl was thinking that Hobby would want to be among the first to enlist, for he possessed a great sense of patriotism, and although she was consoled by the fact that he would never pass for military service, she knew that he would consider himself less of a man somehow in not being able to serve his country in some way. She looked up at Nick and said, "Of course Hobby will be excused because of his disability. And I regret that Nick. He's a loyal American and he wants to do what's best for his country."

"Well, being in the medical field, they might want him anyway," Nick replied. "But then he's married with two children and that will have some bearing. He could serve in the medical corps and not be exposed to real battle."

"I hadn't thought about that," Pearl said. "Even at that, it would not be like serving in battle and feeling a real part in fighting the war."

"There's no telling who will be called before it's over with," Nick said. "If things became bad enough they could call men my age."

"Oh no," Pearl said. "I couldn't bear it if you went away to war Nick."

"Other families feel that way also," Nick said. "But it will become a fact of life for many of them."

- - - - - - - -

Pashey Finch finally rose from the bed, pulled on a dress and walked out on the porch, holding on to a two by four post that helped hold up the roof. Her head was swimming still. She looked out over the community and thought that even the pines seemed to be bowing their limbs. Closer by she noticed the oak leaves still left where they had been blown by the wind to the corner of buildings and they looked black and the cornstalks still left after being bent over by hogs running out made the countryside look more forlorn.

And blackbirds flew over the fields in droves, pitching momentarily, then taking flight again to be replaced by another drove. Maybe it was going to turn cold, she thought. The weather had been unseasonable with little cold weather and frost. She suddenly wanted her children beside her. She felt that there was some protection in numbers and that so long as they were near her no harm could come to them.

She began calling her brood to her, although she didn't see any of them. John was sixteen, but thank God, he was too young to go off to war just yet. But if it lasted long he would be a target later on. Unlike Bud, he was the happy-go-lucky type and too much like her people to have Bud's features and personality.

John came home first. Pashey watched him coming up the path and noticed that he did walk like Walter. "Any more news?" he hollered, cupping his hands so the sound would travel farther. She shook her head.

As he came closer, he said, "Reckon Bud was out there when the bombs fell?"

"Lord, I'm afraid so," his mother said. "Now I've got you to worry about."

"Ma, I ain't old enough to go to war," he said. "I wish I was. I'd shoot some Jap bastard's head off before you could turn around."

"You don't mean that," Pashey said. "Don't you git no such thoughts in your head, John Finch."

- - - - - - - -

Enos Butts' boy, Ham Bone, perhaps said it as well as the people in Bear Grass could say it. He and some of the other boys were outside Stroud's store, leaning up against the side of the building and smoking Golden Grain cigarettes. Ham Bone was nineteen and the two boys younger than him were seventeen and sixteen. So he was a prime target to be drafted. He cut a piece from an oak limb and looked up at the sky and said, "Boys, you've heard me say over and over that I wanted to git out of Bear Grass and see how other folks lived. But I'll have you know I won't never talking about the Japs cause I don't know nothing about 'em, don't care nothing about 'em and hadn't never thought about 'em to tell you the truth. I did sell scrap metal to them and put a few quarters in my pocket. I was thinking about Colorado or Texas or some place like that. But Bear Grass hain't never looked as pretty as it does to me right now. So you know something. I don't want to go nowhere. I hain't never been crazy about farming. But I'd be the best dang farmer you ever saw if I could choose farming or something else. I don't want to go nowhere and I'm homesick already and war's not even been declared yet."

"What you reckon will happen?" Allen Black asked.

"Well, I imagine boys will be signing up tomorrow morning," Ham Bone said. "Boys will have to volunteer or they'll be drafted. And it's not like if we had a choice. When a country goes to war you fight for your country. That's all there is to it."

"But who decides who goes and who stays home?" Robert Williams asked.

"They've got a draft board," Ham Bone said, "the same as they did in World War I. Pa told me about it. The draft board has the power to defer a boy if it thinks the boy's needed to farm. Farming is very important all the time, and 'specially in wartime. They take into account how many boys there are in a family and if there are several large enough to work they'll probably take one of them right off the bat, and if things get bad enough they'll call another."

Robert said, "Even the draft board don't play fair. Pa told me about the draft board too, and he said some farmers got by better than others. He always said there was payoff involved in that too. He said some men with a little pull and a little money kept their boys at home while poor folks like us just saw the boys drafted and yanked off to war. It'll be the same way this time."

Caleb Culpepper walked into the store and ordered a pop. He stood and gulped it down, then belched.

All the men were quiet while he was in the store. None of them spoke to him.

He belched again, wiped his mouth with his hand, and headed on down the road toward Beston.

The boys ran into the store after he left. Ham Bone Butts had an ungodly look on his face and he was wiping at his overalls as if he had something nasty on them. "God damn prick sucker," he said disgustedly.

Coon Edwards laughed and said, "How do you know Ham Bone? Has he been after you?" He rubbed his hand on Ham Bone's leg.

"Hell no," Ham Bone said "Tell you something else, he damn sure better not try it. I'd knock his fucking head off."

"I just don't understand it," Jasper Parker said. "I don't see what no man wants with another. And I don't know where they ever find one that will do that. I shore don't know no men around here that would pull out their pecker for another. Do any of you?"

"Hell no," Gant said. "But we don't never know about the other fellow."

"Boy, he'd just love to go in the army," Ham Bone said. "If he was in with all them soldiers he'd be stuck in the head ever chance he got looking at them dicks and handling them too if he got the chance. But they wouldn't keep that queer long enough to git a GI haircut."

"I don't know of but about three queers around in these parts," Jasper said. "And what I know about them is just what I've heard. But now that we're on the subject I'm going to tell you boys something I never told before. A few years ago I was at Mr. Semps'es at a corn shucking and men were on their knees all around the piles of corn. I'd had a few and won't feeling no pain and I was listening to all the shit the men were slinging and shucking corn up a storm and not paying no attention to what was going on around and all of a sudden I felt a hand on me down there. I looked around right quick and it was that sorry Caleb next to me. I hauled off and cold-cocked him 'fore I knowed what I was doing and he fell over backards like he'd been shot. I got the blood too. It was all over his face when he come up. I could see real good by the lantern light. And that bastard got up from there and high-tailed it." All the men laughed. "Add Jasper to the queer list," somebody said.

- - - - - - - -

Back in Tennessee, Hobby and Robyn received the news with total shock. They sat by the window throughout the afternoon to get all the news bulletins, saying little, each deep in thought.

Finally Hobby said, "I've never regretted being handicapped as much as I do this day. My country is in trouble and I'm not physically able to bear arms and be a foot soldier. I love life Robyn, and you and little John and Heidi are my world. But I want to help protect that world and America. And I may be able to serve in some capacity, but not like the boy that's facing the enemy on the battlefield. And God knows I'm no hero. I'd be scared to death on the battlefield.

"But if we lost our freedom what would there be to live for? To have some foreigner dictating our lives is inconceivable to me."

"I don't like to hear you talk like that Hobby," Robyn said. "But they may call you to some medical unit. Even though you are not a doctor yet, you have valuable experience and many medical men will be needed I'm sure." Tears were in her eyes.

"Well I'm not going to shirk my duty Robyn. You wouldn't be proud of me if I tried to hide behind my disability. Other boys will fight to protect you and the babies and I'll appreciate that, and if I can do something I'll be proud to answer the call."

"They'll sure get some of my brothers too," Robyn said. "It's going to be awful Hobby, no matter how we look at it. There'll be so many sacrifices, so many changes."

They called Jones County and talked with Robyn's parents and Memphis to get Pearl and Nick's comments. Everyone was in a stupor and not quite able to grasp the enormity of the situation, except to say that it would be bad. Everybody was somber, troubled, and unable to console each other.

- - - - - - - -

"I'm really not surprised," Waldo Spence told his wife. Waldo was a Republican and had voted for Herbert Hoover, and had lived to regret it, but he wasn't satisfied with Roosevelt either. "When a man is looked up to as God, you'd better watch out. He may have known more than anybody knew about. I find it hard to believe that a foreign power was ready to attack the United States of America and the leader of this country had no inkling of what was going on. This is awful, Ruth."

"Yes, it's awful," Ruth said. "And the bad part is we're not equipped for a war. We've got to start from scratch building a military machine. That'll mean that our factories and plants will have to be turned into military establishments to build tanks and planes and guns and bullets. We shouldn't ever have gotten into this position. But the country has been in such bad shape it was more than we could do to climb out of the Depression. And we've still got a long way to go."

"And do you know what really worries me Ruth? There's Wilbert Lee, too sorry to take hold of his life and be a productive man. And there he is with two children and a wife, and he'll be protected for a long time because of his family status. It's a shame they won't put a uniform on him and give him a gun and put him out there to help fight the enemy."

"I don't think you should look at it that way," Ruth said. "After all, he is Will and Beth's father, as well as Anne's husband. That means something."

"It doesn't mean an awful lot to me Ruth. W.L. has done so badly as a husband and father I don't have any pity at all for him. We would be better off supporting Anne and the children and have him completely out of our lives."

"Well I'm glad of what little love he does give them," Ruth said.

If she only knew about all of his carrying-ons, Waldo thought, she would be the angriest person in Hallsborough. He was glad he had kept the sordid details to himself. People knew enough just by observation and what people had told others. But all these things were unknown to Ruth.

"He'd have a chance to prove himself," Waldo said. "Do something for his country and finally give people a chance to be proud of him. Plenty of people are sorry, but if they make an about-face and turn their lives around people may not forget but they certainly will forgive. But you know something Ruth, I'd bet anything he wouldn't pass the physical if he were called up."

"You know he would," Ruth said. "He's as healthy a specimen as anybody around. May be a little too fat. Should lose a few pounds. Otherwise, he looks perfect to me."

"So many will die," Waldo said with a sigh. "We don't have a son to lose, but others do, and I hate to think about every boy that will go over there to fight a war on a foreign soil."

- - - - - - - -

As dusk settled over Bear Grass it appeared to be a forlorn world. No children's yells were heard in the neighborhood; only the occasional barking of a dog or the jingle of a bell around a cow's neck; the squeal of a tackle as buckets of water were pulled up from the well. It was a hallowed place that night, more appreciated than in the past for it was home, sweet home spelled out differently than it had ever been to the younger generation. It was threatened and people felt that even the rock of Gibraltar was not strong enough to withstand such a jolt. Clouds settled in and there were no stars. Would foreigners invade America that night on our west coast? Tomorrow would mean war. There was no doubt about it, and it would be a different world forever more

- - - - - - - -

Jasper Parker's boys were right in line for the draft. Ross, the oldest, was nineteen. Prince, next in line, was eighteen, William Earl, third was seventeen and Nelson, the youngest boy, was fifteen.

"They'll git two of them at least," Jasper said to Hettie, his wife, as they sat at the supper table nibbling at their food. "Maybe they'll just git Ross or Prince at first and leave three at home. Nelson's still in school and that ought to mean something to the draft board, depending on who it is, of course."

Jasper found out that Edmund Cox, who lived between Bear Grass and Hallsborough, was on the board and he felt pretty good about him and considered him a reasonable man. And it wasn't long until Ross and Prince were called at the same time for examination.

"Jasper, you ought to go talk to Mr. Cox," Hettie said. "They hain't got no business gitting both boys at the same time. If you don't say nothing they'll probably git both of them. They ort to let one of them stay home, and I shore won't say which. I love one of them just as good as the other and it ain't up to me to say which one goes into battle."

"Do you really think it would help Hettie?" Jasper asked

"I shore God do," Hettie replied.

"How 'bout you going," Jasper said.

"Now ain't that something," Hettie replied as she wiped her mouth with the hem of her apron. "Ain't you man enough to stand up when you've got something to say?"

"Yeah, but folk's would probably say I was trying to put the squeeze on the draft board if I were to do that. I want to do what's right, Hettie."

" Well, I'll go," Hettie said. "Nobody can say anything about a mama that wants to keep her boy out. 'Specially when they's so much to do out in the fields and this country needs farm stuff as bad as any one thing. Them boys can do more good on the farm than they can shooting at people."

Hettie put on a clean dress, took off her apron, balled her hair up fresh and took her Sunday hat from the top of the wardrobe. Jasper was hitching up the mule to the wagon while Hettie dressed. The wagon wheels raised the dust along the road as they traveled to the Cox home.

"He may not be there," Jasper cautioned as they neared the house.

"Naw, he may not," Hettie said. "But we've got to do what we can Jasper. I just want to feel like we're treated right."

"I'm going to stop under the shade of this tree," Jasper said. "You go on up to the house."

Edmund met her at the door. "Good afternoon," he said. "Come in."

"I'm Hettie Parker, Jasper's wife. I believe you know him. I'm here to talk about my boys since both of them got a notice to be examined for the Army."

"Have a seat on the porch," Edmund said as he motioned to a rocker. "I'm ready to hear whatever you have to say."

"Well, my oldest boy is nineteen and the next one is eighteen and both of 'em got a notice yisdiddy to be examined for the Army. Now Jasper and me's willing to do our part Mr. Cox, but I don't think it's fair to take two at one time. Do you?"

"That don't sound quite right," Edmund said.

"I think one of 'em ort to be "ferred" or whatever it is. You just let me git to where I'm supposed to say something right and I'll show my ignorance just as shore as the world. Git all tongue-twisted and everything comes out wrong."

"You mean deferred," Edmund said.

"Yeah, I knowed it was something like that. Anyhow, how about doing that for one of my boys. Jasper ain't able to do what he used to. Bending over and crapping backer just ruins his back, or gitting up corn and throwing it in the wagon from the heap rows just lays him up and he has the pure charleyhorse. And we've got to do all we can to make the stuff for our fighting men as well as the rest of us."

"I'll look into it," Edmund said. "It's very likely that one of the boys will be deferred."

"Thank you, Mr. Cox," Hettie said as she wiped her brow with a handkerchief she had stuck in the bosom of her dress. "Something else I want to ask you, Mr. Cox. I've heard it and I want to know the truth. And I ain't asking about you for I don't believe you'd do such, but is they such a thing as the draft board being bought off if a boy's daddy has got a little something to give the board member?"

"Not to my knowledge," Edmund said. "But I'm not saying that's not possible. You've heard the saying "money talks" and that is very true. And as tight as times are now a few dollars look mighty big in some people's eyes. But to do such a thing with human lives sounds preposterous to me."

"What's that big word?" Hettie asked.

"Preposterous means outrageous, contrary to nature."

"Oh."

"The same way with coupons," Edmund said. "There are black marketers who get plenty of coupons and some people get all the gas they need, all the sugar, all the shoes, even tires."

"Yeah, and it curdles my blood when I see them things," Hettie said. "My young'uns hain't go no coupons for shoes and if we had they wouldn't be no money to buy 'em with. And I can't git used to saccharine tea to save my life. That's the bitterest mess to be sure and the only reason my young'uns will drink tea made with saccharine is that they would have just water otherwise cause there shore ain't no sugar. They're the sugar-lovingest crowd I've ever seen."

"There can come war or pestilence or disasters," Edmund said, "but there will be people who will profit. It's just that way and there doesn't seem any way to stop it. Many people aren't as honest as you are, Mrs. Parker."

"Yeah, but I reckon they's a mean streak in me Mr. Cox, cause I'm always looking at them that's got a little something. Take Wilbur Stroud. I reckon he was about the biggest man around here, and I don't mean just his big belly," she said with a smile. "I had to go to his store to buy lye to make lye soap last week. You have to make it on the full of the moon, you know. And before I got to the store I saw his boy come out of the store like he was in a big hurry and jump into his mobile and take off like a bat out of hell. I thought he'd hit me if I was the last one. And I won't tell you what I liked to of done but I 'speck you can imagine. He took off so fast they was black marks where the tires scraped the road. And I thought about how we were supposed to save all the rubber we could. Course we don't git no new rubber nohow, but he can git another used tire that they do something to and put new treads on them. But you see where it's come loose and is lying all along the highway. But such things make me mad Mr. Edmund. I thought to myself that that boy was running loose just cause his daddy, rest his soul, had been a Bear Grass big shot. No wonder sometimes if I think there ain't a ounce of Christianity in me."

"Ah, but you're one of the good ones, Mrs. Parker," Edmund said as Hettie rose to leave.

"Well, I 'preciate you listening to me Mr. Cox, and whatever you can do about my boys I'll be much obliged and Jasper will too."

"Any preference as to which one to defer?" Edmund asked.

"Lord God no!" Hettie replied. "One's just as important to me as the other and I ain't going around saying eenie meenie miney mo. You just do what you can, you hear?"

"I will," Edmund said as he rose and shook her hand.

- - - - - - - -

Jimmy Joe Edwards had only one boy large enough to work, and he was naturally deferred. And "Coon" Edwards, his son, was as rambunctious as hell. He dreamed about girls all day long and at night too. But they took on wet forms at night. But "Coon" was held back because Jimmy Joe wasn't able to have any kind of automobile. Hell, the days were past when a boy went courting on a buggy with a farting mule. That was old hat, although Jimmy Joe was quick to tell "Coon" all the fun he'd had courting on a buggy.

"I don't want to hear that shit Pa," Coon would say. "You're still living in the past Pa. It just ain't like that no more. And with so many boys off to war them little old girls are out there with them dreamy eyes just waiting for a boy to come by on a mobile to haul them off for a little fun. It looks to me like we could do something to git me some kind of mobile. I seen a good Chevrolet body on stovewood slabs down the road a piece with weeds growed up all around it. And I ain't no expert when it comes to fixing cars, but you know I've tinkered with them all my life. I might be able to find a engine sommers else and the other parts and fix up something to travel on."

"You dream them big dreams "Coon" when you know damn well they ain't a penny to buy that mess. If they was money laying around we wouldn't be in the mess we're in now. How in the hell do you think I'd find the money to buy any such mess?"

"You buy likker sometimes don't you?" "Coon" asked.

"That's different," Jimmy Joe said.

"Well, by God, if you can buy whisky we can find the money for some kind of mobile. Now I don't mind helping farm but I'll be damned if I'll keep hanging around Bear Grass if it's going to keep on being like this. I'll go in the Army first."

"You don't mean that," Jimmy Joe said.

"You just wait and see," "Coon" said. "Hey, we got some beans that'll soon be ready for picking. How about letting me have twenty five dollars or so and I'll come up with something."

"All right, if we git paid enough to have twenty five dollars after paying for the baskets you can have it, seeing as how you're burning up. But I tell you one thing, if they's such a thing as having a mobile that will run, you can git yourself in more trouble in a minute than you can git out of in a lifetime. You'll find out something if you git some little gal knocked up and find a shotgun in your back put there by a mad daddy."

"Don't tell me all that shit Pa," Coon said with a disgusted look. "I'll bet anything I'm the spitting image of you when you were young, and if you'd say the truth you'd admit it." Jimmy Joe didn't answer.

"Another thing about it," Jimmy Joe said, "don't think you can go to town and git a part. You know they ain't making parts for civilian mobiles."

"Pa, if you know the right people, them things can be got too. Don't you know nothing?"

"And I reckon they are your best friends," Jimmy Joe said.

"Naw, but I know some people that know people that can do that."

"Well God bless you," Jimmy Joe said as he scratched at his crotch where red bugs were giving him a fit.

- - - - - - - -

The skies were filled with planes from the military bases scattered across eastern North Carolina. Training exercises were held regularly and where they had drawn a great deal of attention in the early days of the war they became a natural thing in the Tar Heel skies and people seldom watched unless a group of planes was flying in formation or they left trails of smoke in their path.

Mamas wrote to their sons in service, detailing the mundane things back home and love-hungry girls poured out their hearts to the boys that had left them suddenly, with promises to remain true. But youth is restless and absence didn't make the heart grow fonder. Too much was going on at home and the young became restless and many strayed.

A lot of boys and girls in love married before the men were sent overseas, and many of the boys tried to impregnate wives before leaving, hoping a baby would keep their wives true while they were away fighting.

Thousands of girls had babies while their men were overseas and the only thing the men could associate with the babies was the mating ritual. The women who weren't with their GIs in the states sweated through labor, screamed and beat their fists against the walls until birth was apparent and then the doctors placed a mask over their faces and dropped chloroform on the cloths so the pangs of actual birth were not felt. But that was not too far different from men still at home when babies were born. Having babies was woman's work and whether at home or in the hospital, men stayed out of the delivery room. Their greatest association with babies before birth was laying a hand on the woman's stomach and feeling the kicks of the baby and hearing the complaints of the expectant mother.

- - - - - - - -

Hobby was never called into service. He was examined and failed to pass. He was left at home while many of the more experienced doctors were inducted. Orthopedic surgeons were badly needed by the Army to repair GIs who had lost limbs or had mangled limbs as a result of action.

As Waldo Spence had predicted, Wilbert Lee was turned down and was classed 4-F by the draft board. A heart murmur was found upon examination and he carried a secret smile on his face as he left Fort Bragg. He whistled all the way back to Hallsborough on a chartered Greyhound bus.

- - - - - - - -

"Coon" Edwards managed somehow to get the old Chevrolet rolling, and his father was as proud as any member of the family when "Coon" would drive them to Hallsborough once in a while. And Hepzebiah, his mother, said she was shore glad she didn't have to ride on a durn wagon when she had to go to town. About the only time she went to town was in the fall of the year when she had to buy a few pieces of clothing for the young'uns to start to school with anyhow and to buy a bolt of nard homespun to make sheets and pillow cases and slips and things like that for the girls. And occasionally she had to make the boys BVDs when they didn't have any drawers and no money to buy them with.

And "Coon" had him a time on that old car. He'd get buddies from the store and they would ride all over Bear Grass and as far as Hallsborough cruising around if they could get up enough money for gas. It was a sight to see them with their felt hats on, turned up at the front, and their legs stuck out of the Chevrolet windows.

But "Coon" was disappointed with his conquests. Not many of the girls would have anything to do with him, mostly because their parents wouldn't let their girls go off with boys on a car. But "Coon" and the other boys told lies about their escapades. They'd get other boys' mouths watering with their tales about what they'd done the night before. "Coon's" dreams were still mostly of the wet variety.

- - - - - - - -

Quite a few girls from the Bear Grass area had left the farm. They had argued with the old folks until it seemed like there wasn't anything else to do but let them go, especially with a promise of sending money to them every week to help make ends meet. Heck, girls were becoming welders, riveters and all manner of things. And it wasn't like exposing yourself to everybody and making a spectacle of yourself. Women were wearing overalls and coveralls and climbing scaffolds and ladders and on machinery just like men. And they were raking in money and having fun on the side. They were learning the new dances that were coming out. Juke boxes were colorful and loud and every store boasted one. It wasn't unusual to see a group of girls and boys stop at a country store where the lights were bright and the music was blaring. The girls were learning to drink and the boys were trying to get them drunk.

"Boogie Woogie" was a popular song by Jimmy Dorsey and his band, and jitterbugging was the craze, and those boys and girls would have the place shaking while they scampered over the floor with the girls' skirts going up to their waists, in bobby socks and saddle shoes as they twisted over the floor. Heck, there was a home front even if there was a war going on.

- - - - - - - -

Clara Bell dreaded to tell Miss Callie. She had been working for her for seven years, since she was fourteen. Miss Callie had been a good friend and Clara Bell had dreamed big dreams while working at her house.

But things had changed and Clara Bell was caught up in it. She stopped at the clay hill and found a little bit of good clay. "Lawd!" she said to herself. "I'll miss this clay so bad I won't know what to do. Reckon I could git somebody to find me some and mail it to me. But naw, it would dry out and wouldn't be fitten to eat."

She stuck her head in the back door and called," Miss Callie," and she was soon at the door.

"I'se goin' to tell you the bad news right off the bat, Miss Callie" she said with a sigh and rolling those large brown eyes.

"What in the world Clara Bell?" Miss Callie said. "You sound like the world's coming to an end."

"I hates to tell you, Miss Callie, but I won't be working for you no more."

"Why," Miss Callie replied without too much concern.

"I'se goin' off to war too," Clara Bell said. "I mean I'se got me a job in a factory up Nawth and I'll be leaving Bear Grass soon."

"Well I'm glad you've found you a job," Miss Callie said, "and it'll pay a lot more money than you've been used to. I'm happy for you Clara Bell."

"Course I hates to leave you Miss Callie cause you've been mighty good to me. But this plant in Delaware that builds something for airplanes needs girls since they's a shortage of boys. And my Leroy's already been drafted and no telling when I'll see him again if I ever doos. Ain't nothing to stay around Bear Grass for. But that don't mean that I don't like Bear Grass. It's home Miss Callie and I don't know 'bout no other place. Ain't never been no futher than Raleigh and don't you know I'll be a mess way up in Delaware? Is it all the way across the country Miss Callie?"

"No, it's not very far," Miss Callie said, laughing. "Maybe a little over three hundred miles and it's three thousand miles across the country."

"Lawd! This sho is a big country ain't it?" Clara Bell said.

"What kind of work will you be doing?" Miss Callie asked.

"Welding or riveting or something lak dat. Something I ain't never done. But if them other gals can do it I can too. I'll be up on machinery and a good ways off the ground but I won't never scared when I straddled the tier poles in a backer barn. And I'll be wearing men's clothes for you knows it wouldn't never do for a girl to be way up high and men able to look up they's dresses." Clara Bell laughed loudly.

"I tell you this war has changed everything," Miss Callie said.

"It sho has," Clara Bell replied! "But they ain't been many of the hands that work on Mr. Wilbur's place drafted."

"We were able to get most of them deferred to carry on the farming operations," Miss Callie said.

"And I sees Mr. Philip is still around Miss Callie. I knows you are glad your boy hain't gone off to war." She called Philip Mr. now that he was grown up.

"We got Philip deferred to help with the farm too," Miss Callie said.

Clara Bell didn't say a word but she thought: I ain't never seen that white boy even in no field less he had a shotgun on his shoulder going hunting or a fishpole in his hand going down to the water to fish. Peace or war, some folks is able to git by and have it all. Others ain't got a chance.

"And have you heard that Minnie Mae Moore's gone off to war too, Miss Callie?"

"I thought she was at war wherever she was," Miss Callie said with a sneer.

"She's been in Hallsborough a good while," Clara Bell said. "But I heard she got herself cured of that bad disease and went on up the road to a factory job too. I doubts that she'll ever be back in Bear Grass."

"Well, we'll get along just fine without her," Miss Callie replied. Then it dawned on her that she'd really miss Clara Bell. As simple as she was she told her more news, especially gossip that usually turned out to be truth, than anyone in the community.

Clara Bell did the washing as she always did on Wednesday, and as always, looked to see if anybody was watching and smelled of the crotch of Philip's drawers. She did her other chores and scraped paint from Miss Callie's furniture for the last time. She told herself she was glad she was leaving if Miss Callie ever found out what she was doing.

When she finished her work, she came to Miss Callie and put her arms around her and there were tears in her eyes, "I loves you Miss Callie," she said as she patted her on the back. "You bees a good woman and I won't never forget you. I be sending you a Christmas card, hear?"

"That's kind of you Clara Bell," Miss Callie said as she pulled a dollar bill from her apron pocket and placed it in Clara Bell's hand. "I'll miss you but I'll get by. If I find somebody that I like and can trust, I'll let them work, but if I can't I'll just do it myself."

She watched Clara Bell as she walked leisurely down the road. "The war sure has changed things," she said to herself.

Chapter 47

A worldwide financial panic and economic depression began with the October 1929 U.S. stock market crash and the May 1931 failure of the Austrian credit-Anstalt. A credit crunch caused international bankruptcies and unemployment. By 1932 there were twelve million jobless in the U.S., five point six million in Germany, two point seven million in England.

Years of agitation by violent extremism was brought to a head by the Depression. Nazi leader Adolf Hitler was named chancellor by Germany's President Hindenburg in January 1933, and was given dictatorial powers by the Reichstag. By March, opposition parties were disbanded, strikes were banned and all aspects of cultural and religious life were brought under central government and Nazi party control and manipulated by sophisticated propaganda.

Under the Nuremberg Laws severe persecution of the Jews began in 1935. Many Jews, political opponents and others were sent to concentration camps at Dachau where untold numbers died or were killed. Hitler's expansionism began with the reincorporation of the Saar (1935), occupation of the Rhineland (March 1936), and the annexation of Austria (March 1938). At Munich in September 1938, an indecisive Britain and France sanctioned German dismemberment of Czechoslavakia.

In Russia, urbanization and education advanced in 1928. Rapid industrialization was achieved through successive five-year plans. Severe labor discipline was put into effect and there was forced labor. Industry was financed by a decline in living standards and exploitation of agriculture, which was almost totally collectivised by the early 1930s. Millions perished in a series of man-made disasters. Peasant land-owners were eliminated. There was a severe famine in 1932 and 1933. The Great Purge of 1936-1938 saw the suppression of nationalities and poor conditions in labor camps.

Italy's identification with the fascist bloc was sealed in entente with

Hungary and Austria and intervention with 50-75,000 troops in 1934. A pact with Germany and Japan was signed.

Repressive regimes fought for power in East Europe against liberals, socialists, communists, peasants and Nazis. In the destruction of Czechoslavakia, Hungary occupied Southern Slovakia in 1938 and 1939. There was a pro-Nazi regime in the rest of Slovakia. Other boundary disputes - Poland-Lithuania - Bulgaria-Yugoslavia - Romania-Hungary - doomed attempts to build joint fronts against Germany or Russia. Economic depression was severe.

After a period of liberalism in Japan, nativist militarists dominated the government with peasant support. Manchuria was seized in 1932, and a puppet state was set up by (Manchukuo). Adjacent Jehol (inner Mongolia) was occupied in 1933. China proper was invaded in July 1937. Large areas were conquered by October 1938.

In China communist forces left Kuomintang-besieged strongholds in the south in a long march in 1934-1935 to the North. The Kuomintang-besieged strongholds civil war was suspended in January 1937 in the face of threatening Japan.

In Europe, the Nazi-Soviet nonaggression pact in August 1939 freed Germany to attack Poland in September, 1939. Britain and France who had guaranteed Polish independence attacked Finland in November and took the Baltic states. Mobile German forces staged "blitzkrieg" attacks in April, May and June 1940 and conquered neutral Denmark, Norway and the low countries' forces and defeated them.

Russia's counterthrusts from 1941 to 1943 stopped the German advance with U.S. and British Lend-Lease aid, sustaining staggering casualties. The Russians drove the Axis from all of East Europe and the Balkans in the next two years.

The invasion of North Africa in November, Italy in 1943, and Normandy in June 1944 brought U.S. British, Free French and allied troops to Germany by spring 1945, resulting in Germany's surrender on May 7, 1945.

Japan occupied Indochina in September 1940, dominated Thailand in December 1941, as well as Pearl Harbor in December. Also attacked on the same date were Hong Kong and Malaya. Indonesia was attacked in January 1942. Burma was captured in March. The battle of Midway in June 1942 turned back the Japanese advance in the island-hopping battle of Guadalcanal.

All U.S. industries were geared to the war effort and rationing was, in fact, universal. Science was harnessed for the war effort, yielding such innovations as radar, jet planes and synthetic materials. Unscathed U.S. industry, partly staffed by women, helped decide the war.

The recovery was slow. It took time for a nation that had concentrated on winning the war and whose total output was directed mostly toward that goal to restructure its industrial output to supply a civilian population. But World War II was over. The U.S. was a winner and hope soared to the skies.

Chapter 48

T he alarm went off at 7 o'clock and Anne thought it was the telephone ringing. She reached for the receiver, then realized it was the clock. She pushed in the stem, yawned and looked at W.L. who was still sleeping soundly. Turning toward him, she said, "Time to get up, Buster."

W.L. quickly pulled the covers over his head, jerking as he pulled. "I'm not getting up," he said.

"You've got to get up W.L. It's a work day, remember?"

"To hell with a work day. I'm not going to that damn office today and maybe no other day. I've had it, Anne."

"What do you mean W.L.?"

"I mean I'm fed up with your old man and the whole damn bank. I've kissed asses until I'm through. You hear? Through."

"Tell me what's the matter W.L."

"I did some favors for some of my friends and your father has given me hell for weeks. He's accused me of everything you can think of and says I'm not bank material."

"Well, I'm sure Daddy would not accuse you falsely W.L. Daddy is a fair man and he has done a lot for you. You certainly weren't qualified to be a banker and you wouldn't have been except for the fact that you married me. Daddy didn't want me to suffer. You must not think hard of Daddy and I know he is doing what he thinks is best for you. Is that all he's been after you about?"

"Hell no. He says I'm a drunk and that I'm drinking on the job and all that shit." Anne noted that there were two fifths of liquor on the dresser.

"I see you're prepared for the day with all that whisky on the dresser. You know you're not supposed to bring whisky in the house before the children W.L. What has gotten into you?"

Their conversation had awakened Will. He came into the room and crawled into bed with them.

"What the hell?" W.L. asked.

"What's wrong with Daddy, Mama?" Will was crazy about his father.

"Just a bad day, baby," Anne said. "Go get dressed for school and get Beth out of bed too. I will get up and prepare breakfast."

W.L. went to the dresser, uncorked a bottle of whisky and took three swallows straight, then heaved and returned to the bed. His mind was in a state of confusion. He felt the whisky burning in his belly; then there was the light sensation as the alcohol coursed through his body. He had made up his mind what he was going to do but it wasn't going to be as easy to carry out as it had been in planning. The fight with Anne would be the worst thing. He tried to blot out of his mind what the effect would be on Will and Beth. He'd take care of that later.

Anne sent Beth to tell W.L. to get ready for breakfast. Beth ran to the bed and jerked the covers off and W.L. became angry. He grabbed Beth and struck her on her back and she screamed. "What in the hell are you doing girl?" he roared, as Anne and Will ran into the room.

"Daddy beat me," Beth said, crying hard now.

"I didn't hurt the little bitch," W.L. said. "She came in here and jerked the covers off of me. She is becoming a pest."

Anne took Beth in her arms and tried to console her. But Beth was sobbing so hard it was almost impossible for her to catch her breath. "Daddy's drinking Mother. I smelled it on his breath."

"Daddy, what's the matter?" Will asked with tears in his eyes. "What has happened to you? Don't you love us anymore?"

Things were beginning to close in on W.L. He couldn't think straight. Something had to give. "Get the hell out of here, all of you," he said in a loud voice. "I've had it with the old man. I've had it with everybody, including all of you. Do you hear? I'm fed up with the whole cock-eyed world and I'm getting out of this God-forsaken place. There ain't no repenting for me. If there is a God He wouldn't hear nothing I had to say and I don't want to hear anybody's mouths either.

"As for your mother and father, I've always been scum to them and they've hated my guts every day I've been in the family. I really tried to like them too. I tried to kowtow to them and fit myself into a mold they created and one that I didn't fit into. And you, miss high and mighty Anne, I tried to be the big-shot you wanted me to be. And God knows I wanted to be a big shot, but I wanted it my way and on my own terms. I didn't want to be a new creation of the mighty banking family." He went over to the dresser and took another long swill from the bottle, grinning as the whisky went into his stomach, then wiped his face with the back of his hand.

"Youall thought you had me by the balls," W.L. continued. "Everything was cut and dried forevermore. I would work my ass off for the bank and bring the paycheck to my lovely wife and she would dispense it as she saw fit. The children would be brought up properly and old W.L. would be their pawn. But I've got news for you, Miss Anne. I'm getting the hell out of here and out of your life this day. You can kiss me goodbye, forever. I'm off for a new life. I'm leaving you and your mighty father to work out all the details about your future and the children's. And yes, I do love the children but I don't feel like I've ever had a chance to be their father. You and your parents have dictated their lives."

"You're being so unfair W.L.," Anne argued. "It is true that all of us have tried to give you all the advantages you didn't have and to make you a responsible man and a leader in the community. But all that we did is what you yourself had dreamed about all your life. Daddy gave you a responsible job and he provided a comfortable home for us, and it wasn't a handout. He bought the house and allowed us to repay him with no interest. Because of your position you were invited to join the various Hallsborough clubs and you became well-known and don't tell me you weren't happy in that role. Nobody loves to be noticed more than you. You were the same way in high school. You hated a sharecropper's image and my family erased that image. You learned manners and how to speak correctly and you were able to have nice clothes and you are a handsome man, W.L. No man around can match your looks. But somehow, it hurt you rather than helped. You flaunted it before the world and played the part of God. You flirted with all the good-looking women whenever you were in their presence and I don't know what else you have done, but it's plenty, I'm sure."

W.L. had taken the third drink from the bottle by now, and his eyes were becoming glassy. He was able to say anything he felt like saying.

"You're a real bitch, Anne. I mean a first-class bitch. To think that I loved you like a man is supposed to love a woman and how you've turned out. I don't know what I ever saw in those blue eyes and that lovely face of yours. It looks like the face of a devil now."

Anne and the children were crying now with all thoughts of school forgotten and their world falling apart.

"It's whisky talking, W.L." Anne said. "You don't mean what you're saying."

W.L. was slurring his words now. "You—'re wrr-ong, Anne. I'm s-s-s-ay-ing noow wh-a-t I could—'nt say sober. You kn-n-o-w h-h-how it is. A dru-n-k man's wor-ds are a so-o-ber man's thou-u-gh-t-s."

"Where are you going, W.L.?"

"None of your damn business."

"What will you do?"

"I don't care what I do. I don't care if I die. I don't care, period."

"Please don't talk like this W.L. You are destroying me and the children. We love you, W.L. and we can work everything out. I can't stand for you to leave like this."

"It's too late for that kind of talk now, Anne. To-o, lat-e, to-o lat-e, to-o late."

"Is anyone else involved, W.L.?"

"What do you-u mean-n is any-o-ne else in-v-olved? Do you mean a woman? Yes, by golly, there is. And you'd never guess in a hundred years who it is."

"Am I supposed to guess?"

"Hell, no. That's for me to know and you to find out if you can."

"Then that's the reason for all the accusations?"

W.L. had been sitting on the side of the bed, but he rose, took another drink and started pulling on his clothes.

"Aren't you going to take a bath, W.L.?"

"No. I'll stop somewhere on the road and get a room and take a shower. I want to get the hell out of here before I do something foolish."

"You sound threatening W.L."

"Whatever you say."

"It's a pity you aren't more like your half-brother. Hobby is as different from you as night and day."

"Don't bring up that son of a bitch to me, Anne. I hate his guts and you know it and to bring his name up is to get hell in me in an instant."

"I was just making comparisons," Anne said.

"I don't know why in the hell our blood relationship was not kept secret after all those years," W.L. said. "It was always bad enough with the little crippled bastard at best, and I reckon if I had known he was my half brother when we were little I'd have killed the little wimp. He went around looking up to me like he thought I was God and kept himself as close to me as he could get as long as he was in Bear Grass. I began to feel like I was crippled myself. I have never been happier about anything than when they took his little ass off to Tennessee."

"You were jealous W.L. That was your problem."

"Who wouldn't be jealous the way everybody treated Hobby? 'Look at his smile,' they'd say and, 'ain't he the cute one, ' and 'he's pretty enough to be a girl.' "They nauseated me and caused me to hate him more. I was always in competition with Hobby. I had the looks and a sound body, too, and I had everything over Hobby, but nobody seemed to notice."

"You were spoiled, W.L.,"Anne said. "Your mother ruined you from the womb. She tried to make out of you something you were not and she preached your superiority to you as long as you were at home. You just never grew up."

"Well, I'm growing up now. I'm getting the hell out of here. Where is my whisky? You've taken it off the dresser haven't you?"

"You don't need any more whisky W.L. You need to lie down and sleep it off before you do anything."

W.L. got dressed and combed his hair, but he had the look of a wild man. His eyes were bloodshot and his face flushed. He went into the bedroom and began putting things into a suitcase and pulling his suits off the racks.

"I'll help you," Anne said.

"I don't need any help."

Will and Beth had been playing in the yard, happy to be out of school. The leaves on the maple trees in the front yard were beginning to show tints of orange and some had fallen. They had yard rakes pretending to be getting up the leaves but only succeeding in moving them about. A squirrel dashing up an oak tree on the edge of the yard caught their attention. They saw W.L. coming out of the house with one arm filled with clothes and the big suitcase and they ran to him.

"You aren't really leaving are you Daddy?" Will asked, grabbing W.L. by the thigh. Beth joined Will and they pulled him down and kissed him and begged him not to leave, but he paid them little attention. "I'll see you one of these days," he said as he opened the door of the Chevrolet. "Daddy's got places to go and things to do. But you be good, you hear?"

W.L. cranked the car and raced the motor and backed out of the garage. He drove slowly down the hill to the street, entered and mashed on the gas and the tires screeched as the gas exploded in the engine.

Anne ran out immediately after W.L. left. "Has he already gone?" she asked, although a look in the garage told her he was on his way. She had looked for his pistol in the closet where he always kept it, but it wasn't there.

She ran to the house and called Hallsborough First National Bank and asked for her father. When he answered the phone Anne said, "He's gone Daddy, clothes and all."

"What do you mean?"

"I mean W.L. has left and said he wouldn't be back. We are torn all to pieces and the children didn't even go to school. It's been awful, and W.L. is almost drunk. I'm afraid for him to be on the highway and do you know what else Daddy? He has his pistol with him. I've searched the house and it isn't here."

"Keep your composure, my dear," her father said. "This could be the best thing that's happened to you since you married him. He's no good honey, and you know it, although I've tried not to throw it up in your face. W.L. has plenty of sense but he doesn't know how to use it. He's too self-centered to apply his knowledge to the workplace. He has been a bum banker from the start and I'd have thrown him out after the first month if it hadn't been for you. And of course your mother and I worship the children and we could never let you or them down. And don't you worry Anne. Everything will be all right. Your mother and I will be by after the bank closes."

"Thank you Daddy," Anne said. "I just don't know what has happened to W.L. and I wonder whether we have had something to do with what has happened.

"Maybe if we had shown more faith in him he would have done a better job than he has. There's no denying that all of us felt superior to W.L. I wonder if that is simply because he was a sharecropper? If that's the case I don't know why we should have felt that way for there are many people who grew up as sharecroppers that are doing a fine job in the business world. I think maybe we stereotyped them and placed all of them in the same category.

"There were a lot of fine boys and girls that went to Hallsborough High that came from the farm. I really feel sorry for W.L. Daddy and I'm afraid of what he might do in such a frame of mind. You can't imagine how he was this morning - like a wild beast with no reasoning power. I hope nothing happens to him."

"Just hold on darling, and we'll be by later."

"Bye Daddy."

The children came in and sat beside Anne. "Will Daddy be home tonight?" Beth asked.

"I don't know, darling. I hope so." Beth began to cry and Will put his arm around Beth and both of them leaned toward Anne. Will said, "God, please let Daddy come home, and protect him. He's not bad, God."

Once W.L. was gone, Anne's image of him changed immediately. For a long time she had looked at her husband negatively. He had changed so much from the lover he had been during their courtship and the first years of their marriage. He was the most popular boy at Hallsborough High and could have had the pick of most any of the girls, but he had chosen her. With brown, wavy hair and soft brown eyes and a sensuous mouth and narrow face, he was the kind of boy girls wanted to cuddle. He had charm, although she often wondered how this came about. He knew how to flatter a girl and he smiled and teased them and was the center of attention at parties.

Anne had considered herself lucky to have won him over all the other girls at school. She was always jealous of him and of the attention he received from her friends. W.L. was a man girls thought of as being experienced with women, and that only added to his charms. Anne wanted him to herself and their early marriage had been paradise.

He was so handsome and charming and a perfect lover, she thought she was the luckiest girl in the world. She was happy when she became pregnant. W.L. would grow with the bank and over the years he would become one of the pillars of the community. The future was bright. He proved to be a devoted father and showered a lot of love on the children and even helped her around the house sometimes.

That went on until Beth was two. But Anne was slow to take notice and only reviewing it now in retrospect was she able to see it completely. W.L. was often late coming in at night, giving the excuse that he had been at bank meetings or that he had to work late at the office. He was less interested in making love and often gave excuses. She hadn't at the time associated this with philandering.

He was as handsome as ever and a meticulous dresser, but it never dawned on her that he might be dressing for other women. He spent a lot of time in the bathroom primping and washing and brushing his hair but she considered this a good trait. Only now did she realize that he was doing all these things for someone else.

And she couldn't pinpoint the time when she realized that he was drinking to excess. He would bring bottles of whisky home but they would be concealed in a manner so the children wouldn't know what they were and were stored in a cabinet far out of their reach. He would often become a little tipsy before retiring, and it was at those times that he took more interest in love-making, although the alcohol had a negative effect and he couldn't perform sometimes. This angered him and he would take it out on Anne.

She remembered the junior-senior prom and how they danced the night away and the moonlit ride afterward and sitting on the banks of the pond and watching the reflection of the moon in the waters and the gentle ripple as the miniature waves came to shore. She remembered the movies and how they kissed in the balcony and ate popcorn and drank Coca Colas. She remembered all the rides through the country, sometimes going out to Bear Grass and riding up and down the roads, letting people see W.L. with his own car. Abie had saved money from eggs and butter and by selling vegetables in summer had bought W.L. an old Model A Ford.

They had parked in secluded places and W.L. had pleaded with her to go all the way; that they were engaged and that was practically married, and it had almost happened on several occasions. His hands were everywhere and they often touched her breasts. The touch of his mouth on her nipples was almost more than she could bear, but she had held out and remained a virgin on their wedding night. W.L. would become so excited during their petting she had seen wet spots on his pants and had felt his maleness. She loved him so much she wanted to give herself to him and only because of her upbringing was she able to put off sex until they were married.

All of it seemed a world away now.

Meanwhile, W.L. was out on the highway and driving too fast. He was anxious to reach his destination. There was a score to settle and he wouldn't be able to think straight until the mission was carried out. It was a gamble in which he was aware he could be the loser, but it didn't matter about him if everything else was resolved. If he were the winner, there was a bright future ahead. If it failed blood would be shed. He was willing to take that gamble.

He stopped in a small town and bought some cartridges at a hardware store. He carefully checked the caliber of the gun before going to the store, to be sure he had the right bullets.

When he returned to the car he took the pistol from the glove compartment, held it down so it couldn't be seen publicly and loaded the gun with four cartridges, then returned it to the glove compartment.

It had gone on too long. Everything has a beginning and an ending, W.L. reasoned. To drag things out forever gives no solution and no hope.

As he drove farther across state he noticed more color in the trees on the hills. He remembered the days when he had hunted in the marshes and near the pond and how the foliage had looked. He thought about the joy of hunting rabbits, squirrels and birds, and even recalled the nights he and the other boys had gone coon hunting. He remembered the piercing eyes of 'possums when they were looking into a bright light. The cries of the owls and the song of the whippoorwills rang in his ears. Those were happy days, he realized now. Everything about his life had changed since those days.

W.L. was cold sober now. The effects of the whisky were gone and he felt the need of another drink, but realized this was not the time to imbibe. He needed a clear mind to make the long drive. He wouldn't be able to reach his destination today, but he had planned it this way. Morning would be the best time for the confrontation. So when the sun was about an hour from setting, he stopped in a little town and noted the small hotel on the main street. He noticed people going in and out of the stores and walking down the streets. A young boy and girl were walking hand in hand and he remembered the days when he had done the same thing. Although still a young man, he thought of himself as being ancient. There was no youth left. Nothing but a consuming passion. He was heading for an inevitable destiny over which he had no control. There could be no turning back, no matter how hard he might try.

He checked into the hotel, carrying his bag. He had taken the pistol from the car and placed it inside his coat pocket. His pistol was his companion.

He placed his suitcase on a table, hung his suits in the closet and noted they were wrinkled. He removed his shorts, stripped off and took a leisurely shower and dressed. This made him feel better and he realized he was hungry. He went to the dining room and ordered a full meal. It was the first food he had consumed all day. But he was nervous and had a jumpy feeling inside. He couldn't clear his mind.

Why did it have to be such a consuming passion? he thought. Was it because of his jealousy of Hobby? It only came to him in full clarity after Hobby and Robyn were married. Robyn had been nothing more than a worrisome girl when she lived in Bear Grass. There had been nothing to distinguish her from the other girls. She had gone around with stringy hair during the week and had worn ragged dresses with the waist unraveled at times or the hem of her dress hanging. She had been a nuisance. He remembered so well the day he had pulled up the stobs around hers and Arlene's playhouse and how angry Robyn had become. He had ignored both girls completely until Robyn's skirt came up and he saw the blood on her underpants. That had caused him to feel a sensation in his groins for a moment, but he had passed that off also. But all that was before the transformation. He didn't see Robyn Finch for years after she moved to Jones County and had forgotten the entire family. He had classified them with all other sharecroppers and although he was one of them, he didn't think of himself in the same light.

As a matter of fact, he hadn't seen Robyn since they left Bear Grass until the day she and Hobby were married at Whispering Pines Church. And he couldn't believe his eyes. A genuine beauty stood before the altar dressed in white with lace flowing around her and the loveliest face he had ever seen. She looked like no less than an angel. And the strange eyes he suddenly recalled had become pools of mystery that he wanted to penetrate to know their secrets. He realized when he saw Robyn in her wedding gown she had been the only person he had ever really loved. And Hobby had beaten him again. It infuriated him that she would be sleeping with his half-brother and that Hobby, not he, had become the father of their children.

And there had been a transformation in Hobby also. The cripple had had a miracle performed on him and he stood straight and had become a handsome man with blond hair and the same steel-blue eyes he remembered from childhood.

In every respect, Hobby towered over him, even in stature. Now that his leg was straight he stood a good two inches taller, and where W.L. had acquired a beer belly that caused his buttons to pucker when he buttoned his shirts, Hobby was lean and muscular.

It was oppressive in the hotel room. The little fan on the table near his bed oscillated slowly, making a squeaking sound as it made its half-circle. He peeped out the window and hardly nobody was on the streets. One of many little hick places that rolled up the sidewalks at sunset, he told himself. He had always said that about Hallsborough. He picked up the phone and called for a bell hop.

"Yas suh," the young black man said.

"Any whisky around here Big Boy?"

"Lawd man, you knows we got plenty of good whisky, made in the hills Mister. Women too, if you need one."

"Ain't in the mood for that," W.L. replied. "I just need some more liquor sliding down my throat tonight. Tomorrow's when the woman enters the picture, know what I mean?"

"Yas suh," the bell hop replied. "They's a time for that, depending on how that male mind works."

"Bring me a fifth," W.L. said. "Got to clear my mind."

He uncorked the bottle and took a long swill, heaving and burning as if his esophagus were raw as the whisky went down. "Everything's gone to hell and I'm losing touch. My God! Have I got the monkeys? Why am I trembling all over and scared to look out the window and feeling like somebody's watching me? I feel like some crazy son of a bitch sitting here like this."

The whisky was taking effect, and with the amount he had already consumed during the day, it didn't take long for him to fall over on the bed and pass out.

He was either dreaming or having a nightmare. The scene was filled with erotica. There were voluptuous breasts towering over him and panties with flecks of blood showing and he reached out, but nothing was there. He saw a black figure in the distance and Roscoe came to mind. What would Roscoe be doing at such a place? Somehow old Roscoe was always around when such situations arose. Wilbur Stroud stood over him, naked with his hairy body becoming some monster in his mind. Miss Callie was behind him, calling him to come home, pleading with him to put his clothes on and stop acting like a wild man. Wilbur was getting ready to urinate on him and he tried to turn away, but was held captive by some unknown force.

From afar, he saw his mother running toward him, hollering, "Wilbert Lee honey, don't do it. In the name of God, don't do it. You're my baby, Wilbert Lee and you know that. You were always my baby. I've protected you and nobody ever loved you like me. You're back in my womb, Wilbert Lee, where I can always protect you. It's all right about your family. Just you and me count, honey."

"Piss on you!" Wilbert Lee screamed. "You ruined my life and now you are intimidating me in death. You're the devil, old lady. It's because of you I got mixed up with Hobby Turnage. You didn't look after the old man like you ought to or he wouldn't have gone out looking for pig meat."

"Don't say these ugly things to me Wilbert Lee," his mother said as she started running from him. "God help him," he heard her say as she ran down a hill as dark smoke began to rise in the distance.

"She's already in hell," he said as the picture changed to Bear Grass and back to boyhood. It was peaceful and he saw buzzards soaring overhead and the forests below. He was walking with Philip Stroud toward Hallsborough. The golden leaves of fall had become brown and were blowing in the wind, but there was still subtle color around him.

A few leaves still clung to the trees and a brilliant red speck was evident at times, with mostly tans and browns and shades of gray under foot. Philip had outsmarted his old man and they were on their way to town to explore the streets, looking for mischief. He was sixteen and Philip seventeen and they were ready for anything from fighting to "messing around." The skies were blue, the air cool, and life was a paradise. But suddenly there was a billowing storm before him and the scene exploded into terror.

"Why am I experiencing all this terror?" he asked himself. "What am I doing in such a place? I'm W.L. Turner, a respected man back home with a wife and two lovely children. You're the devil, that's who you are. You are tormenting me. I'm no saint, God knows, but I don't deserve this. You're paying me back for everything I've ever done, ain't you? You're getting even because I called Otto Pell a son of a bitch, a big shot in the church that got tangled up with poon tang and gave up God for the same things many men give up God for, family and everything else.

"It's all mixed up with religion. I used to hear the preachers telling about the wages of sin and I laughed in their faces. I heard 'em say God's spirit didn't always strive with man. They'd say 'tonight might be your last chance to come to Christ' and I defied them. Just because I was an atheist and didn't think there was a God was no reason to be treated this way, was it? All of us have a right to our opinions, don't we? But I heard the preachers say 'There is a way that seems right to man, but the end thereof is death.'

"Oh, no, I'm not dying. I'm just preparing to live. Everything is before me. I will begin a new life and I'll change my name and go to a place where nobody knows me and we will build a love nest just like two little birds and everything will be fine. There'll be no more sharecropper shanties and trying to make ends meet working to avoid the ignorant men and women that are always getting up close to me when they see me. I reckon they think because I got out of that shanty I lived in and away from my holy-rolling mama and my screwing-around daddy I got all of it out of my system.

"Well, I didn't. I'm scum to people that matter. They look at me like I'm tainted; that I stink and that I'm too ignorant to associate with them. I hate poor folks. They do stink. How could they not stink when they rub over their nasty bodies with a cloth saturated with a little bit of water and of all things, lye soap most of the time. They ain't even got the money to buy a cake of sweet soap. Their rusty asses don't ever get clean. They wear their drawers for a whole week and anybody knows that human bodies get nasty and the smell is seeping into the underwear. Oh my God, I'm crazy for talking like this."

Then a larger-than-life figure stood before him with his finger pointing directly at his eyes. "I'm watching," the figure said.

He tried to move, to overcome the horror he was experiencing. He strained his body and felt his muscles as they gradually gave him momentum. "I can't stand this anymore," he said as he gradually opened his eyes. He was covered with sweat and more afraid than he'd ever been in his life. What he had experienced were the tortures of hell. He didn't know where he was or why he was there. Reality seemed almost as bad as the nightmare.

Then he remembered. But his mind was still tortured and he told himself he had gone beyond any hope of reforming. It was too late. Too many things had had their impact on him. He had picked up a fairly good vocabulary since he had been in the banking business and he told himself he was schizophrenic; that he had been paranoid since he was a boy; that all the good things that might have come his way had been prohibited by something in his brain that didn't act in the normal manner. He couldn't accept second best at anything. He had excelled in math at Hallsborough High because of that fact. He had made the honor roll most years in school because he couldn't bear to be considered ignorant. He had to try harder to win the prettiest girls in school, to date them and have them always around him as an ego builder. He could no more help that than he could breathing. All those things were absolutely essential to his survival.

He rose from the bed and noted that all the covers were on the floor. Even the case was off the pillow and his car keys that he had placed on the bedside table were lying ten feet away on the floor. But none of this deterred him from his mission. Dawn was breaking over the little town when he looked out the window with a light fog hanging like a cloud over the buildings. A few lights were on in the homes and the street men were collecting the garbage.

"I meet my destiny today," he told himself. He never doubted that he would be able to convince Robyn that their future was linked together by an irreversible force that had been working since their births to bring them together in perfect harmony. Whatever had happened between her and Hobby was only an interlude without any real meaning, just as his and Anne's lives had been joined by marriage but without real substance to withstand the ravages of time. It was destiny at work without any volition on their part.

Robyn could never have really loved Hobby. She had gained her impression of him as a little child and he projected no real male image and even before the forces of nature begin to have their effect on children to make them individuals with individual sexual identities. Something happened in Robyn's mind to cause her to see the crippled Hobby in a different light.

On the other hand, Wilbert Lee had been in puberty before Robyn left the Bear Grass area. His voice was changing. He was growing taller. His body was becoming hairy and he had taken his father's razor and raked across his lips where heavy down was growing. He had also cut his upper lip and the other boys teased him and he replied that they were just jealous because he was becoming a man.

And he daydreamed about Robyn's bloomers with the little flecks of blood on them. He was heavy into masturbation by now and he fantasized about her, satisfying himself momentarily, but the feeling returned over and over and Robyn became his sexual partner two or three times a day. He had heard that masturbation would drive a person crazy and that it was a terrible habit, and this worried him, for it gave him a great sense of pleasure, and he knew even then that he would never be able to forgo the habit. It had too great a hold on him.

He decided he couldn't drink any more whisky, for he was about to begin the end of his mission. Only a few hours from now he would be with his Robyn and by nightfall they would be headed for destinations unknown and there would be only peace and love and a safe haven from the world. Their families would forget in time and go on with their lives. Few people dared to do what he was doing. To him it was a tribute to be able to dare; to relieve himself from situations that brought grief and unhappiness.

Then he had his doubts. "I am as crazy as hell," he said to himself. "I have gone off the deep end and there is no way I'll be able to convince Robyn to go away with me. She has two children, just as I have, and she doesn't have the feeling about life that I have. She's no doubt in love with Hobby, no matter how distasteful it sounds to me. I don't know where I got all my crazy notions; whether from old lady Abie or old man Gant. Must have come from the old lady, since my blood kin with Hobby is through the old man. He laughed aloud, "Old lady Abie sure cooked old man Gant's goose when she learned he had been fooling around with Pearl Turnage. He hasn't had any since."

Time was passing and W.L. dressed, placed his clothes in the suitcase, checking the room to see if he had left anything. Then he took the bag and walked downstairs and checked out of the hotel. He drove to the service station across the street and filled the gasoline tank and had the oil and radiator checked. "Check the tires too," he told the attendant, then added, "how far to Spring Lake?"

"'Bout sixty miles," the attendant replied. "Straight on down the highway."

Cows were grazing peacefully in the meadows as he drove along the highway. People were gathering hay and haybalers were in the fields. W.L. was not very observant of nature, but the brilliant foliage caught his eyes as he drove along. He remembered the color on the ridges in Bear Grass but he didn't like the idea of ever returning to the rural area where he was bred and born.

Forty miles to go and W.L. was becoming fidgety. He felt a twitch in his cheeks and decided he would have to have another drink to steady his nerves before reaching Spring Lake. He fumbled in the glove compartment and found the bottle, uncorked it and listened as the alcohol entered his mouth, burning as it touched his throat. He had been driving on relatively flat terrain, but hills were beginning to appear and in the distance he could see the top of low mountain ranges. The sun was shining brightly but in the distance there was a haze. He'd have to be careful as the elevation rose and the roads became more winding and treacherous. He wasn't used to mountain driving.

What were Will and Beth doing at this moment? Were they in school as if nothing had happened? What had Anne done besides calling her father and crying on his shoulder? Somehow, he wasn't able to associate any of them with his life anymore. He had carefully worked them out over a period of time. He convinced himself they really didn't matter; that just by being Anne's husband and Will and Beth's father was no reason he should feel a lifetime responsibility toward them. Sure, there was the biological factor, but that was true in every aspect of life from the lowest forms to the highest - an egg and a sperm coming together to form a new life - mother nature at work regardless of what forms of life.

A feeling of euphoria settled over him as he neared his destination. He'd have to get a map of the town and find out how to get to the hospital. He reasoned that Hobby and Robyn would be living near the hospital since Hobby spent a lot of his time there. He visualized their home. Robyn would have everything in order with crisp curtains at the windows and bright colors to bring cheerfulness to the rooms. As beautiful as she had become as a woman she wouldn't have her home furnished like the simple place he remembered the Finch place as being. He could see the flowered oilcloth on the table along with the vinegar cruet, the salt and pepper shakers, the jar of hot pepper and the white cloth placed over the table to keep the flies away when it was not in use.

Then there was the sign showing the city limits of Spring Lake, Tennessee, population 5,000. It was a sleepy looking little town, reminiscent of almost any town any place. Trees in the yards were a riot of color with gold and orange predominating from the many maples that shaded bungalow-type homes along the avenues.

He stopped at a filling station and got a map of the town. He located the hospital on the map and turned left at the next stop sign and was soon on the hospital grounds. He had found Robyn's street address in the telephone directory - 119 Chestnut - and he had no trouble finding the street. He stopped at a service station, went to the restroom and took another swill of whisky and hurried back to the car. The time had arrived. There was no more planning. He would soon know his fate.

It was a small cottage at the edge of the hospital grounds and the only house visible since there were many trees and a small stream separating the house from the others. He noted a little bridge spanning the stream and a table and a few chairs sitting under a sycamore tree near the water.

He was shaking as he knocked on the door. It seemed a long time before there was an answer.

"Who is it?" Robyn said.

"Wilbert Lee Turner."

The door opened and Robyn looked at W.L. "What on earth are you doing in Tennessee?" she asked.

"To see you, of course," W.L. replied.

"Come in," Robyn said, all the while observing W.L. and realizing that something was wrong. He didn't look the same. He didn't act the same. It had been a long time since she had seen him, and he wasn't the Wilbert Lee she remembered.

"Seriously, what are you doing in Spring Lake?" Robyn asked. "I'd have thought you would have to work unless you are on vacation and in that event you would have your family with you. What is this all about, Wilbert Lee?"

"Don't you know Robyn?" W.L. asked. "How could you not know? I know that you feel as I do. You see, Robyn, I'm in love with you, completely, uncontrollably. We were destined for each other and whatever has happened was a pure coincidence. I've been in love with you since the first time I saw you. I just wasn't aware of it. In my little-boy days I didn't have the reasoning power to determine what love was. I think I thought of love as hate in those days. I know there was a time when I felt a kind of hatred for you and Arlene and all the other girls. I thought I was superior to you..."

Robyn was sitting in a chair with her arms resting on the dinette table in the kitchen. She rose and started toward the telephone.

"No Robyn," W.L. said. "You can't call Hobby." He rose and took the telephone from her hand and replaced it on the cradle.

"You're talking foolish W.L.," Robyn said. "You're not yourself W.L. and I'm afraid of you. Have you been drinking? Your eyes are all red and bloodshot and there's a funny look in your eyes."

"Don't be afraid my darling," W.L. said. "We can begin a life of paradise today. I've severed all ties back home, Robyn. I've put everything out of my life that has happened before today. This is a new beginning for both of us."

Robyn was crying and drying her tears on the corner of the tablecloth. "Something has happened to your mind. W.L. Please listen to me. You need to go over to the hospital and have yourself admitted and get straightened out. Let me call Hobby and they can have a room ready for you by the time we get there. I'm pregnant W.L. and what you are doing to me could cause me to lose my precious baby. You don't want to be guilty of that, do you?"

"Trust me," W.L. said. "If you only listen to me no harm will come to you. You aren't thinking things out, Robyn. You're not seeing it as I am. But I know that it was me you were in love with all the time you were going with Hobby, and even marrying him for God's sake, and having his babies.

"How could you have done such a thing? You knew Hobby as a little boy and you know there was nothing to attract your attention to him. He was always smiling but all of us just thought of him as a little cripple, some kind of dwarf if you will, in his stooped frame. He didn't represent masculinity, and you can't say that about me. And heaven help the day when I learned he was my half-brother. I don't have to tell you that I always hated the little bastard, and I didn't even know what hate was until after I learned about the old man's philandering.

"I can't stand for you and Hobby to be together a day longer Robyn. I love you with every beat of my heart. You are the only thing in life that matters to me. It has been that way since the day I saw you walk down the aisle at Whispering Pines Church and gave yourself to that pale half-brother of mine. I detested the thought of you and him making love. I was consumed with jealousy. And no matter how much I despised Hobby, he has always looked up to me. He tried to compete with me but I was competing with him in the community. There were always kind words for Hobby but I was some kind of childish son of a bitch to most people in the community. They always said Ma did it to me, and maybe she did. At least she made me feel like somebody rather than a red-neck."

"Please let me call Hobby," Robyn pleaded, but W.L. stood whenever she attempted to reach the telephone.

Robyn could see people working on the hospital grounds and she wanted to raise the window and yell as loudly as she could, but she was deathly afraid of W.L. He was totally insane and drunk as well. The telephone rang one time but W.L. would not let her answer. It would be Hobby calling, as he usually did about midmorning when his work permitted. He would think she was working in the yard perhaps.

"I want you Robyn," W.L. slurred. "I want all of you. You say you are pregnant, but we don't need that child. We can find someone to perform an abortion once we are away from here. I don't want us to start a new life with reminders of the past rising up before us. I will give you a baby, or many babies and they will be that new beginning I'm talking about and something to grow with. Yours and my children just happened. They'll have a father and a mother to look after them. Maybe Hobby and Anne will marry," he said laughing, "and live happily ever afterward."

"You don't know what you are talking about W.L.," Robyn said. "In your deranged state you are saying things that don't make any sense. We can't forget the past nor our obligations to society. If you will lie down for a while and get some sleep maybe you'll see things clearer."

"Don't give me that shit," W.L. replied. "You're beginning to sound like Anne and I can't stomach that. I love you Robyn. You are my sun and my moon and the stars and the sky to me. I think of you every moment, when I'm at work or at play. It has been you with me every day since you were married. All my erotic fantasies are with you. Anne hasn't existed since that day. I am possessed with you as if you had bewitched me. You are Eve, the mother of the human race."

There were beds of mums in the back yard - purple, yellow and white - and they glistened in the morning sunshine. Squirrels ran up and down the oak trees but as Robyn observed them from the kitchen window they were in another world, so close yet so far away. She thought: If I make a move he may attack me but I will be as well off that way or maybe better than staying here. But I can't risk losing my baby. And if something should happen to John and Heidi I couldn't stand that. If Hobby were to come home W.L. would confront him. Still, she had to do something. She rose and started toward the bedroom door, passing W.L. as she stepped swiftly. He stood up and suddenly a gun appeared in his hand. My God, she thought, he's going to kill me.

"Get back over there," W.L. said with a roughness in his voice. "I mean business Robyn, so don't keep crossing me."

"If I promised to leave with you would you let me write a note to Hobby and the children?" she asked, hoping she would somehow be able to get through this dangerous situation without harm.

"No notes," W.L. said. "That wouldn't be breaking all ties and I don't want anything left. I want us to vanish from the face of the earth as far as our families and acquaintenances are concerned. It can't be any other way Robyn. Can't you see that?"

"I can see that you're trying to bend me to your will without any consideration of my feelings. Wilbert Lee, I don't love you. I never loved you. How could I have loved you when you were always teasing and tearing up our playhouses and making fun of all girls in general? All the things that you could have been you were not, not even as a boy. You were a bully then, just as you are now." Her anger was rising up and she had to speak out.

"You don't understand Robyn," W.L. said, his face twitching and his eyes showing that strange look. "This is for keeps, Robyn. We can't go on like this. I either take you with me today or our blood will spill on this spot and we will be together in another life. Come up to me Robyn. I want to touch your flesh, to know you're real."

Robyn hesitated and W.L. took the gun and rubbed it against her breast. "Please, Wilbert Lee, don't defile me," she said as tears spilled down her face. But he had taken his hand and ripped the neckline of her dress and one of her breasts was exposed, firm as a result of pregnancy and with sensitive, red nipples. He took one in his fingers and pressed it until she cried out. "Please Wilbert Lee, think about our past. This is so far from what we were taught and so different from the life we have known it's like being in another world. We have been simple, farm people, poor and with little to guide us except principles taught to us by our parents and the church. This goes against everything we have been taught and you're hurting me." She attempted to pull away.

"If you only knew the depth of my love for you, you would welcome the touch of my hand," W.L. said. "You would want all of me right this instant. We would be in each other's arms this moment, oblivious to the rest of the world. I am consumed with you, my love and I will be the prince of your life if you'll only let me. I can't stand it without you, Robyn. Come with me and let's relive all our childhood and our adult life together. We'll make amends for everything that has gone before. We'll explore the fields and the woods again and listen to the birds sing and wade in the cool waters and swing from the wild grapevines and we'll rest in the meadows where we once ran and I'll love you with all my heart and you will respond likewise. That's the world I want for us, Robyn. That's the only world there is left for us."

I'm going to die this day, Robyn thought. I'm going to die at the hand of a boy I grew up with, whose house I visited, whose parents I knew well. I can't believe what I am experiencing. How could a person have become like this? How could such hatred dwell in the heart of a human being? Why has W.L. hated Hobby so much? Hobby represents all the things W.L. could have been, yet W.L. wanted revenge on Hobby more than anything in the world and he is using me as a way of getting that revenge. He was always spoiled, but who would ever have thought he would become the maniac I am seeing before me?

"You're not seeing things my way at all are you Robyn?" W.L. asked as he rose and went to where his coat was hanging over a chair and retrieved his bottle. He held it to his mouth and guzzled the alcohol down and wiped his mouth with the back of his hand. His tie was twisted and his shirttail almost out.

"I didn't want to get rough with you, my love, but you're tempting me. I'll give you one hour to make up your mind. I imagine Hobby will be coming home for lunch in an hour or so. Everything has to be settled by then." He stood and took the handgun and rubbed her breasts with its muzzle, then forced his mouth to hers and she felt pain as he pressed hard against her lips.

"I feel so sorry for you W.L.," Robyn said between sobs. "You are completely beyond reasoning. I pity your poor soul, to have stooped so low in your thinking that you would do this. Me, a poor farm girl and you also a sharecropper's son, straight from the backwoods of North Carolina, unknown and insignificant, committing a mortal sin in your deranged state. I pity you for allowing whisky to make you do things you wouldn't dare do sober."

He looked into her eyes that intrigued him whenever he saw her face, and fire glowed as her anger swept over her.

"You're just hedging," W.L. said. "You're trying to shame me into giving up, but I won't do it Robyn." He stood over her and she noted that saliva was running from the corners of his mouth. Mucous was running from his nostrils. His hands trembled. His nostrils expanded as he breathed and he was becoming wobbly on his feet.

"Stand up," he ordered. "We're going outside. I saw a stream and a table down in a secluded place as I came in. It's hidden from the hospital grounds and also from the street. I'm taking you there Robyn, for the finale of this tryst. But I can't take you out like this. You would scream if I let you go as you are, and nothing is going to mar this." He found a towel nearby and shredded it into strips. "I'm going to gag you, my dear and it breaks my heart to have to do this. My beloved, this is hurting me more than anything I ever had to do." He took a wide strip of the towel and placed it over her mouth and tied it firmly at the back of her neck. Then he took another strip and tied her hands behind her. "I'll remove all this in due time, my love," he said as a sob rose from his throat.

He opened the door and looked outside to see that no one was nearby. Then he told Robyn to walk out first, as he held the gun to her back. He placed the gun muzzle in her side and told her to walk swiftly across the footbridge and to the table beyond. She obeyed, only pausing as they crossed over the bridge where she and Hobby had stood many times since they had been in Spring Lake and watched the little fish as they swam by and the minnows that played on the top of the water. They had shared their dreams and planned for a bright future. They had talked so many times about Bear Grass and their years spent there and how it had had an impact on their lives. They would recall places they loved best and the scenes that had been most beautiful to them. Whatever their conversation might be, it always included something about Bear Grass. She thought as she walked across the little plank bridge that that was in another world in another lifetime. She sobbed.

We know so little about life, she thought; its beginning, its ending. So miniscule at conception it is less than a speck except for great magnification and a miracle that it even progresses; how little we are able to control our own destinies. The hands of death can ride in a cloudless sky, borne on gentle winds that portend no such evil. Death with its icy hand lurking in disguise under brilliant sunshine on a day when hope can soar to the skies.

Robyn stood facing W.L. He came up to her, took his hand and grabbed the ripped part of her dress and snatched until it was ripped in two. Then he ripped her slip apart and grabbed hold of her panties and pulled them down and they fell at her feet. She stood in shame before him, breasts swollen from pregnancy, a slightly protruding abdomen, her hair falling around her face, her hands bound behind her and her mouth gagged so that she could not give an outcry. He came close and touched her and his body shook violently. He looked into her face, into those mystical, impenetrable eyes that appeared to be looking far beyond the distant hills, and he knew in that instant that he could not reach her so long as there was life in her body. She was a stranger, someone he had never known. And he wanted her more than life.

She hung her head and little sobs, almost inaudible, came from behind the mask. Nothing was left. No husband, no children, no hope. It was going to end without even a struggle, for she had been made powerless by the maniac who stood before her. She prayed.

Wilbert Lee sat down for a moment and rested his elbows on the ground as he observed Robyn in such a state. He felt an orgasm coming on and he stood and pointed the gun at Robyn's heart and cried, "Goodbye my darling. We will soon be together in paradise," and pulled the trigger. He saw her as her legs folded and she sank to the ground as if it were a movie being shown in slow motion. Then he walked to the edge of the stream, placed the muzzle of the gun to his temple and pulled the trigger.

The ground was carpeted with leaves just fallen, still yellow and gold and the blood covered some of them, mixed with his brains, making zig-zag patterns where it ran to the lower levels of the ground.

Chapter 49

Hobby stood by the bedside of his beloved Robyn. There was a pallor of death on her face despite the steady drip of blood into her vein from a bottle attached to a frame near the bed. He looked down at her and violent sobs shook his body. Tears fell on the sheets and he was so out-of-control he stepped to the window and viewed the scene as the sun began to slant westward.

There was a purple tint to the hills and a mist that partially dimmed his view of the higher elevations. But lower down there was a splash of color that spoke something to his soul. It was sedate, yet pleasing to the eye. He took his handkerchief from his pocket and dried his tears and returned to Robyn's bedside. Her thin hand showed purple veins against the whiteness of the skin. He took her hand and held it to his lips.

A nurse came in to check on the flow of blood into Robyn's vein and Hobby asked her whether there had been any change in Robyn's condition while he was out. She said there had not been any change, but that her pulse was stronger, and this gave him new hope.

As he held her hand, he thought of the beauty of their years together, the closeness of their relationship, of their two children - Heidi with the same mysterious eyes as her mother's and the handsome John that somehow reminded him of W.L. They had been such beautiful years and he had never been able to fully appreciate them until now, when there was the possibility that it might all end. It had never been threatened before.

Hobby had a promising future as an orthopedic surgeon. He was in residency in Tennessee, high in the Smoky mountains. He could go far in this field, and no person could more appreciate the healing powers of such miracle workers than he, from his own personal experience. He had been made a whole man by the genius of Dr. William Robards, and he could never forget. Whatever he might be able to do to help others in the same manner would be small compensation for all he had received from this great surgeon's hands.

But he had a complete change of heart as he looked down upon his beautiful Robyn, the source of his greatest joy and the one person in all the world that had made his life complete. From deep within him, hope sprang alive. And it was no longer a time to think of a career. It was a time to follow the dictates of the heart. And with every heartbeat one word reverberated in his mind - HOME.

He couldn't deny it any longer. Medical school had been pleasant and a challenge, and the years had passed swiftly. He had great respect for his fellow classmen and the doctors who had taught them. They were all men of courage with great ambitions and the new graduates would make their marks in the world. Many children were born with deformities that could be corrected by surgery and with the rise in polio cases, their services would be needed to help those with deformities overcome their handicaps and make a place for themselves in society.

But all this paled as he watched his sleeping beauty who had been so much a part of his world, now in a world in which he could not be a part. Both of them had loved their environment in Bear Grass. They had gone back to places of their childhood and renewed memories of days long gone. They had seen a beauty there many others had ignored.

He stood at the foot of the bed and said softly, "We're going home Robyn. We're going home, my love, back to our beginnings. Please open your eyes Robyn and hear what I'm saying. We will return to the place we love best and there will never be any straying again. It's what we've both wanted all the time, yet I was so involved in the medical profession I wouldn't admit it, and you were so loyal and supported me so much you never said what was really in your heart.

"Home is calling us Robyn. It's calling across the hills and the valleys. Listen for it in the breeze, my love. Listen to the melody, like the love songs we have sung together. It's the most beautiful sound I've ever heard. It's all the beautiful sounds that could be joined together to make a perfect harmony.

"Please smile just once for me, my love. Let me know that although you are so far away, you are aware that I'm promising all the things our hearts long for. Please listen to me Robyn. Please open your eyes just once, to let me know that you're still a part of my world.

"Remember the farm? We took our vacation and spent the entire two weeks in Hallsborough and left our hotel room each day and walked over all the places that we loved and remembered with so much nostalgia. Come with me, my love, and we will make it ours. The gates are open and it seems like there's a welcome sign on an old scarecrow nearby. It's pretty leading up to the house and the hay is all shocked and standing in neat rows and the frost sparkles on the brown grass in early morning.

"The corn is in the crib and the hogs are fattening and the chickens are foraging in the green rye all day long. There was a bumper crop this year and the 'simmon beer is already made and the keg is sitting under the shelter. The pecans are falling and you can hear them as they hit the tin roof.

"The horses in the pasture are sleek with their manes flowing in the wind. The colts are running and kicking up their heels and the cows are standing silently and chewing their cuds and I could sit on a wood fence all day and watch the beauty about me.

"Remember the old apple trees we sat under last summer, my love? The leaves were green and the foliage was thick and they were filled with half-grown fruit. I will place a bench there so that we can observe our little paradise and feel as close as we felt that day for as long as we live. When they are pink with blooms, we'll be there for the petals to fall around us. And where the wisteria blooms hung overhead in clusters from the little incline near the creek, we'll add another bench for our trysting place.

A team of physicians entered the room, interrupting his reverie, and Hobby stood aside as they gathered around Robyn. One felt of her pulse. Another pulled the covers down to check on the bandages. A few drops of blood had seeped through. The blood dripping from the bottle into her vein was getting low, and a nurse was summoned and told to get another unit of blood ready. A stethoscope was going over her chest as the doctor listened intently.

"How is she, Doc?" Hobby asked softly.

"Still critically ill," Dr. Wasserman said. "But that is to be expected at this point. She has at least a fifty percent chance of recovering."

But there was a fifty percent chance that she wouldn't live, Hobby thought. Tears flooded his eyes and he again walked to the window where the last rays of daylight were casting their glow over the area. But low on the horizon he saw a star already shining. He told himself that was his Robyn, signalling to him from the sky that everything would be all right.

"God, please help her," he said in a whisper.

As the physicians were leaving, Dr. Wasserman stopped by Hobby's side and offered a word of encouragement. "Don't give up hope," he said. "We've pulled others through who were nearer on the brink than your wife. It will mean a lot if you can think positively. Your wife had a very close call, and the bullet came within an eighth of an inch of severing her spinal cord.

It also punctured her liver. But the bullet went through her entire body and left a clean wound in her back. We feared paralysis, and it's still too early to say for sure there is none. But we believe she will be all right. I hope this will give you a degree of consolation."

"Thank you doctor," Hobby said. "You have helped me a lot."

The room was empty again and a soft light was burning over Robyn's bed. He bent and kissed her pale lips, but she was unresponsive. She lay as if in death, and his spirits were lower than they had ever been in his life.

"You are everything in life to me, my dearest," he sobbed. "You are my sun and my moon, my skies and my world. I'm begging you Robyn, please come back to us. Heidi and John are heartbroken, and their lives have no meaning without you either.

"The little one you were carrying was lost, my love, but there will be others. We are still young. There will be children running over the plantation and they will enjoy all the things we have enjoyed and that have had an indeliable impact on our lives.

"There is no answer for what Wilbert Lee did, Robyn. You know that I worshipped him when I was a boy and I loved him so much I overlooked that part of his nature that was contrary to what I believed. He trampled on all of us and we somehow accepted it, simply because it was Wilbert Lee. I pity his soul.

"We have been exposed to all the realities of life, my love. We have seen the good and the bad, and we haven't judged. If our views differed from those who opposed them, we accepted them as a part of life. We have seen prejudices, discrimination, poverty, hardship, greed, and many loyal, everyday people that strived to lead honest, decent lives.

"It's all a part of life - and death - Robyn. But we have kept the faith. I don't have to say I'm sorry, my dearest, for you have been everything I could ever hope for in a wife, a lover, a mother and a friend. And I know that you know that. It hasn't been perfect, for nothing in life is perfect, but our little differences have only made us love each other more. And it can't end here, Robyn.

"You must return to me, to the world that we love so much. Listen again, my darling. The call is becoming a crescendo. It says for us to return to our heritage and to make a reality out of our dreams.

"Life is changing Robyn. Bear Grass is changing. The great haul-off has already begun. The things we treasured are being thrown away so rapidly they will be gone if we don't take action. Old treasures are lying in junk heaps in woods and on trash dumps. And I hope that in your world which

I cannot penetrate you are having visions of the grandeur of what I am trying to convey to you. It isn't a dream, Robyn. It can be real!

A gurgling sound came from Robyn's throat and there was a frown on her face as if she had eaten something sour, and Hobby panicked. He was almost disoriented as he ran from the room, turning in the wrong direction to reach the nurses' station. "She's dying!" he screamed, and several nurses ran toward Robyn's room. A doctor was nearby and he went in to check on her.

"She's choking on her own fluids," Dr. Best said. "She isn't able to breathe on her own. We've got to do a trachaeotomy immediately." He motioned to the nurses to prepare for the procedure.

"You can stay if you want to Dr. Turnage," Dr. Best said, "but you will probably be better off if you leave the room while we do the procedure. As you know it will only take a few minutes and then your wife will be able to breathe on her own again."

Hobby went into a small sitting room nearby where sobs racked his body. He was beginning to lose hope. His world was falling apart. Despite his positive attitude, there seemed to be a force stronger than his will to make Robyn whole working against him. He had seen it happen before when loved ones placed all their faith in their ability to bring a loved one through during a life-or-death crisis, and in many cases it failed. The cruelty of death haunted his soul.

"I can't make her live, God," he sobbed. "There must be help beyond the realm of man if my Robyn is to survive. I've always believed in a power beyond man although I haven't been a religious person. But I know that you can do anything and I don't doubt your ability to make Robyn a whole woman again if she has anything to offer the world, to say nothing of what she means to our children and me. Please help us, God."

Dr. Best came up to Hobby and told him the trachaeotomy had already been performed and that Robyn was resting better. "This should help," he said.

"Thank you Doctor Best," Hobby replied.

He re-entered Robyn's room and noted that she had been placed in a different position with her face turned to one side. He thought her countenance looked more peaceful, and he found new hope from within.

"I can't give up," he said in a whisper. "I must do everything in my power to reach her, to bring her back to the world that is waiting for her."

He pulled a chair beside her bed, rubbed a hand gently over her face and noted her breathing.

"My darling, the farm is a sure thing if you will return and go with me. It isn't something of the mind. Pearl and Nick are behind us one hundred percent. They made it possible for me to go to college and through medical school. But their one desire is for us to be happy.

"Whatever has been said about my mother, Robyn, she has been an angel to me and no boy could have had a better mother than Pearl has been. Remember how a few boys at Bear Grass School alluded to me as the little crippled bastard? Well, that didn't bother me too much. But when I heard whispers that Pearl was a whore that hurt me to the quick. Pearl was not a whore, and I know that you know that. What happened to her is what happens to many young, inexperienced girls who are caught up in youthful passions without even realizing the consequences. And it doesn't matter how life comes about, it is precious to that person. My life is as precious to me as it would have been if my parents had been married. And Pearl has spent her adult life trying to make up to me for her one mistake. She is royalty in my book. And she has been a wonderful wife to Nick and that man loves me as if I were his own son. He is the kindest man I have ever known, and because he saved his money and didn't have it in the banks when they closed, he has been able to amass a fairly large fortune. He wants to share it with us, my love.

"And you were the sweetest woman that ever lived to have accepted me, knowing my background since you heard everything there was to know about me during our years in Bear Grass. For your family to have accepted me and never to have thrown up my bastardy to me and my mother's mistake means more to me than you can ever know.

"I will never let you down, my dearest. I'm no angel and you know that. I am just a plain, ordinary man who loves more deeply than I can say. I love the simple things in life. I have no desire for wealth Robyn. I don't long for mansions or fine cars or a life of luxury. I'm not made that way. Neither are you. We both appreciate the beauty about us, but the beauty we see comes from within as well as a visual reality.

"That's why you must return from the dreamland that I cannot penetrate, my love. We were so happy during the days when we romped over Mr. Butler's farm, Robyn. We saw all the things we love there - the acres and acres of crops growing in the fields - the well-kept premises and the out-buildings and the tobacco barns one after the other down that long path. We visited the two-story house and were impressed. There are many rooms there, Robyn, and we'll need them for a growing family, plus rooms for Pearl and Nick and Miss Cora and Mr. Tobey when they visit us, or your brothers and sisters. Remember the pegged floors and the wide boards?

Remember how the staircase wound around and the solidness of the structure? Remember the breezeway and the large kitchen and dining room separated from the rest of the house? Remember how we stood and watched the sun set and how the horizon looked that day? There were a few white clouds low in the sky and the sun tinted them pink and it was so peaceful and quiet it seemed that we could have heard a pin drop. Remember how a gentle breeze moved the leaves on the trees and we got a whiff of honeysuckle as we observed the little paradise?

"As I have told you, things are changing Robyn. Tractors have come on the scene and people are getting rid of their mules. Supermarkets have taken over and chickens and hogs and cows are no longer a common sight at country homes. And it's just beginning. It will all be gone one day, my dear. World War II brought new technologies in sight and they have been slow in materializing, but there is a definite trend in the country now. Trailer homes are springing up along all the highways and Bear Grass is losing its identity as a rural community.

"Progress must come and that's the way it should be. But I want us to preserve our heritage, Robyn. While others are changing we will be preserving. Preserving for future generations. The modern trend has not touched Mr. Butler's farm but it is coming."

Weary in spirit, discouraged by Robyn's lack of response, with hope for her recovery fading, he lay his head on her bed and sobbed. He was in this condition when Dr. Wasserman entered the room. The physician placed his hand gently on Hobby's shoulder.

"Dr. Turnage," he said, "you have gone beyond the limit of your endurance. You are rapidly losing any capacity to fight off your burden. You are mentally and physically sick. We will have to intervene to preserve your strength. The room next door is vacant, and I want to put you to bed and enter you as a patient. You need glucose and you must have some sleep. I am taking steps to have you admitted to the hospital and we will get you in shape to cope with your troubles in a few days."

"I can't do it, doctor," Hobby pleaded. "I must be by her bedside."

"I know your feelings," Dr. Wasserman said, "But you've already been here too long. You will be devastated if we don't take immediate action.

"Now you go to the next room and take a shower and don one of the hospital gowns, since I doubt that you have any pajamas here."

"I don't," Hobby replied.

Dr. Wasserman instructed the nurses to begin intravenous feeding, and then give the patient a relaxant to get to sleep. "What he needs more than anything else," the doctor said, "is twenty-four hours of sleep. Then he will need some solid food. I doubt that he's eaten a mouthful of food in the past forty-eight hours."

After Hobby left the room, Cora and Tobey Finch stood silent vigil by their daughter's bedside. Nothing was said. Cora placed her hand over Robyn's and tears came to her eyes. Tobey looked off in the distance. They soon left and two of Robyn's sisters came into the room and broke into tears upon seeing her. They remained only for a moment.

Around-the-clock nurses were ordered for Robyn. Every heartbeat was monitored with constant checks on her blood pressure.

Soon after Hobby was soundly sleeping the nurses noticed a radical drop in Robyn's blood pressure and several doctors were by her bedside in moments.

"I fear internal bleeding," Dr. Wasserman said. "Let's get her to the operating room. We may have to open her up again but God, I hope not. She is barely alive as it is, and if there is further surgery it will only make her weaker and she will have even less resistance."

"I don't think we have a choice," Dr. Stickle said.

The tear in the internal sutures was repaired and Robyn was taken back to her room after two hours in surgery. Dr. Wasserman said it was good that Hobby was sleeping, or there would be another emergency on their hands.

Nurses never left Robyn's bedside. Glucose was kept dripping into her vein and every bodily function was monitored. The nurses administered to Robyn, sometimes crying themselves and shaking their heads. They appeared to be losing her despite all the efforts of the medical profession.

Robyn was still holding on to life four days after she was shot, still in a deep coma, lying perfectly still. Her condition had been so critical there had been no effort to test her thoroughly for paralysis. Since there was no movement her physicians were beginning to fear paralysis more and more as each day went by. But their first concern was to keep her breathing.

Hobby slept soundly for twenty hours. He awakened with glucose dripping into his vein. He started to jump out of bed and hasten to Robyn's room until he realized a needle was attached to his hand. He rang the bell for a nurse, anxious to know how Robyn was doing.

"She's still holding on to life," the nurse told Hobby. "We haven't observed any improvement as yet. I want Dr. Wasserman to talk with you if he is available," she said as she dialed his office number.

"Why?" Hobby asked, fearing that he was being prepared for the worst.

"Dr. Wasserman can explain her condition to you better than I can," the nurse said. "But it's not hopeless, Dr. Turnage," she added.

Dr. Wasserman entered Hobby's room momentarily. He was a kindly man, portly, in his late 50s with a round face, a heavy mustache and warm brown eyes. He inspired trust in his patients.

The doctor greeted Hobby with a handshake and a warm pat on his shoulder. "You've taken quite a nap," he said.

"How long has it been?" Hobby asked.

"Almost around the clock."

"And how is my Robyn?"

"Hobby," the doctor said, "you have been trained in the medical profession and it would be foolish to try to deceive you, and you have known from the start that your wife was critically wounded when she was shot. We have done our utmost to keep her alive, and it seems that we are thwarted in our every effort. To make matters worse, she had internal bleeding and we had to open her up again yesterday and repair some sutures. That has made her weaker, and there has been absolutely no response as to movement, not even her eyelids. So your wife is very near death. All her family has been in since you have been asleep, and even your children stood beside her bed for a moment. We allowed this because we fear she may expire and we didn't want the family to feel they were denied access to her bedside in the event the worst occurs."

Hobby was sobbing and the doctor was silent for a moment. But he felt that he had to say more to Hobby.

"I have never wanted more to save one person's life than your wife's, Hobby. And for more than one reason. In this profession we are confronted with the hard realities of life every day. It is hard to see anyone die, but it is worse when they are young and there is so much promise in life. And I have observed both of you since you have been in residency here at Hope Valley. I have never seen two people more in love than you two. I've watched out my window when you strolled over the grounds and I have noted the worship evident between the two of you, and the tender love you show for your children. And your wife is so incredibly beautiful it would be a tragedy to lose her beauty to this world. I see the promise of a brilliant future for you and you are a handsome young man with everything going for you until this great tragedy struck.

"We are doing everything humanly possible to save your Robyn, Hobby. But I am of the old school and I believe there is hope beyond man. I trust that you will seek out that great physician who can go beyond the powers of mortal men. Look to God, Hobby. He is your greatest hope."

"I tried to reach her through my own efforts," Hobby said between sobs. "I thought that somehow I would be able to penetrate her subconscious and bring her back from a land that I know nothing about. But I too have failed, doctor."

"You don't know that," Dr. Wasserman assured him. "She loves you so much I know if anybody can reach her it is you."

"But I do believe in God," Hobby said. "And I believe in him more since I have faced the crisis of my life than I ever have before. I know that He can bring back my Robyn if it is His will. But I want His will to conform to what I want. I will pray with all my heart and trust that God will hear my prayers and help my poor Robyn."

"You must eat now Hobby," Dr. Wasserman said as he rose to leave. "I won't agree for you to get out of bed until you've consumed a good breakfast - at least two eggs, bacon, toast and coffee, and a large glass of milk. After that, they will remove the glucose and you can dress and go into Robyn's room again."

"Who is looking after the children?" Hobby asked. He had been so obsessed with getting through to Robyn he hadn't thought seriously about John and Heidi.

"Your wife's parents are staying at your house, and other members of the family. They are caring for the children. I have seen to it that they were looked after ever since the tragedy."

"Thank you doctor," Hobby said as he left. "You're a good man and a friend as well as a doctor."

He heard the swishing of the nurses' uniforms as they walked up and down the halls and noted the hospital smells - ether and lysol and the odor of chrysanthemums mingling with all the other hospital smells - something he had been unaware of since Robyn had been wounded. He realized that there was still life and the world was going on, despite his problems.

He ate all his breakfast, although it was nearing the end of daylight. Then the needle was removed from his arm and he dressed. He found fresh clothes in the closet. Cora Finch had brought clean underwear, a starched shirt and another pair of pants and a jacket. He blessed his mother-in-law in his thoughts.

Entering Robyn's room, he found a team of nurses around her. Tubes were protruding from her nostrils and mouth, extending to the floor where fluids were accumulating in glass jugs. Her lips were being moistened with ice and a quill was feeding single drops of water in her mouth. He stood for a moment and watched silently, then left the room and went out on the porch and took a seat in one of the white rocking chairs. The view was beautiful from the porch, with the rolling hills beyond and a panorama of color around him. Leaves in golden hues captured the fading sunlight and sparkled in the distance. The grounds sloped sharply below him. The grass was still green on the lawn and he observed everything about him. It was beautiful, he told himself, but no more so than the land he loved best, his Bear Grass community back home.

People came and went through the hospital doors, but Hobby's thoughts were far from hospitals and sick rooms. He realized only then that he had never been an adult before; that people only mature when they are confronted with situations that demand maturity. He had been a little boy in a little boy's world, accepting all the good things in life and giving no thought to others whose lives may have been affected and changed by events over which they had no control in the same manner his had been changed so suddenly. Hobby became a man that day.

He sat on the porch and watched as daylight faded and lights came on on the grounds. There was a chill in the air but he wasn't cold. The air was invigorating. He rose from the chair and walked down the long flight of steps to the grounds below, strolling slowly, he walked beyond the arc of light that flooded the hospital grounds until he came to a large rock in the edge of the woods. And under a star-studded Tennessee sky, he knelt to pray.

"Dear Father, You have blessed me with the ability to accept my fellowman for what he is without questioning his motives. Now help me to accept You for what You are, my heavenly Father. Don't let me question your motives, Father. In the past I haven't felt that I really needed You, although I always knew You were there. But I was naive, Father. I accepted life in its totality, always being the beneficiary of what I felt was the best that life had to offer. You blessed me without me giving you my loyalty and my love in return. I have been so blind, Father.

"Now I am confronted with a mountain which I cannot climb and I am fully aware of my incapacities. I know that unless You intervene, that which I hold dearest in all the world will depart from me. And if it's Your will, Father, let me hand her over to you this minute and never ask why. Give me the love I will have to have for You in order to do this. I cannot do it on my own. You deserve her, Father. She would be a shining example for Your kingdom. She is at her height, Father. She has made John and Heidi and me so happy, and we want her under any circumstances. But if You will otherwise, let me release my grip on her right this moment and resolve to continue life and to do all that I can to make life good for the two children You have given us. I can't fight it anymore, Father. I leave it all in Your hands."

Pearl and Nick were waiting for him when he returned to the hospital. Hobby had asked them to let him be with Robyn alone and they had acceded to his wishes. Pearl cradled his head in her arms and sighed, "My darling. I'm so very sorry. You are devastated and look so pale. Is there anything I can do?"

"There's nothing anybody can do," Hobby answered. "She is at the brink of death and we must be prepared for whatever comes. If you can break the news to John and Heidi gently that would help. As for myself, I've willed Robyn into the hands of God, and I can accept whatever comes now. I can't fight it any more, Pearl."

"Don't give up hope Hobby," Nick said. "There's still life and nothing is impossible so long as life remains."

"I'm still hoping," Hobby said, "but I'm not demanding that God spare Robyn if it isn't in His plans. I've tried to defy God, and it doesn't work."

They were standing in a hallway between the nurses' station and Robyn's room. A nurse was hurrying toward them, and a lump came into Hobby's throat. "This is it," he said to himself.

"She moved," Miss Slusser said. "She moved an arm on one side and a leg on the other and there was a flutter in her eyes for a moment. We are so pleased, and we wanted you to know as soon as possible."

Hobby's countenance changed in an instant. There was a broad smile on his face and he almost jumped off the floor with excitement. They rushed to Robyn's room but only Hobby and Pearl were allowed to enter. Hobby bent over and kissed Robyn gently on her lips while Pearl held Robyn's hand in hers.

There was another movement and Hobby noticed as her lips parted slightly. He wanted to think there was a smile on her face. Casting his eyes to the floor, he realized that there were fewer fluids dripping into the bottles. Hope soared in his heart.

Dr. Wasserman was soon beside Robyn's bed and Hobby asked him what it all meant.

"It has to mean that there is some improvement," Dr. Wasserman said. "And the fact that there has been movement on both sides indicates that there is no paralysis. And when the fluids stop dripping into the bottles the tubes will be removed and we can feel a lot better about your wife's recovery."

"I'm the happiest man in the world Dr. Wasserman," Hobby said, and the doctor cautioned him that Robyn had a long way to go before they could feel confident of her recovery. "We'll just have to wait and see," he said. "But things are looking up, Hobby and I share some of your happiness with you."

Pearl was smiling and she came around to the side of the bed where Hobby stood and placed her arms around his shoulder. Her every mannerism bespoke pride in this handsome young man that she claimed as her son.

"Hobby, I want you to go home tonight and get some more rest," Dr. Wasserman said. "We can look after your wife better with you out of the room. We are doing all the things possible to help her and she requires constant attention. But what we are doing is benefiting her."

Hobby agreed to go home and he rode with Pearl and Nick since someone else had brought him to the hospital, and he didn't even remember who.

"It is an act of God," Hobby said. "She was dying and all of us knew it, and He heard my prayer. When I was ready to give her up without question He was ready to give her back to me."

The children ran to meet Hobby, holding out their hands and asking him how Mother was. They were delighted when he told them there was some improvement. Bozo, their boxer dog, put his paws on Hobby's stomach with his bit of tail wagging and the Finches came out to greet him. Cora had prepared a big meal and Hobby suddenly had an appetite. He ate heartily and capped it off with a slice of Cora's apple pie a la mode. But his thoughts were on Robyn.

He retired early to comply with the doctor's orders, but sleep did not come. His mind was racing. Now that he believed Robyn's life would be spared, he turned to thoughts of the farm. Many mules would be needed, and mules were a scarcity. He would have to acquire herds of cattle - purebreds - as foundation stock. There would be pastures of horses and he visualized them running over the meadows - light chestnuts with beige manes, palominos, blacks, roans, steel grays - with colts in varying shades.

He would have to round up wagons and carts and tobacco trucks and all manner of farm machinery. The task would be gigantic. Buildings would have to be built to house all the things they would need to make the farm come to life and to portray it realistically.

Arbors would have to planted and fruit trees set out. Beds for flowers would have to be planned. There would have to be landscaping in keeping with the traditional way of life. They would want mass plantings of peach, apple, plum and pear trees in clusters that would color the plantation in spring and which could be seen from the Great House.

Electricity wires would have to be placed underground as would telephone lines.

It would require a giant effort to acquire all the farm machinery and tools he would need for the future. Spare parts would become a big problem for things he would need in most cases were out of production.

He visualized the final result in his mind and it brought a sense of beauty and pleasure to him. He yawned, then realized that he hadn't called about Robyn. It was past midnight but he checked with Third Floor at Hope Valley and was told Robyn was still moving about; that otherwise there was no change. He turned over and slept soundly.

The tubes had been removed from Robyn's throat next morning, but they were still in her nostrils. Hobby stood by her bedside and saw the twitching of her eyelids and he wondered whether she would ever come out of the deep coma. But he didn't lose hope.

He thought about how things were going in Bear Grass since Wilbert Lee had shot Robyn, then taken his own life. He knew it would be a great shock to the community and that it had been the topic of conversation since it all happened. He wondered how the Hallsborough Argus had played the story. He had been so emotionally upset he hadn't given any thought to events after the shooting, except to stand by Robyn's bedside and hope to reach her through his own efforts.

Where was Wilbert Lee's funeral held? At Whispering Pines Church? Were the people back home keeping a check on Robyn's condition? He was unaware of anything that had happened in Bear Grass. He called the house and when Pearl answered he asked her whether people back home were calling about Robyn, and she told him they were getting telephone calls every day and that people in the community were grieving about Robyn and what Wilbert Lee had done.

Hobby returned home and he and Bozo took a stroll down a mountain path and ended up at a little stream where the water sent up a mist as it ran over small rocks in the river. When John and Heidi returned from school he explored the grounds with them, with Bozo running from one to the other in his excitement.

Returning to the hospital after supper, he found Robyn with no tubes attached to her, and Dr. Wasserman assured him that there was definite improvement in her condition. "We believe she's beginning to come out of the coma," he said. Hobby asked how he knew, and the doctor said her eyelids had fluttered earlier in the morning and she had opened her eyes for an instant. "She hasn't spoken, but her lips formed the word "water." That's an indication of consciousness," he said.

Hobby resumed his vigil by Robyn's bedside. He wanted to be there when she regained full consciousness. There was no other way to assure that. The urgency of the situation was over and there were no nurses hovering over Robyn. He wanted to be there to do anything necessary for her.

He was just sitting and watching her, holding one of her hands, when a nurse came in and told him there was a telephone call for him from Wilmington. Who on earth could it be? he thought as he went toward the cubicle where calls were answered.

"Is this Hobby Turnage?" the caller asked.

"Yes," Hobby replied. "Who is calling?"

"Somebody from the past," the voice said. "But I had to call you Hobby to let you know I hāve been thinking about you and Robyn and all the people back in Bear Grass. This is Otto Pell."

"Reverend Pell!" Hobby exclaimed! "So glad to hear from you."

"I thought highly of you as a little boy and a youth, and the Finches were fine people when I was pastor at Whispering Pines. I've thought about those days so many times and they seem now to have been the most rewarding years of my life."

Hobby thought about the scandal that had resulted in Reverend Pell being turned out of the conference, and he realized that this call had to be very painful for the man.

"I'm not a preacher anymore Hobby," Pell said. "But of course you already knew that. Maybell and the children and I live quietly near the beach and our lives are more or less spent in solitude. I fish sometimes, walk along the beach many times, and think all the time. It hasn't been easy, Hobby."

"I'm so sorry to hear that Reverend Pell," Hobby answered. "I was hoping you had found the fulfillment you missed in Bear Grass."

"Conscience is what has done me in," Pell replied. "If I didn't have a conscience I could have found happiness of a sort, as could Maybell, but having to admit that you've broken the laws of society leaves you without the proper essentials to cope with life. But that isn't why I called. It's your problems I'm worried about. I've read the stories about the shooting and Wilbert Lee's suicide and they have touched me more than any one thing since I was a part of the Bear Grass community. I would love to do anything I could to help, although I know of nothing that I could do under the circumstances."

"You have already done more than you realize," Hobby said. "I guess the first time religion registered with me was when I'd hear you preach at Whispering Pines. I wasn't a Christian, but because of you and my grandparents I learned to believe in God. And it has paid off this week, Reverend Pell."

"How?" Pell asked.

"Robyn was dying Reverend Pell. The doctors even told me that and they had tried so desperately to save her. Dr. Wasserman finally told me that Robyn was in the hands of God; that he could act when man could no longer help. I had tried to reach Robyn's subconscious mind by talking to her and trying to bring her back to the world of reality. I failed, but I took the doctor at his word. I was at the end of the trail, with no hope left, and I turned to God - on his terms - and asked him to spare Robyn's life if it was His will, but if it wasn't to take her and let me never question why. The prayer soared through the skies and Robyn took an immediate turn for the better. She's going to be okay Reverend Pell. And you played a part in this, for I believed in you as a preacher and as a man."

"You're so kind, Hobby," Pell replied.

"And we're going back home Reverend Pell. I'm giving up medical practice and we have bought Mr. Butler's farm three miles up the road from where we lived toward Hallsborough. You remember it. There are five thousand acres and I've got big plans for it. I'd love to talk with you about it in person sometime."

"We'll just see about that," Pell said. "But let me say I'm so happy that Robyn is going to be all right and that you're coming back home. Bear Grass is the only place for Hobby Turnage to be."

"And I'm sure you've heard about my leg," Hobby said.

"No, I can't say that I have," Pell replied. "You see, after I left Bear Grass I felt that it would be best to break ties with everybody I knew there and just start over. I wanted to hear from the people, but didn't know any way to do it. I was an outcast when I left, Hobby, and I know it was all so wrong, and I feel that God has forgiven me, but I am a shattered man."

"Well, I have two straight legs now!" Hobby said. "That was almost a miracle also, for you remember how crippled I was."

"I know you're a handsome rascal now," Pell teased, and Hobby smiled and said, "Well" in a tone that implied he felt the same way.

"I'll see you one day," Pell said.

"Maybe you'd even like to live on the farm later on," Hobby suggested.

"Maybe," Pell replied. "But I doubt it Hobby. Anyway we'll see, and I have to go now, but I am overjoyed over Robyn's improvement. I just wanted you to know," and the phone went dead.

He returned to Robyn's bedside and thought more about Otto Pell and all the things that had happened.

He thought about Roscoe Gooch and his antics as a youth and what he did to Minnie Mae Moore, which occurred after he left the community. He remembered reading about the visit of the Klan and Roscoe's beating that cast a pall over the community. And about Wilbur Stroud's death and the petition that helped to end Miss Abie's life.

He remembered the day he and Wilbert Lee were swimming in the creek. Wilbert Lee could jump off the diving board and come up fifty feet farther up the stream. Hobby idolized Wilbert Lee for his litheness, for he had to slide into the water and didn't dare get on the diving board.

Wilbert Lee was diving and doing some fancy swimming while Hobby was swimming slowly in the only manner possible, and he caught cramp in his crippled leg. He was in trouble and Wilbert Lee looked toward him and said, "What in the hell is wrong, Hobby? You're acting like a sissy."

Hobby was struggling and trying to keep from going under. "I've got cramp in my leg Wilbert Lee. Please help me!"

By then Hobby had gone under once and Wilbert Lee finally reached him and took hold of his arm and dragged him to the banks. Hobby was spitting water from his mouth and had a strangling feeling in his throat.

"Thank you," Hobby said, and Wilbert Lee was nonchalant about the whole thing.

"You see, I've saved your life," Wilbert Lee said. "I could have just let you drown, you know." Wilbert Lee's eyes had a strange look.

"You did save my life," Hobby said. "and I'll be grateful to you for as long as I live. You are a hero, Wilbert Lee, and I want everybody to know what you did for me."

"Ah, it was nothing," Wilbert Lee replied.

And to think that the one person he had admired most as a child had done what Wilbert Lee did to Robyn and to himself was almost too much for Hobby to accept. He recognized it now as jealousy. Wilbert Lee had never been able to accept second-best at anything, and Hobby certainly didn't feel that he was superior to Wilbert Lee in any respect. But any accomplishment was taken as a challenge to Wilbert Lee's superiority. The only way Hobby could see it was that Wilbert Lee had always hated him, and when it came out that they were half-brothers it only added to Wilbert Lee's hatred.

It was six years after Hobby had surgery before Wilbert Lee saw him, and he showed shock at seeing Hobby walking in a normal manner. He praised Hobby and told him he had finally become a man, and quite a handsome one, but Hobby sensed that Wilbert Lee felt he was facing his greatest challenge.

Robyn was sleeping soundly and Hobby was beginning to nod. He laid his head on the back of the chair and slept soundly.

It was still dark outside when he woke up. He leaned over Robyn's bed and kissed her lightly on the cheek. He noted more color in her face and his spirits rose.

He walked to the window and looked out upon the hospital grounds. Lights from the city glowed in the distance. He could hear steam as it came into the radiators. A few cars were passing on the street fronting the hospital. He felt that he needed fresh air so he showered and shaved, dressed and walked outside. Heavy frost on the grounds appeared as snow. Two squirrels were chasing each other under the arc of light on the hospital grounds. They darted up a large oak tree and Hobby thought about the big frosts in Bear Grass and going to his rabbit boxes in early morning.

He stopped by the hotel cafeteria and ordered bacon and eggs, grits and coffee. It was good to be eating again. He had gone for three days without taking any kind of nourishment except liquids. And it had been a week since the nightmare began. It seemed like an eternity. Everything preceding the tragedy seemed to have occurred in another world.

He returned to Robyn's room and took his seat beside her bed. She had moved from the position she was in when he left. Her face was toward him and he saw her eyelids flutter and what appeared to be a faint smile on her face. He sat and stared, waiting for the next reaction. It came suddenly. Her eyelids fluttered again and she opened her eyes. He had forgotten how beautiful they were, but suddenly it came back to him. They were the most expressive eyes he had ever seen.

Robyn smiled and held her hand out to him.

"My darling," he said as he stood and embraced her, "You have come back to me."

"What happened?" she asked in a voice almost too weak to hear.

"Don't you know?" Hobby asked.

"I lost my baby," she said and felt of her stomach. Then she discovered the bandages. Tears came to her eyes.

"Why am I bandaged up?" she asked.

Hobby felt that Robyn was trying to evade the real issue; that she must remember having been shot but was trying to put it out of her mind.

"You were shot Robyn," Hobby said, holding her close in his arms. "Wilbert Lee shot you."

"What happened to him?" she asked.

"He took his own life," Hobby said.

Robyn sobbed.

"We thought we were going to lose you," Hobby said. "I've gone through hell Robyn."

Robyn asked for a drink of water and Hobby realized that he should let the doctors know she had regained consciousness. He rang the nurses' bell and when one entered the room she saw that Robyn was awake and alert. She called Dr. Wasserman at home and told him, and he came immediately to the hospital. "I'm so glad you are our Robyn again," the doctor said.

"I'm hungry," Robyn replied.

"Don't you worry dearie," the doctor said. "You will have anything you want to eat today."

"She asked what happened and I told her," Hobby said.

"Good," Dr. Wasserman said. "Now tell me Robyn, were you aware of anything that was happening while you were in a coma? It has been a week, you know."

"It was the most beautiful thing I've ever seen," Robyn replied, her voice becoming stronger now. "It was a paradise, doctor. I don't know if I will ever be able to tell what I experienced. But I was so happy I had no desire to return to anything; just live in the beauty of that world."

"Try to tell us," Hobby said.

"It was like living life again," Robyn explained. "I was back home and everything in my life seemed in perfect order. It was the most beautiful landscape I have ever seen and I was floating on pink clouds and there was a vast space with buildings and trees and picturesque scenes that I will never forget. It was all very simple but oh, so beautiful."

Food was brought in and Robyn winced as she turned toward the tray. She was aware of the bandage and the soreness in her stomach.

"Soft grits and a slice of bacon, light toast and coffee," the nurse said. Robyn felt that she could eat it all, but she felt full when she began eating the grits and was unable to eat the bacon and toast. She did sip the coffee.

"You're tired now and need to rest," the nurse said. "You've already exerted yourself. Let's give you a shot so you can sleep again. There'll be plenty of time to tell about your experience later."

Hobby kissed her and left the room. He was happier than he could ever remember being before. He had lived through his worst fears and the blackest midnight had been replaced with dazzling sunlight. When Robyn awakened again he would give her the details about his plans. He drove home singing, "Oh, What A Beautiful Morning" and the Great Smoky mountains of Tennessee had become his paradise in Bear Grass in his mind as he surveyed the mountainous countryside.

The family had already called the people in Bear Grass and told them the good news. The Finches were preparing to leave for Jones County after they visited Robyn again. Pearl and Nick said they'd be leaving for Memphis the next day, and life would start returning to normal soon. It was all like a dream to Hobby - something that he had imagined and which had never occurred in real life.

Even the farm seemed like a fantasy he had concocted in his mind. And to think that a Greek, a foreigner who had never known anything about farm life, was making all this possible was incredible. He thought about how totally unexpected sources could have the greatest impact on human lives.

But he told himself Nick would never regret his generosity. Nick would supply the money, with not a cent of interest, and Hobby would repay him when the farm began to show a profit. He would never do anything to violate the trust Nick had placed in him.

Hobby returned to the hospital in mid-afternoon and Robyn was awake. Pillows had been placed under her head and she was in a semi-sitting position. Her eyes were warm and luminous and her face was showing pink. Her hair had been combed and it lay in waves on the sides of her pillow. She had never looked more beautiful, dressed in a peach bed jacket, with a touch of lipstick on her lips.

"My, you're pretty," Hobby said as he embraced her.

"Teaser," she replied. "And how are our babies?"

"They're as happy as I am," Hobby replied. "They can't wait for you to return home."

"Are you all right?" Robyn asked.

"Never finer."

"Now catch me up on the news," Robyn said.

"The greatest news I have is about the farm," Hobby said.

"What farm?"

"Ours."

"Where?"

"In Bear Grass, of course."

"Bear Grass?"

"Where else?"

"I don't understand."

"I told you," Hobby said, "but you were in another world. I tried so hard to reach you, Robyn, but I just couldn't."

"Now about the farm."

"We're going home Robyn. I'm giving up medical practice and we're taking over the Butler farm - the one we visited."

"You can't quit medical practice, after all the time you've spent preparing yourself for an orthopedic surgeon."

"After what happened, I suddenly realized that my place in life was to return to Bear Grass," Hobby said. "It was the most compelling force I've ever experienced. I realized that if I were ever able to reach my potential it would have to be back in Bear Grass."

"You're acting too quickly," Robyn said. "Think about this for a while."

"I've thought about it Robyn, and I know that in your heart this is what you want as much as I do."

"Oh, the idea thrills me, for I love Bear Grass as much as you. But I can't see you giving up everything you've worked for."

"Just wait until you hear," Hobby said.

"All right, go," Robyn said.

"It's of such magnitude I don't hardly know how to begin, Robyn. But it's for real. As I said, we're moving to the Butler farm and that's just the start. It will take years to get it like I want it. But it's for the future, my love. It's not just for today, but all the tomorrows.

"We will make the past come to life when everything we have known goes by the wayside. Think what that will mean to future generations. The South as we have known it, is going by the wayside, Robyn. A new South is rising, and it's not all that beautiful. Practices of centuries are being lost and one day all that will be left are memories. But we will preserve it for them, my dear. A day will come when people will search our place out to show a way of life lost forever except for their venture into our world.

"We will keep the countryside just as it is. All the buildings will be preserved. Every privy, every stable, every shelter, every henhouse, every well, every smokehouse. Carts and wagons and mules will still travel the roads and men in overalls will plow the land with sleek mules and chickens will follow the plows to pick up the worms turned up with the soil. There will be hundreds of fruit trees in bloom in spring and the petals will fall all over our domain. I want to preserve every sassafras bush, for they color the ground in autumn. I want every wild grape vine spared, every walnut tree, every house.

"Over a period of time roads will have to be built for easy access by a public that will want to see a lost world. I want the children to be able to see it close up - biddies hatching under their mother - sows with little pigs, newborn calves, mares with their colts, swings under the trees, droves of guineas, ducks on the ponds, geese with their goslings, a sanctuary where birds congregate by the thousand, tree-shaded houses and clean-swept yards, brierberry patches and huckleberry bushes in the woods, row after row of tobacco barns and stacks of wood for curing the leaf and men attending the barns in barning season; lanterns lighting up the night at tobacco shelters, pigs cooking on the coals on special occasions, homemade kites flying in a spring breeze."

"Are you dreaming?" Robyn asked.

"There will be something to see every day of the year, Robyn. Think of the hog-killings when people will be working in the yards. There will be corn-huskings under an autumn moon; wood sawings at night with lanterns for light; ditchings with a dozen or more men cleaning out the debris so the water can flow freely. We'll make syrup every fall and the mule will turn the grist mill that will mash the juice out of the cane and people will be amazed at the sight. There'll be cotton-picking in harvest season and in spring and summer the landscape will be all green when crops are reaching their height.

"It is so beautiful Robyn, so very beautiful it defies description. Think of fall when all the trees on the ridges and the pines in the forests will stand vigil over the lower species that paint the woodlands in shades that artists can't duplicate. Think of the view from the great house. The hay will be shocked and the fields will be smooth and on frosty mornings it will look like a winter wonderland with a dazzling sun sending up golden rays from ice-covered vegetation.

"Think of the times when it snows and the panoramic scene around us. Think of summer when the morning glories put on their show on corn stalks and how the dew captures the entire outline of large spider webs. There will be beds of mums and chrysanthemums in autumn, for they are in keeping with our past. There will be fields of pumpkins on the hillsides that will be visible from the Great House. There will be holly bushes filled with berries. Wash pots will sit on every woodpile and children will play under the spreading trees. The bluebirds and the robins and the cardinals will join the dull-coated birds in the yards and the mockingbirds will sing all day long. The owls will make eerie noises in the night and evenings will be illuminated by silvery moons and tin roofs will sparkle from moonbeams.

"And in our private world, there will be the large kitchen with the windows beside the fireplace where we can enjoy an open fire with a churn of buttermilk on the hearth with our rocking chairs sitting so we can observe the world about us. We can rise in early morning if we choose and see stars low on the horizon and watch the sun come over the trees. But we'll have to observe the sunsets from another location.

"And there will always be the porch inviting us to watch a farm community at work and play. We can see the children playing, including John and Heidi, and the other little ones we will have. And it will be the most beautiful sight at Christmas you ever saw. We'll have a tree that reaches to the ceiling of the large living room, decorated in homemade ornaments and with popcorn strung and winding around the pine or fir or cedar.

"Do you see what I'm seeing my darling? Are you with me? And please don't feel that I'm thinking selfishly. It is because of you this is all possible. I thought I was losing you, Robyn, and my world ended for a time. And it was when you were at your lowest point that the full revelation came to me. There wasn't a moment of choice. It wasn't something I could think over and maybe change my mind. And if you see differently, please tell me right now."

"Somehow it seems I've heard some of the same things before," Robyn replied. "It's like I've lived it before in a sense, and it's in keeping with all the beautiful things I experienced while I was unconscious."

"Then I did reach your subconscious!" Hobby exclaimed. "I sat beside you and talked and my tears fell on your bed sheets and I pleaded with you to hear me. And you did hear, Robyn."

"I left Bear Grass when I was twelve years old and embarked on a new life. But the day I left, I left my heart behind. I accepted another way of life and tried very hard to be happy in my new environment. I became a whole person through surgery and I got a good high school education. I told myself that the only way I could repay society for all it had done for me was to become a healer of the body. I really felt for a time that that was my calling. But try as I might, home was calling me every day. And I will never know why Bear Grass held all the things I've ever loved about life. I wasn't cut out for any kind of life but farming, Robyn. I couldn't farm in my crippled condition and I realized that by the time I left. But it has held something for me no other place on earth could ever hold.

"I regret very much that tragedy had to make me see it in its totality. It breaks my heart that Wilbert Lee chose to take out his hatred for me on you, of all people, then foolishly take his own life. And I wonder sometimes if I failed to try to reach him, to show him a beauty in life I had found and which he would not accept. But hatred poisoned Wilbert Lee's mind and soul."

"I used to think he was the greatest also," Robyn said, "but the day he tore down our playhouse was the day I learned to hate Wilbert Lee. And that's something I can't say about anybody else on earth. He was cruel and deceptive and he felt superior to everybody in Bear Grass and didn't mind stepping on anybody's toes. His was a life of tragedy. Still, I regret that it ended this way."

"Are you willing to go back with me Robyn?" Hobby asked. "Or am I taking over and asking you to do something that you feel is wrong?"

"I can be happy in Bear Grass for the rest of my life," Robyn said. "I was concerned about you and your career and I didn't allow myself to think about living on the farm again. But I am like you in that I found something so beautiful in Bear Grass it has had an impact on me all my life. Yes, I will be happy to return with you, Hobby."

"Then let me finish what I had to say - what has been building in me since you were wounded. I love you with all my heart, all my soul, all that is within me, my dear. Your life is more precious to me than my own, and I will do everything in my power to make you happy for as long as I live. And you will be the main character at our little paradise behind the pines. It's an ideal setting for what I am going to do. The land is in one large tract and the acres fronting the main road are secluded behind large pines for the most part. It will be like entering another world when people turn off the main road.

"And do you remember the little church at the farther end of the property nearer to Hallsborough? I've heard they want to build a new church and are soliciting funds rather than adding on to the present church. I hope to acquire the little church and preserve it as it is. I want it to stay small and humble and a sanctuary for anyone who wants to go there to meditate or to pray. We will patch the ragged plaster, stain the exposed rafters at the top, stain the pews and the lectern, but it will remain just as it is otherwise.

"The plantation will be there forevermore as a testimony to a time that was and will be remembered by millions of people. It is the most important undertaking I could ever take, my dear. It will bring many back to their heritage. It will be something for posterity and a learning institute for the young who will have lost all contact with the way of life we treasure, and which taught us so much about life.

"And the personal rewards are almost beyond comprehension. We'll see the little foxes at play along the edges of the woods; the raccoons by the water's edge; the squirrels playing in the stately oaks; the deer that dart out of the woods occasionally; the bob whites that lay their eggs on the ground and hatch the baby partridges and raise them in the fields about us. We can sit all day sometimes and see the wonders of nature about us. And our neighbors will be people who will tend the fields and make their livings tilling the soil. There'll be parties and barbecues and watermelon cuttings and candy-pullings and dances and people will find fulfillment there they couldn't find anywhere else. I predict that some who are in other businesses and whose roots go back to the soil will want to give up the fast pace and return to the earth and all it has to offer.

"John and Heidi will grow up and realize all the joys we've known. I hope they will want to continue that life after they are educated, but that will be up to them. And there is still time for two or three more babies, Robyn, if you want them. We're still young.

"Not every day will be sunshiny, my dear. We know that the storms will come, that whirlwinds will play over the land sometimes, that thunder will roll and lightning will flash and winds will be furious when the elements seem to vent their passions on us. But it will be a refuge from all those storms. It will be home in the purest sense a place can be home. We will center our lives there and there will be things to enjoy every day.

"We will have modern conveniences, for there is no need to try to live in the past, but they will be concealed so that nothing is changed from the reality of what life has been in the past. All the wiring will be underground and lamps will burn brightly, but the bulbs will be concealed by the old-fashioned lamps we have known, and appliances will be hidden from view with walls or partitions.

"It just has to be Robyn. We've got to preserve it for posterity. We can't let it end, and I've heard of no other person who has such plans in mind. We're still young, Robyn, and we have the time to plan and carry out our dreams while enjoying them. And when decades have gone by, we will become middle aged and then the sunset years will arrive. But we will have lived in a paradise most people only dream of.

"We'll grow old together and there will be so much dazzling beauty for us to behold it is incomprehensible. We will be like children during the years and if adversity comes we will have each other to comfort and minister to our needs.

"And when it is all over, we will have prepared a burial place for us on a hill with shade from the trees and sunshine sometimes, allowing the flowers to grow around the tombs. The wind playing in the trees will create whispers that can be heard by the living sometimes, and overlooking the hill will be pleasant surroundings and a landscape we learned to love before we even started to school. So even the end will be beautiful.

"I remember how we used to whoop and holler when we were children, and how the echoes would come back to us, and the way of life we create will be echoing forevermore as a reminder of a land that was; a simple, humble, pleasant land and the greatest people that ever lived. What we do will be a tribute to them and a testimony to the world that what we had was what the masses are searching for today - peace of mind, a solace from all the cares of the world, a place to collect their thoughts again, to let up and get a new perspective on life.

"All that remains before we begin the most beautiful journey of our life is for you to recover fully, regain your health and vitality, and we'll pack our bags and head for Bear Grass again, our paradise in rural America."

The end

Epilogue

High rise hotels and sprawling motels stand where Bear Grass sharecroppers once farmed the land. The forest where huckleberries once grew and where Nervy Sauls was murdered is a housing development. A manufacturing plant stands where Wilbur Stroud's store was located.

Traffic is heavy along the highway leading to Hallsborough. Eighteen-wheelers and cars speed by on the four-lane that has become a part of the interstate system, beginning far north and going all the way to Miami.

The dog fennel, the cowwitch vines, the maypop plants, and the pines that once formed the silhouette of Bear Grass have long-since been removed. Many of the old-timers have moved away or died.

But very carefully concealed by design and the blessings of nature is the place that Hobby Turnage had the foresight to preserve and the ability to see to its fruition. He dreamed a grandiose dream, never realizing that it would exceed his greatest expectations. Tourists flock there year round by the thousand. But Hobby and his beloved Robyn are now in their sunset years. When tourists pass along the route that takes them over the estate and on to the little church where they worship, they often see a stately gentleman and his lady reclining in comfortable chairs under the trees. Some stop and talk with them and there is always a smile on their faces.

In the library near the church Hobby's book is displayed, which tells the Hobby Turnage story just as it happened.

If you pass along that area in late afternoon and you'll stop for a rest, if there is a lull in traffic you can hear the echoes. They are a recording of Hobby's long-ago call when he would stand out on the veranda as the sun was nearing the treetops, beckoning the children to come home after their long day in the further retreats of his domain.

There is only one month's difference in the age of Gus, Pearl and Nick's son, and John, born to Hobby and Robyn. Two years later came Heidi, the *only girl; one and one half years later, Tobe, and last, Craven. From the age of five they roamed over the back fields to the right of the estate. They explored the forests and the fields, gathered bugs and watched the frogs jump into the pond, often congregating around them and capturing their share.*

Bozo had found a home on the estate and one of his sons had his appearance although the mother was a mixture of hound and collie. His name was Esau and he watched over the boys with a vigilance that was awe-inspiring. If one came too near the water the dog lay down beside him and if anything approached, man or beast, he stood between them and the boys. Hobby and Robyn trusted Esau implicitly.

So Hobby would stand on the veranda with his large fox horn and his call could he heard far and wide. "Gus, John, Tobe, time to come home" and in a few moments there came the bark of a dog, loud and clear, and soon the voices of the boys could be heard in the distance.

Hobby held the horn so that the sound from a building far in the back fields echoed back to him, reverberating over the area. "Esau, Esau, Esau" in quick succession, losing cadence with the reverberations.

"Gus" became the dominant word filling the air waves around the plantation with the passing of the years. Half Greek, son of Nick, he possessed many of Nick's characteristics - the dark hair, soft brown eyes, tall and muscular - but with Hobby's smile and flashing white teeth. There seemed to be something in the chromosomal chain inherited through Pearl that showed up in the offspring. John, Craven and Tobe had the same expression.

Nick and Pearl idolized Gus, but no more so than did Hobby. As they had promised themselves they would do, a day came when Gus was only three that they sold their home in Memphis, left their other holdings in capable hands, and returned to North Carolina to live out their days and to place Gus under Hobby's guidance. And Gus loved it from the moment he arrived at the estate. The wide expanse of grounds, animals and trees seemed to fill something inside that had waited for expression. He and Tobe were explorers, and they were given that freedom to explore at a very early age. And Hobby reveled in their love of the land and the freedom it offered. He saw himself all over again in their enthusiasm.

The boys differed in looks, Tobe with auburn hair and the fairer complexioned of the two, but they were inseparable. Craven would have to wait a few years to join them in their pursuits.

They saw all the beauty Hobby had seen, although in a controlled setting.

All the things that had been dear to Hobby were there to be enjoyed. But he had had to look for them in the wild setting of the Bear Grass of old.

There were places where dog fennel were allowed to grow along garden fences. The road leading to the Great House was lined with golden rods. Rank hard weeds grew around some hogpens. And there were poke berry bushes in some places. The land around a few tobacco barns was allowed to grow up in summer with hard weeds and cowwitch vines, and the vines climbed up the sides of the barns and wrapped themselves around tin smokestacks that towered over the barns. That was to give reality to an era that Hobby froze in time for all generations afterward to visit and to know what life had been like in the 1930s and 1940s.

John made all the family happy when he decided to enter the medical field and pursue a career in orthopedic surgery. He loved Bear Grass and the freedoms it offered, but he lacked that sense of belonging as did the others. He graduated from The University of North Carolina and studied abroad for two years. He is of international renown today. He still visits his Carolina home each year.

Neither was Heidi attracted to the environs of Bear Grass. She married a New Yorker and became a part of society in glittering Manhattan.

Gus, Craven and Tobe attended North Carolina State and majored in animal husbandry. They were interested in subjects that would give them the knowledge to carry on the plantation that Hobby had envisioned.

Nick had to revise his plan to give all of the plantation to Hobby. There had been no way of knowing at the time the agreement was signed that several others would have just as strong an interest as Hobby had had. Turnage Enterprises was formed and every member of the family became a part owner. The same was true of all Nick's other holdings.

They are a very close family but they allow each other room to grow.

The great man, Nick Staphalopoulous, who made it all possible, is only a shell of his former self at age ninety one. Until the age of eighty five he was very alert and took a keen interest in the family and the plantation. He is still revered by the entire clan but they now come into his chambers with sad eyes and stand in reverence by his bedside without speaking.

His hair is snow white and the pallor of his skin gives him the look of a corpse. A sunken mouth reveals the outline of teeth that seem out of place in such a wasted body. Nothing of the man that was remains.

A malignant prostate gland at the age of eighty five left him a eunuch after surgery. So he that had prided himself so much for his manhood was left without any sexuality in his old age. Before the deterioration of the mind set in following his surgery, he would feel down where his manhood had been and smile. The days when he had been amorous had ended at the age of eighty. "I've not missed a thing," he often told himself.

Then came the kidney problems which were diagnosed Brights Disease and his mind began to wander and he'd look at his beloved Pearl sometimes and she was a stranger to him.

Upon their return to North Carolina they had built a home across the county from Bear Grass. There were large columns and spacious grounds and the back sloped down to the river where Nick would imagine sometimes that he was on the Mississippi again, a tie to Tennessee he had not been able to forget. But after his health failed the entire family decided to move he and Pearl to the Great House. Nick needed constant care and there was plenty of help to attend to their needs there. They were given the East wing where morning sunshine filled the room and a view of the grounds with a meadow in the distance and people habitating the road throughout the day. Birds pitch on the windowsills sometimes but they go unnoticed by Nick.

Pearl remains alert at the age of eighty one. Her former beauty has given way to the ravages of time. The once beautiful clear skin is wrinkled and age marks show on her arms and face. But there is still a look of elegance about her. She carries herself well and never goes out without dressing in becoming attire for her age. Her diamonds sparkle on blue-veined hands. She and Robyn visit the malls occasionally and Pearl always has a look of consternation on her face. She tells Robyn people seem to be walking endlessly up and down the crowded place and don't seem to know what they're looking for.

People see Pearl sometimes when she is in public, and all the old timers in Hallsborough know who she is. "I'll bet she was a beauty in her day," is a comment often made.

Pearl spends a lot of her time at Nick's bedside. She'll sit and hold his hand and tears will drop on the sheets. Her love is still as strong as it was when he swept her off her feet in the hills of Tennessee. Then she'll smile when she remembers all the good things that have happened in her lifetime.

"I see it all so clearly now, my darling," she says to Nick sometimes, knowing that her words have no meaning for a mind that doesn't comprehend. "When I was young I thought my generation was forever. I never stopped to think that my parents and their parents were of other generations that had become obsolete with the passing of time. But it's not like I thought at all my love. Look at our fine bunch of children and grandchildren. They now look upon us with pity as we move ever onward toward the sunset. But they too

will pass and life will go on. We're here for a little while, reaching out for all that life has to offer, capturing all the beauty that we can. We're just footprints, my darling. Footprints on the sands of time. But I wouldn't change a thing. We've had our day. Life has been good. Now let us face the sunset and look for the painted clouds at the end of day.